FOUR NOVELS FROM THE INIMITABLE—AND UNMIST.... MASTER OF TERROR AND SUSPENSE:

A story of stunning psychological horror about a group of nice, ordinary kids who learn savage secrets of lust and violence . . . a chilling glimpse into a future America where a macabre marathon is a contest with death . . . an eerie variation on the theme of "Home Sweet Home" . . . and a nightmare vision of a ghoulish game show where you bet your life—literally.

Two of the novels you are about to read—*Rage* and *The Long Walk*—were completed before *Carrie* was even begun. The other two, *Roadwork* and *The Running Man,* were written in between some of Stephen King's most popular bestsellers to date. And each of them is marked by the undeniable fascination of one of the most brilliant imaginations of our time—collected here for a full house of spine-chilling suspense from the man who made shivering believers of us all. . . .

THE BACHMAN BOOKS

FOUR EARLY NOVELS BY STEPHEN KING

THE BACHMAN BOOKS

FOUR EARLY NOVELS BY
STEPHEN KING

Rage
The Long Walk
Roadwork
The Running Man

*With an Introduction,
"Why I Was Bachman"*

A PLUME BOOK

NEW AMERICAN LIBRARY

NEW YORK AND SCARBOROUGH, ONTARIO

NAL BOOKS ARE AVAILABLE AT QUANTITY DISCOUNTS WHEN USED TO
PROMOTE PRODUCTS OR SERVICES. FOR INFORMATION, PLEASE WRITE
TO PREMIUM MARKETING DIVISION, NEW AMERICAN LIBRARY,
1633 BROADWAY, NEW YORK, NEW YORK 10019.

Library of Congress Cataloging in Publication Data

King, Stephen, 1947–
  The Bachman books.

  "With an introduction by Stephen King."
  Reprint of works originally published 1977–1982.
  Contents: Rage—The long walk—Roadwork—[etc.]
  1. Horror tales, American. I. Title.
PS3561.I483A6 1985   813¹.54   85-11411
ISBN 0-453-00507-1
ISBN 0-452-25774-3 (pbk.)

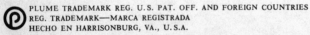 PLUME TRADEMARK REG. U.S. PAT. OFF. AND FOREIGN COUNTRIES
REG. TRADEMARK—MARCA REGISTRADA
HECHO EN HARRISONBURG, VA., U.S.A.
SIGNET, SIGNET CLASSIC, MENTOR, PLUME, MERIDIAN
and NAL BOOKS are published *in the United States* by
New American Library, 1633 Broadway, New York, New York 10019,
in Canada by The New American Library of Canada Limited,
81 Mack Avenue, Scarborough, Ontario M1L 1M8

First Plume (Omnibus) Printing, October, 1985

1 2 3 4 5 6 7 8 9
PRINTED IN THE UNITED STATES OF AMERICA

WHY I WAS BACHMAN
By Stephen King

1

Between 1977 and 1984 I published five novels under the pseudonym of Richard Bachman. These were *Rage* (1977), *The Long Walk* (1979), *Roadwork* (1981), *The Running Man* (1982), and *Thinner* (1984). There were two reasons I was finally linked with Bachman: first, because the first four books, all paperback originals, were dedicated to people associated with my life, and second, because my name appeared on the copyright forms of one book. Now people are asking me why I did it, and I don't seem to have any very satisfactory answers. Good thing I didn't murder anyone, isn't it?

2

I can make a few suggestions, but that's all. The only important thing I ever did in my life for a conscious reason was to ask Tabitha Spruce, the college co-ed I was seeing, if she would marry me. The reason was that I was deeply in love with her. The joke is that love itself is an irrational and indefinable emotion.

Sometimes something just says *Do this* or *Don't do that.* I almost always obey that voice, and when I disobey it I usually rue the day. All I'm saying is that I've got a hunch-player's approach to life. My wife accuses me of being an impossibly picky Virgo and I guess I am in some ways—I usually know at any given time how many pieces of a 500-piece puzzle I've put in, for instance—but I never really planned anything big that I ever did, and that includes the books I've written. I never sat down and wrote page one with anything but the vaguest idea of how things would come out.

One day it occurred to me that I ought to publish *Getting It On,* a novel which Doubleday *almost* published two years before they published *Carrie,* under a pseudonym. It seemed like a good idea so I did it.

Like I say, good thing I didn't kill anybody, huh?

3

In 1968 or 1969, Paul McCartney said a wistful and startling thing in an interview. He said the Beatles had discussed the idea of going out on the road as a bar-band named Randy and the Rockets. They would wear hokey capes and masks à la Count Five, he said, so no one would recognize them, and they would just have a rave-up, like in the old days.

When the interviewer suggested they would be recognized by their voices, Paul seemed at first startled . . . and then a bit appalled.

4

Cub Koda, possibly America's greatest houserocker, once told me this story about Elvis Presley, and like the man said, if it ain't true, it oughtta be. Cub said Elvis told an interviewer something that went like this: *I was like a cow in a pen with a whole bunch of other cows, only I got out somehow. Well, they came and got me and put me in another pen, only this one was bigger and I had it all to myself. I looked around and seen the fences was so high I'd never get out. So I said, "All right, I'll graze."*

5

I wrote five novels before *Carrie*. Two of them were bad, one was indifferent, and I thought two of them were pretty good. The two good ones were *Getting It On* (which became *Rage* when it was finally published) and *The Long Walk. Getting It On* was begun in 1966, when I was a senior in high school. I later found it moldering away in an old box in the cellar of the house where I'd grown up—this rediscovery was in 1970, and I finished the novel in 1971. *The Long Walk* was written in the fall of 1966 and the spring of 1967, when I was a freshman at college.

I submitted *Walk* to the Bennett Cerf/Random House first-novel competition (which has, I think, long since gone the way of the blue suede shoe) in the fall of 1967 and it was promptly rejected with a form note . . . no comment of any kind. Hurt and depressed, sure that the book must really be terrible, I stuck it into the fabled TRUNK, which all novelists, both published and aspiring, carry around. I never submitted it again until Elaine Geiger at New American Library asked if "Dicky" (as we called him) was going to follow up *Rage*. *The Long Walk* went in the TRUNK, but as Bob Dylan says in "Tangled Up in Blue," it never escaped my mind.

None of them has ever escaped my mind—not even the really bad ones.

6

The numbers have gotten very big. That's part of it. I have times when I feel as if I planted a modest packet of words and grew some kind of magic beanstalk . . .or a runaway garden of books (OVER 40 MILLION KING BOOKS IN PRINT!!!, as my publisher likes to trumpet). Or, put it another way—sometimes I feel like Mickey Mouse in *Fantasia*. I knew enough to get the brooms started, but once they start to march, things are never the same.

Am I bitching? No. At least they're very gentle bitches if I am. I have tried my best to follow that other Dylan's advice and sing in my chains like the sea. I mean, I could get down there in the amen corner and crybaby about how tough it is to be Stephen King, but somehow I don't think all those people out there who are a) unemployed or b) busting heavies every week just to keep even with the house payments and the MasterCharge bill would feel a lot of sympathy for me. Nor would I expect it. I'm still married to the same woman, my kids are healthy and bright, and I'm being well paid for doing something I love. So what's to bitch about?

Nothing.

Almost.

7

Memo to Paul McCartney, if he's there: the interviewer was right. They would have recognized your voices, but before you even opened your mouths, they would have recognized George's guitar licks. I did five books as Randy and the Rockets and I've been getting letters asking me if I was Richard Bachman from the very beginning.

My response to this was simplicity itself: I lied.

8

I think I did it to turn the heat down a little bit; to do something as someone other than Stephen King. I think that all novelists are inveterate role-players and it was fun to be someone else for a while—in this case, Richard Bachman. And he *did* develop a personality and a history to go along with the bogus author photo on the back of *Thinner* and the bogus wife (Claudia Inez Bachman) to whom the book is dedicated. Bachman was a fairly unpleasant fellow who was born in New York and spent about ten years in the merchant marine after four years in the Coast Guard. He ultimately settled in rural central New Hampshire, where he wrote at night and tended to his medium-sized dairy farm during the day. The Bachmans had one child, a boy, who died in an unfortunate accident at the age of six (he fell through a well cover and drowned). Three years ago a brain tumor was discovered near the base of Bachman's brain; tricky surgery removed it. And he died suddenly in February of 1985 when the Bangor *Daily News,* my hometown paper, published the story that I was Bachman—a story which I confirmed. Sometimes it was fun to be Bachman, a curmudgeonly recluse à la J. D. Salinger, who never gave interviews and who, on the author questionnaire from New English Library in London, wrote down ''rooster worship'' in the blank provided for religion.

9

I've been asked several times if I did it because I thought I was overpublishing the market as Stephen King. The answer is no. I didn't think I was overpublishing the market . . . but my publishers did. Bachman provided a compromise for both of us. My ''Stephen King publishers'' were like a frigid wifey who only wants to put out once or twice a year, encouraging her endlessly horny hubby to find a call girl. Bachman was where I went when I had to have relief. This does nothing, however, to explain why I've felt this restless need to *publish* what I write when I don't need the dough.

I repeat, good thing I didn't kill someone, huh?

10

I've been asked several times if I did it because I feel typecast as a horror writer. The answer is no. I don't give a shit what people call me as long as I can go to sleep at night.

Nevertheless, only the last of the Bachman books is an out-and-out horror story, and the fact hasn't escaped me. Writing something that was not horror as Stephen King would be perfectly easy, but answering the questions about why I did it would be a pain in the ass. When I wrote straight fiction as Richard Bachman, no one asked the questions. In fact, ha-ha, hardly anyone read the books.

Which leads us to what might be—well, not the reason why that voice spoke up in the first place, but the closest thing to it.

11

You try to make sense of your life. Everybody tries to do that, I think, and part of making sense of things is trying to find reasons . . . or constants . . . things that don't fluctuate.

Everyone does it, but perhaps people who have extraordinarily lucky or unlucky lives do it a little more. Part of you wants to think—or must as least speculate— that you got whopped with the cancer stick because you were one of the bad guys (or one of the good ones, if you believe Durocher's Law). Part of you wants to think that you must have been one hardworking S.O.B. or a real prince or maybe even one of the Sainted Multitude if you end up riding high in a world where people are starving, shooting each other, burning out, bumming out, getting loaded, getting 'Luded.

But there's another part that suggests it's all a lottery, a real-life game-show not much different from "Wheel of Fortune" or "The New Price Is Right" (two of the Bachman books, incidentally, are about game-show-type competitions). It is for some reason depressing to think it was all—or even mostly—an accident. So maybe you try to find out if you could do it again.

Or in my case, if *Bachman* could do it again.

12

The question remains unanswered. Richard Bachman's first four books did not sell well at all, perhaps partly because they were issued without fanfare.

Each month paperback houses issue three types of books: "leaders," which are heavily advertised, stocked in dump-bins (the trade term for those showy cardboard displays you see at the front of your local chain bookstore), and which usually feature fancy covers that have been either die-cut or stamped with foil;"sub-leaders," which are less heavily advertised, less apt to be awarded dump-bins, and less expected to sell millions of copies (two hundred thousand copies sold would be one hell of a good showing for a sub-leader); and just plain books. This third category is the paperback book publishing world's equivalent of trench warfare . . . or cannon fodder. "Just plain books" (the only other term I can think of is sub-sub-leaders, but that is *really* depressing) are rarely hardcover reprints; they are generally backlist books with new covers, genre novels (gothics, Regency romances, westerns, and so on), or series books such as The Survivalist, The Mercenaries, The Sexual Adventures of a Horny Pumpkin . . . you get the idea. And, every now and then, you find genuine *novels* buried in this deep substratum, and the Bachman novels are not the only time such novels have been the work of well-known writers sending out dispatches from deep cover. Donald Westlake published paperback originals under the names Tucker Coe and Richard Stark; Evan Hunter under the name Ed McBain; Gore Vidal under the name Edgar Box. More recently Gordon Lish published an excellent, eerie paperback original called *The Stone Boy* under a pseudonym.

The Bachman novels were "just plain books," paperbacks to fill the drugstore and bus-station racks of America. This was at my request; I wanted Bachman to keep a low profile. So, in that sense, the poor guy had the dice loaded against him from the start.

And yet, little by little, Bachman gained a dim cult following. His final book, *Thinner,* had sold about 28,000 copies in hardcover before a Washington bookstore clerk and writer named Steve Brown got suspicious, went to the Library of Congress, and uncovered my name on one of the Bachman copyright forms. Twenty-eight thousand copies isn't a lot—it's certainly not in best-seller territory—but it's 4,000 copies more than my book *Night Shift* sold in 1978. I had intended Bachman to follow *Thinner* with a rather gruesome suspense novel called *Misery,* and I think that one might have taken "Dicky" onto the best-seller lists. Of course we'll never know now, will we? Richard Bachman, who survived the brain tumor, finally died of a much rarer disease—cancer of the pseudonym. He died with that question—is it work that takes you to the top or is it all just a lottery? —still unanswered.

But the fact that *Thinner* did 28,000 copies when Bachman was the author and *280,000* copies when *Steve King* became the author, might tell you something, huh?

13

There is a stigma attached to the idea of the pen name. This was not so in the past; there was a time when the writing of novels was believed to be a rather low occupation, perhaps more vice than profession, and a pen name thus seemed a perfectly natural and respectable way of protecting one's self (and one's relatives) from embarrassment. As respect for the art of the novel rose, things changed. Both critics and general readers became suspicious of work done by men and women who elected to hide their identities. *If it was good,* the unspoken opinion seems to run, *the guy would have put his real name on it. If he lied about his name, the book must suck like an Electrolux.*

So I want to close by saying just a few words about the worth of these books. Are they good novels? I don't know. Are they honest novels? Yes, I think so. They were honestly meant, anyway, and written with an energy I can only dream about these days *(The Running Man,* for instance, was written during a period of seventy-two hours and published with virtually no changes). Do they suck like an Electrolux? Overall, no. In places . . . wellll . . .

I was not quite young enough when these stories were written to be able to dismiss them as juvenilia. On the other hand, I was still callow enough to believe in oversimple motivations (many of them painfully Freudian) and unhappy endings. The most recent of the Bachman books offered here, *Roadwork,* was written between *'Salem's Lot* and *The Shining,* and was an effort to write a "straight" novel. (I was also young enough in those days to worry about that casual cocktail-party question, "Yes, but when are you going to do something *serious?")* I think it was also an effort to make some sense of my mother's painful death the year before—a lingering cancer had taken her off inch by painful inch. Following this death I was left both grieving and shaken by the apparent senselessness of it all. I suspect *Roadwork* is probably the worst of the lot simply because it tries so hard to be good and to find some answers to the conundrum of human pain.

The reverse of this is *The Running Man,* which may be the best of them because it's nothing but story—it moves with the goofy speed of a silent movie, and anything which is *not* story is cheerfully thrown over the side.

Both *The Long Walk* and *Rage* are full of windy psychological preachments (both textual and subtextual), but there's still a lot of story in those novels—ultimately the reader will be better equipped than the writer to decide if the story is enough to surmount all the failures of perception and motivation.

I'd only add that two of these novels, perhaps even all four, might have been published under my own name if I had been a little more savvy about the publishing business or if I hadn't been preoccupied in the years they were written with first trying to get myself through school and then to support my family. And that I only published them (and am allowing them to be republished now) because they are still my friends; they are undoubtedly maimed in some ways, but they still seem very much alive to me.

14

And a few words of thanks: to Elaine Koster, NAL's publisher (who was Elaine Geiger when these books were first published), who kept "Dicky's" secret so long and successfully; to Carolyn Stromberg, "Dicky's" first editor, who did the same; to Kirby McCauley, who sold the rights and also kept the secret faithfully and well; to my wife, who encouraged me with these just as she did with the others that turned out to be such big and glittery money-makers; and, as always, to you, reader, for your patience and kindness.

Stephen King
Bangor, Maine

SIGNET•451-W7645•$1.50

RAGE

A NOVEL BY
RICHARD BACHMAN

HIS TWISTED MIND TURNED
A QUIET CLASSROOM INTO A
DANGEROUS WORLD OF TERROR.

For Susan Artz
and WGT

So you understand that when we
increase the number of variables,
the axioms themselves never change.
　　　　　—Mrs. Jean Underwood

Teacher, teacher, ring the bell,
My lessons all to you I'll tell,
And when my day at school is through,
I'll know more than aught I knew.
　　　　　—Children's rhyme, c. 1880

Chapter 1

The morning I got it on was nice; a nice May morning. What made it nice was that I'd kept my breakfast down, and the squirrel I spotted in Algebra II.

I sat in the row farthest from the door, which is next to the windows, and I spotted the squirrel on the lawn. The lawn of Placerville High School is a very good one. It does not fuck around. It comes right up to the building and says howdy. No one, at least in my four years at PHS, has tried to push it away from the building with a bunch of flowerbeds or baby pine trees or any of that happy horseshit. It comes right up to the concrete foundation, and there it grows, like it or not. It is true that two years ago at a town meeting some bag proposed that the town build a pavilion in front of the school, complete with a memorial to honor the guys who went to Placerville High and then got bumped off in one war or another. My friend Joe McKennedy was there, and he said they gave her nothing but a hard way to go. I wish I had been there. The way Joe told it, it sounded like a real good time. Two years ago. To the best of my recollection, that was about the time I started to lose my mind.

Chapter 2

So there was the squirrel, running through the grass at 9:05 in the morning, not ten feet from where I was listening to Mrs. Underwood taking us back to the basics of algebra in the wake of a horrible exam that apparently no one had passed except me and Ted Jones. I was keeping an eye on him, I can tell you. The squirrel, not Ted.

On the board, Mrs. Underwood wrote this: $a = 16$. "Miss Cross," she said, turning back. "Tell us what that equation means, if you please."

"It means that a is sixteen," Sandra said. Meanwhile the squirrel ran back and forth in the grass, tail bushed out, black eyes shining bright as buckshot. A nice fat one. Mr. Squirrel had been keeping down more breakfasts than I lately, but this morning's was riding as light and easy as you please. I had no shakes, no acid stomach. I was riding cool.

"All right," Mrs. Underwood said. "Not bad. But it's not the end, is it? No. Would anyone care to elaborate on this fascinating equation?"

I raised my hand, but she called on Billy Sawyer. "Eight plus eight," he blurted.

"Explain."

"I mean it can be . . . " Billy fidgeted. He ran his fingers over the graffiti etched into the surface of his desk; SM L DK, HOT SHIT, TOMMY '73. "See, if you add eight and eight, it means . . . "

"Shall I lend you my thesaurus?" Mrs. Underwood asked, smiling alertly. My stomach began to hurt a little, my breakfast started to move around a little, so I looked back at the squirrel for a while. Mrs. Underwood's smile reminded me of the shark in *Jaws*.

Carol Granger raised her hand. Mrs. Underwood nodded. "Doesn't he mean that eight plus eight also fulfills the equation's need for truth?"

"I don't know *what* he means," Mrs. Underwood said.

A general laugh. "Can you fulfill the equation's truth in any other ways, Miss Granger?"

Carol began, and that was when the intercom said: "Charles Decker to the office, please. Charles Decker. Thank you."

I looked at Mrs. Underwood, and she nodded. My stomach had begun to feel shriveled and old. I got up and left the room. When I left, the squirrel was still scampering.

I was halfway down the hall when I thought I heard Mrs. Underwood coming after me, her hands raised into twisted claws, smiling her big shark smile. *We don't need boys of your type around here . . . boys of your type belong in Greenmantle . . . or the reformatory . . . or the state hospital for the criminally insane . . . so get out! Get out! Get out!*

I turned around, groping in my back pocket for the pipe wrench that was no longer there, and now my breakfast was a hard hot ball inside my guts. But I wasn't afraid, not even when she wasn't there. I've read too many books.

Chapter 3

I stopped in the bathroom to take a whiz and eat some Ritz crackers. I always carry some Ritz crackers in a Baggie. When your stomach's bad, a few crackers can do wonders. One hundred thousand pregnant women can't be wrong. I was thinking about Sandra Cross, whose response in class a few minutes ago had been not bad, but also not the end. I was thinking about how she lost her buttons. She was always losing them—off blouses, off skirts, and the one time I had taken her to a school dance, she had lost the button off the top of her Wranglers and they had almost fallen down. Before she figured out what was happening, the zipper on the front of her jeans had come halfway unzipped, showing a V of flat white panties that was blackly exciting. Those panties were tight, white, and spotless. They were immaculate. They lay against her lower belly with sweet snugness and made little ripples while she moved her body to the beat . . . until she realized what was going on and dashed for the girls' room. Leaving me with a memory of the Perfect Pair of Panties. Sandra was a Nice Girl, and if I had never known it before, I sure-God knew it then, because we all know that the Nice Girls wear the white panties. None of that New York shit is going down in Placerville, Maine.

But Mr. Denver kept creeping in, pushing away Sandra and her pristine panties. You can't stop your mind; the damn thing just keeps right on going. All the same, I felt a great deal of sympathy for Sandy, even though she was never going to figure out just what the quadratic equation was all about. If Mr. Denver and Mr. Grace decided to send me to Greenmantle, I might never see Sandy again. And that would be too bad.

I got up from the hopper, dusted the cracker crumbs down into the bowl, and flushed it. High-school toilets are all the same; they sound like 747s taking off. I've always hated pushing that handle. It makes you sure that the sound is clearly audible in the adjacent classroom and that everybody is thinking: Well, there goes another load. I've always thought a man should be alone with what my mother insisted I call lemonade and chocolate when I was a little kid. The bathroom should be a confessional sort of place. But they foil you. They always foil you. You can't even blow your nose and keep it a secret. Someone's always got to know, someone's always got to peek. People like Mr. Denver and Mr. Grace even get paid for it.

But by then the bathroom door was wheezing shut behind me and I was in the hall again. I paused, looking around. The only sound was the sleepy hive drone that means it's Wednesday again, Wednesday morning, ten past nine, everyone caught for another day in the splendid sticky web of Mother Education.

I went back into the bathroom and took out my Flair. I was going to write something witty on the wall like SANDRA CROSS WEARS WHITE UNDERPANTS, and then I caught sight of my face in the mirror. There were bruised half-moons under my eyes, which looked wide and white and stary. The nostrils were half-flared and ugly. The mouth was a white, twisted line.

I wrote EAT SHIT on the wall until the pen suddenly snapped in my straining fingers. It dropped on the floor and I kicked it.

There was a sound behind me. I didn't turn around. I closed my eyes and breathed slowly and deeply until I had myself under control. Then I went upstairs.

Chapter 4

The administration offices of Placerville High are on the third floor, along with the study hall, the library, and Room 300, which is the typing room. When you push through the door from the stairs, the first thing you hear is that steady clickety-clack. The only time it lets up is when the bell changes the classes or when Mrs. Green has something to say. I guess she usually doesn't say much, because the typewriters hardly ever stop. There are thirty of them in there, a battle-scarred platoon of gray Underwoods. They have them marked with numbers so you know which one is yours. The sound never stops, clickety-clack, clickety-clack, from September to June. I'll always associate that sound with waiting in the outer office of the admin offices for Mr. Denver or Mr. Grace, the original dipso duo. It got to be a lot like those jungle movies where the hero and his safari are pushing deep into darkest Africa, and the hero says: "Why don't they stop those blasted drums?" And when the blasted drums stop he regards the shadowy, rustling foliage and says: "I don't like it. It's too quiet."

I had gotten to the office late just so Mr. Denver would be ready to see me, but the receptionist, Miss Marble, only smiled and said, "Sit down, Charlie. Mr. Denver will be right with you."

So I sat down outside the slatted railing, folded my hands, and waited for Mr. Denver to be right with me. And who should be in the other chair but one of my father's good friends, Al Lathrop. He was giving me the old slick-eye, too, I can tell you. He had a briefcase on his lap and a bunch of sample textbooks beside him. I had never seen him in a suit before. He and my father were a couple of mighty hunters. Slayers of the fearsome sharp-toothed deer and the killer partridge. I had been on a hunting trip once with my father and Al and a couple of my father's other friends. Part of Dad's never-ending campaign to Make a Man Out of My Son.

"Hi, there!" I said, and gave him a big shiteating grin. And I could tell from the way he jumped that he knew all about me.

"Uh, hi, uh, Charlie." He glanced quickly at Miss Marble, but she was going over attendance lists with Mrs. Venson from next door. No help there. He was all alone with Carl Decker's psychotic son, the fellow who had nearly killed the chemistry-physics teacher.

"Sales trip, huh?" I asked him.

"Yeah, that's right." He grinned as best he could. "Just out there selling the old books."

"Really crushing the competition, huh?"

He jumped again. "Well, you win some, you lose some, you know, Charlie."

12

Yeah, I knew that. All at once I didn't want to put the needle in him anymore. He was forty and getting bald and there were crocodile purses under his eyes. He went from school to school in a Buick station wagon loaded with textbooks and he went hunting for a week in November every year with my father and my father's friends, up in the Allagash. And one year I had gone with them. I had been nine, and I woke up and they had been drunk and they had scared me. That was all. But this man was no ogre. He was just forty-baldish and trying to make a buck. And if I had heard him saying he would murder his wife, that was just talk. After all, I was the one with blood on my hands.

But I didn't like the way his eyes were darting around, and for a moment—just a moment—I could have grabbed his windpipe between my hands and yanked his face up to mine and screamed into it: *You and my father and all your friends, you should all have to go in there with me, you should all have to go to Greenmantle with me, because you're all in it, you're all in it, you're all a part of this!*

Instead I sat and watched him sweat and thought about old times.

Chapter 5

I came awake with a jerk out of a nightmare I hadn't had for a long time; a dream where I was in some dark blind alley and something was coming for me, some dark hunched monster that creaked and dragged itself along . . . a monster that would drive me insane if I saw it. Bad dream. I hadn't had it since I was a little kid, and I was a big kid now. Nine years old.

At first I didn't know where I was, except it sure wasn't my bedroom at home. It seemed too close, and it smelled different. I was cold and cramped, and I had to take a whiz something awful.

There was a harsh burst of laughter that made me jerk in my bed—except it wasn't a bed, it was a bag.

"So she's some kind of fucking bag," Al Lathrop said from beyond the canvas wall, "but *fucking's* the operant word there."

Camping, I was camping with my dad and his friends. I hadn't wanted to come.

"Yeah, but how do you git it up, Al? That's what I want to know." That was Scotty Norwiss, another one of Dad's friends. His voice was slurred and furry, and I started to feel afraid again. They were drunk.

"I just turn off the lights and pretend I'm with Carl Decker's wife," Al said, and there was another bellow of laughter that made me cringe and jerk in my sleeping bag. Oh, God, I needed to whiz piss make lemonade whatever you wanted to call it. But I didn't want to go out there while they were drinking and talking.

I turned to the tent wall and discovered I could see them. They were between the tent and the campfire, and their shadows, tall and alien-looking, were cast on the canvas. It was like watching a magic lantern show. I watched the shadow-bottle go from one shadow-hand to the next.

"You know what I'd do if I caught you with my wife?" My dad asked Al.

"Probably ask if I needed any help," Al said, and there was another burst of laughter. The elongated shadow-heads on the tent wall bobbed up and down, back and forth, with insectile glee. They didn't look like people at all. They looked like a bunch of talking praying mantises, and I was afraid.

"No, seriously," my dad said. "Seriously. You know what I'd do if I caught somebody with my wife?"

"What, Carl?" That was Randy Earl.

"You see this?"

A new shadow on the canvas. My father's hunting knife, the one he carried out in the woods, the one I later saw him gut a deer with, slamming it into the deer's guts to the hilt and then ripping upward, the muscles in his forearm bulging, spill-

14

ing out green and steaming intestines onto a carpet of needles and moss. The fire-light and the angle of the canvas turned the hunting knife into a spear.

"You see this son of a bitch? I catch some guy with my wife, I'd whip him over on his back and cut off his accessories."

"He'd pee sitting down to the end of his days, right, Carl?" That was Hubie Levesque, the guide. I pulled my knees up to my chest and hugged them. I've never had to go to the bathroom so bad in my life, before or since.

"You're goddamn right," Carl Decker, my sterling Dad, said.

"Wha' about the woman in the case, Carl?" Al Lathrop asked. He was very drunk. I could even tell which shadow was his. He was rocking back and forth as if he was sitting in a rowboat instead of on a log by the campfire. "Thass what I wanna know. What do you do about a woman who less—lets—someone in the back door? Huh?"

The hunting knife that had turned into a spear moved slowly back and forth. My father said, "The Cherokees used to slit their noses. The idea was to put a cunt right up on their faces so everyone in the tribe could see what part of them got them in trouble."

My hands left my knees and slipped down to my crotch. I cupped my testicles and looked at the shadow of my father's hunting knife moving slowly back and forth. There were terrible cramps in my belly. I was going to whiz in my sleeping bag if I didn't hurry up and go.

"Slit their noses, huh?" Randy said. "That's pretty goddamn good. If they still did that, half the women in Placerville would have a snatch at both ends."

"Not my wife," my father said very quietly, and now the slur in his voice was gone, and the laughter at Randy's joke stopped in mid-roar.

"No, 'course not, Carl," Randy said uncomfortably. "Hey, shit. Have a drink."

My father's shadow tipped the bottle back.

"I wun't slit her nose," Al Lathrop said. "I'd blow her goddamn cheatin' head off."

"There you go," Hubie said. "I'll drink to it."

I couldn't hold it anymore. I squirmed out of the sleeping bag and felt the cold October air bite into my body, which was naked except for a pair of shorts. It seemed like my cock wanted to shrivel right back into my body. And the one thing that kept going around and around in my mind—I was still partly asleep, I guess, and the whole conversation had seemed like a dream, maybe a continuation of the creaking monster in the alley—was that when I was smaller, I used to get into my mom's bed after Dad had put on his uniform and gone off to work in Portland, I used to sleep beside her for an hour before breakfast.

Dark, fear, firelight, shadows like praying mantises. I didn't want to be out in these woods seventy miles from the nearest town with these drunk men. I wanted my mother.

I came out through the tent flap, and my father turned toward me. The hunting knife was still in his hand. He looked at me, and I looked at him. I've never forgotten that, my dad with a reddish beard stubble on his face and a hunting cap cocked on his head and that hunting knife in his hand. All the conversation stopped. Maybe they were wondering how much I had heard. Maybe they were even ashamed.

"What the hell do you want?" my dad asked, sheathing the knife.

"Give him a drink, Carl," Randy said, and there was a roar of laughter. Al laughed so hard he fell over. He was pretty drunk.

"I gotta whiz," I said.

"Then go do it, for Christ's sake," my dad said.

I went over in the grove and tried to whiz. For a long time it wouldn't come out. It was like a hot soft ball of lead in my lower belly. I had nothing but a fingernail's length of penis—the cold had really shriveled it. At last it did come, in a great steaming flood, and when it was all out of me, I went back into the tent and got in my sleeping bag. None of them looked at me. They were talking about the war. They had all been in the war.

My dad got his deer three days later, on the last day of the trip. I was with him. He got it perfectly, in the bunch of muscle between neck and shoulder, and the buck went down in a heap, all grace gone.

We went over to it. My father was smiling, happy. He had unsheathed his knife. I knew what was going to happen, and I knew I was going to be sick, and I couldn't help any of it. He planted a foot on either side of the buck and pulled one of its legs back and shoved the knife in. One quick upward rip, and its guts spilled out on the forest floor, and I turned around and heaved up my breakfast.

When I turned back to him, he was looking at me. He never said anything, but I could read the contempt and disappointment in his eyes. I had seen it there often enough. I didn't say anything either. But if I had been able to, I would have said: *It isn't what you think.*

That was the first and last time I ever went hunting with my dad.

Chapter 6

Al Lathrop was still thumbing through his textbook samples and pretending he was too busy to talk to me when the intercom on Miss Marble's desk buzzed, and she smiled at me as if we had a great and sexy secret. "You can go in now, Charlie."

I got up. "Sell those textbooks, Al."

He gave me a quick, nervous, insincere smile. "I sure will, uh, Charlie."

I went through the slatted gate, past the big safe set into the wall on the right and Miss Marble's cluttered desk on the left. Straight ahead was a door with a frosted glass pane. THOMAS DENVER PRINCIPAL was lettered on the glass. I walked in.

Mr. Denver was looking at *The Bugle,* the school rag. He was a tall, cadaverous man who looked something like John Carradine. He was bald and skinny. His hands were long and full of knuckles. His tie was pulled down, and the top button of his shirt was undone. The skin on his throat looked grizzled and irritated from overshaving.

"Sit down, Charlie."

I sat down and folded my hands. I'm a great old hand-folder. It's a trick I picked up from my father. Through the window behind Mr. Denver I could see the lawn, but not the fearless way it grew right up to the building. I was too high, and it was too bad. It might have helped, like a night-light when you are small.

Mr. Denver put *The Bugle* down and leaned back in his chair. "Kind of hard to see that way, isn't it?" He grunted. Mr. Denver was a crackerjack grunter. If there was a National Grunting Bee, I would put all my money on Mr. Denver. I brushed my hair away from my eyes.

There was a picture of Mr. Denver's family on his desk, which was even more cluttered than Miss Marble's. The family looked well-fed and well-adjusted. His wife was sort of porky, but the two kids were as cute as buttons and didn't look a bit like John Carradine. Two little girls, both blond.

"Don Grace has finished his report, and I've had it since last Thursday, considering his conclusions and his recommendations as carefully as I can. We all appreciate the seriousness of this matter, and I've taken the liberty of discussing the whole thing with John Carlson, also."

"How is he?" I asked.

"Pretty well. He'll be back in a month, I should think."

"Well, that's something."

"It is?" He blinked at me very quickly, the way lizards do.

"I didn't kill him. That's something."

17

"Yes." Mr. Denver looked at me steadily. "Do you wish you had?"

"No."

He leaned forward, drew his chair up to his desk, looked at me, shook his head, and began, "I'm very puzzled when I have to speak the way I'm about to speak to you, Charlie. Puzzled and sad. I've been in the kid business since 1947, and I still can't understand these things. I feel what I have to say to you is right and necessary, but it also makes me unhappy. Because I still can't understand why a thing like this happens. In 1959 we had a very bright boy here who beat a junior-high-school girl quite badly with a baseball bat. Eventually we had to send him to South Portland Correctional Institute. All he could say was that she wouldn't go out with him. Then he would smile." Mr. Denver shook his head.

"Don't bother."

"What?"

"Don't bother trying to understand. Don't lose any sleep over it."

"But why, Charlie? Why did you do that? My God, he was on an operating table for nearly four hours—"

"*Why* is Mr. Grace's question," I said. "He's the school shrink. You, you only ask it because it makes a nice lead-in to your sermon. I don't want to listen to any more sermons. They don't mean *shit* to me. It's *over*. He was going to live or die. He lived. I'm glad. You do what you have to do. What you and Mr. Grace decided to do. But don't you try to understand me."

"Charlie, understanding is part of my job."

"But helping you do your job isn't part of mine," I said. "So let me tell you one thing. To sort of help open the lines of communication, okay?"

"Okay."

I held my hands tightly in my lap. They were trembling. "I'm sick of you and Mr. Grace and all the rest of you. You used to make me afraid and you still make me afraid but now you make me tired too, and I've decided I don't have to put up with that. The way I am, I can't put up with that. What you think doesn't mean anything to me. You're not qualified to deal with me. So just stand back. I'm warning you. You're not qualified."

My voice had risen to a trembling near-shout.

Mr. Denver sighed.

"So you may think, Charlie. But the laws of the state say otherwise. After having read Mr. Grace's report, I think I agree with him that you don't understand yourself or the consequences of what you did in Mr. Carlson's classroom. You are disturbed, Charlie."

You are disturbed, Charlie.

The Cherokees used to slit their noses . . . so everyone in the tribe could see what part of them got them in trouble.

The words echoed greenly in my head, as if at great depths. They were shark words at deep fathoms, jaws words come to gobble me. Words with teeth and eyes.

This is where I started to get it on. I knew it, because the same thing that happened just before I gave Mr. Carlson the business was happening now. My hands stopped shaking. My stomach flutters subsided, and my whole middle felt cool and calm. I felt detached, not only from Mr. Denver and his overshaved neck, but from myself. I could almost float.

Mr. Denver had gone on, something about proper counseling and psychiatric help, but I interrupted him. "Mr. Man, you can go straight to hell."

He stopped and put down the paper he had been looking at so he wouldn't have to look at me. Something from my file, no doubt. The almighty file. The Great American File.

"What?" he said.

"In hell. Judge not, lest ye be judged. Any insanity in your family, Mr. Denver?"

I'll *discuss* this with you, Charlie," he said tightly. "I won't engage in—"

" . . . immoral sex practices," I finished for him. "Just you and me, okay? First one to jack off wins the Putnam Good Fellowship Award. Fill yore hand, pardner. Get Mr. Grace in here, that's even better. We'll have a circle jerk."

"Wh—"

"Don't you get the message? You have to pull it out sometime, right? You owe it to yourself, right? Everybody has to get it on, everybody has to have someone to jack off on. You've already set yourself up as Judge of What's Right for Me. Devils. Demon possession. Why did I hit dat l'il girl wit dat ball bat, Lawd, Lawd? De debbil made me do it, and I'm so *saw-ry*. Why don't you admit it? You get a kick out of peddling my flesh. I'm the best thing that's happened to you since 1959."

He was gawping at me openly. I had him by the short hair, knew it, was savagely proud of it. On the one hand, he wanted to humor me, go along with me, because after all, isn't that what you do with disturbed people? On the other hand, he was in the kid business, just like he told me, and Rule One in the kid business is: Don't Let 'Em Give You No Lip—be fast with the command and the snappy comeback.

"Charlie—"

"Don't bother. I'm trying to tell you I'm tired of being masturbated on. Be a man, for God's sake, Mr. Denver. And if you can't be a man, at least pull up your pants and be a principal."

"Shut up," he grunted. His face had gone bright red. "You're just pretty damn lucky you live in a progressive state and go to a progressive school, young man. You know where you'd be otherwise? Peddling your papers in a reformatory somewhere, serving a term for criminal assault. I'm not sure you don't belong there anyway. You—"

"Thank you," I said.

He stared at me, his angry blue eyes fixed on mine.

"For treating me like a human being even if I had to piss you off to do it. That's real progress." I crossed my legs, being nonchalant. "Want to talk about the panty raids you made the scene at while you were at Big U learning the kid business?"

"Your mouth is filthy," he said deliberately. "And so is your mind."

"Fuck you," I said, and laughed at him.

He went an even deeper shade of scarlet and stood up. He reached slowly over the desk, slowly, slowly, as if he needed oiling, and bunched the shoulder of my shirt in his hand. "You show some respect," he said. He had really blown his cool and was not even bothering to use that really first-class grunt. "You rotten little punk, you show me some respect."

"I could show you my ass and you'd kiss it," I said. "Go on and tell me about the panty raids. You'll feel better. Throw us your panties! Throw us your panties!"

He let go of me, holding his hand away from his body as if a rabid dog had just pooped on it. "Get out," he said hoarsely. "Get your books, turn them in here, and then get out. Your expulsion and transfer to Greenmantle Academy is effective as of Monday. I'll talk to your parents on the telephone. Now get out. I don't want to have to look at you."

I got up, unbuttoned the two bottom buttons on my shirt, pulled the tail out on one side, and unzipped my fly. Before he could move, I tore open the door and staggered into the outer office. Miss Marble and Al Lathrop were conferring at her desk, and they both looked up and winced when they saw me. They had obviously both been playing the great American parlor game of We Don't Really Hear Them, Do We?

"You better get to him," I panted. "We were sitting there talking about panty raids and he just jumped over his desk and tried to rape me."

I'd pushed him over the edge, no mean feat, considering he'd been in the kid business for twenty-nine years and was probably only ten away from getting his gold key to the downstairs crapper. He lunged at me through the door; I danced away from him and he stood there looking furious, silly, and guilty all at once.

"Get somebody to take care of him," I said. "He'll be sweeter after he gets it out of his system." I looked at Mr. Denver, winked, and whispered, "Throw us your panties, right?"

Then I pushed out through the slatted rail and walked slowly out the office door, buttoning my shirt and tucking it in, zipping my fly. There was plenty of time for him to say something, but he didn't say a word.

That's when it really got rolling, because all at once I knew he *couldn't* say a word. He was great at announcing the day's hot lunch over the intercom, but this was a different thing—joyously different. I had confronted him with exactly what he said was wrong with me, and he hadn't been able to cope with that. Maybe he expected us to smile and shake hands and conclude my seven-and-one-half-semester stay at Placerville High with a literary critique of *The Bugle*. But in spite of everything, Mr. Carlson and all the rest, he hadn't really expected any irrational act. Those things were all meant for the closet, rolled up beside those nasty magazines you never show your wife. He was standing back there, vocal cords frozen, not a word left in his mind to say. None of his instructors in Dealing with the Disturbed Child, EdB-211, had ever told him he might someday have to deal with a student who would attack him on a personal level.

And pretty quick he was going to be mad. That made him dangerous. Who knew better than me? I was going to have to protect myself. I was ready, and had been ever since I decided that people might—just *might*, mind you—be following me around and checking up.

I gave him every chance.

I waited for him to charge out and grab me, all the way to the staircase. I didn't want salvation. I was either past that point or never reached it. All I wanted was recognition . . . or maybe for someone to draw a yellow plague circle around my feet.

He didn't come out.

And when he didn't, I went ahead and got it on.

Chapter 7

I went down the staircase whistling; I felt wonderful. Things happen that way sometimes. When everything is at its worst, your mind just throws it all into the wastebasket and goes to Florida for a little while. There is a sudden electric what-the-hell glow as you stand there looking back over your shoulder at the bridge you just burned down.

A girl I didn't know passed me on the second-floor landing, a pimply, ugly girl wearing big horn-rimmed glasses and carrying a clutch of secretarial-type books. On impulse I turned around and looked after her. Yes; yes. From the back she might have been Miss America. It was wonderful.

Chapter 8

The first-floor hall was deserted. Not a soul coming or going. The only sound was the hive drone, the sound that makes all the schoolhouses the same, modern and glass-walled or ancient and stinking of floor varnish. Lockers stood in silent sentinel rows, with a break here and there to make room for a drinking fountain or a classroom door.

Algebra II was in Room 16, but my locker was at the other end of the hall. I walked down to it and regarded it.

My locker. It said so: CHARLES DECKER printed neatly in my hand on a strip of school Con-Tact paper. Each September, during the first home-room period, came the handing out of the blank Con-Tact strips. We lettered carefully, and during the two-minute break between home room and the first class of the new year, we pasted them on. The ritual was as old and as holy as First Communion. On the first day of my sophomore year, Joe McKennedy walked up to me through the crowded hall with his Con-Tact strip pasted on his forehead and a big shiteating grin pasted on his mouth. Hundreds of horrified freshmen, each with a little yellow name tag pinned on his or her shirt or blouse, turned to look at this sacrilege. I almost broke my balls laughing. Of course he got a detention for it, but it made my day. When I think back on it, I guess it made my year.

And there I was, right between ROSANNE DEBBINS and CARLA DENCH, who doused herself in rosewater every morning, which had been no great help in keeping my breakfast where it belonged during the last semester.

Ah, but all that was behind me now.

Gray locker, five feet high, padlocked. The padlocks were handed out at the beginning of the year along with the Con-Tact strips. Titus, the padlock proclaimed itself. Lock me, unlock me. I am Titus, the Helpful Padlock.

"Titus, you old cuffer," I whispered. "Titus, you old cock-knocker."

I reached for Titus, and it seemed to me that my hand stretched to it across a thousand miles, a hand on the end of a plastic arm that elongated painlessly and nervelessly. The numbered surface of Titus' black face looked at me blandly, not condemning but certainly not *approving,* no, not *that,* and I shut my eyes for a moment. My body wrenched through a shudder, pulled by invisible, involuntary, opposing hands.

And when I opened my eyes again, Titus was in my grasp. The chasm had closed.

The combinations on high-school locks are simple. Mine was six to the left, thirty right, and two turns back to zero. Titus was known more for his strength

23

than his intellect. The lock snapped up, and I had him in my hand. I clutched him tightly, making no move to open the locker door.

Up the hall, Mr. Johnson was saying: " . . . and the Hessians, who were paid mercenaries, weren't any too anxious to fight, especially in a countryside where the opportunities for plunder over and above the agreed-upon wages . . . "

"Hessian," I whispered to Titus. I carried him down to the first wastebasket and dropped him in. He looked up at me innocently from a litter of discarded homework papers and old sandwich bags.

" . . . but remember that the Hessians, as far as the Continental Army knew, were formidable German killing machines . . . "

I bent down, picked him up, and put him in my breast pocket, where he made a bulge about the size of a pack of cigarettes.

"Keep it in mind, Titus, you old killing machine," I said, and went back to my locker.

I swung it open. Crumpled up in a sweaty ball at the bottom was my gym uniform, old lunch bags, candy wrappers, a month-old apple core that was browning nicely, and a pair of ratty black sneakers. My red nylon jacket was hung on the coathook, and on the shelf above that were my textbooks, all but Algebra II. Civics, American Government, French Stories and Fables, and Health, that happy Senior gut course, a red, modern book with a high-school girl and boy on the cover and the section on venereal disease neatly clipped by unanimous vote of the School Committee. I started to get it on beginning with the health book, sold to the school by none other than good old Al Lathrop, I hoped and trusted. I took it out, opened it somewhere between "The Building Blocks of Nutrition" and "Swimming Rules for Fun and Safety," and ripped it in two. It came easy. They all came easy except for Civics, which was a tough old Silver Burdett text circa 1946. I threw all the pieces into the bottom of the locker. The only thing left up top was my slide rule, which I snapped in two, a picture of Raquel Welch taped to the back wall (I let it stay), and the box of shells that had been behind my books.

I picked that up and looked at it. The box had originally held Winchester .22 long-rifle shells, but it didn't anymore. I'd put the other shells in it, the ones from the desk drawer in my father's study. There's a deer head mounted on the wall in his study, and it stared down at me with its glassy too-alive eyes as I took the shells and the gun, but I didn't let it bother me. It wasn't the one he'd gotten on the hunting trip when I was nine. The pistol had been in another drawer, behind a box of business envelopes. I doubt if he even remembered it was still there. And as a matter of fact, it wasn't, not anymore. Now it was in the pocket of my jacket. I took it out and shoved it into my belt. I didn't feel much like a Hessian. I felt like Wild Bill Hickok.

I put the shells in my pants pocket and took out my lighter. It was one of those Scripto see-through jobs. I don't smoke myself, but the lighter had kind of caught my fancy. I snapped a light to it, squatted, and set the crap in the bottom of my locker on fire.

The flames licked up greedily from my gym trunks to the lunch bags and candy wrappers to the ruins of my books, carrying a sweaty, athletic smell up to me.

Then, figuring that I had gotten it on as much as I could by myself, I shut the locker door. There were little vents just above where my name was Con-Tact-papered on, and through them I could hear the flames whooshing upward. In a minute little orange flecks were glaring in the darkness beyond the vents, and the gray locker paint started to crack and peel.

A kid came out of Mr. Johnson's room carrying a green bathroom pass. He looked at the smoke belching merrily out of the vents in my locker, looked at me, and hurried down to the bathroom. I don't think he saw the pistol. He wasn't hurrying that fast.

I started down to Room 16. I paused just as I got there, my hand on the door-knob, looking back. The smoke was really pouring out of the vents now, and a dark, sooty stain was spreading up the front of my locker. The Con-Tact paper had turned brown. You couldn't see the letters that made my name anymore.

I don't think there was anything in my brain right then except the usual background static—the kind you get on your radio when it's turned up all the way and tuned to no station at all. My brain had checked to the power, so to speak; the little guy wearing the Napoleon hat inside was showing aces and betting them.

I turned back to Room 16 and opened the door. I was hoping, but I didn't know what.

Chapter 9

" . . . So you understand that when we *increase* the number of variables, the axioms *themselves* never change. For example—"

Mrs. Underwood looked up alertly, pushing her harlequin glasses up on her nose. "Do you have an office pass, Mr. Decker?"

"Yes," I said, and took the pistol out of my belt. I wasn't even sure it was loaded until it went off. I shot her in the head. Mrs. Underwood never knew what hit her, I'm sure. She fell sideways onto her desk and then rolled onto the floor, and that expectant expression never left her face.

Chapter 10

Sanity:

You can go through your whole life telling yourself that life is logical, life is prosaic, life is sane. Above all, sane. And I think it is. I've had a lot of time to think about that. And what I keep coming back to is Mrs. Underwood's dying declaration: *So you understand that when we increase the number of variables, the axioms themselves never change.*

I really believe that.

I think; therefore I am. There are hairs on my face; therefore I shave. My wife and child have been critically injured in a car crash; therefore I pray. It's all logical, it's all sane. We live in the best of all possible worlds, so hand me a Kent for my left, a Bud for my right, turn on *Starsky and Hutch,* and listen to that soft, harmonious note that is the universe turning smoothly on its celestial gyros. Logic and sanity. Like Coca-Cola, it's the real thing.

But as Warner Brothers, John D. MacDonald, and Long Island Dragway know so well, there's a Mr. Hyde for every happy Jekyll face, a dark face on the other side of the mirror. The brain behind that face never heard of razors, prayers, or the logic of the universe. You turn the mirror sideways and see your face reflected with a sinister left-hand twist, half mad and half sane. The astronomers call that line between light and dark the terminator.

The other side says that the universe has all the logic of a little kid in a Halloween cowboy suit with his guts and his trick-or-treat candy spread all over a mile of Interstate 95. This is the logic of napalm, paranoia, suitcase bombs carried by happy Arabs, random carcinoma. This logic eats itself. It says life is a monkey on a stick, it says life spins as hysterically and erratically as the penny you flick to see who buys lunch.

No one looks at that side unless they have to, and I can understand that. You look at it if you hitch a ride with a drunk in a GTO who puts it up to one-ten and starts blubbering about how his wife turned him out; you look at it if some guy decides to drive across Indiana shooting kids on bicycles; you look at it if your sister says "I'm going down to the store for a minute, big guy" and then gets killed in a stickup. You look at it when you hear your dad talking about slitting your mom's nose.

It's a roulette wheel, but anybody who says the game is rigged is whining. No matter how many numbers there are, the principle of that little white jittering ball never changes. Don't say it's crazy. It's all so cool and sane.

And all that weirdness isn't just going on outside. It's in you too, right now,

27

growing in the dark like magic mushrooms. Call it the Thing in the Cellar. Call it the Blow Lunch Factor. Call it the Loony Tunes File. I think of it as my private dinosaur, huge, slimy, and mindless, stumbling around in the stinking swamp of my subconscious, never finding a tarpit big enough to hold it.

But that's me, and I started to tell you about *them,* those bright college-bound students that, metaphorically speaking, walked down to the store to get milk and ended up in the middle of an armed robbery. I'm a documented case, routine grist for the newspaper mill. A thousand newsboys hawked me on a thousand street corners. I had fifty seconds on Chancellor-Brinkley and a column and a half in *Time.* And I stand here before you (metaphorically speaking, again) and tell you I'm perfectly sane. I do have one slightly crooked wheel upstairs, but everything else is ticking along just four-o, thank you very much.

So, *them.* How do you understand *them?* We have to discuss that, don't we?

"Do you have an office pass, Mr. Decker?" she asked me.

"Yes," I said, and took the pistol out of my belt. I wasn't even sure it was loaded until it went off. I shot her in the head. Mrs. Underwood never knew what hit her, I'm sure. She fell sideways onto her desk and then rolled onto the floor, and that expectant expression never left her face.

I'm the sane one: I'm the croupier, I'm the guy who spins the ball against the spin of the wheel. The guy who lays his money on odd/even, the girl who lays her money on black/red . . . what about *them?*

There isn't any division of time to express the marrow of our lives, the time between the explosion of lead from the muzzle and the meat impact, between the impact and the darkness. There's only barren instant replay that shows nothing new.

I shot her; she fell; and there was an indescribable moment of silence, an infinite duration of time, and we all stepped back, watching the ball go around and around, ticking, bouncing, lighting for an instant, going on, heads and tails, red and black, odd and even.

I think that moment ended. I really do. But sometimes, in the dark, I think that hideous random moment is still going on, that the wheel is even yet in spin, and I dreamed all the rest.

What must it be like for a suicide coming down from a high ledge? I'm sure it must be a very sane feeling. That's probably why they scream all the way down.

Chapter 11

If someone had screamed something melodramatic at that precise moment, something like *Oh, my God, he's going to kill us all!* it would have been over right there. They would have bolted like sheep, and somebody aggressive like Dick Keene would have belted me over the head with his algebra book, thereby earning a key to the city and the Good Citizenship Award.

But nobody said a word. They sat in utter stunned silence, looking at me attentively, as if I had just announced that I was going to tell them how they could all get passes to the Placerville Drive-In this Friday night.

I shut the classroom door, crossed the room, and sat behind the big desk. My legs weren't so good. I was almost to the point of sit down or fall down. I had to push Mrs. Underwood's feet out of the way to get my own feet into the kneehole. I put the pistol down on her green blotter, shut her algebra book, and put it with the others that were stacked neatly on the desk's corner.

That was when Irma Bates broke the silence with a high, gobbling scream that sounded like a young tom turkey getting its neck wrung on the day before Thanksgiving. But it was too late; everyone had taken that endless moment to consider the facts of life and death. Nobody picked up on her scream, and she stopped, as if ashamed at screaming while school was in session, no matter how great the provocation. Somebody cleared his throat. Somebody in the back of the room said "Hum!" in a mildly judicial tone. And John "Pig Pen" Dano slithered quietly out of his seat and slumped to the floor in a dead faint.

They looked up at me from the trough of shock.

"This," I said pleasantly, "is known as getting it on."

Footsteps pounded down the hall, and somebody asked somebody else if something had exploded in the chemistry lab. While somebody else was saying he didn't know, the fire alarm went off stridently. Half the kids in the class started to get up automatically.

"That's all right," I said. "It's just my locker. On fire. I set it on fire, that is. Sit down."

The ones that had started to get up sat down obediently. I looked for Sandra Cross. She was in the third row, fourth seat, and she did not seem afraid. She looked like what she was. An intensely exciting Good Girl.

Lines of students were filing out onto the grass; I could see them through the windows. The squirrel was gone, though. Squirrels make lousy innocent bystanders.

29

The door was snatched open, and I picked up the gun. Mr. Vance poked his head in. "Fire alarm," he said. "Everybody . . . Where's Mrs. Underwood?"

"Get out," I said.

He stared at me. He was a very porky man, and his hair was neatly crew cut. It looked as if some landscape artist had trimmed it carefully with hedge clippers. "What? What did you say?"

"Out." I shot at him and missed. The bullet whined off the upper edge of the door, chipping wood splinters.

"Jesus," somebody in the front row said mildly.

Mr. Vance didn't know what was happening. I don't think any of them did. It all reminded me of an article I read about the last big earthquake in California. It was about a woman who was wandering from room to room while her house was being shaken to pieces all around her, yelling to her husband to please unplug the fan.

Mr. Vance decided to go back to the beginning. "There's a fire in the building. Please—"

"Charlie's got a gun, Mr. Vance," Mike Gavin said in a discussing-the-weather tone. "I think you better—"

The second bullet caught him in the throat. His flesh spread liquidly like water spreads when you throw a rock in it. He walked backward into the hall, scratching at his throat, and fell over.

Irma Bates screamed again, but again she had no takers. If it had been Carol Granger, there would have been imitators galore, but who wanted to be in concert with poor old Irma Bates? She didn't even have a boyfriend. Besides, everyone was too busy peeking at Mr. Vance, whose scratching motions were slowing down.

"Ted," I said to Ted Jones, who sat closest to the door. "Shut that and lock it."

"What do you think you're doing?" Ted asked. He was looking at me with a kind of scared and scornful distaste.

"I don't know all the details just yet," I said. "But shut the door and lock it, okay?"

Down the hall someone was yelling: "It's in a locker! It's in a . . . Hey, Pete Vance's had a heart attack! Get some water! Get . . . "

Ted Jones got up, shut the door, and locked it. He was a tall boy wearing wash-faded Levi's and an army shirt with flap pockets. He looked very fine. I had always admired Ted, although he was never part of the circle I traveled in. He drove last year's Mustang, which his father had given him, and didn't get any parking tickets, either. He combed his hair in an out-of-fashion DA, and I bet his was the face that Irma Bates called up in her mind when she sneaked a cucumber out of the refrigerator in the wee hours of the night. With an all-American name like Ted Jones he couldn't very well miss, either. His father was vice-president of the Placerville Bank and Trust.

"Now what?" Harmon Jackson asked. He sounded bewildered.

"Um." I put the pistol down on the blotter again. "Well, somebody try and bring Pig Pen around. He'll get his shirt dirty. Dirtier, I mean."

Sarah Pasterne started to giggle hysterically and clapped her hand over her mouth. George Yannick, who sat close to Pig Pen, squatted down beside him and began to pat his cheeks. Pig Pen moaned, opened his eyes, rolled them, and said, "He shot Book Bags."

There were several hysterical laughs this time. They went off around the room like popping corn. Mrs. Underwood had two plastic briefcases with tartan patterns on them, which she carried into each class. She had also been known as Two-Gun Sue.

Pig Pen settled shakily into his seat, rolled his eyes again, and began to cry.

Somebody pounded up to the door, rattled the knob, and yelled, "Hey! Hey in there!" It looked like Mr. Johnson, who had been talking about the Hessians. I picked up the pistol and put a bullet through the chicken-wired glass. It made a neat little hole beside Mr. Johnson's head, and Mr. Johnson went out of sight like a crash-diving submarine. The class (with the possible exception of Ted) watched all the action with close interest, as if they had stumbled into a pretty good movie by accident.

"Somebody in there's got a gun!" Mr. Johnson yelled. There was a faint bumping sound as he crawled away. The fire alarm buzzed hoarsely on and on.

"Now what?" Harmon Jackson asked again. He was a small boy, usually with a big cockeyed grin on his face, but now he looked helpless, all at sea.

I couldn't think of an answer to that, so I let it pass. Outside, kids were milling restlessly around on the lawn, talking and pointing at Room 16 as the grapevine passed the word among them. After a little bit, some teachers—the men teachers— began shooing them back toward the gymnasium end of the building.

In town the fire whistle on the Municipal Building began to scream, rising and falling in hysterical cycles.

"It's like the end of the world," Sandra Cross said softly.

I had no answer for that, either.

Chapter 12

No one said anything for maybe five minutes—not until the fire engines got to the high school. They looked at me, and I looked at them. Maybe they still could have bolted, and they're still asking me why they didn't. *Why didn't they cut and run, Charlie? What did you do to them?* Some of them ask that almost fearfully, as if I had the evil eye. I don't answer them. I don't answer any questions about what happened that morning in Room 16. But if I told them anything, it would be that they've forgotten what it is to be a kid, to live cheek-by-jowl with violence, with the commonplace fistfights in the gym, brawls at the PAL hops in Lewiston, beatings on television, murders in the movies. Most of us had seen a little girl puke pea soup all over a priest right down at our local drive-in. Old Book Bags wasn't much shakes by comparison.

I'm not taking on any of those things, hey, I'm in no shape for crusades these days. I'm just telling you that American kids labor under a huge life of violence, both real and make-believe. Besides, I was kind of interesting: Hey, Charlie Decker went apeshit today, didja hear? No! Did he? Yeah. Yeah. I was there. It was just like *Bonnie and Clyde,* except Charlie's got zitzes and there wasn't any popcorn.

I know they thought they'd be all right. That's part of it. What I wonder about is this: Were they hoping I'd get somebody else?

Another shrieking sound had joined the fire siren, this one getting closer real fast. Not the cops. It was that hysterical yodeling note that is all the latest rage in ambulances and paramedic vehicles these days. I've always thought the day will come when all the disaster vehicles will get smart and stop scaring the almighty shit out of everyone they're coming to save. When there's a fire or an accident or a natural disaster like me, the red vehicles will rush to the scene accompanied by the amplified sound of the Darktown Strutters playing ''Banjo Rag.'' Someday. Oh, boy.

Chapter 13

Seeing as how it was the school, the town fire department went whole hog. The fire chief came first, gunning into the big semicircular school driveway in his blue bubble-topped Ford Pinto. Behind him was a hook-and-ladder trailing firemen like battle banners. There were two pumpers behind that.

"You going to let them in?" Jack Goldman asked.

"The fire's out there," I said. "Not in here."

"Did you shut ya locka door?" Sylvia Ragan asked. She was a big blond girl with great soft cardiganed breasts and gently rotting teeth.

"Yes."

"Prolly out already, then."

Mike Gavin looked at the scurrying firemen and snickered. "Two of 'em just ran into each other," he said. "Holy moly."

The two downed firemen untangled themselves, and the whole group was preparing to charge into the inferno when two suit-coated figures ran over to them. One was Mr. Johnson, the Human Submarine, and the other was Mr. Grace. They were talking hard and fast to the fire chief.

Great rolls of hose with shiny nozzles were being unreeled from the pumpers and dragged toward the front doors. The fire chief turned around and yelled, "Hold it!" They stood irresolutely on the lawn, their nozzles gripped and held out before them like comic brass phalluses.

The fire chief was still in conference with Mr. Johnson and Mr. Grace. Mr. Johnson pointed at Room 16. Thomas Denver, the Principal with the Amazing Overshaved Neck, ran over and joined the discussion. It was starting to look like a pitcher's mound conference in the last half of the ninth.

"I want to go home!" Irma Bates said wildly.

"Blow it out," I said.

The fire chief had started to gesture toward his knights again, and Mr. Grace shook his head angrily and put a hand on his shoulder. He turned to Denver and said something to him. Denver nodded and ran toward the main doors.

The chief was nodding reluctantly. He went back to his car, rummaged in the back seat, and came up with a really nice Radio Shack battery-powered bullhorn. I bet they had some real tussles back at the fire station about who got to use that. Today the chief was obviously pulling rank. He pointed it at the milling students.

"Please move away from the building. I repeat. Will you please move away from the building. Move up to the shoulder of the highway. Move up to the shoul-

33

der of the highway. We will have buses here to pick you up shortly. School is canceled for—''

Short, bewildered whoop.

''. . . for the remainder of the day. Now, please move away from the building.''

A bunch of teachers—both men and women this time—started herding them up toward the road. They were craning and babbling. I looked for Joe McKennedy but didn't see him anywhere.

''Is it all right to do homework?'' Melvin Thomas asked tremblingly. There was a general laugh. They seemed surprised to hear it.

''Go ahead.'' I thought for a moment and added: ''If you want to smoke, go ahead and do it.''

A couple of them grabbed for their pockets. Sylvia Ragan, doing her lady-of-the-manor bit, fished a battered pack of Camels delicately out of her purse and lit up with leisurely elegance. She blew out a plume of smoke and dropped her match on the floor. She stretched out her legs, not bothering overmuch with the nuisance of her skirt. She looked comfy.

There had to be more, though. I was getting along pretty well, but there had to be a thousand things I wasn't thinking of. Not that it mattered.

''If you've got a friend you want to sit next to, go ahead and change around. But don't try to rush at me or run out the door, please.''

A couple of kids changed next to their buddies, walking quickly and softly, but most of them just sat quiet. Melvin Thomas had opened his algebra book but couldn't seem to concentrate on it. He was staring at me glassily.

There was a faint metallic *chink!* from the upper corner of the room. Somebody had just opened the intercom system.

''Hello,'' Denver said. ''Hello, Room 16.''

''Hello,'' I said.

''Who's that?''

''Charlie Decker.''

Long pause. Finally: ''What's going on down there, Decker?''

I thought it over. ''I guess I'm going berserk,'' I said.

An even longer pause. Then, almost rhetorically: ''What have you done?''

I motioned at Ted Jones. He nodded back at me politely. ''Mr. Denver?''

''Who's that?''

''Ted Jones, Mr. Denver. Charlie has a gun. He's holding us hostage. He's killed Mrs. Underwood. And I think he killed Mr. Vance, too.''

''I'm pretty sure I did,'' I said.

''Oh,'' Mr. Denver said.

Sarah Pasterne giggled again.

''Ted Jones?''

''I'm here,'' Ted told him. He sounded very competent, Ted did, but at the same time distant. Like a first lieutenant who has been to college. You had to admire him.

''Who is in the classroom besides you and Decker?''

"Just a sec," I said. "I'll call the roll. Hold on."

I got Mrs. Underwood's green attendance book and opened it up. "Period two, right?"

"Yeah," Corky said.

"Okay. Here we go. Irma Bates?"

"I want to go *home!*" Irma screamed defiantly.

"She's here," I said. "Susan Brooks?"

"Here."

"Nancy Caskin?"

"Here."

I went through the rest of the roll. There were twenty-five names, and the only absentee was Peter Franklin.

"Has Peter Franklin been shot?" Mr. Denver asked quietly.

"He's got the measles," Don Lordi said. This brought on another attack of the giggles. Ted Jones frowned deeply.

"Decker?"

"Yes."

"Will you let them go?"

"Not right now," I said.

"Why?" There was dreadful concern, a dreadful heaviness in his voice, and for a second I almost caught myself feeling sorry for him. I crushed that quickly. It's like being in a big poker game. Here is this guy who has been winning big all night, he's got a pile of chips that's a mile-high, and all at once he starts to lose. Not a little bit, but a lot, and you want to feel bad for him and his falling empire. But you cram that back and bust him, or you take it in the eye.

So I said, "We haven't finished getting it on down here yet."

"What does that mean?"

"It means stick it," I said. Carol Granger's eyes got round.

"Decker—"

"Call me Charlie. All my friends call me Charlie."

"Decker—"

I held my hand up in front of the class and crossed the fingers in pairs. "If you don't call me Charlie, I'm going to shoot somebody."

Pause.

"Charlie?"

"That's better." In the back row, Mike Gavin and Dick Keene were covering grins. Some of the others weren't bothering to cover them. "You call me Charlie, and I'll call you Tom. That okay, Tom?"

Long, long pause.

"When will you let them go, Charlie? They haven't hurt you."

Outside, one of the town's three black-and-whites and a blue state-police cruiser had arrived. They parked across the road from the high school, and Jerry Kesserling, the chief since Warren Talbot had retired into the local Methodist cemetery in 1975, began directing traffic onto the Oak Hill Pond road.

"Did you hear me, Charlie?"

"Yes. But I can't tell you. I don't know. There are more cops coming, I guess."

"Mr. Wolfe called them," Mr. Denver said. "I imagine there will be a great deal more when they fully appreciate what's going on. They'll have tear gas and Mace, Dec . . . Charlie. Why make it hard on yourself and your classmates?"

"Tom?"

Grudgingly: "What?"

"You get your skinny cracked ass out there and tell them that the minute anyone shoots tear gas or anything else in here, I am going to make them sorry. You tell them to remember who's driving."

"Why? Why are you doing this?" He sounded angry and impotent and frightened. He sounded like a man who has just discovered there is no place left to pass the buck.

"I don't know," I said, "but it sure beats panty raids, Tom. And I don't think it actually concerns you. All I want you to do is trot back out there and tell them what I said. Will you do that, Tom?"

"I have no choice, do I?"

"No, that's right. You don't. And there's something else, Tom."

"What?" He asked it very hesitantly.

"I don't like you very much, Tom, as you have probably realized, but up to now you haven't had to give much of a rip *how* I felt. But I'm out of your filing cabinet now, Tom. Have you got it? I'm not just a record you can lock up at three in the afternoon. Have you got it?" My voice was rising into a scream. "HAVE YOU GOT THAT, TOM? HAVE YOU INTERNALIZED THAT PARTICULAR FACT OF LIFE?"

"Yes, Charlie," he said in a deadly voice. "I have it."

"No you don't, Tom. But you will. Before the day's over, we are going to understand all about the difference between people and pieces of paper in a file, and the difference between doing your job and getting jobbed. What do you think of that, Tommy, my man?"

"I think you're a sick boy, Decker."

"No, you think I'm a sick boy, *Charlie*. Isn't that what you meant to say, Tom?"

"Yes."

"Say it."

"I think you're a sick boy, Charlie." The mechanical, embarrassed rote of a seven-year-old.

"You've got some getting it on to do yourself, Tom. Now, get out there and tell them what I said."

Denver cleared his throat as if he had something else to say, and then the intercom clicked off. A little murmur went through the class. I looked them over very carefully. Their eyes were so cool and somehow detached (shock can do that: you're ejected like a fighter pilot from a humdrum dream of life to a grinding, overloaded slice of the *real* meat, and your brain refuses to make the adjustment; you can only free-fall and hope that sooner or later your chute will open), and a ghost of grammar school came back to me: *Teacher, teacher, ring the bell, My lessons all to you I'll tell, And when my day at school is through, I'll know more than aught I knew.*

I wondered what they were learning today; what I was learning. The yellow school buses had begun to appear, and our classmates were going home to enjoy the festivities on living-room TVs and pocket transistor radios; but in Room 16, education went on.

I rapped the butt of the pistol sharply on the desk. The murmur died. They were watching me as closely as I was watching them. Judge and jury, or jury and defendant? I wanted to cackle.

"Well," I said, "the shit has surely hit the fan. I think we need to talk a little."

"Private?" George Yannick asked. "Just you and us?" He had an intelligent, perky face, and he didn't look frightened.

"Yes."

"You better turn off that intercom, then."

"You bigmouth son of a bitch," Ted Jones said distinctly. George looked at him, wounded.

There was an uncomfortable silence while I got up and pushed the little lever below the speaker from TALK-LISTEN to LISTEN.

I went back and sat down again. I nodded at Ted. "I was thinking of it anyway," I lied. "You shouldn't take on so."

Ted didn't say anything, but he offered me a strange little grin that made me think he might have been wondering about how I might taste.

"Okay," I said to the class at large. "I may be crazy, but I'm not going to shoot anyone for discussing this thing with me. Believe it. Don't be afraid to shoot off your mouths. As long as we don't all talk at once." That didn't look as if it was going to be a problem. "To take the bull by the horns, is there anyone here who really thinks I'm going to just up and murder them?"

A few of them looked uneasy, but nobody said anything.

"Okay. Because I'm not. We're just going to sit around and bug the hell out of everybody."

"Yeah, you sure bugged the hell out of Mrs. Underwood," Ted said. He was still smiling his strange smile.

"I had to. I know that's hard to understand, but . . . I had to. It came down to that. And Mr. Vance. But I want everyone here to take it easy. No one is going to shoot the place up, so you don't have to worry."

Carol Granger raised her hand timidly. I nodded at her. She was smart, smart as a whip. Class president, and a cinch to speak a piece as valedictorian in June— "Our Responsibilities to the Black Race" or maybe "Hopes for the Future." She was already signed up for one of those big-league women's colleges where people always wonder how many virgins there are. But I didn't hold it against her.

"When *can* we go, Charlie?"

I sighed and shrugged my shoulders. "We'll just have to wait and see what happens."

"But my mother will be worried to death!"

"Why?" Sylvia Ragan asked. "She knows where you are, doesn't she?"

General laugh. Except for Ted Jones. He wasn't laughing, and I was going to have to watch that boy. He was still smiling his small, savage smile. He wanted badly to blow everything out of the water—obvious enough. But why? Insanity Prevention Merit Badge? Not enough. Adulation of the community in general—the boy who stood on the burning deck with his finger in the dike? It didn't seem his style. Handsome low profile was Ted's style. He was the only guy I knew who had quit the football team after three Saturdays of glory in his junior year. The guy who wrote sports for the local rag had called him the best running back Placerville High School had ever produced. But he had quit, suddenly and with no explanation. Amazing enough. What was more amazing was the fact that his popularity quotient hadn't lost a point. If anything, Ted became more the local BMOC than ever. Joe McKennedy, who had suffered through four years and one broken nose at left tackle, told me that the only thing Ted would say when the agonized coach demanded an explanation was that football seemed to be a pretty stupid game, and he (Ted) thought that he could find a better way to spend his time. You can see why I respected him, but I was damned if I knew why he wanted me in such a personal way. A little thought on the matter might have helped, but things were going awful fast.

"Are you nuts?" Harmon Jackson asked suddenly.

"I think I must be," I said. "Anyone who kills anyone else is nuts, in my book."

"Well, maybe you ought to give yourself up," Harmon said. "Get some help. A doctor. You know."

"You mean like that Grace?" Sylvia asked. "My God, that creepster. I had to go see him after I threw an inkwell at old lady Green. All he did was look up my dress and try to get me to talk about my sex life."

"Not that you've had any," Pat Fitzgerald said, and there was another laugh.

"And not that it's any business of his or yours," she said haughtily, dropped her cigarette on the floor, and mashed it.

"So what are we going to do?" Jack Goldman asked.

"Just get it on," I said. "That's all."

Out on the lawn, a second town police car had arrived. I guessed that the third one was probably down at Junior's Diner, taking on vital shipments of coffee and doughnuts. Denver was talking with a state trooper in blue pants and one of those almost-Stetsons they wear. Up on the road, Jerry Kesserling was letting a few cars through the roadblock to pick up kids who didn't ride the bus. The cars picked up and then drove hastily away. Mr. Grace was talking to a guy in a business suit that I didn't know. The firemen were standing around and smoking cigarettes and waiting for someone to tell them to put out a fire or go home.

"Has this got anything to do with you beating up Carlson?" Corky asked.

"How should I know what it has to do with?" I asked him irritably. "If I knew what was making me do it, I probably wouldn't have to."

"It's your parents." Susan Brooks spoke up suddenly. "It must be your parents."

Ted Jones made a rude noise.

I looked over at her, surprised. Susan Brooks was one of those girls who never say anything unless called upon, the ones that teachers always have to ask to speak up, please. A very studious, very serious girl. A rather pretty but not terribly bright girl—the kind who isn't allowed to give up and take the general or the commercial courses, because she had a terribly bright older brother or older sister, and teachers expect comparable things from her. In fine, one of those girls who are holding the dirty end of the stick with as much good grace and manners as they can muster. Usually they marry truck drivers and move to the West Coast, where they have kitchen nooks with Formica counters—and they write letters to the Folks Back East as seldom as they can get away with. They make quiet, successful lives for themselves and grow prettier as the shadow of the bright older brother or sister falls away from them.

"My parents," I said, tasting it. I thought about telling them I had been hunting with my dad when I was nine. "My Hunting Trip," by Charles Decker. Subtitle: "Or, How I Overheard My Dad Explain the Cherokee Nose Job." Too revolting.

I snatched a look at Ted Jones, and the rich, coppery aroma of paydirt filled my nostrils. His face was set in a furious, jeering expression, as if someone had just forced a whole lemon into his mouth and then jammed his jaws together. As if someone had dropped a depth charge into his brains and sent some old, sunken hulk into long and ominous psychic vibrations.

"That's what it says in all the psychology books," Susan was going on, all blithely unaware. "In fact . . . " She suddenly became aware of the fact that she was speaking (and in a normal tone of voice, *and* in class) and clammed up. She was wearing a pale-jade-colored blouse, and her bra straps showed through like ghostly, half-erased chalk marks.

"My parents," I said again, and stopped again. I remembered the hunting trip again, but this time I remembered waking up, seeing the moving branches on the tight canvas of the tent (was the canvas tight? you bet it was—my dad put that tent up, and everything he did was tight, no loose screws there), looking at the moving branches, needing to whiz, feeling like a little kid again . . . and remembering something that had happened long ago. I didn't want to talk about that. I hadn't talked about it with Mr. Grace. This was getting it on for real—and besides, there was Ted. Ted didn't care for this at all. Perhaps it was all very important to him. Perhaps Ted could still be . . . helped. I suspected it was much too late for me, but even on that level, don't they say that learning is a good and elegant thing for its own sake? Sure.

Outside, nothing much seemed to be going on. The last town police car had arrived, and, just as I had expected, they were handing out coffee-and. Story time chilluns.

"My parents," I said:

Chapter 14

My parents met at a wedding reception, and although it may have nothing to do with anything—unless you believe in omens—the bride that day was burned to death less than a year later. Her name was Jessie Decker Hannaford. As Jessie Decker, she had been my mom's roommate at the University of Maine, where they were both majoring in political science. The thing that seemed to have happened was this: Jessie's husband went out to a special town meeting, and Jessie went into the bathroom to take a shower. She fell down and hit her head and knocked herself unconscious. In the kitchen, a dish towel fell on a hot stove burner. The house went up like a rocket. Wasn't it a mercy she didn't suffer.

So the only good that came of that wedding was my mother's meeting with Jessie Decker Hannaford's brother. He was an ensign in the Navy. After the reception, he asked my mother if she would like to go dancing. She said yes. They courted for six months, and then they were married. I came along about fourteen months after the nuptials, and I've done the math again and again. As near as I can figure, I was conceived on one of the nights just before or just after my father's sister was being broiled alive in her shower cap. She was my mom's bridesmaid. I've looked at all the wedding pictures, and no matter how often I've looked, it always gives me a weird feeling. There is Jessie holding my mother's bridal train. Jessie and her husband, Brian Hannaford, smiling in the background as my mom and dad cut the wedding cake. Jessie dancing with the minister. And in all the pictures she is only five months away from the shower and the dishrag on the hot stove burner. You wish you could step into one of those Kodachromes and approach her, say: "You're never going to be my aunt Jessie unless you stay out of the shower when your husband is away. Be careful, Aunt Jessie." But you can't go back. For want of a shoe the horse was lost, and all that.

But it happened, which is another way of saying I happened, and that's it. I was an only child; my mother never wanted another. She's very intellectual, my mother. Reads English mysteries, but never by Agatha Christie. Victor Canning and Hammond Innes were always more her cup of tea. Also magazines like *The Manchester Guardian* and *Monocle* and *The New York Review of Books*. My father, who made a career of the Navy and ended up as a recruiter, was more the all-American type. He likes the Detroit Tigers and the Detroit Redwings and wore a black armband the day Vince Lombardi died. No shit. And he reads those Richard Stark novels about Parker, the thief. That always amused the hell out of my mother. She finally broke down and told him that Richard Stark was really Donald Westlake, who writes sort of funny mysteries under his real name. My father tried one and hated it. After that he always acted like Westlake/Stark was his private lapdog who turned against him one night and tried to bite his throat.

My earliest memory is of waking up in the dark and thinking I was dead until I saw the shadows moving on the walls and the ceiling—there was a big old elm outside my window, and the wind would move the branches. This particular night—the first night I remember anything—there must have been a full moon (hunter's moon, do they call it?), because the walls were very bright and the shadows were very dark. The branch shadows looked like great moving fingers. Now when I think of it, they seem like corpse fingers. But I couldn't have thought that then, could I? I was only three. A kid that little doesn't even know what a corpse is.

But there was something coming. I could hear it, down the hall. Something terrible was coming. Coming for me through the darkness. I could hear it, creaking and creaking and creaking.

I couldn't move. Maybe I didn't even want to move. I don't remember about that. I just lay and watched the tree fingers move on the wall and ceiling, and waited for the Creaking Thing to get down to my room and throw open the door.

After a long time—it might have been an hour, or it might only have been seconds—I realized the Creaking Thing wasn't after me at all. Or at least, not yet. It was after Mom and Dad down the hall. The Creaking Thing was in Mom and Dad's room.

I lay there, watching the tree fingers, and listened. Now the whole thing seems so dreamy and far away, like a city must look from a mountaintop where the air is rare, but very real just the same. I can remember the wind shuffling back and forth against the glass of my bedroom window. I can remember wetting myself—it was warm and somehow comforting. And I can remember the Creaking Thing.

After a long, long, *long* time, I can remember my mother's voice, out of breath and irritable, and a little afraid: "Stop now, Carl." Again the creaking, furtive. *"Stop it!"*

A mutter from my father.

From my mother: "I don't care! I don't care if you didn't! Stop it *and let me sleep!"*

So I knew. I went to sleep, but I knew. The Creaking Thing was my father.

Chapter 15

Nobody said anything. Some of them hadn't got the point, if there was one; I wasn't sure. They were still looking at me expectantly, as if awaiting the punch line of a rather good joke.

Others were studying their hands, obviously embarrassed. But Susan Brooks looked altogether radiant and vindicated. It was a very nice thing to see. I felt like a farmer, spreading shit and growing corn.

Still nobody said anything. The clock buzzed away with a vague kind of determination. I looked down at Mrs. Underwood. Her eyes were half-open, glazed, gummy. She looked no more important than a woodchuck I had once blown away with my father's four-ten. A fly was unctuously washing its paws on her forearm. Feeling a little disgusted, I waved it away.

Outside, four more police cars had arrived. Other cars were parked along the shoulder of the highway for as far as I could see beyond the roadblock. Quite a crowd was gathering. I sat back, dry-scrubbed the side of my face with my hand, and looked at Ted. He held up his fists to shoulder height, smiled, and popped up the middle fingers on each one.

He didn't speak, but his lips moved, and I read it easily: *Shit.*

Nobody knew it had been passed but him and me. He looked ready to speak aloud, but I wanted to just keep it between us for a little while. I said:

Chapter 16

My dad has hated me for as long as I can remember.

That's a pretty sweeping statement, and I know how phony it sounds. It sounds petulant and really fantastic—the kind of weapon kids always use when the old man won't come across with the car for your heavy date at the drive-in with Peggy Sue or when he tells you that if you flunk world history the second time through he's going to beat the living hell out of you. In this bright day and age when everybody thinks psychology is God's gift to the poor old anally fixated human race and even the president of the United States pops a trank before dinner, it's really a good way to get rid of those Old Testament guilts that keep creeping up our throats like the aftertaste of a bad meal we overate. If you say your father hated you as a kid, you can go out and flash the neighborhood, commit rape, or burn down the Knights of Pythias bingo parlor and still cop a plea.

But it also means that no one will believe you if it's true. You're the little boy that cried wolf. And for me it is true. Oh, nothing really stunning until after the Carlson thing. I don't think Dad himself really knew it until then. Even if you could dig to the very bottom of his motives, he'd probably say—at the most—that he was hating me for my own good.

Metaphor time in the old corral: To Dad, life was like a precious antique car. Because it is both precious and irreplaceable, you keep it immaculate and in perfect running order. Once a year you take it to the local Old Car Show. No grease is ever allowed to foul the gasoline, no sludge to find its way into the carb, no bolt to loosen on the driveshaft. It must be tuned, oiled, and greased every thousand miles, and you have to wax it every Sunday, just before the pro game on TV. My dad's motto: Keep It Tight and Keep It Right. And if a bird shits on your windshield, you wipe it off before it can dry there.

That was Dad's life, and I was the birdshit on his windshield.

He was a big, quiet man with sandy hair, a complexion that burned easily, and a face that had a vague—but not unpleasant—touch of the simian. In the summertime he always looked angry, with his face sunburned red and his eyes peering belligerently out at you like pale glints of water. Later, after I was ten, he was transferred to Boston and we saw him only on weekends, but before that he was stationed in Portland, and as far as I was concerned, he was like any other nine-to-five father, except that his shirt was khaki instead of white, and his tie was always black.

It says in the Bible that the sins of the fathers are visited upon the sons, and that

43

may be true. But I could also add that the sins of other fathers' sons were visited on me.

Being a recruiting chief was very tough on Dad, and I often thought he would have been much happier stationed out to sea—not to mention how much happier I would have been. For him it was like having to go around and see other people's priceless antique cars driven to rack and ruin, mud-splattered, rust-eaten. He inducted high-school Romeos leaving their pregnant Juliets behind them. He inducted men who didn't know what they were getting into and men who only cared about what they were getting out of. He got the sullen young men who had been made to choose between a bang in the Navy and a bang in South Portland Training and Correction. He got scared bookkeepers who had turned up 1-A and would have done anything to keep away from the gooks in Nam, who were just then beginning their long-running special on Pickled Penis of American Grunt. And he got the slack-jawed dropouts who had to be coached before they could sign their own names and had IQs to match their hat sizes.

And there was me, right there at home, with some budding characteristics attributable to all of the above. Quite a challenge there. And you have to know that he didn't hate me just because I was there; he hated me because he was unequal to the challenge. He might have been if I hadn't been more my mother's child than his, and if my mother and I hadn't both known that. He called me a mamma's boy. Maybe I was.

One day in the fall of 1962 I took it into my head to throw rocks at the storm windows Dad was getting ready to put on. It was early October, a Saturday, and Dad was going at it the way he went at everything, with a step-by-step precision that precluded all error and waste.

First he got all the windows out of the garage (newly painted the spring before, green to match the house trim) and lined them up carefully against the house, one beside each window. I can see him, tall and sunburned and angry-looking, even under the cool October sun, in the vintage October air, which was as cool as kisses. October is such a fine month.

I was sitting on the bottom step of the front porch, playing Quiet and watching him. Every now and then a car would blip by going up Route 9 toward Winsor or down 9 toward Harlow or Freeport. Mom was inside, playing the piano. Something minor—Bach, I think. But then, whatever Mother played usually sounded like Bach. The wind tugged and pushed it, now bringing it to me, now carrying it away. Whenever I hear that piece now, I think about that day. Bach Fugue for Storm Windows in A Minor.

I sat and played Quiet. A 1956 Ford with an out-of-state license plate went by. Up here to shoot partridge and pheasant, probably. A robin landed by the elm tree that threw shadows on my bedroom wall at night, and pecked through the fallen leaves for a worm. My mother played on, right hand rippling the melody, left hand counterpointing it. Mother could play wonderful boogie-woogie when the urge struck her, but it didn't often. She just didn't like it, and it was probably just as well. Even her boogies sounded like Bach wrote them.

All at once it occurred to me how wonderful it would be to break all those storm windows. To break them one by one; the upper panes, and then the lower ones.

You might think it was a piece of revenge, conscious or unconscious, a way to get back at the spit-and-polish, all-hands-on-deck old man. But the truth is, I can't remember putting my father in that particular picture at all. The day was fine and beautiful. I was four. It was a fine October day for breaking windows.

I got up and went out to the soft shoulder and began picking up stones. I was wearing short pants, and I stuffed stones into the front pockets until it must have looked like I was carrying ostrich eggs. Another car went by, and I waved. The driver waved back. The woman beside him was holding a baby.

I went back across the lawn, took a stone out of my pocket, and threw it at the storm window beside the living-room window. I threw it as hard as I could. I missed. I took out another rock, and this time I moved right up on top of that window. A little chill went through my mind, disturbing my thoughts for a tiny moment. I couldn't miss. And didn't.

I went right around the house breaking windows. First the living-room window, then the music-room window. It was propped up against the brick side of the house, and after I broke it I looked in at Mom, playing the piano. She was wearing a sheer blue slip. When she saw me peering in, she jumped a little and hit a sour note, then she gave me a big sweet smile and went on playing. You can see how it was. She hadn't even heard me break the window.

Funny, in a way—there was no sense of doing anything wrong, just of doing something pleasurable. A little kid's selective perception is a strange thing; if the windows had been fastened on, I never would have dreamed of breaking them.

I was regarding the last window, the one outside the den, when a hand fell on my shoulder and turned me around. It was my father. He was mad. I hadn't ever seen him so mad. His eyes were big, and he was biting his tongue between his teeth as if he were having a fit. I cried out, he scared me so bad. It was like your mother coming to the breakfast table with a Halloween mask on.

"Bastard!"

He picked me up in both hands, right hand holding my legs at the ankles and left hand holding my left arm against my chest, and then he threw me on the ground. It was hard—as hard as he could throw, I think. I lay there with all the breath out of me, staring up at the dismay and realization creeping over his face, dissolving the flash of his anger. I was unable to cry or speak or even move my diaphragm. There was a paralyzing pain in my chest and my crotch.

"I didn't mean it," he said, kneeling over me. "You all right? You okay, Chuck?" Chuck was what he called me when we were playing toss in the backyard.

My lungs operated in a spasmodic, lurching gasp. I opened my mouth and let out a huge, screaming bray. The sound scared me, and the next scream was even louder. Tears turned everything to prisms. The sound of the piano stopped.

"You shouldn't have broken those windows," he said. Anger was replacing dismay. "Now, shut up. Be a man, for God's sake."

He jerked me roughly to my feet just as Mom flew around the corner of the house, still in her slip.

"He broke all the storm windows," my father said. "Go put something on."

"What's the matter?" she cried. "Oh, Charlie, did you cut yourself? Where? Show me where!"

"He isn't cut," Dad said disgustedly. "He's afraid he's going to get licked. And he damned well is."

I ran to my mother and pressed my face into her belly, feeling the soft, comforting silk of her slip, smelling her sweet smell. My whole head felt swollen and pulpy, like a turnip. My voice had turned into a cracked donkey bray. I closed my eyes tightly.

"What are you talking about, licking him? He's purple! If you've hurt him, Carl . . ."

"He started to cry when he saw me coming, for Christ's sake."

The voices were coming from high above me, like amplified declarations from mountaintops.

"There's a car coming," he said. "Go inside, Rita."

"Come on, love," my mother said. "Smile for mummy. Big smile." She pushed me away from her stomach and wiped tears from under my eyes. Have you ever had your mother wipe your tears away? About that the hack poets are right. It's one of life's great experiences, right up there with your first ball game and your first wet dream. "There, honey, there. Daddy didn't mean to be cross."

"That was Sam Castinguay and his wife," my father said. "Now you've given that motor-mouth something to talk about. I hope—"

"Come on, Charlie," she said, taking my hand. "We'll have chocolate. In my sewing room."

"The hell you will," Dad said curtly. I looked back at him. His fists were clenched angrily as he stood in front of the one window he had saved. "He'll just puke it up when I whale the tar out of him."

"You'll whale no tar out of anyone," she said. "You've scared him half to death already . . ."

Then he was over to her, not minding her slip anymore, or Sam and his wife. He grabbed her shoulder and pointed to the jagged kitchen storm window. "Look! Look! *He* did that, and now you want to give him chocolate! He's no baby anymore, Rita, it's time for you to stop giving him the tit!"

I cringed against her hip, and she wrenched her shoulder away. White fingermarks stood out on her flesh for a moment and then filled in red.

"Go inside," she said calmly. "You're being quite foolish, Carl."

"I'm going to—"

"Don't tell me what you'll do!" she shouted suddenly, advancing on him. He flinched away instinctively. "Go inside! You've done enough damage! Go inside! Go find some of your friends and have drinks! Go anywhere! *But . . . get out of my sight!*"

"Punishment," he said deliberately. "Did anyone teach you that word in college, or were they too busy filling you full of that liberal bullshit? Next time, he may break something more valuable than a few storm windows. A few times after that, he may break your heart. Wanton destruction—''

''*Get out!*'' she screamed.

I began to cry again, and shrank away from them both. For a moment I stood between, tottering, and then my mother gathered me up. It's all right, honey, she was saying, but I was watching my father, who had turned and was stomping away like a surly little boy. It wasn't until then, until I had seen with what practiced and dreadful ease he had been banished, that I began to dare to hate him back.

While my mother and I were having cocoa in her sewing room, I told her how Dad had thrown me on the ground. I told her Dad had lied.

It made me feel quite wonderful and strong.

Chapter 17

"What happened then?" Susan Brooks asked breathlessly.

"Not much," I said. "It blew over." Now that it was out, I found myself mildly surprised that it had stuck in my throat so long. I once knew a kid, Herk Orville, who ate a mouse. I dared him, and he swallowed it. Raw. It was just a small field-mouse, and it didn't look hurt at all when we found it; maybe it had just died of old age. Anyway, Herk's mom was out hanging clothes, and she just happened to look over at us, sitting in the dirt by the back step. She looked just in time to see the mouse going down Herk's throat, headfirst.

She screamed—what a fright it can give you when a grown-up screams!—and ran over and put her finger down Herk's throat. Herk threw up the mouse, the hamburger he'd eaten for lunch, and some pasty glop that looked like tomato soup. He was just starting to ask his mother what was going on when *she* threw up. And there, in all that puke, that old dead mouse didn't look bad at all. It sure looked better than the rest of the stuff. The moral seemed to be that puking up your past when the present is even worse makes some of the vomitus look nearly tasty. I started to tell them that, and then decided it would only revolt them—like the story of the Cherokee Nose Job.

"Dad was in the doghouse for a few days. That was all. No divorce. No big thing."

Carol Granger started to say something, and that was when Ted stood up. His face was pale as cheese except for two burning patches of red, one above each cheekbone. He was grinning. Did I tell you he wore his hair in a duck's ass cut? Grease, out of style, not cool. But Ted got away with it. In that click of a second when he stood up, he looked like the ghost of James Dean come to get me, and my heart quailed.

"I'm going to take that gun away from you now, tin shit," he said, grinning. His teeth were white and even.

I had to fight hard to keep my voice steady, but I think I did pretty well. "Sit down, Ted."

Ted didn't move forward, but I could see how badly he wanted to. "That makes me sick, you know it? Trying to blame something like this on your *folks.*"

"Did I say I was trying to—?"

"Shut up!" he said in a rising, strident voice. "You killed two people!"

"How really observant of you to notice," I said.

He made a horrible rippling movement with his hands, holding them at waist level, and I knew that in his mind he had just grabbed me and eaten me.

48

"Put that down, Charlie," he said, grinning. "Just put that gun down and fight me fair."

"Why did you quit the football team, Ted?" I asked amiably. It was very hard to sound amiable, but it worked. He looked stunned, suddenly unsure, as if no one but the stolidly predictable coach had ever dared ask him that. He looked as if he had suddenly become aware of the fact that he was the only one standing. It was akin to the look a fellow gets when he realizes his zipper is down, and is trying to think of a nice unobtrusive way to get it back up—so it will look like an act of God.

"Never mind that," he said. "Put down that gun." It sounded melodramatic as hell. Phony. He knew it.

"Afraid for your balls? Your ever-loving sack? Was that it?"

Irma Bates gasped. Sylvia, however, was watching with a certain predatory interest.

"You . . . " He sat down suddenly in his seat, and somebody chuckled in the back of the room. I've always wondered exactly who that was. Dick Keene? Harmon Jackson?

But I saw their faces. And what I saw surprised me. You might even say it shocked me. Because there was pleasure there. There had been a showdown, a verbal shootout, you might say, and I had won. But why did that make them happy? Like those maddening pictures you sometimes see in the Sunday paper—"Why are these people laughing? Turn to page 41." Only, there was no page for me to turn to.

And it's important to know, you know. I've thought and thought, racked whatever brains I have left, and I don't know. Maybe it was only Ted himself, handsome and brave, full of the same natural *machismo* that keeps the wars well-attended. Simple jealousy, then. The need to see everyone at the same level, gargling in the same rat-race choir, to paraphrase Dylan. *Take off your mask, Ted, and sit down with the rest of us regular guys.*

Ted was still staring at me, and I knew well enough that he was unbroken. Only, next time he might not be so direct. Maybe next time he would try me on the flank.

Maybe it's just mob spirit. Jump on the individual.

But I didn't believe that then, and I don't believe it now, although it would explain much. No, the subtle shift from Ted's end of the seesaw to mine could not be dismissed as some mass grunt of emotion. A mob always wipes out the strange one, the sport, the mutant. That was *me*, not Ted. Ted was the exact opposite of those things. He was a boy you would have been proud to have down in the rumpus room with your daughter. No, it was in *Ted*, not in them. It had to be in Ted. I began to feel strange tentacles of excitement in my belly—the way a butterfly collector must feel when he thinks he has just seen a new species fluttering in yon bushes.

"I know why Ted quit football," a voice said slyly. I looked around. It was Pig Pen. Ted had fairly jumped at the sound of his voice. He was beginning to look a wee bit haggard.

"Do tell," I said.

"If you open your mouth, I'll kill you," Ted said deliberately. He turned his grin on Pig Pen.

Pig Pen blinked in a terrified way and licked his lips. He was torn. It was probably the first time in his life that he'd had the ax, and now he didn't know if he dared to grind it. Of course, almost anyone in the room could have told you how he came by any information he had; Mrs. Dano spent her life attending bazaars, rummage sales, church and school suppers, and Mrs. Dano had the longest, shrewdest nose in Gates Falls. I also suspected she held the record for party-line listening in. She could latch on to anyone's dirty laundry before you could say have-you-heard-the-latest-about-Sam-Delacorte.

"I . . . " Pig Pen began, and turned away from Ted as he made an impotent clutching gesture with his hands.

"Go on and tell," Sylvia Ragan said suddenly. "Don't let Golden Boy scare you, hon."

Pig Pen gave her a quivering smile and then blurted out: "Mrs. Jones is an alcoholic. She had to go someplace and dry out. Ted had to help with his family."

Silence for a second.

"I'm going to kill you, Pig Pen," Ted said, getting up. His face was dead pale.

"Now, that's not nice," I said. "You said so yourself. Sit down."

Ted glared at me, and for a moment I thought he was going to break and charge at me. If he had, I would have killed him. Maybe he could see it on my face. He sat back down.

"So," I said. "The skeleton has boogied right out of the closet. Where's she drying out, Ted?"

"Shut up," he said thickly. Some of his hair had fallen across his forehead. It looked greasy. It was the first time it had ever looked that way to me.

"Oh, she's back now," Pig Pen said, and offered Ted a forgiving smile.

"You said you'd kill Pig Pen," I said thoughtfully.

"I *will* kill him," Ted muttered. His eyes were red and baleful.

"Then you can blame it on your parents," I said, smiling. "Won't that be a relief?"

Ted was gripping the edge of his desk tightly. Things weren't going to his liking at all. Harmon Jackson was smiling nastily. Maybe he had an old grudge against Ted.

"Your father drive her to it?" I asked kindly. "How'd it happen? Home late all the time? Supper burned and all that? Nipping on the cooking sherry a little at first? Hi-ho."

"I'll kill you," he moaned.

I was needling him—needling the shit out of him—and no one was telling me to stop. It was incredible. They were all watching Ted with a glassy kind of interest, as if they had expected all along that there were a few maggots under there.

"Must be tough, being married to a big-time bank officer," I said. "Look at it that way. She probably didn't realize she was belting down the hard stuff so heavy.

It can creep up on you, look at it that way. It can get on top of you. And it's not your fault, is it? Hi-ho.''

"Shut up!" he screamed at me.

"There it was, right under your nose, but it just got out of control, am I right? Kind of disgusting, wasn't it? Did she really go to pot, Ted? Tell us. Get rid of it. Kind of just slopping around the house, was she?''

"Shut up! Shut up!"

"Drunk in front of *Dialing for Dollars?* Seeing bugs in the corners? Or was she quiet about it? Did she see bugs? Did she? Did she *go* bugs?''

"Yeah, it was disgusting!" He brayed at me suddenly, through a mouthful of spit. "Almost as disgusting as *you!* Killer! Killer!''

"Did you write her?" I asked softly.

"Why would I write her?" he asked wildly. "Why should I write her? She copped out.''

"And you couldn't play football.''

Ted Jones said clearly, "Drunk *bitch.* ''

Carol Granger gasped, and the spell was broken. Ted's eyes seemed to clear a little. The red light went out of them, and he realized what he had said.

"I'll get you for this, Charlie," he said quietly.

"You might. You might get your chance." I smiled. "A drunken old bitch of a mother. That surely is disgusting, Ted.''

Ted sat silently, staring at me.

It was over, then. We could turn our attention to other things—at least, for the moment. I had a feeling we might be getting back to Ted. Or that he would get back to me.

People moved around restlessly outside.

The clock buzzed.

No one said anything for a long time, or what seemed like a long time. There was a lot to think about now.

Chapter 18

Sylvia Ragan finally broke the silence. She threw back her head and laughed—long, hard, and loud. Several people, including me, jumped. Ted Jones didn't. He was still on his own trip. "You know what I'd like to do after this is over?" she asked.

"What?" Pig Pen asked. He looked surprised that he had spoken up again. Sandra Cross was looking at me gravely. She had her ankles crossed the way pretty girls do when they want to foil boys who want to look up their dresses.

"I'd like to get this in a detective magazine. 'Sixty Minutes of Terror with the Placerville Maniac.' I'd get somebody who writes good to do it. Joe McKennedy or Phil Franks . . . or maybe you, Charlie. How's that bite your banana?" She guffawed, and Pig Pen joined in tentatively. I think he was fascinated by Sylvia's fearlessness. Or maybe it was only her blatant sexuality. She sure didn't have her ankles crossed.

Out on the lawn, two more trooper cars had arrived. The firemen were leaving; the fire alarm had cut out a few minutes ago. Abruptly Mr. Grace disengaged himself from the crowd and started toward the main doors. A light breeze flapped the bottom of his sport coat.

"More company," Corky Herald said.

I got up, went over to the intercom, and switched it back onto TALK-LISTEN. Then I sat down again, sweating a little. Mr. Don-God-Give-Us-Grace was on his way. And he was no lightweight.

A few seconds later there was that hollow *chink!* that means the line is open. Mr. Grace said, "Charlie?" His voice was very calm, very rich, very certain.

"How are you, skinner?" I asked.

"Fine, thanks, Charlie. How are *you?*"

"Keeping my thumb on it," I said agreeably.

Snickers from some of the boys.

"Charlie, we've talked about getting help for you before this. Now, you've committed a pretty antisocial act, wouldn't you agree?"

"By whose standards?"

"Society's standards, Charlie. First Mr. Carlson, now this. Will you let us help you?"

I almost asked him if my co-students weren't a part of society, because no one down here seemed too worked up about Mrs. Underwood. But I couldn't do that. It would have transgressed a set of rules that I was just beginning to grasp.

"How does Ah do it?" I bawled. "Ah already tole dat dere Mr. Denber how

52

sorry Ah is fo' hittin' dat l'il girl wit dat Loosyville Sluggah. Ah wants mah poor haid shrunk! Ah wants mah soul saved an' made white as snow! How does Ah do it, Rev'rund?''

Pat Fitzgerald, who was nearly as black as the ace of spades, laughed and shook his head.

"Charlie, Charlie," Mr. Grace said, as if very sad. "Only you can save your soul now.''

I didn't like that. I stopped shouting and put my hand on the pistol, as if for courage. I didn't like it at all. He had a way of slipping it to you. I'd seen him a lot since I bopped Mr. Carlson with the pipe wrench. He could really slip it in.

"Mr. Grace?''

"What, Charlie?''

"Did Tom tell the police what I said?''

"Don't you mean 'Mr. Denver'?''

"Whatever. Did he . . . ?''

"Yes, he relayed your message.''

"Have they figured out how they're going to handle me yet?''

"I don't know, Charlie. I'm more interested in knowing if you've figured out how you're going to handle yourself.''

Oh, he was slipping it to me, all right. Just like he kept slipping it to me after Mr. Carlson. But then I had to go see him. Now I could turn him off anytime I wanted to. Except I couldn't, and he knew I couldn't. It was too normal to be consistent. And I was being watched by my peerless peers. They were evaluating me.

"Sweating a little?'' I asked the intercom.

"Are you?''

"You guys," I said, an edge of bitterness creeping into my voice. "You're all the same.''

"We are? If so, then we all want to help you.''

He was going to be a much tougher nut to strip than old Tom Denver had been. That was obvious. I called Don Grace up in my mind. Short, dapper little fuck. Bald on top, big muttonchop sideburns, as if to make up for it. He favored tweed coats with suede patches on the elbows. A pipe always stuffed with something that came from Copenhagen and smelled like cowshit. A man with a headful of sharp, prying instruments. A mind-fucker, a head-stud. That's what a shrink is for, my friends and neighbors; their job is to fuck the mentally disturbed and make them pregnant with sanity. It's a bull's job, and they go to school to learn how, and all their courses are variations on a theme: *Slipping It to the Psychos for Fun and Profit, Mostly Profit.* And if you find yourself someday lying on that great analyst's couch where so many have lain before you, I'd ask you to remember one thing: When you get sanity by stud, the child always looks like the father. And they have a very high suicide rate.

But they get you lonely, and ready to cry, they get you ready to toss it all over if they will just promise to go away for a while. What do we have? What do we really have? Minds like terrified fat men, begging the eyes that look up in the bus terminal or the restaurant and threaten to meet ours to look back down, uninterested. We lie awake and picture ourselves in white hats of varying shapes. There's no maidenhead too tough to withstand the seasoned dork of modern psychiatry. But maybe that was okay. Maybe now they would play my game, all these shysters and whores.

"Let us help you, Charlie," Mr. Grace was saying.

"But by letting you help me, I would be helping you." I said it as if the idea had just occurred to me. "Don't want to do that."

"Why, Charlie?"

"Mr. Grace?"

"Yes, Charlie?"

"The next time you ask me a question, I'm going to kill somebody down here."

I could hear Mr. Grace suck wind, as if someone had just told him his son had been in a car crash. It was a very un-self-confident sound. It made me feel very good.

Everyone in the room was looking at me tightly. Ted Jones raised his head slowly, as if he had just awakened. I could see the familiar, hating darkness cloud his eyes. Anne Lasky's eyes were round and frightened. Sylvia Ragan's fingers were doing a slow and dreamy ballet as they rummaged in her purse for another cigarette. And Sandra Cross was looking at me gravely, gravely, as if I were a doctor, or a priest.

Mr. Grace began to speak.

"Watch it!" I said sharply. "Before you say anything, be careful. You aren't playing your game any longer. Understand that. You're playing mine. Statements only. Be very careful. Can you be very careful?"

He didn't say anything about my game metaphor at all. That was when I began to believe I had him.

"Charlie . . ." Was that almost a plea?

"Very good. Do you think you'll be able to keep your job after this, Mr. Grace?"

"Charlie, for God's sake . . ."

"Ever so much better."

"Let them go, Charlie. Save yourself. Please."

"You're talking too fast. Pretty soon a question will pop out, and that'll be the end for somebody."

"Charlie . . ."

"How was your military obligation fulfilled?"

"Wh . . ." Sudden whistling of breath as he cut that off.

"You almost killed somebody," I said. "Careful, Don. I can call you Don, can't I? Sure. Weigh those words, Don."

I was reaching out for him.

I was going to break him.

In that second it seemed as if maybe I could break them all.

"I think I better sign off for the moment, Charlie."

"If you go before I say you can, I'll shoot somebody. What you're going to do is sit there and answer my questions."

The first sweaty desperation, as well concealed as underarm perspiration at the junior prom: "I really mustn't, Charlie. I can't take the responsibility for—"

"Responsibility?" I screamed. "My God, you've been taking the responsibility ever since they let you loose from college! Now you want to cop out the first time your bare ass is showing! But I'm in the driver's seat, and by God you'll pull the cart! Or I'll do just what I said. Do you dig it? *Do you understand me?"*

"I won't play a cheap parlor game with human lives for party favors, Charlie."

"Congratulations to you," I said. "You just described modern psychiatry. That ought to be the textbook definition, Don. Now, let me tell you: you'll take a piss out the window if I tell you to. And God help you if I catch you in a lie. That will get somebody killed too. Ready to bare your soul, Don? Are you on your mark?"

He drew in his breath raggedly. He wanted to ask if I really meant it, but he was afraid I might answer with the gun instead of my mouth. He wanted to reach out quick and shut off the intercom, but he knew he would hear the echo of the shot in the empty building, rolling around in the corridor below him like a bowling ball up a long alley from hell.

"All right," I said. I unbuttoned my shirt cuffs. Out on the lawn, the cops and Tom Denver and Mr. Johnson were standing around restlessly, waiting for the return of their tweedy bull stud. Read my dreams, Sigmund. Squirt 'em with the sperm of symbols and make 'em grow. Show me how we're different from, say, rabid dogs or old tigers full of bad blood. Show me the man hiding between my wet dreams. They had every reason to be confident (although they did not look confident). In the symbolic sense, Mr. Grace was Pathfinder of the Western World. Bull stud with a compass.

Natty Bumppo was breathing raggedly from the little latticed box over my head. I wondered if he'd read any good rapid eye movements lately. I wondered what his own would be like when night finally came.

"All right, Don. Let's get it on."

Chapter 19

"How was your military obligation fulfilled?"

"In the Army, Charlie. This isn't going to accomplish anything."

"In what capacity?"

"As a doctor."

"Psychiatrist?"

"No."

"How long have you been a practicing psychiatrist?"

"Five years."

"Have you ever eaten your wife out?"

"Wh . . . " Terrified, angry pause. "I . . . I don't know the meaning of the phrase."

"I'll rephrase it, then. Have you ever engaged in oral-genital practices with your wife?"

"I won't answer that. You have no right."

"I have all the rights. You have none. Answer, or I'll shoot someone. And remember, if you lie and I catch you in a lie, I'll shoot someone. Have you ever engaged in—?"

"No!"

"How long have you been a practicing psychiatrist?"

"Five years."

"Why?"

"Wh . . . Well, because it fulfills me. As a person."

"Has your wife ever had an affair with another man?"

"No."

"Another woman?"

"*No!*"

"How do you know?"

"She loves me."

"Has your wife ever given you a blow-job, Don?"

"I don't know what you—"

"You know goddamn well what I mean!"

"No, Charlie, I—"

"Ever cheat on an exam in college?"

Pause. "Absolutely not."

"On a quiz?"

"No."

56

I pounced. "Then how can you say your wife has never engaged in oral-genital sex practices with you?"

"I . . . I never . . . Charlie . . . "

"Where did you do your basic training?"

"F-Fort Benning."

"What year?"

"I don't remem—"

"Give me a year or I'm going to shoot somebody down here!"

"Nineteen-fifty-six."

"Were you a grunt?"

"I . . . I don't—".

"Were you a grunt? Were you a dogface?"

"I was . . . I was an officer. First lieu—"

"I didn't ask you for that!" I screamed.

"Charlie . . . Charlie, for God's sake, calm down—"

"What year was your military obligation fulfilled?"

"N-Nineteen-sixty."

"You owe your country six years! You're lying! I'm going to shoot—"

"No!" He cried. "National Guard! I was in the Guard!"

"What was your mother's maiden name?"

"G-G-Gavin."

"Why?"

"Wh . . . I don't know what you m—"

"Why was her maiden name Gavin?"

"Because her father's name was Gavin. Charlie—"

"In what year did you do your basic training?"

"Nineteen-fifty-sev—*six!*"

"You're lying. Caught you, didn't I, Don?"

"No!"

"You started to say fifty-*seven.*"

"I was mixed up."

"I'm going to shoot somebody. In the guts, I think. Yes."

"Charlie, for Jesus' sake!"

"Don't let it happen again. You were a grunt, right? In the Army?"

"Yes—no—I was an officer . . . "

"What was your father's middle name?"

"J-John. Chuh-Charlie, get hold of yourself. D-D-Don't—"

"Ever gobbled your wife, my man?"

"No!"

"You're lying. You said you didn't know what that meant."

"You explained it to me!" He was breathing in fast little grunts. "Let me go, Charlie, let me g—"

"What is your religious denomination?"

"Methodist."

"In the choir?"

"No."

"Did you go to Sunday school?"

"Yes."

"What are the first three words in the Bible?"

Pause. "In the beginning."

"First line of the Twenty-third Psalm?"

"The . . . um . . . The Lord is my shepherd, I shall not want."

"And you first ate your wife in 1956?"

"Yes—no . . . Charlie, let me alone . . . "

"Basic training, what year?"

"Nineteen-fifty-six!"

"You said fifty-seven before!" I screamed. "Here it goes! I'm going to blow someone's head off right now!"

"I said fifty-six, you bastard!" Screaming; out of breath, hysterical.

"What happened to Jonah, Don?"

"He was swallowed by a whale."

"The Bible says big fish, Don. Is that what you meant?"

"Yeah. Big fish. 'Course it was." Pitifully eager.

"Who built the ark?"

"Noah."

"Where did you do your basic?"

"Fort Benning." More confident; familiar ground. He was letting himself be lulled.

"Ever eaten your wife?"

"No."

"What?"

"No!"

"What's the last book in the Bible, Don?"

"Revelations."

"Actually it's just Revelation. No *s*. Right?"

"Right, sure, right."

"Who wrote it?"

"John."

"What was your father's middle name?"

"John."

"Ever get a revelation from your father, Don?"

A strange, high, cackling laugh from Don Grace. Some of the kids blinked uneasily at the sound of that laugh.

"Uh . . . no . . . Charlie . . . I can't say that I ever did."

"What was your mother's maiden name?"

"Gavin."

"Is Christ numbered among the martyrs?"

"Ye-ess . . . " He was too Methodist to really be sure.

"How was he martyred?"

"By the cross. Crucified."

"What did Christ ask God on the cross?"

" 'My God, my God, why hast thou forsaken me?' "

"Don?"

"Yes, Charlie."

"What did you just say?"

"I said 'My God, my God, why . . .' " Pause. "Oh, no, Charlie. That's not fair!"

"You asked a question."

"You tricked me!"

"You just killed someone, Don. Sorry."

"No!"

I fired the pistol into the floor. The whole class, which had been listening with taut, hypnotic attention, flinched. Several people screamed. Pig Pen fainted again, and he struck the floor with a satisfying meat thump. I don't know if the intercom picked it up, but it really didn't matter.

Mr. Grace was crying. Sobbing like a baby.

"Satisfactory," I said to no one in particular. "Very satisfactory."

Things seemed to be progressing nicely.

I let him sob for the best part of a minute; the cops had started toward the school at the sound of the shot, but Tom Denver, still betting on his shrink, held them back, and so *that* was all right. Mr. Grace sounded like a very small child, helpless, hopeless. I had made him fuck himself with his own big tool, like one of those weird experiences you read about in the *Penthouse Forum*. I had taken off his witch doctor's mask and made him human. But I didn't hold it against him. To err is only human, but it's divine to forgive. I believe that sincerely.

"Mr. Grace?" I said finally.

I'm going outside now," he said. And then, with tearful rebelliousness: "And you can't stop me!"

"That's all right," I said tenderly. "The game's over, Mr. Grace. We weren't playing for keepsies this time. No one is dead down here. I shot into the floor."

Breathing silence. Then, tiredly: "How can I believe you, Charlie?"

Because there would have been a stampede.

Instead of saying that, I pointed. "Ted?"

"This is Ted Jones, Mr. Grace," Ted said mechanically.

"Y-Yes, Ted."

"He shot into the floor," Ted said in a robot voice. "Everyone is all right." Then he grinned and began to speak again. I pointed the pistol at him, and he shut his mouth with a snap.

"Thank you, Ted. Thank you, my boy." Mr. Grace began to sob again. After what seemed like a long, long time, he shut the intercom off. A long time after that, he came into view on the lawn again, walking toward the enclave of cops on the lawn, walking in his tweed coat with the suede elbow patches, bald head gleaming, cheeks gleaming. He was walking slowly, like an old man.

It was amazing how much I liked seeing him walk like that.

Chapter 20

"Oh, man," Richard Keene said from the back of the room, and his voice sounded tired and sighing, almost exhausted.

That was when a small, savagely happy voice broke in: "I thought it was great!" I craned my neck around. It was a tiny Dutch doll of a girl named Grace Stanner. She was pretty in a way that attracted the shop-course boys, who still slicked their hair back and wore white socks. They hung around her in the hall like droning bees. She wore tight sweaters and short skirts. When she walked, everything jiggled—as Chuck Berry has said in his wisdom, it's such a sight to see somebody steal the show. Her mom was no prize, from what I understood. She was sort of a pro-am barfly and spent most of her time hanging around at Denny's on South Main, about a half-mile up from what they call the corner here in Placerville. Denny's will never be mistaken for Caesar's Palace. And there are always a lot of small minds in small towns, eager to think like mother, like daughter. Now she was wearing a pink cardigan sweater and a dark green skirt, thigh-high. Her face was alight, elvish. She had raised one clenched fist unconsciously shoulder-high. And there was something crystal and poignant about the moment. I actually felt my throat tighten.

"Go, Charlie! Fuck 'em all!"

A lot of heads snapped around and a lot of mouths dropped open, but I wasn't too surprised. I told you about the roulette ball, didn't I? Sure I did. In some ways—in a lot of ways—it was still in spin. Craziness is only a matter of degree, and there are lots of people besides me who have the urge to roll heads. They go to the stock-car races and the horror movies and the wrestling matches they have in the Portland Expo. Maybe what she said smacked of all those things, but I admired her for saying it out loud, all the same—the price of honesty is always high. She had an admirable grasp of the fundamentals. Besides, she was tiny and pretty.

Irma Bates wheeled on her, face stretched with outrage. It suddenly struck me that what was happening to Irma must be nearly cataclysmic. "Dirty-mouth!"

"Fuck you, too!" Grace shot back at her, smiling. Then, as an afterthought: "Bag!"

Irma's mouth dropped open. She struggled for words; I could see her throat working as she tried them, rejected them, tried more, looking for the words of power that would line Grace's face, drop her breasts four inches toward her belly, pop up varicose veins on those smooth thighs, and turn her hair gray. Surely those words were there someplace, and it was only a matter of finding them. So she

61

struggled, and with her low-slung chin and bulging forehead (both generously sprinkled with blackheads), she looked like a frog.

She finally sprayed out: "They ought to shoot you, just like they'll shoot him, you slut!" She worked for more; it wasn't enough. It couldn't yet express all the horror and outrage she felt for this violent rip in the seam of her universe. "Kill all sluts. Sluts and sluts' daughters!"

The room had been quiet, but now it became absolutely silent. A pool of silence. A mental spotlight had been switched on Irma and Grace. They might have been alone in a pool of light on a huge stage. Up to this last, Grace had been smiling slightly. Now the smile was wiped off.

"What?" Grace asked slowly. "What? What?"

"Baggage! Tramp!"

Grace stood up, as if about to recite poetry. "My-mother-works-in-a-laundry-you-fat-bitch-and-you-better-take-back-what-you-just-said!"

Irma's eyes rolled in caged and desperate triumph. Her neck was slick and shiny with sweat: the anxious sweat of the adolescent damned, the ones who sit home Friday nights and watch old movies on TV and also the clock. The ones for whom the phone is always mute and the voice of the mother is the voice of Thor. The ones who peck endlessly at the mustache shadow between nose and upper lip. The ones who go to see Robert Redford with their girlfriends and then come back alone on another day to see him again, with their palms clutched damply in their laps. The ones who agonize over long, seldom-mailed letters to John Travolta, written by the close, anxious light of Tensor study lamps. The ones for whom time has become a slow and dreamy sledge of doom, bringing only empty rooms and the smell of old sweats. Sure, that neck was slimy with sweat. I wouldn't kid you, any more than I would myself.

She opened her mouth and brayed: "WHORE'S DAUGHTER!"

"Okay," Grace said. She had started up the aisle toward Irma, holding her hands out in front of her like a stage hypnotist's. She had very long fingernails, lacquered the color of pearl. "I'm going to claw your eyes out, cunt."

"Whore's daughter, whore's daughter!" She was almost *singing* it.

Grace smiled. Her eyes were still alight and elvish. She wasn't hurrying up that aisle, but she wasn't lagging, either. No. She was coming right along. She was pretty, as I had never noticed before, pretty and precious. It was as if she had become a secret cameo of herself.

"Okay, Irma," she said. "Here I come. Here I come for your eyes."

Irma suddenly aware, shrank back in her seat.

"Stop," I said to Grace. I didn't pick up the pistol, but I laid my hand on it.

Grace stopped and looked at me inquiringly. Irma looked relieved and also vindicated, as if I had taken on aspects of a justly intervening god. "Whore's daughter," she confided to the class in general. "Missus Stanner has open house every night, just as soon as she gets back from the beerjoint. With *her* as practicing apprentice." She smiled sickly at Grace, a smile that was supposed to convey a superficial, cutting sympathy, and instead only inscribed her own pitiful empty terror. Grace was still looking at me inquiringly.

"Irma?" I asked politely. "Can I have your attention, Irma?"

And when she looked at me, I saw fully what was happening. Her eyes had a glittery yet opaque sheen. Her face was flushed of cheek but waxy of brow. She looked like something you might send your kid out wearing for Halloween. She was blowing up. The whole thing had offended whatever shrieking albino bat it was that passed for her soul. She was ready to go straight up to heaven or dive-bomb down into hell.

"Good," I said when both of them were looking at me. "Now. We have to keep order here. I'm sure you understand that. Without order, what do you have? The jungle. And the best way to keep order is to settle our difficulties in a civilized way."

"Hear, hear!" Harmon Jackson said.

I got up, went to the blackboard, and took a piece of chalk from the ledge. Then I drew a large circle on the tiled floor, perhaps five feet through the middle. I kept a close eye on Ted Jones while I did it, too. Then I went back to the desk and sat down.

I gestured to the circle. "Please, girls."

Grace came forward quickly, precious and perfect. Her complexion was smooth and fair.

Irma sat stony.

"Irma," I said. "Now, Irma. You've made accusations, you know."

Irma looked faintly surprised, as if the idea of accusations had exploded an entirely new train of thought in her mind. She nodded and rose from her seat with one hand cupped demurely over her mouth, as if to stifle a tiny, coquettish giggle. She stepped mincingly up the aisle and into the circle, standing as far away from Grace as was possible, eyes cast demurely down, hands linked together at her waist. She looked ready to sing "Granada" on *The Gong Show.*

I thought randomly: Her father sells cars, doesn't he?

"Very good," I said. "Now, as has been hinted at in church, in school, and even on *Howdy Doody,* a single step outside the circle means death. Understood?"

They understood that. They all understood it. This is not the same as comprehension, but it was good enough. When you stop to think, the whole idea of comprehension has a faintly archaic taste, like the sound of forgotten tongues or a look into a Victorian *camera obscura.* We Americans are much higher on simple understanding. It makes it easier to read the billboards when you're heading into town on the expressway at plus-fifty. To comprehend, the mental jaws have to gape wide enough to make the tendons creak. Understanding, however, can be purchased on every paperback-book rack in America.

"Now," I said. "I would like a minimum of physical violence here. We already have enough of that to think about. I think your mouths and your open hands will be sufficient, girls. I will be the judge. Accepted?"

They nodded.

I reached into my back pocket and brought out my red bandanna. I had bought it at the Ben Franklin five-and-dime downtown, and a couple of times I had worn it to school knotted around my neck, very continental, but I had gotten tired of the effect and put it to work as a snot rag. Bourgeois to the core, that's me.

"When I drop it, you go at it. First lick to you, Grace, as you seem to be the defendant."

Grace nodded brightly. There were roses in her cheeks. That's what my mother always says about someone who has high color.

Irma Bates just looked demurely at my red bandanna.

"Stop it!" Ted Jones snapped. "You said you weren't going to hurt anyone, Charlie. Now, stop it!" His eyes looked desperate. "Just *stop* it!"

For no reason I could fathom, Don Lordi laughed crazily.

"She started it, Ted Jones," Sylvia Ragan said heatedly. "If some Ethiopian jug-diddler called my mother a whore—"

"Whore, dirty whore," Irma agreed demurely.

" . . . I'd claw her fuggin' eyes out!"

"You're crazy!" Ted bellowed at her, his face the color of old brick. "We could stop him! If we all got together, we could—"

"Shut up, Ted," Dick Keene said. "Okay?"

Ted looked around, saw he had neither support nor sympathy, and shut up. His eyes were dark and full of crazy hate. I was glad it was a good long run between his desk and Mrs. Underwood's. I could shoot him in the foot if I had to.

"Ready, girls?"

Grace Stanner grinned a healthy, gutsy grin. "All ready."

Irma nodded. She was a big girl, standing with her legs apart and her head slightly lowered. Her hair was a dirty blond color, done in round curls that looked like toilet-paper rolls.

I dropped my bandanna. It was on.

Grace stood thinking about it. I could almost see her realizing how deep it could be, wondering maybe how far in over her head she wanted to get. In that instant I loved her. No . . . I loved them both.

"You're a fat, bigmouth bitch," Grace said, looking Irma in the eye. "You stink. I mean that. Your body *stinks*. You're a louse."

"Good," I said, when she was done. "Give her a smack."

Grace hauled off and slapped the side of Irma's face. It made a flat whapping noise, like one board striking another. Her sweater pulled up above the waistband of her skirt with the swing of her arm.

Corky Herald went "Unuh!" under his breath.

Irma let out a whoofing grunt. Her head snapped back, her face screwed up. She didn't look demure anymore. There was a large, hectic patch on her left cheek.

Grace threw back her head, drew a sudden knifebreath, and stood ready. Her hair spilled over her shoulders, beautiful and perfect. She waited.

"Irma for the prosecution," I said. "Go ahead, Irma."

Irma was breathing heavily. Her eyes were glazed and offended, her mouth horrified. At that moment she looked like no one's sweet child of morning.

"Whore," she said finally, apparently deciding to stick with a winner. Her lip lifted, fell, and lifted again, like a dog's. "Dirty boy-fucking whore."

I nodded to her.

Irma grinned. She was very big. Her arm, coming around, was like a wall. It rocketed against the side of Grace's face. The sound was a sharp crack.

"Ow!" someone whined.

Grace didn't fall over. The whole side of her face went red, but she didn't fall over. Instead, she smiled at Irma. And Irma flinched. I saw it and could hardly believe it: Dracula had feet of clay, after all.

I snatched a quick look at the audience. They were hung, hypnotized. They weren't thinking about Mr. Grace or Tom Denver or Charles Everett Decker. They were watching, and maybe what they saw was a little bit of their own souls, flashed at them in a cracked mirror. It was fine. It was like new grass in spring.

"Rebuttal, Grace?" I asked.

Grace's lips drew back from her tiny ivory teeth. "You never had a date, that's what's the matter with you. You're ugly. You smell bad. And so all you think about is what other people do, and you have to make it all dirty in your mind. You're a bug."

I nodded to her.

Grace swung, and Irma shied away. The blow struck her only glancingly, but she began to weep with a sudden, slow hopelessness. "Let me out," she groaned. "I don't want to any more, Charlie. Let me *out!*"

"Take back what you said about my mother," Grace said grimly.

"Your mother sucks cocks!" Irma screamed. Her face was twisted; her toilet-roll curls bobbed madly.

"Good," I said. "Go ahead, Irma."

But Irma was weeping hysterically. *"J-J-Je-Jesusss . . . "* she screamed. Her arms came up and covered her face with terrifying slowness. "God I want to be *d-d-d-dead . . . "*

"Say you're sorry," Grace said grimly. "Take it back."

"You suck cocks!" Irma screamed from behind the barricade of her arms.

"Okay," I said. "Let her have it, Irma. Last chance."

This time Irma swung from the heels. I saw Grace's eyes squeeze into slits, saw the muscles of her neck tighten into cords. But the angle of her jaw caught most of the blow and her head shifted only slightly. Still, that whole side of her face was bright red, as if from sunburn.

Irma's whole body jogged and jiggled with the force of her sobs, which seemed to come from a deep well in her that had never been tapped before.

"You haven't got nothing," Grace said. "You *ain't* nothing. Just a fat, stinky pig is what you are."

"Hey, give it to her!" Billy Sawyer yelled. He slammed both fists down heavily on his desk. "Hey, pour it on!"

"You ain't even got any *friends,"* Grace said, breathing hard. "Why do you even bother living?"

Irma let out a thin, reedy wail.

"All done," Grace said to me.

"Okay," I said. "Give it to her."

Grace drew back, and Irma screamed and went to her knees. "Don't h-h-hit me. Don't hit me no more! *Don't you hit me—*"

"Say you're sorry."

"I can't," she wept. "Don't you know I *can't?*"

"You can. You better."

There was no sound for a moment, but the vague buzz of the wall clock. Then Irma looked up, and Grace's hand came down fast, amazingly fast, making a small, ladylike splat against Irma's cheek. It sounded like a shot from a .22.

Irma fell heavily on one hand, her curls hanging in her face. She drew in a huge, ragged breath and screamed, "Okay! All right! I'm sorry!"

Grace stepped back, her mouth half-open and moist, breathing rapidly and shallowly. She raised her hands, palms out, in a curiously dovelike gesture, and pushed her hair away from her cheeks. Irma looked up at her dumbly, unbelievingly. She struggled to her knees again, and for a moment I thought she was going to offer a prayer to Grace. Then she began to weep.

Grace looked at the class, then looked at me. Her breasts were very full, pushing at the soft fabric of her sweater.

"My mother fucks," she said, "and I love her."

The applause started somewhere in the back, maybe with Mike Gavin or Nancy Caskin. But it started and spread until they were all applauding, all but Ted Jones and Susan Brooks. Susan looked too overwhelmed to applaud. She was looking at Gracie Stanner shiningly.

Irma knelt on the floor, her face in her hands. When the applause died (I had looked at Sandra Cross; she applauded very gently, as if in a dream), I said, "Stand up, Irma."

She looked at me wonderingly, her face streaked and shadowed and ravaged, as if she had been in a dream herself.

"Leave her alone," Ted said, each word distinct. .

"Shut up," Harmon Jackson said. "Charlie is doing all right."

Ted turned around in his seat and looked at him. But Harmon did not drop his eyes, as he might have done at another place, another time. They were both on the Student Council together—where Ted, of course, had always been the power.

"Stand up, Irma," I said gently.

"Are you going to shoot me?" she whispered.

"You said you were sorry."

"She made me say it."

"But I bet you are."

Irma looked at me dumbly from beneath the madhouse of her toilet-paper-roll curls. "I've always been sorry," she said. "That's what makes it *s-s-s-so* hard to s-say."

"Do you forgive her?" I asked Grace.

"Huh?" Grace looked at me, a little dazed. "Oh. Yeah. Sure." She walked suddenly back to her seat and sat down, where she looked frowningly at her hands.

"Irma?" I said.

"What?" She was peering at me, doglike, truculent, fearful, pitiful.

"Do you have something you want to say?"

"I don't know."

She stood up a little at a time. Her hands dangled strangely, as if she didn't know exactly what to do with them.

"I think you do."

"You'll feel better when it's off your chest, Irma," Tanis Gannon said. "I always do."

"Leave her alone, fa Chrissake," Dick Keene said from the back of the room.

"I don't want to be let alone," Irma said suddenly. "I want to say it." She brushed back her hair defiantly. Her hands were not dovelike at all. "I'm not pretty. No one likes me. I never had a date. Everything she said is true. There." The words rushed out very fast, and she screwed up her face while she was saying them, as if she were taking nasty medicine.

"Take a little care of yourself," Tanis said. Then, looking embarrassed but still determined: "You know, wash, shave your legs and, uh, armpits. Look nice. I'm no raving beauty, but I don't stay home *every* weekend. You could do it."

"I don't know how!"

Some of the boys were beginning to look uneasy, but the girls were leaning forward. They looked sympathetic now, all of them. They had that confessions-at-the-pajama-party look that every male seems to know and dread.

"Well . . . " Tanis began. Then she stopped and shook her head. "Come back here and sit down."

Pat Fitzgerald snickered. "Trade secrets?"

"That's right."

"Some trade," Corky Herald said. That got laughs. Irma Bates shuttled to the back of the room, where she, Tanis, Anne Lasky, and Susan Brooks started some sort of confabulation. Sylvia was talking softly with Grace, and Pig Pen's eyes were crawling avidly over both of them. Ted Jones was frowning at the air. George Yannick was carving something on the top of his desk and smoking a cigarette—he looked like any busy carpenter. Most of the others were looking out the windows at the cops directing traffic and conferring in desperate-looking little huddles. I could pick out Don Grace, good old Tom Denver, and Jerry Kesserling, the traffic cop.

A bell went off suddenly with a loud bray, making all of us jump. It made the cops outside jump, too. A couple of them pulled their guns.

"Change-of-classes bell," Harmon said.

I looked at the wall clock. It was 9:50. At 9:05 I had been sitting in my seat by the window, watching the squirrel. Now the squirrel was gone, good old Tom Denver was gone, and Mrs. Underwood was really gone. I thought it over and decided I was gone, too.

Chapter 21

Three more state-police cars came, and also a number of citizens from town. The cops tried to shoo them away, with greater or lesser degrees of success. Mr. Frankel, owner and proprietor of Frankel's Jewelry Store & Camera Shop, drove up in his new Pontiac Firebird and jawed for quite a while with Jerry Kesserling. He pushed his horn-rimmed glasses up on his nose constantly as he talked. Jerry was trying to get rid of him, but Mr. Frankel wasn't having any of it. He was also Placerville's second selectman and a crony of Norman Jones, Ted's father.

"My mother got me a ring in his store," Sarah Pasterne said, looking at Ted from the corner of her eye. "It greened my finger the first day."

"My mother says he's a gyp," Tanis said.

"Hey!" Pig Pen gulped. "There's my mother!"

We all looked. Sure enough, there was Mrs. Dano talking with one of the state troopers, her slip hanging a quarter of an inch below the hem of her dress. She was one of those ladies who do fifty percent of their talking with their hands. They fluttered and whipped like flags, and it made me think of autumn Saturdays on the gridiron, somehow: holding . . . clipping . . . illegal tackle. I guess in this case you'd have to say it was illegal holding.

We all knew her by sight as well as by reputation; she headed up a lot of PTA functions and was a member in good standing of the Mothers Club. Go out to a baked-bean supper to benefit the class trip, or to the Sadie Hawkins dance in the gym, or to the senior outing, and you'd be apt to find Mrs. Dano at the door, ready with the old glad hand, grinning like there was no tomorrow, and collecting bits of information the way frogs catch flies.

Pig Pen shifted nervously in his seat, as if he might have to go to the bathroom.

"Hey, Pen, your mudda's callin'," Jack Goldman intoned from the back of the room.

"Let her call," Pig Pen muttered.

The Pen had an older sister, Lilly Dano, who was a senior when we were all freshmen. She had a face that looked a lot like Pig Pen's, which made her nobody's candidate for Teen Queen. A hook-nosed junior named LaFollet St. Armand began squiring her about, and then knocked her up higher than a kite. LaFollet joined the Marines, where they presumably taught him the difference between his rifle and his gun—which was for shooting and which was for fun. Mrs. Dano appeared at no PTA functions for the next two months. Lilly was packed off to an aunt in Boxford, Massachusetts. Shortly after that, Mrs. Dano returned to the same old stand, grinning harder than ever. It's a small-town classic, friends.

"She must be really worried about you," Carol Granger said.

"Who cares?" Pig Pen asked indifferently. Sylvia Ragan smiled at him. Pig Pen blushed.

Nobody said anything for a while. We watched the townspeople mill around beyond the bright yellow crash barricades that were going up. I saw some other mums and dads among them. I didn't see Sandra's mother and father, and I didn't see big Joe McKennedy. Hey, I didn't really expect he'd show up, anyway. Circuses have never been our style.

A newsmobile from WGAN-TV pulled up. One of the guys got out, patting his process neatly into place, and jawed with a cop. The cop pointed across the road. The guy with the process went back to the newsmobile, and two more guys got out and started unloading camera equipment.

"Anybody here got a transistor radio?" I asked.

Three of them raised hands. Corky's was the biggest, a Sony twelve transistor that he carried in his briefcase. It got six bands, including TV, shortwave, and CB. He put it on his desk and turned it on. We were just in time for the ten-o'clock report:

"Topping the headlines, a Placerville High School senior, Charles Everett Decker . . . "

"Everett!" Somebody snickered.

"Shut up," Ted said curtly.

Pat Fitzgerald stuck out his tongue.

" . . . apparently went berserk early this morning and is now holding twenty-four classmates hostage in a classroom of that high school. One person, Peter Vance, thirty-seven, a history teacher at Placerville, is known dead. Another teacher, Mrs. Jean Underwood, also thirty-seven, is feared dead. Decker has commandeered the intercom system and has communicated twice with school authorities. The list of hostages is as follows . . . "

He read down the class list as I had given it to Tom Denver. "I'm on the radio!" Nancy Caskin exclaimed when they reached her name. She blinked and smiled tentatively. Melvin Thomas whistled. Nancy colored and told him to shut up.

" . . . and George Yannick. Frank Philbrick, head of the Maine State Police, has asked that all friends and family stay away from the scene. Decker is presumed dangerous, and Philbrick emphasized that nobody knows at this time what might set him off. "We have to assume that the boy is still on a hair trigger," Philbrick said.

"Want to pull my trigger?" I asked Sylvia.

"Is your safety on?" she asked right back, and the class roared. Anne Lasky laughed with her hands over her mouth, blushing a deep bright red. Ted Jones, our practicing party poop, scowled.

" . . . Grace, Placerville's psychiatrist and guidance counselor, talked to Decker over the intercom system only minutes ago. Grace told reporters that Decker threatened to kill someone in the classroom if Grace did not leave the upstairs office immediately."

"Liar!" Grace Stanner said musically. Irma jumped a little.

"Who does he think he is?" Melvin asked angrily. "Does he think he can get away with that shit?"

" . . . also said that he considers Decker to be a schizophrenic personality, possibly past the point of anything other than borderline rationality. Grace concluded his hurried remarks by saying: 'At this point, Charles Decker might conceivably do anything.' Police from the surrounding towns of . . . "

"Whatta crocka shit!" Sylvia blared. "I'm gonna tell those guys what really went down with that guy when we get outta here! I'm gonna—"

"Shut up and listen!" Dick Keene snapped at her.

" . . . and Lewiston have been summoned to the scene. At this moment, according to Captain Philbrick, the situation is at an impasse. Decker has sworn to kill if tear gas is used, and with the lives of twenty-four children at stake . . . "

"Children," Pig Pen said suddenly. "Children this and children that. They stabbed you in the back, Charlie. Already. Children. Ha. Shit. What do they think is happening? I—"

"He's saying something about—" Corky began.

"Never mind. Turn it off," I said. "This sounds more interesting." I fixed the Pen with my best steely gaze. "What seems to be on yore mind, pard?"

Pig Pen jerked his thumb at Irma. "She thinks she's got it bad," he said. "Her. Heh." He laughed a sudden, erratic laugh. For no particular reason I could make out, he removed a pencil from his breast pocket and looked at it. It was a purple pencil.

"Be-Bop pencil," Pig Pen said. "Cheapest pencils on the face of the earth, that's what I think. Can't sharpen 'em at all. Lead breaks. Every September since I started first grade Ma comes home from the Mammoth Mart with two hundred Be-Bop pencils in a plastic box. And I use 'em, Jesus."

He snapped his purple pencil between his thumbs and stared at it. To tell the truth, I did think it looked like a pretty cheap pencil. I've always used the Eberhard Faber myself.

"Ma," Pig Pen said. "That's Ma for you. Two hundred Be-Bop pencils in a plastic box. You know what her big thing is? Besides all those shitty suppers where they give you a big plate of Hamburger Helper and a paper cup of orange Jell-O full of grated carrots? Huh? She enters contests. That's her hobby. Hundreds of contests. All the time. She subscribes to all the women's magazines and enters the sweepstakes. Why she likes Rinso for all her dainty things in twenty-five words or less. My sister had a kitten once, and Ma wouldn't even let her keep it."

"She the one who got pregnant?" Corky asked.

"Wouldn't even let her keep it," Pig Pen said. "Drownded it in the bathtub when no one would take it. Lilly begged her to at least take it to the vet so it could have gas, and Ma said four bucks for gas was too much to spend on a worthless kitten."

"Oh, poor thing," Susan Brooks said.

"I swear to God, she did it right in the bathtub. All those goddamn pencils. Will she buy me a new shirt? Huh? Maybe for my birthday. I say, 'Ma, you should hear what the kids call me. Ma, for Lord's sake.' I don't even get an allowance, she says she needs it for postage so she can enter her contests. A new shirt for my birthday and a shitload of Be-Bop pencils in a plastic box to take back to school. I tried to get a paper route once, and she put a stop to that. She said there were women of loose virtue who laid in wait for young boys after their husbands went to work.''

''Oh, my *Gawwd!*'' Sylvia bellowed.

''And contests. And PTA suppers. And chaperoning dances. Grabbing on to everybody. Sucking up to them and grinning.''

He looked at me and smiled the oddest smile I had seen all day. And that was going some.

''You know what she said when Lilly had to go away? She said I'd have to sell my car. That old Dodge my uncle gave me when I got my driver's license. I said I wouldn't. I said Uncle Fred gave it to me and I was going to keep it. She said if I wouldn't sell it, she would. She'd signed all the papers, and legally it was hers. She said I wasn't going to get any girl pregnant in the back seat. Me. Get a girl pregnant in the back seat. That's what she said.''

He brandished a broken pencil half. The lead poked out of the wood like a black bone. ''Me. Hah. The last date I had was for the eighth-grade class picnic. I told Ma I wouldn't sell the Dodge. She said I would. I ended up selling it. I knew I would. I can't fight her. She always knows what to say. You start giving her a reason why you can't sell your car, and she says: 'Then how come you stay in the bathroom so long?' Right off the wall. You're talking about the car, and she's talking about the bathroom. Like you're doing something dirty in there. She grinds you.'' He stared out the window. Mrs. Dano was no longer in sight. ''She grinds and grinds and grinds, and she always beats you. Be-Bop pencils that break every time you try to sharpen them. That's how she beats you. That's how she grinds you down. And she's so mean and stupid, she drownded the kitty, just a little kitty, and she's so *stupid* that you know everybody laughs at her behind her back. So what does that make me? Littler and stupider. After a while you feel just like a little kitty that crawled into a plastic box full of Be-Bop pencils and got brought home by mistake.'' The room was dead quiet. Pig Pen had center stage. I don't think he knew it. He looked grubby and pissed off, fists clenched around his broken pencil halves. Outside, a cop had driven a police cruiser onto the lawn. He parked it parallel to the school, and a few more cops ran down behind it, presumably to do secret things. They had riot guns in their hands. ''I don't think I'd mind if she snuffed it,'' Pig Pen said, grinning a small, horrified grin. ''I wish I had your stick, Charlie. If I had your stick, I think I'd kill her myself.''

''You're crazy, too,'' Ted said worriedly. ''God, you're all going crazy right along with him.''

''Don't be such a *creep*, Ted.'' It was Carol Granger. In a way, it was surprising not to find her on Ted's side. I knew he had taken her out a few times before she started with her current steady, and bright establishment types usually stick together. Still, it had been she who had dropped him. To make a very clumsy analogy, I was beginning to suspect that Ted was to my classmates what Eisenhower must always have been to the dedicated liberals of the fifties—you had to like him, that style, that grin, that record, those good intentions, but there was something exasperating and a tiny bit slimy about him. You can see I'm fixated on Ted. . . . Why not? I'm still trying to figure him out. Sometimes it seems that everything that happened on that long morning is just something I imagined, or some half-baked writer's fantasy. But it *did* happen. And sometimes, now, it seems to me that Ted was at the center of it all, not me. It seems that Ted goaded them all into people they were not . . . or into the people they really were. All I know for sure is that Carol was looking at him defiantly, not like a demure valedictorian-to-be due to speak on the problems of the black race. She looked angry and a wee bit cruel.

When I think about the Eisenhower administration, I think about the U-2 incident. When I think about that funny morning, I think about the sweat patches that were slowly spreading under the arms of Ted's khaki shirt.

"When they drag him off, they won't find anything but nut cases," Ted was saying. He looked mistrustfully at Pig Pen, who was glaring sweatily at the halves of his Be-Bop pencil as if they were the only things left in the world. His neck was grimy, but what the hell. Nobody was talking about his neck.

"They grind you down," he whispered. He threw the pencil halves on the floor. He looked at them, then looked up at me. His face was strange and grief-stunned. It made me uncomfortable. "They'll grind you down, too, Charlie. Wait and see if they don't."

There was an uncomfortable silence in the room. I was holding on to the pistol very tightly. Without thinking about it much, I took out the box of shells and put three of them in, filling the magazine again. The handgrip was sweaty. I suddenly realized I had been holding it by the barrel, pointing it at myself, not looking at them. No one had made a break. Ted was sort of hunched over his desk, hands gripping the edge, but he hadn't moved, except in his head. I suddenly thought that touching his skin would be like touching an alligator handbag. I wondered if Carol had ever kissed him, touched him. Probably had. The thought made me want to puke.

Susan Brooks suddenly burst into tears.

Nobody looked at her. I looked at them, and they looked at me. I had been holding the pistol by the barrel. They knew it. They had seen it.

I moved my feet, and one of them kicked Mrs. Underwood. I looked down at her. She had been wearing a casual tartan coat over a brown cashmere sweater. She was beginning to stiffen. Her skin probably felt like an alligator handbag. Rigor, you know. I had left a footmark on her sweater at some point in time. For some reason, that made me think of a picture I had once seen of Ernest Hemingway, standing with one foot on a dead lion and a rifle in his hand and half a dozen grinning black bearers in the background. I suddenly needed to scream. I had taken her life, I had snuffed her, put a bullet in her head and spilled out algebra.

Susan Brooks had put her head down on her desk, the way they used to make us do in kindergarten when it was nap time. She was wearing a powder-blue scarf in her hair. It looked very pretty. My stomach hurt.

"DECKER!"

I cried out and jerked the pistol around toward the windows. It was a state trooper with a battery-powered bullhorn. Up on the hill, the newsmen were grinding away with their cameras. Just grinding away—Pig Pen hadn't been so far wrong, at that.

"COME OUT, DECKER, WITH YOUR HANDS UP!"

"Let me be," I said.

My hands had begun to tremble. My stomach really did hurt. I've always had a lousy stomach. Sometimes I'd get the dry heaves before I went to school in the morning, or when I was taking a girl out for the first time. Once, Joe and I took a couple of girls down to Harrison State Park. It was July, warm and very beautiful. The sky had a dim, very high haze. The girl I was with was named Annmarie. She spelled it all one name. She was very pretty. She wore dark green corduroy shorts and a silk pullover blouse. She had a beach bag. We were going down Route 1 toward Bath, the radio on and playing good rock 'n' roll. Brian Wilson, I remember that, Brian Wilson and the Beach Boys. And Joe was driving his old blue Mercury—he used to call it *De Blue Frawwwg* and then grin his Joe McKennedy grin. All the vents were open. I got sick to my stomach. It was very bad. Joe was talking to his girl. They were talking about surfing, which was certainly compatible with the Beach Boys on the radio. She was a fine-looking girl. Her name was Rosalynn. She was Annmarie's sister. I opened my mouth to say I felt sick, and puked all over the floor. Some of it got on Annmarie's leg, and the look on her face, you couldn't imagine it. Or maybe you could. They all tried to make light of it, brush it off. I let all my guys puke on me on the first date, ha-ha. I couldn't go in swimming that day. My stomach felt too bad. Annmarie sat on the blanket next to me most of the time and got a burn. The girls had packed a picnic lunch. I drank a soda, but I couldn't eat any of the sandwiches. I was thinking about Joe's blue Merc, standing in the sun all day, and how it was going to smell going home. The late Lenny Bruce once said you can't get snot off a suede jacket, and to that I would add one of the other great home truths: you can't get the smell of vomit out of a blue Mercury's upholstery. It's there for weeks, for months, maybe years. And it smelled just about like I thought it would. Everybody just pretended it wasn't there. But it was.

"COME ON OUT, DECKER. WE'RE THROUGH FOOLING AROUND WITH YOU!"

"Stop it! Shut up!" Of course they couldn't hear me. They didn't want to. This was their game.

"Don't like it so well when you can't talk back, do you?" Ted Jones said. "When you can't play any of your smart games."

"Leave me alone." I sounded suspiciously like I was whining.

"They'll wearya out," Pig Pen said. It was the voice of doom. I tried to think about the squirrel, and about the way the lawn grew right up to the building, no fucking around. I couldn't do it. My mind was jackstraws in the wind. The beach that day had been bright and hot. Everybody had a transistor radio, all of them tuned to different stations. Joe and Rosalynn had body-surfed in glass-green waves.

"YOU'VE GOT FIVE MINUTES, DECKER!"

"Go on out," Ted urged. He was gripping the edge of his desk again. "Go out while you've got a chance."

Sylvia whirled on him. "What have you got to be? Some kind of hero? Why? Why? Shit, that's all you'll be, Ted Jones. I'll tell them—"

"Don't tell me what—"

" . . . wearya down, Charlie, grind ya, wait and—"

"DECKER!"

"Go on out, Charlie . . . "

" . . . please, can't you see you're upsetting him—"

"DECKER!"

" . . . PTA suppers and all that lousy . . . "

" . . . cracking up if you'd just let him DECKER! alone grindya wearya down you go Charlie you can't DON'T WANT TO BE FORCED TO SHOOT until you're ready leave him be Ted if you know what all of you shut up good for you COMEOUT . . . "

I swung the pistol up at the windows, holding it in both hands, and pulled the trigger four times. The reports slammed around the room like bowling balls. Window glass blew out in great crackling fistfuls. The troopers dived down out of sight. The cameramen hit the gravel. The clot of spectators broke and ran in all directions. Broken glass shone and twinkled on the green grass outside like diamonds on show-window velvet, brighter gems than any in Mr. Frankel's store.

There was no answering fire. They were bluffing. I knew that; it was my stomach, my goddamn stomach. What else could they do but bluff?

Ted Jones was not bluffing. He was halfway to the desk before I could bring the pistol around on him. He froze, and I knew he thought I was going to shoot him. He was looking right past me into darkness.

"Sit down," I said.

He didn't move. Every muscle seemed paralyzed.

"Sit down."

He began to tremble. It seemed to begin in his legs and spread up his trunk and arms and neck. It reached his mouth, which began to gibber silently. It climbed to his right cheek, which began to twitch. His eyes stayed steady. I have to give him that, and with admiration. One of the few things my father says when he's had a few that I agree with is that kids don't have much balls in this generation. Some of them are trying to start the revolution by bombing U.S. government washrooms, but none of them are throwing Molotov cocktails at the Pentagon. But Ted's eyes, even full of darkness, stayed steady.

"Sit down," I repeated.

He went and sat down.

Nobody in the room had cried out. Several of them had put their hands over their ears. Now they took them away carefully, sampling the noise level of the air, testing it. I looked for my stomach. It was there. I was in control again.

The man with the bullhorn was shouting, but this time he wasn't shouting at me. He was telling the people who had been watching from across the road to get out of the area and be snappy about it. They were doing it. Many of them ran hunched over, like Richard Widmark in a World War II epic.

A quiet little breeze riffled in through the two broken windows. It caught a paper on Harmon Jackson's desk and fluttered it into the aisle. He leaned over and picked it up.

Sandra Cross said, "Tell something else, Charlie."

I felt a weird smile stretch my lips. I wanted to sing the chorus from that folk song, the one about beautiful, beautiful blue eyes, but I couldn't remember the words and probably wouldn't have dared, anyway. I sing like a duck. So I only looked at her and smiled my weird smile. She blushed a little but didn't drop her eyes. I thought of her married to some slob with five two-button suits and fancy pastel toilet paper in the bathroom. It hurt me with its inevitability. They all find out sooner or later how unchic it is to pop your buttons at the Sadie Hawkins dance, or to crawl into the trunk so you can get into the drive-in for free. They stop eating pizza and plugging dimes into the juke down at Fat Sammy's. They stop kissing boys in the blueberry patch. And they always seem to end up looking like the Barbie doll cutouts in *Jack and Jill* magazine. Fold in at Slot A, Slot B, and Slot C. Watch Her Grow Old Before Your Very Eyes. For a second I thought I might actually turn on the waterworks, but I avoided that indignity by wondering if she was wearing white panties today.

It was 10:20. I said:

Chapter 22

I was twelve when Mom got me the corduroy suit. By that time Dad had pretty much given up on me and I was my mother's responsibility. I wore the suit to church on Sundays and to Bible meetings on Thursday nights. With my choice of three snap-on bow ties. Rooty-toot.

But I hadn't expected her to try and make me wear it to that goddamn birthday party. I tried everything. I reasoned with her. I threatened not to go. I even tried a lie—told her the party was off because Carol had the chickenpox. One call to Carol's mother set that straight. Nothing worked. Mom let me run pretty much as I pleased most of the time, but when she got an idea solid in her mind, you were stuck with it. Listen to this: for Christmas one year, my dad's brother gave her this weird jigsaw puzzle. I think Uncle Tom was in collusion with my dad on that one. She did a lot of jigsaws—I helped—and they both thought it was the biggest waste of time on earth. So Tom sent her a five-hundred-piece jigsaw puzzle that had a single blueberry down in the lower-right-hand corner. The rest of the puzzle was solid white, no shades. My father laughed his ass off. "Let's see you do that one, Mother," he said. He always called her "Mother" when he felt a good one had been put over on her, and it never ceased to irritate her. She sat down on Christmas afternoon and spread the puzzle out on her puzzle table in her bedroom—by this time they each had their own. There were TV dinners and pickup lunches for Dad and I on December twenty-sixth and the twenty-seventh, but on the morning of the twenty-eighth, the puzzle was done. She took a Polaroid picture of it to send to Uncle Tom, who lives in Wisconsin. Then she took the puzzle apart and put it away in the attic. That was two years ago, and so far as I know, it's still there. But she did it. My mother is a humorous, literate, pleasant person. She is kind to animals and accordion-playing mendicants. But you didn't cross her, or she could dig in her heels . . . usually somewhere in the groin area.

I was crossing her. I was, in fact, starting to run through my arguments for the fourth time that day, but time had just about run out. The bow tie was clutching my collar like a pink spider with hidden steel legs, the coat was too tight, and she'd even made me put on my square-toed shoes, which were my Sunday best. My father wasn't there, he was down at Gogan's slopping up a few with his good buddies, but if he'd been around he would have said I looked "squared away." I didn't feel like an asshole.

"Listen, Mother—"

"I don't want to hear any more about it, Charlie." I didn't want to hear any more about it either, but since I was the one running for the Shithead of the Year Award, and not her, I felt obliged to give it the old school grunt.

"All I'm trying to tell you is that nobody is going to be wearing a suit to that party, Mom. I called up Joe McKennedy this morning, and he said he was just going to wear—"

"Just shut up about it," she said, very soft, and I did. When my mother says "shut up," she's really mad. She didn't learn "shut up" reading *The Guardian*. "Shut up, or you won't be going anywhere."

But I knew what that meant. "Not going anywhere" would apply to a lot more than Carol Granger's party. It would probably mean movies, the Harlow rec center, and swimming classes for the next month. Mom is quiet, but she carries a grudge when she doesn't get her way. I remembered the jigsaw puzzle, which had borne the whimsical title "Last Berry in the Patch." That puzzle had crossed her, and it hadn't been out of the attic for the last two years. And if you have to know, and maybe some of you do anyway, I had a little crush on Carol. I'd bought her a snotrag with her initials on it and wrapped it myself. Mom offered, but I said no. It wasn't any lousy fifteen-cent hankie, either. Those babies were going in the Lewiston J. C. Penney's for fifty-nine cents, and it had lace all the way around the edge.

"Okay." I grumped at her. "Okay, okay, okay."

"And don't you wise-mouth me, Charlie Decker," she said grimly. "Your father is quite capable of thrashing you yet."

"Don't I know it," I said. "Every time we're in the same room together, he reminds me."

"Charlie . . ."

"I'm on my way," I said quickly, heading it off. "Hang in there, Mom."

"Don't get dirty!" she called after me as I went out the door. "Don't spill any ice cream on your pants! Remember to say thank you when you leave! Say hi to Mrs. Granger!"

I didn't say anything to any of these orders, feeling that to acknowledge might be to encourage. I just jammed the hand that wasn't carrying the package deeper into my pocket and hunched my head.

"Be a gentleman!"

Gawd.

"And remember not to start eating until Carol does!"

Dear Gawd.

I hurried to get out of her sight before she decided to run after me and check to see if I'd peed myself.

But it wasn't a day made to feel bad on. The sky was blue and the sun was just warm enough, and there was a little breeze to chase along at your heels. It was summer vacation, and Carol might even give me a tumble. Of course, I didn't know just what I'd do if Carol *did* give me a tumble—maybe let her ride double on my Schwinn—but I could cross that bridge when I came to it. Perhaps I was even overestimating the negative sex appeal of the corduroy suit. If Carol had a crush on Myron Floren, she was going to love me.

Then I saw Joe and started to feel stupid all over again. He was wearing ragged white Levi's and a T-shirt. I could see him looking me up and down, and I winced. The jacket had little brass buttons with a heralds embossed on them. Rooty-toot.

"Great suit," he said. "You look just like that guy on the Lawrence Belch show. The one with the accordion."

"Myron Floren," I said. "Riiight."

He offered me a stick of gum, and I skinned it.

"My mother's idea." I stuck the gum into my mouth. Black Jack gum. There is no finer. I rolled it across my tongue and chomped. I was feeling better again. Joe was a friend, the only good one I ever had. He never seemed afraid of me, or revolted by my weird mannerisms (when a good idea strikes me, for instance, I have a tendency to walk around with my face screwed up in the most godawful grimaces without even being aware of it—didn't Grace have a field day with that one). I had Joe beat in the brains department, and he had me in the making-friends department. Most kids don't give a hoot in hell for brains; they go a penny a pound, and the kid with the high I.Q. who can't play baseball or at least come in third in the local circle jerk is everybody's fifth wheel. But Joe liked my brains. He never said, but I know he did. And because everyone liked Joe, they had to at least tolerate me. I won't say I worshiped Joe McKennedy, but it was a close thing. He was my mojo.

So there we were, walking along and chewing our Black Jack, when a hand came down on my shoulder like a firecracker. I almost choked on my gum. I stumbled, turned around, and there was Dicky Cable.

Dicky was a squat kid who always somehow reminded me of a lawn mower, a big Briggs & Stratton self-propelling model with the choke stuck open. He had a big square grin, and it was chock-full of big white square teeth that fitted together on the top and bottom like the teeth in two meshing cogs. His teeth seemed to gnash and fume between his lips like revolving mower blades that are moving so fast they seem to stand still. He looked like he ate patrol boys for supper. For all I knew, he did.

"Son of a *gun,* you look *slick!*" He winked elaborately at Joe. "Son of a *gun,* you just look slicker than *owl shit!*" *Whack!* on the back again. I felt very small. About three inches, I'd say. I was scared of him—I think I had a dim idea that I might have to fight him or crawfish before the day was over, and that I would probably crawfish.

"Don't break my back, okay?" I said. But he wouldn't leave it alone. He just kept riding and riding until we got to Carol's house. I knew the worst the minute we went through the door. Nobody was dressed up. Carol was there in the middle of the room, and she looked really beautiful.

It hurt. She looked beautiful and casual, a shadow glass of sophistication over the just-beginning adolescent. She probably still cried and threw tantrums and locked herself in the bathroom, probably still listened to Beatles records and had a picture of David Cassidy, who was big that year, tucked into the corner of her vanity mirror, but none of that showed. And the fact that it didn't show hurt me and made me feel dwarfed. She had a rust-colored scarf tied into her hair. She looked fifteen or sixteen, already filling out in front. She was wearing a brown dress. She was laughing with a bunch of kids and gesturing with her hands.

Dicky and Joe went on over and gave her their presents, and she laughed and nodded and thank-you'd, and my God but she looked nice.

I decided to leave. I didn't want her to see me in my bow tie and my corduroy suit with the little brass buttons. I didn't want to see her talking with Dicky Cable, who looked like a human Lawnboy to me but who seemed to look pretty good to her. I figured I could slip out before anyone got a really good look at me. Like Lamont Cranston, I would just cloud a few minds and then bug out. I had a buck in my pocket from weeding Mrs. Katzentz's flower garden the day before, and I could go to the movies in Brunswick if I could hook a ride, and work up a good head of self-pity sitting there in the dark.

But before I could even find the doorknob, Mrs. Granger spotted me.

It wasn't my day. Imagine a pleated skirt and one of those see-through chiffon blouses on a Sherman tank. A Sherman tank with two gun turrets. Her hair looked like a hurricane, one glump going one way and one glump the other. The two glumps were being held together somehow by a big sateen bow that was poison yellow in color.

"Charlie *Decker!*" she squealed, and spread out arms that looked like loaves of bread. *Big* loaves. I almost chickened and ran for it. She was an avalanche getting ready to happen. She was every Japanese horror monster ever made, all rolled into one, Ghidra, Mothra, Godzilla, Rodan, and Tukkan the Terrible trundling across the Granger living room. But that wasn't the bad part. The bad part was everybody looking at me—you know what I'm talking about.

She gave me a slobbery kiss on the cheek and crowed, "Well, don't you look *nice?*" And for one horribly certain second I expected her to add: "Slicker than *owl shit!*"

Well, I'm not going to torture either you or myself with a blow-by-blow. Where would be the sense? You've got the picture. Three hours of unadulterated hell. Dicky was right there with a "Well, don't you look *nice?*" at every opportunity. A couple of other kids happened over to ask me who died.

Joe was the only one who stuck by me, but even that embarrassed me a little. I could see him telling kids to lay off, and I didn't like it very well. It made me feel like the village idiot.

I think the only one who didn't notice me at all was Carol. It would have bothered me if she had come over and asked me to dance when they put on the records, but it bothered me worse that she didn't. I couldn't dance, but it's the thought that counts.

So I stood around while the Beatles sang "The Ballad of John and Yoko" and "Let It Be," while the Adreizi Brothers sang "We Gotta Get It On Again," while Bobby Sherman sang "Hey, Mr. Sun" in his superbly tuneless style. I was giving my best imitation of a flowerpot. The party, meanwhile, went on. Did it ever. It seemed like it was going to go on eternally, the years flashing by outside like leaves in the wind, cars turning into clumps of rust, houses decaying, parents turning into dust, nations rising and falling. I had a feeling that we would still be there when Gabriel flew overhead, clutching the Judgment trump in one hand and a party favor in the other. There was ice cream, there was a big cake that said HAPPY BIRTHDAY, CAROL in green and red icing, there was more dancing, and a couple of kids wanted to play spin the bottle, but Mrs. Granger laughed a big jolly laugh and said no, ha-ha, no no no. Oh, no.

Finally Carol clapped her hands and said we were all going outside and play follow the leader, the game which asks the burning question: Are you ready for tomorrow's society?

Everybody spilled outside. I could hear them running around and having a good time, or whatever passes for a good time when you're part of a mass puberty cramp. I lingered behind for a minute, half-thinking Carol would stop for a second, but she hurried right by. I went out and stood on the porch watching. Joe was there too, sitting with one leg hooked over the porch railing, and we both watched. Somehow Joe always seems to be where I end up, with one leg hooked over something, watching.

"She's stuck up," he said finally.

"Nah. She's just busy. Lot of people. You know."

"Shit," Joe said.

We were quiet for a minute. Someone yelled, "Hey, Joe!"

"You'll get crap all over that thing if you play," Joe said. "Your mother'll have a kitten."

"She'll have two," I said.

"Come *on*, Joe!" This time it was Carol. She had changed into denims, probably designed by Edith Head, and she looked flushed and pretty. Joe looked at me. He wanted to look out for me, and suddenly I felt more terrified than at any time since I woke up on that hunting trip up north. After a while, being somebody's responsibility makes them hate you, and I was scared that Joe might hate me someday. I didn't know all that then, not at twelve, but I sensed some of it.

"Go on," I said.

"You sure you don't want to—?"

"Yeah. Yeah. I got to get home anyway."

I watched him go, hurt a little that he hadn't offered to come with me, but relieved in a way. Then I started across the lawn toward the street.

Dicky noticed me. "You on your way, pretty boy?"

I should have said something clever like: Yeah. Give my regards to Broadway. Instead I told him to shut up.

He jackrabbited in front of me as if he had been expecting it, that big lawn-mower grin covering the entire lower half of his face. He smelled green and tough, like vines in the jungle. "What was that, pretty boy?"

All of it lumped together, and I felt ugly. Really ugly. I could have spit at Hitler, that's how ugly I felt. "I said shut up. Get out of my way."

[In the classroom, Carol Granger put her hands over her eyes . . . but she didn't tell me to stop. I respected her for that.]

Everyone was staring, but no one was saying anything. Mrs. Granger was in the house, singing "Swanee" at the top of her voice.

"Maybe you think you can shut me up." He ran a hand through his oiled hair.

I shoved him aside. It was like being outside myself. It was the first time I ever felt that way. Someone else, some other me, was in the driver's seat. I was along for the ride, and that was all.

He swung at me; his fist looped down and hit me on the shoulder. It just about paralyzed the big muscle in my arm. Jesus, did that hurt. It was like getting hit with an iceball.

I grabbed him, because I never could box, and shoved him backward across the lawn, that big grin steaming and fuming at me. He dug his heels in and curled an arm around my neck, as if about to kiss me. His other fist started hammering at my back, but it was like someone knocking on a door long ago and far away. We tripped over a pink lawn flamingo and whumped to the ground.

He was strong, but I was desperate. All of a sudden, beating up Dicky Cable was my mission in life. It was what I had been put on earth for. I remembered the Bible story about Jacob wrestling with the angel, and I giggled crazily into Dicky's face. I was on top, and fighting to stay there.

But all at once he slid away from me—he was awful slippery—and he smashed me across the neck with one arm.

I let out a little cry and went over on my belly. He was astride my back in no time. I tried to turn, but I couldn't.

I couldn't. He was going to beat me because I couldn't. It was all senseless and horrible. I wondered where Carol was. Watching, probably. They were all watching. I felt my corduroy coat ripping out under the arms, the buttons with the heralds embossed on them ripping off one by one on the tough loam. But I couldn't turn over.

He was laughing. He grabbed my head and slammed it into the ground like a whiffle ball. "Hey, pretty boy!" *Slam.* Interior stars and the taste of grass in my mouth. Now *I* was the lawnmower. "Hey, pretty boy, don't you look *nice?*" He picked my head up by the hair and slammed it down again. I started to cry.

"Don't you just look dan-dan-*dandy!*" Dicky Cable cried merrily, and hammered my head into the ground again—*fore!* "Don't you just look *woooonder-ful!*"

Then he was off me, because Joe had dragged him off. "That's enough, god-dammit!" he was shouting. "Don't you know that's enough?"

I got up, still crying. There was dirt in my hair. My head didn't hurt enough for me to still be crying, but there it was. I couldn't stop. They were all staring at me with that funny hangdog look kids get when they've gone too far, and I could see they didn't want to look at me and see me crying. They looked at their feet to make sure they were still there. They glanced around at the chain-link fence to make sure no one was stealing it. A few of them glanced over at the swimming pool in the yard next door, just in case someone might be drowning and in need of a quick rescue.

Carol was standing there, and she started to take a step forward. Then she looked around to see if anyone else was stepping forward, and no one else was. Dicky Cable was combing his hair. There was no dirt in it. Carol shuffled her feet. The wind made ripples on her blouse.

Mrs. Granger had stopped singing "Swanee." She was on the porch, her mouth wide open.

Joe came up and put a hand on my shoulder. "Hey, Charlie," he said. "What do you say we go now, huh?"

I tried to shove him away and only made myself fall down. "Leave me alone!" I shouted at him. My voice was hoarse and raw. I was sobbing more than yelling. There was only one button left on the corduroy jacket, and it was hanging by a string. The pants were all juiced up with grass stains. I started to crawl around on the matted earth, still crying, picking up buttons. My face was hot.

Dicky was humming some spry ditty and looking as if he might like to comb his hair again. Looking back, I have to admire him for it. At least he didn't put on a crocodile face about the whole thing.

Mrs. Granger came waddling toward me. "Charlie . . . Charlie, *dear—*"

"Shut up, fat old *bag!*" I screamed. I couldn't see anything. It was all blurred in my eyes, and all the faces seemed to be crowding in on me. All the hands seemed to have claws. I couldn't see to pick up any more buttons. "Fat old *bag!*"

Then I ran away.

I stopped behind an empty house down on Willow Street and just sat there until all the tears dried up. There was dried snot underneath my nose. I spat on my handkerchief and wiped it off. I blew my nose. An alley cat came by, and I tried to pet it. The cat shied from my hand. I knew exactly how he felt.

The suit was pretty well shot, but I didn't care about that. I didn't even care about my mother, although she would probably call Dicky Cable's mother and complain in her cultured voice. But my father. I could see him sitting, looking, carefully poker-faced, saying: *How does the other guy look?*

And my lie.

I sat down for the best part of an hour, planning to go down to the highway and stick out my thumb, hook a ride out of town, and never come back.

But in the end I went home.

Chapter 23

Outside, a regular cop convention was shaping up. Blue trooper cars, white cruisers from the Lewiston P.D., a black-and-white from Brunswick, two more from Auburn. The police responsible for this automotive cornucopia ran hither and yon, ducked over low. More newsmen showed up. They poked cameras equipped with cobralike telephoto lenses over the hoods of their vehicles. Sawhorses had been set up on the road above and below the school, along with double rows of those sooty little kerosene pots—to me those things always look like the bombs of some cartoon anarchist. The DPW people had put up a DETOUR sign. I guess they didn't have anything more appropriate in stock—SLOW! MADMAN AT WORK, for instance. Don Grace and good old Tom were hobnobbing with a huge, blocky man in a state-police uniform. Don seemed almost angry. The big blocky man was listening, but shaking his head. I took him to be Captain Frank Philbrick of the Maine State Police. I wondered if he knew I had a clear shot at him.

Carol Granger spoke up in a trembling voice. The shame on her face was alarming. I hadn't told that story to shame her. "I was just a kid, Charlie." "I know that," I said, and smiled. "You were awful pretty that day. You sure didn't look like a kid."

"I had kind of a crush on Dicky Cable, too."

"After the party and all?"

She looked even more ashamed. "Worse than ever. I went with him to the eighth-grade picnic. He seemed . . . oh, daring, I guess. Wild. At the picnic he . . . you know, he got fresh, and I let him, a little. But that was the only time I went anyplace with him. I don't even know where he is now."

"Placerville Cemetery," Dick Keene said flatly.

It gave me a nasty start. It was as if I had just seen the ghost of Mrs. Underwood. I could still have pointed to the places where Dicky had pounded on me. The idea that he was dead made for a strange, almost dreamy terror in my mind—and I saw a reflection of what I was feeling on Carol's face. *He got fresh, and I let him, a little,* she had said. What, exactly, did that mean to a bright college-bound girl like Carol? Maybe he had kissed her. Maybe he had even gotten her out into the puckerbrush and mapped the virgin territory of her burgeoning chest. At the eighth-grade picnic, God save us all. He had been daring and wild.

"What happened to him?" Don Lordi asked.

Dick spoke slowly. "He got hit by a car. That was really funny. Not ha-ha, you know, but peculiar. He got his driver's license just last October, and he used to drive like a fool. Like a crazy man. I guess he wanted everybody to know he had, you know, balls. It got so that no one would ride with him, hardly. He had this 1966 Pontiac, did all the body work himself. Painted her bottle green, with the ace of spades on the passenger side.''

"Sure, I used to see that around,'' Melvin said. "Over by the Harlow Rec.''

"Put in a Hearst four-shifter all by himself,'' Dick said. "Four-barrel carb, overhead cam, fuel injection. She purred. Ninety in second gear. I was with him one night when he went up the Stackpole Road in Harlow at ninety-five. We go around Brissett's Bend and we start to slide. I hit the floor. You're right, Charlie. He looked weird when he was smiling. I dunno if he looked exactly like a lawn-mower, but he sure looked weird. He just kept grinning and grinning all the time we were sliding. And he goes . . . like, to himself he goes, 'I can hold 'er, I can hold 'er,' over and over again. And he did, I made him stop, and I walked home. My legs were all rubber. A couple of months later he got hit by a delivery truck up in Lewiston while he was crossing Lisbon Street. Randy Milliken was with him, and Randy said he wasn't even drunk or stoned. It was the truck driver's fault entirely. He went to jail for ninety days. But Dicky was dead. Funny.''

Carol looked sick and white. I was afraid she might faint, and so, to take her mind somewhere else, I said, "Was your mother mad at me, Carol?''

"Huh?'' She looked around in that funny, startled way she had.

"I called her a bag. A fat old bag, I think.''

"Oh.'' She wrinkled her nose and then smiled, gratefully, I think, picking up on the gambit. "She was. She sure was. She thought that fight was all your fault.''

"Your mother and my mother used to both be in that club, didn't they?''

"Books and Bridge? Yeah.'' Her legs were still uncrossed, and now her knees were apart a little. She laughed. "I'll tell you the truth, Charlie. I never really cared for your mother, even though I only saw her a couple of times to say hi to. My mother was always talking about how dreadfully *intelligent* Mrs. Decker was, what a very fine *grasp* she had on the novels of Henry James, stuff like that. And what a fine little *gentleman* you were.''

"Slicker than owl shit,'' I agreed gravely. "You know, I used to get the same stuff about you.''

"You did?''

"Sure.'' An idea suddenly rose up and smacked me on the nose. How could I have possibly missed it so long, an old surmiser like me? I laughed with sudden sour delight. "And I bet I know why she was so determined I was going to wear my suit. It's called 'Matchmaking,' or 'Wouldn't They Make a Lovely Couple?' or, 'Think of the Intelligent Offspring.' Played by all the best families, Carol. Will you marry me?''

Carol looked at me with her mouth open. "They were . . . '' She couldn't seem to finish it.

"That's what I think.''

She smiled; a little giggle escaped her. Then she laughed right out loud. It seemed a little disrespectful of the dead, but I let it pass. Although, to tell you the truth, Mrs. Underwood was never far from my mind. After all, I was almost standing on her.

"That big guy's coming," Billy Sawyer said.

Sure enough, Frank Philbrick was striding toward the school, looking neither right nor left. I hoped the news photographers were getting his good side; who knew, he might want to use some of the pix on this year's Xmas cards. He walked through the main door. Down the hall, as if in another world, I could hear his vague steps pause and then go up to the office. It occurred to me in a strange sort of way that he seemed real only inside. Everything beyond the windows was television. They were the show, not me. My classmates felt the same way. It was on their faces.

Silence.

Chink. The intercom.

"Decker?"

"Yes, sir?" I said.

He was a heavy breather. You could hear him puffing and blowing into the mike up there like some large and sweaty animal. I don't like that, never have. My father is like that on the telephone. A lot of heavy breathing in your ear, so you can almost smell the scotch and Pall Malls on his breath. It always seems unsanitary and somehow homosexual.

"This is a very funny situation you've put us all in, Decker."

"I guess it is, sir."

"We don't particularly like the idea of shooting you."

"No, sir, neither do I. I wouldn't advise you to try."

Heavy breathing. "Okay, let's get it out of the henhouse and see what we got in the sack. What's your price?"

"Price?" I said. "Price?" For one loony moment I had the impression he had taken me for an interesting piece of talking furniture—a Morris chair, maybe, equipped to huckster the prospective buyer with all sorts of pertinent info. At first the idea struck me funny. Then it made me mad.

"For letting them go. What do you want? Air time? You got it. Some sort of statement to the papers? You got that." *Snort-snort-snort.* Likewise, *puff-puff-puff.* "But let's do it and get it done before this thing turns into a hairball. But you got to tell us what you want."

"You," I said.

The breath stopped. Then it started again, puffing and blowing. It was starting to really get on my nerves. "You'll have to explain that," he said.

"Certainly, sir," I said. "We can make a deal. Would you like to make a deal? Is that what you were saying?"

No answer. Puff, snort. Philbrick was on the six-o'clock news every Memorial Day and Labor Day, reading a please-drive-safely message off the teleprompter with a certain lumbering ineptitude that was fascinating and almost endearing. I had felt there was something familiar about him, something intimate that smacked of *déjà vu*. Now I could place it. The breathing. Even on TV he sounded like a bull getting ready to mount Farmer Brown's cow in the back forty.

"What's your deal?"

"Tell me something first," I said. "Is there anybody out there who thinks I might just decide to see how many people I can plug down here? Like Don Grace, for instance?"

"That piece of shit," Sylvia said, then clapped a hand over her mouth.

"Who said that?" Philbrick barked.

Sylvia went white.

"Me," I said. "I have certain transsexual tendencies too, sir." I didn't figure he would know what that meant and would be too wary to ask. "Could you answer my question?"

"Some people think you might go the rest of the way out of your gourd, yes," he answered weightily. Somebody at the back of the room tittered. I don't think the intercom picked it up.

"Okay, then," I said. "The deal is this. You be the hero. Come down here. Unarmed. Come inside with your hands on your head. I'll let everybody go. Then I'll blow your fucking head off. Sir. How's that for a deal? You buy it?"

Puff, snort, blow. "You got a dirty mouth, fella. There are girls down there. Young girls."

Irma Bates looked around, startled, as if someone had just called her.

"The deal," I said. "The deal."

"No," Philbrick said. "You'd shoot me and hold on to the hostages." *Puff, snort.* "But I'll come down. Maybe we can figure something out."

"Fella," I said patiently, "if you sign off and I don't see you going out the same door you came in within fifteen seconds, someone in here is just going to swirl down the spout."

Nobody looked particularly worried at the thought of just swirling down the spout.

Puff, puff. "Your chances of getting out of this alive are getting slimmer."

"Frank, my man, none of us get out of it alive. Even my old man knows that."

"Will you come out?"

"No."

"If that's how you feel." He didn't seem upset. "There's a boy named Jones down there. I want to speak with him."

It seemed okay. "You're on, Ted," I told him. "Your big chance, boy. Don't blow it. Folks, this kid is going to dance his balls off before your very eyes."

Ted was looking earnestly at the black grating of the intercom. "This is Ted Jones, sir." On him, "sir" sounded good.

"Is everyone down there still all right, Jones?"

"Yes, sir."

"How do you judge Decker's stability?"

"I think he's apt to do anything, sir," he said, looking directly at me. There was a savage leer in his eyes. Carol looked suddenly angry. She opened her mouth as if to refute, and then, perhaps remembering her upcoming responsibilities as valedictorian and Leading Lamp of the Western World, she closed her mouth with a snap.

"Thank you, Mr. Jones."

Ted looked absurdly pleased at being called mister.

"Decker?"

"Right here."

Snort, snort. "Be seeing you."

"I better see you," I said. "Fifteen seconds." Then, as an afterthought: "Philbrick?"

"Yeah?"

"You've got a shitty habit, you know it? I've noticed it on all those TV drive-safely pitches that you do. You breathe in people's ears. You sound like a stallion in heat, Philbrick. That's a shitty habit. You also sound like you're reading off a teleprompter, even when you're not. You ought to take care of stuff like that. You might save a life."

Philbrick puffed and snorted thoughtfully.

"Screw, buddy," he said, and the intercom clicked off.

Exactly twelve seconds later he came out the front door, striding stolidly along. When he got to the cars that had been driven onto the lawn, there was another conference. Philbrick gestured a lot.

Nobody said anything. Pat Fitzgerald was chewing a fingernail thoughtfully. Pig Pen had taken out another pencil and was studying it. And Sandra Cross was looking at me steadily. There seemed to be a kind of mist between us that made her glow.

"What about sex?" Carol said suddenly, and when everyone looked at her, she colored.

"Male," Melvin said, and a couple of the jocks in the back of the room haw-hawed.

"What do you mean?" I asked.

Carol looked very much as if she wished her mouth had been stitched closed. "I thought when someone started to act . . . well . . . you know, strangely . . . " She stopped in confusion, but Susan Brooks sprang to the ramparts.

"That's right," she said. "And you all ought to stop grinning. Everyone thinks sex is so *dirty*. That's half what's the matter with all of us. We *worry* about it." She looked protectively at Carol.

"That's what I meant," Carol said. "Are you . . . well, did you have some bad experience?"

"Nothing since that time I went to bed with Mom," I said blandly.

An expression of utter shock struck her face, and then she saw I was joking. Pig Pen snickered dolefully and went on looking at his pencil.

"No, really," she said.

"Well," I said, frowning. "I'll tell about my sex life if you'll tell about yours."

"Oh . . . . " She looked shocked again, but in a pleasant way.

Gracie Stanner laughed. "Cough up, Carol." I had always gotten a murky impression that there was no love lost between those two girls, but now Grace seemed genuinely to be joking—as if some understood but never-mentioned inequality had been erased.

" 'Ray, 'ray," Corky Herald said, grinning.

Carol was blushing furiously. "I'm sorry I asked."

"Go on," Don Lordi said. "It won't hurt."

"Everybody would tell," Carol said. "I know the way bo . . . the way people talk around."

"Secrets," Mike Gavin whispered hoarsely, "give me more secrets." Everybody laughed, but it was getting to be no laughing matter.

"You're not being *fair,*" Susan Brooks said.

"That's right," I said. "Let's drop it."

"Oh . . . never mind," Carol said. "I'll talk. I'll tell you something."

It was my turn to be surprised. Everybody looked at her expectantly. I didn't really know what they expected to hear—a bad case of penis envy, maybe, or Ten Nights with a Candle. I figured they were in for a disappointment, whatever it was. No whips, no chains, no night sweats. Small-town virgin, fresh, bright, pretty, and someday maybe she would blow Placerville and have a real life. Sometimes they change in college. Some of them discover existentialism and anomie and hash pipes. Sometimes they only join sororities and continue with the same sweet dream that began in junior high school, a dream so common to the pretty small-town virgins that it almost could have been cut from a Simplicity pattern, like a jumper or a Your Yummy Summer blouse or play skirt. There's a whammy on bright girls and boys. If the bright ones have a twisted fiber, it shows. If they don't, you can figure them as easily as square roots. Girls like Carol have a steady boyfriend and enjoy a little necking (but, as the Tubes say, "Don't Touch Me There"), nothing overboard. It's okay, I guess. You'd expect more, but, so sorry please, there just isn't. Bright kids are like TV dinners. That's all right. I don't carry a big stick on that particular subject. Smart girls are just sort of dull.

And Carol Granger had that image. She went steady with Buck Thorne (the perfect American name). Buck was the center of the Placerville High Greyhounds, which had posted an 11–0 record the previous fall, a fact that Coach Bob "Stone Balls" Stoneham made much of at our frequent school-spirit assemblies.

Thorne was a good-natured shit who weighed in at a cool two-ten; not exactly the brightest thing on two feet (but college material, of course), and Carol probably had no trouble keeping him in line. I've noticed that pretty girls make the best lion tamers, too. Besides, I always had an idea that Buck Thorne thought the sexiest thing in the world was a quarterback sneak right up the middle.

"I'm a virgin," Carol said defiantly, startling me up out of my thoughts. She crossed her legs as if to prove it symbolically, then abruptly uncrossed them. "And I don't think it's so bad, either. Being a virgin is like being bright."

"It is?" Grace Stanner asked doubtfully.

"You have to work at it," Carol said. "That's what I meant, you have to work at it." The idea seemed to please her. It scared the hell out of me.

"You mean Buck never . . . "

"Oh, he used to want to. I suppose he still does. But I made things pretty clear to him early in the game. And I'm not frigid or anything, or a puritan. It's just that . . . " She trailed off, searching.

"You wouldn't want to get pregnant," I said.

"No!" she said almost contemptuously. "I know all about that." With something like shock I realized she was angry and upset because she was. Anger is a very difficult emotion for a programmed adolescent to handle. "I don't live in books all the time. I read all about birth control in . . . " She bit her lip as the contradiction of what she was saying struck her.

"Well," I said. I tapped the stock of the pistol lightly on the desk blotter. "This is serious, Carol. Very serious. I think a girl should know why she's a virgin, don't you?"

"I *know* why!"

"Oh." I nodded helpfully. Several girls were looking at her with interest. "Because . . . "

Silence. Faintly, the sound of Jerry Kesserling using his whistle to direct traffic.

"Because . . . "

She looked around. Several of them flinched and looked down at their desks. Just then I would have given my house and lot, as the old farmers say, to know just how many virgins we had in here. "And you don't all have to *stare* at me! I didn't ask you to *stare* at me! I'm not going to talk about it! I don't *have* to talk about it!"

She looked at me bitterly.

"People tear you down, that's it. They grind you if you let them, just like Pig Pen said. They all want to pull you down to their level and make you dirty. Look at what they are doing to you, Charlie."

I wasn't sure they had done anything to me just yet, but I kept my mouth shut.

"I was walking along Congress Street in Portland just before Christmas last year. I was with Donna Taylor. We were buying Christmas presents. I'd just bought my sister a scarf in Porteus-Mitchell, and we were talking about it and laughing. Just silly stuff. We were giggling. It was about four o'clock and just starting to get dark. It was snowing. All the colored lights were on, and the shop windows were full of glitter and packages . . . pretty . . . and there was one of those Salvation Army Santa Clauses on the corner by Jones's Book Shop. He was ringing his bell and smiling. I felt good. I felt really good. It was like the Christmas spirit, and all that. I was thinking about getting home and having hot chocolate with whipped cream on top of it. And then this old car drove by, and whoever was driving cranked his window down and yelled, *'Hi, cunt!'* "

Anne Lasky jumped. I have to admit that the word did sound awfully funny coming out of Carol Granger's mouth.

"Just like that," she said bitterly. "It was all wrecked. Spoiled. Like an apple you thought was good and then bit into a worm hole. 'Hi, cunt.' As if that was all there was, no person, just a huh-h-h . . . '' Her mouth pulled down in a trembling, agonized grimace. ''And that's like being bright, too. They want to stuff things into your head until it's all filled up. It's a different hole, that's all. That's all.''

Sandra Cross's eyes were half-closed, as if she dreamed. ''You know,'' she said. ''I feel funny. I feel . . . ''

I wanted to jump up and tell her to keep her mouth shut, tell her not to incriminate herself in this fool's parade, but I couldn't. Repeat, *couldn't*. If I didn't play by my rules, who would?

''I feel like this is all,'' she said.

''Either all brains or all cunt,'' Carol said with brittle good humor. ''Doesn't leave room for much else, does it?''

''Sometimes,'' Sandra said, ''I feel very empty.''

''I . . . '' Carol began, and then looked at Sandra, startled. ''You do?''

''Sure.'' She looked thoughtfully out the broken windows. ''I like to hang out clothes on windy days. Sometimes that's all I feel like. A sheet on the line. You try to get interested in things . . . Politics, the school . . . I was on the Student Council last semester . . . but it's not real, and it's awfully dull. And there aren't a lot of minorities or anything around here to fight for, or . . . well, you know. Important things. And so I let Ted do that to me.''

I looked carefully at Ted, who was looking at Sandra with his face frozen. A great blackness began to drizzle down on me. I felt my throat close.

''It wasn't so hot,'' Sandra said. ''I don't know what all the shouting's about. It's . . . '' She looked at me, her eyes widening, but I could hardly see her. But I could see Ted. He was very clear. In fact, he seemed to be lit by a strange golden glow that stood out in the new clotted darkness like a halo, a supernormal aura.

I raised the pistol very carefully in both hands.

For a moment I thought about the inner caves of my body, the living machines that run on and on in the endless dark.

I was going to shoot him, but they shot me first.

Chapter 24

I know what happened now, although I didn't then.

They had the best sharpshooter in the state out there, a state policeman named Daniel Malvern, from Kent's Hill. There was a picture of him in the Lewiston *Sun* after everything was all over. He was a small man with a crew cut. He looked like an accountant. They had given him a huge Mauser with a telescopic sight. Daniel Malvern took the Mauser to a gravel pit several miles away, test-fired it, and then brought it back and walked down to one of the cruisers parked on the lawn with the rifle stuffed down his pants leg. He rested in the prone position behind the front fender, in deep shadow. He gauged the windage with a wet thumb. Nil. He peered through the telescopic sight. Through the 30X cross-hatched lens, I must have looked as big as a bulldozer. There was not even any window glass to throw a glare, because I had broken it earlier when I fired the pistol to make them stop using the bullhorn. An easy shot. But Dan Malvern took his time. After all, it was probably the most important shot of his life. I was not a clay pigeon; my guts were going to splatter all over the blackboard behind me when the bullet made its mushrooming exit. Crime Does Not Pay. Loony Bites the Dust. And when I half-rose, half-leaned over Mrs. Underwood's desk to put a bullet in Ted Jones, Dan's big chance came. My body half-twisted toward him. He fired his weapon and put the bullet exactly where he had hoped and expected to put it: through my breast pocket, which lay directly over the living machine of my heart.

Where it struck the hard steel of Titus, the Helpful Padlock.

Chapter 25

I held on to the pistol.

The impact of the slug knocked me straight backward against the blackboard, where the chalk ledge bit cruelly into my back. Both of my cordovan loafers flew off. I hit the floor on my fanny. I didn't know what had happened. There was too much all at once. A huge auger of pain drilled my chest, followed by sudden numbness. The ability to breathe stopped. Spots flashed in front of my eyes.

Irma Bates was screaming. Her eyes were closed, her fists were clenched, and her face was a hectic, patched red with effort. It was far away and dreamy, coming from a mountain or a tunnel.

Ted Jones was getting out of his seat again, floating really, in a slow and dreamy motion. This time he was going for the door. "They got the son of a bitch!" His voice sounded incredibly slow and draggy, like a 78-RPM record turned down to 33⅓. "They got the crazy—"

"Sit down."

He didn't hear me. I wasn't surprised. I could hardly hear myself. I didn't have any wind to talk with. He was reaching for the doorknob when I fired the pistol. The bullet slammed into the wood beside his head, and he shied away. When he turned around, his face was a stew of changing emotions: white astonishment, agonized unbelief, and twisted, murdering hate.

"You can't . . . you're . . . "

"Sit down." A little better. Perhaps six seconds had gone by since I had been knocked on my ass. "Stop yelling, Irma."

"You're shot, Charlie," Grace Stanner said calmly.

I looked outside. The cops were rushing the building. I fired twice and made myself breathe. The auger struck again, threatening to explode my chest with pain. *"Get back! I'll shoot them!"*

Frank Philbrick stopped and looked around wildly. He seemed to want a telephone call from Jesus. He looked confused enough to try and carry on with it, so I fired again, up in the air. It was his turn to go a hundred miles in his head during half a second. "Get back!" he yelled. "Get the Christ back!"

They retreated, getting back even quicker than they had gotten down.

Ted Jones was edging toward me. That boy was simply not part of the real universe. "Do you want me to shoot your weenie off?" I asked.

He stopped, but that terrifying, twisted expression was still on his face. "You're dead," he hissed. "Lie down, God damn you."

"Sit down, Ted."

The pain in my chest was a live thing, horrible. The left side of my rib cage felt as if it had been struck by Maxwell's silver hammer. They were staring at me, my captive class, with expressions of preoccupied horror. I didn't dare look down at myself because of what I might see. The clock said 10:55.

"DECKER!"

"Sit down, Ted."

He lifted his lip in an unconscious facial gesture that made him look like a slat-sided hound that I had seen lying mortally wounded beside a busy street when I was just a kid. He thought about it, and then he sat down. He had a good set of sweat circles started under his armpits.

"DECKER! MR. DENVER IS GOING UP TO THE OFFICE!"

It was Philbrick on the bullhorn, and not even the asexual sexuality of the amplification could hide how badly he was shaken up. An hour before, it would have pleased me—fulfilled me—in a savage way, but now I felt nothing.

"HE WANTS TO TALK TO YOU!"

Tom walked out from behind one of the police cars and started across the lawn, walking slowly, as if he expected to be shot at any second. Even at a distance, he looked ten years older. Not even that could please me. Not even that.

I got up a little at a time, fighting the pain, and stepped into my loafers. I almost fell, and had to clutch the desk with my free hand for support.

"Oh, Charlie," Sylvia moaned.

I fully loaded the pistol again, this time keeping it pointed toward them (I don't think even Ted knew it couldn't be fired with the clip sprung), doing it slowly so I could put off looking down at myself for as long as possible. My chest throbbed and ached. Sandra Cross seemed lost again in whatever fuzzy dream it was that she contemplated.

The clip snapped back into place, and I looked down at myself almost casually. I was wearing a neat blue shirt (I've always been fond of solid colors), and I expected to see it matted with my blood. But it wasn't.

There was a large dark hole, dead center through my breast pocket, which was on the left. An uneven scattering of smaller holes radiated out from all around it, like one of those solar-system maps that show the planets going around the sun. I reached inside the pocket very carefully. That was when I remembered Titus, whom I had rescued from the wastebasket. I pulled him out very carefully. The class went *"Aaahhh!"* as if I had just sawed a lady in half or pulled a hundred-dollar bill out of Pig Pen's nose. None of them asked why I was carrying my combination lock in my pocket. I was glad. Ted was looking at Titus bitterly, and suddenly I was very angry at Ted. And I wondered how he would like to eat poor old Titus for his lunch.

The bullet had smashed through the hard, high-density plastic dial, sending high-speed bits of shrapnel out through my shirt. Not one of them had touched my flesh. The steel behind the face had caught the slug, had turned it into a deadly lead blossom with three bright petals. The whole lock was twisted, as if by fire. The semicircular lock bar had been pulled like taffy. The back side of the lock had bulged but not broken through.*

Chink! on the intercom.

"Charlie?"

"Just a minute, Tom. Don't rush me."

"Charlie, you have to—"

"Shut the fuck up."

I unbuttoned my shirt and opened it. The class went *"Aaahhh!"* again. Titus was imprinted on my chest in angry purple, and the flesh had been mashed into an indentation that looked deep enough to hold water. I didn't like to look at it, any more than I liked to look at the old drunk with the bag of flesh below his nose, the one that always hung around Gogan's downtown. It made me feel nauseated. I closed my shirt.

"Tom, those bastards tried to shoot me."

"They didn't mean—"

"Don't tell me what they didn't mean to do!" I screamed at him. There was a crazy note in my voice that made me feel even sicker. "You get your old cracked ass out there and tell that motherfucker Philbrick he almost had a bloodbath down here, have you got it?"

"Charlie . . . " He was whining.

"Shut up, Tom. I'm through fooling with you. I'm in the driver's seat. Not you, not Philbrick, not the superintendent of schools, not God. Have you got it?"

"Charlie, let me explain."

"HAVE YOU GOT IT?"

"Yes, but—"

"All right. We've got that straight. So you go back and give him a message, Tom. Tell him that I don't want to see him or anyone else out there make a move during the next hour. No one is going to come in and talk on this goddamn intercom, and no one else is going to try and shoot me. At noon I want to talk to Philbrick again. Can you remember all that, Tom?"

"Yes, Charlie. All right, Charlie." He sounded relieved and foolish. "They just wanted me to tell you it was a mistake, Charlie. Somebody's gun went off by accident and—"

"One other thing, Tom. Very important."

"What, Charlie?"

"You need to know where you stand with that guy Philbrick, Tom. He gave

---

* It was a year and a half later when I saw that commercial on TV for the first time. The one where the guy with the rifle takes aim at the padlock nailed to the board. You even get a look through the telescopic sight at the padlock—a Yale, a Master, I don't know which. The guy pulls the trigger. And you see that lock jump and dent and mash, and it looked in that commercial just the way old Titus looked when I took him out of my pocket. They show it happening in regular motion, and then they show it in slow motion, and the first and only time I saw it, I leaned down between my legs and puked between my ankles. They took me away. They took me back to my room. And the next day my pet shrink here looked at a note and said, "They tell me you had a setback yesterday, Charlie. Want to talk about it?" But I couldn't talk about it. I've never been able to talk about it. Until now.

you a shovel and told you to walk behind the ox cart, and you're doing it. I gave him a chance to put his ass on the line, and he wouldn't do it. Wake up, Tom. Assert yourself.''

"Charlie, you have to understand what a terrible position you're putting us all in.''

"Get out, Tom.''

He clicked off. We all watched him come out through the main doors and start back toward the cars. Philbrick came over to him and put a hand on his arm. Tom shook it off. A lot of the kids smiled at that. I was past smiling. I wanted to be home in my bed and dreaming all of this.

"Sandra,'' I said. "I believe you were telling us about your *affaire de coeur* with Ted.''

Ted threw a dark glance at me. "You don't want to say anything, Sandy. He's just trying to make all of us look dirty like he is. He's sick and full of germs. Don't let him infect you with what he's got.''

She smiled. She was really radiant when she smiled like a child. I felt a bitter nostalgia, not for her, exactly, or for any imagined purity (Dale Evans panties and all that), but for something I could not precisely put my hand on. Her, maybe. Whatever it was, it made me feel ashamed.

"But I want to,'' she said. "I want to get it on, too. I always have.''

It was eleven o'clock on the nose. The activity outside seemed to have died. I was sitting well back from the windows now. I thought Philbrick would give me my hour. He wouldn't dare do anything else now. I felt better, the pain in my chest receding a little. But my head felt very strange, as if my brains were running without coolant and overheating like a big hot rod engine in the desert. At times I was almost tempted to feel (foolish conceit) that I was holding them myself, by sheer willpower. Now I know, of course, that nothing could have been further from the truth. I had one real hostage that day, and his name was Ted Jones.

"We just did it,'' Sandra said, looking down at her desk and tracing the engravings there with a shaped thumbnail. I could see the part in her hair. She parted it on the side, like a boy. "Ted asked me to go to the Wonderland dance with him, and I said I would. I had a new formal.'' She looked at me reproachfully. "*You* never asked me, Charlie.''

Could it be that I was shot in the padlock only ten minutes ago? I had an insane urge to ask them if it had really happened. How strange they all were!

"So we went to that, and afterward we went to the Hawaiian Hut. Ted knows the man who runs it and got us cocktails. Just like the grown-ups.'' It was hard to tell if there was sarcasm in her voice or not.

Ted's face was carefully blank, but the others were looking at him as if they were seeing a strange bug. Here was a kid, one of their own, who knew the man who runs it. Corky Herald was obviously chewing it and not liking it.

"I didn't think I'd like the drinks, because everybody says liquor tastes horrible at first, but I did. I had a gin fizz, and it tickled my nose.'' She looked pensively in front of her. "There were little straws in it, red ones, and I didn't know if you drank through them or just stirred your drink with them, until Ted told me. It was a very nice time. Ted talked about how nice it was playing golf at Poland Springs. He said he'd take me sometime and teach me the game, if I wanted.''

Ted was curling and uncurling his lip again, doglike.

"He wasn't, you know, fresh or anything. He kissed me good night, though, and he wasn't a bit nervous about it. Some boys are just miserable all the way home, wondering if they should try to kiss you good night or not. I always kissed them, just so they wouldn't feel bad. If they were yucky, I just pretended I was licking a letter.''

I remembered the first time I took Sandy Cross out, to the regular Saturday-night dance at the high school. I had been miserable all the way home, wondering if I should kiss her good night or not. I finally didn't.

"After that, we went out three more times. Ted was very nice. He could always think of funny things to say, but he never told dirty jokes or anything, you know, like that. We did some necking, and that was all. Then I didn't see him to go out with for a long time, not until this April. He asked me if I wanted to go to the Rollerdrome in Lewiston.''

I had wanted to ask her to go to the Wonderland dance with me, but I hadn't dared. Joe, who always got dates when he wanted them, kept saying why don't you, and I kept getting more nervous and kept telling him to fuck off. Finally I got up the stuff to call her house, but I had to hang up the telephone after one ring and run to the bathroom and throw up. As I told you, my stomach is bad.

"We were having a pretty blah time, when all of a sudden these kids got into an argument on the middle of the floor,'' Sandra said. "Harlow boys and Lewiston boys, I think. Anyway, a big fight started. Some of them were fighting on their roller skates, but most of them had taken them off. The man who runs it came out and said if they didn't stop, he was going to close. People were getting bloody noses and skating around and kicking people that had fallen down, and punching and yelling horrible things. And all the time, the jukebox was turned up real loud, playing Rolling Stones music.''

She paused, and then went on: "Ted and I were standing in one corner of the floor, by the bandstand. They have live music on Saturday nights, you know. This one boy skated by, wearing a black jacket. He had long hair and pimples. He laughed and waved at Ted when he went by and yelled, 'Fuck her, buddy, I did!' And Ted just reached out and popped him upside the head. The kid went skating right into the middle part of the rink and tripped over some kid's shoes and fell on his head. Anyway, Ted was looking at me, and his eyes were, you know, almost bugging out of his head. He was grinning. You know, that's really the only time I ever really saw Ted grin, like he was having a good time.

"Ted goes to me, 'I'll be right back,' and he walks across the rink to that inside part where the kid who said that was still getting up. Ted grabbed him by the back of the jacket and . . . I don't know . . . started to yank him back and forth . . . and the kid couldn't turn around . . . and Ted just kept yanking him back and forth, and that kid's head was bouncing, and then his jacket ripped right down the middle. And he goes, 'I'll kill you for ripping my best jacket, you m.f.' So Ted hit him again, and the kid fell down, and Ted threw the piece of his jacket he was holding right down on top of him. Then he came back to where I was standing, and we left. We drove out into Auburn to a gravel pit he knew about. It was on that road to Lost Valley, I think. Then we did it. In the back seat."

She was tracing the graffiti on her desk again. "It didn't hurt very much. I thought it would, but it didn't. It was nice." She sounded as if she were discussing a Walt Disney feature film, one of those with all the cute little animals. Only, this one was starring Ted Jones as the Bald-Headed Woodchuck.

"He didn't use one of those things like he said he would, but I didn't get pregnant or anything."

Slow red was beginning to creep out of the collar of Ted's khaki army shirt, spreading up his neck and over his cheeks. His face remained fumingly expressionless.

Sandra's hands made slow, languorous gestures. I suddenly knew that her natural habitat would be in a porch hammock at the very August height of summer, temperature ninety-two in the shade, reading a book (or perhaps just staring out at the heat shimmer rising over the road), a can of Seven-Up beside her with an elbow straw in it, dressed in cool white short-shorts and a brief halter with the straps pushed down, small diamonds of sweat stippled across the upper swell of her breasts and her lower stomach. . . .

"He apologized afterward. He acted uncomfortable, and I felt a little bad for him. He kept saying he would marry me if . . . you know, if I got preggers. He was really upset. And I go, 'Well, let's not buy trouble, Teddy,' and he goes, 'Don't call me that, it's a baby name.' I think he was surprised I did it with him. And I didn't get preggers. There just didn't seem to be that much to it.

"Sometimes I feel like a doll. Not really real. You know it? I fix my hair, and every now and then I have to hem a skirt, or maybe I have to baby-sit the kids when Mom and Dad go out. And it all just seems very fake. Like I could peek behind the living-room wall and it would be cardboard, with a director and a cameraman getting ready for the next scene. Like the grass and the sky were painted on canvas flats. Fake." She looked at me earnestly. "Did you ever feel like that, Charlie?"

I thought about it very carefully. "No," I said. "I can't remember that ever crossing my mind, Sandy."

"It crossed mine. Even more after with Ted. But I didn't get pregnant or anything. I used to think every girl got pregnant the first time, without fail. I tried to imagine what it would be like, telling my parents. My father would get real mad and want to know who the son of a bee was, and my mother would cry and say, 'I thought we raised you right.' That would have been *real*. But after a while I stopped thinking about that. I couldn't even remember exactly what it felt like, having him . . . well, inside me. So I went back to the Rollerdrome."

The room was totally silent. Never in her wildest dreams could Mrs. Underwood have hoped to command such attention as Sandra Cross commanded now.

"This boy picked me up. I let him pick me up." Her eyes had picked up a strange sparkle. "I wore my shortest skirt. My powder-blue one. And a thin blouse. Later on, we went out back. And *that* seemed real. He wasn't polite at all. He was sort of . . . jerky. I didn't know him at all. I kept thinking that maybe he was one of those sex maniacs. That he might have a knife. That he might make me take dope. Or that I might get pregnant. I felt *alive*."

Ted Jones had finally turned and was looking at Sandra with an almost woodcut expression of horror and dead revulsion. It all seemed like a dream—something out of *le moyen age*, a dark passion play.

"That was Saturday night, and the band was playing. You could hear it out in the parking lot, but kind of faint. The Rollerdrome doesn't look like much from the back, just all boxes and crates piled up, and trashcans full of Coke bottles. I was scared, but I was excited, too. He was breathing really fast and holding on to my wrist tight, as if he expected me to try to get away. He . . ."

Ted made a horrid gagging sound. It was hard to believe that anyone in my peer group could be touched so painfully by anything other than the death of a parent. Again I admired him.

"He had an old black car, and it made me think of how my mother used to tell me when I was just little that sometimes strange men want you to get in the car with them and you should never do it. That excited me too. I can remember thinking: What if he kidnaps me and takes me to some old shack in the country and holds me for ransom? He opened the back door, and I got in. He started to kiss me. His mouth was all greasy, like he'd been eating pizza. They sell pizza inside for twenty cents a slice. He started to feel me up, and I could see he was smudging pizza on my blouse. Then we were lying down, and I pulled my skirt up for him—"

"*Shut up!*" Ted cried out with savage suddenness. He brought both fists crashing down on his desk, and everybody jumped. "*You rotten whore! You can't tell that in front of people! Shut your mouth or I'll shut it for you! You—*"

"You shut up, Teddy, or I'll knock your teeth down your fucking throat," Dick Keene said coldly. "You got yours, didn't you?"

Ted gaped at him. The two of them shot a lot of pool together down at the Harlow Rec, and sometimes went cruising in Ted's car. I wondered if they would be hanging out together when this was all over. I had my doubts.

"He didn't smell very nice," Sandra continued, as if there had been no interruption at all. "But he was hard. And bigger than Ted. Not circumcised, either. I remember that. It looked like a plum when he pushed it out of, you know, his foreskin. I thought it might hurt even, though I wasn't a virgin anymore. I thought the police might come and arrest us. I knew they walked through the parking lot to make sure no one was stealing hubcaps or anything.

"And a funny thing started to happen inside me, before he even got my pants down. I never felt anything so good. Or so *real*." She swallowed. Her face was flushed. "He touched me with his hand, and I went. Just like that. And the funny thing was, he didn't even get to do it. He was trying to get it in and I was trying to help him and it kept rubbing against my leg and all of a sudden . . . you know.

And he just laid there on top of me for a minute, and then he said in my ear: 'You little bitch. You did that on purpose,' And that was all.''

She shook her head vaguely. ''But it was very real. I can remember everything—the music, the way he smiled, the sound his zipper made when he opened it—everything.''

She smiled at me, that strange, dreamy smile.

''But this has been better, Charlie.''

And the strange thing was, I couldn't tell if I felt sick or not. I didn't think I did, but it was really too close to call. I guess when you turn off the main road, you have to be prepared to see some funny houses. ''How do people know they're real?'' I muttered.

''What, Charlie?''

''Nothing.''

I looked at them very carefully. They didn't look sick, any of them. There was a healthy sheen on every eye. There was something in me (maybe it came over on the *Mayflower*) that wanted to know: *How could she let that beyond the walls of herself? How could she say that?* But there was nothing in the faces that I saw to echo that thought. There would have been in Philbrick's face. In good old Tom's face. Probably not in Don Grace's, but he would have been thinking it. Secretly, all the evening news shows notwithstanding, I'd held the belief that things change but people don't. It was something of a horror to begin realizing that all those years I'd been playing baseball on a soccer field. Pig Pen was still studying the bitter lines of his pencil. Susan Brooks only looked sweetly sympathetic. Dick Keene had a half-interested, half-lustful expression on his face. Corky's head was furrowed and frowning as he wrestled with it. Gracie looked slightly surprised, but that was all. Irma Bates merely looked vapid. I don't think she had recovered from seeing me shot. Were the lives of all our elders so plain that Sandy's story would have made lurid reading for them? Or were all of theirs so strange and full of terrifying mental foliage that their classmate's sexual adventure was on a level with winning a pinball replay? I didn't want to think about it. I was in no position to be reviewing moral implications.

Only Ted looked sick and horrified, and he no longer counted.

''I don't know what's going to happen,'' Carol Granger said, mildly worried. She looked around. ''I'm afraid all of this changes things. I don't like it.'' She looked at me accusingly. ''I liked the way things were going, Charlie. I don't want things to change after this is over.''

''Heh,'' I said.

But that kind of comment had no power over the situation. Things had gotten out of control. There was no real way that could be denied anymore. I had a sudden urge to laugh at all of them, to point out that I had started out as the main attraction and had ended up as the sideshow.

''I have to go to the bathroom,'' Irma Bates said suddenly.

''Hold it,'' I said. Sylvia laughed.

''Turnabout is fair play,'' I said. ''I promised to tell you about my sex life. In all actuality, there isn't very much to tell about, unless you read palms. However, there is one little story which you might find interesting.''

Sarah Pasterne yawned, and I felt a sudden, excruciating urge to blow her head off. But number two must try harder, as they say in the rent-a-car ads. Some cats drive faster, but Decker vacuums all the psychic cigarette butts from the ashtrays of your mind.

I was suddenly reminded of that Beatles song that starts off: ''I read the news today, oh boy . . . ''

I told them:

Chapter 26

In the summer before my junior year at Placerville, Joe and I drove up to Bangor to spend a weekend with Joe's brother, who had a summer job working for the Bangor Sanitation Department. Pete McKennedy was twenty-one (a fantastic age, it seemed to me; I was struggling through the open sewer that is seventeen) and going to the University of Maine, where he was majoring in English.

It looked like it was going to be a great weekend. On Friday night I got drunk for the first time in my life, along with Pete and Joe and one or two of Pete's friends, and I wasn't even very hungover the next day. Pete didn't work Saturdays, so he took us up to the campus and showed us around. It's really very pretty up there in summer, although on a Saturday in July there weren't many pretty coeds to look at. Pete told us that most of the summer students took off for Bar Harbor or Clear Lake on weekends.

We were just getting ready to go back to Pete's place when he saw a guy he knew slouching down toward the steam-plant parking lot.

"Scragg!" He yelled. "Hey, Scragg!"

Scragg was a big guy wearing paint-splattered, faded jeans and a blue workshirt. He had a drooping sand-colored mustache and was smoking an evil-looking little black cigar that he later identified as the Original Smoky Perote. It smelled like slowly burning underwear.

"How's it hanging?" He asked.

"Up a foot," Pete said. "This is my brother, Joe, and his buddy Charlie Decker," he introduced. "Scragg Simpson."

"Howdy-doody," Scragg said, shaking hands and dismissing us. "What you doing tonight, Peter?"

"Thought the three of us might go to a movie."

"Doan do that, Pete," Scragg said with a grin. "Doan do that, baby."

"What's better?" Pete asked, also grinning.

"Dana Collette's throwing a party at this camp her folks own out near Schoodic Point. There's gonna be about forty million unattached ladies there. Bring dope."

"Does Larry Moeller have any grass?" Pete asked.

"Last I knew, he had a shitload. Foreign, domestic, local . . . everything but filter tips."

Pete nodded. "We'll be there, unless the creek rises."

Scragg nodded and waved a hand as he prepared to resume his version of that ever-popular form of campus locomotion, the Undergraduate Slouch. "Meet-cha," he said to Joe and me.

We went down to see Jerry Moeller, who Pete said was the biggest dope dealer in the Orono-Oldtown-Stillwater triangle. I kept my cool about it, as if I were one of the original Placerville jones men, but privately I was excited and pretty apprehensive. As I remember it, I sort of expected to see Jerry sitting naked on the john with a piece of rubber flex tied off below his elbow and a hypo dangling from the big forearm vein. And watching the rise and fall of ancient Atlantis in his navel.

He had a small apartment in Oldtown, which borders the campus on one side. Oldtown is a small city with three distinctions: its paper mill; its canoe factory; and twelve of the roughest honky-tonks in this great smiling country. It also has an encampment of real reservation Indians, and most of them look at you as if wondering how much hair you might have growing out of your asshole and whether or not it would be worth scalping.

Jerry turned out to be not an ominous jones-man type holding court amid the reek of incense and Ravi Shankar music, but a small guy with a constant wedge-of-lemon grin. He was fully clothed and in his right mind. His only ornament was a bright yellow button which bore the message GOLDILOCKS LOVED IT. Instead of Ravi and His Incredible Boinging Sitar, he had a large collection of bluegrass music. When I saw his Greenbriar Boys albums, I asked him if he'd ever heard the Tarr Brothers—I've always been a country-and-bluegrass nut. After that, we were off. Pete and Joe just sat around looking bored until Jerry produced what looked like a small cigarette wrapped in brown paper.

"You want to light it?" he asked Pete.

Pete lit it. The smell was pungent, almost tart, and very pleasant. He drew it deep, held the smoke, and passed the j on to Joe, who coughed most of it out.

Jerry turned back to me. "You ever heard the Clinch Mountain Boys?"

I shook my head. "Heard of them, though."

"You gotta listen to this," he said. "Boy, is it horny." He put an LP with a weird label on the stereo. The j came around to me. "You smoke cigarettes?" Jerry asked me paternally.

I shook my head.

"Then draw slow, or you'll lose it."

I drew slow. The smoke was sweet, rather heavy, acrid, dry. I held my breath and passed the j on to Jerry. The Clinch Mountain Boys started in on "Blue Ridge Breakdown."

Half an hour later we had progressed through two more joints and were listening to Flatt and Scruggs charge through a little number called "Russian Around." I was about ready to ask when I should start feeling stoned when I realized I could actually visualize the banjo chords in my mind. They were bright, like long steel threads, and shuttling back and forth like looms. They were moving rapidly, but I could follow them if I concentrated deeply. I tried to tell Joe about it, but he only looked at me in a puzzled, fuzzy way. We both laughed. Pete was looking at a picture of Niagara Falls on the wall very closely.

We ended up sticking around until almost five o'clock, and when we left, I was wrecked out of my mind. Pete bought an ounce of grass from Jerry, and we took off for Schoodic. Jerry stood in the doorway of his apartment and waved good-bye and yelled for me to come back and bring some of my records.

That's the last really happy time I can remember.

It was a long drive down to the coast. All three of us were still very high, and although Pete had no trouble driving, none of us could seem to talk without getting the giggles. I remember asking Pete once what this Dana Collette who was throwing the party looked like, and he just leered. That made me laugh until I thought my stomach was going to explode. I could still hear bluegrass playing in my head.

Pete had been to a party out there in the spring, and we only took one wrong turn finding it. It was at the end of a narrow mile of gravel marked PRIVATE ROAD. You could hear the heavy bass signature of the music a quarter-mile from the cabin. There were so many cars stacked up that we had to walk from just about that point.

Pete parked and we got out. I was starting to feel unsure of myself and self-conscious again (partly the residue of the pot and partly just me), worried about how young and stupid I would probably look to all these college people. Jerry Moeller had to be one in a hundred. I decided I would just stick close to Joe and keep my mouth closed.

As it turned out, I could have saved the worry. The place was packed to the rafters with what seemed like a million people, every one of them drunk, stoned, or both. The smell of marijuana hung on the air like a heavy mist, along with wine and hot bods. The place was a babble of conversation, loud rock music, and laughter. There were two lights dangling from the ceiling, one red, one blue. That rounds off the first impression the place gave me—it was like the funhouse at Old Orchard Beach.

Scragg waved at us from across the room.

"Pete!" someone squealed, almost in my ear. I jerked and almost swallowed my tongue.

It was a short, almost pretty girl with bleached hair and the shortest dress I have ever seen—it was a bright fluorescent orange that looked almost alive in the weird lighting.

"Hi, Dana!" Pete shouted over the noise. "This is my brother, Joe, and one of his buddies, Charlie Decker."

She said hi to both of us. "Isn't it a great party?" she asked me. When she moved, the hem of her dress swirled around the lace bottoms of her panties.

I said it was a great party.

"Did you bring any goodies, Pete?" Pete grinned and held up his Baggie of weed. Her eyes sparkled. She was standing next to me, her hip pressed casually against mine. I could feel her bare thigh. I began to get as horny as a bull moose.

"Bring it over here," she said.

We found a relatively unoccupied corner behind one of the stereo speakers, and Dana produced a huge scrolled water pipe from a low bookshelf that was fairly groaning with Hesse, Tolkien, and Reader's Digest condensed books. The latter belonged to the parents, I assumed. We toked up. The grass was much smoother in the water pipe, and I could hold the smoke better. I began to get very high indeed. My head was filling up with helium. People came and went. Introductions, which I promptly forgot, were made. The thing that I liked best about the introductions was that, every time a stray wandered by, Dana would bounce up to grab him or her. And when she did, I could look straight up her dress to where the Heavenly Home was sheathed in the gauziest of blue nylon. People changed records. I watched them come and go (some of them undoubtedly talking of Michelangelo, or Ted Kennedy or Kurt Vonnegut). A woman asked me if I had read Susan Brownmiller's *Women Rapists*. I said no. She told me it was very tight. She crossed her fingers in front of her eyes to show me how tight it was and then wandered off. I watched the fluorescent poster on the far wall, which showed a guy in a T-shirt sitting in front of a TV. The guy's eyeballs were slowly dripping down his cheeks, and there was a big cheese-eating grin on his face. The poster said: SHEEEIT! FRIDAY NIGHT AND I'M STONED AGAIN!

I watched Dana cross and uncross her legs. A few filaments of pubic hair, nine shades darker than the bleach job, had strayed out of the lacy leg bands. I don't think I have ever been that horny. I doubt if I will ever be that horny again. I had an organ which felt large enough and long enough to pole-vault on. I began to wonder if the male sex organ can explode.

She turned to me and suddenly whispered in my ear. My stomach heated up twenty degrees instantly, as if I had been eating chili. A moment before, she had been talking to Pete and to some joker I remembered being nonintroduced to. Then she was whispering in my ear, her breath tickling the dark channel. "Go on out the back door," she said. "There." She pointed.

It was hard to comprehend, so I just followed her finger. Yes, there was the door. The door was real and the door was earnest. It had one hell of a knob on it. I chuckled, convinced that I had just thought a particularly witty thought. She laughed lightly in my ear and said, "You've been looking up my dress all night. What does that mean?" And before I could say anything, she kissed my cheek softly and gave me a little shove to get me going.

I looked around for Joe, but I didn't see him anyplace. Sorry, Joe. I got up and heard both my knees pop. My legs were stiff from sitting in the same position so long. I had an urge to untuck my shirt and cover up the huge bulge in my jeans. I had an urge to tiptoe across the room. I had an urge to cackle wildly and announce to the general attendance that Charles Everett Decker earnestly believed that he was about to get screwed; that—to drop a bad pun—Charles Everett Decker was about to rip off his maiden piece.

I didn't do any of those things.

I went out the back door.

I was so stoned and so horny that I almost fell twenty feet to the tiny white shingle of beach that was down below. The back of the cabin overlooked a sudden rocky drop to a postage-stamp inlet. A flight of weather-washed steps led down. I walked carefully, holding on to the railing. My feet felt a thousand miles away. The music sounded distant on this side, blending and almost being covered by the rhythmic sound of the waves.

There was a slip of a moon and a ghost of a breeze. The scene was so frozenly beautiful that for a moment I thought I had walked into a black-and-white picture postcard. The cabin behind and above was only a dim blur. The trees climbed on both sides, pines and spruces that sloped off to naked rock headland—twin spurs of it, which cupped the crescent-shaped beach where the waves licked. Straight ahead was the Atlantic, pinpointed with uncertain nets of light from the moon. I could see the faintest curve of an island far out to the left, and wondered who walked there that night besides the wind. It was a lonesome thought, and it made me shiver a little.

I slipped off my shoes and waited for her.

I don't know how long it was before she came. I didn't have any wristwatch and was too stoned to be able to judge in any case. And after a little while, unease began to creep in. Something about the shadow of trees on the wet, packed sand, and the sound of the wind. Maybe the ocean itself, a big thing, a mean mother-humper full of unseen life and all those little pricks of light. Maybe the cold feel of the sand under my bare feet. Maybe none of those things, maybe all of them and more. But by the time she put her hand on my shoulder, I had lost my erection. Wyatt Earp striding into the OK Corral with no sixgun.

She turned me around, stood on tiptoe, kissed me. I could feel the warmth of her thighs, but now it was nothing special to me. "I saw you looking at me," is what she said. "Are you nice? Can you be nice?"

"I can try," I told her, feeling a little absurd. I touched her breasts, and she held me close. But my erection was still gone.

"Don't tell Pete," she said, taking me by the hand. "He'd kill me. We've got a . . . kind of a thing."

She led me underneath the back steps, where the grass was cool and matted with aromatic pine needles. The shadows made cold venetian blinds on her body as she slipped out of her dress.

"This is so crazy," she said, and she sounded excited.

Then we were rolling together and my shirt was off. She was working at the snap on the front of my jeans. But my cock was still on coffee break. She touched me, sliding her hand inside my underpants, and the muscles down there jerked— not in pleasure or in revulsion, but in a kind of terror. Her hand felt like rubber, cold and impersonal and antiseptic.

"Come on," she whispered. "Come on, come on, come *on* . . . "

I tried to think of something sexy, anything sexy. Looking up Darleen Andreissen's skirt in study hall and her knowing it and letting me. Maynard Quinn's pack of dirty French playing cards. I thought of Sandy Cross in sexy black underwear, and that started to move something around down there . . . and then, of all things to come cruising out of my imagination, I saw my father with his hunting knife, talking about the Cherokee Nose Job.

["The *what*?" Corky Herald asked. I explained the Cherokee Nose Job. "Oh," Corky said. I went on.]

That did it. Everything collapsed into noodledom again. And after that, there was nothing. And nothing. And nothing. My jeans had joined my shirt. My underpants were somewhere down around my ankles. She was quivering underneath me, I could feel her, like the plucked string of a musical instrument. I reached down and took hold of my penis and shook it as if to ask what was wrong with it. But Mr. Penis wasn't talking. I let my hand wander around to the warm junction of her thighs. I could feel her pubic hair, a little kinky, shockingly like my own. I slid an exploratory finger into her, thinking: *This is the place. This is the place men like my father joke about on hunting trips and in barber shops. Men kill for this. Force it open. Steal it or bludgeon it. Take it . . . or leave it.*

"Where is it?" Dana whispered in a high, breathless voice. "Where is it? Where . . . ?"

So I tried. But it was like that old joke about the guy that tried to jam a marshmallow into the piggy bank. Nothing. And all the time I could hear the soft sound of the ocean grounding on the beach, like the soundtrack of a sappy movie.

Then I rolled off. "I'm sorry." My voice was shockingly loud, rasping.

I could hear her sigh. It was a short sound, an irritated sound. "All right," she said. "It happens."

"Not to me," I said, as if this was the first time in several thousand sexual encounters that my equipment had malfunctioned. Dimly I could hear Mick Jagger and the Stones shouting out "Hot Stuff." One of life's little ironies. I still felt wrecked, but it was a cold feeling, depthless. The cold certainty that I was queer crept over me like rising water. I had read someplace that you didn't have to have any overt homosexual experience to be queer; you could just be that way and never know it until the queen in your closet leaped out at you like Norman Bates's mom in *Psycho,* a grotesque mugger prancing and mincing in Mommy's makeup and Mommy's shoes.

"It's just as well," she said. "Pete—"

"Look, I'm sorry."

She smiled, but it looked manufactured. I've wondered since if it was or not. I'd like to believe it was a real smile. "It's the dope. I bet you're a hell of a lover when things are right."

"Fuck," I said, and shivered at the dead sound in my own voice.

"No." She sat up. "I'm going back in. Wait until I'm gone awhile before you come up."

I wanted to tell her to wait, to let me try it again, but I knew I couldn't, not if all the seas dried up and the moon turned to zinc oxide. She zipped into her dress and was gone, leaving me there under the steps. The moon watched me closely, perhaps to see if I might cry. I didn't. After a little while I got my clothes straightened around and most of last fall's leaves brushed off me. Then I went back upstairs. Pete and Dana were gone. Joe was over in a corner, making out with a really stunning girl who had her hands in his mop of blond hair. I sat down and waited for the party to be over. Eventually it was.

By the time the three of us got back to Bangor, dawn had already pulled most of her tricks out of her bag and a red edge of sun was peering down at us from between the smokestacks of beautiful downtown Brewer. None of us had much to say. I felt tired and grainy and not able to tell how much damage had been done to me. I had a leaden feeling that it was more than I really needed.

We went upstairs, and I fell into the tiny daybed in the living room. The last thing I saw before I went to sleep was bars of sunlight falling through the venetian blinds and onto the small throw rug by the radiator.

I dreamed about the Creaking Thing. It was almost the same as when I was small, I in my bed, the moving shadows of the tree outside on the ceiling, the steady, sinister sound. Only, this time the sound kept getting closer and closer, until the door of the bedroom burst open with an awful crack like the sound of doom.

It was my father. My mother was in his arms. Her nose had been slit wide open, and blood streamed down her cheeks like war paint.

"You want her?" he said. "Here, take her, you worthless good-for-nothing. Take her."

He threw her on the bed beside me and I saw that she was dead, and that's when I woke up screaming. With an erection.

Chapter 27

Nobody had anything to say after that one, not even Susan Brooks. I felt tired. There didn't seem to be a great deal left to say. Most of them were looking outside again, but there wasn't anything to see that hadn't been there an hour before—actually less, because all of the pedestrians had been shooed away. I decided Sandra's sex story had been better. There had been an orgasm in hers.

Ted Jones was staring at me with his usual burning intensity (I thought, however, that revulsion had given way entirely to hate, and that was mildly satisfying). Sandra Cross was off in her own world. Pat Fitzgerald was carefully folding a cheap piece of study-hall math paper into an aerodynamically unsound aircraft.

Suddenly Irma Bates said defiantly, "I have to go to the *bathroom*!"

I sighed. It sounded a great deal like the way I remember Dana Collette's sigh at Schoodic Point. "Go, then."

She looked at me unbelievingly. Ted blinked. Don Lordi snickered.

"You'd shoot me."

I looked at her. "Do you need to go to the crapper or not?"

"I can hold it," she said sulkily.

I blew out my cheeks, the way my father does when he's put out. "Well, either go or stop wiggling around in your seat. We don't need a puddle underneath your desk."

Corky went haw-haw at that. Sarah Pasterne looked shocked.

As if to spite me, Irma got up and walked with flat-footed vigor toward the door. I had gained at least one point: Ted was staring at her instead of me. Once there, she paused uncertainly, hand over the knob. She looked like someone who has just gotten an electric shock while adjusting the TV rabbit ears and is wondering whether or not to try again.

"You won't shoot me?"

"Are you going to the bathroom or not?" I asked. I wasn't sure if I was going to shoot her. I was still disturbed by (jealous of?) the fact that Sandra's story seemed to have so much more power than my own. In some undefined way, they had gained the upper hand. I had the crazy feeling that instead of my holding them, it was the other way around. Except for Ted, of course. We were all holding Ted.

Maybe I was going to shoot her. I certainly didn't have anything to lose. Maybe it would even help. Maybe I could get rid of the crazy feeling that I had waked up in the middle of a new dream.

She opened the door and went out. I never raised the gun off the blotter. The door closed. We could hear her feet moving off down the hall, not picking up tempo, not breaking into a run. They were all watching the door, as if something completely unbelievable had poked its head through, winked, and then withdrawn.

For myself, I had a strange feeling of relief, a feeling so tenuous that I could never explain it.

The footfalls died out.

Silence. I waited for someone else to ask to go to the bathroom. I waited to see Irma Bates dash crazily out of the front doors and right onto the front pages of a hundred newspapers. It didn't happen.

Pat Fitzgerald rattled the wings of his plane. It was a loud sound.

"Throw that goddamn thing away," Billy Sawyer said irritably. "You can't make a paper plane out of study-hall paper." Pat made no move to throw the goddamn thing away. Billy didn't say anything else.

New footfalls, coming toward us.

I lifted up the pistol and pointed it toward the door. Ted was grinning at me, but I don't think he knew it. I looked at his face, at the flat, conventionally good looking planes of his cheeks, at the forehead, barricading all those memories of summer country-club days, dances, cars, Sandy's breasts, calmness, ideals of rightness; and suddenly I knew what the last order of business was; perhaps it had been the only order of business all along; and more importantly, I knew that his eye was the eye of a hawk and his hand was stone. He could have been my own father, but that didn't matter. He and Ted were both remote and Olympian: gods. But my arms were too tired to pull down temples. I was never cut out to be Samson.

His eyes were so clear and so straight, so frighteningly purposeful—they were politician's eyes.

Five minutes before, the sound of the footfalls wouldn't have been bad, do you see? Five minutes before, I could have welcomed them, put the gun down on the desk blotter and gone to meet them, perhaps with a fearful backward glance at the people I was leaving behind me. But now it was the steps themselves that frightened me. I was afraid Philbrick had decided to take me up on my offer—that he had come to shut off the main line and leave our business unfinished.

Ted Jones grinned hungrily.

The rest of us waited, watching the door. Pat's fingers had frozen on his paper plane. Dick Keene's mouth hung open, and in that moment I could see for the first time the family resemblance between him and his brother Flapper, a borderline IQ case who had graduated after six long years in Placerville. Flapper was now doing postgraduate work at Thomaston State Prison, doing doctoral work in laundry maintenance and advanced spoon sharpening.

An unformed shadow rose up on the glass, the way it does when the surface is pebbly and opaque. I lifted the pistol to high port and got ready. I could see the class out of the corner of my right eye, watching with absorbed fascination, the way you watch the last reel of a James Bond movie, when the body count really soars.

A clenched sound, sort of a whimper, came out of my throat.

The door opened, and Irma Bates came back in. She looked around peevishly, not happy to find everyone staring at her. George Yannick began to giggle and said, ''Guess who's coming to dinner.'' It didn't make anyone else laugh; it was George's own private yuck. The rest of us just went on staring at Irma.

''What are you looking at me for?'' she asked crossly, holding the knob. ''People do go to the bathroom, didn't you know that?'' She shut the door, went to her seat, and sat down primly.

It was almost noon.

Chapter 28

Frank Philbrick was right on time. *Chink,* and he was on the horn. He didn't seem to be puffing and blowing as badly, though. Maybe he wanted to placate me. Or maybe he'd thought over my advice on his speaking voice and had decided to take it. Stranger things have happened. God knows.

"Decker?"

"I'm here."

"Listen, that stray shot that came through the window wasn't intentional. One of the men from Lewiston—"

"Let's not even bother, Frank," I said. "You're embarrassing me and you're embarrassing these people down here, who saw what happened. If you've got any integrity at all, and I'm sure you do, you're probably embarrassing yourself."

Pause. Maybe he was collecting his temper. "Okay. What do you want?"

"Not much. Everybody comes out at one o'clock this afternoon. In exactly"— I checked the wall clock—"fifty-seven minutes by the clock down here. Without a scratch. I guarantee it."

"Why not now?"

I looked at them. The air felt heavy and nearly solemn, as if between us we had written a contract in someone's blood.

I said carefully, "We have a final piece of business down here. We have to finish getting it on."

"What is it?"

"It doesn't concern you. But we all know what it is." There wasn't a pair of eyes that showed uncertainty. They knew, all right, and that was good, because it would save time and effort. I felt very tired.

"Now, listen carefully, Philbrick, so we have no misunderstanding, while I describe the last act of this little comedy. In about three minutes, someone is going to pull down all the shades in here."

"No way they are, Decker." He sounded very tough.

I let the air whistle through my teeth. What an amazing man he was. No wonder he screwed up all his drive-safely spiels. "When are you going to get it through your head that I'm in charge?" I asked him. "Someone is going to pull the shades, Philbrick, and it won't be me. So if you shoot someone, you can pin your badge to your ass and kiss them both good-bye."

Nothing.

"Silence gives consent," I said, trying to sound merry. I didn't feel merry. "I'm not going to be able to see what you're doing either, but don't get any clever ideas.

111

If you do, some of these people are going to get hurt. If you sit until one, every-thing will be fine again and you'll be the big brave policeman everybody knows you are. Now, how 'bout it?''

He paused for a long time. "I'm damned if you *sound* crazy," he said finally.

"How about it?''

"How do I know you're not going to change your mind, Decker? What if you want to try for two o'clock? Or three?''

"How about it?'' I asked inexorably.

Another pause. "All right. But if you hurt any of those kids . . . ''

"You'll take away my Junior Achiever card. I know. Go away, Frank.''

I could feel him wanting to say something warm, wonderful, and witty, some-thing that would summarize his position for the ages, something like: Fuck off, Decker, or: Cram it up y'ass, Decker; but he didn't quite dare. There were, after all, young girls down here. "One o'clock,'' he repeated. The intercom went dead. A moment later he was walking across the grass.

"What nasty little masturbation fantasies have you got lined up now, Charlie?'' Ted asked, still grinning.

"Why don't you just cool it, Ted?'' Harmon Jackson asked remotely.

"Who will volunteer to close the shades?'' I asked. Several hands went up. I pointed to Melvin Thomas and said, "Do it slowly. They're probably nervous.''

Melvin did it slowly. With the canvas shades pulled all the way down to the sills, the room took on a half-dreamlike drabness. Lackluster shadows clustered in the corners like bats that hadn't been getting enough to eat. I didn't like it. The shadows made me feel very jumpy indeed.

I pointed to Tanis Gannon, who sat in the row of seats closest to the door. "Will you favor us with the lights?''

She smiled shyly, like a deb, and went to the light switches. A moment later we had cold fluorescents, which were not much better than the shadows. I wished for the sun and the sight of blue sky, but said nothing. There was nothing to say. Tanis went back to her seat and smoothed her skirt carefully behind her thighs as she sat down.

"To use Ted's adequate phrase,'' I said, "there is only one masturbation fan-tasy left before we get down to business—or two halves of one whole, if you want to look at it that way. That is the story of Mr. Carlson, our late teacher of chemistry and physics, the story that good old Tom Denver managed to keep out of the papers but which, as the saying goes, remains in our hearts.

"And how my father and I got it on following my suspension.''

I looked at them, feeling a dull, horrid ache in the back of my skull. Somewhere it had all slipped out of my hands. I was reminded of Mickey Mouse as the sor-cerer's apprentice in the old Disney cartoon *Fantasia*. I had brought all the brooms to life, but now where was the kindly old magician to say abracadabra backwards and make them go back to sleep?

Stupid, stupid.

Pictures whirled in front of my eyes, hundreds of them, fragments from dreams, fragments from reality. It was impossible to separate one from the other. Lunacy is when you can't see the seams where they stitched the world together anymore. I supposed there was still a chance that I might wake up in my bed, safe and still at least half-sane, the black, irrevocable step not taken (or at least not yet), with all the characters of this particular nightmare retreating back into their subconscious caves. But I wasn't banking on it.

Pat Fitzgerald's brown hands worked on his paper plane like the sad, moving fingers of death itself.

I said:

Chapter 29

There was no one reason why I started carrying the pipe wrench to school.

Now, even after all of this, I can't isolate the major cause. My stomach was hurting all the time, and I used to imagine people were trying to pick fights with me even when they weren't. I was afraid I might collapse during physical-education calisthenics, and wake up to see everybody around me in a ring, laughing and pointing . . . or maybe having a circle jerk. I wasn't sleeping very well. I'd been having some goddamn funny dreams, and it scared me, because quite a few of them were wet dreams, and they weren't the kind that you're supposed to wake up after with a wet sheet. There was one where I was walking through the basement of an old castle that looked like something out of an old Universal Pictures movie. There was a coffin with the top up, and when I looked inside I saw my father with his hands crossed on his chest. He was neatly decked out—pun intended, I guess—in his dress Navy uniform, and there was a stake driven into his crotch. He opened his eyes and smiled at me. His teeth were fangs. In another one my mother was giving me an enema and I was begging her to hurry because Joe was outside waiting for me. Only, Joe was there, looking over her shoulder, and he had his hands on her breasts while she worked the little red rubber bulb that was pumping soapsuds into my ass. There were others, featuring a cast of thousands, but I don't want to go into them. It was all Napoleon XIV stuff.

I found the pipe wrench in the garage, in an old toolbox. It wasn't a very big piece, but there was a rust-clotted socket on one end. And it hefted heavy in my hand. It was winter then, and I used to wear a big bulky sweater to school every day. I have an aunt that sends me two of those every year, birthday and Christmas. She knits them, and they always come down below my hips. So I started to carry the pipe wrench in my back pocket. It went everyplace with me. If anyone ever noticed, they never said. For a little while, it evened things up, but not for long. There were days when I came home feeling like a guitar string that has been tuned five octaves past its proper position. On those days I'd say hi to Mom, then go upstairs and either weep or giggle into my pillow until it felt as if all my guts were going to blow up. That scared me. When you do things like that, you are ready for the loony bin.

The day that I almost killed Mr. Carlson was the third of March. It was raining, and the last of the snow was just trickling away in nasty little rivulets. I guess I don't have to go into what happened, because most of you were there and saw it. I had the pipe wrench in my back pocket. Carlson called me up to do a problem

114

on the board, and I've always hated that—I'm lousy in chemistry. It made me break out in a sweat every time I had to go up to that board.

It was something about weight-stress on an inclined plane, I forget just what, but I fucked it all up. I remember thinking he had his fucking gall, getting me up here in front of everybody to mess around with an inclined-plane deal, which was really a physics problem. He probably had it left over from his last class. And he started to make fun of me. He was asking me if I remembered what two and two made, if I'd ever heard of long division, wonderful invention, he said, ha-ha, a regular Henny Youngman. When I did it wrong for the third time he said, "Well, that's just *woonderful*, Charlie. *Woooonderful*." He sounded just like Dicky Cable. He sounded so much like him that I turned around fast to look. He sounded so much like him that I reached for my back pocket where that pipe wrench was tucked away, before I even thought. My stomach was all drawn up tight, and I thought I was just going to lean down and blow my cookies all over the floor.

I hit the back pocket with my hand, and the pipe wrench fell out. It hit the floor and clanged.

Mr. Carlson looked at it. "Now, just what is *that*?" he asked, and started to reach for it.

"Don't touch it," I said, and reached down and grabbed it for myself.

"Let me see it, Charlie." He put his hand out for it.

I felt as if I were going in twelve different directions at once. Part of my mind was screaming at me—really, actually screaming, like a child in a dark room where there are horrible, grinning boogeymen.

"Don't," I said. And everybody was *looking* at me. All of them *staring*.

"You can give it to me or you can give it to Mr. Denver," he said.

And then a funny thing happened to me . . . except, when I think about it, it wasn't funny at all. There must be a line in all of us, a very clear one, just like the line that divides the light side of a planet from the dark. I think they call that line the terminator. That's a very good word for it. Because at one moment I was freaking out, and at the next I was as cool as a cucumber.

"I'll give it to you, skinner," I said, and thumped the socket end into my palm. "Where do you want it?"

He looked at me with his lips pursed. With those heavy tortoiseshell glasses he wore, he looked like some kind of bug. A very stupid kind. The thought made me smile. I thumped the business end of the wrench into my palm again.

"All right, Charlie," he said. "Give that thing to me and then go up to the office. I'll come up after class."

"Eat shit," I said, and swung the pipe wrench behind me. It thocked against the slate skin of the blackboard, and little chips flew out. There was yellow chalk dust on the socket end, but it didn't seem any worse for the encounter. Mr. Carlson, on the other hand, winced as though it had been his mother I'd hit instead of some fucking torture-machine blackboard. It was quite an insight into his character, I can tell you. So I hit the blackboard again. And again.

"*Charlie!*"

"It's a treat . . . to beat your meat . . . on the Mississippi mud," I sang, whacking the blackboard in time. Every time I hit it, Mr. Carlson jumped. Every time Mr. Carlson jumped, I felt a little better. Transitional action analysis, baby. Dig it. The Mad Bomber, that poor sad sack from Waterbury, Connecticut, must have been the most well-adjusted American of the last quarter-century.

"Charlie, I'll see that you're suspen—"

I turned around and began to whack away at the chalk ledge. I had already made a hell of a hole in the board itself; it wasn't such a tough board at that, not once you had its number. Erasers and chalk fell on the floor, puffing up dust. I was just on the brink of realizing you could have anybody's number if you held a big enough stick when Mr. Carlson grabbed me.

I turned around and hit him. Just once. There was a lot of blood. He fell on the floor, and his tortoiseshell glasses fell off and skated about eight feet. I think that's what broke the spell, the sight of those glasses sliding across the chalk-dusty floor, leaving his face bare and defenseless, looking the way it must look when he was asleep. I dropped the pipe wrench on the floor and walked out without looking back. I went upstairs and told them what I had done.

Jerry Kesserling picked me up in a patrol car and they sent Mr. Carlson to Central Maine General Hospital, where an X ray showed that he had a hairline fracture just above the frontal lobe. I understand they picked four splinters of bone out of his brain. A few dozen more, and they could have put them together with airplane glue so they spelled ASSHOLE and given it to him for his birthday with my compliments.

There were conferences. Conferences with my father, with good old Tom, with Don Grace, and with every possible combination and permutation of the above. I conferenced with everybody but Mr. Fazio, the janitor. Through it all my father kept admirably calm—my mother would come out of the house and was on tranquilizers—but every now and then during these civilized conversations, he would turn an icy, speculative eye on me that I knew eventually we would be having our own conference. He could have killed me cheerfully with his bare hands. In a simpler time, he might have done it.

There was a very touching apology to a bandage-wrapped, black-eyed Mr. Carlson and his stony-eyed wife (" . . . distraught . . . haven't been myself . . . sorrier than I can say . . . "), but I got no apology for being badgered in front of the chemistry class as I stood sweating at the blackboard with all the numbers looking like fifth-century Punic. No apology from Dicky Cable or Dana Collette. Or from your Friendly Neighborhood Creaking Thing who told me through tight lips on the way home from the hospital that he wanted to see me out in the garage after I had changed my clothes.

I thought about that as I took off my sport jacket and my best slacks and put on jeans and an old chambray workshirt. I thought about not going—just heading off down the road instead. I thought about just going out and taking it. Something in me rebelled at that. I had been suspended. I had spent five hours in a holding cell in Placerville Center before my father and my hysterical mother ("Why did you do it, Charlie? Why? Why?'') forked over the bail money—the charges, at the joint agreement of the school, the cops, and Mr. Carlson (not his wife; she had been hoping I'd get at least ten years), had been dropped later.

One way or the other, I thought my father and I owed each other something. And so I went out to the garage.

It's a musty, oil-smelling place, but completely trim. Shipshape. It's his place, and he keeps it that way. A place for everything, and everything in its place. Yo-ho-ho, matey. The riding lawnmower placed neatly with its nose against the wall. The gardening and landscaping tools neatly hung up on nails. Jar tops nailed to the roof beams so jars of nails could be screwed into them at eye level. Stacks of old magazines neatly tied up with twine—*Argosy, Bluebook, True, Saturday Evening Post*. The ranch wagon neatly parked facing out.

He was standing there in an old faded pair of twill khakis and a hunting shirt. For the first time, I noticed how old he was starting to look. His belly had always been as flat as a two-by-four, but now it was bulging out a little—too many beers down at Gogan's. There seemed to be more veins in his nose burst out into little purple deltas under the skin, and the lines around his mouth and eyes were deeper.

"What's your mother doing?" he asked me.

"Sleeping," I said. She had been sleeping a lot, with the help of a Librium prescription. Her breath was sour and dry with it. It smelled like dreams gone rancid.

"Good," he said, nodding. "That's how we want it, isn't it?"

He started taking off his belt.

"I'm going to take the hide off you," he said.

"No," I said. "You're not."

He paused, the belt half out of the loops. "What?"

"If you come at me with that thing, I'm going to take it away from you," I said. My voice was trembling and uneven. "I'm going to do it for the time you threw me on the ground when I was little and then lied about it to Mom. I'm going to do it for every time you belted me across the face for doing something wrong, without giving me a second chance. I'm going to do it for that hunting trip when you said you'd slit her nose open if you ever caught her with another man."

He had gone a deadly pale. Now it was his voice trembling. "You gutless, spineless wonder. Do you think you can blame this on me? You go tell that to that pansy psychiatrist if you want to, that one with the pipe. Don't try it on me."

"You stink," I said. "You fucked up your marriage and you fucked up your only child. You come on and try to take me if you think you can. I'm out of school. Your wife's turning into a pillhead. You're nothing but a boozehound." I was crying. "You come on and try it, you dumb fuck."

"You better stop it, Charlie," he said. "Before I stop just wanting to punish you and start wanting to kill you."

"Go ahead and try," I said, crying harder. "I've wanted to kill you for thirteen years. I hate your guts. You suck."

So then he came at me like something out of a slave-exploitation movie, one end of his Navy-issue belt wrapped in his fist, the other end, the buckle end, dangling down. He swung it at me, and I ducked. It went by my shoulder and hit the hood of his Country Squire wagon with a hard clank, scoring the finish. His tongue was caught between his teeth, and his eyes were bulging. He looked the way he had that day I broke the storm windows. Suddenly I wondered if that was the way he looked when he made love to my mother (or what passed for it); if that's what she had to look up at while she was pinned under him. The thought froze me with such a bolt of disgusted revelation that I forgot to duck the next one.

The buckle came down alongside my face, ripped into my cheek, pulling it open in a long furrow. It bled a lot. It felt like the side of my face and neck had been doused in warm water.

"Oh, God," he said. "Oh, God, Charlie."

My eye had watered shut on that side, but I could see him coming toward me with the other. I stepped to meet him and grabbed the end of the belt and pulled. He wasn't expecting it. It jerked him off balance, and when he started to run a little to catch it back, I tripped him up and he thumped to the oil-stained concrete floor. Maybe he had forgotten I wasn't four anymore, or nine years old and cowering in a tent, having to take a whiz while he yucked it up with his friends. Maybe he had forgotten or never knew that little boys grow up remembering every blow and word of scorn, that they grow up and want to eat their fathers alive.

A harsh little grunt escaped him as he hit the concrete. He opened his hands to break his fall, and I had the belt. I doubled it and brought it down on his broad khaki ass. It made a loud smack, and it probably didn't hurt much, but he cried out in surprise, and I smiled. It hurt my cheek to smile. He had really beaten the shit out of my cheek.

He got up warily. "Charlie, put that down," he said. "Let's take you to the doctor and get that stitched up."

"You better say yes-sir to the Marines you see if your own kid can knock you down," I said.

That made him mad, and he lunged at me, and I hit him across the face with the belt. He put his hands up to his face, and I dropped the belt and hit him in the stomach as hard as I could. The air whiffled out of him, and he doubled over. His belly was soft, even softer than it had looked. I didn't know whether to feel disgust or pity suddenly. It occurred to me that the man I really wanted to hurt was safely out of my reach, standing behind a shield of years.

He straightened up, looking pale and sick. There was a red mark across his forehead where I had hit him with the belt.

"Okay," he said, and turned around. He pulled a hardhead rake off the wall. "If that's how you want it."

I reached out beside me and pulled the hatchet off the wall and held it up with one hand.

"That's how I want it," I said. "Take one step, and I'll cut your head off, if I can."

So we stood there, trying to figure out if we meant it. Then he put the rake back, and I put the hatchet back. There was no love in it, no love in the way we looked at each other. He didn't say, *If you'd had the guts to do that five years ago, none of this would have happened, son . . . come on, I'll take you down to Gogan's and buy you a beer in the back room.* And I didn't say I was sorry. It happened because I got big enough, that was all. None of it changed anything. Now I wish it was him I'd killed, if I had to kill anyone. This thing on the floor between my feet is a classic case of misplaced aggression.

"Come on," he said. "Let's get that stitched up."

"I can drive myself."

"I'll drive you."

And so he did. We went down to the emergency room in Brunswick, and the doctor put six stitches in my cheek, and I told him that I had tripped over a chunk of stove wood in the garage and cut my cheek on a fireplace screen my dad was blacking. We told Mom the same thing. And that was the end of it. We never discussed it again. He never tried to tell me what to do again. We lived in the same house, but we walked in wide circles around each other, like a pair of old toms. If I had to guess, I'd say he'll get along without me very well . . . like the song says.

During the second week of April they sent me back to school with the warning that my case was still under consideration and I would have to go see Mr. Grace every day. They acted like they were doing me a favor. Some favor. It was like being popped back into the cabinet of Dr. Caligari.

It didn't take as long to go bad this time. The way people looked at me in the halls. The way I knew they were talking about me in the teachers' rooms. The way nobody would even talk to me anymore except Joe. And I wasn't very cooperative with Grace.

Yes, folks, things got bad very fast indeed, and they went from bad to worse. But I've always been fairly quick on the uptake, and I don't forget many lessons that I've learned well. I certainly learned the lesson about how you could get anyone's number with a big enough stick. My father picked up the hardhead rake, presumably planning to trepan my skull with it, but when I picked up the hatchet, he put it back.

I never saw that pipe wrench again, but what the fuck. I didn't need that anymore, because that stick wasn't big enough. I'd known about the pistol in my father's desk for ten years. Near the end of April I started to carry it to school.

Chapter 30

I looked up at the wall clock. It was 12:30. I drew in all my mental breath and got ready to sprint down the homestretch.

"So ends the short, brutal saga of Charles Everett Decker," I said. "Questions?"

Susan Brooks said very quietly in the dim room, "I'm sorry for you, Charlie." It was like the crack of damnation.

Don Lordi was looking at me in a hungry way that reminded me of *Jaws* for the second time that day. Sylvia was smoking the last cigarette in her pack. Pat Fitzgerald labored on his plane, crimping the paper wings, the usual funny-sly expression gone from his face, replaced by something that was wooden and carved. Sandra Cross still seemed to be in a pleasant daze. Even Ted Jones seemed to have his mind on other matters, perhaps on a door he had forgotten to latch when he was ten, or a dog he might once have kicked.

"If that's all, then it brings us to the final order of business in our brief but enlightening stay together," I said. "Have you learned anything today? Who knows the final order of business? Let's see."

I watched them. There was nothing. I was afraid it wouldn't come, couldn't come. So tight, so frozen, all of them. When you're five and you hurt, you make a big noise unto the world. At ten you whimper. But by the time you make fifteen you begin to eat the poisoned apples that grow on your own inner tree of pain. It's the Western Way of Enlightenment. You begin to cram your fists into your mouth to stifle the screams. You bleed on the inside. But they had gone so far . . .

And then Pig Pen looked up from his pencil. He was smiling a small, red-eyed smile, the smile of a ferret. His hand crept up into the air, the fingers still clenched around his cheap writing instrument. Be-bop-a-lula, she's my baby.

So then it was easier for the rest of them. One electrode begins to arc and sputter, and—*yoiks!*—look, professor, the monster walks tonight.

Susan Brooks put her hand up next. Then there were several together: Sandra raised hers, Grace Stanner raised hers—delicately—and Irma Bates did likewise. Corky. Don. Pat. Sarah Pasterne. Some smiling a little, most of them solemn. Tanis. Nancy Caskin. Dick Keene and Mike Gavin, both renowned in the Placerville Greyhounds' backfield. George and Harmon, who played chess together in study hall. Melvin Thomas. Anne Lasky. At the end all of them were up—all but one.

I called on Carol Granger, because I thought she deserved her moment. You would have thought that she might have had the most trouble making the switch, crossing the terminator, so to speak, but she had done it almost effortlessly, like a girl shedding her clothes in the bushes after dusk had come to the class picnic.

"Carol?" I said. "What's the answer?"

She thought about how to word it. She put a finger up to the small dimple beside her mouth as she thought, and there was a furrow in her milk-white brow.

"We have to help," she said. "We have to help show Ted where he has gone wrong."

That was a very tasteful way to put it, I thought.

"Thank you, Carol," I said.

She blushed.

I looked at Ted, who had come back to the here and now. He was glaring again, but in kind of a confused way.

"I think the best thing," I said, "would be if I became a sort of combination judge and public attorney. Everyone else can be witnesses; and of course, you're the defendant, Ted."

Ted laughed wildly. "You," he said. "Oh, Jesus, Charlie. Who do you think you are? You're crazy as a bat."

"Do you have a statement?" I asked him.

"You're not going to play tricks with me, Charlie. I'm not saying a darn thing. I'll save my speech for when we get out of here." His eyes swept his classmates accusingly and distrustfully. "And I'll have a lot to say."

"You know what happens to squealers, Rocco," I said in a tough Jimmy Cagney voice. I brought the pistol up suddenly, pointed it at his head, and screamed "BANG!"

Ted shrieked in surprise.

Anne Lasky laughed merrily.

"Shut up!" Ted yelled at her.

"Don't you tell *me* to shut up," she said. "What are you so afraid of?"

"What . . . ?" His jaw dropped. The eyes bulged. In that moment I felt a great deal of pity for him. The Bible says the snake tempted Eve with the apple. What would have happened if he had been forced to eat it himself?

Ted half-rose from his seat, trembling. "What am I . . . ? What am I . . . ?" He pointed a shivering finger at Anne, who did not cringe at all. "YOU GODDAMN SILLY BITCH! HE HAS GOT A GUN! HE IS CRAZY! HE HAS SHOT TWO PEOPLE! DEAD! HE IS HOLDING US HERE!"

"Not me, he isn't," Irma said. "I could have walked right out."

"We've learned some very good things about ourselves, Ted," Susan said coldly. "I don't think you're being very helpful, closing yourself in and trying to be superior. Don't you realize that this could be the most meaningful experience of our lives?"

"He's a killer," Ted said tightly. "He killed two people. This isn't TV. Those people aren't going to get up and go off to their dressing rooms to wait for the next take. They're *really dead.* He *killed* them."

"Soul killer!" Pig Pen hissed suddenly.

"Where the fuck do you think you get off?" Dick Keene asked. "All this just shakes the shit out of your tight little life, doesn't it? You didn't think anybody'd find out about you banging Sandy, did you? Or your mother. Ever think about her? You think you're some kind of white knight. I'll tell you what you are. You're a cocksucker."

"Witness! Witness!" Grace cried merrily, waving her hand. "Ted Jones buys girlie magazines. I've seen him in Ronnie's Variety doing it."

"Beat off much, Ted?" Harmon asked. He was smiling viciously.

"And you were a Star Scout," Pat said dolorously.

Ted twitched from them like a bear that has been tied to a post for the villagers' amusement. *"I don't masturbate!"* he yelled.

"Right," Corky said disgustedly.

"I bet you really stink in bed," Sylvia said. She looked at Sandra. "Did he stink in bed?"

"We didn't do it in bed," Sandra said. "We were in a car. And it was over so quick . . . "

"Yeah, that's what I figured."

"All right," Ted said. His face was sweaty. He stood up. "I'm walking out of here. You're all crazy. I'll tell them . . . " He stopped and added with a strange and touching irrelevancy, "I never meant what I said about my mother." He swallowed. "You can shoot me, Charlie, but you can't stop me. I'm going out."

I put the gun down on the blotter. "I have no intention of shooting you, Ted. But let me remind you that you haven't really done your duty."

"That's right," Dick said, and after Ted had taken two steps toward the door, Dick came out of his seat, took two running steps of his own, and collared him. Ted's face dissolved into utter amazement.

"Hey, Dick," he said.

"Don't you Dick me, you son of a bitch."

Ted tried to give him an elbow in the belly, and then his arms were pinned behind him, one by Pat and one by George Yannick.

Sandra Cross got slowly out of her seat and walked to him, demurely, like a girl on a country road. Ted's eyes were bulging, half-mad. I could taste what was coming, the way you can taste thunderheads before summer rain . . . and the hail that comes with it sometimes.

She stopped before him, and an expression of sly, mocking devotion crossed her face and was gone. She put a hand out, touched the collar of his shirt. The muscles of his neck bunched as he jerked away from her. Dick and Pat and George held him like springs. She reached slowly inside the open collar of the khaki shirt and began to pull it open, popping the buttons. There was no sound in the room but the tiny, flat tic-tic as the buttons fell to the floor and rolled. He was wearing no undershirt. His flesh was bare and smooth. She moved as if to kiss it, and he spit in her face.

Pig Pen smiled from over Sandra's shoulder, the grubby court jester with the king's paramour. "I could put your eyes out," he said. "Do you know that? Pop them out just like olives. *Poink! Poink!*"

"*Let me go!* Charlie, make them let me—"

"He cheats," Sarah Pasterne said loudly. "He always looks at my answer sheet in French. Always."

Sandra stood before him, now looking down, a sweet, murmurous smile barely curving the bow of her lips. The first two fingers of her right hand touched the slick spittle on her cheek lightly.

"Here," Billy Sawyer whispered. "Here's something for you, handsome." He crept up behind Ted on tippy-toe and suddenly pulled his hair.

Ted screamed.

"He cheats on the laps in gym, too," Don said harshly. "You really quit football because you dint have no sauce, dintchoo?"

"Please," Ted said. "Please, Charlie." He had begun to grin oddly, and his eyeballs were shiny with tears. Sylvia had joined the little circle around him. She might have been the one who goosed him, but I couldn't really see.

They were moving around him in a slow kind of dance that was nearly beautiful. Fingers pinched and pulled, questions were asked, accusations made. Irma Bates pushed a ruler down the back of his pants. Somehow his shirt was ripped off and flew to the back of the room in two tatters. Ted was breathing in great, high whoops. Anne Lasky began to rub the bridge of his nose with an eraser. Corky scurried back to his desk like a good mouse, found a bottle of Carter's ink, and dumped it in his hair. Hands flew out like birds and rubbed it in briskly.

Ted began to weep and talk in strange, unconnected phrases.

"Soul brother?" Pat Fitzgerald asked. He was smiling, whacking Ted's bare shoulders lightly with a notebook in cadence. "Be my soul brother? That right? Little Head Start? Little free lunch? That right? Hum? Hum? Brothers? Be soul brothers?"

"Got your Silver Star, hero," Dick said, and raised his knee, placing it expertly in the big muscle of Ted's thigh.

Ted screamed. His eyes bulged and rolled toward me, the eyes of a horse staved on a high fence. "*Please . . . pleeeese, Charlie . . . pleeeeeeeeee—*" And then Nancy Caskin stuffed a large wad of notebook paper into his mouth. He tried to spit it out, but Sandra rammed it back in.

"That will teach you to spit," she said reproachfully.

Harmon knelt and pulled off one of his shoes. He rubbed it in Ted's inky hair and then slammed the sole against Ted's chest. It left a huge, grotesque footprint.

"Admit one!" he crowed.

Tentatively, almost demurely, Carol stepped on Ted's stockinged foot and twisted her heel. Something in his foot snapped. Ted blubbered.

He sounded like he was begging somewhere behind the paper, but you couldn't really tell. Pig Pen darted in spiderlike and suddenly bit his nose.

There was a sudden black pause. I noticed that I had turned the pistol around so that the muzzle was pointed at my head, but of course that would not be at all cricket. I unloaded it and put it carefully in the top drawer, on top of Mrs. Underwood's plan book. I was quite confident that this had not been in today's lesson plan at all.

They were smiling at Ted, who hardly looked human at all anymore. In that brief flick of time, they looked like gods, young, wise, and golden. Ted did not look like a god. Ink ran down his cheeks in blue-black teardrops. The bridge of his nose was bleeding, and one eye glared disjointedly toward no place. Paper protruded through his teeth. He breathed in great white snuffles of air.

I had time to think: *We have got it on. Now we have got it all the way on.*

They fell on him.

Chapter 31

I had Corky pull up the shades before they left. He did it with quick, jerky motions. There were now what seemed like hundreds of cruisers out there, thousands of people. It was three minutes of one.

The sunlight hurt my eyes.

"Good-bye," I said.

"Good-bye," Sandra said.

They all said good-bye, I think, before they went out. Their footfalls made a funny, echoy noise going down the hall. I closed my eyes and imagined a giant centipede wearing Georgia Giants on each of its one hundred feet. When I opened them again, they were walking across the bright green of the lawn. I wished they had used the sidewalk; even after all that had happened, it was still a hell of a lawn.

The last thing I remember seeing of them was that their hands were streaked with black ink.

People enveloped them.

One of the reporters, throwing caution to the winds, eluded three policemen and raced down to where they were, pell-mell.

The last one to be swallowed up was Carol Granger. I thought she looked back, but I couldn't tell for sure. Philbrick started to walk stolidly toward the school. Flashbulbs were popping all over the place.

Time was short. I went over to where Ted was leaning against the green cinderblock wall. He was sitting with his legs splayed out below the bulletin board, which was full of notices from the Mathematical Society of America, which nobody ever read, Peanuts comic strips (the acme of humor, in the late Mrs. Underwood's estimation), and a poster showing Bertrand Russell and a quote: "Gravity alone proves the existence of God." But any undergraduate in creation could have told Bertrand that it has been conclusively proved that there is no gravity; the earth just sucks.

I squatted beside Ted. I pulled the crumpled wad of math paper out of his mouth and laid it aside. Ted began to drool.

"Ted."

He looked past me, over my shoulder.

"Ted," I said, and patted his cheek gently.

He shrank away. His eyes rolled wildly.

"You're going to get better," I said. "You're going to forget this day ever happened."

Ted made mewling sounds.

125

"Or maybe you won't. Maybe you'll go on from here, Ted. Build from this. Is that such an impossible idea?"

It was, for both of us. And being so close to Ted had begun to make me very nervous.

The intercom chinked open. It was Philbrick. He was puffing and blowing again.

"Decker?"

"Right here."

"Come out with your hands up."

I sighed. "You come down and get me, Philbrick, old sport. I'm pretty goddamn tired. This psycho business is a hell of a drain on the glands."

"All right," he said, tough. "They'll be shooting in the gas canisters in just about one minute."

"Better not," I said. I looked at Ted. Ted didn't look back; he just kept on looking into emptiness. Whatever he saw there must have been mighty tasty, because he was still drooling down his chin. "You forgot to count noses. There's still one of them down here. He's hurt." That was something of an understatement.

His voice was instantly wary. "Who?"

"Ted Jones."

"How is he hurt?"

"Stubbed his toe."

"He's not there. You're lying."

"I wouldn't lie to you, Philbrick, and jeopardize our beautiful relationship."

No answer. Puff, snort, blow.

"Come on down," I invited. "The gun is unloaded. It's in a desk drawer. We can play a couple of cribbage hands, then you can take me out and tell all the papers how you did it single-handed. You might even make the cover of *Time* if we work it right."

Chink. He was off the horn.

I closed my eyes and put my face in my hands. All I saw was gray. Nothing but gray. Not even a flash of white light. For no reason at all, I thought of New Year's Eve, when all those people crowd into Times Square and scream like jackals as the lighted ball slides down the pole, ready to shed its thin party glare on three hundred and sixty-five new days in this best of all possible worlds. I have always wondered what it would be like to be caught in one of those crowds, screaming and not able to hear your own voice, your individuality momentarily wiped out and replaced with the blind empathic overslop of the crowd's lurching, angry anticipation, hip to hip and shoulder to shoulder with no one in particular.

I began to cry.

When Philbrick stepped through the door, he glanced down at the drooling Ted-thing and then up at me. "What in the name of God did you . . . ?" he began.

I made as if to grab something behind Mrs. Underwood's desktop row of books and plants. "Here it comes, you shit cop!" I screamed.

He shot me three times.

Chapter 32

CHARLES EVERETT DECKER, convicted in Superior Court this day, August 27, 1976, of the willful murder of *Jean Alice Underwood,* and also convicted this day, August 27, 1976, of the willful murder of *John Downes Vance,* both human beings.

It has been determined by five state psychiatrists that Charles Everett Decker cannot at this time be held accountable for his actions, by reason of insanity. It is therefore the decision of this court that he be remanded to the Augusta State Hospital, where he will be held in treatment until such time as he can be certified responsible to answer for his acts.

To this writ have I set my hand.

(Signed)

(Judge) Samuel K. N. Deleavney

In other words, until shit sticks on the moon, baby.

Chapter 33

FROM: Dr. Andersen
TO: Rich Gossage, Admin. Wing
SUBJECT: Theodore Jones

Rich,

Am still loath to try the shock treatments on this boy, altho I can't explain it even to myself—call it hunch. Of course I can't justify hunch to the board of directors, or to Jones's uncle, who is footing the bill, which, in a private institution like Woodlands, don't come cheap, as we both know. If there is no movement in the next four to six weeks, we'll go on with the standard electroshock therapy, but for now I would like to run the standard drug schedule again, plus a few not so standard—I am thinking of both synthetic mescaline and psyilocybin, if you concur. Will Greenberger has had a great deal of success with semicatatonic patients as you know, and these two hallucinogens have played a major part in his therapy.

Jones is such a strange case—goddammit, if we only could be sure what had gone on in that classroom after that Decker individual had the shades pulled down!

Diagnosis hasn't changed. Flat-line catatonic state w/some signs of deterioration.

I might as well admit to you up front, Rich, that I am not as hopeful for this boy as I once was.

November 3, 1976

Chapter 34

December 5, 1976

Dear Charlie,

They tell me you can have mail now, so I thought I would drop you a line. Maybe you noticed this is postmarked Boston—your old buddy finally made the Big Time, and I'm taking sixteen hours here at B.U. (that stands for Bullshit Unlimited). It's all pretty slushy except for my English class. The instructor assigned us a book called *The Postman Always Rings Twice* that was really good, and I got an A on the exam. It's by James Cain, did you ever read it? I'm thinking about majoring in English, how's that for a laugh? Must be your influence. And you were always the brains of the combination.

I saw your mom just before I left Placerville, and she said you were just about all healed up and the last of the drains were out three weeks ago. I was sure glad to hear it. She said you aren't talking much. That doesn't sound like you, skinner. It would sure be a loss to the world if you clammed up and just scrunched in a corner all day.

Although I haven't been home since the semester started, Sandy Cross wrote me a letter with a lot of news about all the people at home. (Will the bastards censor this part? I bet they read all your mail.) Sandy herself decided not to go to college this year. She's just sort of hanging around, waiting for something to happen, I guess. I might as well tell you that I dated her a couple of times last summer, but she just seemed kind of distant. She asked me to say "hi" to you, so "hi" from Sandy.

Maybe you know what happened to Pig Pen, no one in town can believe it, about him and Dick Keene [following has been censored as possibly upsetting to patient], so you can never tell what people are going to do, can you?

Carol Granger's validictory (sp?) speech was reprinted by *Seventeen* magazine. As I remember, it was on "Self-Integrity and a Normal Response to It," or some such happy horseshit. We would have had some fun ranking that one out, right, Charlie?

Oh, yeah, and Irma Bates is going out with some "hippie" from Lewiston. I guess they were even in a demonstration when Robt. Dole came to Portland to campaign in the presidential election stuff. They were arrested and then let go when Dole flew out. Mrs. Bates must be having birds about it. Can't you just see Irma trying to brain Robt. Dole with a Gus Hall campaign sign? Ha-

ha, that just kills me. We would have had some laughs over that one, too, Charlie. God, I miss your old cracked ass sometimes.

Gracie Stanner, that cute little chick, is going to get married, and that's also a local sensation. It boggles the mind. [Following has been censored as possibly upsetting to patient.] Anyway, you can never tell what sort of monkey-shines people are going to get up to, right?

Well, guess that's all for now. I hope they are treating you right, Ferd, as you've got to be out of there as soon as they'll let you. And if they start letting you have visitors, I want you to know that I will be the first in line.

There are a lot of us pulling for you, Charlie. Pulling hard.

People haven't forgotten. You know what I mean.

You have to believe that.

With love, your friend,

Joe McK.

Chapter 35

I haven't had any bad dreams for two weeks, almost. I do lots of jigsaw puzzles. They give me custard and I hate it, but I eat it just the same. They think I like it. So I have a secret again. Finally I have a secret again.

My mom sent me the yearbook. I haven't unwrapped it yet, but maybe I will. Maybe next week I will. I think I could look at all the senior pictures and not tremble a bit. Pretty soon. Just as soon as I can make myself believe that there won't be any black streaks on their hands. That their hands will be clean. With no ink. Maybe next week I'll be completely sure of that.

About the custard: it's only a little secret, but having a secret makes me feel better. Like a human being again.

That's the end. I have to turn off the light now. Good night.

SIGNET•451-J8754•$1.95

IN A FUTURE AMERICA,
THE MARATHON IS
THE ULTIMATE SPORTS
COMPETITION—
A NOVEL OF CHILLING,
MACABRE POSSIBILITY

THE

LONG
WALK

BY
RICHARD BACHMAN
AUTHOR OF RAGE

This is for Jim Bishop
and Burt Hatlen and Ted Holmes.

"To me the Universe was all void of Life, or Purpose, of Volition, even of Hostility; it was one huge, dead, immeasurable Steam-engine, rolling on, in its dead indifference, to grind me limb from limb. O vast, gloomy, solitary Golgotha, and Mill of Death! Why was the Living banished thither companionless, conscious? Why, if there is no Devil; nay, unless the Devil is your God?"

—Thomas Carlyle

"I would encourage every American to walk as often as possible. It's more than healthy; it's fun."

—John F. Kennedy (1962)

"The pump don't work
'Cause the vandals took the handle."

—Bob Dylan

PART ONE

Starting Out

Chapter 1

"Say the secret word and win a hundred dollars.
George, who are our first contestants?
George . . . ? Are you there, George?"
—Groucho Marx
You Bet Your Life

An old blue Ford pulled into the guarded parking lot that morning, looking like a small, tired dog after a hard run. One of the guards, an expressionless young man in a khaki uniform and a Sam Browne belt, asked to see the blue plastic ID card. The boy in the back seat handed it to his mother. His mother handed it to the guard. The guard took it to a computer terminal that looked strange and out of place in the rural stillness. The computer terminal ate the card and flashed this on its screen:

GARRATY RAYMOND DAVIS
RD 1 POWNAL MAINE
ANDROSGOGGIN COUNTY
ID NUMBER *49–801–89*
OK-OK-OK

The guard punched another button and all of this disappeared, leaving the terminal screen smooth and green and blank again. He waved them forward.

"Don't they give the card back?" Mrs. Garraty asked. "Don't they—"

"No, Mom," Garraty said patiently.

"Well, I don't like it," she said, pulling forward into an empty space. She had been saying it ever since they set out in the dark of two in the morning. She had been moaning it, actually.

"Don't worry," he said without hearing himself. He was occupied with looking and with his own confusion of anticipation and fear. He was out of the car almost before the engine's last asthmatic wheeze—a tall, well-built boy wearing a faded army fatigue jacket against the eight o'clock spring chill.

His mother was also tall, but too thin. Her breasts were almost nonexistent: token nubs. Her eyes were wandering and unsure, somehow shocked. Her face was an invalid's face. Her iron-colored hair had gone awry under the complication of clips that was supposed to hold it in place. Her dress hung badly on her body as if she had recently lost a lot of weight.

"Ray," she said in that whispery conspirator's voice that he had come to dread. "Ray, listen—"

141

He ducked his head and pretended to tuck in his shirt. One of the guards was eating Crations from a can and reading a comic book. Garraty watched the guard eating and reading and thought for the ten thousandth time: It's all *real.* And now, at last, the thought began to swing some weight.

"There's still time to change your mind—"

The fear and anticipation cranked up a notch.

"No, there's no time for that," he said. "The backout date was yesterday."

Still in that low conspirator's voice that he hated: "They'd understand, I know they would. The Major—"

"The Major would—" Garraty began, and saw his mother wince. "You know what the Major would do, Mom."

Another car had finished the small ritual at the gate and had parked. A boy with dark hair got out. His parents followed and for a moment the three of them stood in conference like worried baseball players. He, like some of the other boys, was wearing a light packsack. Garraty wondered if he hadn't been a little stupid not to bring one himself.

"You won't change your mind?"

It was guilt, guilt taking the face of anxiety. Although he was only sixteen, Ray Garraty knew something about guilt. She felt that she had been too dry, too tired, or maybe just too taken up with her older sorrows to halt her son's madness in its seedling stage—to halt it before the cumbersome machinery of the State with its guards in khaki and its computer terminals had taken over, binding himself more tightly to its insensate self with each passing day, until yesterday, when the lid had come down with a final bang.

He put a hand on her shoulder. "This is my idea, Mom. I know it wasn't yours. I—" He glanced around. No one was paying the slightest attention to them. "I love you, but this way is best, one way or the other."

"It's not," she said, now verging on tears. "Ray, it's not, if your father was here, he'd put a stop to—"

"Well, he's not, is he?" He was brutal, hoping to stave off her tears . . . what if they had to drag her off? He had heard that sometimes that happened. The thought made him feel cold. In a softer voice he said, "Let it go now, Mom. Okay?" He forced a grin. "Okay," he answered for her.

Her chin was still trembling, but she nodded. Not all right, but too late. There was nothing anyone could do.

A light wind soughed through the pines. The sky was pure blue. The road was just ahead and the simple stone post that marked the border between America and Canada. Suddenly his anticipation was greater than his fear, and he wanted to get going, get the show on the road.

"I made these. You can take them, can't you? They're not too heavy, are they?" She thrust a foil-wrapped package of cookies at him.

"Yeah." He took them and then clutched her awkwardly, trying to give her what she needed to have. He kissed her cheek. Her skin was like old silk. For a moment he could have cried himself. Then he thought of the smiling, mustachioed face of the Major and stepped back, stuffing the cookies into the pocket of his fatigue jacket.

"G'bye, Mom."

"Goodbye, Ray. Be a good boy."

She stood there for a moment and he had a sense of her being very light, as if even the light puffs of breeze blowing this morning might send her sailing away like a dandelion gone to seed. Then she got back into the car and started the engine. Garraty stood there. She raised her hand and waved. The tears were flowing now. He could see them. He waved back and then as she pulled out he just stood there with his arms at his sides, conscious of how fine and brave and alone he must look. But when the car had passed back through the gate, forlornness struck him and he was only a sixteen-year-old boy again, alone in a strange place.

He turned back toward the road. The other boy, the dark-haired one, was watching his folks pull out. He had a bad scar along one cheek. Garraty walked over to him and said hello.

The dark-haired boy gave him a glance. "Hi."

"I'm Ray Garraty," he said, feeling mildly like an asshole.

"I'm Peter McVries."

"You all ready?" Garraty asked.

McVries shrugged. "I feel jumpy. That's the worst."

Garraty nodded.

The two of them walked toward the road and the stone marker. Behind them, other cars were pulling out. A woman began screaming abruptly. Unconsciously, Garraty and McVries drew closer together. Neither of them looked back. Ahead of them was the road, wide and black.

"That composition surface will be hot by noon," McVries said abruptly. "I'm going to stick to the shoulder."

Garraty nodded. McVries looked at him thoughtfully.

"What do you weigh?"

"Hundred and sixty."

"I'm one-sixty-seven. They say the heavier guys get tired quicker, but I think I'm in pretty good shape."

To Garraty, Peter McVries looked rather more than that—he looked awesomely fit. He wondered who *they* were that said the heavier guys got tired quicker, almost asked, and decided not to. The Walk was one of those things that existed on apocrypha, talismans, legend.

McVries sat down in the shade near a couple of other boys, and after a moment, Garraty sat beside him. McVries seemed to have dismissed him entirely. Garraty looked at his watch. It was five after eight. Fifty-five minutes to go. Impatience and anticipation came back, and he did his best to squash them, telling himself to enjoy sitting while he could.

All of the boys were sitting. Sitting in groups and sitting alone; one boy had climbed onto the lowest branch of a pine overlooking the road and was eating what looked like a jelly sandwich. He was skinny and blond, wearing purple pants and a blue chambray shirt under an old green zip sweater with holes in the elbows. Garraty wondered if the skinny ones would last or burn out quickly.

The boys he and McVries had sat down next to were talking.

"I'm not hurrying," one of them said. "Why should I? If I get warned, so what? You just adjust, that's all. Adjustment is the key word here. Remember where you heard that first."

He looked around and discovered Garraty and McVries.

"More lambs to the slaughter. Hank Olson's the name. Walking is my game." He said this with no trace of a smile at all.

Garraty offered his own name. McVries spoke his own absently, still looking off toward the road.

"I'm Art Baker," the other said quietly. He spoke with a very slight Southern accent. The four of them shook hands all around.

There was a moment's silence, and McVries said, "Kind of scary, isn't it?"

They all nodded except Hank Olson, who shrugged and grinned. Garraty watched the boy in the pine tree finish his sandwich, ball up the waxed paper it had been in, and toss it onto the soft shoulder. He'll burn out early, he decided. That made him feel a little better.

"You see that spot right by the marker post?" Olson said suddenly.

They all looked. The breeze made moving shadow-patterns across the road. Garraty didn't know if he saw anything or not.

"That's from the Long Walk the year before last," Olson said with grim satisfaction. "Kid was so scared he just froze up at nine o'clock."

They considered the horror of it silently.

"Just couldn't move. He took his three warnings and then at 9:02 AM they gave him his ticket. Right there by the starting post."

Garraty wondered if his own legs would freeze. He didn't think so, but it was a thing you wouldn't know for sure until the time came, and it was a terrible thought. He wondered why Hank Olson wanted to bring up such a terrible thing.

Suddenly Art Baker sat up straight. "Here he comes."

A dun-colored jeep drove up to the stone marker and stopped. It was followed by a strange, tread-equipped vehicle that moved much more slowly. There were toy-sized radar dishes mounted on the front and back of this halftrack. Two soldiers lounged on its upper deck, and Garraty felt a chill in his belly when he looked at them. They were carrying army-type heavy-caliber carbine rifles.

Some of the boys got up, but Garraty did not. Neither did Olson or Baker, and after his initial look, McVries seemed to have fallen back into his own thoughts. The skinny kid in the pine tree was swinging his feet idly.

The Major got out of the jeep. He was a tall, straight man with a deep desert tan that went well with his simple khakis. A pistol was strapped to his Sam Browne belt, and he was wearing reflector sunglasses. It was rumored that the Major's eyes were extremely light-sensitive, and he was never seen in public without his sunglasses.

"Sit down, boys," he said. "Keep Hint Thirteen in mind." Hint Thirteen was "Conserve energy whenever possible."

Those who had stood sat down. Garraty looked at his watch again. It said 8:16, and he decided it was a minute fast. The Major always showed up on time. He thought momentarily of setting it back a minute and then forgot it.

"I'm not going to make a speech," the Major said, sweeping them with the blank lenses that covered his eyes. "I give my congratulations to the winner among your number, and my acknowledgments of valor to the losers."

He turned to the back of the jeep. There was a living silence. Garraty breathed deep of the spring air. It would be warm. A good day to walk.

The Major turned back to them. He was holding a clipboard. "When I call your name, please step forward and take your number. Then go back to your place until it is time to begin. Do this smartly, please."

"You're in the army now," Olson whispered with a grin, but Garraty ignored it. You couldn't help admiring the Major. Garraty's father, before the Squads took him away, had been fond of calling the Major the rarest and most dangerous monster any nation can produce, a society-supported sociopath. But he had never seen the Major in person.

"Aaronson."

A short, chunky farmboy with a sunburned neck gangled forward, obviously awed by the Major's presence, and took his large plastic 1. He fixed it to his shirt by the pressure strip and the Major clapped him on the back.

"Abraham."

A tall boy with reddish hair in jeans and a T-shirt. His jacket was tied about his waist schoolboy style and flapped wildly around his knees. Olson sniggered.

"Baker, Arthur."

"That's me," Baker said, and got to his feet. He moved with deceptive leisure, and he made Garraty nervous. Baker was going to be tough. Baker was going to last a long time.

Baker came back. He had pressed his number 3 onto the right breast of his shirt.

"Did he say anything to you?" Garraty asked.

"He asked me if it was commencing to come off hot down home," Baker said shyly. "Yeah, he . . . the Major talked to me."

"Not as hot as it's gonna commence getting up here," Olson cracked.

"Baker, James," the Major said.

It went on until 8:40, and it came out right. No one had ducked out. Back in the parking lot, engines started and a number of cars began pulling out—boys from the backup list who would now go home and watch the Long Walk coverage on TV. It's on, Garraty thought, it's really on.

When his turn came, the Major gave him number 47 and told him "Good luck." Up close he smelled very masculine and somehow overpowering. Garraty had an almost insatiable urge to touch the man's leg and make sure he was real.

Peter McVries was 61. Hank Olson was 70. He was with the Major longer than the rest. The Major laughed at something Olson said and clapped him on the back.

"I told him to keep a lot of money on short call," Olson said when he came back. "And he told me to give 'em hell. Said he liked to see someone who was raring to rip. Give 'em hell, boy, he said."

"Pretty good," McVries said, and then winked at Garraty. Garraty wondered what McVries had meant, winking like that. Was he making fun of Olson?

The skinny boy in the tree was named Stebbins. He got his number with his head down, not speaking to the Major at all, and then sat back at the base of his tree. Garraty was somehow fascinated with the boy.

Number 100 was a red-headed fellow with a volcanic complexion. His name was Zuck. He got his number and then they all sat and waited for what would come next.

Then three soldiers from the halftrack passed out wide belts with snap pockets. The pockets were filled with tubes of high-energy concentrate pastes. More soldiers came around with canteens. They buckled on the belts and slung the canteens. Olson slung his belt low on his hips like a gunslinger, found a Waifa chocolate bar, and began to eat it. "Not bad," he said, grinning. He swigged from his canteen, washing down the chocolate, and Garraty wondered if Olson was just fronting, or if he knew something Garraty did not.

The Major looked them over soberly. Garraty's wristwatch said 8:56—how had it gotten so late? His stomach lurched painfully.

"All right, fellows, line up by tens, please. No particular order. Stay with your friends, if you like."

Garraty got up. He felt numb and unreal. It was as if his body now belonged to someone else.

"Well, here we go," McVries said at his elbow. "Good luck, everyone."

"Good luck to you," Garraty said surprised.

McVries said: "I need my fucking head examined." He looked suddenly pale and sweaty, not so awesomely fit as he had earlier. He was trying to smile and not making it. The scar stood out on his cheek like a wild punctuation mark.

Stebbins got up and ambled to the rear of the ten wide, ten deep queue. Olson, Baker, McVries, and Garraty were in the third row. Garraty's mouth was dry. He wondered if he should drink some water. He decided against it. He had never in his life been so aware of his feet. He wondered if he might freeze and get his ticket on the starting line. He wondered if Stebbins would fold early—Stebbins with his jelly sandwich and his purple pants. He wondered if *he* would fold up first. He wondered what it would feel like if—

His wristwatch said 8:59.

The Major was studying a stainless steel pocket chronometer. He raised his fingers slowly, and everything hung suspended with his hand. The hundred boys watched it carefully, and the silence was awful and immense. The silence was everything.

Garraty's watch said 9:00, but the poised hand did not fall.

Do it! Why doesn't he *do* it?

He felt like screaming it out.

Then he remembered that his watch was a minute fast—you could set your watch by the Major, only he hadn't, he had forgotten.

The Major's fingers dropped. "Luck to all," he said. His face was expressionless and the reflector sunglasses hid his eyes. They began to walk smoothly, with no jostling.

Garraty walked with them. He hadn't frozen. Nobody froze. His feet passed beyond the stone marker, in parade-step with McVries on his left and Olson on his right. The sound of feet was very loud.

This is *it*, this is *it*, this is *it*.

A sudden insane urge to stop came to him. Just to see if they really meant business. He rejected the thought indignantly and a little fearfully.

They came out of the shade and into the sun, the warm spring sun. It felt good. Garraty relaxed, put his hands in his pockets, and kept step with McVries. The group began to spread out, each person finding his own stride and speed. The half-track clanked along the soft shoulder, throwing thin dust. The tiny radar dishes turned busily, monitoring each Walker's speed with a sophisticated on-board computer. Low speed cutoff was exactly four miles an hour.

"Warning! Warning 88!"

Garraty started and looked around. It was Stebbins. Stebbins was 88. Suddenly he was sure Stebbins was going to get his ticket right here, still in sight of the starting post.

"Smart." It was Olson.

"What?" Garraty asked. He had to make a conscious effort to move his tongue.

"The guy takes a warning while he's still fresh and gets an idea of where the limit is. And he can sluff it easy enough—you walk an hour without getting a fresh warning, you lose one of the old ones. You know that."

"Sure I know it," Garraty said. It was in the rule book. They gave you three warnings. The fourth time you fell below four miles an hour you were . . . well, you were out of the Walk. But if you had three warnings and could manage to walk for three hours, you were back in the sun again.

"So now he knows," Olson said. "And at 10:02, he's in the clear again."

Garraty walked on at a good clip. He was feeling fine. The starting post dropped from sight as they breasted a hill and began descending into a long, pine-studded valley. Here and there were rectangular fields with the earth just freshly turned.

"Potatoes, they tell me," McVries said.

"Best in the world," Garraty answered automatically.

"You from Maine?" Baker asked.

"Yeah, downstate." He looked up ahead. Several boys had drawn away from the main group, making perhaps six miles an hour. Two of them were wearing identical leather jackets, with what looked like eagles on the back. It was a temptation to speed up, but Garraty refused to be hurried. "Conserve energy whenever possible"—Hint 13.

"Does the road go anywhere near your hometown?" McVries asked.

"About seven miles to one side. I guess my mother and my girlfriend will come to see me." He paused and added carefully: "If I'm still walking, of course."

"Hell, there won't be twenty-five gone when we get downstate," Olson said.

A silence fell among them at that. Garraty knew it wasn't so, and he thought Olson did, too.

Two other boys received warnings, and in spite of what Olson had said, Garraty's heart lurched each time. He checked back on Stebbins. He was still at the rear, and eating another jelly sandwich. There was a third sandwich jutting from the pocket of his ragged green sweater. Garraty wondered if his mother had made them, and he thought of the cookies his own mother had given him—pressed on him, as if warding off evil spirits.

"Why don't they let people watch the start of a Long Walk?" Garraty asked.

"Spoils the Walkers' concentration," a sharp voice said.

Garraty turned his head. It was a small dark, intense-looking boy with the number 5 pressed to the collar of his jacket. Garraty couldn't remember his name. "Concentration?" he said.

"Yes." The boy moved up beside Garraty. "The Major has said it is very important to concentrate on calmness at the beginning of a Long Walk." He pressed his thumb reflectively against the end of his rather sharp nose. There was a bright red pimple there. "I agree. Excitement, crowds, TV later. Right now all we need to do is focus." He stared at Garraty with his hooded dark brown eyes and said it again. "Focus."

"All I'm focusing on is pickin' 'em up and layin' 'em down," Olson said.

5 looked insulted. "You have to pace yourself. You have to focus on yourself. You have to have a Plan. I'm Gary Barkovitch, by the way. My home is Washington, D.C."

"I'm John Carter," Olson said. "My home is Barsoom, Mars."

Barkovitch curled his lip in contempt and dropped back.

"There's one cuckoo in every clock, I guess," Olson said.

But Garraty thought Barkovitch was thinking pretty clearly—at least until one of the guards called out "Warning! Warning 5!" about five minutes later.

"I've got a stone in my shoe!" Barkovitch said waspishly.

The soldier didn't reply. He dropped off the halftrack and stood on the shoulder of the road opposite Barkovitch. In his hand he held a stainless steel chronometer just like the Major's. Barkovitch stopped completely and took off his shoe. He shook a tiny pebble out of it. Dark, intense, his olive-sallow face shiny with sweat, he paid no attention when the soldier called out, "Second warning, 5." Instead, he smoothed his sock carefully over the arch of his foot.

"Oh-oh," Olson said. They had all turned around and were walking backward.

Stebbins, still at the tag end, walked past Barkovitch without looking at him. Now Barkovitch was all alone, slightly to the right of the white line, retying his shoe.

"Third warning, 5. Final warning."

There was something in Garraty's belly that felt like a sticky ball of mucus. He didn't want to look, but he couldn't look away. He wasn't conserving energy whenever possible by walking backward, but he couldn't help that, either. He could almost feel Barkovitch's seconds shriveling away to nothing.

"Oh, boy," Olson said. "That dumb shit, he's gonna get his ticket."

But then Barkovitch was up. He paused to brush some road dirt from the knees of his pants. Then he broke into a trot, caught up with the group, and settled back into his walking pace. He passed Stebbins, who still didn't look at him, and caught up with Olson.

He grinned, brown eyes glittering. "See? I just got myself a rest. It's all in my Plan."

"Maybe you think so," Olson said, his voice higher than usual. "All I see that you got is three warnings. For your lousy minute and a half you got to walk three . . . fucking . . . *hours*. And why in hell did you need a rest? We just started, for Chrissake!"

Barkovitch looked insulted. His eyes burned at Olson. "We'll see who gets his ticket first, you or me," he said. "It's all in my Plan."

"Your Plan and the stuff that comes out of my asshole bear a suspicious resemblance to each other," Olson said, and Baker chuckled.

With a snort, Barkovitch strode past them.

Olson couldn't resist a parting shot. "Just don't stumble, buddy. They don't warn you again. They just . . . "

Barkovitch didn't even look back and Olson gave up, disgusted.

At thirteen past nine by Garraty's watch (he had taken the trouble to set it back the one minute), the Major's jeep breasted the hill they had just started down. He came past them on the shoulder opposite the pacing halftrack and raised a battery-powered loudhailer to his lips.

"I'm pleased to announce that you have finished the first mile of your journey, boys. I'd also like to remind you that the longest distance a full complement of Walkers has ever covered is seven and three-quarters miles. I'm hoping you'll better that."

The jeep spurted ahead. Olson appeared to be considering this news with startled, even fearful, wonder. Not even eight miles, Garraty thought. It wasn't nearly as far as he would have guessed. He hadn't expected anyone—not even Stebbins—to get a ticket until late afternoon at least. He thought of Barkovitch. All he had to do was fall below speed once in the next hour.

"Ray?" It was Art Baker. He had taken off his coat and slung it over one arm. "Any particular reason you came on the Long Walk?"

Garraty unclipped his canteen and had a quick swallow of water. It was cool and good. It left beads of moisture on his upper lip and he licked them off. It was good, good to feel things like that.

"I don't really know," he said truthfully.

"Me either." Baker thought for a moment. "Did you go out for track or anything? In school?"

"No."

"Me either. But I guess it don't matter, does it? Not now."

"No, not now," Garraty asked.

Conversation lulled. They passed through a small village with a country store and a gas station. Two old men sat on folding lawn-chairs outside the gas station, watching them with hooded and reptilian old men's eyes. On the steps of the country store, a young woman held up her tiny son so he could see them. And a couple of older kids, around twelve, Garraty judged, watched them out of sight wistfully.

Some of the boys began to speculate about how much ground they had covered. The word came back that a second pacer halftrack had been dispatched to cover the half a dozen boys in the vanguard . . . they were now completely out of sight. Someone said they were doing seven miles an hour. Someone else said it was ten. Someone told them authoritatively that a guy up ahead was flagging and had been warned twice. Garraty wondered why they weren't catching up to him if that was true.

Olson finished the Waifa chocolate bar he had started back at the border and drank some water. Some of the others were also eating, but Garraty decided to wait until he was really hungry. He had heard the concentrates were quite good. The astronauts got them when they went into space.

A little after ten o'clock, they passed a sign that said LIMESTONE 10 MI. Garraty thought about the only Long Walk his father had ever let him go to. They went to Freeport and watched them walk through. His mother had been with them. The Walkers were tired and hollow-eyed and barely conscious of the cheering and the waving signs and the constant hoorah as people cheered on their favorites and those on whom they had wagered. His father told him later that day that people lined the roads from Bangor on. Up-country it wasn't so interesting, and the road was strictly cordoned off—maybe so they could concentrate on being calm, as Barkovitch had said. But as time passed, it got better, of course.

When the Walkers passed through Freeport that year they had been on the road over seventy-two hours. Garraty had been ten and overwhelmed by everything. The Major had made a speech to the crowd while the boys were still five miles out of town. He began with Competition, progressed to Patriotism, and finished with something called the Gross National Product—Garraty had laughed at that, because to him gross meant something nasty, like boogers. He had eaten six hotdogs and when he finally saw the Walkers coming he had wet his pants.

One boy had been screaming. That was his most vivid memory. Every time he put his foot down he had screamed: *I can't. I CAN'T. I can't. I CAN'T.* But he went on walking. They all did, and pretty soon the last of them had gone past L.L. Bean's on U.S. 1 and out of sight. Garraty had been mildly disappointed at not seeing anyone get a ticket. They had never gone to another Long Walk. Later that night Garraty had heard his father shouting thickly at someone into the telephone, the way he did when he was being drunk or political, and his mother in the background, her conspiratorial whisper, begging him to stop, please stop, before someone picked up the party line.

Garraty drank some more water and wondered how Barkovitch was making it.

They were passing more houses now. Families sat out on their front lawns, smiling, waving, drinking Coca-Colas.

"Garraty," McVries said. "My, my, look what you got."

A pretty girl of about sixteen in a white blouse and red-checked pedal pushers was holding up a big Magic Marker sign: GO-GO-GARRATY NUMBER 47 *We Love You Ray* "Maine's Own."

Garraty felt his heart swell. He suddenly knew he was going to win. The unnamed girl proved it.

Olson whistled wetly, and began to slide his stiff index finger rapidly in and out of his loosely curled fist. Garraty thought that was a pretty goddam sick thing to be doing.

To hell with Hint 13. Garraty ran over to the side of the road. The girl saw his number and squealed. She threw herself at him and kissed him hard. Garraty was suddenly, sweatily aroused. He kissed back vigorously. The girl poked her tongue into his mouth twice, delicately. Hardly aware of what he was doing, he put one hand on a round buttock and squeezed gently.

"Warning! Warning 47!"

Garraty stepped back and grinned. "Thanks."

"Oh . . . oh . . . oh *sure!*" Her eyes were starry.

He tried to think of something else to say, but he could see the soldier opening his mouth to give him the second warning. He trotted back to his place, panting a little and grinning. He felt a little guilty after Hint 13 just the same, though.

Olson was also grinning. "For that I would have taken three warnings."

Garraty didn't answer, but he turned around and walked backward and waved to the girl. When she was out of sight he turned around and began to walk firmly. An hour before his warning would be gone. He must be careful not to get another one. But he felt good. He felt fit. He felt like he could walk all the way to Florida. He started to walk faster.

"Ray." McVries was still smiling. "What's your hurry?"

Yeah, that was right. Hint 6: Slow and easy does it. "Thanks."

McVries went on smiling. "Don't thank me too much. I'm out to win, too."

Garraty stared at him, disconcerted.

"I mean, let's not put this on a Three Musketeers basis. I like you and it's obvious you're a big hit with the pretty girls. But if you fall over, I won't pick you up."

"Yeah." He smiled back, but his smile felt lame.

"On the other hand," Baker drawled softly, "we're all in this together and we might as well keep each other amused."

McVries smiled. "Why not?"

They came to an upslope and saved their breath for walking. Halfway up, Garraty took off his jacket and slung it over his shoulder. A few moments later they passed someone's discarded sweater lying on the road. Someone, Garraty thought, is going to wish they had that tonight. Up ahead, a couple of the point Walkers were losing ground.

Garraty concentrated on picking them up and putting them down. He still felt good. He felt strong.

Chapter 2

"Now you have the money, Ellen and
that's yours to keep. Unless, of course,
you'd like to trade it for what's behind the curtain."
—Monty Hall
Let's Make a Deal

"I'm Harkness. Number 49. You're Garraty. Number 47. Right?"

Garraty looked at Harkness, who wore glasses and had a crewcut. Harkness's face was red and sweaty. "That's right."

Harkness had a notebook. He wrote Garraty's name and number in it. The script was strange and jerky, bumping up and down as he walked. He ran into a fellow named Collie Parker who told him to watch where the fuck he was going. Garraty suppressed a smile.

"I'm taking down everyone's name and number," Harkness said. When he looked up, the midmorning sun sparkled on the lenses of his glasses, and Garraty had to squint to see his face. It was 10:30, and they were 8 miles out of Limestone, and they had only 1.75 miles to go to beat the record of the farthest distance traveled by a complete Long Walk group.

"I suppose you're wondering why I'm writing down everyone's name and number," Harkness said.

"You're with the Squads," Olson cracked over his shoulder.

"No, I'm going to write a book," Harkness said pleasantly. "When this is all over, I'm going to write a book."

Garraty grinned. "If you win you're going to write a book, you mean."

Harkness shrugged. "Yes, I suppose. But look at this: a book about the Long Walk from an insider's point of view could make me a rich man."

McVries burst out laughing. "If you win, you won't need a book to make you a rich man, will you?"

Harkness frowned. "Well . . . I suppose not. But it would still make one heck of an interesting book, I think."

They walked on, and Harkness continued taking names and numbers. Most gave them willingly enough, joshing him about the great book.

Now they had come six miles. The word came back that it looked good for breaking the record. Garraty speculated briefly on why they should want to break the record anyhow. The quicker the competition dropped out, the better the odds became for those remaining. He supposed it was a matter of pride. The word also came back that thundershowers were forecast for the afternoon—someone had a transistor radio, Garraty supposed. If it was true, it was bad news. Early May thundershowers weren't the warmest.

They kept walking.

McVries walked firmly, keeping his head up and swinging his arms slightly. He had tried the shoulder, but fighting the loose soil there had made him give it up. He hadn't been warned, and if the knapsack was giving him any trouble or chafing, he showed no sign. His eyes were always searching the horizon. When they passed small clusters of people, he waved and smiled his thin-lipped smile. He showed no signs of tiring.

Baker ambled along, moving in a kind of knee-bent shuffle that seemed to cover the ground when you weren't looking. He swung his coat idly, smiled at the pointing people, and sometimes whistled a low snatch of some tune or other. Garraty thought he looked like he could go on forever.

Olson wasn't talking so much anymore, and every few moments he would bend one knee swiftly. Each time Garraty could hear the joint pop. Olson was stiffening up a little, Garraty thought, beginning to show six miles of walking. Garraty judged that one of his canteens must be almost empty. Olson would have to pee before too long.

Barkovitch kept up the same jerky pace, now ahead of the main group as if to catch up with the vanguard Walkers, now dropping back toward Stebbins's position on drag. He lost one of his three warnings and gained it back five minutes later. Garraty decided he must like it there on the edge of nothing.

Stebbins just kept on walking off by himself. Garraty hadn't seen him speak to anybody. He wondered if Stebbins was lonely or tired. He still thought Stebbins would fold up early—maybe first—although he didn't know why he thought so. Stebbins had taken off the old green sweater, and he carried the last jelly sandwich in his hand. He looked at no one. His face was a mask.

They walked on.

The road was crossed by another, and policemen were holding up traffic as the Walkers passed. They saluted each Walker, and a couple of the boys, secure in their immunity, thumbed their noses. Garraty didn't approve. He smiled and nodded to acknowledge the police and wondered if the police thought they were all crazy.

The cars honked, and then some woman yelled out to her son. She had parked beside the road, apparently waiting to make sure her boy was still along for the Walk.

"Percy! *Percy!*"

It was 31. He blushed, then waved a little, and then hurried on with his head slightly bent. The woman tried to run out into the road. The guards on the top deck of the halftrack stiffened, but one of the policemen caught her arm and restrained her gently. Then the road curved and the intersection was out of sight.

They passed across a wooden-slatted bridge. A small brook gurgled its way underneath. Garraty walked close to the railing, and looking over he could see, for just a moment, a distorted image of his own face.

They passed a sign which read LIMESTONE 7 MI. and then under a rippling banner which said LIMESTONE IS PROUD TO WELCOME THE LONG WALKERS. Garraty figured they had to be less than a mile from breaking the record.

Then the word came back, and this time the word was about a boy named Curley, number 7. Curley had a charley horse and had already picked up his first warning. Garraty put on some speed and came even with McVries and Olson. "Where is he?"

Olson jerked his thumb at a skinny, gangling boy in bluejeans. Curley had been trying to cultivate sideburns. The sideburns had failed. His lean and earnest face was now set in lines of terrific concentration, and he was staring at his right leg. He was favoring it. He was losing ground and his face showed it.

"Warning! Warning 7!"

Curley began to force himself faster. He was panting a little. As much from fear as from his exertions, Garraty thought. Garraty lost all track of time. He forgot everything but Curley. He watched him struggle, realizing in a numb sort of way that this might be his struggle an hour from now or a day from now.

It was the most fascinating thing he had ever seen.

Curley fell back slowly, and several warnings were issued to others before the group realized they were adjusting to his speed in their fascination. Which meant Curley was very close to the edge.

"Warning! Warning 7! Third warning, 7!"

"I've got a charley horse!" Curley shouted hoarsely. "It ain't no fair if you've got a charley horse!"

He was almost beside Garraty now. Garraty could see Curley's adam's apple going up and down. Curley was massaging his leg frantically. And Garraty could smell panic coming off Curley in waves, and it was like the smell of a ripe, freshly cut lemon.

Garraty began to pull ahead of him, and the next moment Curley exclaimed: "Thank God! She's loosening!"

No one said anything. Garraty felt a grudging disappointment. It was mean, and unsporting, he supposed, but he wanted to be sure someone got a ticket before he did. Who wants to bow out first?

Garraty's watch said five past eleven now. He supposed that meant they had beaten the record, figuring two hours times four miles an hour. They would be in Limestone soon. He saw Olson flex first one knee, then the other, again. Curious, he tried it himself. His knee joints popped audibly, and he was surprised to find how much stiffness had settled into them. Still, his feet didn't hurt. That was something.

They passed a milk truck parked at the head of a small dirt feeder road. The milkman was sitting on the hood. He waved good-naturedly. "Go to it, boys!"

Garraty felt suddenly angry. Felt like yelling. *Why don't you just get up off your fat ass and go to it with us?* But the milkman was past eighteen. In fact, he looked well past thirty. He was old.

"Okay, everybody, take five," Olson cracked suddenly, and got some laughs.

The milk truck was out of sight. There were more roads now, more policemen and people honking and waving. Someone threw confetti. Garraty began to feel important. He was, after all, "Maine's Own."

Suddenly Curley screamed. Garraty looked back over his shoulder. Curley was doubled over, holding his leg and screaming. Somehow, incredibly, he was still walking, but very slowly. Much too slowly.

Everything went slowly then, as if to match the way Curley was walking. The soldiers on the back of the slow-moving halftrack raised their guns. The crowd gasped, as if they hadn't known this was the way it was, and the Walkers gasped, as if they hadn't known, and Garraty gasped with them, but of course he had known, of course they had all known, it was very simple, Curley was going to get his ticket.

The safeties clicked off. Boys scattered from around Curley like quail. He was suddenly alone on the sunwashed road.

"It isn't fair!" he screamed. "It just isn't *fair!*"

The walking boys entered a leafy glade of shadow, some of them looking back, some of them looking straight ahead, afraid to see. Garraty was looking. He had to look. The scatter of waving spectators had fallen silent as if someone had simply clicked them all off.

"It isn't—"

Four carbines fired. They were very loud. The noise traveled away like bowling balls, struck the hills, and rolled back.

Curley's angular, pimply head disappeared in a hammersmash of blood and brains and flying skull-fragments. The rest of him fell forward on the white line like a sack of mail.

99 now, Garraty thought sickly. 99 bottles of beer on the wall and if one of those bottles should happen to fall . . . oh Jesus . . . oh Jesus . . .

Stebbins stepped over the body. His foot slid a little in some of the blood, and his next step with that foot left a bloody track, like a photograph in an *Official Detective* magazine. Stebbins didn't look down at what was left of Curley. His face didn't change expression. Stebbins, you bastard, Garraty thought, you were supposed to get your ticket first, didn't you know? Then Garraty looked away. He didn't want to be sick. He didn't want to vomit.

A woman beside a Volkswagen bus put her face in her hands. She made odd noises in her throat, and Garraty found he could look right up her dress to her underpants. Her blue underpants. Inexplicably, he found himself aroused again. A fat man with a bald head was staring at Curley and rubbing frantically at a wart beside his ear. He wet his large, thick lips and went on looking and rubbing the wart. He was still looking when Garraty passed him by.

They walked on. Garraty found himself walking with Olson, Baker, and McVries again. They were almost protectively bunched up. All of them were looking straight ahead now, their faces carefully expressionless. The echoes of the carbines seemed to hang in the air still. Garraty kept thinking about the bloody footprint that Stebbins's tennis shoe had left. He wondered if it was still tracking red, almost turned his head to look, then told himself not to be a fool. But he couldn't help wondering. He wondered if it had hurt Curley. He wondered if Curley had felt the gas-tipped slugs hitting home or if he had just been alive one second and dead the next.

But of course it had hurt. It had hurt before, in the worst, rupturing way, knowing there would be no more you but the universe would roll on just the same, unharmed and unhampered.

The word came back that they had made almost nine miles before Curley bought his ticket. The Major was said to be as pleased as punch. Garraty wondered how anyone could know where the hell the Major was.

He looked back suddenly, wanting to know what was being done with Curley's body, but they had already rounded another curve. Curley was out of sight.

"What have you got in that packsack?" Baker asked McVries suddenly. He was making an effort to be strictly conversational, but his voice was high and reedy, near to cracking.

"A fresh shirt," McVries said. "And some raw hamburger."

"Raw hamburger—" Olson made a sick face.

"Good fast energy in raw hamburger," McVries said.

"You're off your trolley. You'll puke all over the place."

McVries only smiled.

Garraty kind of wished he had brought some raw hamburger himself. He didn't know about fast energy, but he liked raw hamburger. It beat chocolate bars and concentrates. Suddenly he thought of his cookies, but after Curley he wasn't very hungry. After Curley, could he really have been thinking about eating raw hamburger?

The word that one of the Walkers had been ticketed out ran through the spectators, and for some reason they began to cheer even more loudly. Thin applause crackled like popcorn. Garraty wondered if it was embarrassing, being shot in front of people, and guessed by the time you got to that you probably didn't give a tin whistle. Curley hadn't looked as if he gave a tin whistle, certainly. Having to relieve yourself, though. That would be bad. Garraty decided not to think about that.

The hands on his watch now stood firmly straight up at noon. They crossed a rusty iron bridge spanning a high, dry gorge, and on the other side was a sign reading: ENTERING LIMESTONE CITY LIMITS—WELCOME, LONG WALKERS!

Some of the boys cheered, but Garraty saved his breath.

The road widened and the Walkers spread across it comfortably, the groups loosening up a little. After all, Curley was three miles back now.

Garraty took out his cookies, and for a moment turned the foil package over in his hands. He thought homesickly of his mother, then stuffed the feeling aside.

He would see Mom and Jan in Freeport. That was a promise. He ate a cookie and felt a little better.

"You know something?" McVries said.

Garraty shook his head. He took a swig from his canteen and waved at an elderly couple sitting beside the road with a small cardboard GARRATY sign.

"I have no idea what I'll want if I do win this," McVries said. "There's nothing that I really need. I mean, I don't have a sick old mother sitting home or a father on a kidney machine, or anything. I don't even have a little brother dying gamely of leukemia." He laughed and unstrapped his canteen

"You've got a point there," Garraty agreed.

"You mean I *don't* have a point there. The whole thing is pointless."

"You don't really mean that," Garraty said confidently. "If you had it to do all over again—"

"Yeah, yeah, I'd still do it, but—"

"Hey!" The boy ahead of them, Pearson, pointed. "Sidewalks!"

They were finally coming into the town proper. Handsome houses set back from the road looked down at them from the vantage of ascending green lawns. The lawns were crowded with people, waving and cheering. It seemed to Garraty that almost all of them were sitting down. Sitting on the ground, on lawn chairs like the old men back at the gas station, sitting on picnic tables. Even sitting on swings and porch gliders. He felt a touch of jealous anger.

Go ahead and wave your asses off. I'll be damned if I'll wave back anymore. Hint 13. Conserve energy whenever possible.

But finally he decided he was being foolish. People might decide he was getting snotty. He was, after all, "Maine's Own." He decided he would wave to all the people with GARRATY signs. And to all the pretty girls.

Sidestreets and cross-streets moved steadily past. Sycamore Street and Clark Avenue, Exchange Street and Juniper Lane. They passed a corner grocery with a Narragansett beer sign in the window, and a five-and-dime plastered with pictures of the Major.

The sidewalks were lined with people, but thinly lined. On the whole, Garraty was disappointed. He knew the real crowds would come further down the line, but it was still something of a wet firecracker. And poor old Curley had missed even this.

The Major's jeep suddenly spurted out of a sidestreet and began pacing the main group. The vanguard was still some distance ahead.

A tremendous cheer went up. The Major nodded and smiled and waved to the crowd. Then he made a neat left-face and saluted the boys. Garraty felt a thrill go straight up his back. The Major's sunglasses glinted in the early afternoon sunlight.

The Major raised the battery-powered loudhailer to his lips. "I'm proud of you, boys. Proud!"

From somewhere behind Garraty a voice said softly but clearly: "Diddly shit."

Garraty turned his head, but there was no one back there but four or five boys watching the Major intently (one of them realized he was saluting and dropped his hand sheepishly), and Stebbins. Stebbins did not even seem to be looking at the Major.

The jeep roared ahead. A moment later the Major was gone again.

They reached downtown Limestone around twelve-thirty. Garraty was disappointed. It was pretty much of a one-hydrant town. There was a business section and three used-car lots and a McDonalds and a Burger King and a Pizza Hut and an industrial park and that was Limestone.

"It isn't very big, is it?" Baker said.

Olson laughed.

"It's probably a nice place to live," Garraty said defensively.

"God spare me from nice places to live," McVries said, but he was smiling.

"Well, what turns you on," Garraty said lamely.

By one o'clock, Limestone was a memory. A small swaggering boy in patched denim overalls walked along with them for almost a mile, then sat down and watched them go by.

The country grew hillier. Garraty felt the first real sweat of the day coming out on him. His shirt was patched to his back. On his right, thunderheads were forming, but they were still far away. There was a light, circulating breeze, and that helped a little.

"What's the next big town, Garraty?" McVries asked.

"Caribou, I guess." He was wondering if Stebbins had eaten his last sandwich yet. Stebbins had gotten into his head like a snatch of pop music that goes around and around until you think you're going to go crazy with it. It was one-thirty. The Long Walk had progressed through eighteen miles.

"How far's that?" Garraty wondered what the record was for miles walked with only one Walker punched out. Eighteen miles seemed pretty good to him. Eighteen miles was a figure a man could be proud of. I walked eighteen miles. Eighteen.

"I said—" McVries began patiently.

"Maybe thirty miles from here."

"Thirty," Pearson said. "Jesus."

"It's a bigger town than Limestone," Garraty said. He was still feeling defensive, God knew why. Maybe because so many of these boys would die here, maybe all of them. Probably all of them. Only six Long Walks in history had ended over the state line in New Hampshire, and only one had gotten into Massachusetts, and the experts said that was like Hank Aaron hitting seven hundred and thirty home runs, or whatever it was . . . a record that would never be equaled. Maybe he would die here, too. Maybe he would. But that was different. Native soil. He had an idea the Major would like that. "He died on his native soil."

He tipped his canteen up and found it was empty. "Canteen!" he called. "47 calling for a canteen!"

One of the soldiers jumped off the halftrack and brought over a fresh canteen. When he turned away, Garraty touched the carbine slung over the soldier's back. He did it furtively. But McVries saw him.

"Why'd you do that?"

Garraty grinned and felt confused. "I don't know. Like knocking on wood, maybe."

"You're a dear boy, Ray," McVries said, and then put on some speed and caught up with Olson, leaving Garraty to walk alone, feeling more confused than ever.

Number 93—Garraty didn't know his name—walked past him on Garraty's right. He was staring down at his feet and his lips moved soundlessly as he counted his paces. He was weaving slightly.

"Hi," Garraty said.

93 cringed. There was a blankness in his eyes, the same blankness that had been in Curley's eyes while he was losing his fight with the charley horse. He's tired, Garraty thought. He knows it, and he's scared. Garraty suddenly felt his stomach tip over and right itself slowly.

Their shadows walked alongside them now. It was quarter of two. Nine in the morning, cool, sitting on the grass in the shade, was a month back.

At just before two, the word came back again. Garraty was getting a firsthand lesson in the psychology of the grapevine. Someone found something out, and suddenly it was all over. Rumors were created by mouth-to-mouth respiration. It looks like rain. Chances are it's going to rain. It's gonna rain pretty soon. The guy with the radio says it's gonna shit potatoes pretty quick. But it was funny how often the grapevine was right. And when the word came back that someone was slowing up, that someone was in trouble, the grapevine was always right.

This time the word was that number 9, Ewing, had developed blisters and had been warned twice. Lots of boys had been warned, but that was normal. The word was that things looked bad for Ewing.

He passed the word to Baker, and Baker looked surprised. "The black fella?" Baker said. "So black he looks sorta blue?"

Garraty said he didn't know if Ewing was black or white.

"Yeah, he's black," Pearson said. He pointed to Ewing. Garraty could see tiny jewels of perspiration gleaming in Ewing's natural. With something like horror, Garraty observed that Ewing was wearing sneakers.

Hint 3: Do not, repeat, *do not* wear sneakers. Nothing will give you blisters faster than sneakers on a Long Walk.

"He rode up with us," Baker said. "He's from Texas."

Baker picked up his pace until he was walking with Ewing. He talked with Ewing for quite a while. Then he dropped back slowly to avoid getting warned himself. His face was bleak. "He started to blister up two miles out. They started to break back in Limestone. He's walkin' in pus from broken blisters."

They all listened silently. Garraty thought of Stebbins again. Stebbins was wearing tennis shoes. Maybe Stebbins was fighting blisters right now.

"Warning! Warning 9! This is your third warning, 9!"

The soldiers were watching Ewing carefully now. So were the Walkers. Ewing was in the spotlight. The back of his T-shirt, startlingly white against his black skin, was sweat-stained gray straight down the middle. Garraty could see the big muscles in his back ripple as he walked. Muscles enough to last for days, and Baker said he was walking in pus. Blisters and charley horses. Garraty shivered. Sudden death. All those muscles, all the training, couldn't stop blisters and charley horses. What in the name of God had Ewing been thinking about when he put on those P.F. Flyers?

Barkovitch joined them. Barkovitch was looking at Ewing, too. "Blisters!" He made it sound like Ewing's mother was a whore. "What the hell can you expect from a dumb nigger? Now I ask you."

"Move away," Baker said evenly, "or I'll poke you."

"It's against the rules," Barkovitch said with a smirk. "Keep it in mind, cracker." But he moved away. It was as if he took a small poison cloud with him.

Two o'clock became two-thirty. Their shadows got longer. They walked up a long hill, and at the crest Garraty could see low mountains, hazy and blue, in the distance. The encroaching thunderheads to the west were darker now, and the breeze had stiffened, making his flesh goosebump as the sweat dried on him.

A group of men clustered around a Ford pickup truck with a camper on the back cheered them crazily. The men were all very drunk. They all waved back at the men, even Ewing. They were the first spectators they had seen since the swaggering little boy in the patched overalls.

Garraty broke open a concentrate tube without reading the label and ate it. It tasted slightly porky. He thought about McVries's hamburger. He thought about a great big chocolate cake with a cherry on the top. He thought about flapjacks. For some crazy reason he wanted a cold flapjack full of apple jelly. The cold lunch his mother always made when he and his father went hunting in November.

Ewing bought a hole about ten minutes later.

He was clustered in with a group of boys when he fell below speed for the last time. Maybe he thought the boys would protect him. The soldiers did their job well. The soldiers were experts. They pushed the other boys aside. They dragged Ewing over to the shoulder. Ewing tried to fight, but not much. One of the soldiers pinned Ewing's arms behind him while the other put his carbine up to Ewing's head and shot him. One leg kicked convulsively.

"He bleeds the same color as anyone else," McVries said suddenly. It was very loud in the stillness after the single shot. His adam's apple bobbed, and something clicked in his throat.

Two of them gone now. The odds infinitesimally adjusted in favor of those remaining. There was some subdued talk, and Garraty wondered again what they did with the bodies.

You wonder too goddam much! he shouted at himself suddenly.

And realized he was tired.

PART TWO

Going Down the Road

Chapter 3

"You will have thirty seconds, and
please remember that your answer must
be in the form of a question."
                                        —Art Fleming
                                        Jeopardy

It was three o'clock when the first drops of rain fell on the road, big and dark and round. The sky overhead was tattered and black, wild and fascinating. Thunder clapped hands somewhere above the clouds. A blue fork of lightning went to earth somewhere up ahead.

Garraty had donned his coat shortly after Ewing had gotten his ticket, and now he zipped it and turned up his collar. Harkness, the potential author, had carefully stowed his notebook in a Baggie. Barkovitch had put on a yellow vinyl rainhat. There was something incredible about what it did to his face, but you would have been hard put to say just what. He peered out from beneath it like a truculent lighthouse keeper.

There was a stupendous crack of thunder. "Here it comes!" Olson cried.

The rain came pouring down. For a few moments it was so heavy that Garraty found himself totally isolated inside an undulating shower curtain. He was immediately soaked to the skin. His hair became a dripping pelt. He turned his face up into the rain, grinning. He wondered if the soldiers could see them. He wondered if a person might conceivably—

While he was still wondering, the first vicious onslaught let up a little and he could see again. He looked over his shoulder at Stebbins. Stebbins was walking hunched over, his hands hooked against his belly, and at first Garraty thought he had a cramp. For a moment Garraty was in the grip of a strong panicky feeling, nothing at all like he had felt when Curley and Ewing bought it. He didn't want Stebbins to fold up early anymore.

Then he saw Stebbins was only protecting the last half of his jelly sandwich, and he faced forward again, feeling relieved. He decided Stebbins must have a pretty stupid mother not to wrap his goddam sandwiches in foil, just in case of rain.

Thunder cracked stridently, artillery practice in the sky. Garraty felt exhilarated, and some of his tiredness seemed to wash away with the sweat from his body. The rain came again, hard and pelting, and finally let off into a steady drizzle. Overhead, the clouds began to tatter.

Pearson was now walking beside him. He hitched up his pants. He was wearing

163

jeans that were too big for him and he hitched up his pants often. He wore horn-rimmed glasses with lenses like the bottoms of Coke bottles, and now he whipped them off and began to clean them on the tail of his shirt. He goggled in that myopic, defenseless way that people with very poor eyesight have when their glasses are off. "Enjoy your shower, Garraty?"

Garraty nodded. Up ahead, McVries was urinating. He was walking backward while he did it, spraying the shoulder considerably away from the others.

Garraty looked up at the soldiers. They were wet, too, of course, but if they were uncomfortable, they didn't show it. Their faces were perfectly wooden. I wonder what it feels like, he thought, just to shoot someone down. I wonder if it makes them feel powerful. He remembered the girl with the sign, kissing her, feeling her ass. Feeling her smooth underpants under her pedal pushers. That had made him feel powerful.

"That guy back there sure doesn't say much, does he?" Baker said suddenly. He jerked a thumb at Stebbins. Stebbins's purple pants were almost black now that they were soaked through.

"No. No, he doesn't."

McVries pulled a warning for slowing down too much to zip up his fly. They pulled even with him, and Baker repeated what he had said about Stebbins.

"He's a loner, so what?" McVries said, and shrugged. "I think—"

"Hey," Olson broke in. It was the first thing he had said in some time, and he sounded queer. "My legs feel funny."

Garraty looked at Olson closely and saw the seedling panic in his eyes already. The look of bravado was gone. "How funny?" he asked.

"Like the muscles are all turning . . . baggy."

"Relax," McVries said. "It happened to me a couple of hours ago. It passes off."

Relief showed in Olson's eyes. "Does it?"

"Yeah, sure it does."

Olson didn't say anything, but his lips moved. Garraty thought for a moment he was praying, but then he realized he was just counting his paces.

Two shots rang out suddenly. There was a cry, then a third shot.

They looked and saw a boy in a blue sweater and dirty white clamdiggers lying facedown in a puddle of water. One of his shoes had come off. Garraty saw he had been wearing white athletic socks. Hint 12 recommended them.

Garraty stepped over him, not looking too closely for holes. The word came back that this boy had died of slowing down. Not blisters or a charley horse, he had just slowed down once too often and got a ticket.

Garraty didn't know his name or number. He thought the word would come back on that, but it never did. Maybe nobody knew. Maybe he had been a loner like Stebbins.

Now they were twenty-five miles into the Long Walk. The scenery blended into a continuous mural of woods and fields, broken by an occasional house or a cross-roads where waving, cheering people stood in spite of the dying drizzle. One old lady stood frozenly beneath a black umbrella, neither waving nor speaking nor smiling. She watched them go by with gimlet eyes. There was not a sign of life or movement about her except for the wind-twitched hem of her black dress. On the middle finger of her right hand she wore a large ring with a purple stone. There was a tarnished cameo at her throat.

They crossed a railroad track that had been abandoned long ago—the rails were rusty and witch-grass was growing in the cinders between the ties. Somebody stumbled and fell and was warned and got up and went on walking with a bleeding knee.

It was only nineteen miles to Caribou, but dark would come before that. No rest for the wicked, Garraty thought, and that struck him funny. He laughed.

McVries looked at him closely. "Getting tired?"

"No," Garraty said. "I've been tired for quite a while now." He looked at McVries with something like animosity. "You mean you're not?"

McVries said, "Just go on dancing with me like this forever, Garraty, and I'll never tire. We'll scrape our shoes on the stars and hang upside down from the moon."

He blew Garraty a kiss and walked away.

Garraty looked after him. He didn't know what to make of McVries.

By quarter of four the sky had cleared and there was a rainbow in the west, where the sun was sitting below gold-edged clouds. Slanting rays of the late afternoon sunlight colored the newly turned fields they were passing, making the furrows sharp and black where they contoured around the long, sloping hills.

The sound of the halftrack was quiet, almost soothing. Garraty let his head drop forward and semi-dozed as he walked. Somewhere up ahead was Freeport. Not tonight or tomorrow, though. Lot of steps. Long way to go. He found himself still with too many questions and not enough answers. The whole Walk seemed nothing but one looming question mark. He told himself that a thing like this must have some deep meaning. Surely it was so. A thing like this must provide an answer to every question; it was just a matter of keeping your foot on the throttle. Now if he could only—

He put his foot down in a puddle of water and started fully awake again. Pearson looked at him quizzically and pushed his glasses up on his nose. "You know that guy that fell down and cut himself when we were crossing the tracks?"

"Yeah. It was Zuck, wasn't it?"

"Yeah. I just heard he's still bleeding."

"How far to Caribou, Maniac?" somebody asked him. Garraty looked around. It was Barkovitch. He had tucked his rainhat into his back pocket where it flapped obscenely.

"How the hell should I know?"

"You live here, don't you?"

"It's about seventeen miles," McVries told him. "Now go peddle your papers, little man."

Barkovitch put on his insulted look and moved away.

"He's some hot ticket," Garraty said.

"Don't let him get under your skin," McVries replied. "Just concentrate on walking him into the ground."

"Okay, coach."

McVries patted Garraty on the shoulder. "You're going to win this one for the Gipper, my boy."

"It seems like we've been walking forever, doesn't it?"

"Yeah."

Garraty licked his lips, wanting to express himself and not knowing just how. "Did you ever hear that bit about a drowning man's life passing before his eyes?"

"I think I read it once. Or heard someone say it in a movie."

"Have you ever thought that might happen to us? On the Walk?"

McVries pretended to shudder. "Christ, I hope not."

Garraty was silent for a moment and then said, "Do you think . . . never mind. The hell with it."

"No, go on. Do I think what?"

"Do you think we could live the rest of our lives on this road? That's what I meant. The part we would have had if we hadn't . . . you know."

McVries fumbled in his pocket and came up with a package of Mellow cigarettes. "Smoke?"

"I don't."

"Neither do I," McVries said, and then put a cigarette into his mouth. He found a book of matches with a tomato sauce recipe on it. He lit the cigarette, drew smoke in, and coughed it out. Garraty thought of Hint 10: Save your wind. If you smoke ordinarily, try not to smoke on the Long Walk.

"I thought I'd learn," McVries said defiantly.

"It's crap, isn't it?" Garraty said sadly.

McVries looked at him, surprised, and then threw the cigarette away. "Yeah," he said. "I think it is."

The rainbow was gone by four o'clock. Davidson, 8, dropped back with them. He was a good-looking boy except for the rash of acne on his forehead. "That guy Zuck's really hurting," Davidson said. He had had a packsack the last time Garraty saw him, but he noticed that at some point Davidson had cast it away.

"Still bleeding?" McVries asked.

"Like a stuck pig." Davidson shook his head. "It's funny the way things turn out, isn't it? You fall down any other time, you get a little scrape. He needs stitches." He pointed to the road. "Look at that."

Garraty looked and saw tiny dark spots on the drying hardtop. "Blood?"

"It ain't molasses," Davidson said grimly.

"Is he scared?" Olson asked in a dry voice.

"He says he doesn't give a damn," Davidson said. "But *I'm* scared." His eyes were wide and gray. "I'm scared for all of us."

They kept on walking. Baker pointed out another Garraty sign.

"Hot shit," Garraty said without looking up. He was following the trail of

Zuck's blood, like Dan'l Boone tracking a wounded Indian. It weaved slowly back and forth across the white line.

"McVries," Olson said. His voice had gotten softer in the last couple of hours. Garraty had decided he liked Olson in spite of Olson's brass-balls outer face. He didn't like to see Olson getting scared, but there could be no doubt that he was.

"What?" McVries said.

"It isn't going away. That baggy feeling I told you about. It isn't going away."

McVries didn't say anything. The scar on his face looked very white in the light of the setting sun.

"It feels like my legs could just collapse. Like a bad foundation. That won't happen, will it? Will it?" Olson's voice had gotten a little shrill.

McVries didn't say anything.

"Could I have a cigarette?" Olson asked. His voice was low again.

"Yeah. You can keep the pack."

Olson lit one of the Mellows with practiced ease, cupping the match, and thumbed his nose at one of the soldiers watching him from the halftrack. "They've been giving me the old hairy eyeball for the last hour or so. They've got a sixth sense about it." He raised his voice again. "You like it, don't you, fellas? You like it, right? That goddam right, is it?"

Several of the Walkers looked around at him and then looked away quickly. Garraty wanted to look away too. There was hysteria in Olson's voice. The soldiers looked at Olson impassively. Garraty wondered if the word would go back on Olson pretty quick, and couldn't repress a shudder.

By four-thirty they had covered thirty miles. The sun was half-gone, and it had turned blood red on the horizon. The thunderheads had moved east, and overhead the sky was a darkening blue. Garraty thought about his hypothetical drowning man again. Not so hypothetical at that. The coming night was like water that would soon cover them.

A feeling of panic rose in his gullet. He was suddenly and terribly sure that he was looking at the last daylight in his life. He wanted it to stretch out. He wanted it to last. He wanted the dusk to go on for hours.

"Warning! Warning 100! Your third warning, 100!"

Zuck looked around. There was a dazed, uncomprehending look in his eyes. His right pantsleg was caked with dried blood. And then, suddenly, he began to sprint. He weaved through the Walkers like a broken-field runner carrying a football. He ran with that same dazed expression on his face.

The halftrack picked up speed. Zuck heard it coming and ran faster. It was a queer, shambling, limping run. The wound on his knee broke open again, and as he burst into the open ahead of the main pack, Garraty could see the drops of fresh blood splashing and flying from the cuff of his pants. Zuck ran up the next rise, and for a moment he was starkly silhouetted against the red sky, a galvanic black shape, frozen for a moment in midstride like a scarecrow in full flight. Then he was gone and the halftrack followed. The two soldiers that had dropped off it trudged along with the boys, their faces empty.

Nobody said a word. They only listened. There was no sound for a long time. An incredibly, unbelievably long time. Only a bird, and a few early May crickets, and somewhere behind them, the drone of a plane.

Then there was a single sharp report, a pause, then a second.

"Making sure," someone said sickly.

When they got up over the rise they saw the halftrack sitting on the shoulder half a mile away. Blue smoke was coming from its dual exhaust pipes. Of Zuck there was no sign. No sign at all.

"Where's the Major?" someone screamed. The voice was on the raw edge of panic. It belonged to a bulletheaded boy named Gribble, number 48. "I want to see the Major, goddammit! Where is he?"

The soldiers walking along the verge of the road did not answer. No one answered.

"Is he making another speech?" Gribble stormed. "Is that what he's doing? Well, he's a *murderer!* That's what he is, a *murderer!* I . . . I'll tell him! You think I won't? I'll tell him to his face! I'll tell him *right to his face!*" In his excitement he had fallen below the pace, almost stopping, and the soldiers became interested for the first time.

"Warning! Warning 48!"

Gribble faltered to a stop, and then his legs picked up speed. He looked down at his feet as he walked. Soon they were up to where the halftrack waited. It began to crawl along beside them again.

At about 4:45, Garraty had supper—a tube of processed tuna fish, a few Snappy Crackers with cheese spread, and a lot of water. He had to force himself to stop there. You could get a canteen anytime, but there would be no fresh concentrates until tomorrow morning at nine o'clock . . . and he might want a midnight snack. Hell, he might *need* a midnight snack.

"It may be a matter of life and death," Baker said, "but it sure isn't hurtin' your appetite any."

"Can't afford to let it," Garraty answered. "I don't like the idea of fainting about two o'clock tomorrow morning."

Now there was a genuinely unpleasant thought. You wouldn't know anything, probably. Wouldn't feel anything. You'd just wake up in eternity.

"Makes you think, doesn't it?" Baker said softly.

Garraty looked at him. In the fading daylight, Baker's face was soft and young and beautiful. "Yeah. I've been thinking about a whole hell of a lot of things."

"Such as?"

"Him, for one," Garraty said, and jerked his head toward Stebbins, who was still walking along at the same pace he had been walking at when they started out. His pants were drying on him. His face was shadowy. He was still saving his last half-sandwich.

"What about him?"

"I wonder why he's here, why he doesn't say anything. And whether he'll live or die."

"Garraty, we're all going to die."

"But hopefully not tonight," Garraty said. He kept his voice light, but a shudder suddenly wracked him. He didn't know if Baker saw it or not. His kidneys contracted. He turned around, unzipped his fly, and began walking backward.

"What do you think about the Prize?" Baker asked.

"I don't see much sense thinking about it," Garraty said, and began to urinate. He finished, zipped his fly, and turned around again, mildly pleased that he had accomplished the operation without drawing a warning.

"I think about it," Baker said dreamily. "Not so much the Prize itself as the money. All that money."

"Rich men don't enter the Kingdom of Heaven," Garraty said. He watched his feet, the only things that were keeping him from finding out if there really was a Kingdom of Heaven or not.

"Hallelujah," Olson said. "There'll be refreshments after the meetin'."

"You a religious fella?" Baker asked Garraty.

"No, not particularly. But I'm no money freak."

"You might be if you grew up on potato soup and collards," Baker said. "Sidemeat only when your daddy could afford the ammunition."

"Might make a difference," Garraty agreed, and then paused, wondering whether to say anything else. "But it's never really the important thing." He saw Baker looking at him uncomprehendingly and a little scornfully.

"You can't take it with you, that's your next line," McVries said.

Garraty glanced at him. McVries was wearing that irritating, slanted smile again. "It's true, isn't it?" he said. "We don't bring anything into the world and we sure as shit don't take anything out."

"Yes, but the period in between those two events is more pleasant in comfort, don't you think?" McVries said.

"Oh, comfort, shit," Garraty said. "If one of those goons riding that overgrown Tonka toy over there shot you, no doctor in the world could revive you with a transfusion of twenties or fifties."

"I ain't dead," Baker said softly.

"Yeah, but you could be." Suddenly it was very important to Garraty that he put this across. "What if you won? What if you spent the next six weeks planning what you were going to do with the cash—never mind the Prize, just the cash—and what if the first time you went out to buy something, you got flattened by a taxicab?"

Harkness had come over and was now walking beside Olson. "Not me, babe," he said. "First thing I'd do is buy a whole fleet of Checkers. If I win this, I may never walk again."

"You don't understand," Garraty said, more exasperated than ever. "Potato soup or sirloin tips, a mansion or a hovel, once you're dead that's it, they put you on a cooling board like Zuck or Ewing and that's it. You're better to take it a day at a time, is all I'm saying. If people just took it a day at a time, they'd be a lot happier."

"Oh, such a golden flood of bullshit," McVries said.

"Is that so?" Garraty cried. "How much planning are you doing?"

"Well, right now I've sort of adjusted my horizons, that's true—"

"You bet it is," Garraty said grimly. "The only difference is we're involved in dying right now."

Total silence followed that. Harkness took off his glasses and began to polish them. Olson looked a shade paler. Garraty wished he hadn't said it; he had gone too far.

Then someone in back said quite clearly: "Hear, hear!"

Garraty looked around, sure it was Stebbins even though he had never heard Stebbins's voice. But Stebbins gave no sign. He was looking down at the road.

"I guess I got carried away," Garraty muttered, even though he wasn't the one who had gotten carried away. That had been Zuck. "Anyone want a cookie?"

He handed the cookies around, and it got to be five o'clock. The sun seemed to hang suspended halfway over the horizon. The earth might have stopped turning. The three or four eager beavers who were still ahead of the pack had dropped back until they were less than fifty yards ahead of the main group.

It seemed to Garraty that the road had become a sly combination of upgrades with no corresponding downs. He was thinking that if that were true they'd all end up breathing through oxygen faceplates before long when his foot came down on a discarded belt of food concentrates. Surprised, he looked up. It had been Olson's. His hands were twitching at his waist. There was a look of frowning surprise on his face.

"I dropped it," he said. "I wanted something to eat and I dropped it." He laughed, as if to show what a silly thing that had been. The laugh stopped abruptly. "I'm hungry," he said.

No one answered. By that time everyone had gone by and there was no chance to pick it up. Garraty looked back and saw Olson's food belt lying across the broken white passing line.

"I'm hungry," Olson repeated patiently.

The Major likes to see someone who's raring to rip, wasn't that what Olson had said when he came back from getting his number? Olson didn't look quite so raring to rip anymore. Garraty looked at the pockets of his own belt. He had three tubes of concentrate left, plus the Snappy Crackers and the cheese. The cheese was pretty cruddy, though.

"Here," he said, and gave Olson the cheese.

Olson didn't say anything, but he ate the cheese.

"Musketeer," McVries said, with that same slanted grin.

By five-thirty the air was smoky with twilight. A few early lightning bugs flitted aimlessly through the air. A groundfog had curdled milkily in the ditches and lower gullies of the fields. Up ahead someone asked what happened if it got so foggy you walked off the road by mistake.

Barkovitch's unmistakable voice came back quickly and nastily: "What do you think, Dumbo?"

Four gone, Garraty thought. Eight and a half hours on the road and only four gone. There was a small, pinched feeling in his stomach. I'll never outlast all of them, he thought. Not *all* of them. But on the other hand, why not? Someone had to.

Talk had faded with the daylight. The silence that set in was oppressive. The encroaching dark, the groundmist collecting into small, curdled pools . . . for the first time it seemed perfectly real and totally unnatural, and he wanted either Jan or his mother, some woman, and he wondered what in the hell he was doing and how he ever could have gotten involved. He could not even kid himself that everything had not been up front, because it had been. And he hadn't even done it alone. There were currently ninety-five other fools in this parade.

The mucus ball was in his throat again, making it hard to swallow. He realized that someone up ahead was sobbing softly. He had not heard the sound begin, and no one had called his attention to it; it was as if it had been there all along.

Ten miles to Caribou now, and at least there would be lights. The thought cheered Garraty a little. It was okay after all, wasn't it? He was alive, and there was no sense thinking ahead to a time when he might not be. As McVries had said, it was all a matter of adjusting your horizons.

At quarter of six the word came back on a boy named Travin, one of the early leaders who was now falling slowly back through the main group. Travin had diarrhea. Garraty heard it and couldn't believe it was true, but when he saw Travin he knew that it was. The boy was walking and holding his pants up at the same time. Every time he squatted he picked up a warning, and Garraty wondered sickly why Travin didn't just let it roll down his legs. Better to be dirty than dead.

Travin was bent over, walking like Stebbins with his sandwich, and every time he shuddered Garraty knew that another stomach cramp was ripping through him. Garraty felt disgusted. There was no fascination in this, no mystery. It was a boy with a bellyache, that was all, and it was impossible to feel anything but disgust and a kind of animal terror. His own stomach rolled queasily.

The soldiers were watching Travin very carefully. Watching and waiting. Finally Travin half-squatted, half-fell, and the soldiers shot him with his pants down. Travin rolled over and grimaced at the sky, ugly and pitiful. Someone retched noisily and was warned. It sounded to Garraty as if he was spewing his belly up whole.

"He'll go next," Harkness said in a businesslike way.

"Shut up," Garraty choked thickly. "Can't you just shut up?"

No one replied. Harkness looked ashamed and began to polish his glasses again. The boy who vomited was not shot.

They passed a group of cheering teenagers sitting on a blanket and drinking Cokes. They recognized Garraty and gave him a standing ovation. It made him feel uncomfortable. One of the girls had very large breasts. Her boyfriend was watching them jiggle as she jumped up and down. Garraty decided that he was turning in to a sex maniac.

"Look at them jahoobies," Pearson said. "Dear, dear me."

Garraty wondered if she was a virgin, like he was.

They passed by a still, almost perfectly circular pond, faintly misted over. It looked like a gently clouded mirror, and in the mysterious tangle of water plants growing around the edge, a bullfrog croaked hoarsely. Garraty thought the pond was one of the most beautiful things he had ever seen.

"This is one hell of a big state," Barkovitch said someplace up ahead.

"That guy gives me a royal pain in the ass," McVries said solemnly. "Right now my one goal in life is to outlast him."

Olson was saying a Hail Mary.

Garraty looked at him, alarmed.

"How many warnings has he got?" Pearson asked.

"None that I know of," Baker said.

"Yeah, but he don't look so good."

"At this point, none of us do," McVries said.

Another silence fell. Garraty was aware for the first time that his feet hurt. Not just his legs, which had been troubling him for some time, but his feet. He noticed that he had been unconsciously walking on the outside of the soles, but every now and then he put a foot down flat and winced. He zipped his jacket all the way up and turned the collar against his neck. The air was still damp and raw.

"Hey! Over there!" McVries said cheerfully.

Garraty and the others looked to the left. They were passing a graveyard situated atop a small grassy knoll. A fieldstone wall surrounded it, and now the mist was creeping slowly around the leaning gravestones. An angel with a broken wing stared at them with empty eyes. A nuthatch perched atop a rust flaking flagholder left over from some patriotic holiday and looked them over perkily.

"Our first boneyard," McVries said. "It's on your side, Ray, you lose all your points. Remember that game?"

"You talk too goddam much," Olson said suddenly.

"What's wrong with graveyards, Henry, old buddy? A fine and private place, as the poet said. A nice watertight casket—"

"Just shut up!"

"Oh, pickles," McVries said. His scar flashed very white in the dying daylight. "You don't really mind the thought of dying, do you, Olson? Like the poet also said, it ain't the dying, it's laying in the grave so long. Is that what's bugging you, booby?" McVries began to trumpet. "Well, cheer up, Charlie! There's a brighter day com—"

"Leave him alone," Baker said quietly.

"Why should I? He's busy convincing himself he can crap out any time he feels like it. That if he just lays down and dies, it won't be as bad as everyone makes out. Well, I'm not going to let him get away with it."

"If he doesn't die, you will," Garraty said.

"Yeah, I'm remembering," McVries said, and gave Garraty his tight, slanted smile . . . only this time there was absolutely no humor in it at all. Suddenly

McVries looked furious, and Garraty was almost afraid of him. "He's the one that's forgetting. This turkey here."

"I don't want to do it anymore," Olson said hollowly. "I'm sick of it."

"Raring to rip," McVries said, turning on him. "Isn't that what you said? Fuck it, then. Why don't you just fall down and die then?"

"Leave him alone," Garraty said.

"Listen, Ray—"

"No, you listen. One Barkovitch is enough. Let him do it his own way. No musketeers, remember."

McVries smiled again. "Okay, Garraty. You win."

Olson didn't say anything. He just kept picking them up and laying them down.

Full dark had come by six-thirty. Caribou, now only six miles away, could be seen on the horizon as a dim glow. There were few people along the road to see them into town. They seemed to have all gone home to supper. The mist was chilly around Ray Garraty's feet. It hung over the hills in ghostly limp banners. The stars were coming brighter overhead, Venus glowing steadily, the Dipper in its accustomed place. He had always been good at the constellations. He pointed out Cassiopeia to Pearson, who only grunted.

He thought about Jan, his girl, and felt a twinge of guilt about the girl he had kissed earlier. He couldn't remember exactly what that girl had looked like anymore, but she had excited him. Putting his hand on her ass like that had excited him—what would have happened if he had tried to put his hand between her legs? He felt a clockspring of pressure in his groin that made him wince a little as he walked.

Jan had long hair, almost to her waist. She was sixteen. Her breasts were not as big as those of the girl who had kissed him. He had played with her breasts a lot. It drove him crazy. She wouldn't let him make love to her, and he didn't know how to make her. She wanted to, but she wouldn't. Garraty knew that some boys could do that, could get a girl to go along, but he didn't seem to have quite enough personality—or maybe not quite enough *will*—to convince her. He wondered how many of the others here were virgins. Gribble had called the Major a murderer. He wondered if Gribble was a virgin. He decided Gribble probably was.

They passed the Caribou city limits. There was a large crowd there, and a news truck from one of the networks. A battery of lights bathed the road in a warm white glare. It was like walking into a sudden warm lagoon of sunlight, wading through it, and then emerging again.

A fat newspaperman in a three-piece suit trotted along with them, poking his long-reach microphone at different Walkers. Behind him, two technicians busily unreeled a drum of electric cable.

"How do you feel?"

"Okay. I guess I feel okay."

"Feeling tired?"

"Yeah, well, you know. Yeah. But I'm still okay."

"What do you think your chances are now?"

"I dunno . . . okay, I guess. I still feel pretty strong."

He asked a big bull of a fellow, Scramm, what he thought of the Long Walk. Scramm grinned, said he thought it was the biggest fucking thing he'd ever seen, and the reporter made snipping motions with his fingers at the two technicians. One of them nodded back wearily.

Shortly afterward he ran out of microphone cable and began wending his way back toward the mobile unit, trying to avoid the tangles of unreeled cord. The crowd, drawn as much by the TV crew as by the Long Walkers themselves, cheered enthusiastically. Posters of the Major were raised and lowered rhythmically on sticks so raw and new they were still bleeding sap. When the cameras panned over them, they cheered more frantically than ever and waved to Aunt Betty and Uncle Fred.

They rounded a bend and passed a small shop where the owner, a little man wearing stained whites, had set up a soft drink cooler with a sign over it which read: ON THE HOUSE FOR THE LONG WALKERS!! COURTESY OF "EV'S" MARKET! A police cruiser was parked close by, and two policemen were patiently explaining to Ev, as they undoubtedly did every year, that it was against the rules for spectators to offer any kind of aid or assistance—including soft drinks—to the Walkers.

They passed by the Caribou Paper Mills, Inc., a huge, soot-blackened building on a dirty river. The workers were lined up against the cyclone fences, cheering good-naturedly and waving. A whistle blew as the last of the Walkers—Stebbins—passed by, and Garraty, looking back over his shoulder, saw them trooping inside again.

"Did he ask you?" a strident voice inquired of Garraty. With a feeling of great weariness, Garraty looked down at Gary Barkovitch.

"Did who ask me what?"

"The reporter, Dumbo. Did he ask you how you felt?"

"No, he didn't get to me." He wished Barkovitch would go away. He wished the throbbing pain in the soles of his feet would go away.

"They asked me," Barkovitch said. "You know what I told them?"

"Huh-uh."

"I told them I felt great," Barkovitch said aggressively. The rainhat was still flopping in his back pocket. "I told them I felt real strong. I told them I felt prepared to go on forever. And do you know what else I told them?"

"Oh, shut up," Pearson said.

"Who asked you, long, tall and ugly?" Barkovitch said.

"Go away," McVries said. "You give me a headache."

Insulted once more, Barkovitch moved on up the line and grabbed Collie Parker. "Did he ask you what—"

"Get out of here before I pull your fucking nose off and make you eat it," Collie Parker snarled. Barkovitch moved on quickly. The word on Collie Parker was that he was one mean son of a bitch.

"That guy drives me up the wall," Pearson said.

"He'd be glad to hear it," McVries said. "He likes it. He also told that reporter that he planned to dance on a lot of graves. He means it, too. That's what keeps him going."

"Next time he comes around I think I'll trip him," Olson said. His voice sounded dull and drained.

"Tut-tut," McVries said. "Rule 8, no interference with your fellow Walkers."

"You know what you can do with Rule 8," Olson said with a pallid smile.

"Watch out," McVries grinned, "you're starting to sound pretty lively again."

By 7 PM the pace, which had been lagging very close to the minimum limit, began to pick up a little. It was cool and if you walked faster you kept warmer. They passed beneath a turnpike overpass, and several people cheered them around mouthfuls of Dunkin' Donuts from the glass-walled shop situated near the base of the exit ramp.

"We join up with the turnpike someplace, don't we?" Baker asked.

"In Oldtown," Garraty said. "Approximately one hundred and twenty miles."

Harkness whistled through his teeth.

Not long after that, they walked into downtown Caribou. They were forty-four miles from their starting point.

Chapter 4

"The ultimate game show would be one
where the losing contestant was killed."
—Chuck Barris
Game show creator
MC of *The Gong Show*

Everyone was disappointed with Caribou.

It was just like Limestone.

The crowds were bigger, but otherwise it was just another mill-pulp-and-service town with a scattering of stores and gas stations, one shopping center that was having, according to the signs plastered everywhere, OUR ANNUAL WALK-IN FOR VALUES SALE!, and a park with a war memorial in it. A small, evil-sounding high school band struck up the National Anthem, then a medley of Sousa marches, and then, with taste so bad it was almost grisly, *Marching to Pretoria*.

The same woman who had made a fuss at the crossroads so far back turned up again. She was still looking for Percy. This time she made it through the police cordon and right onto the road. She pawed through the boys, unintentionally tripping one of them up. She was yelling for her Percy to come home now. The soldiers went for their guns, and for a moment it looked very much as if Percy's mom was going to buy herself an interference ticket. Then a cop got an armlock on her and dragged her away. A small boy sat on a KEEP MAINE TIDY barrel and ate a hotdog and watched the cops put Percy's mom in a police cruiser. Percy's mom was the high point of going through Caribou.

"What comes after Oldtown, Ray?" McVries asked.

"I'm not a walking roadmap," Garraty said irritably. "Bangor, I guess. Then Augusta. Then Kittery and the state line, about three hundred and thirty miles from here. Give or take. Okay? I'm picked clean."

Somebody whistled. "Three hundred and thirty miles."

"It's unbelievable," Harkness said gloomily.

"The whole damn thing is unbelievable," McVries said. "I wonder where the Major is?"

"Shacked up in Augusta," Olson said.

They all grinned, and Garraty reflected how strange it was about the Major, who had gone from God to Mammon in just ten hours.

Ninety-five left. But that wasn't even the worst anymore. The worst was trying

176

to visualize McVries buying it, or Baker. Or Harkness with his silly book idea. His mind shied away from the thought.

Once Caribou was behind them, the road became all but deserted. They walked through a country crossroads with a single lightpole rearing high above, spotlighting them and making crisp black shadows as they passed through the glare. Far away a train whistle hooted. The moon cast a dubious light on the groundfog, leaving it pearly and opalescent in the fields.

Garraty took a drink of water.

"Warning! Warning 12! This is your final warning, 12!"

12 was a boy named Fenter who was wearing a souvenir T-shirt which read I RODE THE MT. WASHINGTON COG RAILWAY. Fenter was licking his lips. The word was that his foot had stiffened up on him badly. When he was shot ten minutes later, Garraty didn't feel much. He was too tired. He walked around Fenter. Looking down he saw something glittering in Fenter's hand. A St. Christopher's medal.

"If I get out of this," McVries said abruptly, "you know what I'm going to do?"

"What?" Baker asked.

"Fornicate until my cock turns blue. I've never been so horny in my life as I am right this minute, at quarter of eight on May first."

"You mean it?" Garraty asked.

"I do," McVries assured. "I could even get horny for you, Ray, if you didn't need a shave."

Garraty laughed.

"Prince Charming, that's who I am," McVries said. His hand went to the scar on his cheek and touched it. "Now all I need is a Sleeping Beauty. I could awake her with a biggy sloppy soul kiss and the two of us would ride away into the sunset. At least as far as the nearest Holiday Inn."

"Walk," Olsen said listlessly.

"Huh?"

"Walk into the sunset."

"Walk into the sunset, okay," McVries said. "True love either way. Do you believe in true love, Hank dear?"

"I believe in a good screw," Olson said, and Art Baker burst out laughing.

"I believe in true love," Garraty said, and then felt sorry he had said it. It sounded naive.

"You want to know why I don't?" Olson said. He looked up at Garraty and grinned a scary, furtive grin. "Ask Fenter. Ask Zuck. They know."

"That's a hell of an attitude," Pearson said. He had come out of the dark from someplace and was walking with them again. Pearson was limping, not badly, but very obviously limping.

"No, it's not," McVries said, and then, after a moment, he added cryptically: "Nobody loves a deader."

"Edgar Allan Poe did," Baker said. "I did a report on him in school and it said he had tendencies that were ne-necro—"

"Necrophiliac," Garraty said.

"Yeah, that's right."

"What's that?" Pearson asked.

"It means you got an urge to sleep with a dead woman," Baker said. "Or a dead man, if you're a woman."

"Or if you're a fruit," McVries put in.

"How the hell did we get on this?" Olson croaked. "Just how in the hell did we get on the subject of screwing dead people? It's fucking repulsive."

"Why not?" A deep, somber voice said. It was Abraham, 2. He was tall and disjointed-looking; he walked in a perpetual shamble. "I think we all might take a moment or two to stop and think about whatever kind of sex life there may be in the next world."

"I get Marilyn Monroe," McVries said. "You can have Eleanor Roosevelt, Abe old buddy."

Abraham gave him the finger. Up ahead, one of the soldiers droned out a warning.

"Just a second now. Just one motherfucking second here." Olson spoke slowly, as if he wrestled with a tremendous problem in expression. "You're all off the subject. All off."

"The Transcendental Quality of Love, a lecture by the noted philosopher and Ethiopian jug-rammer Henry Olson," McVries said. "Author of *A Peach Is Not a Peach without a Pit* and other works of—"

"Wait!" Olson cried out. His voice was as shrill as broken glass. "You wait just one goddam second! Love is a put-on! It's nothing! One big fat el zilcho! You got it?"

No one replied. Garraty looked out ahead of him, where the dark charcoal hills met the star-punched darkness of the sky. He wondered if he couldn't feel the first faint twinges of a charley horse in the arch of his left foot. I want to sit down, he thought irritably. Damn it all, I want to sit down.

"Love is a fake!" Olson was blaring. "There are three great truths in the world and they are a good meal, a good screw, and a good shit, and that's *all!* And when you get like Fenter and Zuck—"

"Shut up," a bored voice said, and Garraty knew it was Stebbins. But when he looked back, Stebbins was only looking at the road and walking along near the left-hand edge.

A jet passed overhead, trailing the sound of its engines behind it and chalking a feathery line across the night sky. It passed low enough for them to be able to see its running lights, pulsing yellow and green. Baker was whistling again. Garraty let his eyelids drop mostly shut. His feet moved on their own.

His half-dozing mind began to slip away from him. Random thoughts began to chase each other lazily across its field. He remembered his mother singing him an Irish lullaby when he was very small . . . something about cockles and mussels, alive, alive-o. And her face, so huge and beautiful, like the face of an actress on a movie screen. Wanting to kiss her and be in love with her for always. When he grew up, he would marry her.

This was replaced by Jan's good-humored Polish face and her dark hair that streamed nearly to her waist. She was wearing a two-piece bathing suit beneath a short beach coat because they were going to Reid Beach. Garraty himself was wearing a ragged pair of denim shorts and his zoris.

Jan was gone. Her face became that of Jimmy Owens, the kid down the block from them. He had been five and Jimmy had been five and Jimmy's mother had caught them playing Doctor's Office in the sandpit behind Jimmy's house. They both had boners. That's what they called them—boners. Jimmy's mother had called his mother and his mother had come to get him and had sat him down in her bedroom and had asked him how he would like it if she made him go out and walk down the street with no clothes on. His dozing body contracted with the groveling embarrassment of it, the deep shame. He had cried and begged, not to make him walk down the street with no clothes on . . . and not to tell his father.

Seven years old now. He and Jimmy Owens peering through the dirt-grimed window of the Burr's Building Materials office at the naked lady calendars, knowing what they were looking at but not really knowing, feeling a crawling shameful exciting pang of something. Of something. There had been one blond lady with a piece of blue silk draped across her hips and they had stared at it for a long, long time. They argued about what might be down there under the cloth. Jimmy said he had seen his mother naked. Jimmy said he knew. Jimmy said it was hairy and cut open. He had refused to believe Jimmy, because what Jimmy said was disgusting.

Still he was sure that ladies must be different from men down there and they had spent a long purple summer dusk discussing it, swatting mosquitoes and watching a scratch baseball game in the lot of the moving van company across the street from Burr's. He could feel, actually *feel* in the half-waking dream the sensation of the hard curb beneath his fanny.

The next year he had hit Jimmy Owens in the mouth with the barrel of his Daisy air rifle while they were playing guns and Jimmy had to have four stitches in his upper lip. A year after that they had moved away. He hadn't meant to hit Jimmy in the mouth. It had been an accident. Of that he was quite sure, even though by then he had known Jimmy was right because he had seen his own mother naked (he had not meant to see her naked—it had been an accident). They were hairy down there. Hairy and cut open.

Shhh, it isn't a tiger, love, only your teddy bear, see? . . . Cockles and mussels, alive, alive-o . . . Mother loves her boy . . . Shhh . . . Go to sleep . . .

"Warning! Warning 47!"

An elbow poked him rudely in the ribs. "That's you, boy. Rise and shine." McVries was grinning at him.

"What time is it?" Garraty asked thickly.

"Eight thirty-five."

"But I've been—"

"—dozing for hours," McVries said. "I know the feeling."

"Well, it sure seemed that way."

"It's your mind," McVries said, "using the old escape hatch. Don't you wish your feet could?"

"I use Dial," Pearson said, pulling an idiotic face. "Don't you wish everybody did?"

Garraty thought that memories were like a line drawn in the dirt. The further back you went the scuffier and harder to see that line got. Until finally there was nothing but smooth sand and the black hole of nothingness that you came out of. The memories were in a way like the road. Here it was real and hard and tangible. But that early road, that nine in the morning road, was far back and meaningless.

They were almost fifty miles into the Walk. The word came back that the Major would be by in his jeep to review them and make a short speech when they actually got to the fifty-mile point. Garraty thought that was most probably horseshit.

They breasted a long, steep rise, and Garraty was tempted to take his jacket off again. He didn't. He unzipped it, though, and then walked backward for a minute. The lights of Caribou twinkled at him, and he thought about Lot's wife, who had looked back and turned into a pillar of salt.

"Warning! Warning 47! Second warning, 47!"

It took Garraty a moment to realize it was him. His second warning in ten minutes. He started to feel afraid again. He thought of the unnamed boy who had died because he had slowed down once too often. Was that what he was doing?

He looked around. McVries, Harkness, Baker and Olson were all staring at him. Olson was having a particularly good look. He could make out the intent expression on Olson's face even in the dark. Olson had outlasted six. He wanted to make Garraty lucky seven. He wanted Garraty to die.

"See anything green?" Garraty asked irritably.

"No," Olson said, his eyes sliding away. "Course not."

Garraty walked with determination now, his arms swinging aggressively. It was twenty to nine. At twenty to eleven—eight miles down the road—he would be free again. He felt an hysterical urge to proclaim he could do it, they needn't send the word back on him, they weren't going to watch him get a ticket . . . at least not yet.

The groundfog spread across the road in thin ribbons, like smoke. The shapes of the boys moved through it like dark islands somehow set adrift. At fifty miles into the Walk they passed a small, shut-up garage with a rusted-out gas pump in front. It was little more than an ominous, leaning shape in the fog. The clear fluorescent light from a telephone booth cast the only glow. The Major didn't come. No one came.

The road dipped gently around a curve, and then there was a yellow road sign ahead. The word came back, but before it got to Garraty he could read the sign for himself:

STEEP GRADE   TRUCKS USE LOW GEAR

Groans and moans. Somewhere up ahead Barkovitch called out merrily: "Step into it, brothers! Who wants to race me to the top?"

"Shut your goddam mouth, you little freak," someone said quietly.

"Make me, Dumbo!" Barkovitch shrilled. "Come on up here and make me!"

"He's crackin'," Baker said.

"No," McVries replied. "He's just stretching. Guys like him have an awful lot of stretch."

Olson's voice was deadly quiet. "I don't think I can climb that hill. Not at four miles an hour."

The hill stretched above them. They were almost to it now. With the fog it was impossible to see the top. For all we know, it might just go up forever, Garraty thought.

They started up.

It wasn't as bad, Garraty discovered, if you stared down at your feet as you walked and leaned forward a little. You stared strictly down at the tiny patch of pavement between your feet and it gave you the impression that you were walking on level ground. Of course, you couldn't kid yourself that your lungs and the breath in your throat weren't heating up, because they were.

Somehow the word started coming back—some people still had breath to spare, apparently. The word was that this hill was a quarter of a mile long. The word was it was two miles long. The word was that no Walker had ever gotten a ticket on this hill. The word was that three boys had gotten tickets here just last year. And after that, the word stopped coming back.

"I can't do it," Olson was saying monotonously. "I can't do it anymore." His breath was coming in doglike pants. But he kept on walking and they all kept on walking. Little grunting noises and soft, plosive breathing became audible. The only other sounds were Olson's chant, the scuff of many feet, and the grinding, ratcheting sound of the halftrack's engine as it chugged along beside them.

Garraty felt the bewildered fear in his stomach grow. He could actually die here. It wouldn't be hard at all. He had screwed around and had gotten two warnings on him already. He couldn't be much over the limit right now. All he had to do was slip his pace a little and he'd have number three—final warning. And then . . .

"Warning! Warning 70!"

"They're playing your song, Olson," McVries said between pants. "Pick up your feet. I want to see you dance up this hill like Fred Astaire."

"What do you care?" Olson asked fiercely.

McVries didn't answer. Olson found a little more inside himself and managed to pick it up. Garraty wondered morbidly if the little more Olson had found was his last legs. He also wondered about Stebbins, back there tailing the group. How are you, Stebbins? Getting tired?

Up ahead, a boy named Larson, 60, suddenly sat down on the road. He got a warning. The other boys split and passed around him, like the Red Sea around the Children of Israel.

"I'm just going to rest for a while, okay?" Larson said with a trusting, shell-shocked smile. "I can't walk anymore right now, okay?" His smile stretched wider, and he turned it on the soldier who had jumped down from the halftrack with his rifle unslung and the stainless steel chronometer in his hand.

"Warning, 60," the soldier said. "Second warning."

"Listen, I'll catch up," Larson hastened to assure him. "I'm just resting. A guy can't walk all the time. Not *all* the time. Can he, fellas?'' Olson made a little moaning noise as he passed Larson, and shied away when Larson tried to touch his pants cuff.

Garraty felt his pulse beating warmly in his temples. Larson got his third warning . . . now he'll understand, Garraty thought, now he'll get up and start flogging it.

And at the end, Larson did realize, apparently. Reality came crashing back in. ''Hey!'' Larson said behind them. His voice was high and alarmed. ''Hey, just a second, don't do that, I'll get up. Hey, don't! D—''

The shot. They walked on up the hill.

''Ninety-three bottles of beer left on the shelf,'' McVries said softly.

Garraty made no reply. He stared at his feet and walked and focused all of his concentration on getting to the top without that third warning. It couldn't go on much longer, this monster hill. Surely not.

Up ahead someone uttered a high, gobbling scream, and then the rifles crashed in unison.

''Barkovitch,'' Baker said hoarsely. ''That was Barkovitch, I'm sure it was.''

''Wrong, redneck!'' Barkovitch yelled out of the darkness. ''One hundred per cent dead wrong!''

They never did see the boy who had been shot after Larson. He had been part of the vanguard and he was dragged off the road before they got there. Garraty ventured a look up from the pavement, and was immediately sorry. He could see the top of the hill—just barely. They still had the length of a football field to go. It looked like a hundred miles. No one said anything else. Each of them had retreated into his own private world of pain and effort. Seconds seemed to telescope into hours.

Near the top of the hill, a rutted dirt road branched off the main drag, and a farmer and his family stood there. They watched the Walkers go past—an old man with a deeply seamed brow, a hatchet-faced woman in a bulky cloth coat, three teenaged children who all looked half-witted.

''All he needs . . . is a pitchfork,'' McVries told Garraty breathlessly. Sweat was streaming down McVries's face. ''And . . . Grant Wood . . . to paint him.''

Someone called out: ''Hiya, Daddy!''

The farmer and the farmer's wife and the farmer's children said nothing. The cheese stands alone, Garraty thought crazily. Hi-ho the dairy-o, the cheese stands alone. The farmer and his family did not smile. They did not frown. They held no signs. They did not wave. They watched. Garraty was reminded of the Western movies he had seen on all the Saturday afternoons of his youth, where the hero was left to die in the desert and the buzzards came and circled overhead. They were left behind, and Garraty was glad. He supposed the farmer and his wife and the three half-witted children would be out there around nine o'clock next May first . . . and the next . . . and the next. How many boys had they seen shot? A dozen? Two? Garraty didn't like to think of it. He took a pull at his canteen, sloshed the water around in his mouth, trying to cut through the caked saliva. He spit the mouthful out.

The hill went on. Up ahead Toland fainted and was shot after the soldier left beside him had warned his unconscious body three times. It seemed to Garraty that they had been climbing the hill for at least a month now. Yes, it had to be a month at least, and that was a conservative estimate because they had been walking for just over three years. He giggled a little, took another mouthful of water, sloshed it around in his mouth, and then swallowed it. No cramps. A cramp would finish him now. But it could happen. It could happen because someone had dipped his shoes in liquid lead while he wasn't looking.

Nine gone, and a third of them had gotten it right here on this hill. The Major had told Olson to give them hell, and if this wasn't hell, it was a pretty good approximation. A pretty good . . .

Oh boy—

Garraty was suddenly aware that he felt quite giddy, as if he might faint himself. He brought one hand up and slapped himself across the face, backward and forward, hard.

"You all right?" McVries asked.

"Feel faint."

"Pour your . . . " Quick, whistling breath, " . . . canteen over your head."

Garraty did it. I christen thee Raymond Davis Garraty, pax vobiscum. The water was very cold. He stopped feeling faint. Some of the water trickled down inside his shirt in freezing cold rivulets. "Canteen! 47!" he shouted. The effort of the shout left him feeling drained all over again. He wished he had waited awhile.

One of the soldiers jog-trotted over to him and handed him a fresh canteen. Garraty could feel the soldier's expressionless marble eyes sizing him up. "Get away," he said rudely, taking the canteen. "You get paid to shoot me, not to look at me."

The soldier went away with no change of expression. Garraty made himself walk a little faster.

They kept climbing and no one else got it and then they were at the top. It was nine o'clock. They had been on the road twelve hours. It didn't mean anything. The only thing that mattered was the cool breeze blowing over the top of the hill. And the sound of a bird. And the feel of his damp shirt against his skin. And the memories in his head. Those things mattered, and Garraty clung to them with desperate awareness. They were his things and he still had them.

"Pete?"

"Yeah."

"Man, I'm glad to be alive."

McVries didn't answer. They were on the downslope now. Walking was easy.

"I'm going to try hard to stay alive," Garraty said, almost apologetically.

The road curved gently downward. They were still a hundred and fifteen miles from Oldtown and the comparative levelness of the turnpike.

"That's the idea, isn't it?" McVries asked finally. His voice sounded cracked and cobwebby, as if it had issued from a dusty cellar.

Neither of them said anything for a while. No one was talking. Baker ambled steadily along—he hadn't drawn a warning yet—with his hands in his pockets, his head nodding slightly with the flatfooted rhythm of his walk. Olson had gone back to Hail Mary, full of grace. His face was a white splotch in the darkness. Harkness was eating.

"Garraty," McVries said.

"I'm here."

"You ever see the end of a Long Walk?"

"No, you?"

"Hell, no. I just thought, you being close to it and all—"

"My father hated them. He took me to one as a what-do-you-call-it, object lesson. But that was the only time."

"I saw."

Garraty jumped at the sound of that voice. It was Stebbins. He had pulled almost even with them, his head still bent forward, his blond hair flapping around his ears like a sickly halo.

"What was it like?" McVries asked. His voice was younger somehow.

"You don't want to know," Stebbins said.

"I asked, didn't I?"

Stebbins made no reply. Garraty's curiosity about him was stronger than ever. Stebbins hadn't folded up. He showed no signs of folding up. He went on without complaint and hadn't been warned since the starting line.

"Yeah, what's it like?" he heard himself asking.

"I saw the end four years ago," Stebbins said. "I was thirteen. It ended about sixteen miles over the New Hampshire border. They had the National Guard out and sixteen Federal Squads to augment the State Police. They had to. The people were packed sixty deep on both sides of the road for fifty miles. Over twenty people were trampled to death before it was all over. It happened because people were trying to move with the Walkers, trying to see the end of it. I had a front-row seat. My dad got it for me."

"What does your dad do?" Garraty asked.

"He's in the Squads. And he had it figured just right. I didn't even have to move. The Walk ended practically in front of me."

"What happened?" Olson asked softly.

"I could hear them coming before I could see them. We all could. It was one big soundwave, getting closer and closer. And it was still an hour before they got close enough to see. They weren't looking at the crowd, either of the two that were left. It was like they didn't even know the crowd was there. What they were looking at was the road. They were hobbling along, both of them. Like they had been crucified and then taken down and made to walk with the nails still through their feet."

They were all listening to Stebbins now. A horrified silence had fallen like a rubber sheet.

"The crowd was yelling at them, almost as if they could still hear. Some were yelling one guy's name, and some were yelling the other guy's, but the only thing that really came through was this *Go . . . Go . . . Go* chant. I was getting shoved around like a beanbag. The guy next to me either pissed himself or jacked off in his pants, you couldn't tell which.

"They walked right past me. One of them was a big blond with his shirt open. One of his shoe soles had come unglued or unstitched or whatever, and it was flapping. The other guy wasn't even wearing his shoes anymore. He was in his stocking feet. His socks ended at his ankles. The rest of them . . . why, he'd just walked them away, hadn't he? His feet were purple. You could see the broken blood vessels in his feet. I don't think he really felt it anymore. Maybe they were able to do something with his feet later, I don't know. Maybe they were."

"Stop. For God's sake, stop it." It was McVries. He sounded dazed and sick.

"You wanted to know," Stebbins said, almost genially. "Didn't you say that?"

No answer. The halftrack whined and clattered and spurted along the shoulder, and somewhere farther up someone drew a warning.

"It was the big blond that lost. I saw it all. They were just a little past me. He threw both of his arms up, like he was Superman. But instead of flying he just fell flat on his face and they gave him his ticket after thirty seconds because he was walking with three. They were both walking with three.

"Then the crowd started to cheer. They cheered and they cheered and then they could see that the kid that won was trying to say something. So they shut up. He had fallen on his knees, you know, like he was going to pray, only he was just crying. And then he crawled over to the other boy and put his face in that big blond kid's shirt. Then he started to say whatever it was he had to say, but we couldn't hear it. He was talking into the dead kid's shirt. He was telling the dead kid. Then the soldiers rushed out and told him he had won the Prize, and asked him how he wanted to start."

"What did he say?" Garraty asked. It seemed to him that with the question he had laid his whole life on the line.

"He didn't say anything to them, not then," Stebbins said. "He was talking to the dead kid. He was telling the dead kid something, but we couldn't hear it."

"What happened then?" Pearson asked.

"I don't remember," Stebbins said remotely.

No one said anything. Garraty felt a panicked, trapped sensation, as if someone had stuffed him into an underground pipe that was too small to get out of. Up ahead a third warning was given out and a boy made a croaking, despairing sound, like a dying crow. Please God, don't let them shoot anyone now, Garraty thought. I'll go crazy if I hear the guns now. Please God, please God.

A few minutes later the guns rammed their steel-death sound into the night. This time it was a short boy in a flapping red and white football jersey. For a moment Garraty thought Percy's mom would not have to wonder or worry anymore, but it wasn't Percy—it was a boy named Quincy or Quentin or something like that.

Garraty didn't go crazy. He turned around to say angry words at Stebbins—to ask him, perhaps, how it felt to inflict a boy's last minutes with such a horror—but Stebbins had dropped back to his usual position and Garraty was alone again.

They walked on, the ninety of them.

Chapter 5

"You did not tell the truth and so
you will have to pay the consequences."
—Bob Barker
Truth or Consequences

At twenty minutes of ten on that endless May first, Garraty sluffed one of his two warnings. Two more Walkers had bought it since the boy in the football jersey. Garraty barely noticed. He was taking a careful inventory of himself.

One head, a little confused and crazied up, but basically okay. Two eyes, grainy. One neck, pretty stiff. Two arms, no problem there. One torso, okay except for a gnawing in his gut that concentrates couldn't satisfy. Two damn tired legs. Muscles aching. He wondered how far his legs would carry him on their own—how long before his brain took them over and began punishing them, making them work past any sane limit, to keep a bullet from crashing into its own bony cradle. How long before the legs began to kink and then to bind up, to protest and finally to seize up and stop.

His legs were tired, but so far as he could tell, still pretty much okay.

And two feet. Aching. They were tender, no use denying it. He was a big boy. Those feet were shifting a hundred and sixty pounds back and forth. The soles ached. There were occasional strange shooting pains in them. His left great toe had poked through his sock (he thought of Stebbins's tale and felt a kind of creeping horror at that), and had begun to rub uncomfortably against his shoe. But his feet were working, there were still no blisters on them, and he felt his feet were still pretty much okay, too.

Garraty, he pep-talked himself, you're in good shape. Twelve guys dead, twice that many maybe hurting bad by now, but you're okay. You're going good. You're great. You're alive.

Conversation, which had died violently at the end of Stebbins's story, picked up again. Talking was what living people did. Yannick, 98, was discussing the ancestry of the soldiers on the halftrack in an overloud voice with Wyman, 97. Both agreed that it was mixed, colorful, hirsute, and bastardized.

Pearson, meanwhile, abruptly asked Garraty: "Ever have an enema?"

"Enema?" Garraty repeated. He thought about it. "No. I don't think so."

"Any of you guys?" Pearson asked. "Tell the truth, now."

"I did," Harkness said, and chuckled a little. "My mother gave me one after Halloween once when I was little. I ate pretty near a whole shopping bag of candy."

186

"Did you like it?" Pearson pressed.

"Hell, no! Who in *hell* would like a half a quart of warm soapsuds up your—"

"My little brother," Pearson said sadly. "I asked the little snot if he was sorry I was going and he said no because Ma said he could have an enema if he was good and didn't cry. He loves 'em."

"That's sickening," Harkness said loudly.

Pearson looked glum. "I thought so, too."

A few minutes later Davidson joined the group and told them about the times he got drunk at the Steubenville State Fair and crawled into the hoochie-kooch tent and got biffed in the head by a big fat momma wearing nothing but a G-string. When Davidson told her (so he said) that he was drunk and thought it was the tattooing tent he was crawling into, the red hot big fat momma let him feel her up for a while (so he said). He had told her he wanted to get a Stars and Bars tattooed on his stomach.

Art Baker told them about a contest they'd had back home, to see who could light the biggest fart, and this hairy-assed old boy named Davey Popham had managed to burn off almost all the hair on his ass and the small of his back as well. Smelled like a grassfire, Baker said. This got Harkness laughing so hard he drew a warning.

After that, the race was on. Tall story followed tall story until the whole shaky structure came tumbling down. Someone else was warned, and not long after, the other Baker (James) bought a ticket. The good humor went out of the group. Some of them began to talk about their girlfriends, and the conversation became stumbling and maudlin. Garraty said nothing about Jan, but as tired ten o'clock came rolling in, a black coalsack splattered with milky groundmist, it seemed to him that she was the best thing he had ever known.

They passed under a short string of mercury streetlights, through a closed and shuttered town, all of them subdued now, speaking in low murmurs. In front of the Shopwell near the far end of this wide place in the road a young couple sat asleep on a sidewalk bench with their heads leaning together. A sign that could not be read dangled between them. The girl was very young—she looked no more than fourteen—and her boyfriend was wearing a sport shirt that had been washed too many times to ever look very sporty again. Their shadows in the street made a merge that the Walkers passed quietly over.

Garraty glanced back over his shoulder, quite sure that the rumble of the half-track must have awakened them. But they still slept, unaware that the Event had come and passed them by. He wondered if the girl would catch what-for from her old man. She looked awfully young. He wondered if their sign was for Go-Go Garraty, "Maine's Own." Somehow he hoped not. Somehow the idea was a little repulsive.

He ate the last of his concentrates and felt a little better. There was nothing left for Olson to cadge off him now. It was funny about Olson. Garraty would have bet six hours ago that Olson was pretty well done in. But he was still walking, and now without warnings. Garraty supposed a person could do a lot of things when his life was at stake. They had come about fifty-four miles now.

The last of the talk died with the nameless town. They marched in silence for an hour or so, and the chill began to seep into Garraty again. He ate the last of his mom's cookies, balled up the foil, and pitched it into the brush at the side of the road. Just another litterbug on the great tomato plant of life.

McVries had produced a toothbrush of all things from his small packsack and was busy dry-brushing his teeth. It all goes on, Garraty thought wonderingly. You burp, you say excuse me. You wave back at the people who wave to you because that's the polite thing to do. No one argues very much with anyone else (except for Barkovitch) because that's also the polite thing to do. It all goes on.

Or did it? He thought of McVries sobbing at Stebbins to shut up. Of Olson taking his cheese with the dumb humility of a whipped dog. It all seemed to have a heightened intensity about it, a sharper contrast of colors and light and shadow.

At eleven o'clock, several things happened almost at once. The word came back that a small plank bridge up ahead had been washed out by a heavy afternoon thunderstorm. With the bridge out, the Walk would have to be temporarily stopped. A weak cheer went up through the ragged ranks, and Olson, in a very soft voice, muttered "Thank God."

A moment later Barkovitch began to scream a flood of profanity at the boy next to him, a squat, ugly boy with the unfortunate name of Rank. Rank took a swing at him—something expressly forbidden by the rules—and was warned for it. Barkovitch didn't even break stride. He simply lowered his head and ducked under the punch and went on yelling.

"Come on, you sonofabitch! I'll dance on your goddam grave! Come on, Dumbo, pick up your feet! Don't make it too easy for me!"

Rank threw another punch. Barkovitch nimbly stepped around it, but tripped over the boy walking next to him. They were both warned by the soldiers, who were now watching the developments carefully but emotionlessly—like men watching a couple of ants squabbling over a crumb of bread, Garraty thought bitterly.

Rank started to walk faster, not looking at Barkovitch. Barkovitch himself, furious at being warned (the boy he had tripped over was Gribble, who had wanted to tell the Major he was a murderer), yelled at him: "Your mother sucks cock on 42nd Street, Rank!"

With that, Rank suddenly turned around and charged Barkovitch.

Cries of "Break it up!" and "Cut the shit!" filled the air, but Rank took no notice. He went for Barkovitch with his head down, bellowing.

Barkovitch sidestepped him. Rank went stumbling and pinwheeling across the soft shoulder, skidded in the sand, and sat down with his feet splayed out. He was given a third warning.

"Come on, Dumbo!" Barkovitch goaded. "Get up!"

Rank did get up. Then he slipped somehow and fell over on his back. He seemed dazed and woozy.

The third thing that happened around eleven o'clock was Rank's death. There was a moment of silence when the carbines sighted in, and Baker's voice was loud and clearly audible: "There, Barkovitch, you're not a pest anymore. Now you're a murderer."

The guns roared. Rank's body was thrown into the air by the force of the bullets. Then it lay still and sprawled, one arm on the road.

"It was his own fault!" Barkovitch yelled. "You saw him, he swung first! Rule 8! Rule 8!"

No one said anything.

"Go fuck yourselves! All of you!"

McVries said easily: "Go on back and dance on him a little, Barkovitch. Go entertain us. Boogie on him a little bit, Barkovitch."

"Your mother sucks cock on 42nd Street too, scarface," Barkovitch said hoarsely.

"Can't wait to see your brains all over the road," McVries said quietly. His hand had gone to the scar and was rubbing, rubbing, rubbing. "I'll cheer when it happens, you murdering little bastard."

Barkovitch muttered something else under his breath. The others had shied away from him as if he had the plague and he was walking by himself.

They hit sixty miles at about ten past eleven, with no sign of a bridge of any kind. Garraty was beginning to think the grapevine had been wrong this time when they cleared a small hill and looked down into a pool of light where a small crowd of hustling, bustling men moved.

The lights were the beams of several trucks, directed at a plank bridge spanning a fast-running rill of water. "Truly I love that bridge," Olson said, and helped himself to one of McVries's cigarettes. "Truly."

But as they drew closer, Olson made a soft, ugly sound in his throat and pitched the cigarette away into the weeds. One of the bridge's supports and two of the heavy butt planks had been washed away, but the Squad up ahead had been working diligently. A sawed-off telephone pole had been planted in the bed of the stream, anchored in what looked like a gigantic cement plug. They hadn't had a chance to replace the butts, so they had put down a big convoy-truck tailgate in their place. Makeshift, but it would serve.

"The Bridge of San Loois Ray," Abraham said. "Maybe if the ones up front stomp a little, it'll collapse again."

"Small chance," Pearson said, and then added in a breaking, weepy voice, "Aw, *shit!*"

The vanguard, down to three or four boys, was on the bridge now. Their feet clumped hollowly as they crossed. Then they were on the other side, walking without looking back. The halftrack stopped. Two soldiers jumped out and kept pace with the boys. On the other side of the bridge, two more fell in with the vanguard. The boards rumbled steadily now.

Two men in corduroy coats leaned against a big asphalt-spattered truck marked HIGHWAY REPAIR. They were smoking. They wore green gumrubber boots.

They watched the Walkers go by. As Davidson, McVries, Olson, Pearson, Harkness, Baker, and Garraty passed in a loose sort of group one of them flicked his cigarette end over end into the stream and said: "That's him. That's Garraty."

"Keep goin', boy!" the other yelled. "I got ten bucks on you at twelve-to-one!"

Garraty noticed a few sawdusty lengths of telephone pole in the back of the truck. They were the ones who had made sure he was going to keep going, whether he liked it or not. He raised one hand to them and crossed the bridge. The tailgate that had replaced the butt planks clunked under his shoes and then the bridge was behind them. The road doglegged, and the only reminder of the rest they'd almost had was a wedge-shaped swath of light on the trees at the side of the road. Soon that was gone, too.

"Has a Long Walk ever been stopped for anything?" Harkness asked.

"I don't think so," Garraty said. "More material for the book?"

"No," Harkness said. He sounded tired. "Just personal information."

"It stops every year," Stebbins said from behind them. "Once."

There was no reply to that.

About half an hour later, McVries came up beside Garraty and walked with him in silence for a little while. Then, very quietly, he said: "Do you think you'll win, Ray?"

Garraty considered it for a long, long time.

"No," he said finally. "No, I . . . no."

The stark admission frightened him. He thought again about buying a ticket, no, buying a *bullet,* of the final frozen half-second of total knowledge, seeing the bottomless bores of the carbines swing toward him. Legs frozen. Guts crawling and clawing. Muscles, genitals, brain all cowering away from the oblivion a bloodbeat away.

He swallowed dryly. "How about yourself?"

"I guess not," McVries said. "I stopped thinking I had any real chance around nine tonight. You see, I . . . " He cleared his throat. "It's hard to say, but . . . I went into it with my eyes open, you know?" He gestured around himself at the other boys. "Lots of these guys didn't, you know? I knew the odds. But I didn't figure on *people*. And I don't think I ever realized the real gut truth of what this is. I think I had the idea that when the first guy got so he couldn't cut it anymore they'd aim the guns at him and pull the triggers and little pieces of paper with the word BANG printed on them would . . . would . . . and the Major would say April Fool and we'd all go home. Do you get what I'm saying at all?"

Garraty thought of his own rending shock when Curley had gone down in a spray of blood and brains like oatmeal, brains on the pavement and the white line. "Yes," he said. "I know what you're saying."

"It took me a while to figure it out, but it was faster after I got around that mental block. Walk or die, that's the moral of this story. Simple as that. It's not survival of the physically fittest, that's where I went wrong when I let myself get into this. If it was, I'd have a fair chance. But there are weak men who can lift cars if their wives are pinned underneath. The brain, Garraty.'' McVries's voice had dropped to a hoarse whisper. ''It isn't man or God. It's something . . . in the brain.''

A whippoorwill called once in the darkness. The groundfog was lifting.

''Some of these guys will go on walking long after the laws of biochemistry and handicapping have gone by the boards. There was a guy last year that crawled for two miles at four miles an hour after both of his feet cramped up at the same time, you remember reading about that? Look at Olson, he's worn out but he keeps going. That goddam Barkovitch is running on high-octane hate and he just keeps going and he's as fresh as a daisy. I don't think I can do that. I'm not tired—not really tired—yet. But I will be.'' The scar stood out on the side of his haggard face as he looked ahead into the darkness. ''And I think . . . when I get tired enough . . . I think I'll just sit down.''

Garraty was silent, but he felt alarmed. Very alarmed.

''I'll outlast Barkovitch, though,'' McVries said, almost to himself. ''I can do that, by Christ.''

Garraty glanced at his watch and saw it was 11:30. They passed through a deserted crossroads where a sleepy-looking constable was parked. The possible traffic he had been sent out to halt was nonexistent. They walked past him, out of the bright circle of light thrown by the single mercury lamp. Darkness fell over them like a coalsack again.

''We could slip into the woods now and they'd never see us,'' Garraty said thoughtfully.

''Try it,'' Olson said. ''They've got infrared sweepscopes, along with forty other kinds of monitoring gear, including high-intensity microphones. They hear everything we're saying. They can almost pick up your heartbeat. And they see you like daylight, Ray.''

As if to emphasize his point, a boy behind them was given second warning.

''You take all the fun outta livin','' Baker said softly. His faint Southern drawl sounded out of place and foreign to Garraty's ears.

McVries had walked away. The darkness seemed to isolate each of them, and Garraty felt a shaft of intense loneliness. There were mutters and half-yelps every time something crashed through the woods they were going past, and Garraty realized with some amusement that a late evening stroll through the Maine woods could be no picnic for the city boys in the crew. An owl made a mysterious noise somewhere to their left. On the other side something rustled, was still, rustled again, was still, and then made a crashing break for less populated acreage. There was another nervous cry of ''What was that?''

Overhead, capricious spring clouds began to scud across the sky in mackerel shapes, promising more rain. Garraty turned up his collar and listened to the sound of his feet pounding the pavement. There was a trick to that, a subtle mental adjustment, like having better night vision the longer you were in the dark. This morning the sound of his feet had been lost to him. They had been lost in the tramp of ninety-nine other pairs, not to mention the rumble of the halftrack. But now he heard them easily. His own particular stride, and the way his left foot scraped the pavement every now and then. It seemed to him that the sound of his footfalls had become as loud to his ears as the sound of his own heartbeat. Vital, life and death sound.

His eyes felt grainy, trapped in their sockets. The lids were heavy. His energy seemed to be draining down some sinkhole in the middle of him. Warnings were droned out with monotonous regularity, but no one was shot. Barkovitch had shut up. Stebbins was a ghost again, not even visible in back of them.

The hands on his watch read 11:40.

On up toward the hour of witches, he thought. When churchyards yawn and give up their moldy dead. When all good little boys are sacked out. When wives and lovers have given up the carnal pillowfight for the evening. When passengers sleep uneasy on the Greyhound to New York. When Glenn Miller plays uninterrupted on the radio and bartenders think about putting the chairs up on the tables, and—

Jan's face came into his mind again. He thought of kissing her at Christmas, almost half a year ago, under the plastic mistletoe his mother always hung from the big light globe in the kitchen. Stupid kid stuff. Look where you're standing. Her lips had been surprised and soft, not resisting. A nice kiss. One to dream on. His first real kiss. He did it again when he took her home. They had been standing in her driveway, standing in the silent grayness of falling Christmas snow. That had been something more than a nice kiss. His arms around her waist. Her arms around his neck, locked there, her eyes closed (he had peeked), the soft feel of her breasts—muffled up in her coat, of course—against him. He had almost told her he loved her then, but no . . . that would have been too quick.

After that, they taught each other. She taught him that books were sometimes just to be read and discarded, not studied (he was something of a grind, which amused Jan, and her amusement first exasperated him and then he also saw the funny side of it). He taught her to knit. That had been a funny thing. His father, of all people, had taught him how to knit . . . before the Squads got him. His father had taught Garraty's father, as well. It was something of a male tradition in the clan Garraty, it seemed. Jan had been fascinated by the pattern of the increases and decreases, and she left him behind soon enough, overstepping his laborious scarves and mittens to sweaters, cableknits, and finally to crocheting and even the tatting of doilies, which she gave up as ridiculous as soon as the skill was mastered.

He had also taught her how to rhumba and cha-cha, skills he had learned on endless Saturday mornings at Mrs. Amelia Dorgens's School for Modern Dance . . . that had been his mother's idea, one he had objected to strenuously. His mother had stuck to her guns, thank God.

He thought now of the patterns of light and shadow on the nearly perfect oval of her face, the way she walked, the lift and fall of her voice, the easy, desirable swing of one hip, and he wondered in terror what he was doing here, walking down this dark road. He wanted her now. He wanted to do it all over again, but differently. Now, when he thought of the Major's tanned face, the salt-and-pepper mustache, the mirrored sunglasses, he felt a horror so deep it made his legs feel rubbery and weak. Why am I here? he asked himself desperately, and there was no answer, so he asked the question again: Why am—

The guns crashed in the darkness, and there was the unmistakable mailsack thud of a body falling on the concrete. The fear was on him again, the hot, throat-choking fear that made him want to run blindly, to dive into the bushes and just keep on running until he found Jan and safety.

McVries had Barkovitch to keep him going. He would concentrate on Jan. He would walk to Jan. They reserved space for Long Walkers' relatives and loved ones in the front lines. He would see her.

He thought about kissing that other girl and was ashamed.

How do you know you'll make it? A cramp . . . blisters . . . a bad cut or a nosebleed that just won't quit . . . a big hill that was just too big and too long. How do you know you'll make it?

I'll make it, I'll make it.

"Congratulations," McVries said at his shoulder, making him jump.

"Huh?"

"It's midnight. We live to fight another day, Garraty."

"And many of 'em," Abraham added. "For me, that is. Not that I begrudge you, you understand."

"A hundred and five miles to Oldtown, if you care," Olson put in tiredly.

"Who gives a shit about Oldtown?" McVries demanded. "You ever been there, Garraty?"

"No."

"How about Augusta? Christ, I thought that was in Georgia."

"Yeah, I've been in Augusta. It's the state capital—"

"Regional," Abraham said.

"And the Corporate Governor's mansion, and a couple of traffic circles, and a couple of movies—"

"You have those in Maine?" McVries asked.

"Well, it's a small state capital, okay?" Garraty said, smiling.

"Wait'll we hit Boston," McVries said.

There were groans.

From up ahead there came cheers, shouts, and catcalls. Garraty was alarmed to hear his own name called out. Up ahead, about half a mile away, was a ramshackle farmhouse, deserted and fallen down. But a battered Klieg light had been plugged in somewhere, and a huge sign, lettered with pine boughs across the front of the house read:

GARRATY'S OUR MAN!!!
Aroostook County Parents' Association

"Hey, Garraty, where's the parents?" someone yelled.

"Back home making kids," Garraty said, embarrassed. There could be no doubt that Maine was Garraty country, but he found the signs and cheers and the gibes of the others all a little mortifying. He had found—among other things—in the last

fifteen hours that he didn't much crave the limelight. The thought of a million people all over the state rooting for him and laying bets on him (at twelve-to-one, the
highway worker had said . . . was that good or bad?) was a little scary.

"You'd think they would have left a few plump, juicy parents lying around
somewhere," Davidson said.

"Poontang from the PTA?" Abraham asked.

The ribbing was halfhearted and didn't last very long. The road killed most ribbing very quickly. They crossed another bridge, this time a cement one that
spanned a good-sized river. The water rippled below them like black silk. A few
crickets chirred cautiously, and around fifteen past midnight, a spatter of light,
cold rain fell.

Up ahead, someone began to play a harmonica. It didn't last long (Hint 6: Conserve Wind), but it was pretty for the moment it lasted. It sounded a little like *Old
Black Joe,* Garraty thought. Down in de cornfiel', here dat mournful soun'. All
de darkies am aweeping, Ewing's in de cole, cole groun'.

No, that wasn't *Old Black Joe,* that tune was some other Stephen Foster racist
classic. Good old Stephen Foster. Drank himself to death. So did Poe, it had been
reputed. Poe the necrophiliac, the one who had married his fourteen-year-old cousin. That made him a pedophile as well. All-around depraved fellows, he and Stephen Foster both. If only they could have lived to see the Long Walk, Garraty
thought. They could have collaborated on the world's first Morbid Musical. *Mas-
sa's on De Cold, Cold Road,* or *The Tell-Tale Stride,* or—

Up ahead someone began to scream, and Garraty felt his blood go cold. It was
a very young voice. It was not screaming words. It was only screaming. A dark
figure broke from the pack, pelted across the shoulder of the road in front of the
halftrack (Garraty could not even remember when the halftrack had rejoined their
march after the repaired bridge), and dived for the woods. The guns roared. There
was a rending crash as a dead weight fell through the juniper bushes and underbrush to the ground. One of the soldiers jumped down and dragged the inert form
up by the hands. Garraty watched apathetically and thought, even the horror wears
thin. There's a surfeit even of death.

The harmonica player started in satirically on *Taps* and somebody—Collie Parker, by the sound—told him angrily to shut the fuck up. Stebbins laughed. Garraty
felt suddenly furious with Stebbins, and wanted to turn to him and ask him how
he'd like someone laughing at his death. It was something you'd expect of Barkovitch. Barkovitch had said he'd dance on a lot of graves, and there were sixteen
he could dance on already.

I doubt that he'll have much left of his feet to dance with, Garraty thought. A
sharp twinge of pain went through the arch of his right foot. The muscle there tightened heart-stoppingly, then loosened. Garraty waited with his heart in his mouth
for it to happen again. It would hit harder. It would turn his foot into a block of
useless wood. But it didn't happen.

"I can't walk much further," Olson croaked. His face was a white blur in the
darkness. No one answered him.

The darkness. Goddam the darkness. It seemed to Garraty they had been buried alive in it. Immured in it. Dawn was a century away. Many of them would never see the dawn. Or the sun. They were buried six feet deep in the darkness. All they needed was the monotonous chanting of the priest, his voice muffled but not entirely obscured by the new-packed darkness, above which the mourners stood. The mourners were not even aware that they were *here,* they were *alive,* they were screaming and scratching and clawing at the coffin-lid darkness, the air was flaking and rusting away, the air was turning into poison gas, hope fading until hope itself was a darkness, and above all of it the nodding chapel-bell voice of the priest and the impatient, shuffling feet of mourners anxious to be off into the warm May sunshine. Then, overmastering that, the sighing, shuffling chorus of the bugs and the beetles, squirming their way through the earth, come for the feast.

I could go crazy, Garraty thought. I could go right the fuck off my rocker.

A little breeze soughed through the pines.

Garraty turned around and urinated. Stebbins moved over a little, and Harkness made a coughing, snoring sound. He was walking half-asleep.

Garraty became acutely conscious of all the little sounds of life: someone hawked and spat, someone else sneezed, someone ahead and to the left was chewing something noisily. Someone asked someone else softly how he felt. There was a murmured answer. Yannick was singing at a whisper level, soft and very much off-key.

Awareness. It was all a function of awareness. But it wasn't forever.

"Why did I get into this?" Olson suddenly asked hopelessly, echoing Garraty's thoughts not so many minutes ago. "Why did I let myself in for this?"

No one answered him. No one had answered him for a long time now. Garraty thought it was as if Olson were already dead.

Another light spatter of rain fell. They passed another ancient graveyard, a church next door, a tiny shopfront, and then they were walking through a small New England community of small, neat homes. The road crosshatched a miniature business section where perhaps a dozen people had gathered to watch them pass. They cheered, but it was a subdued sound, as if they were afraid they might wake their neighbors. None of them was young, Garraty saw. The youngest was an intense-eyed man of about thirty-five. He was wearing rimless glasses and a shabby sport coat, pulled against him to protect against the chill. His hair stuck up in back, and Garraty noted with amusement that his fly was half-unzipped.

"Go! Great! Go! Go! Oh, great!" he chanted softly. He waved one soft plump hand ceaselessly, and his eyes seemed to burn over each of them as they passed.

On the far side of the village a sleepy-eyed policeman held up a rumbling trailer truck until they had passed. There were four more streetlights, an abandoned, crumbling building with EUREKA GRANGE NO. 81 written over the big double doors at the front, and then the town was gone. For no reason Garraty could put a finger on, he felt as if he had just walked through a Shirley Jackson short story.

McVries nudged him. "Look at that dude," he said.

"That dude" was a tall boy in a ridiculous loden-green trenchcoat. It flapped around his knees. He was walking with his arms wrapped around his head like a gigantic poultice. He was weaving unsteadily back and forth. Garraty watched him closely, with a kind of academic interest. He couldn't recall ever having seen this particular Walker before . . . but of course the darkness changed faces.

The boy stumbled over one of his own feet and almost fell down. Then he went on walking. Garraty and McVries watched him in fascinated silence for perhaps ten minutes, losing their own aches and tiredness in the trenchcoated boy's struggle. The boy in the trenchcoat didn't make a sound, not a groan or a moan.

Finally he did fall over and was warned. Garraty didn't think the boy would be able to get up, but he did. Now he was walking almost with Garraty and the boys around him. He was an extremely ugly boy, with the number 45 pressure-taped to his coat.

Olson whispered, "What's the matter with you?" but the boy seemed not to hear. They got that way, Garraty had noticed. Complete withdrawal from everything and everyone around them. Everything but the road. They stared at the road with a kind of horrid fascination, as if it were a tightrope they had to walk over an endless, bottomless chasm.

"What's your name?" he asked the boy, but there was no answer. And he found himself suddenly spitting the question at the boy over and over, like an idiot litany that would save him from whatever fate was coming for him out of the darkness like a black express freight. "What's your name, huh? What's your name, what's your name, what's—"

"Ray." McVries was tugging at his sleeve.

"He won't tell me, Pete, make him tell me, make him say his name—"

"Don't bother him," McVries said. "He's dying, don't bother him."

The boy with 45 on his trenchcoat fell over again, this time on his face. When he got up, there were scratches on his forehead, slowly welling blood. He was behind Garraty's group now, but they heard it when he got his final warning.

They passed through a hollow of deeper darkness that was a railroad overpass. Rain dripped somewhere, hollow and mysterious in this stone throat. It was very damp. Then they were out again, and Garraty saw with gratitude that there was a long, straight, flat stretch ahead.

45 fell down again. Footsteps quickened as boys scattered. Not long after, the guns roared. Garraty decided the boy's name must not have been important anyway.

Chapter 6

"And now our contestants are in the isolation booths."
—Jack Barry
Twenty-One

Three-thirty in the morning.

To Ray Garraty it seemed the longest minute of the longest night of his entire life. It was low tide, dead ebb, the time when the sea washes back, leaving slick mudflats covered with straggled weed, rusty beer cans, rotted prophylactics, broken bottles, smashed buoys, and green-mossed skeletons in tattered bathing trunks. It was dead ebb.

Seven more had gotten tickets since the boy in the trenchcoat. At one time, around two in the morning, three had gone down almost together, like dried cornshocks in the first hard autumn wind. They were seventy-five miles into the Walk, and there were twenty-four gone.

But none of that mattered. All that mattered was dead ebb. Three-thirty and the dead ebb. Another warning was given, and shortly after, the guns crashed once more. This time the face was a familiar one. It was 8, Davidson, who claimed he had once sneaked into the hoochie-kooch tent at the Steubenville State Fair.

Garraty looked at Davidson's white, blood-spattered face for just a moment and then he looked back at the road. He looked at the road quite a lot now. Sometimes the white line was solid, sometimes it was broken, and sometimes it was double, like streetcar tracks. He wondered how people could ride over this road all the other days of the year and not see the pattern of life and death in that white paint. Or did they see, after all?

The pavement fascinated him. How good and easy it would be to sit on that pavement. You'd start by squatting, and your stiff knee-joints would pop like toy air-pistols. Then you'd put bracing hands back on the cool, pebbled surface and snuggle your buttocks down, you'd feel the screaming pressure of your one hundred and sixty pounds leave your feet . . . and then to lie down, just fall backward and lie there, spread-eagled, feeling your tired spine stretch . . . looking up at the encircling trees and the majestic wheel of the stars . . . not hearing the warnings, just watching the sky and waiting . . . waiting . . .

Yeah.

Hearing the scatter of footsteps as Walkers moved out of the line of fire, leaving him alone, like a sacrificial offering. Hearing the whispers. It's Garraty, hey, it's Garraty getting a ticket! Perhaps there would be time to hear Barkovitch laugh as

197

he strapped on his metaphorical dancing shoes one more time. The swing of the carbines zeroing in, then—

He tore his glance forcibly from the road and stared blearily at the moving shadows around him, then looked up at the horizon, hunting for even a trace of dawn light. There was none, of course. The night was still dark.

They had passed through two or three more small towns, all of them dark and closed. Since midnight they had passed maybe three dozen sleepy spectators, the die-hard type who grimly watch in the New Year each December 31st, come hell or high water. The rest of the last three and a half hours was nothing but a dream montage, an insomniac's half-sleeping wakemare.

Garraty looked more closely at the faces around him, but none seemed familiar. An irrational panic stole over him. He tapped the shoulder of the Walker in front of him. "Pete? Pete, that you?"

The figure slipped away from him with an irritated grunt and didn't look back. Olson had been on his left, Baker on his right, but now there was no one at all on his left side and the boy to his right was much chubbier than Art Baker.

Somehow he had wandered off the road and fallen in with a bunch of late-hiking Boy Scouts. They would be looking for him. Hunting for him. Guns and dogs and Squads with radar and heat-tracers and—

Relief washed over him. That was Abraham, up ahead and at four o'clock. All he'd had to do was turn his head a little. The gangling form was unmistakable.

"Abraham!" he stage-whispered. "Abraham, you awake?"

Abraham muttered something.

"I said, you awake?"

"Yes goddammit Garraty lea'me alone."

At least he was still with them. That feeling of total disorientation passed away.

Someone up ahead was given a third warning and Garraty thought, I don't have any! I could sit down for a minute or a minute and a half. I could—

But he'd never get up.

Yes I would, he answered himself. Sure I would, I'd just—

Just die. He remembered promising his mother that he would see her and Jan in Freeport. He had made the promise lightheartedly, almost carelessly. At nine o'clock yesterday morning, his arrival in Freeport had been a foregone conclusion. But it wasn't a game anymore, it was a three-dimensional reality, and the possibility of walking into Freeport on nothing but a pair of bloody stumps seemed a horribly possible possibility.

Someone else was shot down . . . behind him, this time. The aim was bad, and the unlucky ticket-holder screamed hoarsely for what seemed a very long time before another bullet cut off the sound. For no reason at all Garraty thought of bacon, and heavy, sour spit came into his mouth and made him feel like gagging. Garraty wondered if twenty-six down was an unusually high or an unusually low number for seventy-five miles into a Long Walk.

His head dropped slowly between his shoulders, and his feet carried them forward on their own. He thought about a funeral he had gone to as a boy. It had been

Freaky D'Allessio's funeral. Not that his real name had been Freaky, his real name had been George, but all the kids in the neighborhood called him Freaky because his eyes didn't quite jibe . . .

He could remember Freaky waiting to be picked up for baseball games, always coming in dead last, his out-of-kilter eyes switching hopefully from one team captain to the other like a spectator at a tennis match. He always played deep center field, where not too many balls were hit and he couldn't do much damage; one of his eyes was almost blind, and he didn't have enough depth perception to judge any balls hit to him. Once he got under one and jabbed his glove at a hunk of thin air while the ball landed on his forehead with an audible *bonk!* like a cantaloupe being whocked with the handle of a kitchen knife. The threads on the ball left an imprint dead square on his forehead for a week, like a brand.

Freaky was killed by a car on U.S. 1 outside of Freeport. One of Garraty's friends, Eddie Klipstein, saw it happen. He held kids in thrall for six weeks, Eddie Klipstein did, telling them about how the car hit Freaky D'Allessio's bike and Freaky went up over the handlebars, knocked spang out of his shitkicker boots by the impact, both of his legs trailing out behind him in crippled splendor as his body flew its short, wingless flight from the seat of his Schwinn to a stone wall where Freaky landed and spread his head like a dollop of wet glue on the rocks.

He went to Freaky's funeral, and before they got there he almost lost his lunch wondering if he would see Freaky's head spread in the coffin like a glob of Elmer's Glue, but Freaky was all fixed up in his sport coat and tie and his Cub Scouts attendance pin, and he looked ready to step out of his coffin the moment someone said baseball. The eyes that didn't jibe were closed, and in general Garraty felt pretty relieved.

That had been the only dead person he had ever seen before all of this, and it had been a clean, neat dead person. Nothing like Ewing, or the boy in the loden trenchcoat, or Davidson with blood on his livid, tired face.

It's sick, Garraty thought with dismal realization. It's just sick.

At quarter to four he was given first warning, and he slapped himself twice smartly across the face, trying to make himself wake up. His body felt chilled clear through. His kidneys dragged at him, but at the same time he felt that he didn't quite have to pee yet. It might have been his imagination, but the stars in the east seemed a trifle paler. With real amazement it occurred to him that at this time yesterday he had been asleep in the back of the car as they drove up toward the stone marking post at the border. He could almost see himself stretched out on his back, *sprawling* there, not even *moving*. He felt an intense longing to be back there. Just to bring back yesterday morning.

Ten of four now.

He looked around himself, getting a superior, lonely kind of gratification from knowing he was one of the few fully awake and aware. It was definitely lighter now, light enough to make out snatches of features in the walking silhouettes. Baker was up ahead—he could tell it was Art by the flapping red-striped shirt—and McVries was near him. He saw Olson was off to the left, keeping pace with the halftrack, and was surprised. He was sure that Olson had been one of those to get tickets during the small hours of the morning, and had been relieved that he hadn't had to see Hank go down. It was too dark even now to see how he looked, but Olson's head was bouncing up and down in time to his stride like the head of a rag doll.

Percy, whose mom kept showing up, was back by Stebbins now. Percy was walking with a kind of lopsided roll, like a long-time sailor on his first day ashore. He also spotted Gribble, Harkness, Wyman, and Collie Parker. Most of the people he knew were still in it.

By four o'clock there was a brightening band on the horizon, and Garraty felt his spirits lift. He stared back at the long tunnel of the night in actual horror, and wondered how he ever could have gotten through it.

He stepped up his pace a little, approaching McVries, who was walking with his chin against his breast, his eyes half-open but glazed and vacant, more asleep than awake. A thin, delicate cord of saliva hung from the corner of his mouth, picking up the first tremulous touch of dawn with pearly, beautiful fidelity. Garraty stared at this strange phenomenon, fascinated. He didn't want to wake McVries out of his doze. For the time being it was enough to be close to someone he liked, someone else who had made it through the night.

They passed a rocky, steeply slanting meadow where five cows stood gravely at a bark-peeled pole fence, staring out at the Walkers and chewing thoughtfully. A small dog tore out of a farmyard and barked at them ratchetingly. The soldiers on the halftrack raised their guns to high port, ready to shoot the animal if he interfered with any Walker's progress, but the dog only chased back and forth along the shoulder, bravely voicing defiance and territoriality from a safe distance. Someone yelled thickly at him to shut up, goddammit.

Garraty became entranced with the coming dawn. He watched as the sky and the land lightened by degrees. He watched the white band on the horizon deepen to a delicate pink, then red, then gold. The guns roared once more before the last of the night was finally banished, but Garraty barely heard. The first red arc of sun was peering over the horizon, faded behind a fluff of cloud, then came again in an onslaught. It looked to be a perfect day, and Garraty greeted it only half-coherently by thinking: Thank God I can die in the daylight.

A bird twitted sleepily. They passed another farmhouse where a man with a beard waved at them after putting down a wheelbarrow filled with hoes, rakes, and planting-seed.

A crow cawed raucously off in the shadowy woods. The first heat of the day touched Garraty's face gently, and he welcomed it. He grinned and yelled loudly for a canteen.

McVries twitched his head oddly, like a dog interrupted in a dream of cat-chasing, and then looked around with muddy eyes. "My God, daylight. Daylight, Garraty. What time?"

Garraty looked at his watch and was surprised to find it was quarter of five. He showed McVries the dial.

"How many miles? Any idea?"

"About eighty, I make it. And twenty-seven down. We're a quarter of the way home, Pete."

"Yeah." McVries smiled. "That's right, isn't it?"

"Damn right."

"You feel better?" Garraty asked.

"About one thousand per cent."

"So do I. I think it's the daylight."

"My God, I bet we see some people today. Did you read that article in *World's Week* about the Long Walk?"

"Skimmed it," Garraty said. "Mostly to see my name in print."

"Said that over two billion dollars gets bet on the Long Walk every year. Two *billion!*"

Baker had awakened from his own doze and had joined them. "We used to have a pool in my high school," he said. "Everybody'd kick in a quarter, and then we'd each pick a three-digit number out of a hat. And the guy holdin' the number closest to the last mile of the Walk, he got the money."

"Olson!" McVries yelled over cheerily. "Just think of all the cash riding on you, boy! Think of the people with a bundle resting right on your skinny ass!"

Olson told him in a tired, washed-out voice that the people with a bundle wagered on his skinny ass could perform two obscene acts upon themselves, the second proceeding directly from the first. McVries, Baker, and Garraty laughed.

"Be a lotta pretty girls on the road today," Baker said, eyeing Garraty roguishly.

"I'm all done with that stuff," Garraty said. "I got a girl up ahead. I'm going to be a good boy from now on."

"Sinless in thought, word, and deed," McVries said sententiously.

Garraty shrugged. "See it any way you like," he said.

"Chances are a hundred to one against you ever having a chance to do more than wave to her again," McVries said flatly.

"Seventy-three to one now."

"Still pretty high."

But Garraty's good humor was solid. "I feel like I could walk forever," he said blandly. A couple of the Walkers around him grimaced.

They passed an all-night gas station and the attendant came out to wave. Just about everyone waved back. The attendant was calling encouragement to Wayne, 94, in particular.

"Garraty," McVries said quietly.

"What?"

"I couldn't tell all the guys that bought it. Could you?"

"No."

"Barkovitch?"

"No. Up ahead. In front of Scramm. See him?"

McVries looked. "Oh. Yeah, I think I do."

"Stebbins is still back there, too."

"Not surprised. Funny guy, isn't he?"

"Yeah."

There was silence between them. McVries sighed deeply, then unshouldered his knapsack and pulled out some macaroons. He offered one to Garraty, who took one. "I wish this was over," he said. "One way or the other."

They ate their macaroons in silence.

"We must be halfway to Oldtown, huh?" McVries said. "Eighty down, eighty to go?"

"I guess so," Garraty said.

"Won't get there until tonight, then."

The mention of night made Garraty's flesh crawl. "No," he said. Then, abruptly: "How'd you get that scar, Pete?"

McVries's hand went involuntarily to his cheek and the scar. "It's a long story," he said briefly.

Garraty took a closer look at him. His hair was rumpled and clotty with dust and sweat. His clothes were limp and wrinkled. His face was pallid and his eyes were deeply circled in their bloodshot orbs.

"You look like shit," he said, and suddenly burst out laughing.

McVries grinned. "You don't exactly look like a deodorant ad yourself, Ray."

They both laughed then, long and hysterically, clutching each other and trying to keep walking at the same time. It was as good a way as any to put an end to the night once and for all. It went on until Garraty and McVries were both warned. They stopped laughing and talking then, and settled into the day's business.

Thinking, Garraty thought. That's the day's business. Thinking. Thinking and isolation, because it doesn't matter if you pass the time of day with someone or not; in the end, you're alone. He seemed to have put in as many miles in his brain as he had with his feet. The thoughts kept coming and there was no way to deny them. It was enough to make you wonder what Socrates had thought about right after he had tossed off his hemlock cocktail.

At a little past five o'clock they passed their first clump of bona fide spectators, four little boys sitting crosslegged like Indians outside a pup tent in a dewy field. One was still wrapped up in his sleeping bag, as solemn as an Eskimo. Their hands went back and forth like timed metronomes. None of them smiled.

Shortly afterward, the road forked into another, larger road. This one was a smooth, wide expanse of asphalt, three lanes wide. They passed a truck-stop restaurant, and everyone whistled and waved at the three young waitresses sitting on the steps, just to show them they were still starchy. The only one who sounded halfway serious was Collie Parker.

"Friday night," Collie yelled loudly. "Keep it in mind. You and me, Friday night."

Garraty thought they were all acting a little immature, but he waved politely and the waitresses seemed not to mind. The Walkers spread out across the wider road as more of them came fully awake to the May 2nd morning sunshine. Garraty caught sight of Barkovitch again and wondered if Barkovitch wasn't really one of the smart ones. With no friends you had no grief.

A few minutes later the word came back, and this time the word was a knock-knock joke. Bruce Pastor, the boy just in front of Garraty, turned around to Garraty and said, "Knock, knock, Garraty."

"Who's there?"

"Major."

"Major who?"

"Major buggers his mother before breakfast," Bruce Pastor said, and laughed uproariously. Garraty chuckled and passed it back to McVries, who passed it to Olson. When the joke came back the second time, the Major was buggering his grandmother before breakfast. The third time he was buggering Sheila, the Bedlington terrier that appeared with him in so many of his press releases.

Garraty was still laughing over that one when he noticed that McVries's laughter had tapered off and disappeared. He was staring with an odd fixity at the wooden-faced soldiers atop the halftrack. They were staring back impassively.

"You think that's *funny?*" he yelled suddenly. The sound of his shout cut cleanly through the laughter and silenced it. McVries's face was dark with suffused blood. The scar stood out in dead white contrast, like a slashed exclamation mark, and for one fear-filled moment Garraty thought he was having a stroke.

"Major buggers *himself,* that's what I think!" McVries cried hoarsely. "You guys, you probably bugger each other. Pretty funny, huh? Pretty funny, you bunch of motherfuckers, right? Pretty goddam *FUNNY, am I right?*"

Other Walkers stared uneasily at McVries and then eased away.

McVries suddenly ran at the halftrack. Two of the three soldiers raised their guns to high port, ready, but McVries halted, halted dead, and raised his fists at them, shaking them above his head like a mad conductor.

"Come on down here! Put down those rifles and come on down here! I'll show you what's funny!"

"Warning," one of them said in a perfectly neutral voice. "Warning 61. Second warning."

Oh my God, Garraty thought numbly. He's going to get it and he's so close . . . so close to them . . . he'll fly through the air just like Freaky D'Allessio.

McVries broke into a run, caught up with the halftrack, stopped, and spat on the side of it. The spittle cut a clean streak through the dust on the side of the halftrack.

"Come on!" McVries screamed. *"Come on down here! One at a time or all at once, I don't give a shit!"*

"Warning! Third Warning, 61, final warning."

"Fuck your warnings!"

Suddenly, unaware he was going to do it, Garraty turned and ran back, drawing his own warning. He only heard it with some back part of his mind. The soldiers were drawing down on McVries now. Garraty grabbed McVries's arm. "Come on."

"Get out of here, Ray, I'm gonna fight them!"

Garraty put out his hands and gave McVries a hard, flat shove. "You're going to get shot, you asshole."

Stebbins passed them by.

McVries looked at Garraty, seeming to recognize him for the first time. A second later Garraty drew his own third warning, and he knew McVries could only be seconds away from his ticket.

"Go to hell," McVries said in a dead, washed-out voice. He began to walk again.

Garraty walked with him. "I thought you were going to buy it, that's all," he said.

"But I didn't, thanks to the musketeer," McVries said sullenly. His hand went to the scar. "Fuck, we're all going to buy it."

"Somebody wins. It might be one of us."

"It's a fake," McVries said, his voice trembling. "There's no winner, no Prize. They take the last guy out behind a barn somewhere and shoot him too."

"Don't be so fucking stupid!" Garraty yelled at him furiously. "You don't have the slightest idea what you're sa—"

"Everyone loses," McVries said. His eyes peered out of the dark cave of his sockets like baleful animals. They were walking by themselves. The other Walkers were keeping away, at least for the time being. McVries had shown red, and so had Garraty, in a way—he had gone against his own best interest when he ran back to McVries. In all probability he had kept McVries from being number twenty-eight.

"Everyone loses," McVries repeated. "You better believe it."

They walked over a railroad track. They walked under a cement bridge. On the other side they passed a boarded-up Dairy Queen with a sign that read: WILL RE-OPEN FOR SEASON JUNE 5.

Olson drew a warning.

Garraty felt a tap on his shoulder and turned around. It was Stebbins. He looked no better or worse than he had the night before. "Your friend there is jerked at the Major," he said.

McVries showed no sign of hearing.

"I guess so, yeah," Garraty said. "I myself have passed the point where I'd want to invite him home for tea."

"Look behind us."

Garraty did. A second halftrack had rolled up, and as he looked, a third fell in behind it, coming in off a side road.

"The Major's coming," Stebbins said, "and everybody will cheer." He smiled, and his smile was oddly lizardlike. "They don't really hate him yet. Not yet. They just think they do. They think they've been through hell. But wait until tonight. Wait until *tomorrow*."

Garraty looked at Stebbins uneasily. "What if they hiss and boo and throw canteens at him, or something?"

"Are you going to hiss and boo and throw your canteen?"

"No."

"Neither will anyone else. You'll see."

"Stebbins?"

Stebbins raised his eyebrows.

"You think you'll win, don't you?"

"Yes," Stebbins said calmly. "I'm quite sure of it." And he dropped back to his usual position.

At 5:25 Yannick bought his ticket. And at 5:30 AM, just as Stebbins had predicted, the Major came.

There was a winding, growling roar as his jeep bounced over the crest of the hill behind them. Then it was roaring past them, along the shoulder. The Major was standing at full attention. As before, he was holding a stiff, eyes-right salute. A funny chill of pride went through Garraty's chest.

Not all of them cheered. Collie Parker spat on the ground. Barkovitch thumbed his nose. And McVries only looked, his lips moving soundlessly. Olson appeared not to notice at all as the Major went by; he was back to looking at his feet.

Garraty cheered. So did Percy What's-His-Name and Harkness, who wanted to write a book, and Wyman and Art Baker and Abraham and Sledge, who had just picked up his second warning.

Then the Major was gone, moving fast. Garraty felt a little ashamed of himself. He had, after all, wasted energy.

A short time later the road took them past a used car lot where they were given a twenty-one-horn salute. An amplified voice roaring out over double rows of fluttering plastic pennants told the Walkers—and the spectators—that no one outtraded McLaren's Dodge. Garraty found it all a little disheartening.

"You feel any better?" he asked McVries hesitantly.

"Sure," McVries said. "Great. I'm just going to walk along and watch them drop all around me. What fun it is. I just did all the division in my head—math was my good subject in school—and I figure we should be able to make at least three hundred and twenty miles at the rate we're going. That's not even a record distance."

"Why don't you just go and have it on someplace else if you're going to talk like that, Pete," Baker said. He sounded strained for the first time.

"Sorry, Mum," McVries said sullenly, but he shut up.

The day brightened. Garraty unzipped his fatigue jacket. He slung it over his shoulder. The road was level here. It was dotted with houses, small businesses, and occasional farms. The pines that had lined the road last night had given way to Dairy Queens and gas stations and little crackerbox ranchos. A great many of the ranchos were FOR SALE. In two of the windows Garraty saw the familiar signs: MY SON GAVE HIS LIFE IN THE SQUADS.

"Where's the ocean?" Collie Parker asked Garraty. "Looks like I was back in Illy-noy."

"Just keep walking," Garraty said. He was thinking of Jan and Freeport again. Freeport was on the ocean. "It's there. About a hundred and eight miles south."

"Shit," said Collie Parker. "What a dipshit state this is."

Parker was a big-muscled blond in a polo shirt. He had an insolent look in his eye that not even a night on the road had been able to knock out. "Goddam trees everyplace! Is there a city in the whole damn place?"

"We're funny up here," Garraty said. "We think it's fun to breathe real air instead of smog."

"Ain't no smog in Joliet, you fucking hick," Collie Parker said furiously. "What are you laying on me?"

"No smog but a lot of hot air," Garraty said. He was angry.

"If we was home, I'd twist your balls for that."

"Now boys," McVries said. He had recovered and was his old sardonic self again. "Why don't you settle this like gentlemen? First one to get his head blown off has to buy the other one a beer."

"I hate beer," Garraty said automatically.

Parker cackled. "You fucking bumpkin," he said, and walked away.

"He's buggy," McVries said. "Everybody's buggy this morning. Even me. And it's a beautiful day. Don't you agree, Olson?"

Olson said nothing.

"Olson's got bugs, too," McVries confided to Garraty. "Olson! Hey, Hank!"

"Why don't you leave him alone?" Baker asked.

"Hey *Hank!*" McVries shouted, ignoring Baker. "Wanna go for a walk?"

"Go to hell," Olson muttered.

"What?" McVries cried merrily, cupping a hand to his ear. "Wha choo say, bo?"

"Hell! *Hell!*" Olson screamed. "Go to hell!"

"Is *that* what you said." McVries nodded wisely.

Olson went back to looking at his feet, and McVries tired of baiting him . . . if that was what he was doing.

Garraty thought about what Parker had said. Parker was a bastard. Parker was a big drugstore cowboy and Saturday night tough guy. Parker was a leather jacket hero. What did he know about Maine? He had lived in Maine all his life, in a little town called Porterville, just west of Freeport. Population 970 and not so much as a blinker light and just what's so damn special about Joliet, Illy-noy anyway?

Garraty's father used to say Porterville was the only town in the county with more graveyards than people. But it was a clean place. The unemployment was high, the cars were rusty, and there was plenty of screwing around going on, but it was a clean place. The only action was Wednesday Bingo at the grange hall (last game a coverall for a twenty-pound turkey and a twenty-dollar bill), but it was clean. And it was quiet. What was wrong with that?

He looked at Collie Parker's back resentfully. You missed out, buddy, that's all. You take Joliet and your candy-store ratpack and your mills and you jam them. Jam them crossways, if they'll fit.

He thought about Jan again. He needed her. I love you, Jan, he thought. He wasn't dumb, and he knew she had become more to him than she actually was. She had turned into a life-symbol. A shield against the sudden death that came from the halftrack. More and more he wanted her because she symbolized the time when he could have a piece of ass—his own.

It was quarter of six in the morning now. He stared at a clump of cheering housewives bundled together near an intersection, small nerve-center of some unknown village. One of them was wearing tight slacks and a tighter sweater. Her face was plain. She wore three gold bracelets on her right wrist that clinked as she waved. Garraty could hear them clink. He waved back, not really thinking about it. He was thinking about Jan, who had come up from Connecticut, who had seemed so smooth and self-confident, with her long blond hair and her flat shoes. She alnost always wore flats because she was so tall. He met her at school. It went slow, but finally it clicked. God, had it clicked.

"Garraty?"

"Huh?"

It was Harkness. He looked concerned. "I got a cramp in my foot, man. I don't know if I can walk on it." Harkness's eyes seemed to be pleading for Garraty to do something.

Garraty didn't know what to say. Jan's voice, her laughter, the tawny caramel-colored sweater and her cranberry-red slacks, the time they took his little brother's sled and ended up making out in a snowbank (before she put snow down the back of his parka) . . . those things were life. Harkness was death. By now Garraty could smell it.

"I can't help you," Garraty said. "You have to do it yourself."

Harkness looked at him in panicked consternation, and then his face turned grim and he nodded. He stopped, kneeled, and fumbled off his loafer.

"Warning! Warning 49!"

He was massaging his foot now. Garraty had turned around and was walking backwards to watch him. Two small boys in Little League shirts with their baseball gloves hung from their bicycle handlebars were also watching him from the side of the road, their mouths hung open.

"Warning! Second warning, 49!"

Harkness got up and began to limp onward in his stocking foot, his good leg already trying to buckle with the extra weight it was bearing. He dropped his shoe, grabbed for it, got two fingers on it, juggled it, and lost it. He stopped to pick it up and got his third warning.

Harkness's normally florid face was now fire-engine red. His mouth hung open in a wet, sloppy O. Garraty found himself rooting for Harkness. Come on, he thought, come on, catch up. Harkness, you can.

Harkness limped faster. The Little League boys began to pedal along, watching him. Garraty turned around frontward, not wanting to watch Harkness anymore. He stared straight ahead, trying to remember just how it had felt to kiss Jan, to touch her swelling breast.

A Shell station came slowly up on the right. There was a dusty, fender-dented pickup parked on the tarmac, and two men in red-and-black-checked hunting shirts sitting on the tailgate, drinking beer. There was a mailbox at the end of a rutted dirt driveway, its lid hanging open like a mouth. A dog was barking hoarsely and endlessly somewhere just out of sight.

The carbines came slowly down from high port and found Harkness.

There was a long, terrible moment of silence, and then they went back up again to high port, all according to the rules, according to the book. Then they came down again. Garraty could hear Harkness's hurried, wet breathing.

The guns went back up, then down, then slowly back up to high port.

The two Little Leaguers were still keeping pace. "Get outta here!" Baker said suddenly, hoarsely. "You don't want to see this. Scat!"

They looked with flat curiosity at Baker and kept on. They had looked at Baker as if he was some kind of fish. One of them, a small, bulletheaded kid with a wiffle haircut and dish-sized eyes, blipped the horn bolted to his bike and grinned. He wore braces, and the sun made a savage metal glitter in his mouth.

The guns came back down. It was like some sort of dance movement, like a ritual. Harkness rode the edge. Read any good books lately? Garraty thought insanely. This time they're going to shoot you. Just one step too slow—

Eternity.

Everything frozen.

Then the guns went back up to high port.

Garraty looked at his watch. The second hand swung around once, twice, three times. Harkness caught up to him, passed him by. His face was set and rigid. His eyes looked straight ahead. His pupils were contracted to tiny points. His lips had a faint bluish cast, and his fiery complexion had faded to the color of cream, except for two garish spots of color, one on each cheek. But he was not favoring the bad foot anymore. The cramp had loosened. His stocking foot slapped the road rhythmically. How long can you walk without your shoes? Garraty wondered.

He felt a loosening in his chest all the same, and heard Baker let out his breath. It was stupid to feel that way. The sooner Harkness stopped walking, the sooner he could stop walking. That was the simple truth. That was logic. But something went deeper, a truer, more frightening logic. Harkness was a part of the group that Garraty was a part of, a segment of his subclan. Part of a magic circle that Garraty belonged to. And if one part of that circle could be broken, any part of it could be broken.

The Little Leaguers biked along with them for another two miles before losing interest and turning back. It was better, Garraty thought. It didn't matter if they had looked at Baker as though he were something in a zoo. It was better for them to be cheated of their death. He watched them out of sight.

Up ahead, Harkness had formed a new one-man vanguard, walking very rapidly, almost running. He looked neither right nor left. Garraty wondered what he was thinking.

Chapter 7

"I like to think I'm quite an engaging bloke, really.
People I meet consider I'm schizophrenic
just because I'm completely different offscreen
than I am before the cameras . . . "
—Nicholas Parsons
Sale of the Century
(British version)

Scramm, 85, did not fascinate Garraty because of his flashing intelligence, because Scramm wasn't all that bright. He didn't fascinate Garraty because of his moon face, his crew cut, or his build, which was mooselike. He fascinated Garraty because he was married.

"Really?" Garraty asked for the third time. He still wasn't convinced Scramm wasn't having him on. "You're really married?"

"Yeah." Scramm looked up at the early morning sun with real pleasure. "I dropped out of school when I was fourteen. There was no point to it, not for me. I wasn't no troublemaker, just not able to make grades. And our history teacher read us an article about how schools are overpopulated. So I figured why not let somebody who can learn sit in, and I'll get down to business. I wanted to marry Cathy anyway."

"How old were you?" Garraty asked, more fascinated than ever. They were passing through another small town, and the sidewalks were lined with signs and spectators, but he hardly noticed. Already the watchers were in another world, not related to him in any way. They might have been behind a thick plate-glass shield.

"Fifteen," Scramm answered. He scratched his chin, which was blue with beard stubble.

"No one tried to talk you out of it?"

"There was a guidance counselor at school, he gave me a lot of shit about sticking with it and not being a ditch digger, but he had more important things to do besides keep me in school. I guess you could say he gave me the soft sell. Besides, somebody has to dig ditches, right?"

He waved enthusiastically at a group of little girls who were going through a spastic cheerleader routine, pleated skirts and scabbed knees flying.

"Anyhow, I never did dig no ditch. Never dug a one in my whole career. Went to work for a bedsheet factory out in Phoenix, three dollars an hour. Me and Cathy, we're happy people." Scramm smiled. "Sometimes we'll be watching TV and Cath will grab me and say, 'We're happy people, honey.' She's a peach."

"You got any kids?" Garraty asked, feeling more and more that this was an insane discussion.

"Well, Cathy's pregnant right now. She said we should wait until we had enough in the bank to pay for the delivery. When we got up to seven hundred, she said go, and we went. She caught pregnant in no time at all." Scramm looked sternly at Garraty. "My kid's going to college. They say dumb guys like me never have smart kids, but Cathy's smart enough for both of us. Cathy finished high school. I made her finish. Four night courses and then she took the H.S.E.T. My kid's going to as much college as he wants."

Garraty didn't say anything. He couldn't think of anything to say. McVries was off to the side, in close conversation with Olson. Baker and Abraham were playing a word game called Ghost. He wondered where Harkness was. Far out of sight, anyway. That was Scramm, too. Really out of sight. Hey Scramm, I think you made a bad mistake. Your wife, she's *pregnant,* Scramm, but that doesn't win you any special favors around here. Seven hundred in the bank? You don't spell *pregnant* with just three numbers, Scramm. And no insurance company in the world would touch a Long Walker.

Garraty stared at and through a man in a hound's tooth jacket who was deliriously waving a straw hat with a stringy brim.

"Scramm, what happens if you buy it?" he asked cautiously.

Scramm smiled gently. "Not me. I feel like I could walk forever. Say, I wanted to be in the Long Walk ever since I was old enough to want anything. I walked eighty miles just two weeks ago, no sweat."

"But suppose something should happen—"

But Scramm only chuckled.

"How old's Cathy?"

"About a year older than me. Almost eighteen. Her folks are with her now, there in Phoenix."

It sounded to Garraty as if Cathy Scramm's folks knew something Scramm himself did not.

"You must love her a lot," he said, a little wistfully.

Scramm smiled, showing the stubborn last survivors of his teeth. "I ain't looked at anyone else since I married her. Cathy's a peach."

"And you're doing this."

Scramm laughed. "Ain't it fun?"

"Not for Harkness," Garraty said sourly. "Go ask him if he thinks it's fun."

"You don't have any grasp of the consequences," Pearson said, falling in between Garraty and Scramm. "You *could* lose. You have to admit you *could* lose."

"Vegas odds made me the favorite just before the Walk started," Scramm said. "Odds-on."

"Sure," Pearson said glumly. "And you're in shape, too, anyone can see that." Pearson himself looked pale and peaked after the long night on the road. He glanced disinterestedly at the crowd gathered in a supermarket parking lot they were just passing. "Everyone who wasn't in shape is dead now, or almost dead. But there's still seventy-two of us left."

"Yeah, but . . . " A thinking frown spread over the broad circle of Scramm's face. Garraty could almost hear the machinery up there working: slow, ponderous, but in the end as sure as death and as inescapable as taxes. It was somehow awesome.

"I don't want to make you guys mad," Scramm said. "You're good guys. But you didn't get into this thinking of winning out and getting the Prize. Most of these guys don't know why they got into it. Look at that Barkovitch. He ain't in it to get no Prize. He's just walkin' to see other people die. He lives on it. When someone gets a ticket, he gets a little more go-power. It ain't enough. He'll dry up just like a leaf on a tree."

"And me?" Garraty asked.

Scramm looked troubled. "Aw, hell . . . "

"No, go on."

"Well, the way I see it, you don't know why you're walking, either. It's the same thing. You're going now because you're afraid, but . . . that's not enough. That wears out." Scramm looked down at the road and rubbed his hands together. "And when it wears out, I guess you'll buy a ticket like all the rest, Ray."

Garraty thought about McVries saying, *When I get tired . . . really tired . . . why, I guess I will sit down.*

"You'll have to walk a long time to walk me down," Garraty said, but Scramm's simple assessment of the situation had scared him badly.

"I," Scramm said, "am ready to walk a long time."

Their feet rose and fell on the asphalt, carrying them forward, around a curve, down into a dip and then over a railroad track that was metal grooves in the road. They passed a closed fried clam shack. Then they were out in the country again.

"I understand what it is to die, I think," Pearson said abruptly. "Now I do, anyway. Not death itself, I still can't comprehend that. But dying. If I stop walking, I'll come to an end." He swallowed, and there was a click in his throat. "Just like a record after the last groove." He looked at Scramm earnestly. "Maybe it's like you say. Maybe it's not enough. But . . . I don't want to die."

Scramm looked at him almost scornfully. "You think just knowing about death will keep you from dying?"

Pearson smiled a funny, sick little smile, like a businessman on a heaving boat trying to keep his dinner down. "Right now that's about all that's keeping me going." And Garraty felt a huge gratefulness, because his defenses had not been reduced to that. At least, not yet.

Up ahead, quite suddenly and as if to illustrate the subject they had been discussing, a boy in a black turtleneck sweater suddenly had a convulsion. He fell on the road and began to snap and sunfish and jackknife viciously. His limbs jerked and flopped. There was a funny gargling noise in his throat, *aaa-aaa-aaa*, a sheeplike sound that was entirely mindless. As Garraty hurried past, one of the fluttering hands bounced against his shoe and he felt a wave of frantic revulsion. The boy's eyes were rolled up to the whites. There were splotches of foam splattered on his lips and chin. He was being second-warned, but of course he was beyond hearing, and when his two minutes were up they shot him like a dog.

Not long after that they reached the top of a gentle grade and stared down into the green, unpopulated country ahead. Garraty was grateful for the cool morning breeze that slipped over his fast-perspiring body.

"That's some view," Scramm said.

The road could be seen for perhaps twelve miles ahead. It slid down the long slope, ran in flat zigzags through the woods, a blackish-gray charcoal mark across a green swatch of crepe paper. Far ahead it began to climb again, and faded into the rosy-pink haze of early morning light.

"This might be what they call the Hainesville Woods," Garraty said, not too sure. "Truckers' graveyard. Hell in the wintertime."

"I never seen nothing like it," Scramm said reverently. "There isn't this much green in the whole state of Arizona."

"Enjoy it while you can," Baker said, joining the group. "It's going to be a scorcher. It's hot already and it's only six-thirty in the morning."

"Think you'd get used to it, where you come from," Pearson said, almost resentfully.

"You don't get used to it," Baker said, slinging his light jacket over his arm. "You just learn to live with it."

"I'd like to build a house up here," Scramm said. He sneezed heartily, twice, sounding a little like a bull in heat. "Build it right up here with my own two hands, and look at the view every morning. Me and Cathy. Maybe I will someday, when this is all over."

Nobody said anything.

By 6:45 the ridge was above and behind them, the breeze mostly cut off, and the heat already walked among them. Garraty took off his own jacket, rolled it, and tied it securely about his waist. The road through the woods was no longer deserted. Here and there early risers had parked their cars off the road and stood or sat in clumps, cheering, waving, and holding signs.

Two girls stood beside a battered MG at the bottom of one dip. They were wearing tight summer shorts, middy blouses, and sandals. There were cheers and whistles. The faces of these girls were hot, flushed, and excited by something ancient, sinuous, and, to Garraty, erotic almost to the point of insanity. He felt animal lust rising in him, an aggressively alive thing that made his body shake with a palsied fever all its own.

It was Gribble, the radical among them, that suddenly dashed at them, his feet kicking up spurts of dust along the shoulder. One of them leaned back against the hood of the MG and spread her legs slightly, tilting her hips at him. Gribble put his hands over her breasts. She made no effort to stop him. He was warned, hesitated, and then plunged against her, a jamming, hurtling, frustrated, angry, frightened figure in a sweaty white shirt and cord pants. The girl hooked her ankles around Gribble's calves and put her arms lightly around his neck. They kissed.

Gribble took a second warning, then a third, and then, with perhaps fifteen seconds of grace left, he stumbled away and broke into a frantic, shambling run. He fell down, picked himself up, clutched at his crotch and staggered back onto the road. His thin face was hectically flushed.

"Couldn't," he was sobbing. "Wasn't enough time and she wanted me to and I couldn't . . . I . . ." He was weeping and staggering, his hands pressed against his crotch. His words were little more than indistinct wails.

"So you gave them their little thrill," Barkovitch said. "Something for them to talk about in Show and Tell tomorrow."

"Just shut up!" Gribble screamed. He dug at his crotch. "It hurts, I got a cramp—"

"Blue balls," Pearson said. "That's what he's got."

Gribble looked at him through the stringy bangs of black hair that had fallen over his eyes. He looked like a stunned weasel. "It hurts," he muttered again. He dropped slowly to his knees, hands pressed into his lower belly, head drooping, back bowed. He was shivering and snuffling and Garraty could see the beads of sweat on his neck, some of them caught in the fine hairs on the nape—what Garraty's own father had always called quackfuzz.

A moment later and he was dead.

Garraty turned his head to look at the girls, but they had retreated inside their MG. They were nothing but shadow-shapes.

He made a determined effort to push them from his mind, but they kept creeping back in. How must it have been, dry-humping that warm, willing flesh? Her thighs had twitched, my God, they had *twitched,* in a kind of spasm, orgasm, oh God, the uncontrollable urge to squeeze and caress . . . and most of all to feel that heat . . . *that heat*

He felt himself go. That warm, shooting flow of sensation, warming him. Wetting him. Oh Christ, it would soak through his pants and someone would notice. Notice and point a finger and ask him how he'd like to walk around the neighborhood with no clothes on, walk naked, walk . . . and walk . . . and walk . . .

Oh Jan I love you really I love you, he thought, but it was confused, all mixed up in something else.

He retied his jacket about his waist and then went on walking as before, and the memory dulled and browned very quickly, like a Polaroid negative left out in the sun.

The pace stepped up. They were on a steep downhill grade now, and it was hard to walk slowly. Muscles worked and pistoned and squeezed against each other. The sweat rolled freely. Incredibly, Garraty found himself wishing for night again. He looked over at Olson curiously, wondering how he was making it.

Olson was staring at his feet again. The cords in his neck were knotted and ridged. His lips were drawn back in a frozen grin.

"He's almost there now," McVries said at his elbow, startling him. "When they start half-hoping someone will shoot them so they can rest their feet, they're not far away."

"Is that right?" Garraty asked crossly. "How come everybody else around here knows so much more about it than me?"

"Because you're so sweet," McVries said tenderly, and then he sped up, letting his legs catch the downgrade, and passed Garraty by.

Stebbins. He hadn't thought about Stebbins in a long time. He turned his head to look for Stebbins. Stebbins was there. The pack had strung out coming down the long hill, and Stebbins was about a quarter of a mile back, but there was no mistaking those purple pants and that chambray workshirt. Stebbins was still tailing the pack like some thin vulture, just waiting for them to fall—

Garraty felt a wave of rage. He had a sudden urge to rush back and throttle Stebbins. There was no rhyme or reason to it, but he had to actively fight the compulsion down.

By the time they had reached the bottom of the grade, Garraty's legs felt rubbery and unsteady. The state of numb weariness his flesh had more or less settled into was broken by unexpected darning-needles of pain that drove through his feet and legs, threatening to make his muscles knot and cramp. And Jesus, he thought, why not? They had been on the road for twenty-two hours. Twenty-two hours of nonstop walking, it was unbelievable.

"How do you feel now?" he asked Scramm, as if the last time he had asked him had been twelve hours ago.

"Fit and fine," Scramm said. He wiped the back of his hand across his nose, sniffed, and spat. "Just as fit and fine as can be."

"You sound like you're getting a cold."

"Naw, it's the pollen. Happens every spring. Hay fever. I even get it in Arizona. But I never catch colds."

Garraty opened his mouth to reply when a hollow, *poom-poom* sound echoed back from far ahead. It was rifle fire. The word came back. Harkness had burnt out.

There was an odd, elevatorish sensation in Garraty's stomach as he passed the word on back. The magic circle was broken. Harkness would never write his book about the Long Walk. Harkness was being dragged off the road someplace up ahead like a grain bag or was being tossed into a truck, wrapped securely in a canvas bodybag. For Harkness, the Long Walk was over.

"Harkness," McVries said. "Ol' Harkness bought a ticket to see the farm."

"Why don't you write him a poime?" Barkovitch called over.

"Shut up, killer," McVries answered absently. He shook his head. "Ol' Harkness, sonofabitch."

"I ain't no killer!" Barkovitch screamed. "I'll dance on your grave, scarface! I'll—"

A chorus of angry shouts silenced him. Muttering, Barkovitch glared at McVries. Then he began to stalk on a little faster, not looking around.

"You know what my uncle did?" Baker said suddenly. They were passing through a shady tunnel of overleafing trees, and Garraty was trying to forget about Harkness and Gribble and think only of the coolness.

"What?" Abraham asked.

"He was an undertaker," Baker said.

"Good deal," Abraham said disinterestedly.

"When I was a kid, I always used to wonder," Baker said vaguely. He seemed to lose track of his thought, then glanced at Garraty and smiled. It was a peculiar smile. "Who'd embalm him, I mean. Like you wonder who cuts the barber's hair or who operates on the doctor for gallstones. See?"

"It takes a lot of gall to be a doctor," McVries said solemnly.

"You know what I mean."

"So who got the call when the time came?" Abraham asked.

"Yeah," Scramm added. "Who did?"

Baker looked up at the twining, heavy branches under which they were passing, and Garraty noticed again that Baker now looked exhausted. Not that we don't all look that way, he added to himself.

"Come on," McVries said. "Don't keep us hanging. Who buried him?"

"This is the oldest joke in the world," Abraham said. "Baker says, whatever made you think he was dead?"

"He is, though," Baker said. "Lung cancer. Six years ago."

"Did he smoke?" Abraham asked, waving at a family of four and their cat. The cat was on a leash. It was a Persian cat. It looked mean and pissed off.

"No, not even a pipe," Baker said. "He was afraid it would give him cancer."

"Oh, for Christ's sake," McVries said, "who *buried* him? Tell us so we can discuss world problems, or baseball, or birth control or something."

"I think birth control *is* a world problem," Garraty said seriously. "My girl-friend is a Catholic and—"

"*Come on!*" McVries bellowed. "Who the fuck buried your grandfather, Baker?"

"My uncle. He was my uncle. My grandfather was a lawyer in Shreveport. He—"

"I don't give a shit," McVries said. "I don't give a shit if the old gentleman had three cocks, I just want to know who buried him so we can get *on*."

"Actually, nobody buried him. He wanted to be cremated."

"Oh my aching balls," Abraham said, and then laughed a little.

"My aunt's got his ashes in a ceramic vase. At her house in Baton Rouge. She tried to keep the business going—the undertaking business—but nobody much seemed to cotton to a lady undertaker."

"I doubt if that was it," McVries said.

"No?"

"No. I think your uncle jinxed her."

"Jinx? How do you mean?" Baker was interested.

"Well, you have to admit it wasn't a very good advertisement for the business."

"What, dying?"

"No," McVries said. "Getting cremated."

Scramm chuckled stuffily through his plugged nose. "He's got you there, old buddy."

"I expect he might," Baker said. He and McVries beamed at each other.

"Your uncle," Abraham said heavily, "bores the tits off me. And might I also add that he—"

At that moment, Olson began begging one of the guards to let him rest.

He did not stop walking, or slow down enough to be warned, but his voice rose and fell in a begging, pleading, totally craven monotone that made Garraty crawl with embarrassment for him. Conversation lagged. Spectators watched Olson with horrified fascination. Garraty wished Olson would shut up before he gave the rest of them a black eye. He didn't want to die either, but if he had to he wanted to go out without people thinking he was a coward. The soldiers stared over Olson, through him, around him, wooden-faced, deaf and dumb. They gave an occasional warning, though, so Garraty supposed you couldn't call them dumb.

It got to be quarter to eight, and the word came back that they were just six miles short of one hundred miles. Garraty could remember reading that the largest number to ever complete the first hundred miles of a Long Walk was sixty-three. They looked a sure bet to crack that record; there were still sixty-nine in this group. Not that it mattered, one way or the other.

Olson's pleas rose in a constant, garbled litany to Garraty's left, somehow seeming to make the day hotter and more uncomfortable than it was. Several of the boys had shouted at Olson, but he seemed either not to hear or not to care.

They passed through a wooden covered bridge, the planks rumbling and bumping under their feet. Garraty could hear the secretive flap and swoop of the barn swallows that had made their homes among the rafters. It was refreshingly cool, and the sun seemed to drill down even hotter when they reached the other side. Wait till later if you think it's hot now, he told himself. Wait until you get back into open country. Boy howdy.

He yelled for a canteen, and a soldier trotted over with one. He handed it to Garraty wordlessly, then trotted back. Garraty's stomach was also growling for food. At nine o'clock, he thought. Have to keep walking until then. Be damned if I'm going to die on an empty stomach.

Baker cut past him suddenly, looked around for spectators, saw none, dropped his britches and squatted. He was warned. Garraty passed him, but heard the soldier warn him again. About twenty seconds after that he caught up with Garraty and McVries again, badly out of breath. He was cinching his pants.

"Fastest crap I *evah* took!" he said, badly out of breath.

"You should have brought a catalogue along," McVries said.

"I never could go very long without a crap," Baker said. "Some guys, hell, they crap once a week. I'm a once-a-day man. If I don't crap once a day, I take a laxative."

"Those laxatives will ruin your intestines," Pearson said.

"Oh, shit," Baker scoffed.

McVries threw back his head and laughed.

Abraham twisted his head around to join the conversation. "My grandfather never used a laxative in his life and he lived to be—"

"You kept records, I presume," Pearson said.

"You wouldn't be doubting my grandfather's word, would you?"

"Heaven forbid." Pearson rolled his eyes.

"Okay. My grandfather—"

"Look," Garraty said softly. Not interested in either side of the laxative argument, he had been idly watching Percy What's-His-Name. Now he was watching him closely, hardly believing what his eyes were seeing. Percy had been edging closer and closer to the side of the road. Now he was walking on the sandy shoulder. Every now and then he snapped a tight, frightened glance at the soldiers on top of the halftrack, then to his right, at the thick screen of trees less than seven feet away.

"I think he's going to break for it," Garraty said.

"They'll shoot him sure as hell," Baker said. His voice had dropped to a whisper.

"Doesn't look like anyone's watching him," Pearson replied.

"Then for God's sake, don't tip them!" McVries said angrily. "You bunch of dummies! Christ!"

For the next ten minutes none of them said anything sensible. They aped conversation and watched Percy watching the soldiers, watching and mentally gauging the short distance to the thick woods.

"He hasn't got the guts," Pearson muttered finally, and before any of them could answer, Percy began walking, slowly and unhurriedly, toward the woods. Two steps, then three. One more, two at the most, and he would be there. His jeans-clad legs moved unhurriedly. His sun-bleached blond hair ruffled just a little in a light puff of breeze. He might have been an Explorer Scout out for a day of bird-watching.

There were no warnings. Percy had forfeited his right to them when his right foot passed over the verge of the shoulder. Percy had left the road, and the soldiers had known all along. Old Percy What's-His-Name hadn't been fooling anybody. There was one sharp, clean report, and Garraty jerked his eyes from Percy to the soldier standing on the back deck of the halftrack. The soldier was a sculpture in clean, angular lines, the rifle nestled into the hollow of his shoulder, his head half-cocked along the barrel.

Then his head swiveled back to Percy again. Percy was the real show, wasn't he? Percy was standing with both his feet on the weedy border of the pine forest now. He was as frozen and as sculpted as the man who had shot him. The two of them together would have been a subject for Michelangelo, Garraty thought. Percy stood utterly still under a blue springtime sky. One hand was pressed to his chest, like a poet about to speak. His eyes were wide, and somehow ecstatic.

A bright seepage of blood ran through his fingers, shining in the sunlight. Old Percy What's-Your-Name. Hey Percy, your mother's calling. Hey Percy, does your mother know you're out? Hey Percy, what kind of silly sissy name is that,

Percy, Percy, aren't you cute? Percy transformed into a bright, sunlit Adonis counterpointed by the savage, duncolored huntsman. And one, two, three coin-shaped splatters of blood fell on Percy's travel-dusty black shoes, and all of it happened in a space of only three seconds. Garraty did not take even two full steps and he was not warned, and oh Percy, what *is* your mother going to say? Do you, tell me, *do* you really have the *nerve* to die?

Percy did. He pitched forward, struck a small, crooked sapling, rolled through a half-turn, and landed face-up to the sky. The grace, the frozen symmetry, they were gone now. Percy was just dead.

"Let this ground be seeded with salt," McVries said suddenly, very rapidly. "So that no stalk of corn or stalk of wheat shall ever grow. Cursed be the children of this ground and cursed be their loins. Also cursed be their hams and hocks. Hail Mary full of grace, let us blow this goddam place."

McVries began to laugh.

"Shut up," Abraham said hoarsely. "Stop talking like that."

"All the world is God," McVries said, and giggled hysterically. "We're *walking* on the Lord, and back there the flies are *crawling* on the Lord, in fact the flies are also the Lord, so blessed be the fruit of thy womb Percy. Amen, hallelujah, chunky peanut butter. Our father, which art in tinfoil, hallow'd be thy name."

"I'll hit you!" Abraham warned. His face was very pale. "I will, Pete!"

"A *praaayin'* man!" McVries gibed, and he giggled again. "Oh my suds and body! Oh my sainted *hat!*"

"I'll hit you if you don't shut up!" Abraham bellowed.

"Don't," Garraty said, frightened. "Please don't fight. Let's . . . be nice."

"Want a party favor?" Baker asked crazily.

"Who asked you, you goddam redneck?"

"He was awful young to be on this hike," Baker said sadly. "If he was fourteen, I'll smile 'n' kiss a pig."

"Mother spoiled him," Abraham said in a trembling voice. "You could tell." He looked around at Garraty and Pearson pleadingly. "You could tell, couldn't you?"

"She won't spoil him anymore," McVries said.

Olson suddenly began babbling at the soldiers again. The one who had shot Percy was now sitting down and eating a sandwich. They walked past eight o'clock. They passed a sunny gas station where a mechanic in greasy coveralls was hosing off the tarmac.

"Wish he'd spray us with some of that," Scramm said. "I'm as hot as a poker."

"We're all hot," Garraty said.

"I thought it never got hot in Maine," Pearson said. He sounded more tired than ever. "I thought Maine was s'posed to be cool."

"Well then, now you know different," Garraty said shortly.

"You're a lot of fun, Garraty," Pearson said. "You know that? You're really a lot of fun. Gee, I'm glad I met you."

McVries laughed.

"You know what?" Garraty replied.

"What?"

"You got skidmarks in your underwear," Garraty said. It was the wittiest thing he could think of at short notice.

They passed another truck stop. Two or three big rigs were pulled in, hauled off the highway no doubt to make room for the Long Walkers. One of the drivers was standing anxiously by his rig, a huge refrigerator truck, and feeling the side. Feeling the cold that was slipping away in the morning sun. Several of the waitresses cheered as the Walkers trudged by, and the trucker who had been feeling the side of his refrigerator compartment turned and gave them the finger. He was a huge man with a red neck bulling its way out of a dirty T-shirt.

"Now why'd he wanna do that?" Scramm cried. "Just a rotten old sport!"

McVries laughed. "That's the first honest citizen we've seen since this clambake got started, Scramm. Man, do I love him!"

"Probably he's loaded up with perishables headed for Montreal," Garraty said. "All the way from Boston. We forced him off the road. He's probably afraid he'll lose his job—or his rig, if he's an independent."

"Isn't that tough?" Collie Parker brayed. "Isn't that too goddam tough? They only been tellin' people what the route was gonna be for two months or more. Just another goddam hick, that's all!"

"You seem to know a lot about it," Abraham said to Garraty.

"A little," Garraty said, staring at Parker. "My father drove a rig before he got . . . before he went away. It's a hard job to make a buck in. Probably that guy back there thought he had time to make it to the next cutoff. He wouldn't have come this way if there was a shorter route."

"He didn't have to give us the finger," Scramm insisted. "He didn't have to do that. By God, his rotten old tomatoes ain't life and death, like this is."

"Your father took off on your mother?" McVries asked Garraty.

"My dad was Squaded," Garraty said shortly. Silently he dared Parker—or anyone else—to open his mouth, but no one said anything.

Stebbins was still walking last. He had no more than passed the truck stop before the burly driver was swinging back up into the cab of his jimmy. Up ahead, the guns cracked out their single word. A body spun, flipped over, and lay still. Two soldiers dragged it over to the side of the road. A third tossed them a bodybag from the halftrack.

"I had an uncle that was Squaded," Wyman said hesitantly. Garraty noticed that the tongue of Wyman's left shoe had worked out from beneath the lacings and was flapping obscenely.

"No one but goddam fools get Squaded," Collie Parker said clearly.

Garraty looked at him and wanted to feel angry, but he dropped his head and stared at the road. His father had been a goddam fool, all right. A goddam drunkard who could not keep two cents together in the same place for long no matter what he tried his hand at, a man without the sense to keep his political opinions to himself. Garraty felt old and sick.

"Shut your stinking trap," McVries said coldly.

"You want to try and make m—"

"No, I don't want to try and make you. Just shut up, you sonofabitch."

Collie Parker dropped back between Garraty and McVries. Pearson and Abraham moved away a little. Even the soldiers straightened, ready for trouble. Parker studied Garraty for a long moment. His face was broad and beaded with sweat, his eyes still arrogant. Then he clapped Garraty briefly on the arm.

"I got a loose lip sometimes. I didn't mean nothing by it. Okay?" Garraty nodded wearily, and Parker shifted his glance to McVries. "Piss on you, Jack," he said, and moved up again toward the vanguard.

"What an unreal bastard," McVries said glumly.

"No worse than Barkovitch," Abraham said. "Maybe even a little better."

"Besides," Pearson added, "what's getting Squaded? It beats the hell out of getting dead, am I right?"

"How would you know?" Garraty asked. "How would any of us know?"

His father had been a sandy-haired giant with a booming voice and a bellowing laugh that had sounded to Garraty's small ears like mountains cracking open. After he lost his own rig, he made a living driving Government trucks out of Brunswick. It would have been a good living if Jim Garraty could have kept his politics to himself. But when you work for the Government, the Government is twice as aware that you're alive, twice as ready to call in a Squad if things seem a little dicky around the edges. And Jim Garraty had not been much of a Long Walk booster. So one day he got a telegram and the next day two soldiers turned up on the doorstep and Jim Garraty had gone with them, blustering, and his wife had closed the door and her cheeks had been pale as milk and when Garraty asked his mother where Daddy was going with the soldier mens, she had slapped him hard enough to make his mouth bleed and told him to shut up, shut up. Garraty had never seen his father since. It had been eleven years. It had been a neat removal. Odorless, sanitized, pasteurized, sanforized, and dandruff-free.

"I had a brother that was in law trouble," Baker said. "Not the Government, just the law. He stole himself a car and drove all the way from our town to Hattiesburg, Mississippi. He got two years' suspended sentence. He's dead now."

"Dead?" The voice was a dried husk, wraithlike. Olson had joined them. His haggard face seemed to stick out a mile from his body.

"He had a heart attack," Baker said. "He was only three years older than me. Ma used to say he was her cross, but he only got into bad trouble that once. I did worse. I was a night rider for three years."

Garraty looked over at him. There was shame in Baker's tired face, but there was also dignity there, outlined against a dusky shaft of sunlight poking through the trees.

"That's a Squading offense, but I didn't care. I was only twelve when I got into it. Ain't hardly nothing but kids who go night-riding now, you know. Older heads are wiser heads. They'd tell us to go to it and pat our heads, but they weren't out to get Squaded, not them. I got out after we burnt a cross on some black man's lawn. I was scairt green. And ashamed, too. Why does anybody want to go burning a cross on some black man's lawn? Jesus Christ, that stuff's history, ain't it? Sure it is." Baker shook his head vaguely. "It wasn't right."

At that moment the rifles went again.

"There goes one more," Scramm said. His voice sounded clogged and nasal, and he wiped his nose with the back of his hand.

"Thirty-four," Pearson said. He took a penny out of one pocket and put it in the other. "I brought along ninety-nine pennies. Every time someone buys a ticket, I put one of 'em in the other pocket. And when—"

"That's gruesome!" Olson said. His haunted eyes stared balefully at Pearson. "Where's your death watch? Where's your voodoo dolls?"

Pearson didn't say anything. He studied the fallow field they were passing with anxious embarrassment. Finally he muttered, "I didn't mean to say anything about it. It was for good luck, that was all."

"It's dirty," Olson croaked. "It's *filthy.* It's—"

"Oh, quit it," Abraham said. "Quit getting on my nerves."

Garraty looked at his watch. It was twenty past eight. Forty minutes to food. He thought how nice it would be to go into one of those little roadside diners that dotted the road, snuggle his fanny against one of the padded counter stools, put his feet up on the rail (oh God, the relief of just that!) and order steak and fried onions, with a side of French fries and a big dish of vanilla ice cream with strawberry sauce for dessert. Or maybe a big plate of spaghetti and meatballs, with Italian bread and peas swimming in butter on the side. And milk. A whole pitcher of milk. To hell with the tubes and the canteens of distilled water. Milk and solid food and a place to sit and eat it in. Would that be fine?

Just ahead a family of five—mother, father, boy, girl, and white-haired grandmother—were spread beneath a large elm, eating a picnic breakfast of sandwiches and what looked like hot cocoa. They waved cheerily at the Walkers.

"Freaks," Garraty muttered.

"What was that?" McVries asked.

"I said I want to sit down and have something to eat. Look at those people. Fucking bunch of pigs."

"You'd be doing the same thing," McVries said. He waved and smiled, saving the biggest, flashiest part of the smile for the grandmother, who was waving back and chewing—well, gumming was closer to the truth—what looked like an egg salad sandwich.

"The hell I would. Sit there and eat while a bunch of starving—"

"Hardly starving, Ray. It just feels that way."

"*Hungry,* then—"

"Mind over matter," McVries incanted. "Mind over matter, my young friend." The incantation had become a seamy imitation of W.C. Fields.

"To hell with you. You just don't want to admit it. Those people, they're animals. They want to see someone's brains on the road, that's why they turn out. They'd just as soon see yours."

"That isn't the point," McVries said calmly. "Didn't you say you went to see the Long Walk when you were younger?"

"Yes, when I didn't know any better!"

"Well, that makes it okay, doesn't it?" McVries uttered a short, ugly-sounding laugh. "Sure they're animals. You think you just found out a new principle? Sometimes I wonder just how naive you really are. The French lords and ladies used to screw after the guillotinings. The old Romans used to stuff each other during the gladiatorial matches. That's entertainment, Garraty. It's nothing new." He laughed again. Garraty stared at him, fascinated.

"Go on," someone said. "You're at second base, McVries. Want to try for third?"

Garraty didn't have to turn. It was Stebbins, of course. Stebbins the lean Buddha. His feet carried him along automatically, but he was dimly aware that they felt swollen and slippery, as if they were filling with pus.

"Death is great for the appetites," McVries said. "How about those two girls and Gribble? They wanted to see what screwing a dead man felt like. Now for Something Completely New and Different. I don't know if Gribble got much out of it, but they sure as shit did. It's the same with anybody. It doesn't matter if they're eating or drinking or sitting on their cans. They like it better, they feel it and taste it better because they're watching dead men.

"But even that's not the real point of this little expedition, Garraty. The point is, they're the smart ones. *They're* not getting thrown to the lions. *They're* not staggering along and hoping they won't have to take a shit with two warnings against them. You're dumb, Garraty. You and me and Pearson and Barkovitch and Stebbins, we're all dumb. Scramm's dumb because he thinks he understands and he doesn't. Olson's dumb because he understood too much too late. They're animals, all right. But why are you so goddam sure that makes us human beings?"

He paused, badly out of breath.

"There," he said. "You went and got me going. Sermonette No. 342 in a series of six thousand, et cetera, et cetera. Probably cut my lifespan by five hours or more."

"Then why are you doing it?" Garraty asked him. "If you know that much, and if you're that sure, why are you doing it?"

"The same reason we're all doing it," Stebbins said. He smiled gently, almost lovingly. His lips were a little sunparched; otherwise, his face was still unlined and seemingly invincible. "We want to die, that's why we're doing it. Why else, Garraty? Why else?"

Chapter 8

"Three-six-nine, the goose drank wine
The monkey chewed tobacco on the streetcar line
The line broke
The monkey got choked
And they all went to heaven in a little rowboat . . . "
—Children's rhyme

Ray Garraty cinched the concentrate belt tightly around his waist and firmly told himself he would eat absolutely nothing until nine-thirty at least. He could tell it was going to be a hard resolution to keep. His stomach gnawed and growled. All around him Walkers were compulsively celebrating the end of the first twenty-four hours on the road.

Scramm grinned at Garraty through a mouthful of cheese spread and said something pleasant but untranslatable. Baker had his vial of olives—real olives—and was popping them into his mouth with machine-gun regularity. Pearson was jamming crackers mounded high with tuna spread into his mouth, and McVries was slowly eating chicken spread. His eyes were half-lidded, and he might have been in extreme pain or at the pinnacle of pleasure.

Two more of them had gone down between eight-thirty and nine; one of them had been the Wayne that the gas jockey had been cheering for a ways back. But they had come ninety-nine miles with just thirty-six gone. Isn't that wonderful, Garraty thought, feeling the saliva spurt in his mouth as McVries mopped the last of the chicken concentrate out of the tube and then cast the empty aside. Great. I hope they all drop dead right now.

A teenager in pegged jeans raced a middle-aged housewife for McVries's empty tube, which had stopped being something useful and had begun its new career as a souvenir. The housewife was closer but the kid was faster and he beat her by half a length. "Thanks!" he hollered to McVries, holding the bent and twisted tube aloft. He scampered back to his friends, still waving it. The housewife eyed him sourly.

"Aren't you eating anything?" McVries asked.

"I'm making myself wait."

"For what?"

"Nine-thirty."

McVries eyed him thoughtfully. "The old self-discipline bit?"

Garraty shrugged, ready for the backlash of sarcasm, but McVries only went on looking at him.

"You know something?" McVries said finally.

"What?"

"If I had a dollar . . . *just* a dollar, mind you . . . I think I'd put it on you, Garraty. I think you've got a chance to win this thing."

Garraty laughed self-consciously. "Putting the whammy on me?"

"The what?"

"The whammy. Like telling a pitcher he's got a no-hitter going."

"Maybe I am," McVries said. He put his hands out in front of him. They were shaking very slightly. McVries frowned at them in a distracted sort of concentration. It was a half-lunatic sort of gaze. "I hope Barkovitch buys out soon," he said.

"Pete?"

"What?"

"If you had it to do all over again . . . if you knew you could get this far and still be walking . . . would you do it?"

McVries put his hands down and stared at Garraty. "Are you kidding? You must be."

"No, I'm serious."

"Ray, I don't think I'd do it again if the Major put his pistol up against my nates. This is the next thing to suicide, except that a regular suicide is quicker."

"True," Olson said. "How true." He smiled a hollow, concentration-camp smile that made Garraty's belly crawl.

Ten minutes later they passed under a huge red-and-white banner that proclaimed: 100 MILES!! CONGRATULATIONS FROM THE JEFFERSON PLANTATION CHAMBER OF COMMERCE! CONGRATULATIONS TO THIS YEAR'S "CENTURY CLUB" LONG WALKERS!!

"I got a place where they can put their Century Club," Collie Parker said. "It's long and brown and the sun never shines there."

Suddenly the spotty stands of second-growth pine and spruce that had bordered the road in scruffy patches were gone, hidden by the first real crowd they had seen. A tremendous cheer went up, and that was followed by another and another. It was like surf hammering on rocks. Flashbulbs popped and dazzled. State police held the deep ranks of people back, and bright orange nylon restraining ropes were strung along the soft shoulders. A policeman struggled with a screaming little boy. The boy had a dirty face and a snotty nose. He was waving a toy glider in one hand and an autograph book in the other.

"Jeez!" Baker yelled. "Jeez, look at 'em, just look at 'em all!"

Collie Parker was waving and smiling, and it was not until Garraty closed up with him a little that he could hear him calling in his flat Midwestern accent: "Glad to seeya, ya goddam bunch of fools!" A grin and a wave. "Howaya, Mother McCree, you goddam bag. Your face and my ass, what a match. Howaya, howaya?"

Garraty clapped his hands over his mouth and giggled hysterically. A man in the first rank waving a sloppily lettered sign with Scramm's name on it had popped his fly. A row back a fat woman in a ridiculous yellow sunsuit was being ground between three college students who were drinking beer. Stone-ground fatty, Garraty thought, and laughed harder.

You're going to have hysterics, oh my God, don't let it get you, think about Gribble . . . and don't . . . don't let . . . don't . . .

But it was happening. The laughter came roaring out of him until his stomach was knotted and cramped and he was walking bent-legged and somebody was hollering at him, screaming at him over the roar of the crowd. It was McVries. "Ray! *Ray!* What is it? You all right?"

"They're funny!" He was nearly weeping with laughter now. "Pete, Pete, they're so funny, it's just . . . just . . . that they're so *funny!*"

A hard-faced little girl in a dirty sundress sat on the ground, pouty-mouthed and frowning. She made a horrible face as they passed. Garraty nearly collapsed with laughter and drew a warning. It was strange—in spite of all the noise he could still hear the warnings clearly.

I could die, he thought. I could just die laughing, wouldn't that be a scream?

Collie was still smiling gaily and waving and cursing spectators and newsmen roundly, and that seemed funniest of all. Garraty fell to his knees and was warned again. He continued to laugh in short, barking spurts, which were all his laboring lungs would allow.

"He's gonna puke!" someone cried in an ecstasy of delight. "Watch 'im, Alice, he's gonna puke!"

"Garraty! Garraty for God's sake!" McVries was yelling. He got an arm around Garraty's back and hooked a hand into his armpit. Somehow he yanked him to his feet and Garraty stumbled on.

"Oh God," Garraty gasped. "Oh Jesus Christ they're killing me. I . . . I can't . . . " He broke into loose, trickling laughter once more. His knees buckled. McVries ripped him to his feet once more. Garraty's collar tore. They were both warned. That's my last warning, Garraty thought dimly. I'm on my way to see that fabled farm. Sorry, Jan, I . . .

"Come on, you turkey, I can't lug you!" McVries hissed.

"I can't do it," Garraty gasped. "My wind's gone, I—"

McVries slapped him twice quickly, forehand on the right cheek, backhand on the left. Then he walked away quickly, not looking back.

The laughter had gone out of him now but his gut was jelly, his lungs empty and seemingly unable to refill. He staggered drunkenly along, weaving, trying to find his wind. Black spots danced in front of his eyes, and a part of him understood how close to fainting he was. His one foot fetched against his other foot, he stumbled, almost fell, and somehow kept his balance.

If I fall, I die. I'll never get up.

They were watching him. The crowd was watching him. The cheers had died away to a muted, almost sexual murmur. They were waiting for him to fall down.

He walked on, now concentrating only on putting one foot out in front of the other. Once, in the eighth grade, he had read a story by a man named Ray Bradbury, and this story was about the crowds that gather at the scenes of fatal accidents, about how these crowds always have the same faces, and about how they seem to know whether the wounded will live or die. I'm going to live a little longer, Garraty told them. I'm going to live. I'm going to live a little longer.

He made his feet rise and fall to the steady cadence in his head. He blotted everything else out, even Jan. He was not aware of the heat, or of Collie Parker, or of Freaky D'Allessio. He was not even aware of the steady dull pain in his feet and the frozen stiffness of the hamstring muscles behind his knees. The thought pounded in his mind like a big kettledrum. Like a heartbeat. *Live a little longer. Live a little longer. Live a little longer.* Until the words themselves became meaningless and signified nothing.

It was the sound of the guns that brought him out of it.

In the crowd-hushed stillness the sound was shockingly loud and he could hear someone screaming. Now you know, he thought, you live long enough to hear the sound of the guns, long enough to hear yourself screaming—

But one of his feet kicked a small stone then and there was pain and it wasn't him that had bought it, it was 64, a pleasant, smiling boy named Frank Morgan. They were dragging Frank Morgan off the road. His glasses were dragging and bouncing on the pavement, still hooked stubbornly over one ear. The left lens had been shattered.

"I'm not dead," he said dazedly. Shock hit him in a warm blue wave, threatening to turn his legs to water again.

"Yeah, but you ought to be," McVries said.

"You saved him," Olson said, turning it into a curse. "Why did you do that? *Why did you do that?*" His eyes were as shiny and as blank as doorknobs. "I'd kill you if I could. I hate you. You're gonna die, McVries. You wait and see. God's gonna strike you dead for what you did. God's gonna strike you dead as dogshit." His voice was pallid and empty. Garraty could almost smell the shroud on him. He clapped his own hands over his mouth and moaned through them. The truth was that the smell of the shroud was on all of them.

"Piss on you," McVries said calmly. "I pay my debts, that's all." He looked at Garraty. "We're square, man. It's the end, right?" He walked away, not hurrying, and was soon only another colored shirt about twenty yards ahead.

Garraty's wind came back, but very slowly, and for a long time he was sure he could feel a stitch coming in his side . . . but at last that faded. McVries had saved his life. He had gone into hysterics, had a laughing jag, and McVries had saved him from going down. We're square, man. It's the end, right? All right.

"God will punish him," Hank Olson was blaring with dead and unearthly assurance. "God will strike him down."

"Shut up or I'll strike you down myself," Abraham said.

The day grew yet hotter, and small, quibbling arguments broke out like brushfires. The huge crowd dwindled a little as they walked out of the radius of TV cameras and microphones, but it did not disappear or even break up into isolated knots of spectators. The crowd had come now, and the crowd was here to stay.

The people who made it up merged into one anonymous Crowd Face, a vapid, eager visage that duplicated itself mile by mile. It peopled doorsteps, lawns, driveways, picnic areas, gas station tarmacs (where enterprising owners had charged admission), and, in the next town they passed through, both sides of the street and the parking lot of the town's supermarket. The Crowd Face mugged and gibbered and cheered, but always remained essentially the same. It watched voraciously as Wyman squatted to make his bowels work. Men, women, and children, the Crowd Face was always the same, and Garraty tired of it quickly.

He wanted to thank McVries, but somehow doubted that McVries wanted to be thanked. He could see him up ahead, walking behind Barkovitch. McVries was staring intently at Barkovitch's neck.

Nine-thirty came and passed. The crowd seemed to intensify the heat, and Garraty unbuttoned his shirt to just above his belt buckle. He wondered if Freaky D'Allessio had known he was going to buy a ticket before he did. He supposed that knowing wouldn't have really changed things for him, one way or the other.

The road inclined steeply, and the crowd fell away momentarily as they climbed up and over four sets of east/west railroad tracks that ran below, glittering hotly in their bed of cinders. At the top, as they crossed the wooden bridge, Garraty could see another belt of woods ahead, and the built-up, almost suburban area through which they had just passed to the right and left.

A cool breeze played over his sweaty skin, making him shiver. Scramm sneezed sharply three times.

"I *am* getting a cold," he announced disgustedly.

"That'll take the starch right out of you," Pearson said. "That's a bitch."

"I'll just have to work harder," Scramm said.

"You must be made of steel," Pearson said. "If I had a cold I think I'd roll right over and die. That's how little energy I've got left."

"Roll over and die now!" Barkovitch yelled back. "Save some energy!"

"Shut up and keep walking, killer," McVries said immediately.

Barkovitch looked around at him. "Why don't you get off my back, McVries? Go walk somewhere else."

"It's a free road. I'll walk where I damn well please."

Barkovitch hawked, spat, and dismissed him.

Garraty opened one of his food containers and began to eat cream cheese on crackers. His stomach growled bitterly at the first bite, and he had to fight himself to keep from wolfing everything. He squeezed a tube of roast beef concentrate into his mouth, swallowing steadily. He washed it down with water and then made himself stop there.

They walked by a lumberyard where men stood atop stacks of planks, silhouetted against the sky like Indians, waving to them. Then they were in the woods again and silence seemed to fall with a crash. It was not silent, of course; Walkers talked, the halftrack ground along mechanically, somebody broke wind, somebody laughed, somebody behind Garraty made a hopeless little groaning sound. The sides of the road were still lined with spectators, but the great "Century Club" crowd had disappeared and it seemed quiet by comparison. Birds sang in the high-crowned trees, the furtive breeze now and then masked the heat for a moment or two, sounding like a lost soul as it soughed through the trees. A brown squirrel froze on a high branch, tail bushed out, black eyes brutally attentive, a nut caught between his ratlike front paws. He chittered at them, then scurried higher up and disappeared. A plane droned far away, like a giant fly.

To Garraty it seemed that everyone was deliberately giving him the silent treatment. McVries was still walking behind Barkovitch. Pearson and Baker were talking about chess. Abraham was eating noisily and wiping his hands on his shirt. Scramm had torn off a piece of his T-shirt and was using it as a hanky. Collie Parker was swapping girls with Wyman. And Olson . . . but he didn't even want to look at Olson, who seemed to want to implicate everyone else as an accessory in his own approaching death.

So he began to drop back, very carefully, just a little at a time (very mindful of his three warnings), until he was in step with Stebbins. The purple pants were dusty now. There were dark circles of sweat under the armpits of the chambray shirt. Whatever else Stebbins was, he wasn't Superman. He looked up at Garraty for a moment, lean face questioning, and then he dropped his gaze back to the road. The knob of spine at the back of his neck was very prominent.

"How come there aren't more people?" Garraty asked hesitantly. "Watching, I mean."

For a moment he didn't think Stebbins was going to answer. But finally he looked up again, brushed the hair off his forehead and replied, "There will be. Wait awhile. They'll be sitting on roofs three deep to look at you."

"But somebody said there was billions bet on this. You'd think they'd be lined up three deep the whole way. And that there'd be TV coverage—"

"It's discouraged."

"Why?"

"Why ask me?"

"Because you *know*," Garraty said, exasperated.

"How do you know?"

"Jesus, you remind me of the caterpillar in *Alice in Wonderland*, sometimes," Garraty said. "Don't you ever just talk?"

"How long would you last with people screaming at you from both sides? The body odor alone would be enough to drive you insane after a while. It would be like walking three hundred miles through Times Square on New Year's Eve."

"But they *do* let them watch, don't they? Someone said it was one big crowd from Oldtown on."

"I'm not the caterpillar, anyway," Stebbins said with a small, somehow secretive smile. "I'm more the white rabbit type, don't you think? Except I left my gold watch at home and no one has invited me to tea. At least, to the best of my knowledge, no one has. Maybe that's what I'll ask for when I win. When they ask me what I want for my Prize, I'll say, 'Why, I want to be invited home for tea.' "

"Goddammit!"

Stebbins smiled more widely, but it was still only an exercise in lip-pulling. "Yeah, from Oldtown or thereabouts the damper is off. By then no one is thinking very much about mundane things like B.O. And there's continuous TV coverage from Augusta. The Long Walk is the national pastime, after all."

"Then why not here?"

"Too soon," Stebbins said. "Too soon."

From around the next curve the guns roared again, startling a pheasant that rose from the underbrush in an electric uprush of beating feathers. Garraty and Stebbins rounded the curve, but the bodybag was already being zipped up. Fast work. He couldn't see who it had been.

"You reach a certain point," Stebbins said, "when the crowd ceases to matter, either as an incentive or a drawback. It ceases to be there. Like a man on a scaffold, I think. You burrow away from the crowd."

"I think I understand that," Garraty said. He felt timid.

"If you understood it, you wouldn't have gone into hysterics back there and needed your friend to save your ass. But you will."

"How far do you burrow, I wonder?"

"How deep are you?"

"I don't know."

"Well, that's something you'll get to find out, too. Plumb the unplumbed depths of Garraty. Sounds almost like a travel ad, doesn't it? You burrow until you hit bedrock. Then you burrow *into* the bedrock. And finally you get to the bottom. And then you buy out. That's my idea. Let's hear yours."

Garraty said nothing. Right at present, he had no ideas.

The Walk went on. The heat went on. The sun hung suspended just above the line of trees the road cut its way through. Their shadows were stubby dwarves. Around ten o'clock, one of the soldiers disappeared through the back hatch of the halftrack and reappeared with a long pole. The upper two thirds of the pole was shrouded in cloth. He closed the hatch and dropped the end of the pole into a slot in the metal. He reached under the cloth and did something . . . fiddled something, probably a stud. A moment later a large, dun-colored sun umbrella popped up. It shaded most of the halftrack's metal surface. He and the other two soldiers currently on duty sat cross-legged in the army-drab parasol's shade.

"You rotten sonsabitches!" somebody screamed. "My Prize is gonna be your public castration!"

The soldiers did not seem exactly struck to the heart with terror at the thought. They continued to scan the Walkers with their blank eyes, referring occasionally to their computerized console.

"They probably take this out on their wives," Garraty said. "When it's over."

"Oh, I'm sure they do," Stebbins said, and laughed.

Garraty didn't want to walk with Stebbins anymore, not right now. Stebbins made him uneasy. He could only take Stebbins in small doses. He walked faster, leaving Stebbins by himself again. 10:02. In twenty-three minutes he could drop a warning, but for now he was still walking with three. It didn't scare him the way he had thought it would. There was still the unshakable, blind assurances that this organism Ray Garraty could not die. The others could die, they were extras in the movie of his life, but not Ray Garraty, star of that long-running hit film, *The Ray Garraty Story.* Maybe he would eventually come to understand the untruth of that emotionally as well as intellectually . . . maybe that was the final depth of which Stebbins had spoken. It was a shivery, unwelcome thought.

Without realizing it, he had walked three quarters of the way through the pack. He was behind McVries again. There were three of them in a fatigue-ridden conga line: Barkovitch at the front, still trying to look cocky but flaking a bit around the edges; McVries with his head slumped, hands half-clenched, favoring his left foot a little now; and, bringing up the rear, the star of *The Ray Garraty Story* himself. And how do I look? he wondered.

He rubbed a hand up the side of his cheek and listened to the rasp his hand made against his light beard-stubble. Probably he didn't look all that snappy himself.

He stepped up his pace a little more until he was walking abreast of McVries, who looked over briefly and then back at Barkovitch. His eyes were dark and hard to read.

They climbed a short, steep, and savagely sunny rise and then crossed another small bridge. Fifteen minutes went by, then twenty. McVries didn't say anything. Garraty cleared his throat twice but said nothing. He thought that the longer you went without speaking, the harder it gets to break the silence. Probably McVries was pissed that he had saved his ass now. Probably McVries had repented of it. That made Garraty's stomach quiver emptily. It was all hopeless and stupid and pointless, most of all that, so goddam pointless it was really pitiful. He opened his mouth to tell McVries that, but before he could, McVries spoke.

"Everything's all right." Barkovitch jumped at the sound of his voice and McVries added, "Not you, killer. Nothing's ever going to be all right for you. Just keep striding."

"Eat my meat," Barkovitch snarled.

"I guess I caused you some trouble," Garraty said in a low voice.

"I told you, fair is fair, square is square, and quits are quits," McVries said evenly. "I won't do it again. I want you to know that."

"I understand that," Garraty said. "I just—"

"Don't hurt me!" someone screamed. "Please don't hurt me!"

It was a redhead with a plaid shirt tied around his waist. He had stopped in the middle of the road and he was weeping. He was given first warning. And then he raced toward the halftrack, his tears cutting runnels through the sweaty dirt on his face, red hair glinting like a fire in the sun. "Don't . . . I can't . . . please . . . my mother . . . I can't . . . don't . . . no more . . . my feet . . . " He was trying to scale the side, and one of the soldiers brought the butt of his carbine down on his hands. The boy cried out and fell in a heap.

He screamed again, a high, incredibly thin note that seemed sharp enough to shatter glass and what he was screaming was:

"My feeeeeeeeeeeeeeeeeeeeeeeeeeeeeeeeeeee—"

"Jesus," Garraty muttered. "Why doesn't he stop that?" The screams went on and on.

"I doubt if he can," McVries said clinically. "The back treads of the halftrack ran over his legs."

Garraty looked and felt his stomach lurch into his throat. It was true. No wonder the redheaded kid was screaming about his feet. They had been obliterated.

"Warning! Warning 38!"

"—eeeeeeeeeeeeeeeeeeeeeeeeee—"

"I want to go home," someone behind Garraty said very quietly. "Oh Christ, do I ever want to go home."

A moment later the redheaded boy's face was blown away.

"I'm gonna see my girl in Freeport," Garraty said rapidly. "And I'm not gonna have any warnings and I'm gonna kiss her, God I miss her, God, *Jesus,* did you see his *legs?* They were still warning him, Pete, like they thought he was gonna get up and *walk*—"

"Another boy has gone ober to dat Silver City, lawd, lawd," Barkovitch intoned.

"Shut up, killer," McVries said absently. "She pretty, Ray? Your girl?"

"She's beautiful. I love her."

McVries smiled. "Gonna marry her?"

"Yeah," Garraty babbled. "We're gonna be Mr. and Mrs. Norman Normal, four kids and a collie dog, his *legs,* he didn't have any *legs,* they ran over him, they can't run *over* a guy, that isn't in the rules, somebody ought to report that, somebody—"

"Two boys and two girls, that what you're gonna have?"

"Yeah, yeah, she's beautiful, I just wish I hadn't—"

"And the first kid will be Ray Junior and the dog'll have a dish with its name on it, right?"

Garraty raised his head slowly, like a punchdrunk fighter. "Are you making fun of me? Or what?"

"No!" Barkovitch exclaimed. "He's *shitting* on you, boy! And don't you forget it. But I'll dance on his grave for you, don't worry." He cackled briefly.

"Shut up, killer," McVries said. "I'm not dumping on you, Ray. Come on, let's get away from the killer, here."

"Shove it up your ass!" Barkovitch screamed after them.

"She love you? Your girl? Jan?"

"Yeah, I think so," Garraty said.

McVries shook his head slowly. "All of that romantic horseshit . . . you know, it's true. At least, for some people for some short time, it is. It was for me. I felt like you." He looked at Garraty. "You still want to hear about the scar?"

They rounded a bend and a camperload of children squealed and waved.

"Yes," Garraty said.

"Why?" He looked at Garraty, but his suddenly naked eyes might have been searching himself.

"I want to help you," Garraty said.

McVries looked down at his left foot. "Hurts. I can't wiggle the toes very much anymore. My neck is stiff and my kidneys ache. My girl turned out to be a bitch, Garraty. I got into this Long Walk shit the same way that guys used to get into the Foreign Legion. In the words of the great rock and roll poet, I gave her my heart, she tore it apart, and who gives a fart."

Garraty said nothing. It was 10:30. Freeport was still far.

"Her name was Priscilla," McVries said. "You think you got a case? I was the original Korny Kid, Moon-June was my middle name. I used to kiss her fingers. I even took to reading Keats to her out in back of the house, when the wind was right. Her old man kept cows, and the smell of cowshit goes, to put it in the most delicate way, in a peculiar fashion with the works of John Keats. Maybe I should have read her Swinburne when the wind was wrong." McVries laughed.

"You're cheating what you felt," Garraty said.

"Ah, you're the one faking it, Ray, not that it matters. All you remember is the Great Romance, not all the times you went home and jerked your meat after whispering words of love in her shell-pink ear."

"You fake your way, I'll fake mine."

McVries seemed not to have heard. "These things, they don't even bear the weight of conversation," he said. "J. D. Salinger . . . John Knowles . . . even James Kirkwood and that guy Don Bredes . . . they've destroyed being an adolescent, Garraty. If you're a sixteen-year-old boy, you can't discuss the pains of adolescent love with any decency anymore. You just come off sounding like fucking Ron Howard with a hardon."

McVries laughed a little hysterically. Garraty had no idea what McVries was talking about. He was secure in his love for Jan, he didn't feel in the least self-conscious about it. Their feet scuffed on the road. Garraty could feel his right heel wobbling. Pretty soon the nails would let go, and he would shed the shoeheel like dead skin. Behind them, Scramm had a coughing fit. It was the Walk that bothered Garraty, not all this weird shit about romantic love.

"But that doesn't have anything to do with the story," McVries said, as if reading his mind. "About the scar. It was last summer. We both wanted to get away from home, away from our parents, and away from the smell of all that cowshit so the Great Romance could bloom in earnest. So we got jobs working for a pajama factory in New Jersey. How does that grab you, Garraty? A pj factory in New Jersey.

"We got separate apartments in Newark. Great town, Newark, on a given day you can smell all the cowshit in New Jersey in Newark. Our parents kicked a little, but with separate apartments and good summer jobs, they didn't kick too much. My place was with two other guys, and there were three girls in with Pris. We left on June the third in my car, and we stopped once around three in the afternoon at a motel and got rid of the virginity problem. I felt like a real crook. She didn't really want to screw, but she wanted to please me. That was the Shady Nook motel. When we were done I flushed that Trojan down the Shady Nook john and washed out my mouth with a Shady Nook paper cup. It was all very romantic, very ethereal.

"Then it was on to Newark, smelling the cowshit and being so sure it was *different* cowshit. I dropped her at her apartment and then went on to my own. The next Monday we started in at the Plymouth Sleepwear factory. It wasn't much like the movies, Garraty. It stank of raw cloth and my foreman was a bastard and during lunch break we used to throw baling hooks at the rats under the fabric bags. But I didn't mind because it was love. See? It was love."

He spat dryly into the dust, swallowed from his canteen, then yelled for another one. They were climbing a long, curve-banked hill now, and his words came in out-of-breath bursts.

"Pris was on the first floor, the showcase for all the idiot tourists who didn't have anything better to do than go on a guided tour of the place that made their jam-jams. It was nice down where Pris was. Pretty pastel walls, nice modern machinery, air conditioning. Pris sewed on buttons from seven till three. Just think, there are men all over the country wearing pj's held up by Priscilla's buttons. There is a thought to warm the coldest heart.

"I was on the fifth floor. I was a bagger. See, down in the basement they dyed the raw cloth and sent it up to the fifth floor in these warm-air tubes. They'd ring a bell when the whole lot was done, and I'd open my bin and there'd be a whole shitload of loose fiber, all the colors of the rainbow. I'd pitchfork it out, put it in two-hundred-pound sacks, and chain-hoist the sacks onto a big pile of other sacks for the picker machine. They'd separate it, the weaving machines wove it, some other guys cut it and sewed it into pajamas, and down there on that pretty pastel first floor Pris put on the buttons while the dumbass tourists watched her and the other girls through this glass wall . . . just like the people are watching us today. Am I getting through to you at all, Garraty?"

"The scar," Garraty reminded.

"I keep wandering away from that, don't I?" McVries wiped his forehead and unbuttoned his shirt as they breasted the hill. Waves of woods stretched away before them to a horizon poked with mountains. They met the sky like interlocking jigsaw pieces. Perhaps ten miles away, almost lost in the heat-haze, a fire tower jutted up through the green. The road cut through it all like a sliding gray serpent.

"At first, the joy and bliss was Keatsville all the way. I screwed her three more times, all at the drive-in with the smell of cowshit coming in through the car window from the next pasture. And I could never get all of the loose fabric out of my hair no matter how many times I shampooed it, and the worst thing was she was getting away from me, going beyond me I loved her, I really did, I knew it and there was no way I could tell her anymore so she'd understand. I couldn't even screw it into her. There was always that smell of cowshit.

"The thing of it was, Garraty, the factory was on piecework. That means we got lousy wages, but a percentage for all we did over a certain minimum. I wasn't a very good bagger. I did about twenty-three bags a day, but the norm was usually right around thirty. And this did not endear me to the rest of the boys, because I was fucking them up. Harlan down in the dyehouse couldn't make piecework because I was tying up his blower with full bins. Ralph on the picker couldn't make piecework because I wasn't shifting enough bags over to him. It wasn't pleasant. They saw to it that it wasn't pleasant. You understand?''

"Yeah,'' Garraty said. He wiped the back of his hand across his neck and then wiped his hand on his pants. It made a dark stain.

"Meanwhile, down in buttoning, Pris was keeping herself busy. Some nights she'd talk for hours about her girlfriends, and it was usually the same tune. How much this one was making. How much that one was making. And most of all, how much she was making. And she was making plenty. So I got to find out how much fun it is to be in competition with the girl you want to marry. At the end of the week I'd go home with a check for $64.40 and put some Cornhusker's Lotion on my blisters. She was making something like ninety a week, and socking it away as fast as she could run to the bank. And when I suggested we go someplace dutch, you would have thought I'd suggested ritual murder.

"After a while I stopped screwing her. I'd like to say I stopped going to bed with her, it's more pleasant, but we never had a bed to go to. I couldn't take her to my apartment, there were usually about sixteen guys there drinking beer, and there were always people at her place—that's what she said, anyway—and I couldn't afford another motel room and I certainly wasn't going to suggest we go dutch on *that,* so it was just screwing in the back seat at the drive-in. And I could tell she was getting disgusted. And since I knew it and since I had started to hate her even though I still loved her, I asked her to marry me. Right then. She started wriggling around, trying to put me off, but I made her come out with it, yes or no.''

"And it was no.''

"Sure it was no. 'Pete, we can't afford it. What would my mom say. Pete, we have to wait.' Pete this and Pete that and all the time the real reason was her money, the money she was making sewing on buttons.''

"Well, you were damned unfair to ask her.''

"Sure I was unfair!'' McVries said savagely. "I knew that. I wanted to make her feel like a greedy, self-centered little bitch because she was making me feel like a failure.''

His hand crept up to the scar.

"Only she didn't have to make me *feel* like a failure, because I *was* a failure. I didn't have anything in particular going for me except a cock to stick in her and she wouldn't even make me feel like a man by refusing that.''

The guns roared behind them.

"Olson?'' McVries asked.

"No. He's still back there.''

"Oh . . . ''

"The scar,'' Garraty reminded.

"Oh, why don't you let it alone?''

"You saved my life.''

"Shit on you."

"The scar."

"I got into a fight," McVries said finally, after a long pause. "With Ralph, the guy on the picker. He blacked both my eyes and told me I better take off or he'd break my arms as well. I turned in my time and told Pris that night that I'd quit. She could see what I looked like for herself. She understood. She said that was probably best. I told her I was going home and I asked her to come. She said she couldn't. I said she was nothing but a slave to her fucking buttons and that I wished I'd never seen her. There was just so much poison inside me, Garraty. I told her she was a fool and an unfeeling bitch that couldn't see any further than the goddam bank book she carried around in her purse. Nothing I said was fair, but . . . there was some truth in all of it, I guess. Enough. We were at her apartment. That was the first time I'd ever been there when all her roommates were out. They were at the movies. I tried to take her to bed and she cut my face open with a letter-opener. It was a gag letter-opener, some friend of hers sent it to her from England. It had Paddington Bear on it. She cut me like I was trying to rape her. Like I was germs and I'd infect her. Am I giving you the drift, Ray?"

"Yes, I'm getting it," Garraty said. Up ahead a white station wagon with the words WHGH NEWSMOBILE lettered on the side was pulled off the road. As they drew near, a balding man in a shiny suit began shooting them with a big newsreel ciné camera. Pearson, Abraham, and Jensen all clutched their crotches with their left hand and thumbed their noses with their right. There was a Rockettelike precision about this little act of defiance that bemused Garraty.

"I cried," McVries said. "I cried like a baby. I got down on my knees and held her skirt and begged her to forgive me, and all the blood was getting on the floor, it was a basically disgusting scene, Garraty. She gagged and ran off into the bathroom. She threw up. I could hear her throwing up. When she came out, she had a towel for my face. She said she never wanted to see me again. She was crying. She asked me why I'd done that to her, hurt her like that. She said I had no right. There I was, Ray, with my face cut wide open and she's asking *me* why I hurt *her*."

"Yeah."

"I left with the towel still on my face. I had twelve stitches and that's the story of the fabulous scar and aren't you happy?"

"Have you ever seen her since?"

"No," McVries said. "And I have no real urge to. She seems very small to me now, very far away. Pris at this point in my life is no more than a speck on the horizon. She really was mental, Ray. Something . . . her mother, maybe, her mother was a lush . . . something had fixed her on the subject of money. She was a real miser. Distance lends perspective, they say. Yesterday morning Pris was still very important to me. Now she's nothing. That story I just told you, I thought that would hurt. It didn't hurt. Besides, I doubt if all that shit really has anything to do with why I'm here. It just made a handy excuse at the time."

"What do you mean?"

"Why are you here, Garraty?"

"I don't know." His voice was mechanical, doll-like. Freaky D'Allessio hadn't been able to see the ball coming—his eyes weren't right, his depth perception was screwed—it had hit him in the forehead, and branded him with stitches. And later (or earlier . . . all of his past was mixed up and fluid now) he had hit his best friend in the mouth with the barrel of an air rifle. Maybe he had a scar like McVries. Jimmy. He and Jimmy had been playing doctor.

"You don't know," McVries said. "You're dying and you don't know why."

"It's not important after you're dead."

"Yeah, maybe," McVries said, "but there's one thing you ought to know, Ray, so it won't all be so pointless."

"What's that?"

"Why, that you've been had. You mean you really didn't know that, Ray? You really didn't?"

Chapter 9

"Very good, Northwestern, now here is
your ten-point tossup question."
                    —Allen Ludden
                    College Bowl

At one o'clock, Garraty took inventory again.

One hundred and fifteen miles traveled. They were forty-five miles north of Oldtown, a hundred and twenty-five miles north of Augusta, the state capital, one hundred and fifty to Freeport (or more . . . he was terribly afraid there were more than twenty-five miles between Augusta and Freeport), probably two-thirty to the New Hampshire border. And the word was that this Walk was sure to go that far.

For a long while—ninety minutes or so—no one at all had been given a ticket. They walked, they half-listened to the cheers from the sidelines, and they stared at mile after monotonous mile of piney woods. Garraty discovered fresh twinges of pain in his left calf to go with the steady, wooden throbbing that lived in both of his legs, and the low-key agony that was his feet.

Then, around noon, as the day's heat mounted toward its zenith, the guns began to make themselves heard again. A boy named Tressler, 92, had a sunstroke and was shot as he lay unconscious. Another boy suffered a convulsion and got a ticket as he crawdaddied on the road, making ugly noises around his swallowed tongue. Aaronson, 1, cramped up in both feet and was shot on the white line, standing like a statue, his face turned up to the sun in neck-straining concentration. And at five minutes to one, another boy Garraty did not know had a sunstroke.

This is where I came in, Garraty thought, walking around the twitching, mumbling form on the road where the rifles sight in, seeing the jewels of sweat in the exhausted and soon-to-be-dead boy's hair. This is where I came in, can't I leave now?

The guns roared, and a covey of high school boys sitting in the scant shade of a Scout camper applauded briefly.

"I wish the Major would come through," Baker said pettishly. "I want to see the Major."

"What?" Abraham asked mechanically. He had grown gaunter in the last few hours. His eyes were sunk deeper in their sockets. The blue suggestion of a beard patched his face.

"So I can piss on him," Baker said.

"Relax," Garraty said. "Just relax." All three of his warnings were gone now.

"*You* relax," Baker said. "See what it gets you."

"You've got no right to hate the Major. He didn't *force* you."

"*Force me?* FORCE me? He's *KILLING* me, that's all!''

"It's still not—"

"Shut up," Baker said curtly, and Garraty shut. He rubbed the back of his neck briefly and stared up into the whitish-blue sky. His shadow was a deformed huddle almost beneath his feet. He turned up his third canteen of the day and drained it.

Baker said: "I'm sorry. I surely didn't mean to shout. My feet—"

"Sure," Garraty said.

"We're all getting this way," Baker said. "I sometimes think that's the worst part."

Garraty closed his eyes. He was very sleepy.

"You know what I'd like to do?" Pearson said. He was walking between Garraty and Baker.

"Piss on the Major," Garraty said. "Everybody wants to piss on the Major. When he comes through again we'll gang up on him and drag him down and all unzip and drown him in—"

"That isn't what I want to do." Pearson was walking like a man in the last stages of conscious drunkenness. His head made half-rolls on his neck. His eyelids snapped up and down like spastic windowblinds. "It's got nothin' to do with the Major. I just want to go into the next field and lay down and close my eyes. Just lay there on my back in the wheat—"

"They don't grow wheat in Maine," Garraty said. "It's hay."

"—in the hay, then. And compose myself a poem. While I go to sleep."

Garraty fumbled in his new foodbelt and found nothing in most of the pouches. Finally he happened on a waxpac of Saltines and began washing them down with water. "I feel like a sieve," he said. "I drink it and it pops out on my skin two minutes later."

The guns roared again and another figure collapsed gracelessly, like a tired jack-in-the-box.

"Fordy fibe," Scramm said, joining them. "I don't thing we'll even get to Pordland ad this rade."

"You don't sound so good," Pearson said, and there might have been careful optimism in his voice.

"Luggy for me I god a good codstitution," Scramm said cheerfully. "I thing I'be rudding a fever now."

"Jesus, how do you keep going?" Abraham asked, and there was a kind of religious fear in his voice.

"Me? Talk about *me?*" Scramm said. "Look at *hib!* How does he keep going? Thad's what I'd like to know!" And he cocked his thumb at Olson.

Olson had not spoken for two hours. He had not touched his newest canteen. Greedy glances were shot at his foodbelt, which was also almost untouched. His eyes, darkly obsidian, were fixed straight ahead. His face was speckled by two days of beard and it looked sickly vulpine. Even his hair, frizzed up in back and hanging across his forehead in front, added to the overall impression of ghoulishness. His lips were parched dry and blistering. His tongue hung over his bottom lip like a dead serpent on the lip of a cave. Its healthy pinkness had disappeared. It was dirty-gray now. Road-dust clung to it.

He's there, Garraty thought, sure he is. Where Stebbins said we'd all go if we stuck with it long enough. How deep inside himself is he? Fathoms? Miles? Light-years? How deep and how dark? And the answer came back to him: Too deep to see out. He's hiding down there in the darkness and it's too deep to see out.

"Olson?" he said softly. "Olson?"

Olson didn't answer. Nothing moved but his feet.

"I wish he'd put his tongue in at least," Pearson whispered nervously.

The Walk went on.

The woods melted back and they were passing through another wide place in the road. The sidewalks were lined with cheering spectators. Garraty signs again predominated. Then the woods closed in again. But not even the woods could hold the spectators back now. They were beginning to line the soft shoulders. Pretty girls in shorts and halters. Boys in basketball shorts and muscle shirts.

Gay holiday, Garraty thought.

He could no longer wish he wasn't here; he was too tired and numb for retrospect. What was done was done. Nothing in the world would change it. Soon enough, he supposed, it would even become too much of an effort to talk to the others. He wished he could hide inside himself like a little boy rolled up inside a rug, with no more worries. Then everything would be much simpler.

He had wondered a great deal about what McVries had said. That they had all been swindled, rooked. But that couldn't be right, he insisted stubbornly to himself. One of them had not been swindled. One of them was going to swindle everyone else . . . wasn't that right?

He licked his lips and drank some water.

They passed a small green sign that informed them the Maine turnpike was forty-four miles hence.

"That's it," he said to no one in particular. "Forty-four miles to Oldtown."

No one replied and Garraty was just considering taking a walk back up to McVries when they came to another intersection and a woman began to scream. The traffic had been roped off, and the crowd pressed eagerly against the barriers and the cops manning them. They waved their hands, their signs, their bottles of suntan lotion.

The screaming woman was large and red-faced. She threw herself against one of the waist-high sawhorse barriers, toppling it and yanking a lot of the bright yellow guard-rope after it. Then she was fighting and clawing and screaming at the policemen who held her. The cops were grunting with effort.

I know her, Garraty thought. Don't I know her?

The blue kerchief. The belligerent, gleaming eyes. Even the navy dress with the crooked hem. They were all familiar. The woman's screams had become incoherent. One pinwheeling hand ripped stripes of blood across the face of one of the cops holding her—*trying* to hold her.

Garraty passed within ten feet of her. As he walked past, he knew where he had seen her before—she was Percy's mom, of course. Percy who had tried to sneak into the woods and had snuck right into the next world instead.

"I want m'boy!" she hollered. "I want m'boy!"

The crowd cheered her enthusiastically and impartially. A small boy behind her spat on her leg and then darted away.

Jan, Garraty thought. I'm walking to you, Jan, fuck this other shit, I swear to God I'm coming. But McVries had been right. Jan hadn't wanted him to come. She had cried. She had begged him to change his mind. They could wait, she didn't want to lose him, please Ray, don't be dumb, the Long Walk is nothing but murder—

They had been sitting on a bench beside the bandstand. It had been a month ago, April, and he had his arm around her. She had been wearing the perfume he had gotten her for her birthday. It seemed to bring out the secret girl-smell of her, a dark smell, fleshy and heady. I have to go, he had told her. I have to, don't you understand, I have to.

Ray, you don't understand what you're doing. Ray, please don't. I love you.

Well, he thought now, as he walked on down the road, she was right about that. I sure didn't understand what I was doing.

But I don't understand it even now. That's the hell of it. The pure and simple hell of it.

"Garraty?"

He jerked his head up, startled. He had been half-asleep again. It was McVries, walking beside him.

"How you feeling?"

"Feeling?" Garraty said cautiously. "All right, I guess. I guess I'm all right."

"Barkovitch is cracking," McVries said with quiet joy. "I'm sure of it. He's talking to himself. And he's limping."

"You're limping, too," Garraty said. "So's Pearson. So am I."

"My foot hurts, that's all. But Barkovitch . . . he keeps rubbing his leg. I think he's got a pulled muscle."

"Why do you hate him so much? Why not Collie Parker? Or Olson? Or all of us?"

"Because Barkovitch knows what he's doing."

"He plays to win, do you mean?"

"You don't know what I mean, Ray."

"I wonder if you do yourself," Garraty said. "Sure he's a bastard. Maybe it takes a bastard to win."

"Good guys finish last?"

"How the hell should I know?"

They passed a clapboard one-room schoolhouse. The children stood out in the play yard and waved. Several boys stood atop the jungle gym like sentries, and Garraty was reminded of the men in the lumberyard a ways back.

"Garraty!" One of them yelled. "Ray Garraty! Gar-ra-*tee!*" A small boy with a tousled head of hair jumped up and down on the top level of the jungle gym, waving with both arms. Garraty waved back halfheartedly. The boy flipped over, hung upside down by the backs of his legs, and continued to wave. Garraty was a little relieved when he and the schoolyard were out of sight. That last had been a little too strenuous to bear thinking about for long.

Pearson joined them. "I've been thinking."

"Save your strength," McVries said.

"Feeble, man. That is feeble."

"What have you been thinking about?" Garraty asked.

"How tough it's going to be for the second-to-last guy."

"Why so tough?" McVries asked.

"Well . . . " Pearson rubbed his eyes, then squinted at a pine tree that had been struck by lightning some time in the past. "You know, to walk down everybody, absolutely *everybody* but that last guy. There ought to be a runner-up Prize, that's what I think."

"What?" McVries asked flatly.

"I dunno."

"How about his life?" Garraty asked.

"Who'd walk for that?"

"Nobody, before the Walk started, maybe. But right now I'd be happy enough with just that, the hell with the Prize, the hell with having my every heart's desire. How about you?"

Pearson thought about it for a long time. "I just don't see the sense of it," he said at last, apologetically.

"You tell him, Pete," Garraty said.

"Tell him what? He's right. The whole banana or no banana at all."

"You're crazy," Garraty said, but without much conviction. He was very hot and very tired, and there were the remotest beginnings of a headache in back of his eyes. Maybe this is how sunstroke starts, he thought. Maybe that would be the best way, too. Just go down in a dreamy, slow-motion half-knowingness, and wake up dead.

"Sure," McVries said amiably. "We're all crazy or we wouldn't be here. I thought we'd thrashed that out a long time ago. We want to die, Ray. Haven't you got that through your sick, thick head yet? Look at Olson. A skull on top of a stick. Tell me he doesn't want to die. You can't. Second place? It's bad enough that even one of us has got to get gypped out of what he really wants."

"I don't know about all that fucking psychohistory," Pearson said finally. "I just don't think anyone should get to cop out second."

Garraty burst out laughing. "You're nuts," he said.

McVries also laughed. "Now you're starting to see it my way. Get a little more sun, stew your brain a little more, and we'll make a real believer out of you."

The Walk went on.

The sun seemed neatly poised on the roof of the world. The mercury reached seventy-nine degrees (one of the boys had a pocket thermometer) and eighty trembled in its grasp for a few broiling minutes. Eighty, Garraty thought. Eighty. Not that hot.

In July the mercury would go ten degrees higher. Eighty. Just the right temperature to sit in the backyard under an elm tree eating a chicken salad on lettuce. Eighty. Just the ticket for belly-flopping into the nearest piece of the Royal River, oh Jesus, wouldn't that feel good. The water was warm on the top, but down by your feet it was cold and you could feel the current pull at you just a little and there were suckers by the rocks, but you could pick 'em off if you weren't a pussy. All that water, bathing your skin, your hair, your crotch. His hot flesh trembled as he thought about it. Eighty. Just right for shucking down to your swim trunks and laying up in the canvas hammock in the backyard with a good book. And maybe drowse off. Once he had pulled Jan into the hammock with him and they had lain there together, swinging and necking until his cock felt like a long hot stone against his lower belly. She hadn't seemed to mind. Eighty. Christ in a Chevrolet, eighty degrees.

Eighty. Eightyeightyeighty. Make it nonsense, make it gone.

"I'd never been so hod id by whole life," Scramm said through his plugged nose. His broad face was red and dripping sweat. He had stripped off his shirt and bared his shaggy torso. Sweat was running all over him like small creeks in spring flow.

"You better put your shirt back on," Baker said. "You'll catch a chill when the sun starts to go down. Then you'll really be in trouble."

"This goddab code," Scramm said. "I'be burding ub."

"It'll rain," Baker said. His eyes searched the empty sky. "It has to rain."

"It doesn't have to do a goddam thing," Collie Parker said. "I never seen such a fucked-up state."

"If you don't like it, why don't you go on home?" Garraty asked, and giggled foolishly.

"Stuff it up your ass."

Garraty forced himself to drink just a little from his canteen. He didn't want water cramps. That would be a hell of a way to buy out. He'd had them once, and once had been enough. He had been helping their next-door neighbors, the El-wells, get in their hay. It was explosively hot in the loft of the Elwells' barn, and they had been throwing up the big seventy-pound bales in a fireman's relay. Garraty had made the tactical mistake of drinking three dipperfuls of the ice-cold water Mrs. Elwell had brought out. There had been sudden blinding pain in his chest and belly and head, he had slipped on some loose hay and had fallen bonelessly out of the loft and into the truck. Mr. Elwell held him around the middle with his work-callused hands while he threw up over the side, weak with pain and shame. They had sent him home, a boy who had flunked one of his first manhood tests, hayrash on his arms and chaff in his hair. He had walked home, and the sun had beaten down on the back of his sunburned neck like a ten-pound hammer.

He shivered convulsively, and his body broke out momentarily in heat-bumps. The headache thumped sickishly behind his eyes . . . how easy it would be to let go of the rope.

He looked over at Olson. Olson was there. His tongue was turning blackish. His face was dirty. His eyes stared blindly. I'm not like him. Dear God, not like him. Please, I don't want to go out like Olson.

"This'll take the starch out," Baker said gloomily. "We won't make it into New Hampshire. I'd bet money on it."

"Two years ago they had sleet," Abraham said. "*They* made it over the border. Four of 'em did, anyway."

"Yeah, but the heat's different," Jensen said. "When you're cold you can walk faster and get warmed up. When you're hot you can walk slower . . . and get iced. What can you do?"

"No justice," Collie Parker said angrily. "Why couldn't they have the goddam Walk in Illinois, where the ground's flat?"

"I like Baine," Scramm said. "Why do you swear so buch, Parger?"

"Why do you have to wipe so much snot out of your nose?" Parker asked. "Because that's the way I am, that's why. Any objections?"

Garraty looked at his watch, but it was stopped at 10:16. He had forgotten to wind it. "Anybody got the time?" he asked.

"Lemme see." Pearson squinted at his watch. "Just happast an asshole, Garraty."

Everyone laughed. "Come on," he said. "My watch stopped."

Pearson looked again. "It's two after two." He looked up at the sky. "That sun isn't going to set for a long time."

The sun was poised malevolently over the fringe of woods. There was not enough angle on it yet to throw the road into the shade, and wouldn't be for another hour or two. Far off to the south, Garraty thought he could see purple smudges that might be thunderheads or only wishful thinking.

Abraham and Collie Parker were lackadaisically discussing the merits of four-barrel carbs. No one else seemed much disposed to talk, so Garraty wandered off by himself to the far side of the road, waving now and then to someone, but not bothering as a rule.

The Walkers were not spread out as much as they had been. The vanguard was in plain sight: two tall, tanned boys with black leather jackets tied around their waists. The word was that they were queer for each other, but Garraty believed that like he believed the moon was green cheese. They didn't look effeminate, and they seemed like nice enough guys . . . not that either one of those things had much to do with whether or not they were queer, he supposed. And not that it was any of his business if they were. But . . .

Barkovitch was behind the leather boys and McVries was behind him, staring intently at Barkovitch's back. The yellow rainhat still dangled out of Barkovitch's back pocket, and he didn't look like he was cracking to Garraty. In fact, he thought with a painful twinge, McVries was the one who looked bushed.

Behind McVries and Barkovitch was a loose knot of seven or eight boys, the kind of carelessly knit confederation that seemed to form and reform during the course of the Walk, new and old members constantly coming and going. Behind them was a smaller group, and behind that group was Scramm, Pearson, Baker, Abraham, Parker, and Jensen. His group. There had been others with it near the start, and now he could barely remember their names.

There were two groups behind his, and scattered through the whole raggle-taggle column like pepper through salt were the loners. A few of them, like Olson, were withdrawn and catatonic. Others, like Stebbins, seemed to genuinely prefer their own company. And almost all of them had that intent, frightened look stamped on their faces. Garraty had come to know that look so well.

The guns came down and bore on one of the loners he had been looking at, a short, stoutish boy who was wearing a battered green silk vest. It seemed to Garraty that he had collected his final warning about half an hour ago. He threw a short, terrified glance at the guns and stepped up his pace. The guns lost their dreadful interest in him, at least for the time being.

Garraty felt a sudden incomprehensible rise in spirits. They couldn't be much more than forty miles from Oldtown and civilization now—if you wanted to call a mill, shoe, and canoe town civilization. They'd pull in there sometime late tonight, and get on the turnpike. The turnpike would be smooth sailing, compared to this. On the turnpike you could walk on the grassy median strip with your shoes off if you wanted. Feel the cold dew. Good Christ, that would be great. He mopped his brow with his forearm. Maybe things were going to turn out okay after all. The purple smudges were a little closer, and they were definitely thunderheads.

The guns went off and he didn't even jump. The boy in the green silk vest had bought a ticket, and he was staring up at the sun. Not even death was that bad, maybe. Everybody, even the Major himself, had to face it sooner or later. So who was swindling who, when you came right down to it? He made a mental note to mention that to McVries the next time they spoke.

He picked up his heels a little and made up his mind to wave to the next pretty girl he saw. But before there was a pretty girl, there was the little Italian man.

He was a caricature Italian man, a small guy with a battered felt hat and a black mustache that curled up at the ends. He was beside an old station wagon with the back hatch standing open. He was waving and grinning with incredibly white, incredibly square teeth.

An insulating mat had been laid on the bottom of the station wagon's cargo compartment. The mat had been piled high with crushed ice, and peeking through the ice in dozens of places, like wide pink peppermint grins, were wedges of watermelon.

Garraty felt his stomach flop over twice, exactly like a snap-rolling high diver. A sign on top of the station wagon read: DOM L'ANTIO LOVES ALL LONG WALKERS—FREE WATERMELON!!!

Several of the Walkers, Abraham and Collie Parker among them, broke for the shoulder at a dogtrot. All were warned. They were doing better than four an hour, but they were doing it in the wrong direction. Dom L'Antio saw them coming and laughed—a crystal, joyous, uncomplicated sound. He clapped his hands, dug into the ice, and came out with double handfuls of pink grinning watermelons. Garraty felt his mouth shrivel with want. But they won't let him, he thought. Just like they wouldn't let the storekeeper give the sodas. And then: But oh God, it'd taste good. Would it be too much, God, for them to be a little slow with the hook this time? Where did he get watermelon this time of year, anyway?

The Long Walkers milled outside the restraining ropes, the small crowd around

Dom went mad with happiness, second warnings were parceled out, and three State Troopers appeared miraculously to restrain Dom, whose voice came loud and clear:

"Whatcha mean? Whatcha mean I can't? These my wat'amelon, you dumb cop! I wanna give, I gonna give, hey! what you t'ink? Get offa my case, you hardass!"

One of the Troopers made a grab for the watermelons Dom held in his hands. Another buttonhooked around him and slammed the cargo door of the wagon shut.

"You bastards!" Garraty screamed with all his force. His shriek sped through the bright day like a glass spear, and one of the Troopers looked around, startled and . . . well, almost hangdog.

"Stinking sonsofbitches!" Garraty shrieked at them. "I wish your mothers had miscarried you stinking *whoresons!*"

"You tell 'em Garraty!" someone else yelled, and it was Barkovitch, grinning like a mouthful of tenpenny nails and shaking both of his fists at the State Troopers. "You tell—"

But they were all screaming now, and the Troopers were not handpicked Long Walk soldiers fresh off the National Squads. Their faces were red and embarrassed, but all the same they were hustling Dom and his double handfuls of cool pink grins away from the sidelines at double time.

Dom either lost his English or gave it up. He began to yell fruity Italian curses. The crowd booed the State Troopers. A woman in a floppy straw sunhat threw a transistor radio at one of them. It hit him in the head and knocked off his cap. Garraty felt sorry for the Trooper but continued to scream curses. He couldn't seem to help it. That word "whoresons," he hadn't thought anybody ever used a word like that outside of books.

Just as it seemed that Dom L'Antio would be removed from their view for good, the little Italian slipped free and dashed back toward them, the crowd parting magically for him and closing—or trying to—against the police. One of the Troopers threw a flying tackle at him, caught him around the knees, and spilled him forward. At the last instant of balance Dom let his beautiful pink grins fly in a wide-swinging throw.

"DOM L'ANTIO LOVES YOU ALL!" he cried.

The crowd cheered hysterically. Dom landed headfirst in the dirt, and his hands were cuffed behind him in a trice. The watermelon slices arced and pinwheeled through the bright air, and Garraty laughed aloud and raised both hands to the sky and shook his fists triumphantly as he saw Abraham catch one with nonchalant deftness.

Others were third-warned for stopping to pick up chunks of watermelon, but amazingly, no one was shot and five—no, six, Garraty saw—of the boys had ended up with watermelon. The rest of them alternately cheered those who had managed to get some of it, or cursed the wooden-faced soldiers, whose expressions were now satisfyingly interpreted to hold subtle chagrin.

"I love everybody!" Abraham bellowed. His grinning face was streaked with pink watermelon juice. He spat three brown seeds into the air.

"Goddam," Collie Parker said happily. "I'm goddamned, goddam if I ain't."

He drove his face into the watermelon, gobbled hungrily, then busted his piece in two. He threw half of it over to Garraty, who almost fumbled it in his surprise. "There ya go, hicksville!" Collie shouted. "Don't say I never gave ya nothin', ya goddam rube!"

Garraty laughed. "Go fuck yourself," he said. The watermelon was cold, cold. Some of the juice got up his nose, some more ran down his chin, and oh sweet heaven in his throat, running down his throat.

He only let himself eat half. "Pete!" he shouted, and tossed the remaining chunk to him.

McVries caught it with a flashy backhand, showing the sort of stuff that makes college shortstops and, maybe, major league ballplayers. He grinned at Garraty and ate the melon.

Garraty looked around and felt a crazy joy breaking through him, pumping at his heart, making him want to run around in circles on his hands. Almost everyone had gotten a scrap of the melon, even if it was no more than a scrap of the pink meat clinging to a seed.

Stebbins, as usual, was the exception. He was looking at the road. There was nothing in his hands, no smile on his face.

Screw him, Garraty thought. But a little of the joy went out of him nevertheless. His feet felt heavy again. He knew that it wasn't that Stebbins hadn't gotten any. Or that Stebbins didn't want any. Stebbins didn't need any.

2:30 PM. They had walked a hundred and twenty-one miles. The thunderheads drifted closer. A cool breeze sprang up, chill against Garraty's hot skin. It's going to rain again, he thought. Good.

The people at the sides of the road were rolling up blankets, catching flying bits of paper, reloading their picnic baskets. The storm came flying lazily at them, and all at once the temperature plummeted and it felt like autumn. Garraty buttoned his shirt quickly.

"Here it comes again," he told Scramm. "Better get your shirt on."

"Are you kidding?" Scramm grinned. "This is the besd I've feld all day!"

"It's gonna be a boomer!" Parker yelled gleefully.

They were on top of a gradually slanting plateau, and they could see the curtain of rain beating across the woods toward them below the purple thunderheads. Directly above them the sky had gone a sick yellow. A tornado sky, Garraty thought. Wouldn't that be the living end. What would they do if a tornado just came tearing ass down the road and carried them all off to Oz in a whirling cloud of dirt, flapping shoeleather, and whirling watermelon seeds?

He laughed. The wind ripped the laugh out of his mouth.

"McVries!"

McVries angled to meet him. He was bent into the wind, his clothes plastered against his body and streaming out behind him. The black hair and the white scar etched against his tanned face made him look like a weathered, slightly mad sea captain astride the bridge of his ship.

"What?" he bellowed.

"Is there a provision in the rules for an act of God?"

McVries considered. "No, I don't think so." He began buttoning his jacket.

"What happens if we get struck by lightning?"

McVries threw back his head and cackled. "We'll be dead!"

Garraty snorted and walked away. Some of the others were looking up into the sky anxiously. This was going to be no little shower, the kind that had cooled them off after yesterday's heat. What had Parker said? A boomer. Yes, it certainly was going to be a boomer.

A baseball cap went cartwheeling between his legs, and Garraty looked over his shoulder and saw a small boy looking after it longingly. Scramm grabbed it and tried to scale it back to the kid, but the wind took it in a big boomerang arc and it wound up in a wildly lashing tree.

Thunder whacked. A white-purple tine of lightning jabbed the horizon. The comforting sough of the wind in the pines had become a hundred mad ghosts, flapping and hooting.

The guns cracked, a small popgun sound almost lost in the thunder and the wind. Garraty jerked his head around, the premonition that Olson had finally bought his bullet strong upon him. But Olson was still there, his flapping clothes revealing how amazingly fast the weight had melted off him. Olson had lost his jacket somewhere; the arms that poked out of his short shirtsleeves were bony and as thin as pencils.

It was somebody else who was being dragged off. The face was small and exhausted and very dead beneath the whipping mane of his hair.

"If it was a tailwind we could be in Oldtown by four-thirty!" Barkovitch said gleefully. He had his rainhat jammed down over his ears, and his sharp face was joyful and demented. Garraty suddenly understood. He reminded himself to tell McVries. Barkovitch was crazy.

A few minutes later the wind suddenly dropped off. The thunder faded to a series of thick mutters. The heat sucked back at them, clammy and nearly unbearable after the rushy coolness of the wind.

"What happened to it?" Collie Parker brayed. "Garraty! Does this goddam state punk out on its rainstorms, too?"

"I think you'll get what you want," Garraty said. "I don't know if you'll want it when you get it, though."

"Yoo-hoo! Raymond! Raymond Garraty!"

Garraty's head jerked up. For one awful moment he thought it was his mother, and visions of Percy danced through his head. But it was only an elderly, sweet-faced lady peeping at him from beneath a *Vogue* magazine she was using as a rain-hat.

"Old bag," Art Baker muttered at his elbow.

"She looks sweet enough to me. Do you know her?"

"I know the type," Baker said balefully. "She looks just like my Aunt Hattie. She used to like to go to funerals, listen to the weeping and wailing and carryings-ons with just that same smile. Like a cat that got into the aigs."

"She's probably the Major's mother," Garraty said. It was supposed to be funny, but it fell flat. Baker's face was strained and pallid under the fading light in the rushing sky.

"My Aunt Hattie had nine kids. Nine, Garraty. She buried four of 'em with just that same look. Her own young. Some folks like to see other folks die. I can't understand that, can you?"

"No," Garraty said. Baker was making him uneasy. The thunder had begun to roll its wagons across the sky again. "Your Aunt Hattie, is she dead now?"

"No." Baker looked up at the sky. "She's down home. Probably out on the front porch in her rockin' chair. She can't walk much anymore. Just sittin' and rockin' and listenin' to the bulletins on the radio. And smilin' each time she hears the new figures." Baker rubbed his elbows with his palms. "You ever see a cat eat its own kittens, Garraty?"

Garraty didn't reply. There was an electric tension in the air now, something about the storm poised above them, and something more. Garraty could not fathom it. When he blinked his eyes he seemed to see the out-of-kilter eyes of Freaky D'Allessio looking back at him from the darkness.

Finally he said to Baker: "Does everybody in your family study up on dying?"

Baker smiled pallidly. "Well, I was turnin' over the idea of going to mortician's school in a few years. Good job. Morticians go on eating even in a depression."

"I always thought I'd get into urinal manufacture," Garraty said. "Get contracts with cinemas and bowling alleys and things. Sure-fire. How many urinal factories can there be in the country?"

"I don't think I'd still want to be a mortician," Baker said. "Not that it matters."

A huge flash of lightning tore across the sky. A gargantuan clap of thunder followed. The wind picked up in jerky gusts. Clouds raced across the sky like crazed privateers across an ebony nightmare sea.

"It's coming," Garraty said. "It's coming, Art."

"Some people say they don't care," Baker said suddenly. " 'Something simple, that's all I want when I go, Don.' That's what they'd tell him. My uncle. But most of 'em care plenty. That's what he always told me. They say, 'Just a pine box will do me fine.' But they end up having a big one . . . with a lead sleeve if they can afford it. Lots of them even write the model number in their wills."

"Why?" Garraty asked.

"Down home, most of them want to be buried in mausoleums. Aboveground. They don't want to be underground 'cause the water table's so high where I come from. Things rot quick in the damp. But if you're buried aboveground, you got the rats to worry about. Big Louisiana bayou rats. Graveyard rats. They'd gnaw through one of them pine boxes in zip flat."

The wind pulled at them with invisible hands. Garraty wished the storm would come on and come. It was like an insane merry-go-round. No matter who you talked to, you came around to this damned subject again.

"Be fucked if I'd do it," Garraty said. "Lay out fifteen hundred dollars or something just to keep the rats away after I was dead."

"I dunno," Baker said. His eyes were half-lidded, sleepy. "They go for the soft parts, that's what troubles my mind. I could see 'em worryin' a hole in my own coffin, then makin' it bigger, finally wrigglin' through. And goin' right for my eyes like they was jujubes. They'd eat my eyes and then I'd be part of that rat. Ain't that right?''

"I don't know," Garraty said sickly.

"No thanks. I'll take that coffin with the lead sleeve. Every time.''

"Although you'd only actually need it the once," Garraty said with a horrified little giggle.

"That *is* true," Baker agreed solemnly.

Lightning forked again, an almost pink streak that left the air smelling of ozone. A moment later the storm smote them again. But it wasn't rain this time. It was hail.

In a space of five seconds they were being pelted by hailstones the size of small pebbles. Several of the boys cried out, and Garraty shielded his eyes with one hand. The wind rose to a shriek. Hailstones bounced and smashed against the road, against faces and bodies.

Jensen ran in a huge, rambling circle, eyes covered, feet stumbling and rebounding against each other, in a total panic. He finally blundered off the shoulder, and the soldiers on the halftrack pumped half a dozen rounds into the undulating curtain of hail before they could be sure. Goodbye, Jensen, Garraty thought. Sorry, man.

Then rain began to fall through the hail, sluicing down the hill they were climbing, melting the hail scattered around their feet. Another wave of stones hit them, more rain, another splatter of hail, and then the rain was falling in steady sheets, punctuated by loud claps of thunder.

"Goddam!" Parker yelled, striding up to Garraty. His face was covered with red blotches, and he looked like a drowned water rat. "Garraty, this is without a doubt—"

"—yeah, the most fucked-up state in the fifty-one," Garraty finished. "Go soak your head."

Parker threw his head back, opened his mouth, and let the cold rain patter in. "I am, goddammit, I am!"

Garraty bent himself into the wind and caught up with McVries. "How does this grab you?" he asked.

McVries clutched himself and shivered. "You can't win. Now I wish the sun was out."

"It won't last long," Garraty said, but he was wrong. As they walked into four o'clock, it was still raining.

Chapter 10

"Do you know *why* they call me the Count?
Because I love to count! Ah-hah-hah."
—The Count
Sesame Street

There was no sunset as they walked into their second night on the road. The rainstorm gave way to a light, chilling drizzle around four-thirty. The drizzle continued on until almost eight o'clock. Then the clouds began to break up and show bright, coldly flickering stars.

Garraty pulled himself closer together inside his damp clothes and did not need a weatherman to know which way the wind blew. Fickle spring had pulled the balmy warmth that had come with them this far from beneath them like an old rug.

Maybe the crowds provided some warmth. Radiant heat, or something. More and more of them lined the road. They were huddled together for warmth but were undemonstrative. They watched the Walkers go past and then went home or hurried on to the next vantage point. If it was blood the crowds were looking for, they hadn't gotten much of it. They had lost only two since Jensen, both of them younger boys who had simply fainted dead away. That put them exactly halfway. No . . . really more than half. Fifty down, forty-nine to go.

Garraty was walking by himself. He was too cold to be sleepy. His lips were pressed together to keep the tremble out of them. Olson was still back there; halfhearted bets had gone round to the effect that Olson would be the fiftieth to buy a ticket, the halfway boy. But he hadn't. That signal honor had gone to 13, Roger Fenum. Unlucky old 13. Garraty was beginning to think that Olson would go on indefinitely. Maybe until he starved to death. He had locked himself safely away in a place beyond pain. In a way he supposed it would be poetic justice if Olson won. He could see the headlines: LONG WALK WON BY DEAD MAN!

Garraty's toes were numb. He wiggled them against the shredded inner linings of his shoes and could feel nothing. The real pain was not in his toes now. It was in his arches. A sharp, blatting pain that knifed up into his calves each time he took a step. It made him think of a story his mother had read him when he was small. It was about a mermaid who wanted to be a woman. Only she had a tail and a good fairy or someone said she could have legs if she wanted them badly enough. Every step she took on dry land would be like walking on knives, but she could have them if she wanted them, and she said yeah, okay, and that was the Long Walk. In a nutshell—

250

"Warning! Warning 47!"

"I hear you," Garraty snapped crossly, and picked up his feet.

The woods were thinner. The real northern part of the state was behind them. They had gone through two quietly residential towns, the road cutting them lengthwise and the sidewalks packed with people that were little more than shadows beneath the drizzle-diffused streetlamps. No one cheered much. It was too cold, he supposed. Too cold and too dark and Jesus Christ now he had another warning to walk off and if that wasn't a royal pisser, nothing was.

His feet were slowing again and he forced himself to pick them up. Somewhere quite far up ahead Barkovitch said something and followed it up with a short burst of his unpleasant laughter. He could hear McVries's response clearly: "Shut up, killer." Barkovitch told McVries to go to hell, and now he seemed quite upset by the whole thing. Garraty smiled wanly in the darkness.

He had dropped back almost to the tail of the column and reluctantly realized he was angling toward Stebbins again. Something about Stebbins fascinated him. But he decided he didn't particularly care what that something was. It was time to give up wondering about things. There was no percentage in it. It was just another royal pisser.

There was a huge, luminescent arrow ahead in the dark. It glowed like an evil spirit. Suddenly a brass band struck up a march. A good-sized band, by the sound. There were louder cheers. The air was full of drifting fragments, and for a crazy moment Garraty thought it was snowing. But it wasn't snow. It was confetti. They were changing roads. The old one met the new one at a right angle and another Maine Turnpike sign announced that Oldtown was now a mere sixteen miles away. Garraty felt a tentative feeler of excitement, maybe even pride. After Oldtown he knew the route. He could have traced it on the palm of his hand.

"Maybe it's your edge. I don't think so, but maybe it is."

Garraty jumped. It was as if Stebbins had pried the lid off his mind and peeked down inside.

"What?"

"It's your country, isn't it?"

"Not up here. I've never been north of Greenbush in my life, except when we drove up to the marker. And we didn't come this way." They left the brass band behind them, its tubas and clarinets glistening softly in the moist night.

"But we go through your hometown, don't we?"

"No, but close by it."

Stebbins grunted. Garraty looked down at Stebbins's feet and saw with surprise that Stebbins had removed his tennis shoes and was wearing a pair of soft-looking moccasins. His shoes were tucked into his chambray shirt.

"I'm saving the tennis shoes," Stebbins said, "just in case. But I think the mocs will finish it."

"Oh."

They passed a radio tower standing skeletal in an empty field. A red light pulsed as regular as a heartbeat at its tip.

"Looking forward to seeing your loved ones?"

"Yes, I am," Garraty said.

"What happens after that?"

"Happens?" Garraty shrugged. "Keep on walking down the road, I guess. Unless you are all considerate enough to buy out by then."

"Oh, I don't think so," Stebbins said, smiling remotely. "Are you sure you won't be walked out? After you see them?"

"Man, I'm not sure of anything," Garraty said. "I didn't know much when I started, and I know less now."

"You think you have a chance?"

"I don't know that either. I don't even know why I bother talking to you. It's like talking to smoke."

Far ahead, police sirens howled and gobbled in the night.

"Somebody broke through to the road up ahead where the police are spread thinner," Stebbins said. "The natives are getting restless, Garraty. Just think of all the people diligently making way for you up ahead."

"For you too."

"Me too," Stebbins agreed, then didn't say anything for a long time. The collar of his chambray workshirt flapped vacuously against his neck. "It's amazing how the mind operates the body," he said at last. "It's amazing how it can take over and dictate to the body. Your average housewife may walk up to sixteen miles a day, from icebox to ironing board to clothesline. She's ready to put her feet up at the end of the day but she's not exhausted. A door-to-door salesman might do twenty. A high school kid in training for football walks twenty-five to twenty-eight . . . that's in one day from getting up in the morning to going to bed at night. All of them get tired, but none of them get exhausted."

"Yeah."

"But suppose you told the housewife: today you must walk sixteen miles before you can have your supper."

Garraty nodded. "She'd be exhausted instead of tired."

Stebbins said nothing. Garraty had the perverse feeling that Stebbins was disappointed in him.

"Well . . . wouldn't she?"

"Don't you think she'd have her sixteen miles in by noon so she could kick off her shoes and spend the afternoon watching the soaps? I do. Are you tired, Garraty?"

"Yeah," Garraty said shortly. "I'm tired."

"Exhausted?"

"Well, I'm getting there."

"No, you're not getting exhausted yet, Garraty." He jerked a thumb at Olson's silhouette. "*That's* exhausted. He's almost through now."

Garraty watched Olson, fascinated, almost expecting him to drop at Stebbins's word. "What are you driving at?"

"Ask your cracker friend, Art Baker. A mule doesn't like to plow. But he likes

carrots. So you hang a carrot in front of his eyes. A mule without a carrot gets
exhausted. A mule with a carrot spends a long time being tired. You get it?''

''No.''

Stebbins smiled again. ''You will. Watch Olson. He's lost his appetite for the
carrot. He doesn't quite know it yet, but he has. Watch Olson, Garraty. You can
learn from Olson.''

Garraty looked at Stebbins closely, not sure how seriously to take him. Stebbins
laughed aloud. His laugh was rich and full—a startling sound that made other
Walkers turn their heads. ''Go on. Go talk to him, Garraty. And if he won't talk,
just get up close and have a good look. It's never too late to learn.''

Garraty swallowed. ''Is it a very important lesson, would you say?''

Stebbins stopped laughing. He caught Garraty's wrist in a strong grip. ''The
most important lesson you'll ever learn, maybe. The secret of life over death. Reduce that equation and you can afford to die, Garraty. You can spend your life like
a drunkard on a spree.''

Stebbins dropped his hand. Garraty massaged his wrist slowly. Stebbins seemed
to have dismissed him again. Nervously, Garraty walked away from him, and toward Olson.

It seemed to Garraty that he was drawn toward Olson on an invisible wire. He
flanked him at four o'clock. He tried to fathom Olson's face.

Once, a long time ago, he had been frightened into a long night of wakefulness
by a movie starring—who? It had been Robert Mitchum, hadn't it? He had been
playing the role of an implacable Southern revival minister who had also been a
compulsive murderer. In silhouette, Olson looked a little bit like him now. His
form had seemed to elongate as the weight sloughed off him. His skin had gone
scaly with dehydration. His eyes had sunk into hollowed sockets. His hair flew
aimlessly on his skull like wind-driven cornsilk.

Why, he's nothing but a robot, nothing but an automaton, really. Can there still
be an Olson in there hiding? No. He's gone. I am quite sure that the Olson who
sat on the grass and joked and told about the kid who froze on the starting line and
bought his ticket right there, that Olson is gone. This is a dead clay thing.

''Olson?'' he whispered.

Olson walked on. He was a shambling haunted house on legs. Olson had fouled
himself. Olson smelled bad.

''Olson, can you talk?''

Olson swept onward. His face was turned into the darkness, and he *was* moving,
yes he *was* moving. Something was going on here, something was still ticking
over, but—

Something, yes, there was *something,* but what?

They breasted another rise. The breath came shorter and shorter in Garraty's
lungs until he was panting like a dog. Tiny vapors of steam rose from his wet
clothes. There was a river below them, lying in the dark like a silver snake. The
Stillwater, he imagined. The Stillwater passed near Oldtown. A few halfhearted
cheers went up, but not many. Further on, nestled against the far side of the river's

dogleg (maybe it was the Penobscot, after all), was a nestle of lights. Oldtown. A smaller nestle of light on the other side would be Milford and Bradley. Oldtown. They had made it to Oldtown.

"Olson," he said. "That's Oldtown. Those lights are Oldtown. We're getting there, fellow."

Olson made no answer. And now he could remember what had been eluding him and it was nothing so vital after all. Just that Olson reminded him of the Flying Dutchman, sailing on and on after the whole crew had disappeared.

They walked rapidly down a long hill, passed through an S-curve, and crossed a bridge that spanned, according to the sign, Meadow Brook. On the far side of this bridge was another STEEP HILL TRUCKS USE LOW GEAR sign. There were groans from some of the Walkers.

It was indeed a steep hill. It seemed to rise above them like a toboggan slide. It was not long; even in the dark they could see the summit. But it was steep, all right. Plenty steep.

They started up.

Garraty leaned into the slope, feeling his grip on his respiration start to trickle away almost at once. Be panting like a dog at the top, he thought . . . and then thought, if I *get* to the top. There was a protesting clamor rising in both legs. It started in his thighs and worked its way down. His legs were screaming at him that they simply weren't going to do this shit any longer.

But you will, Garraty told them. You will or you'll die.

I don't care, his legs answered back. Don't care if I do die, do die, do die.

The muscles seemed to be softening, melting like Jell-O left out in a hot sun. They trembled almost helplessly. They twitched like badly controlled puppets.

Warnings cracked out right and left, and Garraty realized he would be getting one for his very own soon enough. He kept his eyes fixed on Olson, forcing himself to match his pace to Olson's. They would make it together, up over the top of this killer hill, and then he would get Olson to tell him his secret. Then everything would be jake and he wouldn't have to worry about Stebbins or McVries or Jan or his father, no, not even about Freaky D'Allessio, who had spread his head on a stone wall beside U.S. 1 like a dollop of glue.

What was it, a hundred feet on? Fifty? What?

Now he was panting.

The first gunshots rang out. There was a loud, yipping scream that was drowned by more gunshots. And at the brow of the hill they got one more. Garraty could see nothing in the dark. His tortured pulse hammered in his temples. He found that he didn't give a fuck who had bought it this time. It didn't matter. Only the pain mattered, the tearing pain in his legs and lungs.

The hill rounded, flattened, and rounded still more on the downslope. The far side was gently sloping, perfect for regaining wind. But that soft jelly feeling in his muscles didn't want to leave. My legs are going to collapse, Garraty thought calmly. They'll never take me as far as Freeport. I don't think I can make it to Oldtown. I'm dying, I think.

A sound began to beat its way into the night then, savage and orgiastic. It was a voice, it was many voices, and it was repeating the same thing over and over:

Garraty! Garraty! GARRATY! GARRATY! GARRATY!

It was God or his father, about to cut the legs out from under him before he could learn the secret, the secret, the secret of—

Like thunder: *GARRATY! GARRATY! GARRATY!*

It wasn't his father and it wasn't God. It was what appeared to be the entire student body of Oldtown High School, chanting his name in unison. As they caught sight of his white, weary, and strained face, the steady beating cry dissolved into wild cheering. Cheerleaders fluttered pompoms. Boys whistled shrilly and kissed their girls. Garraty waved back, smiled, nodded, and craftily crept closer to Olson.

"Olson," he whispered. "Olson."

Olson's eyes might have flickered a tiny bit. A spark of life like the single turn of an old starter in a junked automobile.

"Tell me how, Olson," he whispered. "Tell me what to do."

The high school girls and boys (did I once go to high school? Garraty wondered, was that a dream?) were behind them now, still cheering rapturously.

Olson's eyes moved jerkily in their sockets, as if long rusted and in need of oil. His mouth fell open with a nearly audible clunk.

"That's it," Garraty whispered eagerly. "Talk. Talk to me, Olson. Tell me. Tell me."

"Ah," Olson said. "Ah. Ah."

Garraty moved even closer. He put a hand on Olson's shoulder and leaned into an evil nimbus of sweat, halitosis, and urine.

"Please," Garraty said. "Try hard."

"Ga. Go. God. God's garden—"

"God's garden," Garraty repeated doubtfully. "What about God's garden, Olson?"

"It's full. Of. Weeds," Olson said sadly. His head bounced against his chest. "I."

Garraty said nothing. He could not. They were going up another hill now and he was panting again. Olson did not seem to be out of breath at all.

"I don't. Want. To die," Olson finished.

Garraty's eyes were soldered to the shadowed ruin that was Olson's face. Olson turned creakily toward him.

"Ah?" Olson raised his lolling head slowly. "Ga. Ga. Garraty?"

"Yes, it's me."

"What time is it?"

Garraty had rewound and reset his watch earlier. God knew why. "It's quarter of nine."

"No. No later. Than that?" Mild surprise washed over Olson's shattered old man's face.

"Olson—" He shook Olson's shoulder gently and Olson's whole frame seemed to tremble, like a gantry in a high wind. "What's it all about?" Suddenly Garraty cackled madly. "What's it all about, Alfie?"

Olson looked at Garraty with calculated shrewdness.

"Garraty," he whispered. His breath was like a sewer-draught.

"What?"

"What time is it?"

"Dammit!" Garraty shouted at him. He turned his head quickly, but Stebbins was staring down at the road. If he was laughing at Garraty, it was too dark to see.

"Garraty?"

"What?" Garraty said more quietly.

"Je. Jesus will save you."

Olson's head came up all the way. He began to walk off the road. He was walking at the halftrack.

"Warning. Warning 70!"

Olson never slowed. There was a ruinous dignity about him. The gabble of the crowd quieted. They watched, wide-eyed.

Olson never hesitated. He reached the soft shoulder. He put his hands over the side of the halftrack. He began to clamber painfully up the side.

"Olson!" Abraham yelled, startled. "Hey, that's Hank Olson!"

The soldiers brought their guns around in perfect four-part harmony. Olson grabbed the barrel of the closest and yanked it out of the hands that held it as if it had been an ice-cream stick. It clattered off into the crowd. They shrank from it, screaming, as if it had been a live adder.

Then one of the other three guns went off. Garraty saw the flash at the end of the barrel quite clearly. He saw the jerky ripple of Olson's shirt as the bullet entered his belly and then punched out the back.

Olson did not stop. He gained the top of the halftrack and grabbed the barrel of the gun that had just shot him. He levered it up into the air as it went off again.

"Get 'em!" McVries was screaming savagely up ahead. "Get 'em, Olson! Kill 'em! Kill 'em!"

The other two guns roared in unison and the impact of the heavy-caliber slugs sent Olson flying off the halftrack. He landed spread-eagled on his back like a man nailed to a cross. One side of his belly was a black and shredded ruin. Three more bullets were pumped into him. The guard Olson had disarmed had produced another carbine (effortlessly) from inside the halftrack.

Olson sat up. He put his hands against his belly and stared calmly at the poised soldiers on the deck of the squat vehicle. The soldiers stared back.

"You bastards!" McVries sobbed. "You bloody bastards!"

Olson began to get up. Another volley of bullets drove him flat again.

Now there was a sound from behind Garraty. He didn't have to turn his head to know it was Stebbins. Stebbins was laughing softly.

Olson sat up again. The guns were still trained on him, but the soldiers did not shoot. Their silhouettes on the halftrack seemed almost to indicate curiosity.

Slowly, reflectively, Olson gained his feet, hands crossed on his belly. He seemed to sniff the air for direction, turned slowly in the direction of the Walk, and began to stagger along.

"Put him out of it!" a shocked voice screamed hoarsely. "For Christ's sake put him out of it!"

The blue snakes of Olson's intestines were slowly slipping through his fingers. They dropped like link sausages against his groin, where they flapped obscenely. He stopped, bent over as if to retrieve them (*retrieve* them, Garraty thought in a near ecstasy of wonder and horror), and threw up a huge glut of blood and bile. He began to walk again, bent over. His face was sweetly calm.

"Oh my God," Abraham said, and turned to Garraty with his hands cupped over his mouth. Abraham's face was white and cheesy. His eyes were bulging. His eyes were frantic with terror. "Oh my God, Ray, what a fucking gross-out, oh Jesus!" Abraham vomited. Puke sprayed through his fingers.

Well, old Abe has tossed his cookies, Garraty thought remotely. That's no way to observe Hint 13, Abe.

"They gut-shot him," Stebbins said from behind Garraty. "They'll do that. It's deliberate. To discourage anybody else from trying the old Charge of the Light Brigade number."

"Get away from me," Garraty hissed. "Or I'll knock your block off!"

Stebbins dropped back quickly.

"Warning! Warning 88!"

Stebbins's laugh drifted softly to him.

Olson went to his knees. His head hung between his arms, which were propped on the road.

One of the rifles roared, and a bullet clipped asphalt beside Olson's left hand and whined away. He began to climb slowly, wearily, to his feet again. They're playing with him, Garraty thought. All of this must be terribly boring for them, so they are playing with Olson. Is Olson fun, boys? Is Olson keeping you amused?

Garraty began to cry. He ran over to Olson and fell on his knees beside him and held the tired, hectically hot face against his chest. He sobbed into the dry, bad-smelling hair.

"Warning! Warning 47!"

"Warning! Warning 61!"

McVries was pulling at him. It was McVries again. "Get up, Ray, get up, you can't help him, for God's sake get up!"

"It's not *fair!*" Garraty wept. There was a sticky smear of Olson's blood on his cheekbone. "It's just not fair!"

"I know. Come on. Come on."

Garraty stood up. He and McVries began walking backward rapidly, watching Olson, who was on his knees. Olson got to his feet. He stood astride the white line. He raised both hands up into the sky. The crowd sighed softly.

"I DID IT *WRONG!*" Olson shouted tremblingly, and then fell flat and dead.

The soldiers on the halftrack put another two bullets in him and then dragged him busily off the road.

"Yes, that's that."

They walked quietly for ten minutes or so, Garraty drawing a low-key comfort just from McVries's presence. "I'm starting to see something in it, Pete," he said at last. "There's a pattern. It isn't all senseless."

"Yeah? Don't count on it."

"He talked to me, Pete. He wasn't dead until they shot him. He was *alive.*" Now it seemed that was the most important thing about the Olson experience. He repeated it. *"Alive."*

"I don't think it makes any difference," McVries said with a tired sigh. "He's just a number. Part of the body count. Number fifty-three. It means we're a little closer and that's all it means."

"You don't really think that."

"Don't tell me what I think and what I don't!" McVries said crossly. "Leave it alone, can't you?"

"I put us about thirteen miles outside of Oldtown," Garraty said.

"Well hot shit!"

"Do you know how Scramm is?"

"I'm not his doctor. Why don't you scram yourself?"

"What the hell's eating you?"

McVries laughed wildly. "Here we are, here we are and you want to know what's *eating* me! I'm worried about next year's income taxes, that's what's eating me. I'm worried about the price of grain in South Dakota, that's what's eating me. Olson, his *guts* were falling out, Garraty, at the end he was walking with his *guts falling out,* and that's eating me, that's *eating* me—" He broke off and Garraty watched him struggle to keep from vomiting. Abruptly McVries said, "Scramm's poor."

"Is he?"

"Collie Parker felt his forehead and said he was burning up. He's talking funny. About his wife, about Phoenix, Flagstaff, weird stuff about the Hopis and the Navajos and kachina dolls . . . it's hard to make out."

"How much longer can he go?"

"Who can say. He still might outlast us all. He's built like a buffalo and he's trying awful hard. Jesus, am I tired."

"What about Barkovitch?"

"He's wising up. He knows a lot of us'll be glad to see him buy a ticket to see the farm. He's made up his mind to outlast me, the nasty little fucker. He doesn't like me shagging him. Tough shit, right, I know." McVries uttered his wild laugh again. Garraty didn't like the sound of it. "He's scared, though. He's easing up on the lungpower and going to leg-power."

"We all are."

"Yeah. Oldtown coming up. Thirteen miles?"

"That's right."

"Can I say something to you, Garraty?"

"Sure. I'll carry it with me to the grave."

"I suppose that's true."

Someone near the front of the crowd set off a firecracker, and both Garraty and McVries jumped. Several women screeched. A burly man in the front row said "Goddammit!" through a mouthful of popcorn.

"The reason all of this is so horrible," McVries said, "is because it's just trivial. You know? We've sold ourselves and traded our souls on trivialities. Olson, he was trivial. He was magnificent, too, but those things aren't mutually exclusive. He was magnificent and trivial. Either way, or both, he died like a bug under a microscope."

"You're as bad as Stebbins," Garraty said resentfully.

"I wish Priscilla had killed me," McVries said. "At least that wouldn't have been—"

"Trivial," Garraty finished.

"Yes. I think—"

"Look, I want to doze a little if I can. You mind?"

"No. I'm sorry." McVries sounded stiff and offended.

"*I'm* sorry," Garraty said. "Look, don't take it to heart. It's really—"

"Trivial," McVries finished. He laughed his wild laugh for the third time and walked away. Garraty wished—not for the first time—that he had made no friends on the Long Walk. It was going to make it hard. In fact, it was already hard.

There was a sluggish stirring in his bowels. Soon they would have to be emptied. The thought made him grind his mental teeth. People would point and laugh. He would drop his shit in the street like a mongrel hound and afterward people would gather it up in paper napkins and put it in bottles for souvenirs. It seemed impossible that people would do such things, but he knew it happened.

Olson with his guts falling out.

McVries and Priscilla and the pajama factory.

Scramm, glowing fever-bright.

Abraham . . . what price stovepipe hat, audience?

Garraty's head dropped. He dozed. The Walk went on.

Over hill, over dale, over stile and mountain. Over ridge and under bridge and past my lady's fountain. Garraty giggled in the dimming recesses of his brain. His feet pounded the pavement and the loose heel flapped looser, like an old shutter on a dead house.

I think, therefore I am. First-year Latin class. Old tunes in a dead language. Ding-dong-bell-pussy's-down-the-well. Who pushed her in? Little Jackie Flynn.

I *exist,* therefore I am.

Another firecracker went off. There were whoops and cheers. The halftrack ground and clattered and Garraty listened for the sound of his number in a warning and dozed deeper.

Daddy, I wasn't glad when you had to go, but I never really missed you when you were gone. Sorry. But that's not the reason I'm here. I have no subconscious urge to kill myself, sorry Stebbins. So sorry but—

The guns again, startling him awake, and there was the familiar mailsack thud of another boy going home to Jesus. The crowd screamed its horror and roared its approval.

"Garraty!" a woman squealed. "Ray *Garraty!*" Her voice was harsh and scabbed. "We're *with* you, boy! *We're with you Ray!*"

Her voice cut through the crowd and heads turned, necks craned, so that they could get a better look at Maine's Own. There were scattered boos drowned in a rising cheer.

The crowd took up the chant again. Garraty heard his name until it was reduced to a jumble of nonsense syllables that had nothing to do with him.

He waved briefly and dozed again.

Chapter 11

"Come on, assholes! You want to live forever?"
—Unknown World War I
Top Sergeant

They passed into Oldtown around midnight. They switched through two feeder roads, joined Route 2, and went through the center of town.

For Ray Garraty the entire passage was a blurred, sleep-hazed nightmare. The cheering rose and swelled until it seemed to cut off any possibility of thought or reason. Night was turned into glaring, shadowless day by flaring arc-sodium lamps that threw a strange orange light. In such a light even the most friendly face looked like something from a crypt. Confetti, newspaper, shredded pieces of telephone book, and long streamers of toilet paper floated and soared from second- and third-story windows. It was a New York tickertape parade in Bush League U.S.A.

No one died in Oldtown. The orange arc-lamps faded and the crowd depleted a little as they walked along the Stillwater River in the trench of morning. It was May 3rd now. The ripe smell of paper mill smote them. A juicy smell of chemicals, woodsmoke, polluted river, and stomach cancer waiting to happen. There were conical piles of sawdust higher than the buildings downtown. Heaped stacks of pulpwood stood to the sky like monoliths. Garraty dozed and dreamed his shadowy dreams of relief and redemption and after what seemed to be an eternity, someone began jabbing him in the ribs. It was McVries.

"Wassamatter?"

"We're going on the turnpike," McVries said. He was excited. "The word's back. They got a whole sonofabitchin' color guard on the entrance ramp. We're gonna get a four-hundred-gun salute!"

"Into the valley of death rode the four hundred," Garraty muttered, rubbing the sleepy-seeds out of his eyes. "I've heard too many three-gun salutes tonight. Not interested. Lemme sleep."

"That isn't the point. After *they* get done, we're gonna give *them* a salute."

"We are?"

"Yeah. A forty-six-man raspberry."

Garraty grinned a little. It felt stiff and uncertain on his lips. "That right?"

"It certainly is. Well . . . a forty-man raspberry. A few of the guys are pretty far gone now."

Garraty had a brief vision of Olson, the human Flying Dutchman.

"Well, count me in," he said.

"Bunch up with us a little, then."

Garraty picked it up. He and McVries moved in tighter with Pearson, Abraham, Baker and Scramm. The leather boys had further shortened their vanguard.

"Barkovitch in on it?" Garraty asked.

McVries snorted. "He thinks it's the greatest idea since pay toilets."

Garraty clutched his cold body a little tighter to himself and let out a humorless little giggle. "I bet he's got a hell of a wicked raspberry."

They were paralleling the turnpike now. Garraty could see the steep embankment to his right, and the fuzzy glow of more arc-sodiums—bone-white this time—above. A distance ahead, perhaps half a mile, the entrance ramp split off and climbed.

"Here we come," McVries said.

"Cathy!" Scramm yelled suddenly, making Garraty start. "I ain't gave up yet, Cathy!" He turned his blank, fever-glittering eyes on Garraty. There was no recognition in them. His cheeks were flushed, his lips cracked with fever blisters.

"He ain't so good," Baker said apologetically, as if he had caused it. "We been givin' him water every now and again, also sort of pourin' it over his head. But his canteen's almost empty, and if he wants another one, he'll have to holler for it himself. It's the rules."

"Scramm," Garraty said.

"Who's that?" Scramm's eyes rolled wildly in their sockets.

"Me. Garraty."

"Oh. You seen Cathy?"

"No," Garraty said uncomfortably. "I—"

"Here we come," McVries said. The crowd's cheers rose in volume again, and a ghostly green sign came out of the darkness: INTERSTATE 95 AUGUSTA PORTLAND PORTSMOUTH POINTS SOUTH.

"That's us," Abraham whispered. "God help us an' points south."

The exit ramp tilted up under their feet. They passed into the first splash of light from the overhead arcs. The new paving was smoother beneath their feet, and Garraty felt a familiar lift-drop of excitement.

The soldiers of the color guard had displaced the crowd along the upward spiral of the ramp. They silently held their rifles to high port. Their dress uniforms gleamed resplendently; their own soldiers in their dusty halftrack looked shabby by comparison.

It was like rising above a huge and restless sea of noise and into the calm air. The only sound was their footfalls and the hurried pace of their breathing. The entrance ramp seemed to go on forever, and always the way was fringed by soldiers in scarlet uniforms, their arms held in high-port salute.

And then, from the darkness somewhere, came the Major's electronically amplified voice: "Pre-*sent* harms!"

Weapons slapped flesh.

"Salute *ready!*"

Guns to shoulders, pointed skyward above them in a steely arch. Everyone in-

stinctively huddled together against the crash which meant death—it had been Pav-
loved into them.

"Fire!"

Four hundred guns in the night, stupendous, ear-shattering. Garraty fought down
the urge to put his hands to his head.

"Fire!"

Again the smell of powder smoke, acrid, heavy with cordite. In what book did
they fire guns over the water to bring the body of a drowned man to the surface?

"My head," Scramm moaned. "Oh Jesus my head aches."

"Fire!"

The guns exploded for the third and last time.

McVries immediately turned around and walked backward, his face going a
spotty red with the effort it cost him to shout. "Pre-*sent* harms!"

Forty tongues pursed forty sets of lips.

"Salute *ready!*"

Garraty drew breath into his lungs and fought to hold it.

"Fire!"

It was pitiful, really. A pitiful little noise of defiance in the big dark. It was not
repeated. The wooden faces of their color guard did not change, but seemed all
the same to indicate a subtle reproach.

"Oh, screw it," said McVries. He turned around and began to walk frontwards
again, with his head down.

The pavement leveled off. They were on the turnpike. There was a brief vision
of the Major's jeep spurting away to the south, a flicker of cold fluorescent light
against black sunglasses, and then the crowd closed in again, but farther from them
now, for the highway was four lanes wide, five if you counted the grassy median
strip.

Garraty angled to the median quickly, and walked in the close-cropped grass,
feeling the dew seep through his cracked shoes and paint his ankles. Someone was
warned. The turnpike stretched ahead, flat and monotonous, stretches of concrete
tubing divided by this green inset, all of it banded together by strips of white light
from the arc-sodiums above. Their shadows were sharp and clear and long, as if
thrown by a summer moon.

Garraty tipped his canteen up, swigged deep, recapped it, and began to doze
again. Eighty, maybe eighty-four miles to Augusta. The feel of the wet grass was
soothing . . .

He stumbled, almost fell, and came awake with a jerk. Some fool had planted
pines on the median strip. He knew it was the state tree, but wasn't that taking it
a little far? How could they expect you to walk on the grass when there were—

They didn't, of course.

Garraty moved over to the left lane, where most of them were walking. Two
more halftracks had rattled onto the turnpike at the Orono entrance to fully cover
the forty-six Walkers now left. They didn't expect you to walk on the grass. Another joke on you, Garraty old sport. Nothing vital, just another little disappoint-

ment. Trivial, really. Just . . . don't dare wish for anything, and don't count on anything. The doors are closing. One by one, they're closing.

"They'll drop out tonight," he said. "They'll go like bugs on a wall tonight."

"I wouldn't count on it," Collie Parker said, and now he sounded worn and tired—subdued at last.

"Why not?"

"It's like shaking a box of crackers through a sieve, Garraty. The crumbs fall through pretty fast. Then the little pieces break up and they go, too. But the big crackers"—Parker's grin was a crescent flash of saliva-coated teeth in the darkness—"the *whole* crackers have to bust off a crumb at a time."

"But such a long way to walk . . . still . . . "

"I still want to live," Parker said roughly. "So do you, don't shit me, Garraty. You and that guy McVries can walk down the road and bullshit the universe and each other, so what, it's all a bunch of phony crap but it passes the time. But don't shit me. The bottom line is you still want to live. So do most of the others. They'll die slow. They'll die one piece at a time. I may get it, but right now I feel like I could walk all the way to New Orleans before I fell down on my knees for those wet ends in their kiddy car."

"Really?" He felt a wave of despair wash over him. "Really?"

"Yeah, really. Settle down, Garraty. We still got a long way to go." He strode away, up to where the leather boys, Mike and Joe, were pacing the group. Garraty's head dropped and he dozed again.

His mind began to drift clear of his body, a huge sightless camera full of unexposed film snapping shuttershots of everything and anything, running freely, painlessly, without friction. He thought of his father striding off big in green rubber boots. He thought of Jimmy Owens, he had hit Jimmy with the barrel of his air rifle, and yes he had meant to, because it had been Jimmy's idea, taking off their clothes and touching each other had been Jimmy's idea, it had been Jimmy's idea. The gun swinging in a glittering arc, a glittering *purposeful* arc, the splash of blood ("I'm sorry Jim oh jeez you need a bandaid") across Jimmy's chin, helping him into the house . . . Jimmy hollering . . . hollering.

Garraty looked up, half-stupefied and a little sweaty in spite of the night chill. Someone had hollered. The guns were centered on a small, nearly portly figure. It looked like Barkovitch. They fired in neat unison, and the small, nearly portly figure was thrown across two lanes like a limp laundry sack. The bepimpled moon face was not Barkovitch's. To Garraty the face looked rested, at peace.

He found himself wondering if they wouldn't all be better off dead, and shied away from the thought skittishly. But wasn't it true? The thought was inexorable. The pain in his feet would double, perhaps treble before the end came, and the pain seemed insupportable now. And it was not even pain that was the worst. It was the death, the constant death, the stink of carrion that had settled into his nostrils. The crowd's cheers were a constant background to his thoughts. The sound lulled him. He began to doze again, and this time it was the image of Jan that came. For a while he had forgotten all about her. In a way, he thought disjointedly, it was better to doze than to sleep. The pain in his feet and his legs seemed to belong to someone else to whom he was tethered only loosely, and with just a little effort he could regulate his thoughts. Put them to work for him.

He built her image slowly in his mind. Her small feet. Her sturdy but completely feminine legs—small calves swelling to full earthy peasant thighs. Her waist was small, her breasts full and proud. The intelligent, rounded planes of her face. Her long blond hair. Whore's hair he thought it for some reason. Once he had told her that—it had simply slipped out and he thought she would be angry, but she had not replied at all. He thought she had been secretly pleased . . .

It was the steady, reluctant contraction in his bowels that raised him this time. He had to grit his teeth to keep walking at speed until the sensation had passed. The fluorescent dial on his watch said it was almost one o'clock.

Oh God, please don't make me have to take a crap in front of all these people. Please God. I'll give You half of everything I get if I win, only please constipate me. Please. Please. Pl—

His bowels contracted again, strongly and hurtfully, perhaps affirming the fact that he was still essentially healthy in spite of the pounding his body had taken. He forced himself to go on until he had passed out of the merciless glare of the nearest overhead. He nervously unbuckled his belt, paused, then, grimacing, shoved his pants down with one hand held protectively across his genitals, and squatted. His knees popped explosively. The muscles in his thighs and calves protested screamingly and threatened to knot as they were bullied unwillingly in a new direction.

"Warning! Warning 47!"

"John! Hey Johnny, look at that poor bastard over there."

Pointing fingers, half-seen and half-imagined in the darkness. Flashbulbs popped and Garraty turned his head away miserably. Nothing could be worse than this. Nothing.

He almost fell on his back and managed to prop himself up with one arm.

A squealing, girlish voice: "I *see* it! I see his *thing!*"

Baker passed him without a glance.

For a terrifying moment he thought it was all going to be for nothing anyway—a false alarm—but then it was all right. He was able to take care of business. Then, with a grunting half-sob, he rose to his feet and stumbled into a half-walk, half-run, cinching his pants tight again, leaving part of him behind to steam in the dark, eyed avidly by a thousand people—bottle it! put it on your mantel! The shit of a man with his life laid straight out in the line! *This is it, Betty, I told you we had something special in the game room . . . right up here, over the stereo. He was shot twenty minutes later . . .*

He caught up with McVries and walked beside him, head down.

"Tough?" McVries asked. There was unmistakable admiration in his voice.

"Real tough," Garraty said, and let out a shivery, loosening sigh. "I knew I forgot something."

"What?"

"I left my toilet paper home."

McVries cackled. "As my old granny used to say, if you ain't got a cob, then just let your hips slide a little freer."

Garraty burst out laughing, a clear, hearty laugh with no hysteria in it. He felt lighter, looser. No matter how things turned out, he wouldn't have to go through *that* again.

"Well, you made it," Baker said, falling in step.

"Jesus," Garraty said, surprised. "Why don't all you guys just send me a get-well card, or something?"

"It's no fun, with all those people staring at you," Baker said soberly. "Listen, I just heard something. I don't know if I believe it. I don't know if I even *want* to believe it."

"What is it?" Garraty asked.

"Joe and Mike? The leather-jacket guys everybody thought was queer for each other? They're Hopis. I think that was what Scramm was trying to tell us before, and we weren't gettin' him. But . . . see . . . what I hear is that they're brothers."

Garraty's jaw dropped.

I walked up and took a good look at 'em," Baker was going on. "And I'll be goddamned if they don't *look* like brothers."

"That's twisted," McVries said angrily. "That's fucking twisted! Their folks ought to be Squaded for allowing something like that!"

You ever know any Indians?" Baker asked quietly.

"Not unless they came from Passaic," McVries said. He still sounded angry.

"There's a Seminole reservation down home, across the state line," Baker said. "They're funny people. They don't think of things like 'responsibility' the same way we do. They're proud. And poor. I guess those things are the same for the Hopis as they are for the Seminoles. And they know how to die."

"None of that makes it right," McVries said.

"They come from New Mexico," Baker said.

"It's an abortion," McVries said with finality, and Garraty tended to agree.

Talk flagged all up and down the line, partially because of the noise from the crowd. but more, Garraty suspected, because of the very monotony of the turnpike itself. The hills were long and gradual, barely seeming like hills. Walkers dozed, snorted fitfully, and seemed to pull their belts tighter and resign themselves to a long, barely understood bitterness ahead. The little clots of society dissolved into threes, twos, solitary islands.

The crowd knew no fatigue. They cheered steadily with one hoarse voice, they waved unreadable placards. Garraty's name was shouted with monotonous frequency, but blocs of out-of-staters cheered briefly for Barkovitch, Pearson, Wyman. Other names blipped past and were gone with the speeding velocity of snow across a television screen.

Firecrackers popped and spluttered in strings. Someone threw a burning road flare into the cold sky and the crowd scattered, screaming, as it pinwheeled down to hiss its glaring purple light into the dirt of a gravel shoulder beyond the break-down lane. There were other crowd standouts. A man with an electric bullhorn who alternately praised Garraty and advertised his own candidacy to represent the second district; a woman with a big crow in a small cage which she hugged jealously to her giant bosom; a human pyramid made out of college boys in University of New Hampshire sweatshirts; a hollow-cheeked man with no teeth in an Uncle Sam suit wearing a sign which said: WE GAVE AWAY THE PANAMA CANAL TO THE COMMUNIST NIGGERS. But otherwise the crowd seemed as dull and bland as the turnpike itself.

Garraty dozed on fitfully, and the visions in his head were alternately of love and horror. In one of the dreams a low and droning voice asked over and over again: *Are you experienced? Are you experienced? Are you experienced?* and he could not tell if it was the voice of Stebbins or of the Major.

Chapter 12

"I went down the road, the road was muddy.
I stubbed my toe, my toe was bloody.
You all here?"
—Child's hide-and-seek rhyme

Somehow it had got around to nine in the morning again.

Ray Garraty turned his canteen over his head, leaning back until his neck popped. It had only just warmed up enough so you could no longer see your breath, and the water was frigid, driving back the constant drowsiness a little.

He looked his traveling companions over. McVries had a heavy scrub of beard now, as black as his hair. Collie Parker looked haggard but tougher than ever. Baker seemed almost ethereal. Scramm was not so flushed, but he was coughing steadily—a deep, thundering cough that reminded Garraty of himself, long ago. He had had pneumonia when he was five.

The night had passed in a dream-sequence of odd names on the reflectorized overhead signs. Veazie. Bangor. Hermon. Hampden. Winterport. The soldiers had made only two kills, and Garraty was beginning to accept the truth of Parker's cracker anthology.

And now bright daylight had come again. The little protective groups had re-formed, Walkers joking about beards but not about feet . . . never about feet. Garraty had felt several small blisters break on his right heel during the night, but the soft, absorbent sock had buffered the raw flesh somewhat. Now they had just passed a sign that read AUGUSTA 48 PORTLAND 117.

"It's further than you said," Pearson told him reproachfully. He was horribly haggard, his hair hanging lifelessly about his cheeks.

"I'm not a walking roadmap," Garraty said.

"Still . . . it's your state."

"Tough."

"Yeah, I suppose so." There was no rancor in Pearson's tired voice. "Boy, I'd never do this again in a hundred thousand years."

"You should live so long."

"Yeah." Pearson's voice dropped. "I've made up my mind, though. If I get so tired and I can't go on, I'm gonna run over there and dive into the crowd. They won't dare shoot. Maybe I can get away."

"It'd be like hitting a trampoline," Garraty said. "They'll bounce you right back onto the pavement so they can watch you bleed. Don't you remember Percy?"

268

"Percy wasn't thinkin'. Just trying to walk off into the woods. They beat the dog out of Percy, all right." He looked curiously at Garraty. "Aren't you tired, Ray?"

"Shit, no." Garraty flapped his thin arms with mock grandeur. "I'm coasting, couldn't you tell?"

"I'm in bad shape," Pearson said, and licked his lips. "I'm havin' a hard job just thinking straight. And my legs feel like they got harpoons in them all the way up to—"

McVries came up behind them. "Scramm's dying," he said bluntly.

Garraty and Pearson said "Huh?" in unison.

"He's got pneumonia," McVries said.

Garraty nodded. "I was afraid it might be that."

"You can hear his lungs five feet away. It sounds like somebody pumped the Gulf Stream through them. If it gets hot again today, he'll just burn up."

"Poor bastard," Pearson said, and the tone of relief in his voice was both unconscious and unmistakable. "He could have taken us all, I think. And he's married. What's his wife gonna do?"

"What *can* she do?" Garraty asked.

They were walking fairly close to the crowd, no longer noticing the outstretched hands that strove to touch them—you got to know your distance after fingernails had taken skin off your arm once or twice. A small boy whined that he wanted to go home.

"I've been talking to everybody," McVries said. "Well, just about everybody. I think the winner should do something for her."

"Like what?" Garraty asked.

"That'll have to be between the winner and Scramm's wife. And if the bastard welshes, we can all come back and haunt him."

"Okay," Pearson said. "What's to lose?"

"Ray?"

"All right. Sure. Have you talked to Gary Barkovitch?"

"That prick? He wouldn't give his mother artificial respiration if she was drowning."

"I'll talk to him," Garraty said.

"You won't get anywhere."

"Just the same. I'll do it now."

"Ray, why don't you talk to Stebbins, too? You seem to be the only one he talks to."

Garraty snorted. "I can tell you what he'll say in advance."

"No?"

"He'll say why. And by the time he gets done, I won't have any idea."

"Skip him then."

"Can't." Garraty began angling toward the small, slumped figure of Barkovitch. "He's the only guy that still thinks he's going to win."

Barkovitch was in a doze. With his eyes nearly closed and the faint peachfuzz that coated his olive cheeks, he looked like a put-upon and badly used teddy bear. He had either lost his rainhat or thrown it away.

"Barkovitch."

Barkovitch snapped awake. "Wassamatter? Whozat? Garraty?"

"Yes. Listen, Scramm's dying."

"Who? Oh, right. Beaver-brains over there. Good for him."

"He's got pneumonia. He probably won't last until noon."

Barkovitch looked slowly around at Garraty with his bright black shoebutton eyes. Yes, he looked remarkably like some destructive child's teddy bear this morning. "Look at you there with your big earnest face hanging out, Garraty. What's your pitch?"

"Well, if you didn't know, he's married, and—"

Barkovitch's eyes widened until it seemed they were in danger of falling out. *"Married? MARRIED? ARE YOU TELLING ME THAT NUMBSKULL IS—"*

"Shut up, you asshole! He'll hear you!"

"I don't give a sweet fuck! He's crazy!" Barkovitch looked over at Scramm, outraged. *"WHAT DID YOU THINK YOU WERE DOING, NUMBNUTS, PLAYING GIN RUMMY?"* he screamed at the top of his lungs. Scramm looked around blearily at Barkovitch, and then raised his hand in a halfhearted wave. He apparently thought Barkovitch was a spectator. Abraham, who was walking near Scramm, gave Barkovitch the finger. Barkovitch gave it right back, and then turned to Garraty. Suddenly he smiled.

"Aw, goodness," he said. "It shines from your dumb hick face, Garraty. Passing the hat for the dying guy's wifey, right? Ain't that cute."

"Count you out, huh?" Garraty said stiffly. "Okay." He started to walk away.

Barkovitch's smile wobbled at the edges. He grabbed Garraty's sleeve. "Hold on, hold on. I didn't say no, did I? Did you hear me say no?"

"No—"

"No, course I didn't." Barkovitch's smile reappeared, but now there was something desperate in it. The cockiness was gone. "Listen, I got off on the wrong foot with you guys. I didn't mean to. Shit, I'm a good enough guy when you get to know me, I'm always gettin' off on the wrong foot, I never had much of a crowd back home. In my school, I mean. Christ, I don't know why. I'm a good enough guy when you get to know me, as good as anyone else, but I always just, you know, seem to get off on the wrong foot. I mean a guy's got to have a couple of friends on a thing like this. It's no good to be alone, right? Jesus *Christ,* Garraty, you know that. That Rank. He started it, Garraty. He wanted to tear my ass. Guys, they always want to tear my ass. I used to carry a switchblade back at my high school on account of guys wanting to tear my ass. That Rank. I didn't mean for him to *croak,* that wasn't the idea at all. I mean, it wasn't my fault. You guys just saw the end of it, not the way he was . . . ripping my ass, you know . . . " Barkovitch trailed off.

"Yeah, I guess so," Garraty said, feeling like a hypocrite. Maybe Barkovitch could rewrite history for himself, but Garraty remembered the Rank incident too clearly. "Well, what do you want to do, anyway? You want to go along with the deal?"

"Sure, sure." Barkovitch's hand tightened convulsively on Garraty's sleeve, pulling it like the emergency-stop cord on a bus. "I'll send her enough bread to keep her in clover the rest of her life. I just wanted to tell you . . . make you see . . . a guy's got to have some friends . . . a guy's got to have a crowd, you know? Who wants to die hated, if you got to die, that's the way I look at it. I . . . I . . ."

"Sure, right." Garraty began to drop back, feeling like a coward, still hating Barkovitch but somehow feeling sorry for him at the same time. "Thanks a lot." It was the touch of human in Barkovitch that scared him. For some reason it scared him. He didn't know why.

He dropped back too fast, got a warning, and spent the next ten minutes working back to where Stebbins was ambling along.

"Ray Garraty," Stebbins said. "Happy May 3rd, Garraty."

Garraty nodded cautiously. "Same goes both ways."

"I was counting my toes," Stebbins said companionably. "They are fabulously good company because they always add up the same way. What's on your mind?"

So Garraty went through the business about Scramm and Scramm's wife for the second time, and halfway through another boy got his ticket (HELL'S ANGELS ON WHEELS stenciled on the back of his battered jeans jacket) and made it all seem rather meaningless and trite. Finished, he waited tensely for Stebbins to start anatomizing the idea.

"Why not?" Stebbins said amiably. He looked up at Garraty and smiled. Garraty could see that fatigue was finally making its inroads, even in Stebbins.

"You sound like you've got nothing to lose," he said.

"That's right," Stebbins said jovially. "None of us really has anything to lose. That makes it easier to give away."

Garraty looked at Stebbins, depressed. There was too much truth in what he said. It made their gesture toward Scramm look small.

"Don't get me wrong, Garraty old chum. I'm a bit weird, but I'm no old meanie. If I could make Scramm croak any faster by withholding my promise, I would. But I can't. I don't know for sure, but I'll bet every Long Walk finds some poor dog like Scramm and makes a gesture like this, Garraty, and I'll further bet it always comes at just about this time in the Walk, when the old realities and mortalities are starting to sink in. In the old days, before the Change and the Squads, when there were still millionaires, they used to set up foundations and build libraries and all that good shit. Everyone wants a bulwark against mortality, Garraty. Some people can kid themselves that it's their kids. But none of those poor lost children"— Stebbins swung one thin arm to indicate the other Walkers and laughed, but Garraty thought he sounded sad—"they're never even going to leave any bastards." He winked at Garraty. "Shock you?"

"I . . . I guess not."

"You and your friend McVries stand out in this motley crew, Garraty. I don't understand how either of you got here. I'm willing to bet it runs deeper than you think, though. You took me seriously last night, didn't you? About Olson."

"I suppose so," Garraty said slowly.

Stebbins laughed delightedly. "You're the bee's knees, Ray. Olson had no secrets."

"I don't think you were ribbing last night."

"Oh, yes. I was."

Garraty smiled tightly. "You know what I think? I think you had some sort of insight and now you want to deny it. Maybe it scared you."

Stebbins's eyes went gray. "Have it how you like it, Garraty. It's your funeral. Now what say you flake off? You got your promise."

"You want to cheat it. Maybe that's your trouble. You like to think the game is rigged. But maybe it's a straight game. That scare you, Stebbins?"

"Take off."

"Go on, admit it."

"I admit nothing, except your own basic foolishness. Go ahead and tell yourself it's a straight game." Thin color had come into Stebbins's cheeks. "Any game looks straight if everyone is being cheated at once."

"You're all wet," Garraty said, but now his voice lacked conviction. Stebbins smiled briefly and looked back down at his feet.

They were climbing out of a long, swaybacked dip, and Garraty felt sweat pop out on him as he hurried back up through the line to where McVries, Pearson, Abraham, Baker, and Scramm were bundled up together—or, more exactly, the others were bundled around Scramm. They looked like worried seconds around a punchy fighter.

"How is he?" Garraty asked.

"Why ask them?" Scramm demanded. His former husky voice had been reduced to a mere whisper. The fever had broken, leaving his face pallid and waxy.

"Okay, I'll ask you."

"Aw, not bad," Scramm said. He coughed. It was a raspy, bubbling sound that seemed to come from underwater. "I'm not so bad. It's nice, what you guys are doing for Cathy. A man likes to take care of his own, but I guess I wouldn't be doing right to stand on my pride. Not the way things are now."

"Don't talk so much," Pearson said, "you'll wear yourself out."

"What's the difference? Now or later, what's the difference?" Scramm looked at them dumbly, then shook his head slowly from side to side. "Why'd I have to get sick? I was going good, I really was. Odds-on favorite. Even when I'm tired I like to walk. Look at folks, smell the air . . . why? Is it God? Did God do it to me?"

"I don't know," Abraham said.

Garraty felt the death-fascination coming over him again, and was repulsed. He tried to shake it off. It wasn't fair. Not when it was a friend.

"What time is it?" Scramm asked suddenly, and Garraty was eerily reminded of Olson.

"Ten past ten," Baker said.

"Just about two hundred miles down the road," McVries added.

"My feet ain't tired," Scramm said. "That's something."

A little boy was screaming lustily on the sidelines. His voice rose above the low crowd rumble by virtue of pure shrillness. "Hey Ma! Look at the big guy! Look at that moose, Ma! Hey Ma! Look!"

Garraty's eyes swept the crowd briefly and picked out the boy in the first row. He was wearing a Randy the Robot T-shirt and goggling around a half-eaten jam sandwich. Scramm waved at him.

"Kids're nice," he said. "Yeah. I hope Cathy has a boy. We both wanted a boy. A girl would be all right, but you guys know . . . a boy . . . he keeps your name and passes it on. Not that Scramm's such a great name." He laughed, and Garraty thought of what Stebbins had said, about bulwarks against mortality.

An apple-cheeked Walker in a droopy blue sweater dropped through them, bringing the word back. Mike, of Mike and Joe, the leather boys, had been struck suddenly with gut cramps.

Scramm passed a hand across his forehead. His chest rose and fell in a spasm of heavy coughing that he somehow walked through. "Those boys are from my neck of the woods," he said. "We all coulda come together if I'd known. They're Hopis."

"Yeah," Pearson said. "You told us."

Scramm looked puzzled. "Did I? Well, it don't matter. Seems like I won't be making the trip alone, anyway. I wonder—"

An expression of determination settled over Scramm's face. He began to step up his pace. Then he slowed again for a moment and turned around to face them. It seemed calm now, settled. Garraty looked at him, fascinated in spite of himself.

"I don't guess I'll be seeing you guys again." There was nothing in Scramm's voice but simple dignity. "Goodbye."

McVries was the first to respond. "Goodbye, man," he said hoarsely. "Good trip."

"Yeah, good luck," Pearson said, and then looked away.

Abraham tried to speak and couldn't. He turned away, pale, his lips writhing.

"Take it easy," Baker said. His face was solemn.

"Goodbye," Garraty said through frozen lips. "Goodbye, Scramm, good trip, good rest."

"Good rest?" Scramm smiled a little. "The real Walk may still be coming."

He sped up until he had caught up with Mike and Joe, with their impassive faces and their worn leather jackets. Mike had not allowed the cramps to bow him over. He was walking with both hands pressed against his lower belly. His speed was constant.

Scramm talked with them.

They all watched. It seemed that the three of them conferred for a very long time.

"Now what the hell are they up to?" Pearson whispered fearfully to himself.

Suddenly the conference was over. Scramm walked a ways distant from Mike and Joe. Even from back here Garraty could hear the ragged bite of his cough. The soldiers were watching all three of them carefully. Joe put a hand on his brother's shoulder and squeezed it hard. They looked at each other. Garraty could discern no emotion on their bronzed faces. Then Mike hurried a little and caught up with Scramm.

A moment later Mike and Scramm did an abrupt about-face and began to walk toward the crowd, which, sensing the sharp tang of fatality about them, shrieked, unclotted, and backed away from them as if they had the plague.

Garraty looked at Pearson and saw his lips tighten.

The two boys were warned, and as they reached the guardrails that bordered the road, they about-faced smartly and faced the oncoming halftrack. Two middle fingers stabbed the air in unison.

"I fucked your mother and she sure was fine!" Scramm cried.

Mike said something in his own language.

A tremendous cheer went up from the Walkers, and Garraty felt weak tears beneath his eyelids. The crowd was silent. The spot behind Mike and Scramm was barren and empty. They took second warning, then sat down together, cross-legged, and began to talk together calmly. And that was pretty goddamned strange, Garraty thought as they passed by, because Scramm and Mike did not seem to be talking in the same language.

He did not look back. None of them looked back, not even after it was over.

"Whoever wins better keep his word," McVries said suddenly. "He just better."

No one said anything.

Chapter 13

"Joanie Greenblum, *come on down!*"
—Johnny Olsen
The New Price Is Right

Two in the afternoon.

"You're cheating, you fuck!" Abraham shouted.

"I'm not cheating," Baker said calmly. "That's a dollar forty you owe me, turkey."

"I don't pay cheaters." Abraham clutched the dime he had been flipping tightly in his hand.

"And I usually don't match dimes with guys that call me that," Baker said grimly, and then smiled. "But in your case, Abe, I'll make an exception. You have so many winning ways I just can't help myself."

"Shut up and flip," Abraham said.

"Oh please don't take that tone of voice to me," Baker said abjectly, rolling his eyes. "I might fall over in a dead faint!" Garraty laughed.

Abraham snorted and flicked his dime, caught it, and slapped it down on his wrist. "You match me."

"Okay." Baker flipped his dime higher, caught it more deftly and, Garraty was sure, palmed it on edge.

"You show first this time," Baker said.

"Nuh-uh. I showed first last time."

"Oh shit, Abe, I showed first three times in a row before *that*. Maybe you're the one cheating."

Abraham muttered, considered, and then revealed his dime. It was tails, showing the Potomac River framed in laurel leaves.

Baker raised his hand, peeked under it, and smiled. His dime also showed tails. "That's a dollar *fifty* you owe me."

"My *God* you must think I'm dumb!" Abraham hollered. "You think I'm some kind of idiot, right? Go on and admit it! Just taking the rube to the cleaners, right?"

Baker appeared to consider.

"Go on, go on!" Abraham bellowed. "I can take it!"

"Now that you put it to me," Baker said, "whether or not you're a rube never entered my mind. That you're an ijit is pretty well established. As far as taking you to the cleaners"—he put a hand on Abraham's shoulder—"that, my friend, is a certainty."

275

"Come on," Abraham said craftily. "Double or nothing for the whole bundle. And this time *you* show first."

Baker considered. He looked at Garraty. "Ray, would you?"

"Would I what?" Garraty had lost track of the conversation. His left leg had begun to feel decidedly strange.

"Would you go double or nothing against this here fella?"

"Why not? After all, he's too dumb to cheat *you.*"

"Garraty, I thought you were my friend," Abraham said coldly.

"Okay, dollar fifty, double or nothing," Baker said, and that was when the monstrous pain bolted up Garraty's left leg, making all the pain of the last thirty hours seem like a mere whisper in comparison.

"My leg, my leg, my leg!" he screamed, unable to help himself.

"Oh, Jesus, Garraty," Baker had time to say—nothing in his voice but mild surprise, and then they had passed beyond him, it seemed that they were all passing him as he stood here with his left leg turned to clenched and agonizing marble, passing him, leaving him behind.

"Warning! Warning 47!"

Don't panic. If you panic now you've had the course.

He sat down on the pavement, his left leg stuck out woodenly in front of him. He began to massage the big muscles. He tried to knead them. It was like trying to knead ivory.

"Garraty?" It was McVries. He sounded scared . . . surely that was only an illusion? "What is it? Charley horse?"

"Yeah, I guess so. Keep going. It'll be all right."

Time. Time was speeding up for him, but everyone else seemed to have slowed to a crawl, to the speed of an instant replay on a close play at first base. McVries was picking up his pace slowly, one heel showing, then the other, a glint from the worn nails, a glimpse of cracked and tissue-thin shoeleather. Barkovitch was passing by slowly, a little grin on his face, a wave of tense quiet came over the crowd slowly, moving outward in both directions from where he had sat down, like great glassy combers headed for the beach. My second warning, Garraty thought, my second warning's coming up, come on leg, come on goddam leg. I don't want to buy a ticket, what do you say, come on, gimme a break.

"Warning! Second warning, 47!"

Yeah, I know, you think I can't keep score, you think I'm sitting here trying to get a suntan?

The knowledge of death, as true and unarguable as a photograph, was trying to get in and swamp him. Trying to paralyze him. He shut it out with a desperate coldness. His thigh was excruciating agony, but in his concentration he barely felt it. A minute left. No, fifty seconds now, no, forty-five, it's dribbling away, my time's going.

With an abstract, almost professorly expression on his face, Garraty dug his fingers into the frozen straps and harnesses of muscle. He kneaded. He flexed. He talked to his leg in his head. Come on, come on, come on, goddam thing. His fingers began to ache and he did not notice that much either. Stebbins passed him and murmured something. Garraty did not catch what it was. It might have been good luck. Then he was alone, sitting on the broken white line between the travel lane and the passing lane.

All gone. The carny just left town, pulled stakes in the middle of everything and blew town, no one left but this here kid Garraty to face the emptiness of flattened candy wrappers and squashed cigarette butts and discarded junk prizes.

All gone except one soldier, young and blond and handsome in a remote sort of way. His silver chronometer was in one hand, his rifle in the other. No mercy in that face.

"Warning! Warning 47! Third warning, 47!"

The muscle was not loosening at all. He was going to die. After all this, after ripping his guts out, that was the fact, after all.

He let go of his leg and stared calmly at the soldier. He wondered who was going to win. He wondered if McVries would outlast Barkovitch. He wondered what a bullet in the head felt like, if it would just be sudden darkness or if he would actually feel his thoughts being ripped apart.

The last few seconds began to drain away.

The cramp loosened. Blood flowed back into the muscle, making it tingle with needles and pins, making it warm. The blond soldier with the remotely handsome face put away the pocket chronometer. His lips moved soundlessly as he counted down the last few seconds.

But I can't get up, Garraty thought. It's too good just to sit. Just sit and let the phone ring, the hell with it, why didn't I take the phone off the hook?

Garraty let his head fall back. The soldier seemed to be looking down at him, as if from the mouth of a tunnel or over the lip of a deep well. In slow motion he transferred the gun to both hands and his right forefinger kissed over the trigger, then curled around it and the barrel started to come around. The soldier's left hand was solid on the stock. A wedding band caught a glimmer of sun. Everything was slow. So slow. Just . . . hold the phone.

This, Garraty thought.

This is what it's like. To die.

The soldier's right thumb was rotating the safety catch to the off position with exquisite slowness. Three scrawny women were directly behind him, three weird sisters, hold the phone. Just hold the phone a minute longer, I've got something to die here. Sunshine, shadow, blue sky. Clouds rushing up the highway. Stebbins was just a back now, just a blue workshirt with a sweatstain running up between the shoulder blades, goodbye, Stebbins.

Sounds thundered in on him. He had no idea if it was his imagination, or heightened sensibility, or simply the fact of death reaching out for him. The safety catch snapped off with a sound like a breaking branch. The rush of indrawn air between his teeth was the sound of a wind tunnel. His heartbeat was a drum. And there was a high singing, not in his ears but between them, spiraling up and up, and he was crazily sure that it was the actual sound of brainwaves—

He scrambled to his feet in a convulsive flying jerk, screaming. He threw himself into an accelerating, gliding run. His feet were made of feathers. The finger of the soldier tightened on the trigger and whitened. He glanced down at the solid-state computer on his waist, a gadget that included a tiny but sophisticated sonar device. Garraty had once read an article about them in *Popular Mechanix*. They could read out a single Walker's speed as exactly as you would have wanted, to four numbers to the right of the decimal point.

The soldier's finger loosened.

Garraty slowed to a very fast walk, his mouth cottony dry, his heart pounding at triphammer speed. Irregular white flashes pulsed in front of his eyes, and for a sick moment he was sure he was going to faint. It passed. His feet, seemingly furious at being denied their rightful rest, screamed at him rawly. He gritted his teeth and bore the pain. The big muscle in his left leg was still twitching alarmingly, but he wasn't limping. So far.

He looked at his watch. It was 2:17 PM. For the next hour he would be less than two seconds from death.

"Back to the land of the living," Stebbins said as he caught up.

"Sure," Garraty said numbly. He felt a sudden wave of resentment. They would have gone on walking even if he had bought his ticket. No tears shed for him. Just a name and number to be entered in the official records—GARRATY, RAYMOND, #47, ELIMINATED 218th MILE. And a human-interest story in the state newspapers for a couple of days. GARRATY DEAD; "MAINE'S OWN" BECOMES 61ST TO FALL!

"I hope I win," Garraty muttered.

"Think you will?"

Garraty thought of the blond soldier's face. It had shown as much emotion as a plate of potatoes.

"I doubt it," he said. "I've already got three strikes against me. That means you're out, doesn't it?"

"Call the last one a foul tip," Stebbins said. He was regarding his feet again.

Garraty picked his own feet up, his two-second margin like a stone in his head. There would be no warning this time. Not even time for someone to say, you better pick it up, Garraty, you're going to draw one.

He caught up with McVries, who glanced around. "I thought you were out of it, kiddo," McVries said.

"So did I."

"That close?"

"About two seconds, I think."

McVries pursed a silent whistle. "I don't think I'd like to be in your shoes right now. How's the leg?"

"Better. Listen, I can't talk. I'm going up front for a while."

"It didn't help Harkness any."

Garraty shook his head. "I have to make sure I'm topping the speed."

"All right. You want company?"

"If you've got the energy."

McVries laughed. "I got the time if you got the money, honey."

"Come on, then. Let's pick it up while I've still got the sack for it."

Garraty stepped up his pace until his legs were at the point of rebellion, and he and McVries moved quickly through the front-runners. There was a space between the boy who had been walking second, a gangling, evil-faced boy named Harold Quince, and the survivor of the two leather boys. Joe. Closer to, his complexion was startlingly bronzed. His eyes stared steadily at the horizon, and his features were expressionless. The many zippers on his jacket jingled, like the sound of far-away music.

"Hello, Joe," McVries said, and Garraty had an hysterical urge to add, whad-daya know?

"Howdy," Joe said curtly.

They passed him and then the road was theirs, a wide double-barreled strip of composition concrete stained with oil and broken by the grassy median strip, bordered on both sides by a steady wall of people.

"Onward, ever onward," McVries said. "Christian soldiers, marching as to war. Ever hear that one, Ray?"

"What time is it?"

McVries glanced at his watch. "2:20. Look, Ray, if you're going to—"

"God, is that all? I thought—" He felt panic rising in his throat, greasy and thick. He wasn't going to be able to do it. The margin was just too tight.

"Look, if you keep thinking about the time, you're gonna go nuts and try to run into the crowd and they'll shoot you dog-dead. They'll shoot you with your tongue hanging out and spit running down your chin. Try to forget about it."

"I can't." Everything was bottling up inside him, making him feel jerky and hot and sick. "Olson . . . Scramm . . . they died. Davidson died. I can die too, Pete. I believe it now. It's breathing down my fucking back!"

"Think about your girl. Jan, what's-her-face. Or your mother. Or your goddam kitty-cat. Or don't think about anything. Just pick 'em up and put 'em down. Just keep on walking down the road. Concentrate on that."

Garraty fought for control of himself. Maybe he even got a little. But he was unraveling just the same. His legs didn't want to respond smoothly to his mind's commands anymore, they seemed as old and as flickery as ancient lightbulbs.

"He won't last much longer," a woman in the front row said quite audibly.

"Your tits won't last much longer!" Garraty snapped at her, and the crowd cheered him.

"They're screwed up," Garraty muttered. "They're really screwed up. Perverted. What time is it, McVries?"

"What was the first thing you did when you got your letter of confirmation?" McVries asked softly. "What did you do when you knew you were really in?"

Garraty frowned, wiped his forearm quickly across his forehead, and then let his mind free of the sweaty, terrifying present to that sudden, flashing moment.

"I was by myself. My mother works. It was a Friday afternoon. The letter was in the mailbox and it had a Wilmington, Delaware, postmark, so I knew that had to be it. But I was sure it said I'd flunked the physical or the mental or both. I had to read it twice. I didn't go into any fits of joy, but I was pleased. Real pleased. And confident. My feet didn't hurt then and my back didn't feel like somebody had shoved a rake with a busted handle into it. I was one in a million. I wasn't bright enough to realize the circus fat lady is, too.''

He broke off for a moment, thinking, smelling early April.

''I couldn't back down. There were too many people watching. I think it must work the same with just about everyone. It's one of the ways they tip the game, you know. I let the April 15th backout date go by and the day after that they had a big testimonial dinner for me at the town hall—all my friends were there and after dessert everyone started yelling Speech! Speech! And I got out and mumbled something down at my hands about how I was gonna do the best I could if I got in, and everyone applauded like mad. It was like I'd laid the fucking Gettysburg Address on their heads. You know what I mean?''

''Yes, I know,'' McVries said, and laughed—but his eyes were dark.

Behind them the guns thunderclapped suddenly. Garraty jumped convulsively and nearly froze in his tracks. Somehow he kept walking. Blind instinct this time, he thought. What about next time?

''Son of a bitch,'' McVries said softly. ''It was Joe.''

''What time is it?'' Garraty asked, and before McVries could answer he remembered that he was wearing a watch of his own. It was 2:38. Christ. His two-second margin was like an iron dumbbell on his back.

''No one tried to talk you out of it?'' McVries asked. They were far out beyond the rest now, better than a hundred yards beyond Harold Quince. A soldier had been dispatched to keep tabs on them. Garraty was very glad it wasn't the blond guy. ''No one tried to talk you into using the April 31st backout?''

''Not at first. My mother and Jan and Dr. Patterson—he's my mother's special friend, you know, they've been keeping company for the last five years or so—they just kind of soft-pedaled it at first. They were pleased and proud because most of the kids in the country over twelve take the tests but only one in fifty passes. And that still leaves thousands of kids and they can use two hundred—one hundred Walkers and a hundred backups. And there's no skill in getting picked, you know that.''

''Sure, they draw the names out of that cocksucking drum. Big TV spectacular.'' McVries's voice cracked a little.

''Yeah. The Major draws the two hundred names, but the names're all they announce. You don't know if you're a Walker or just a backup.''

''And no notification of which you are until the final backout date itself,'' McVries agreed, speaking of it as if the final backout date had been years ago instead of only four days. ''Yeah, they like to stack the deck their way.''

Somebody in the crowd had just released a flotilla of balloons. They floated up to the sky in a dissolving arc of reds, blues, greens, yellows. The steady south wind carried them away with taunting, easy speed.

"I guess so," Garraty said. "We were watching the TV when the Major drew the names. I was number seventy-three out of the drum. I fell right out of my chair. I just couldn't believe it."

"No, it can't be *you*," McVries agreed. "Things like that always happen to the other guy."

"Yeah, that's the feeling. That's when everybody started in on me. It wasn't like the first backout date when it was all speeches and pie in the sky by-and-by. Jan . . ."

He broke off. Why not? He'd told everything else. It didn't matter. Either he or McVries was going to be dead before it was over. Probably both of them. "Jan said she'd go all the way with me, any time, any way, as often as I wanted if I'd take the April 31st backout. I told her that would make me feel like an opportunist and a heel, and she got mad at me and said it was better than feeling dead, and then she cried a lot. And begged me." Garraty looked up at McVries. "I don't know. Anything else she could have asked me, I would have tried to do it. But this one thing . . . I couldn't. It was like there was a stone caught in my throat. After a while she knew I couldn't say Yes, okay, I'll call the 800 number. I think she started to understand. Maybe as well as I did myself, which God knows wasn't— isn't—very well.

"Then Dr. Patterson started in. He's a diagnostician, and he's got a wicked logical mind. He said, 'Look here, Ray. Figuring in the Prime group and the back-ups, your chance of survival is fifty-to-one. Don't do this to your mother, Ray.' I was polite with him for as long as I could, but finally I told him to just kiss off. I said I figured the odds on him ever marrying my mother were pretty long, but I never noticed him backing off because of that."

Garraty ran both hands through the straw-thatch of his hair. He had forgotten about the two-second margin.

"God, didn't he get mad. He ranted and raved and told me if I wanted to break my mother's heart to just go ahead. He said I was as insensitive as a . . . a wood tick, I think that's what he said, insensitive as a wood tick, maybe it's a family saying of his or something, I don't know. He asked me how it felt to be doing the number on my mom and on a nice girl like Janice. So I countered with my own unarguable logic."

"Did you," McVries said, smiling. "What was that?"

"I told him if he didn't get out I was going to hit him."

"What about your mother?"

"She didn't say much at all. I don't think she could believe it. And the thought of what I'd get if I won. The Prize—everything you want for the rest of your life— that sort of blinded her, I think. I had a brother, Jeff. He died of pneumonia when he was six, and—it's cruel—but I don't know how we'd've gotten along if he'd've lived. And . . . I guess she just kept thinking I'd be able to back out of it if I did turn out to be Prime. The Major is a nice man. That's what she said. I'm sure he'd let you out of it if he understood the circumstances. But they Squad them just as fast for trying to back out of a Long Walk as they do for talking against it. And then I got the call and I knew I was a Walker. I was Prime.''

''I wasn't.''

''No?''

''No. Twelve of the original Walkers used the April 31st backout. I was number twelve, backup. I got the call just past 11 PM four days ago.''

''Jesus! Is that so?''

''Uh-huh. That close.''

''Doesn't it make you . . . bitter?''

McVries only shrugged.

Garraty looked at his watch. It was 3:02. It was going to be all right. His shadow, lengthening in the afternoon sun, seemed to move a little more confidently. It was a pleasant, brisk spring day. His leg felt okay now.

''Do you still think you might just . . . sit down?'' he asked McVries. ''You've outlasted most of them. Sixty-one of them.''

''How many you or I have outlasted doesn't matter, I think. There comes a time when the will just runs out. Doesn't matter what I *think*, see? I used to have a good time smearing away with oil paints. I wasn't too bad, either. Then one day—bingo. I didn't taper off, I just stopped. Bingo. There was no urge to go on even another minute. I went to bed one night liking to paint and when I woke up it was nowhere.''

''Staying alive hardly qualifies as a hobby.''

''I don't know about that. How about skin divers? Big-game hunters? Mountain climbers? Or even some half-witted millworker whose idea of a good time is picking fights on Saturday night? All of those things reduce staying alive to a hobby. Part of the game.''

Garraty said nothing.

''Better pick it up some,'' McVries said gently. ''We're losing speed. Can't have that.''

Garraty picked it up.

''My dad has a half-ownership in a drive-in movie theater,'' McVries said. ''He was going to tie me and gag me down in the cellar under the snack concession to keep me from coming, Squads or no Squads.''

''What did you do? Just wear him down?''

''There was no time for that. When the call came, I had just ten hours. They laid on an airplane and a rental car at the Presque Isle airport. He ranted and raved and I just sat there and nodded and agreed and pretty soon there was a knock on the door and when my mom opened it, two of the biggest, meanest-looking soldiers you ever saw were standing on the porch. Man, they were so ugly they could have stopped clocks. My dad took one look at them and said, 'Petie, you better go upstairs and get your Boy Scout pack.' '' McVries jolted the pack up and down on his shoulders and laughed at the memory. ''And just about the next thing any of us knew, we were on that plane, even my little sister Katrina. She's only four. We landed at three in the morning and drove up to the marker. And I think Katrina was the only one who really understood. She kept saying 'Petie's going on an adventure.' " McVries flapped his hands in an oddly uncompleted way. "They're staying at a motel in Presque Isle. They didn't want to go home until it was over. One way or the other."

Garraty looked at his watch. It was 3:20.

"Thanks," he said.

"For saving your life again?" McVries laughed merrily.

"Yes, that's just right."

"Are you sure that would be any kind of a favor?"

"I don't know." Garraty paused. "I'll tell you something though. It's never going to be the same for me. The time limit thing. Even when you're walking with no warnings, there's only two minutes between you and the inside of a cemetery fence. That's not much time."

As if on cue, the guns roared. The holed Walker made a high, gobbling sound, like a turkey grabbed suddenly by a silent-stepping farmer. The crowd made a low sound that might have been a sigh or a groan or an almost sexual outletting of pleasure.

"No time at all," McVries agreed.

They walked. The shadows got longer. Jackets appeared in the crowd as if a magician had conjured them out of a silk hat. Once Garraty caught a warm whiff of pipesmoke that brought back a hidden, bittersweet memory of his father. A pet dog escaped from someone's grasp and ran out into the road, red plastic leash dragging, tongue lolling out pinkly, foam flecked on its jaws. It yipped, chased drunkenly after its stubby tail, and was shot when it charged drunkenly at Pearson, who swore bitterly at the soldier who had shot it. The force of the heavy-caliber bullet drove it to the edge of the crowd where it lay dull-eyed, panting, and shivering. No one seemed anxious to claim it. A small boy got past the police, wandered out into the left lane of the road, and stood there, weeping. A soldier advanced on him. A mother screamed shrilly from the crowd. For one horrified moment Garraty thought the soldier was going to shoot the kid as the dog had been shot, but the soldier merely swept the little boy indifferently back into the crowd.

At 6:00 PM the sun touched the horizon and turned the western sky orange. The air turned cold. Collars were turned up. Spectators stamped their feet and rubbed their hands together.

Collie Parker registered his usual complaint about the goddam Maine weather.

By quarter of nine we'll be in Augusta, Garraty thought. Just a hop, skip, and a jump from there to Freeport. Depression dropped over him. What then? Two minutes you'll have to see her, unless you should miss her in the crowd—God forbid. Then what? Fold up?

He was suddenly sure Jan and his mother wouldn't be there anyway. Just the kids he had gone to school with, anxious to see the suicidal freak they had unknowingly nurtured among them. And the Ladies' Aid. They would be there. The Ladies' Aid had given him a tea two nights before the Walk started. In that antique time.

"Let's start dropping back," McVries said. "We'll do it slow. Get together with Baker. We'll walk into Augusta together. The original Three Musketeers. What do you say, Garraty?"

"All right," Garraty said. It sounded good.

They dropped back a little at a time, eventually leaving the sinister-faced Harold Quince to lead the parade. They knew they were back with their own people when Abraham, out of the gathering gloom, asked: "You finally decide to come back and visit the po' folks?"

"Je-sus, he really does look like him," McVries said, staring at Abraham's weary, three-day-bearded face. "Especially in this light."

"Fourscore and seven years ago," Abraham intoned, and for an eerie moment it was as if a spirit had inhabited seventeen-year-old Abraham. "Our fathers set forth on this continent . . . ah, bullshit. I forget the rest. We had to learn it in eighth grade history if we wanted an A."

"The face of a founding father and the mentality of a syphilitic donkey," McVries said sadly. "Abraham, how did you get into a balls-up like this?"

"Bragged my way in," Abraham said promptly. He started to go on and the guns interrupted him. There was the familiar mailsack thud.

"That was Gallant," Baker said, looking back. "He's been walking dead all day."

"Bragged his way into it," Garraty mused, and then laughed.

"Sure." Abraham ran a hand up one cheek and scratched the cavernous hollow under one eye. "You know the essay test?"

They all nodded. An essay, *Why Do You Feel Qualified to Participate in the Long Walk?*, was a standard part of the Mentals section of the exam. Garraty felt a warm trickle on his right heel and wondered if it was blood, pus, sweat, or all of the above. There seemed to be no pain, although his sock felt ragged back there.

"Well, the thing was," Abraham said, "I didn't feel particularly qualified to participate in anything. I took the exam completely on the spur of the moment. I was on my way to the movies and I just happened past the gym where they were having the test. You have to show your Work Permit card to get in, you know. I just happened to have mine with me that day. If I hadn't, I wouldn't have bothered to go home and get it. I just would have gone on to the movies and I wouldn't be here right now, dying in such jolly company."

They considered this silently.

"I took the physical and then I zipped through the objective stuff and then I see this three-page blank at the end of the folder. 'Please answer this question as objectively and honestly as you can, using not more than 1500 words,' oh holy shit, I think. The rest of it was sort of fun. What a bunch of fucked-up questions."

"Yeah, how often do you have a bowel movement?" Baker said dryly. "Have you ever used snuff?"

"Yeah, yeah, stuff like that," Abraham agreed. "I'd forgotten all about that stupid snuff question. I just zipped along, bullshitting in good order, you know, and I come to this essay about why I feel qualified to participate. I couldn't think of a thing. So finally some bastard in an army coat strolls by and says, 'Five minutes. Will everyone finish up, please?' So I just put down, 'I feel qualified to participate in the Long Walk because I am one useless S.O.B and the world would be better off without me, unless I happened to win and get rich in which case I would buy a Van Go to put in every room of my manshun and order up sixty high-class horrs and not bother anybody.' I thought about that for about a minute, and then I put in parenthesis: '(I would give all my sixty high-class horrs old-age pensions, too.)' I thought that would really screw 'em up. So a month later—I'd forgotten all about the whole thing—I get a letter saying I qualified. I damn near creamed my jeans.''

''And you went through with it?'' Collie Parker demanded.

''Yeah, it's hard to explain. The thing was, everybody thought it was a big joke. My girlfriend wanted to have the letter photographed and get it turned into a T-shirt down at the Shirt Shack, like she thought I'd pulled the biggest practical joke of the century. It was like that with everybody. I'd get the big glad hand and somebody was always saying something like, 'Hey Abe, you really tweaked the Major's balls, din'tchoo?' It was so funny I just kept on going. I'll tell you,'' Abraham said, smiling morbidly, ''it got to be a real laff riot. Everybody thought I was just gonna go on tweaking the Major's balls to the very end. Which was what I did. Then one morning I woke up and I was in. I was a Prime Walker, sixteenth out of the drum, as a matter of fact. So I guess it turned out the Major was tweaking *my* balls.''

An abortive little cheer went through the Walkers, and Garraty glanced up. A huge reflector sign overhead informed them: AUGUSTA 10.

''You could just die laughing, right?'' Collie said.

Abraham looked at Parker for a long time. ''The Founding Father is not amused,'' he said hollowly.

Chapter 14

"And remember, if you use your hands,
   or gesture with any part of your body,
   or use any part of the word, you will forfeit
   your chance for the ten thousand dollars.
Just give a list. Good luck.''
      —Dick Clark
         The Ten Thousand Dollar Pyramid

They had all pretty much agreed that there was little emotional stretch or recoil left
in them. But apparently, Garraty thought tiredly as they walked into the roaring
darkness along U.S. 202 with Augusta a mile behind them, it was not so. Like a
badly treated guitar that has been knocked about by an unfeeling musician, the
strings were not broken but only out of tune, discordant, chaotic.

Augusta hadn't been like Oldtown. Oldtown had been a phony hick New York.
Augusta was some new city, a once-a-year city of crazy revelers, a party-down
city full of a million boogying drunks and cuckoo birds and out-and-out maniacs.

They had heard Augusta and seen Augusta long before they had reached Augusta. The image of waves beating on a distant shore recurred to Garraty again and
again. They heard the crowd five miles out. The lights filled the sky with a bub-
blelike pastel glow that was frightening and apocalyptic, reminding Garraty of pictures he had seen in the history books of the German air-blitz of the American East
Coast during the last days of World War II.

They stared at each other uneasily and bunched closer together like small boys
in a lightning storm or cows in a blizzard. There was a raw redness in that swelling
sound of Crowd. A hunger that was numbing. Garraty had a vivid and scary image
of the great god Crowd clawing its way out of the Augusta basin on scarlet spider-
legs and devouring them all alive.

The town itself had been swallowed, strangled, and buried. In a very real sense
there was no Augusta, and there were no more fat ladies, or pretty girls, or pomp-
ous men, or wet-crotched children waving puffy clouds of cotton candy. There
was no bustling Italian man here to throw slices of watermelon. Only Crowd, a
creature with no body, no head, no mind. Crowd was nothing but a Voice and an
Eye, and it was not surprising that Crowd was both God and Mammon. Garraty
felt it. He knew the others were feeling it. It was like walking between giant electrical pylons, feeling the tingles and shocks stand every hair on end, making the
tongue jitter nuttily in the mouth, making the eyes seem to crackle and shoot off

286

sparks as they rolled in their beds of moisture. Crowd was to be pleased. Crowd was to be worshiped and feared. Ultimately, Crowd was to be made sacrifice unto.

They plowed through ankle-deep drifts of confetti. They lost each other and found each other in a sheeting blizzard of magazine streamers. Garraty snatched a paper out of the dark and crazy air at random and found himself looking at a Charles Atlas body-building ad. He grabbed another one and was brought face-to-face with John Travolta.

And at the height of the excitement, at the top of the first hill on 202, overlooking the mobbed turnpike behind and the gorged and glutted town at their feet, two huge purple-white spotlights split the air ahead of them and the Major was there, drawing away from them in his jeep like an hallucination, holding his salute ramrod stiff, incredibly, fantastically oblivious of the crowd in the gigantic throes of its labor all around him.

And the Walkers—the strings were not broken on their emotions, only badly out-of-tune. They had cheered wildly with hoarse and totally unheard voices, the thirty-seven of them that were left. The crowd could not know they were cheering but somehow they did, somehow they understood that the circle between death-worship and death-wish had been completed for another year and the crowd went completely loopy, convulsing itself in greater and greater paroxysms. Garraty felt a stabbing, needling pain in the left side of his chest and was still unable to stop cheering, even though he understood he was driving at the very brink of disaster.

A shifty-eyed Walker named Milligan saved them all by falling to his knees, his eyes squeezed shut and his hands pressed to his temples, as if he were trying to hold his brains in. He slid forward on the end of his nose, abrading the tip of it on the road like soft chalk on a rough blackboard—how amazing, Garraty thought, that kid's wearing his nose away on the road—and then Milligan was mercifully blasted. After that the Walkers stopped cheering. Garraty was badly scared by the pain in his chest that was subsiding only partially. He promised that was the end of the craziness.

"We getting close to your girl?" Parker asked. He had not weakened, but he had mellowed. Garraty liked him okay now.

"About fifty miles. Maybe sixty. Give or take."

"You're one lucky sonofabitch, Garraty," Parker said wistfully.

"I am?" He was surprised. He turned to see if Parker was laughing at him. Parker wasn't.

"You're gonna see your girl and your mother. Who the hell am I going to see between now and the end? No one but these pigs." He gestured with his middle finger at the crowd, which seemed to take the gesture as a salute and cheered him deliriously. "I'm homesick," he said. "And scared." Suddenly he screamed at the crowd: *"Pigs! You pigs!"* They cheered him more loudly than ever.

"I'm scared, too. And homesick. I . . . I mean *we* . . . " He groped. "We're all too far away from home. The road keeps us away. I may see them, but I won't be able to touch them."

"The rules say—"

"I know what the rules say. Bodily contact with anyone I wish, as long as I don't leave the road. But it's not the same. There's a wall."

"Fuckin' easy for you to talk. You're going to see them, just the same."

"Maybe that'll only make it worse," McVries said. He had come quietly up behind them. They had just passed under a blinking yellow warning flasher at the Winthrop intersection. Garraty could see it waxing and waning on the pavement after they had passed it, a fearful yellow eye, opening and closing.

"You're all crazy," Parker said amiably. "I'm getting out of here." He put on a little speed and had soon nearly disappeared into the blinking shadows.

"He thinks we're queer for each other," McVries said, amused.

"He *what?*" Garraty's head snapped up.

"He's not such a bad guy," McVries said thoughtfully. He cocked a humorous eye at Garraty. "Maybe he's even half-right. Maybe that's why I saved your ass. Maybe I'm queer for you."

"With a face like mine? I thought you perverts liked the willowy type." Still, he was suddenly uneasy.

Suddenly, shockingly, McVries said: "Would you let me jerk you off?"

Garraty hissed in breath. "What the hell—"

"Oh, shut up," McVries said crossly. "Where do you get off with all this self-righteous shit? I'm not even going to make it any easier by letting you know if I'm joking. What say?"

Garraty felt a sticky dryness in his throat. The thing was, he wanted to be touched. Queer, not queer, that didn't seem to matter now that they were all busy dying. All that mattered was McVries. He didn't want McVries to touch him, not that way.

"Well, I suppose you did save my life—" Garraty let it hang.

McVries laughed. "I'm supposed to feel like a heel because you owe me something and I'm taking advantage? Is that it?"

"Do what you want," Garraty said shortly. "But quit playing games."

"Does that mean yes?"

"Whatever you want!" Garraty yelled. Pearson, who had been staring, nearly hypnotized, at his feet, looked up, startled. "Whatever you goddam want!" Garraty yelled.

McVries laughed again. "You're all right, Ray. Never doubt it." He clapped Garraty's shoulder and dropped back.

Garraty stared after him, mystified.

"He just can't get enough," Pearson said tiredly.

"Huh?"

"Almost two hundred and fifty miles," Pearson groaned. "My feet are like lead with poison inside them. My back's burning. And that screwed-up McVries doesn't have enough yet. He's like a starving man gobbling up laxatives."

"He wants to be hurt, do you think?"

"Jesus, what do you think? He ought to be wearing a BEAT ME HARD sign. I wonder what he's trying to make up for."

"I don't know," Garraty said. He was going to add something else, but saw Pearson wasn't listening anymore. He was watching his feet again, his weary features drawn in lines of horror. He had lost his shoes. The dirty white athletic socks on his feet made gray-white arcs in the darkness.

They passed a sign that said LEWISTON 32 and a mile beyond that an arched electric sign that proclaimed GARRATY 47 in lightbulb lettering.

Garraty wanted to doze but was unable. He knew what Pearson meant about his back. His own spine felt like a blue rod of fire. The muscles at the backs of his legs were open, flaming sores. The numbness in his feet was being replaced by an agony much more sharp and defined than any that had gone before. He was no longer hungry, but he ate a few concentrates anyway. Several Walkers were nothing but flesh-covered skeletons—concentration-camp horrors. Garraty didn't want to get like that . . . but of course he was, anyway. He ran a hand up his side and played the xylophone on his ribs.

"I haven't heard from Barkovitch lately," he said in an effort to raise Pearson from his dreadful concentration—it was altogether too much like Olson reincarnated.

"No. Somebody said one of his legs went stiff on him coming through Augusta."

"That right?"

"That's what they said."

Garraty felt a sudden urge to drop back and look at Barkovitch. He was hard to find in the dark and Garraty drew a warning, but finally he spotted Barkovitch, now back in the rear echelon. Barkovitch was scurrying gimpily along, his face set in strained lines of concentration. His eyes were slitted down to a point where they looked like dimes seen edge-on. His jacket was gone. He was talking to himself in a low, strained monotone.

"Hello, Barkovitch," Garraty said.

Barkovitch twitched, stumbled, and was warned . . . third warning. "There!" Barkovitch screamed shrewishly. "There, see what you did? Are you and your hotshit friends satisfied?"

"You don't look so good," Garraty said.

Barkovitch smiled cunningly. "It's all a part of the Plan. You remember when I told you about the Plan? Didn't believe me. Olson didn't. Davidson neither. Gribble neither." Barkovitch's voice dropped to a succulent whisper, pregnant with spit. "Garraty, I daaanced on their graves!"

"Your leg hurt?" Garraty asked softly. "Say, isn't that awful."

"Just thirty-five left to walk down. They're all going to fall apart tonight. You'll see. There won't be a dozen left on the road when the sun comes up. You'll see. You and your diddy-bop friends, Garraty. All dead by morning. Dead by *midnight.*"

Garraty felt suddenly very strong. He knew that Barkovitch would go soon now. He wanted to break into a run, bruised kidneys and aching spine and screaming feet and all, run and tell McVries he was going to be able to keep his promise.

"What will you ask for?" Garraty said aloud. "When you win?"

Barkovitch grinned gleefully as if he had been waiting for the question. In the uncertain light his face seemed to crumple and squeeze as if pushed and pummeled by giant hands. "Plastic feet," he whispered. "Plaaastic feet, Garraty. I'm just gonna have these ones cut off, fuck 'em if they can't take a joke. I'll have new plastic feet put on and put these ones in a laundromat washing machine and watch them go around and around and around—"

"I thought maybe you'd wish for friends," Garraty said sadly. A heady sense of triumph, suffocating and enthralling, roared through him.

"Friends?"

"Because you don't have any," Garraty said pityingly. "We'll all be glad to see you die. No one's going to miss *you*, Gary. Maybe I'll walk behind you and spit on your brains after they blow them all over the road. Maybe I'll do that. Maybe we all will." It was crazy, crazy, as if his whole head was flying off, it was like when he had swung the barrel of the air rifle at Jimmy, the blood . . . Jimmy screamed . . . his whole head had gone heat-hazy with the savage, primitive justice of it.

"Don't hate me," Barkovitch was whining, "why do you want to hate me? I don't want to die any more than you do. What do you want? Do you want me to be sorry? I'll be sorry! I . . . I . . . "

"We'll all spit in your brains," Garraty said crazily. "Do you want to touch me too?"

Barkovitch looked at him palely, his eyes confused and vacant.

"I . . . I'm sorry," Garraty whispered. He felt degraded and dirty. He hurried away from Barkovitch. Damn you McVries, he thought, why? Why?

All at once the guns roared, and there were two of them falling down dead at once and one of them *had* to be Barkovitch, *had* to be. And this time it was his fault, he was the murderer.

Then Barkovitch was laughing. Barkovitch was cackling, higher and madder and even more audible than the madness of the crowd. "Garraty! Gaaarrratee! I'll dance on your grave, Garraty! I'll *daaaance*—"

"Shut up!" Abraham yelled. "Shut up, you little prick!"

Barkovitch stopped, then began to sob.

"Go to hell," Abraham muttered.

"Now you did it," Collie Parker said reproachfully. "You made him cry, Abe, you bad boy. He's gonna go home and tell his mommy."

Barkovitch continued to sob. It was an empty, ashy sound that made Garraty's skin crawl. There was no hope in it.

"Is little uggy-wuggy gonna tell Mommy?" Quince called back. "Ahhhh, Barkovitch, ain't that too *bad*?"

Leave him alone, Garraty screamed out in his mind, leave him alone, you have no idea how bad he's hurting. But what kind of lousy hypocritical thought was that? He wanted Barkovitch to die. Might as well admit it. He wanted Barkovitch to crack up and croak off.

And Stebbins was probably back there in the dark laughing at them all.

He hurried, caught up with McVries, who was ambling along and staring idly at the crowd. The crowd was staring back at him avidly.

"Why don't you help me decide?" McVries said.

"Sure. What's the topic for decision?"

"Who's in the cage. Us or them."

Garraty laughed with genuine pleasure. "All of us. And the cage is in the Major's monkey house."

McVries didn't join in Garraty's laughter. "Barkovitch is going over the high side, isn't he?"

"Yes, I think so."

"I don't want to see it anymore. It's lousy. And it's a cheat. You build it all around something . . . set yourself on something . . . and then you don't want it. Isn't it too bad the great truths are all such lies?"

"I never thought much about it. Do you realize it's almost ten o'clock?"

"It's like practicing pole-vaulting all your life and then getting to the Olympics and saying, 'What the hell do I want to jump over that stupid bar for?' "

"Yeah."

"You almost could care, right?" McVries said, nettled.

"It's getting harder to work me up," Garraty admitted. He paused. Something had been troubling him badly for some time now. Baker had joined them. Garraty looked from Baker to McVries and then back again. "Did you see Olson's . . . did you see his hair? Before he bought it?"

"What about his hair?" Baker asked.

"It was going gray."

"No, that's crazy," McVries said, but he suddenly sounded very scared. "No, it was dust or something."

"It was gray," Garraty said. "It seems like we've been on this road forever. It was Olson's hair getting . . . getting that way that made me think of it first, but . . . maybe this is some crazy kind of immortality." The thought was terribly depressing. He stared straight ahead into the darkness, feeling the soft wind against his face.

"I walk, I did walk, I will walk, I will have walked," McVries chanted. "Shall I translate into Latin?"

We're suspended in time, Garraty thought.

Their feet moved but they did not. The cherry cigarette glows in the crowd, the occasional flashlight or flaring sparkler might have been stars, weird low constellations that marked their existence ahead and behind, narrowing into nothing both ways.

"Bruh," Garraty said, shivering. "A guy could go crazy."

"That's right," Pearson agreed, and then laughed nervously. They were starting up a long, twisting hill. The road was now expansion-jointed concrete, hard on the feet. It seemed to Garraty that he felt every pebble through the paper-thinness of his shoes. The frisky wind had scattered shallow drifts of candy wrappers, popcorn boxes, and other assorted muck in their way. At some places they almost had to fight their way through. It's not fair, Garraty thought self-pityingly.

"What's the layout up ahead?" McVries asked him apologetically.

Garraty closed his eyes and tried to make a map in his head. "I can't remember all the little towns. We come to Lewiston, that's the second-biggest city in the state, bigger than Augusta. We go right down the main drag. It used to be Lisbon Street, but now it's Cotter Memorial Avenue. Reggie Cotter was the only guy from Maine to ever win the Long Walk. It happened a long time ago."

"He died, didn't he?" Baker said.

"Yeah. He hemorrhaged in one eye and finished the Walk half-blind. It turned out he had a blood clot on his brain. He died a week or so after the Walk." And in a feeble effort to remove the onus, Garraty repeated: "It was a long time ago."

No one spoke for a while. Candy wrappers crackled under their feet like the sound of a faraway forest fire. A cherry bomb went off in the crowd. Garraty could see a faint lightness on the horizon that was probably the twin cities of Lewiston and Auburn, the land of Dussettes and Aubuchons and Lavesques, the land of *Nous parlons français ici*. Suddenly Garraty had a nearly obsessive craving for a stick of gum.

"What's after Lewiston?"

"We go down Route 196, then along 126 to Freeport, where I'm going to see my mom and my girl. That's also where we get on U.S. 1. And that's where we stay until it's over."

"The big highway," McVries muttered.

"Sure."

The guns blasted and they all jumped.

"It was Barkovitch or Quince," Pearson said. "I can't tell . . . one of them's still walking . . . it's—"

Barkovitch laughed out of the darkness, a high, gobbling sound, thin and terrifying. "Not yet, you whores! I ain't gone yet! Not *yeeeeeettttttt* . . . "

His voice kept climbing and climbing. It was like a fire whistle gone insane. And Barkovitch's hands suddenly went up like startled doves taking flight and Barkovitch ripped out his own throat.

"My *Jesus!*" Pearson wailed, and threw up over himself.

They fled from him, fled and scattered ahead and behind, and Barkovitch went on screaming and gobbling and clawing and walking, his feral face turned up to the sky, his mouth a twisted curve of darkness.

Then the fire-whistle sound began to fail, and Barkovitch failed with it. He fell down and they shot him, dead or alive.

Garraty turned around and walked forward again. He was dimly grateful that he hadn't been warned. He saw a carbon copy of his horror on the faces of all about him. The Barkovitch part of it was over. Garraty thought it did not bode well for the rest of them, for their future on this dark and bloody road.

"I don't feel good," Pearson said. His voice was flat. He dry-retched and walked doubled over for a moment. ''Oh. Not so good. Oh God. I don't. Feel. So good. Oh.''

McVries looked straight ahead. ''I think . . . I wish I were insane,'' he said thoughtfully.

Only Baker said nothing. And that was odd, because Garraty suddenly got a whiff of Louisiana honeysuckle. He could hear the croak of the frogs in the bottoms. He could feel the sweaty, lazy hum of cicadas digging into the tough cypress bark for their dreamless seventeen-year sleep. And he could see Baker's aunt rocking back and forth, her eyes dreamy and smiley and vacant, sitting on her porch and listening to the static and hum and faraway voices on an old Philco radio with a chipped and cracked mahogany cabinet. Rocking and rocking and rocking. Smiling, sleepy. Like a cat that has been into the cream and is well satisfied.

Chapter 15

Daylight came in creeping through a white, muted world of fog. Garraty was walking by himself again. He no longer even knew how many had bought it in the night. Five, maybe. His feet had headaches. Terrible migraines. He could feel them swelling each time he put his weight on them. His buttocks hurt. His spine was icy fire. But his feet had headaches and the blood was coagulating in them and swelling them and turning the veins to *al dente* spaghetti.

And still there was a worm of excitement growing in his guts: they were now only thirteen miles out of Freeport. They were in Porterville now, and the crowd could barely see them through the dense fog, but they had been chanting his name rhythmically since Lewiston. It was like the pulse of a giant heart.

Freeport and Jan, he thought.

"Garraty?" The voice was familiar but washed out. It was McVries. His face was a furry skull. His eyes were glittering feverishly. "Good morning," McVries croaked. "We live to fight another day."

"Yeah. How many got it last night, McVries?"

"Six." McVries dug a jar of bacon spread out of his belt and began to finger it into his mouth. His hands were shaking badly. "Six since Barkovitch." He put the jar back with an old man's palsied care. "Pearson bought it."

"Yeah?"

"There's not many of us left, Garraty. Only twenty-six."

"No, not many." Walking through the fog was like walking through weightless clouds of mothdust.

"Not many of *us*, either. The Musketeers. You and me and Baker and Abraham. Collie Parker. And Stebbins. If you want to count him in. Why not? Why the fuck not? Let's count Stebbins in, Garraty. Six Musketeers and twenty spear-carriers."

"Do you still think I'll win?"

"Does it always get this foggy up here in the spring?"

"What's that mean?"

"No, I don't think you'll win. It's Stebbins, Ray. Nothing can wear him down,

294

he's like diamonds. The word is Vegas likes him nine-to-one now that Scramm's out of it. Christ, he looks almost the same now as when we started.''

Garraty nodded as if expecting this. He found his tube of beef concentrate and began to eat it. What he wouldn't have given for some of McVries's long-gone raw hamburger.

McVries snuffled a little and wiped a hand across his nose. ''Doesn't it seem strange to you? Being back on your home stomping grounds after all of this?''

Garraty felt the worm of excitement wriggle and turn again. ''No,'' he said. ''It seems like the most natural thing in the world.''

They walked down a long hill, and McVries glanced up into white drive-in screen nothing. ''The fog's getting worse.''

''It's not fog,'' Garraty said. ''It's rain now.''

The rain fell softly, as if it had no intention of stopping for a very long time.

'Where's Baker?''

''Back there someplace,'' McVries said.

Without a word—words were almost unnecessary now—Garraty began dropping back. The road took them past a traffic island, past the rickety Porterville Rec Center with its five lanes of candlepins, past a dead black Government Sales building with a large MAY IS CONFIRM-YOUR-SEX MONTH sign in the window.

In the fog Garraty missed Baker and ended up walking beside Stebbins. Hard like diamonds, McVries had said. But this diamond was showing some small flaws, he thought. Now they were walking parallel to the mighty and dead-polluted Androscoggin River. On the other side the Porterville Weaving Company, a textile mill reared its turrets into the fog like a filthy medieval castle.

Stebbins didn't look up, but Garraty knew Stebbins knew he was there. He said nothing, foolishly determined to make Stebbins say the first word. The road curved again. For a moment the crowd was gone as they crossed the bridge spanning the Androscoggin. Beneath them the water boiled along, sullen and salty, dressed with cheesy yellow foam.

''Well?''

''Save your breath for a minute,'' Garraty said. ''You'll need it.''

They came to the end of the bridge and the crowd was with them again as they swung left and started up the Brickyard Hill. It was long, steep, and banked. The river was dropping away below them on the left, and on their right was an almost perpendicular upslope. Spectators clung to trees, to bushes, to each other, and chanted Garraty's name. Once he had dated a girl who lived on Brickyard Hill, a girl named Carolyn. She was married now. Had a kid. She might have let him, but he was young and pretty dumb.

From up ahead Parker was giving a whispery, out-of-breath *goddam!* that was barely audible over the crowd. Garraty's legs quivered and threatened to go to jelly, but this was the last big hill before Freeport. After that it didn't matter. If he went to hell he went to hell. Finally they breasted it (Carolyn had nice breasts, she often wore cashmere sweaters) and Stebbins, panting just a little, repeated: ''Well?''

The guns roared. A boy named Charlie Field bowed out of the Walk.

"Well, nothing," Garraty said. "I was looking for Baker and found you instead. McVries says he thinks you'll win."

"McVries is an idiot," Stebbins said casually. "You really think you'll see your girl, Garraty? In all these people?"

"She'll be in the front," Garraty said. "She's got a pass."

"The cops'll be too busy holding everybody back to get her through to the front."

"That isn't true," Garraty said. He spoke sharply because Stebbins had articulated his own deep fear. "Why do you want to say a thing like that?"

"It's really your mother you want to see anyway."

Garraty recoiled sharply. "What?"

"Aren't you going to marry her when you grow up, Garraty? That's what most little boys want."

"You're crazy!"

"Am I?"

"Yes!"

"What makes you think you deserve to win, Garraty? You're a second-class intellect, a second-class physical specimen, and probably a second-class libido. Garraty, I'd bet my dog and lot you never slipped it to that girl of yours."

"Shut your goddam mouth!"

"Virgin, aren't you? Maybe a little bit queer in the bargain? Touch of the lavender? Don't be afraid. You can talk to Papa Stebbins."

"I'll walk you down if I have to walk to Virginia, you cheap fuck!" Garraty was shaking with anger. He could not remember being so angry in his whole life.

"That's okay," Stebbins said soothingly. "I understand."

"Motherfucker! You!—"

"Now *there's* an interesting word. What made you use *that* word?"

For a moment Garraty was sure he must throw himself on Stebbins or faint with rage, yet he did neither. "If I have to walk to Virginia," he repeated. "If I have to walk all the way to Virginia."

Stebbins stretched up on his toes and grinned sleepily. "*I* feel like I could walk all the way to Florida, Garraty."

Garraty lunged away from him, hunting for Baker, feeling the anger and rage die into a throbbing kind of shame. He supposed Stebbins thought he was an easy mark. He supposed he was.

Baker was walking beside a boy Garraty didn't know. His head was down, his lips moving a little.

"Hey, Baker," Garraty said.

Baker started, then seemed to shake himself all over, like a dog. "Garraty," he said. "You."

"Yea, me."

"I was having a dream—an awful real one. What time?"

Garraty checked. "Almost twenty to seven."

"Will it rain all day, you think?"

"I . . . *uh!*" Garraty lurched forward, momentarily off balance. "My damn shoeheel came off," he said.

"Get rid of 'em both," Baker advised. "The nails will get to pokin' through. And you have to work harder when you're off balance."

Garraty kicked off one shoe and it went end over end almost to the edge of the crowd, where it lay like a small crippled puppy. The hands of Crowd groped for it eagerly. One snared it, another took it away, and there was a violent, knotted struggle over it. His other shoe would not kick off; his foot had swelled tight inside it. He knelt, took his warning, untied it, and took it off. He considered throwing it to the crowd and then left it lying on the road instead. A great and irrational wave of despair suddenly washed over him and he thought: *I have lost my shoes. I have lost my shoes.*

The pavement was cold against his feet. The ripped remains of his stockings were soon soaked. Both feet looked strange, oddly lumpish. Garraty felt despair turn to pity for his feet. He caught up quickly with Baker, who was also walking shoeless. "I'm about done in," Baker said simply.

"We all are."

"I get to remembering all the nice things that ever happened to me. The first time I took a girl to a dance and there was this big ole drunk fella that kep tryin' to cut in and I took him outside and whipped his ass for him. I was only able to because he was so drunk. And that girl looked at me like I was the greatest thing since the internal combustion engine. My first bike. The first time I read *The Woman in White,* by Wilkie Collins . . . that's my favorite book, Garraty, should anyone ever ask you. Sittin' half asleep by some mudhole with a fishin' line and catchin' crawdaddies by the thousands. Layin' in the backyard and sleepin' with a *Popeye* funnybook over my face. I think about those things, Garraty. Just lately. Like I was old and gettin' senile."

The early morning rain fell silverly around them. Even the crowd seemed quieter, more withdrawn. Faces could be seen again, blurrily, like faces behind rainy panes of glass. They were pale, sloe-eyed faces with brooding expressions under dripping hats and umbrellas and spread newspaper tents. Garraty felt a deep ache inside him and it seemed it would be better if he could cry out, but he could not, any more than he could comfort Baker and tell him it was all right to die. It might be, but then again, it might not.

"I hope it won't be dark," Baker said. "That's all I hope. If there is an . . . an after, I hope it's not dark. And I hope you can *remember.* I'd hate to wander around in the dark forever, not knowing who I was or what I was doin' there, or not even knowing that I'd ever had anything different."

Garraty began to speak, and then the gunshots silenced him. Business was picking up again. The hiatus Parker had so accurately predicted was almost over. Baker's lips drew up in a grimace.

"That's what I'm most afraid of. That sound. Why did we do it, Garraty? We must have been insane."

"I don't think there was any good reason."

"All we are is mice in a trap."

The Walk went on. Rain fell. They walked past the places that Garraty knew— tumbledown shanties where no one lived, an abandoned one-room schoolhouse that had been replaced by the new Consolidated building, chicken houses, old trucks up on blocks, newly harrowed fields. He seemed to remember each field, each house. Now he tingled with excitement. The road seemed to fly by. His legs seemed to gain a new and spurious springiness. But maybe Stebbins was right— maybe she wouldn't be there. It had to be considered and prepared for, at least.

The word came back through the thinned ranks that there was a boy near the front who believed he had appendicitis.

Garraty would have boggled at this earlier, but now he couldn't seem to care about anything except Jan and Freeport. The hands on his watch were racing along with a devilish life of their own. Only five miles out now. They had passed the Freeport town line. Somewhere up ahead Jan and his mother were already standing in front of Woolman's Free Trade Center Market, as they had arranged it.

The sky brightened somewhat but remained overcast. The rain turned to a stubborn drizzle. The road was now a dark mirror, black ice in which Garraty could almost see the twisted reflection of his own face. He passed a hand across his forehead. It felt hot and feverish. Jan, oh Jan. You must know I—

The boy with the hurting side was 59, Klingerman. He began to scream. His screams quickly became monotonous. Garraty thought back to the one Long Walk he had seen—also in Freeport—and the boy who had been monotonously chanting *I can't. I can't. I can't.*

Klingerman, he thought, shut ya trap.

But Klingerman kept on walking, and he kept on screaming, hands laced over his side, and Garraty's watch hands kept on racing. It was eight-fifteen now. You'll be there, Jan, right? Right. Okay. I don't know what you mean anymore, but I know I'm still alive and that I need you to be there, to give me a sign, maybe. Just be there. Be there.

Eight-thirty.

"We gettin' close to this goddam town, Garraty?" Parker hollered.

"What do *you* care?" McVries jeered. "You sure don't have a girl waiting for you."

"I got girls everywhere, you dumb hump," Parker said. "They take one look at this face and cream in their silks." The face to which he referred was now haggard and gaunt, just a shadow of what it had been.

Eight forty-five.

"Slow down, fella," McVries said as Garraty caught up with him and started to pass by. "Save a little for tonight."

"I can't. Stebbins said she wouldn't be there. That they wouldn't have a man to spare to help her through. I have to find out. I have to—"

"Just take it easy is all I'm saying. Stebbins would get his own mother to drink a Lysol cocktail if it would help him win. Don't listen to him. She'll be there. It makes great PR, for one thing."

"But—"

"But me no buts, Ray. Slow down and live."

"You can just cram your fucking platitudes!" Garraty shouted. He licked his lips and put a shaky hand to his face. "I . . . I'm sorry. That was uncalled for. Stebbins also said I really only wanted to see my mother anyway."

"Don't you want to see her?"

"Of course I want to see her! What the hell do you think I—no—yes—I don't know. I had a friend once. And he and I—we—we took off our clothes—and she—she—"

"Garraty," McVries said, and put out a hand to touch his shoulder. Klingerman was screaming very loudly now. Somebody near the front lines asked him if he wanted an Alka-Seltzer. This sally brought general laughter. "You're falling apart, Garraty. Settle down. Don't blow it."

"*Get off my back!*" Garraty screamed. He crammed one fist against his lips and bit down on it. After a second he said, "Just get off me."

"Okay. Sure."

McVries strode away. Garraty wanted to call him back but couldn't.

Then, for the fourth time, it was nine o'clock in the morning. They turned left and the crowd was again below the twenty-four of them as they crossed the 295 overpass and into the town of Freeport. Up ahead was the Dairy Joy where he and Jan sometimes used to stop after the movies. They turned right and were on U.S. 1, what somebody had called the big highway. Big or small, it was the last highway. The hands on Garraty's watch seemed to jump out at him. Downtown was straight ahead. Woolman's was on the right. He could just see it, a squat and ugly building hiding behind a false front. The tickertape was starting to fall again. The rain made it sodden and sticky, lifeless. The crowd was swelling. Someone turned on the town fire siren, and its wails mixed and blended with Klingerman's. Klingerman and the Freeport fire siren sang a nightmarish duet.

Tension filled Garraty's veins, stuffed them full of copper wire. He could hear his heart thudding, now in his guts, now in his throat, now right between the eyes. Two hundred yards. They were screaming his name again (*RAY-RAY-ALL-THE-WAY!*) but he had not seen a familiar face in the crowd yet.

He drifted over to the right until the clutching hands of Crowd were inches from him—one long and brawny arm actually twitched the cloth of his shirt, and he jumped back as if he had almost been drawn into a threshing machine—and the soldiers had their guns on him, ready to let fly if he tried to disappear into the surge of humanity. Only a hundred yards to go now. He could see the big brown Woolman's sign, but no sign of his mother or of Jan. God, oh God God, Stebbins had been right . . . and even if they were here, how was he going to see them in this shifting, clutching mass?

A shaky groan seeped out of him, like a disgorged strand of flesh. He stumbled and almost fell over his own loose legs. Stebbins had been right. He wanted to stop here, to not go any further. The disappointment, the sense of loss, was so staggering it was hollow. What was the point? What was the point now?

Fire siren blasting, Crowd screaming, Klingerman shrieking, rain falling, and his own little tortured soul, flapping through his head and crashing blindly off its walls.

I can't go on. Can't, can't, can't. But his feet stumbled on. *Where am I? Jan? Jan? . . . JAN!*

He saw her. She was waving the blue silk scarf he had gotten her for her birthday, and the rain shimmered in her hair like gems. His mother was beside her, wearing her plain black coat. They had been jammed together by the mob and were being swayed helplessly back and forth. Over Jan's shoulder a TV camera poked its idiot snout.

A great sore somewhere in his body seemed to burst. The infection ran out of him in a green flood. He burst into a shambling, pigeon-toed run. His ripped socks flapped and slapped his swollen feet.

"Jan! Jan!"

He could hear the thought but not the words in his mouth. The TV camera tracked him enthusiastically. The din was tremendous. He could see her lips form his name, and he had to reach her, had to—

An arm brought him up short. It was McVries. A soldier speaking through a sexless bullhorn was giving them both first warning.

"Not into the crowd!" McVries's lips were against Garraty's ear and he was shouting. A lancet of pain pierced into Garraty's head.

"Let me go!"

"I won't let you kill yourself, Ray!"

"Let me go goddammit!"

"Do you want to die in her arms? Is that it?"

The time was fleeting. She was crying. He could see the tears on her cheeks. He wrenched free of McVries. He started for her again. He felt hard, angry sobs coming up from inside him. He wanted sleep. He would find it in her arms. He loved her.

Ray, I love you.

He could see the words on her lips.

McVries was still beside him. The TV camera glared down. Now, peripherally, he could see his high school class, and they were unfurling a huge banner and somehow it was his own face, his yearbook photo, blown up to Godzilla size, he was grinning down at himself as he cried and struggled to reach her.

Second warning, blared from the loudhailer like the voice of God.

Jan—

She was reaching out to him. Hands touching. Her cool hand. Her tears—

His mother. Her hands, reaching—

He grasped them. In one hand he held Jan's hand, in the other his mother's hand. He touched them. It was done.

It was done until McVries's arm came down around his shoulder again, cruel McVries.

"Let me *go!* Let me *go!*"

"Man, you must really hate her!" McVries screamed in his ear. "What do you want? To die knowing they're both stinking with your blood? Is that what you want? For Christ's sake, come on!"

He struggled, but McVries was strong. Maybe McVries was even right. He looked at Jan and now her eyes were wide with alarm. His mother made shooing gestures. And on Jan's lips he could read the words like a damnation: *Go on! Go on!*

Of course I must go on, he thought dully. I am Maine's Own. And in that second he hated her, although if he had done anything, it was no more than to catch her—and his mother—in the snare he had laid for himself.

Third warning for him and McVries, rolling majestically like thunder; the crowd hushed a little and looked on with wet-eyed eagerness. Now there was panic written on the faces of Jan and his mother. His mother's hands flew to her face, and he thought of Barkovitch's hands flying up to his neck like startled doves and ripping out his own throat.

"If you've got to do it, do it around the next corner, you cheap shit!" McVries cried.

He began to whimper. McVries had beaten him again. McVries was very strong. "All right," he said, not knowing if McVries could hear him or not. He began to walk. "All right, all right, let me loose before you break my collarbone." He sobbed, hiccuped, wiped his nose.

McVries let go of him warily, ready to grab him again.

Almost as an afterthought, Garraty turned and looked back, but they were already lost in the crowd again. He thought he would never forget that look of panic rising in their eyes, that feeling of trust and sureness finally kicked brutally away. He got nothing but half a glimpse of a waving blue scarf.

He turned around and faced forward again, not looking at McVries, and his stumbling, traitorous feet carried him on and they walked out of town.

Chapter 16

"The blood has begun to flow! Liston is staggering!
Clay is rocking him with combinations! . . .
boring in! Clay is killing him! Clay is killing him!
Ladies and gentlemen, Liston is down!
Sonny Liston is down! Clay is dancing . . .
waving . . . yelling into the crowd!
Oh, ladies and gentlemen, I don't know how
to describe this scene!"

—Radio Commentator
Second Clay-Liston Fight

Tubbins had gone insane.

Tubbins was a short boy with glasses and a faceful of freckles. He wore hip-hanging bluejeans that he had been constantly hitching up. He hadn't said much, but he had been a nice enough sort before he went insane.

"WHORE!" Tubbins babbled to the rain. He had turned his face up into it, and the rain dripped off his specs onto his cheeks and over his lips and down off the end of his blunted chin. "THE WHORE OF BABYLON HAS COME AMONG US! SHE LIES IN THE STREETS AND SPREADS HER LEGS ON THE FILTH OF COBBLESTONES! VILE! VILE! BEWARE THE WHORE OF BABYLON! HER LIPS DRIP HONEY BUT HER HEART IS GALL AND WORMWOOD—"

"And she's got the clap," Collie Parker added tiredly. "Jeezus, he's worse than Klingerman." He raised his voice. "Drop down dead, Tubby!"

"WHOREMONGER AND WHOREMASTER!" shrieked Tubbins. "VILE! UNCLEAN!"

"Piss on him," Parker muttered. "I'll kill him myself if he don't shut up." He passed trembling skeletal fingers across his lips, dropped them to his belt, and spent thirty seconds making them undo the clip that held his canteen to his belt. He almost dropped it getting it to his mouth, and then spilled half of it. He began to weep weakly.

It was three in the afternoon. Portland and South Portland were behind them. About fifteen minutes ago they had passed under a wet and flapping banner that proclaimed that the New Hampshire border was only 44 miles away.

Only, Garraty thought. *Only*, what a stupid little word that is. Who was the idiot who took it into his head that we needed a stupid little word like that?

He was walking next to McVries, but McVries had spoken only in monosyl-

302

lables since Freeport. Garraty hardly dared speak to him. He was indebted again, and it shamed him. It shamed him because he knew he would not help McVries if the chance came. Now Jan was gone, his mother was gone. Irrevocably and for eternity. Unless he won. And now he wanted to win very badly.

It was odd. This was the first time he could remember wanting to win. Not even at the start, when he had been fresh (back when dinosaurs walked the earth), had he consciously *wanted* to win. There had only been the challenge. But the guns didn't produce little red flags with BANG written on them. It wasn't baseball or Giant Step; it was all real.

Or had he known it all along?

His feet seemed to hurt twice as badly since he had decided he wanted to win, and there were stabbing pains in his chest when he drew long breaths. The sensation of fever was growing—perhaps he had picked something up from Scramm.

He wanted to win, but not even McVries could carry him over the invisible finish line. He didn't think he was going to win. In the sixth grade he had won his school's spelling bee and had gone on to the district spelldown, but the district spellmaster wasn't Miss Petrie, who let you take it back. Softhearted Miss Petrie. He had stood there, hurt, unbelieving, sure there must have been some mistake, but there had been none. He just hadn't been good enough to make the cut then, and he wasn't going to be good enough now. Good enough to walk most of them down, but not all. His feet and legs had gone beyond numb and angry rebellion, and now mutiny was just a step away.

Only three had gone down since they left Freeport. One of them had been the unfortunate Klingerman. Garraty knew what the rest of them were thinking. It was too many tickets issued for them to just quit, any of them. Not with only twenty left to walk over. They would walk now until their bodies or minds shook apart.

They passed over a bridge spanning a placid little brook, its surface lightly pocked by the rain. The guns roared, the crowd cheered, and Garraty felt the stubborn cranny of hope in the back of his brain open an infinitesimal bit more.

"Did your girl look good to you?"

It was Abraham, looking like a victim of the Bataan March. For some inconceivable reason he had shucked both his jacket and his shirt, leaving his bony chest and stacked ribcage bare.

"Yeah," Garraty said. "I hope I can make it back to her."

Abraham smiled. "Hope? Yeah, I'm beginning to remember how to spell that word, too." It was like a mild threat. "Was that Tubbins?"

Garraty listened. He heard nothing but the steady roar of the crowd. "Yeah, by God it was. Parker put the hex on him, I guess."

"I keep telling myself," Abraham said, "that all I got to do is to continue putting one foot in front of the other."

"Yeah."

Abraham looked distressed. "Garraty . . . this is a bitch to say . . . "

"What's that?"

Abraham was quiet for a long time. His shoes were big heavy Oxfords that looked horrendously heavy to Garraty (whose own feet were now bare, cold, and scraping raw). They clopped and dragged on the pavement, which had now expanded to three lanes. The crowd did not seem so loud or quite so terrifyingly close as it had ever since Augusta.

Abraham looked more distressed than ever. "It's a bitch. I just don't know how to say it."

Garraty shrugged, bewildered. "I guess you just say it."

"Well, look. We're getting together on something. All of us that are left."

"Scrabble, maybe?"

"It's a kind of a . . . a promise."

"Oh yeah?"

"No help for anybody. Do it on your own or don't do it."

Garraty looked at his feet. He wondered how long it had been since he was hungry, and he wondered how long it would be before he fainted if he didn't eat something. He thought that Abraham's Oxfords were like Stebbins—those shoes could carry him from here to the Golden Gate Bridge without so much as a busted shoelace . . . at least they looked that way.

"That sounds pretty heartless," he said finally.

"It's gotten to be a pretty heartless situation." Abraham wouldn't look at him.

"Have you talked to all the others about this?"

"Not yet. About a dozen."

"Yeah, it's a real bitch. I can see how hard it is for you to talk about."

"It seems to get harder rather than easier."

"What did they say?" He knew what they said, what were they supposed to say?

"They're for it."

Garraty opened his mouth, then shut it. He looked at Baker up ahead. Baker was wearing his jacket, and it was soaked. His head was bent. One hip swayed and jutted awkwardly. His left leg had stiffened up quite badly.

"Why'd you take off your shirt?" he asked Abraham suddenly.

"It was making my skin itch. It was raising hives or something. It was a synthetic, maybe I have an allergy to synthetic fabrics, how the hell should I know? What do you say, Ray?"

"You look like a religious penitent or something."

"What do you say? Yes or no?"

"Maybe I owe McVries a couple." McVries was still close by, but it was impossible to tell if he could hear their conversation over the din of the crowd. Come on, McVries, he thought. Tell him I don't owe you anything. Come on, you son of a bitch. But McVries said nothing.

"All right, count me in," Garraty said.

"Cool."

Now I'm an animal, nothing but a dirty, tired, stupid animal. You did it. You sold it out.

"If you try to help anybody, we can't hold you back. That's against the rules. But we'll shut you out. And you'll have broken your promise."

"I won't try."

"Same goes for anyone who tries to help you."

"Yuh."

"It's nothing personal. You know that, Ray. But we're down against it now."

"Root hog or die."

"That's it."

"Nothing personal. Just back to the jungle."

For a second he thought Abraham was going to get pissed, but his quickly drawn-in breath came out in a harmless sigh. Maybe he was too tired to get pissed. "You agreed. I'll hold you to that, Ray."

"Maybe I should get all high-flown and say I'll keep my promise because my word is my bond," Garraty said. "But I'll be honest. I want to see you get that ticket, Abraham. The sooner the better."

Abraham licked his lips. "Yeah."

"Those look like good shoes, Abe."

"Yeah. But they're too goddam heavy. You buy for distance, you gain the weight."

"Just ain't no cure for the summertime blues, is there?"

Abraham laughed. Garraty watched McVries. His face was unreadable. He might have heard. He might not have. The rain fell in steady straight lines, heavier now, colder. Abraham's skin was fishbelly white. Abraham looked more like a convict with his shirt off. Garraty wondered if anyone had told Abraham he didn't stand a dog's chance of lasting the night with his shirt off. Twilight already seemed to be creeping in. McVries? Did you hear us? I sold you down, McVries. Musketeers forever.

"Ah, I don't want to die this way," Abraham said. He was crying. "Not in public with people rooting for you to get up and walk another few miles. It's so fucking mindless. Just fucking *mindless*. This has about as much dignity as a mongoloid idiot strangling on his own tongue and shitting his pants at the same time."

It was quarter past three when Garraty gave his no help promise. By six that evening, only one more had gotten a ticket. No one talked. There seemed to be an uncomfortable conspiracy afoot to ignore the last fraying inches of their lives, Garraty thought, to just pretend it wasn't happening. The groups—what pitiful little remained of them—had broken down completely. Everyone had agreed to Abraham's proposal. McVries had. Baker had. Stebbins had laughed and asked Abraham if he wanted to prick his finger so he could sign in blood.

It was growing very cold. Garraty began to wonder if there really was such a thing as a sun, or if he had dreamed it. Even Jan was a dream to him now—a summer dream of a summer that never was.

Yet he seemed to see his father ever more clearly. His father with the heavy shock of hair he himself had inherited, and the big, meaty truck-driver's shoulders.

His father had been built like a fullback. He could remember his father picking him up, swinging him dizzyingly, rumpling his hair, kissing him. Loving him.

He hadn't really seen his mother back there in Freeport at all, he realized sadly, but she had been there—in her shabby black coat, "for best," the one that showed the white snowfall of dandruff on the collar no matter how often she shampooed. He had probably hurt her deeply by ignoring her in favor of Jan. Perhaps he had even meant to hurt her. But that didn't matter now. It was past. It was the future that was unraveling, even before it was knit.

You get in deeper, he thought. It never gets shallower, just deeper, until you're out of the bay and swimming into the ocean. Once all of this had looked simple. Pretty funny, all right. He had talked to McVries and McVries had told him the first time he had saved him out of pure reflex. Then, in Freeport, it had been to prevent an ugliness in front of a pretty girl he would never know. Just as he would never know Scramm's wife, heavy with child. Garraty had felt a pang at the thought, and sudden sorrow. He had not thought of Scramm in such a long time. He thought McVries was quite grown-up, really. He wondered why *he* hadn't managed to grow up any.

The Walk went on. Towns marched by.

He fell into a melancholy, oddly satisfying mood that was shattered quite suddenly by an irregular rattle of gunfire and hoarse screams from the crowd. When he looked around he was stunned to see Collie Parker standing on top of the halftrack with a rifle in his hands.

One of the soldiers had fallen off and lay staring up at the sky with empty, expressionless eyes. There was a neat blue hole surrounded by a corona of powder burns in the center of his forehead.

"Goddam bastards!" Parker was screaming. The other soldiers had jumped from the halftrack. Parker looked out over the stunned Walkers. "Come on, you guys! Come on! We can—"

The Walkers, Garraty included, stared at Parker as if he had begun to speak in a foreign language. And now one of the soldiers who had jumped when Parker swarmed up the side of the 'track now carefully shot Collie Parker in the back.

"Parker!" McVries screamed. It was as if he alone understood what had happened, and a chance that might have been missed. "Oh, no! *Parker!*"

Parker grunted as if someone had hit him in the back with a padded Indian club. The bullet mushroomed and there was Collie Parker, standing on top of the halftrack with his guts all over his torn khaki shirt and blue jeans. One hand was frozen in the middle of a wide, sweeping gesture, as if he was about to deliver an angry philippic.

"God.

"Damn," Parker said.

He fired the rifle he had wrenched away from the dead soldier twice into the road. The slugs snapped and whined, and Garraty felt one of them tug air in front of his face. Someone in the crowd screamed in pain. Then the gun slid from Parker's hands. He made an almost military half-turn and then fell to the road where he lay on his side, panting rapidly like a dog that has been struck and mortally wounded by a passing car. His eyes blazed. He opened his mouth and struggled through blood for some coda.

"You. Ba. Bas. Bast. Ba." He died, staring viciously at them as they passed by.

"What happened?" Garraty cried out to no one in particular. "What *happened* to him?"

"He snuck up on 'em," McVries said. "That's what happened. He must have known he couldn't make it. He snuck right up behind 'em and caught 'em asleep at the switch." McVries's voice hoarsened. "He wanted us all up there with him, Garraty. And I think we could have done it."

"What are you talking about?" Garraty asked, suddenly terrified.

"You don't know?" McVries asked. "You don't *know?*"

"Up there with him? . . . What? . . . "

"Forget it. Just forget it."

McVries walked away. Garraty had a sudden attack of the shivers. He couldn't stop them. He didn't know what McVries was talking about. He didn't want to know what McVries was talking about. Or even think about it.

The Walk went on.

By nine o'clock that night the rain had stopped, but the sky was starless. No one else had gone down, but Abraham had begun to moan inarticulately. It was very cold, but no one offered to give Abraham something to wear. Garraty tried to think of it as poetic justice, but it only made him feel sick. The pain within him had turned into a sickness, a rotten sick feeling that seemed to be growing in the hollows of his body like a green fungus. His concentrate belt was nearly full, but it was all he could do to eat a small tube of tuna paste without gagging.

Baker, Abraham, and McVries. His circle of friends had come down to those three. And Stebbins, if he was anyone's friend. Acquaintance, then. Or demigod. Or devil. Or whatever. He wondered if any of them would be here by morning, and if he would be alive to know.

Thinking such things, he almost ran into Baker in the dark. Something clinked in Baker's hands.

"What you doing?" Garraty asked.

"Huh?" Baker looked up blankly.

"What're you doing?" Garraty repeated patiently.

"Counting my change."

"How much you got?"

Baker clinked the money in his cupped hands and smiled. "Dollar twenty-two," he said.

Garraty grinned. "A fortune. What you going to do with it?"

Baker didn't smile back. He looked into the cold darkness dreamily. "Git me one of the big ones," he said. His light Southern drawl had thickened appreciably. "Git me a lead-lined one with pink silk insides and a white satin headpillow." He blinked his empty doorknob eyes. "Wouldn't never rot then, not till Judgment Trump, when we are as we were. Clothed in flesh incorruptible."

Garraty felt a warm trickle of horror. "Baker? Have you gone nuts, Baker?"

"You cain't beat it. We-uns was all crazy to try. You cain't beat the rottenness of it. Not in this world. Lead-lined, that's the ticket . . . "

"If you don't get hold of yourself, you'll be dead by morning."

Baker nodded. His skin was drawn tight over his cheekbones, giving him the aspect of a skull. "That's the ticket. I wanted to die. Didn't you? Isn't that why?"

"Shut up!" Garraty yelled. He had the shakes again.

The road sloped sharply up then, cutting off their talk. Garraty leaned into the hill, cold and hot, his spine hurting, his chest hurting. He was sure his muscles would flatly refuse to support him much longer. He thought of Baker's lead-lined box, sealed against the dark millennia, and wondered if it would be the last thing he ever thought of. He hoped not, and struggled for some other mental track.

Warnings cracked out sporadically. The soldiers on the halftrack were back up to the mark; the one Parker had killed had been unobtrusively replaced. The crowd cheered monotonously. Garraty wondered how it would be, to lie in the biggest, dustiest library silence of all, dreaming endless, thoughtless dreams behind gummed-down eyelids, dressed forever in your Sunday suit. No worries about money, success, fear, joy, pain, sorrow, sex, or love. Absolute zero. No father, mother, girlfriend, lover. The dead are orphans. No company but the silence like a moth's wing. An end to the agony of movement, to the long nightmare of going down the road. The body in peace, stillness, and order. The perfect darkness of death.

How would that be? Just how would that be?

And suddenly his roiling, agonized muscles, the sweat running down his face, even the pain itself—seemed very sweet and real. Garraty tried harder. He struggled to the top of the hill and gasped raggedly all the way down the far side.

At 11:40 Marty Wyman bought his hole. Garraty had forgotten all about Wyman, who hadn't spoken or gestured for the last twenty-four hours. He didn't die spectacularly. He just lay down and got shot. And someone whispered, that was Wyman. And someone else whispered, that's eighty-three, isn't it? And that was all.

By midnight they were only eight miles from the New Hampshire border. They passed a drive-in theater, a huge white oblong in the darkness. A single slide blazed from the screen: THE MANAGEMENT OF THIS THEATRE SALUTES THIS YEAR'S LONG WALKERS! At 12:20 in the morning it began to rain again, and Abraham began to cough—the same kind of wet, ragged cough that had gotten Scramm not long before he bought out. By one o'clock the rain had become a hard, steady downpour that stung Garraty's eyes and made his body ache with a kind of internal ague. The wind drove at their backs.

At quarter past the hour, Bobby Sledge tried to scutter quietly into the crowd under the cover of the dark and the driving rain. He was holed quickly and efficiently. Garraty wondered if the blond soldier who had almost sold him his ticket had done it. He knew the blond was on duty; he had seen his face clearly in the glare from the drive-in spotlights. He wished heartily that the blond had been the one Parker had ticketed.

At twenty of two Baker fell down and hit his head on the paving. Garraty started to go to him without even thinking. A hand, still strong, clamped on his arm. It was McVries. Of course it would have to be McVries.

"No," he said. "No more musketeers. And now it's real."

They walked on without looking back.

Baker collected three warnings, and then the silence stretched out interminably. Garraty waited for the guns to come down, and when they didn't, he checked his watch. Over four minutes had passed. Not long after, Baker walked past him and McVries, not looking at anything. There was an ugly, trickling wound on his forehead, but his eyes looked saner. The vacuous, dazed look was gone.

A little before two AM they crossed into New Hampshire amid the greatest pandemonium yet. Cannons went off. Fireworks burst in the rainy sky, lighting a multitude that stretched away as far as the eye could see in a crazy feverlight. Competing brass bands played martial airs. The cheers were thunder. A great overhead airburst traced the Major's face in fire, making Garraty think numbly of God. This was followed by the face of the New Hampshire Provo Governor, a man known for having stormed the German nuclear base in Santiago nearly singlehanded back in 1953. He had lost a leg to radiation poisoning.

Garraty dozed again. His thoughts grew incoherent. Freaky D'Allessio was crouched beneath the rocking chair of Baker's aunt, curled in a tiny coffin. His body was that of a plump Cheshire cat. He was grinning toothily. Faintly, in the fur between his slightly off-center green eyes, were the healed brand-marks of an old baseball wound. They were watching Garraty's father being led to an unmarked black van. One of the soldiers flanking Garraty's father was the blond soldier. Garraty's father was wearing only undershorts. The other soldier looked back over his shoulder and for a moment Garraty thought it was the Major. Then he saw it was Stebbins. He looked back and the Cheshire cat with Freaky's head had disappeared—all but the grin, which hung crescently in the air under the rocker like the outside edge of a watermelon . . .

The guns were shooting again, God, they were shooting at him now, he felt the air from that one, it was over, all over—

He snapped full awake and took two running steps, sending jolts of pain all the way up from his feet to his groin before he realized they had been shooting at someone else, and the someone else was dead, facedown in the rain.

"Hail Mary," McVries muttered.

"Full of grace," Stebbins said from behind them. He had moved up, moved up for the kill, and he was grinning like the Cheshire cat in Garraty's dream. "Help me win this stock-car race."

"Come on," McVries said. "Don't be a wise-ass."

"My ass is no wiser than your ass," Stebbins said solemnly.

McVries and Garraty laughed—a little uneasily.

"Well," Stebbins said, "maybe a little."

"Pick 'em up, put 'em down, shut your mouth," McVries chanted. He passed a shaky hand across his face and walked on, eyes straight ahead, his shoulders like a broken bow.

One more bought out before three o'clock—shot down in the rain and windy darkness as he went to his knees somewhere near Portsmouth. Abraham, coughing steadily, walked in a hopeless glitter of fever, a kind of death-glow, a brightness that made Garraty think of streaking meteorites. He was going to burn up instead of burning out—that was how tight it had gotten now.

Baker walked with steady, grim determination, trying to get rid of his warnings before they got rid of him. Garraty could just make him out through the slashing rain, limping along with his hands clenched at his sides.

And McVries was caving in. Garraty was not sure when it had begun; it might have happened in a second, while his back was turned. At one moment he had still been strong (Garraty remembered the clamp of McVries fingers on his lower arm when Baker had fallen), and now he was like an old man. It was unnerving.

Stebbins was Stebbins. He went on and on, like Abraham's shoes. He seemed to be favoring one leg slightly, but it could have been Garraty's imagination.

Of the other ten, five seemed to have drawn into that special netherworld that Olson had discovered—one step beyond pain and the comprehension of what was coming to them. They walked through the rainy dark like gaunt ghosts, and Garraty didn't like to look at them. They were the walking dead.

Just before dawn, three of them went down at once. The mouth of the crowd roared and belched anew with enthusiasm as the bodies spun and thumped like chunks of cut cordwood. To Garraty it seemed the beginning of a dreadful chain reaction that might sweep through them and finish them all. But it ended. It ended with Abraham crawling on his knees, eyes turned blindly up to the halftrack and the crowd beyond, mindless and filled with confused pain. They were the eyes of a sheep caught in a barbed wire fence. Then he fell on his face. His heavy Oxfords drummed fitfully against the wet road and then stopped.

Shortly after, the aqueous symphony of dawn began. The last day of the Walk came up wet and overcast. The wind howled down the almost-empty alley of the road like a lost dog being whipped through a strange and terrible place.

PART THREE

The Rabbit

Chapter 17

"Mother! Mother! Mother! Mother!"
—The Reverend Jim Jones,
at the moment of his apostasy

The concentrates were being passed out for the fifth and last time. It took only one of the soldiers to pass them out now. There were only nine Walkers left. Some of them looked at the belts dully, as if they had never seen such things, and let them slide out of their hands like slippery snakes. It took Garraty what seemed like hours to make his hands go through the complicated ritual of snapping the belt closed around his waist, and the thought of eating made his cramped and shriveled stomach feel ugly and nauseated.

Stebbins was now walking beside him. My guardian angel, Garraty thought wryly. As Garraty watched, Stebbins smiled widely and crammed two crackers smeared with peanut butter into his mouth. He ate noisily. Garraty felt sick.

"Wassa matter?" Stebbins asked around his sticky mouthful. "Can't take it?"

"What business is it of yours?"

Stebbins swallowed with what looked to Garraty like real effort. "None. If you faint from malnutrition, all the better for me."

"We're going to make it into Massachusetts, I think," McVries said sickly.

Stebbins nodded. "The first Walk to do it in seventeen years. They'll go crazy."

"How do you know so much about the Long Walk?" Garraty asked abruptly.

Stebbins shrugged. "It's all on record. They don't have anything to be ashamed of. Now do they?"

"What'll you do if you win, Stebbins?" McVries asked.

Stebbins laughed. In the rain, his thin, fuzzed face, lined with fatigue, looked lionlike. "What do *you* think? Get a big yella Cadillac with a purple top and a color TV with stereo speakers for every room of the house?"

"I'd expect," McVries said, "that you'd donate two or three hundred grand to the Society for Intensifying Cruelty to Animals."

"Abraham looked like a sheep," Garraty said abruptly. "Like a sheep caught on barbed wire. That's what I thought."

They passed under a huge banner that proclaimed they were now only fifteen miles from the Massachusetts border—there was really not much of New Hampshire along U.S. 1, only a narrow neck of land separating Maine and Massachusetts.

313

"Garraty," Stebbins said amiably, "why don't you go have sex with your mother?"

"Sorry, you're not pushing the right button anymore." He deliberately selected a bar of chocolate from his belt and crammed it whole into his mouth. His stomach knotted furiously, but he swallowed the chocolate. And after a short, tense struggle with his own insides, he knew he was going to keep it down. "I figure I can walk another full day if I have to," he said casually, "and another two if I need to. Resign yourself to it, Stebbins. Give up the old psy-war. It doesn't work. Have some more crackers and peanut butter."

Stebbins's mouth pursed tightly—just for a moment, but Garraty saw it. He had gotten under Stebbins's skin. He felt an incredible surge of elation. The mother lode at last.

"Come on, Stebbins," he said. "Tell us why *you're* here. Seeing as how we won't be together much longer. Tell us. Just between the three of us, now that we know you're not Superman."

Stebbins opened his mouth and with shocking abruptness he threw up the crackers and peanut butter he had eaten, almost whole and seemingly untouched by digestive juices. He staggered, and for only the second time since the Walk began, he was warned.

Garraty felt hard blood drumming in his head. "Come on, Stebbins. You've thrown up. Now own up. Tell us."

Stebbins's face had gone the color of old cheesecloth, but he had his composure back. "Why am I here? You want to know?"

McVries was looking at him curiously. No one was near; the closest was Baker, who was wandering along the edge of the crowd, looking intently into its mass face.

"Why am I here or why do I walk? Which do you want to know?"

"I want to know everything," Garraty said. It was only the truth.

"I'm the rabbit," Stebbins said. The rain fell steadily, dripping off their noses, hanging in droplets on their earlobes like earrings. Up ahead a barefoot boy, his feet purple patchworks of burst veins, went to his knees, crawled along with his head bobbing madly up and down, tried to get up, fell, and finally made it. He plunged onward. It was Pastor, Garraty noted with some amazement. Still with us.

"I'm the rabbit," Stebbins repeated. "You've seen them, Garraty. The little gray mechanical rabbits that the greyhounds chase at the dog races. No matter how fast the dogs run, they can never quite catch the rabbit. Because the rabbit isn't flesh and blood and they are. The rabbit, he's just a cutout on a stick attached to a bunch of cogs and wheels. In the old days, in England, they used to use a real rabbit, but sometimes the dogs caught it. More reliable the new way."

"He fooled me."

Stebbins's pale blue eyes stared into the falling rain.

"Maybe you could even say . . . he conjured me. He changed me into a rabbit. Remember the one in *Alice in Wonderland?* But maybe you're right, Garraty.

Time to stop being rabbits and grunting pigs and sheep and to be people . . . even if we can only rise to the level of whoremasters and the perverts in the balconies of the theaters on 42nd Street.'' Stebbins's eyes grew wild and gleeful, and now he looked at Garraty and McVries—and they flinched away from that stare. Stebbins was crazy. In that instant there could be no doubt of it. Stebbins was totally mad.

His low-pitched voice rose to a pulpit shout.

''How come I know so much about the Long Walk? I know all about the Long Walk! I ought to! *The Major is my father, Garraty! He's my father!*''

The crowd's voice rose in a mindless cheer that was mountainous and mindless in its intensity; they might have been cheering what Stebbins had said, if they could have heard it. The guns blasted. That was what the crowd was cheering. The guns blasted and Pastor rolled over dead.

Garraty felt a crawling in his guts and scrotum.

''Oh my God,'' McVries said. ''Is it true?'' He ran his tongue over his cracked lips.

''It's true,'' Stebbins said, almost genially, ''I'm his bastard. You see . . . I didn't think he knew. I didn't think he knew I was his son. That was where I made my mistake. He's a randy old sonofabitch, is the Major. I understand he's got dozens of little bastards. What I wanted was to spring it on him—spring it on the world. Surprise, surprise. And when I won, the Prize I was going to ask for was to be taken into my father's house.''

''But he knew *everything?*'' McVries whispered.

''He made me his rabbit. A little gray rabbit to make the rest of the dogs run faster . . . and further. And I guess it worked. We're going to make it into Massachusetts.''

''And now?'' Garraty asked.

Stebbins shrugged. ''The rabbit turns out to be flesh and blood after all. I walk. I talk. And I suppose if all this doesn't end soon, I'll be crawling on my belly like a reptile.''

They passed under a heavy brace of power lines. A number of men in climbing boots clung to the support posts, above the crowd, like grotesque praying mantises.

''What time is it?'' Stebbins asked. His face seemed to have melted in the rain. It had become Olson's face, Abraham's face, Barkovitch's face . . . then, terribly, Garraty's own face, hopeless and drained, sunken and crenellated in on itself, the face of a rotten scarecrow in a long-since-harvested field.

''It's twenty until ten,'' McVries said. He grinned—a ghostly imitation of his old cynical grin. ''Happy day five to you, suckers.''

Stebbins nodded. ''Will it rain all day, Garraty?''

''Yeah, I think so. It looks that way.''

Stebbins nodded slowly. ''I think so, too.''

''Well, come on in out of the rain,'' McVries said suddenly.

''All right. Thanks.''

They walked on, somehow in step, although all three of them were bent forever in different shapes by the pains that pulled them.

When they crossed into Massachusetts, they were seven: Garraty, Baker, McVries, a struggling, hollow-eyed skeleton named George Fielder, Bill Hough ("pronounce that Huff," he had told Garraty much earlier on), a tallish, muscular fellow named Milligan who did not seem to be in really serious shape yet, and Stebbins.

The pomp and thunder of the border crossing slowly passed behind them. The rain continued, constant and monotonous. The wind howled and ripped with all the young, unknowing cruelty of spring. It lifted caps from the crowd and whirled them, saucerlike, in brief and violent arcs across the whitewash-colored sky.

A very short while ago—just after Stebbins had made his confession—Garraty had experienced an odd, light lifting of his entire being. His feet seemed to remember what they had once been. There was a kind of frozen cessation to the blinding pains in his back and neck. It was like climbing up a final sheer rock face and coming out on the peak—out of the shifting mist of clouds and into the cold sunshine and the bracing, undernourished air . . . with noplace to go but down, and that at flying speed.

The halftrack was a little ahead of them. Garraty looked at the blond soldier crouched under the big canvas umbrella on the back deck. He tried to project all the ache, all the rainsoaked misery out of himself and into the Major's man. The blond stared back at him indifferently.

Garraty glanced over at Baker and saw that his nose was bleeding badly. Blood painted his cheeks and dripped from the line of his jaw.

"He's going to die, isn't he?" Stebbins said.

"Sure," McVries answered. "They've all been dying, didn't you know?"

A hard gust of wind sheeted rain across them, and McVries staggered. He drew a warning. The crowd cheered on, unaffected and seemingly impervious. At least there had been fewer firecrackers today. The rain had put a stop to that happy bullshit.

The road took them around a big, banked curve, and Garraty felt his heart lurch. Faintly he heard Milligan mutter, "Good Jesus!"

The road was sunk between two sloping hills. The road was like a cleft between two rising breasts. The hills were black with people. The people seemed to rise above them and around them like the living walls of a huge dark slough.

George Fielder came abruptly to life. His skull-head turned slowly this way and that on his pipestem neck. "They're going to eat us up," he muttered. "They're gonna fall in on us and eat us up."

"I think not," Stebbins said shortly. "There has never been a—"

"They're gonna eat us up! Eat us up! Eatusup! Up! Up! Eatusupeatusup—" George Fielder whirled around in a huge, rambling circle, his arms flapping madly. His eyes blazed with mousetrap terror. To Garraty he looked like one of those video games gone crazy.

"Eatusupeatusupeatusup—"

He was screeching at the top of his voice, but Garraty could barely hear him. The waves of sound from the hills beat down on them like hammers. Garraty could not even hear the gunshots when Fielder bought out; only the savage scream from the throat of Crowd. Fielder's body did a gangling but strangely graceful rhumba in the center of the road, feet kicking, body twitching, shoulders jerking. Then, apparently too tired to dance anymore, he sat down, legs spread wide, and he died that way, sitting up, his chin tucked down on his chest like a tired little boy caught by the sandman at playtime.

"Garraty," Baker said. "Garraty, I'm bleeding." The hills were behind them now and Garraty could hear him—badly.

"Yeah," he said. It was a struggle to keep his voice level. Something inside Art Baker had hemorrhaged. His nose was gushing blood. His cheeks and neck were lathered with gore. His shirt collar was soaked with it.

"It's not bad, is it?" Baker asked him. He was crying with fear. He knew it was bad.

"No, not too bad," Garraty said.

"The rain feels so warm," Baker said. "I know it's only rain, though. It's only rain, right, Garraty?"

"Right," Garraty said sickly.

"I wish I had some ice to put on it," Baker said, and walked away. Garraty watched him go.

Bill Hough ("you pronounce that Huff") bought a ticket at quarter of eleven, and Milligan at eleven-thirty, just after the Flying Deuces precision-flying team rocketed overhead in six electric blue F-111s. Garraty had expected Baker to go before either of them. But Baker continued on, although now the whole top half of his shirt was soaked through.

Garraty's head seemed to be playing jazz. Dave Brubeck, Thelonius Monk, Cannonball Adderly—the Banned Noisemakers that everybody kept under the table and played when the party got noisy and drunk.

It seemed that he had once been loved, once he himself had loved. But now it was just jazz and the rising drumbeat in his head and his mother had only been stuffed straw in a fur coat, Jan nothing but a department store dummy. It was over. Even if he won, if he managed to outlast McVries and Stebbins and Baker, it was over. He was never going home again.

He began to cry a little bit. His vision blurred and his feet tangled up and he fell down. The pavement was hard and shockingly cold and unbelievably restful. He was warned twice before he managed to pick himself up, using a series of drunken, crablike motions. He got his feet to work again. He broke wind—a long, sterile rattle that seemed to bear no relationship at all to an honest fart.

Baker was zigging and zagging drunkenly across the road and back. McVries and Stebbins had their heads together. Garraty was suddenly very sure they were plotting to kill him, the way someone named Barkovitch had once killed a faceless number named Rank.

He made himself walk fast and caught up with them. They made room for him wordlessly. (You've stopped talking about me, haven't you? But you were. Do you think I don't know? Do you think I am nuts?), but there was a comfort. He wanted to be with them, stay with them, until he died.

They passed a sign now which seemed to summarize to Garraty's dumbly wondering eyes all the screaming insanity there might be in the universe, all the idiot whistling laughter of the spheres, and this sign read: 49 MILES TO BOSTON! WALKERS YOU CAN MAKE IT! He would have shrieked with laughter if he had been able. Boston! The very sound was mythic, rich with unbelievability.

Baker was beside him again. "Garraty?"

"What?"

"Are we in?"

"Huh?"

"In, are we in? Garraty, *please.*"

Baker's eyes pleaded. He was an abattoir, a raw-blood machine.

"Yeah. We're in. We're in, Art." He had no idea what Baker was talking about.

"I'm going to die now, Garraty."

"All right."

"If you win, will you do something for me? I'm scairt to ask anyone else." And Baker made a sweeping gesture at the deserted road as if the Walk was still rich with its dozens. For a chilling moment Garraty wondered if maybe they were all there still, walking ghosts that Baker could now see in his moment of extremis.

"Anything."

Baker put a hand on Garraty's shoulder, and Garraty began weeping uncontrollably. It seemed that his heart would burst out of his chest and weep its own tears.

Baker said, "Lead-lined."

"Walk a little bit longer," Garraty said through his tears. "Walk a little longer, Art."

"No—I can't."

"All right."

"Maybe I'll see you, man," Baker said, and wiped slick blood from his face absently.

Garraty lowered his head and wept.

"Don't watch 'em do it," Baker said. "Promise me that, too."

Garraty nodded, beyond speech.

"Thanks. You've been my friend, Garraty." Baker tried to smile. He stuck his hand blindly out, and Garraty shook it with both of his.

"Another time, another place," Baker said.

Garraty put his hands over his face and had to bend over to keep walking. The sobs ripped out of him and made him ache with a pain that was far beyond anything the Walk had been able to inflict.

He hoped he wouldn't hear the shots. But he did.

Chapter 18

"I proclaim this year's Long Walk at an end.
Ladies and gentlemen—citizens—behold
your winner!"

—The Major

They were forty miles from Boston.

"Tell us a story, Garraty," Stebbins said abruptly. "Tell us a story that will take our minds off our troubles." He had aged unbelievably; Stebbins was an old man.

"Yeah," McVries said. He also looked ancient and wizened. "A story, Garraty."

Garraty looked from one to the other dully, but he could see no duplicity in their faces, only the bone-weariness. He was falling off his own peak now; all the ugly, dragging pains were rushing back in.

He closed his eyes for a long moment. When he opened them, the world had doubled and came only reluctantly back into focus. "All right," he said.

McVries clapped his hands solemnly, three times. He was walking with three warnings; Garraty had one; Stebbins, none.

"Once upon a time—"

"Oh, who wants to hear a fucking fairy story?" Stebbins asked.

McVries giggled a little.

"You'll hear what I want to tell you!" Garraty said shrewishly. "You want to hear it or not?"

Stebbins stumbled against Garraty. Both he and Stebbins were warned. "I s'pose a fairy story's better than no story at all."

"It's not a fairy story, anyway. Just because it's in a world that never was doesn't mean it's a fairy story. It doesn't mean—"

"Are you gonna tell it or not?" McVries asked pettishly.

"Once upon a time," Garraty began, "there was a white knight that went out into the world on a Sacred Quest. He left his castle and walked through the Enchanted Forest—"

"Knights ride," Stebbins objected.

"Rode through the Enchanted Forest, then. *Rode.* And he had many strange adventures. He fought off thousands of trolls and goblins and a whole shitload of wolves. All right? And he finally got to the king's castle and asked permission to take Gwendolyn, the famous Lady Fair, out walking."

319

McVries cackled.

"The king wasn't digging it, thinking no one was good enough for his daughter Gwen, the world-famous Lady Fair, but the Lady Fair loved the White Knight so much that she threatened to run away into the Wildwoods if . . . if . . . " A wave of dizziness rode over him darkly, making him feel as if he were floating. The roar of the crowd came to him like the boom of the sea down a long, cone-shaped tunnel. Then it passed, but slowly.

He looked around. McVries's head had dropped, and he was walking at the crowd, fast asleep.

"Hey!" Garraty shouted. "Hey, Pete! *Pete!*"

"Let him alone," Stebbins said. "You made the promise like the rest of us."

"Fuck you," Garraty said distinctly, and darted to McVries's side. He touched McVries's shoulders, setting him straight again. McVries looked up at him sleepily and smiled. "No, Ray. It's time to sit down."

Terror pounded Garraty's chest. "No! No way!"

McVries looked at him for a moment, then smiled again and shook his head. He sat down, cross-legged on the pavement. He looked like a world-beaten monk. The scar on his cheek was a white slash in the rainy gloom.

"No!" Garraty screamed.

He tried to pick McVries up, but, thin as he was, McVries was much too heavy. McVries wouldn't even look at him. His eyes were shut. And suddenly two of the soldiers were wrenching McVries away from him. They were putting their guns to McVries's head.

"No!" Garraty screamed again. *"Me! Me! Shoot me!"*

But instead, they gave him his third warning.

McVries opened his eyes and smiled again. The next instant, he was gone.

Garraty walked unknowingly now. He stared blankly at Stebbins, who stared back at him curiously. Garraty was filled with a strange, roaring emptiness.

"Finish the story," Stebbins said. "Finish the story, Garraty."

"No," Garraty said. "I don't think so."

"Let it go, then," Stebbins said, and smiled winningly. "If there are such things as souls, his is still close. You could catch up."

Garraty looked at Stebbins and said, "I'm going to walk you into the ground."

Oh, Pete, he thought. He didn't even have any tears left to cry.

"Are you?" Stebbins said. "We'll see."

By eight that evening they were walking through Danvers, and Garraty finally knew. It was almost done, because Stebbins could not be beaten.

I spent too much time thinking about it. McVries, Baker, Abraham . . . they didn't think about it, they just did it. As if it were natural. And it *is* natural. In a way, it's the most natural thing in the world.

He shambled along, bulge-eyed, jaw hanging agape, rain swishing in. For a misty, shutterlike moment he thought he saw someone he knew, knew as well as himself, weeping and beckoning in the dark ahead, but it was no use. He couldn't go on.

He would just tell Stebbins. He was up ahead a little, limping quite a bit now, and looking emaciated. Garraty was very tired, but he was no longer afraid. He felt calm. He felt okay. He made himself go faster until he could put a hand on Stebbins's shoulder. "Stebbins," he said.

Stebbins turned and looked at Garraty with huge, floating eyes that saw nothing for a moment. Then recognition came and he reached out and clawed at Garraty's shirt, pulling it open. The crowd screamed its anger at this interference, but only Garraty was close enough to see the horror in Stebbins's eyes, the horror, the darkness, and only Garraty knew that Stebbins's grip was a last despairing reach for rescue.

"Oh Garraty!" he cried, and fell down.

Now the sound of the crowd was apocalyptic. It was the sound of mountains falling and breaking, the earth shattering. The sound crushed Garraty easily beneath it. It would have killed him if he had heard it. But he heard nothing but his own voice.

"Stebbins?" he said curiously. He bent and somehow managed to turn Stebbins over. Stebbins still stared at him, but the despair had already skimmed over. His head rolled bonelessly on his neck.

He put a cupped hand in front of Stebbins's mouth. "Stebbins?" he said again.

But Stebbins was dead.

Garraty lost interest. He got to his feet and began to walk. Now the cheers filled the earth and fireworks filled the sky. Up ahead, a jeep roared toward him.

No vehicles on the road, you damn fool. That's a capital offense, they can shoot you for that.

The Major stood in the jeep. He held a stiff salute. Ready to grant first wish, every wish, any wish, death wish. The Prize.

Behind him, they finished by shooting the already-dead Stebbins, and now there was only him, alone on the road, walking toward where the Major's jeep had stopped diagonally across the white line, and the Major was getting out, coming to him, his face kind and unreadable behind the mirror sunglasses.

Garraty stepped aside. He was not alone. The dark figure was back, up ahead, not far, beckoning. He knew that figure. If he could get a little closer, he could make out the features. Which one hadn't he walked down? Was it Barkovitch? Collie Parker? Percy What'shisname? Who was it?

"GARRATY!" the crowd screamed deliriously. *"GARRATY, GARRATY, GARRATY!"*

Was it Scramm? Gribble? Davidson?

A hand on his shoulder. Garraty shook it off impatiently. The dark figure beckoned, beckoned in the rain, beckoned for him to come and walk, to come and play the game. And it was time to get started. There was still so far to walk.

Eyes blind, supplicating hands held out before him as if for alms, Garraty walked toward the dark figure.

And when the hand touched his shoulder again, he somehow found the strength to run.

SIGNET•451-E9668•$2.25

ROADWORK

HIS LIFE
WAS IN THE PATH
OF THE WRECKING
BALL...BUT HE
WOULDN'T
BUDGE

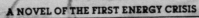

A NOVEL OF THE FIRST ENERGY CRISIS

BY RICHARD BACHMAN

AUTHOR OF THE LONG WALK & RAGE

In memory of Charlotte Littlefield.
Proverbs 31:10–28.

Prologue

I don't know why. You don't know why.
Most likely God don't know why, either.
It's just Government business, that's all.
—Man-in-the-street interview
    concerning Viet Nam, circa 1967

But Viet Nam was over and the country was getting on.

On this hot August afternoon in 1972, the WHLM Newsmobile was parked near Westgate at the end of the Route 784 expressway. There was a small crowd around a bunting-covered podium that had been hurriedly tossed together; the bunting was thin flesh on a skeleton of naked planks. Behind it, at the top of a grassy embankment, were the highway tollbooths. In front of it, open, marshy land stretched toward the suburban hem of the city's outskirts.

A young reporter named Dave Albert was doing a series of man-on-the-street interviews while he and his co-workers waited for the mayor and the governor to arrive for the ground-breaking ceremony.

He held the microphone toward an elderly man wearing tinted spectacles.

"Well," the elderly man said, looking tremulously into the camera, "I think it's a great thing for the city. We've needed this a long time. It's . . . a great thing for the city." He swallowed, aware that his mind was broadcasting echos of itself, helpless to stop, hypnotized by the grinding, Cyclopean eye of posterity. "Great," he added limply.

"Thank you, sir. Thank you very much."

"Do you think they'll use it? On the news tonight?"

Albert flashed a professional, meaningless smile. "Hard to tell, sir. There's a good chance."

His sound man pointed up to the tollgate turnaround, where the governor's Chrysler Imperial had just pulled up, winking and gleaming like a chrome-inlaid eight ball in the summer sunshine. Albert nodded back, held up a single finger. He and the cameraman approached a guy in a white shirt with rolled-up sleeves. The guy was looking moodily at the podium.

"Would you mind stating your opinion of all this, Mr. . . . ?"

"Dawes. No, I don't mind." His voice was low, pleasant.

"Speed," the cameraman murmured.

The man in the white shirt said, still pleasantly, "I think it's a piece of shit."

The cameraman grimaced. Albert nodded, looking at the man in the white shirt reproachfully, and then made cutting gestures with the first two fingers of his right hand.

The elderly gentleman was looking at this tableau with real horror. Above, up by the tollbooths, the governor was getting out of his Imperial. His green tie was resplendent in the sun.

The man in the white shirt said politely: "Will that be on the six or eleven o'clock news?"

"Ho-ho, fella, you're a riot," Albert said sourly, and walked away to catch the governor. The cameraman trailed after him. The man in the white shirt watched the governor as he came carefully down the grassy slope.

Albert met the man in the white shirt again seventeen months later, but since neither of them remembered that they had met before, it might as well have been the first time.

329

PART ONE

November

Late last night the rain was knocking on my window
I moved across the darkened room and in the lampglow
I thought I saw down in the street
The spirit of the century
Telling us that we're all standing on the border.
—Al Stewart

November 20, 1973

He kept doing things without letting himself think about them. Safer that way. It was like having a circuit breaker in his head, and it thumped into place every time part of him tried to ask: *But why are you doing this?* Part of his mind would go dark. Hey Georgie, who turned out the lights? Whoops, I did. Something screwy in the wiring, I guess. Just a sec. Reset the switch. The lights go back on. But the thought is gone. Everything is fine. Let us continue, Freddy—where were we?

He was walking to the bus stop when he saw the sign that said:

AMMO HARVEY'S GUN SHOP AMMO
Remington   Winchester   Colt   Smith & Wesson
HUNTERS WELCOME

It was snowing a little out of a gray sky. It was the first snow of the year and it landed on the pavement like white splotches of baking soda, then melted. He saw a little boy in a red knitted cap go by with his mouth open and his tongue out to catch a flake. It's just going to melt, Freddy, he thought at the kid, but the kid went on anyway, with his head cocked back at the sky.

He stopped in front of Harvey's Gun Shop, hesitating. There was a rack of late edition newspapers outside the door, and the headline said:

SHAKY CEASE-FIRE HOLDS

Below that, on the rack, was a smudged white sign that said:

PLEASE PAY FOR YOUR PAPER!
THIS IS AN HONOR RACK, DEALER MUST PAY FOR ALL PAPERS

It was warm inside. The shop was long but not very wide. There was only a single aisle. Inside the door on the left was a glass case filled with boxes of ammunition. He recognized the .22 cartridges immediately, because he'd had a .22 single-shot rifle as a boy in Connecticut. He had wanted that rifle for three years and when he finally got it he couldn't think of anything to do with it. He shot at cans for a while, then shot a blue jay. The jay hadn't been a clean kill. It sat in the snow surrounded by a pink blood stain, its beak slowly opening and closing. After that he had put the rifle up on hooks and it had stayed there for three years until he sold it to a kid up the street for nine dollars and a carton of funny books.

The other ammunition was less familiar. Thirty-thirty, thirty-ought-six, and some that looked like scale-model howitzer shells. What animals do you kill with those? he wondered. Tigers? Dinosaurs? Still it fascinated him, sitting there inside the glass case like penny candy in a stationery store.

The clerk or proprietor was talking to a fat man in green pants and a green fatigue shirt. The shirt had flap pockets. They were talking about a pistol that was lying on top of another glass case, dismembered. The fat man thumbed back the slide and they both peered into the oiled chamber. The fat man said something and the clerk or proprietor laughed.

"Autos always jam? You got that from your father, Mac. Admit it."

"Harry, you're full of bullshit up to your eyebrows."

You're full of it, Fred, he thought. Right up to your eyebrows. You know it, Fred?

Fred said he knew it.

On the right was a glass case that ran the length of the shop. It was full of rifles on pegs. He was able to pick out the double-barreled shotguns, but everything else was a mystery to him. Yet some people—the two at the far counter, for example— had mastered this world as easily as he had mastered general accounting in college.

He walked further into the store and looked into a case filled with pistols. He saw some air guns, a few .22's, a .38 with a wood-grip handle, .45's, and a gun he recognized as a .44 Magnum, the gun Dirty Harry had carried in that movie. He had heard Ron Stone and Vinnie Mason talking about that movie at the laundry, and Vinnie had said: They'd never let a cop carry a gun like that in the city. You can blow a hole in a man a mile away with one of those.

The fat man, Mac, and the clerk or proprietor, Harry (as in Dirty Harry), had the gun back together.

"You give me a call when you get that Menschler in," Mac said.

"I will . . . but your prejudice against autos is irrational," Harry said. (He decided Harry must be the proprietor—a clerk would never call a customer irrational.) "Have you got to have the Cobra next week?"

"I'd like it," Mac said.

"I don't promise."

"You never do . . . but you're the best goddam gunsmith in the city, and you know it."

"Of course I do."

Mac patted the gun on top of the glass case and turned to go. Mac bumped into him—*Watch it, Mac. Smile when you do that*—and then went on to the door. The paper was tucked under Mac's arm, and he could read:

SHAKY CEA

Harry turned to him, still smiling and shaking his head. "Can I help you?"

"I hope so. But I warn you in advance, I know nothing about guns."

Harry shrugged. "There's a law you should? Is it for someone else? For Christmas?"

"Yes, that's just right," he said, seizing on it. "I've got this cousin—Nick, his name is. Nick Adams. He lives in Michigan and he's got yea guns. You know. Loves to hunt, but it's more than that. It's sort of a, well, a—"

"Hobby?" Harry asked, smiling.

"Yes, that's it." He had been about to say *fetish*. His eyes dropped to the cash register, where an aged bumper sticker was pasted on. The bumper sticker said:

IF GUNS ARE OUTLAWED, ONLY OUTLAWS WILL HAVE GUNS

He smiled at Harry and said, "That's very true, you know."

"Sure it is," Harry said. "This cousin of yours . . ."

"Well, it's kind of a one-upmanship type of thing. He knows how much I like boating and I'll be damned if he didn't up and give me an Evinrude sixty-horsepower motor last Christmas. He sent it by REA express. I gave him a hunting jacket. I felt sort of like a horse's ass."

Harry nodded sympathetically.

"Well, I got a letter from him about six weeks ago, and he sounds just like a kid with a free pass to the circus. It seems that he and about six buddies chipped in together and bought themselves a trip to this place in Mexico, sort of like a free-fire zone—"

"A no-limit hunting preserve?"

"Yeah, that's it." He chuckled a little. "You shoot as much as you want. They stock it, you know. Deer, antelope, bear, bison. Everything."

"Was it Boca Rio?"

"I really don't remember. I think the name was longer than that."

Harry's eyes had gone slightly dreamy. "That guy that just left and myself and two others went to Boca Rio in 1965. I shot a zebra. A goddam zebra! I got it mounted in my game room at home. That was the best time I ever had in my life, bar none. I envy your cousin."

"Well, I talked it over with my wife," he said, "and she said go ahead. We had a very good year at the laundry. I work at the Blue Ribbon Laundry over in Western."

"Yes, I know where that is."

He felt that he could go on talking to Harry all day, for the rest of the year, embroidering the truth and the lies into a beautiful, gleaming tapestry. Let the world go by. Fuck the gas shortage and the high price of beef and the shaky ceasefire. Let there be talk of cousins that never were, right, Fred? Right on, Georgie.

"We got the Central Hospital account this year, as well as the mental institution, and also three new motels."

"Is the Quality Motor Court on Franklin Avenue one of yours?"

"Yes, it is."

"I've stayed there a couple of times," Harry said. "The sheets were always very clean. Funny, you never think about who washes the sheets when you stay at a motel."

"Well, we had a good year. And so I thought, maybe I can get Nick a rifle and a pistol. I know he's always wanted a .44 Magnum, I've heard him mention that one—''

Harry brought the Magnum up and laid it carefully on top of the glass case. He picked it up. He liked the heft of it. It felt like business.

He put it back down on the glass case.

"The chambering on that—" Harry began.

He laughed and held up a hand. "Don't sell me. I'm sold. An ignoramus always sells himself. How much ammunition should I get with that?"

Harry shrugged. "Get him ten boxes, why don't you? He can always get more. The price on that gun is two-eighty-nine plus tax, but I'm going to give it to you for two-eighty, ammo thrown in. How's that?"

"Super," he said, meaning it. And then, because something more seemed required, he added: "It's a handsome piece."

"If it's Boca Rio, he'll put it to good use."

"Now the rifle—"

"What does he have?"

He shrugged and spread his hands. "I'm sorry. I really don't know. Two or three shotguns, and something he calls an auto-loader—"

"Remington?" Harry asked him so quickly that he felt afraid; it was as if he had been walking in waist-deep water that had suddenly shelved off.

"I think it was. I could be wrong."

"Remington makes the best," Harry said, and nodded, putting him at ease again. "How high do you want to go?"

"Well, I'll be honest with you. The motor probably cost him four hundred. I'd like to go at least five. Six hundred tops."

"You and this cousin really get along, don't you?"

"We grew up together," he said sincerely. "I think I'd give my right arm to Nick, if he wanted it."

"Well, let me show you something," Harry said. He picked a key out of the bundle on his ring and went to one of the glass cabinets. He opened it, climbed up on a stool, and brought down a long, heavy rifle with an inlaid stock. "This may be a little higher than you want to go, but it's a beautiful gun." Harry handed it to him.

"What is it?"

"That's a four-sixty Weatherbee. Shoots heavier ammunition than I've got here in the place right now. I'd have to order however many rounds you wanted from Chicago. Take about a week. It's a perfectly weighted gun. The muzzle energy on that baby is over eight thousand pounds . . . like hitting something with an airport limousine. If you hit a buck in the head with it, you'd have to take the tail for a trophy."

"I don't know," he said, sounding dubious even though he had decided he wanted the rifle. "I know Nick wants trophies. That's part of—"

"Sure it is," Harry said, taking the Weatherbee and chambering it. The hole looked big enough to put a carrier pigeon in. "Nobody goes to Boca Rio for meat.

So your cousin gutshoots. With this piece, you don't have to worry about tracking the goddam animal for twelve miles through the high country, the animal suffering the whole time, not to mention you missing dinner. This baby will spread his insides over twenty feet."

"How much?"

"Well, I'll tell you. I can't move it in town. Who wants a freaking anti-tank gun when there's nothing to go after anymore but pheasant? And if you put them on the table, it tastes like you're eating exhaust fumes. It retails for nine-fifty, wholesales for six-thirty. I'd let you have it for seven hundred."

"That comes to . . . almost a thousand bucks."

"We give a ten percent discount on orders over three hundred dollars. That brings it back to nine." He shrugged. "You give that gun to your cousin, I guarantee he hasn't got one. If he does, I'll buy it back for seven-fifty. I'll put that in writing, that's how sure I am."

"No kidding?"

"Absolutely. Absolutely. Of course, if it's too steep, it's too steep. We can look at some other guns. But if he's a real nut on the subject, I don't have anything else he might not have two of."

"I see." He put a thoughtful expression on his face. "Have you got a telephone?"

"Sure, in the back. Want to call your wife and talk it over?"

"I think I better."

"Sure. Come on."

Harry led him into a cluttered back room. There was a bench and a scarred wooden table littered with gun guts, springs, cleaning fluid, pamphlets, and labeled bottles with lead slugs in them.

"There's the phone," Harry said.

He sat down, picked up the phone, and dialed while Harry went back to get the Magnum and put it in a box.

"Thank you for calling the WDST Weatherphone," the bright, recorded voice said. "This afternoon, snow flurries developing into light snow late this evening—"

"Hi, Mary?" he said. "Listen, I'm in this place called Harvey's Gun Shop. Yeah, about Nicky. I got the pistol we talked about, no problem. There was one right in the showcase. Then the guy showed me this rifle—"

"—clearing by tomorrow afternoon. Lows tonight will be in the thirties, tomorrow in the mid to upper forties. Chance of precipitation tonight—"

"—so what do you think I should do?" Harry was standing in the doorway behind him; he could see the shadow.

"Yeah," he said. "I know that."

"Thank you for dialing the WDST Weatherphone, and be sure to watch Newsplus-Sixty with Bob Reynolds each weekday evening at six o'clock for a weather update. Good-bye."

"You're not kidding. I *know* it's a lot."

"Thank you for calling the WDST Weatherphone. This afternoon, snow flurries developing into—"

"You sure, honey?"

"Chance of precipitation tonight eight percent, tomorrow—"

"Well, okay." He turned on the bench, grinned at Harry, and made a circle with his right thumb and forefinger. "He's a nice guy. Said he'd guarantee me Nick didn't have one."

"—by tomorrow afternoon. Lows tonight—"

"I love you too, Mare. Bye." He hung up. Jesus, Freddy, that was neat. It was, George. It was.

He got up. "She says go if I say okay. I do."

Harry smiled. "What are you going to do if he sends you a Thunderbird?"

He smiled back. "Return it unopened."

As they walked back out Harry asked, "Check or charge?"

"American Express, if it's okay."

"Good as gold."

He got his card out. On the back, written on the special strip, it said:

BARTON GEORGE DAWES

"You're sure the shells will come in time for me to ship everything to Fred?"

Harry looked up from the credit blank. "Fred?"

His smile expanded. "Nick is Fred and Fred is Nick," he said. "Nicholas Frederic Adams. It's kind of a joke about the name. From when we were kids."

"Oh." He smiled politely as people do when the joke is in and they are out. "You want to sign here?"

He signed.

Harry took another book out from under the counter, a heavy one with a steel chain punched through the upper left corner, near the binding. "And your name and address here for the federals."

He felt his fingers tighten on the pen. "Sure," he said. "Look at me, I never bought a gun in my life and I'm mad." He wrote his name and address in the book:

Barton George Dawes 1241 Crestallen Street West

"They're into everything," he said.

"This is nothing to what they'd like to do," Harry said.

"I know. You know what I heard on the news the other day? They want a law that says a guy riding on a motorcycle has to wear a mouth protector. A *mouth* protector, for God's sake. Now is it the government's business if a man wants to chance wrecking his bridgework?"

"Not in my book it isn't," Harry said, putting his book under the counter.

"Or look at that highway extension they're building over in Western. Some snot-nose surveyor says 'It's going through here' and the state sends out a bunch of letters and the letters say, 'Sorry, we're putting the 784 extension through here. You've got a year to find a new house.' "

"It's a goddam shame."

"Yes, it is. What does 'eminent domain' mean to someone who's lived in the frigging house for twenty years? Made love to their wife there and brought their kid up there and come home to there from trips? That's just something from a law book that they made up so they can crook you better."

Watch it, watch it. But the circuit breaker was a little slow and some of it got through.

"You okay?" Harry asked.

"Yeah. I had one of those submarine sandwiches for lunch, I should know better. They give me gas like hell."

"Try one of these," Harry said, and took a roll of pills from his breast pocket. Written on the outside was:

ROLAIDS

"Thanks," he said. He took one off the top and popped it into his mouth, never minding the bit of lint on it. Look at me, I'm in a TV commercial. Consumes forty-seven times its own weight in excess stomach acid.

"They always do the trick for me," Harry said.

"About the shells—"

"Sure. A week. No more than two. I'll get you seventy rounds."

"Well, why don't you keep these guns right here? Tag them with my name or something. I guess I'm silly, but I really don't want them in the house. That's silly, isn't it?"

"To each his own," Harry said equably.

"Okay. Let me write down my office number. When those bullets come in—"

"Cartridges," Harry interrupted. "Cartridges or shells."

"Cartridges," he said, smiling. "When they come in, give me a ring. I'll pick the guns up and make arrangements about shipping them. REA will ship guns, won't they?"

"Sure. Your cousin will have to sign for them on the other end, that's all."

He wrote his name on one of Harry's business cards. The card said:

Harold Swinnerton   849-6330

HARVEY'S GUN SHOP

Ammunition   Antique Guns

"Say," he said. "If you're Harold, who's Harvey?"

"Harvey was my brother. He died eight years ago."

"I'm sorry."

"We all were. He came down here one day, opened up, cleared the cash register, and then dropped dead of a heart attack. One of the sweetest men you'd ever want to meet. He could bring down a deer at two hundred yards."

He reached over the counter and they shook.

"I'll call," Harry promised.

"Take good care."

He went out into the snow again, past SHAKY CEASE-FIRE HOLDS. It was coming down a little harder now, and his gloves were home.

What were you doing in there, George?

Thump, the circuit breaker.

By the time he got to the bus stop, it might have been an incident he had read about somewhere. No more.

Crestallen Street West was a long, downward-curving street that had enjoyed a fair view of the park and an excellent view of the river until progress had intervened in the shape of a high-rise housing development. It had gone up on Westfield Avenue two years before and had blocked most of the view.

Number 1241 was a split-level ranch house with a one-car garage beside it. There was a long front yard, now barren and waiting for snow—real snow—to cover it. The driveway was asphalt, freshly hot-topped the previous spring.

He went inside and heard the TV, the new Zenith cabinet model they had gotten in the summer. There was a motorized antenna on the roof which he had put up himself. She had not wanted that, because of what was supposed to happen, but he had insisted. If it could be mounted, he had reasoned, it could be dismounted when they moved. Bart, don't be silly. It's just extra expense . . . just extra work for you. But he had outlasted her, and finally she said she would "humor" him. That's what she said on the rare occasions when he cared enough about something to force it through the sticky molasses of her arguments. All right, Bart. This time I'll "humor" you.

At the moment she was watching Merv Griffin chat with a celebrity. The celebrity was Lorne Green, who was talking about his new police series, *Griff.* Lorne was telling Merv how much he loved doing the show. Soon a black singer (a negress songstress, he thought) who no one had ever heard of would come on and sing a song. "I left My Heart in San Francisco," perhaps.

"Hi, Mary," he called.

"Hi, Bart."

Mail on the table. He flipped through it. A letter to Mary from her slightly psycho sister in Baltimore. A Gulf credit card bill—thirty-eight dollars. A checking account statement: 49 debits, 9 credits, $954.47 balance. A good thing he had used American Express at the gun shop.

"The coffee's hot," Mary called. "Or did you want a drink?"

"Drink," he said. "I'll get it."

Three other pieces of mail: An overdue notice from the library. *Facing the Lions,* by Tom Wicker. Wicker had spoken to a Rotary luncheon a month ago, and he was the best speaker they'd had in years.

A personal note from Stephan Ordner, one of the managerial bigwigs in Amroco, the corporation that now owned the Blue Ribbon almost outright. Ordner wanted him to drop by and discuss the Waterford deal—would Friday be okay, or was he planning to be away for Thanksgiving? If so, give a call. If not, bring Mary.

Carla always enjoyed the chance to see Mary and blah-blah and bullshit-bullshit, etc., *et al.*

And another letter from the highway department.

He stood looking down at it for a long time in the gray afternoon light that fell through the windows, and then put all the mail on the sideboard. He made himself a scotch-rocks and took it into the living room.

Merv was still chatting with Lorne. The color on the new Zenith was more than good; it was nearly occult. He thought, if our ICBM's are as good as our color TV, there's going to be a hell of a big bang someday. Lorne's hair was silver, the most impossible shade of silver conceivable. *Boy, I'll snatch you bald-headed,* he thought, and chuckled. It had been one of his mother's favorite sayings. He could not say why the image of Lorne Green bald-headed was so amusing. A light attack of belated hysteria over the gun shop episode, maybe.

Mary looked up, a smile on her lips. "A funny?"

"Nothing," he said. "Just my thinks."

He sat down beside her and pecked her cheek. She was a tall woman, thirty-eight now, and at that crisis of looks where early prettiness is deciding what to be in middle age. Her skin was very good, her breasts small and not apt to sag much. She ate a lot, but her conveyor-belt metabolism kept her slim. She would not be apt to tremble at the thought of wearing a bathing suit on a public beach ten years from now, no matter how the gods decided to dispose of the rest of her case. It made him conscious of his own slight bay window. Hell, Freddy, every executive has a bay window. It's a success symbol, like a Delta 88. That's right, George. Watch the old ticker and the cancer-sticks and you'll see eighty yet.

"How did it go today?" she asked.

"Good."

"Did you get out to the new plant in Waterford?"

"Not today."

He hadn't been out to Waterford since late October. Ordner knew it—a little bird must have told him—and hence the note. The site of the new plant was a vacated textile mill, and the smart mick realtor handling the deal kept calling him. We have to close this thing out, the smart mick realtor kept telling him. You people aren't the only ones over in Westside with your fingers in the crack. I'm going as fast as I can, he told the smart mick realtor. You'll have to be patient.

"What about the place in Crescent?" she asked him. "The brick house."

"It's out of our reach," he said. "They're asking forty-eight thousand."

"For that place?" she asked indignantly. "Highway robbery!"

"It sure is." He took a deep swallow of his drink. "What did old Bea from Baltimore have to say?"

"The usual. She's into consciousness-raising group hydrotherapy now. Isn't that a sketch? Bart—"

"It sure is," he said quickly.

"Bart, we've got to get moving on this. January twentieth is coming, and we'll be out in the street."

"I'm going as fast as I can," he said. "We just have to be patient."

"That little Colonial on Union Street—"

"—is sold." he finished, and drained his drink.

"Well that's what I mean," she said, exasperated. "That would have been perfectly fine for the two of us. With the money the city's allowing us for this house and lot, we could have been ahead."

"I didn't like it."

"You don't seem to like very much these days," she said with surprising bitterness. "He didn't like it," she told the TV. The negress songstress was on now, singing "Alfie."

"Mary, I'm doing all I can."

She turned and looked at him earnestly. "Bart, I know how you feel about this house—"

"No you don't," he said. "Not at all."

November 21, 1973

A light skim of snow had fallen over the world during the night, and when the bus doors chuffed open and he stepped onto the sidewalk, he could see the tracks of the people who had been there before him. He walked down Fir Street from the corner, hearing the bus pull away behind him with its tiger purr. Then Johnny Walker passed him, headed out for his second pickup of the morning. Johnny waved from the cab of his blue and white laundry van, and he waved back. It was a little after eight o'clock.

The laundry began its day at seven when Ron Stone, the foreman, and Dave Radner, who ran the washroom, got there and ran up the pressure on the boiler. The shirt girls punched in at seven-thirty, and the girls who ran the speed ironer came in at eight. He hated the downstairs of the laundry where the brute work went on, where the exploitation went on, but for some perverse reason the men and women who worked there liked him. They called him by his first name. And with a few exceptions, he liked them.

He went in through the driver's loading entrance and threaded through the baskets of sheets from last night that the ironer hadn't run yet. Each basket was covered tightly with plastic to keep the dust off. Down front, Ron Stone was tightening the drive belt on the old Milnor single-pocket while Dave and his helper, a college dropout named Steve Pollack, were loading the industrial Washex machines with motel sheets.

"Bart!" Ron Stone greeted him. He bellowed everything; thirty years of talking to people over the combined noises of dryers, ironers, shirt presses, and washers on extract had built the bellow into his system. "This son of a bitch Milnor keeps seizing up. The program's so far over to bleach now that Dave has to run it on manual. And the extract keeps cutting out.''

"We've got the Kilgallon order," he soothed. "Two more months—"

"In the Waterford plant?''

"Sure," he said, a little giddy.

"Two more months and I'll be ready for the nuthatch," Stone said darkly. "And switching over . . . it's gonna be worse than a Polish army parade.''

"The orders will back up, I guess.''

"Back up! We won't get dug out for three months. Then it'll be summer.''

He nodded, not wanting to go on with it. "What are you running first?''

"Holiday Inn.''

"Get a hundred pounds of towels in with every load. You know how they scream for towels.''

"Yeah, they scream for everything.''

"How much you got?''

"They marked in six hundred pounds. Mostly from the Shriners. Most of them stayed over Monday. Cummyest sheets I ever seen. Some of em'd stand on end.''

He nodded toward the new kid, Pollack. "How's he working out?'' The Blue Ribbon had a fast turnover in washroom helpers. Dave worked them hard and Ron's bellowing made them nervous, then resentful.

"Okay so far," Stone said. "Do you remember the last one?''

He remembered. The kid had lasted three hours.

"Yeah, I remember. What was his name?''

Ron Stone's brow grew thundery. "I don't remember. Baker? Barker? Something like that. I saw him at the Stop and Shop last Friday, handing out leaflets about a lettuce boycott or something. That's something, isn't it? A fellow can't hold a job, so he goes out telling everyone how fucking lousy it is that America can't be like Russia. That breaks my heart.''

"You'll run Howard Johnson next?''

Stone looked wounded. "We always run it first thing.''

"By nine?''

"Bet your ass.''

Dave waved to him, and he waved back. He went upstairs, through dry-cleaning, through accounting, and into his office. He sat down behind his desk in his swivel chair and pulled everything out of the in box to read. On his desk was a plaque that said:

THINK!
It May Be A New Experience

He didn't care much for that sign but he kept it on his desk because Mary had given it to him—when? Five years back? He sighed. The salesmen that came through thought it was funny. They laughed like hell. But then if you showed a salesman a picture of starving kids or Hitler copulating with the Virgin Mary, he would laugh like hell.

Vinnie Mason, the little bird who had undoubtedly been chirruping in Steve Ordner's ear, had a sign on his desk that said:

Thimk

Now what kind of sense did that make, Thimk? Not even a salesman would laugh at that, right, Fred? Right, George—kee-rect. There were heavy diesel rumblings outside, and he swiveled his chair around to look. The highway people were getting ready to start another day. A long flatbed with two bulldozers on top of it was going by the laundry, followed by an impatient line of cars.

From the third floor, over dry-cleaning, you could watch the progress of the construction. It cut across the Western business and residential sections like a long brown incision, an operation scar poulticed with mud. It was already across Guilder Street, and it had buried the park on Hebner Avenue where he used to take Charlie when he was small . . . no more than a baby, really. What was the name of the park? He didn't know. Just the Hebner Avenue Park I guess, Fred. There was a Little League ball park and a bunch of teeter-totters and a duck pond with a little house in the middle of it. In the summertime, the roof of the little house was always covered with bird shit. There had been swings, too. Charlie got his first swing experience in the Hebner Avenue Park. What do you think of that, Freddy old kid old sock? Scared him at first and he cried and then he liked it and when it was time to go home he cried because I took him off. Wet his pants all over the car seat coming home. Was that really fourteen years ago?

Another truck went by, carrying a payloader.

The Garson Block had been demolished about four months ago; that was three or four blocks west of Hebner Avenue. A couple of office buildings full of loan companies and a bank or two, the rest dentists and chiropractors and foot doctors. That didn't matter so much, but Christ it had hurt to see the old Grand Theater go. He had seen some of his favorite movies there, in the early fifties. *Dial M for Murder,* with Ray Milland. *The Day the Earth Stood Still,* with Michael Rennie. That one had been on TV just the other night and he had meant to watch it and then fell asleep right in front of the fucking TV and never woke up until the national anthem. He had spilled a drink on the rug and Mary had had a bird over that, too.

The Grand, though—that had really been something. Now they had these new-breed movie theaters out in the suburbs, crackerjack little buildings in the middle of four miles of parking lot. Cinema I, Cinema II, Cinema III, Screening Room, Cinema MCMXLVII. He had taken Mary to one out in Waterford to see *The Godfather* and the tickets were $2.50 a crack and inside it looked like a fucking bowling alley. No balcony. But the Grand had had a marble floor in the lobby and a balcony and an ancient, lovely, grease-clotted popcorn machine where a big box cost a dime. The character who tore your ticket (which had cost you sixty cents) wore a red uniform, like a doorman, and he was at least six hundred. And he always croaked the same thing. "Hopeya enjoy da show." Inside, the auditorium glass chandelier overhead. You never wanted to sit under it, because if it ever fell on you they'd have to scrape you up with a putty knife. The Grand was—

He looked at his wristwatch guiltily. Almost forty minutes had gone by. Christ, that was bad news. He had just lost forty minutes, and he hadn't even been *thinking* that much. Just about the park and the Grand Theater.

Is there something wrong with you, Georgie?

There might be, Fred. I guess maybe there might be.

He wiped his fingers across his cheek under his eye and saw by the wetness on them that he had been crying.

He went downstairs to talk to Peter, who was in charge of deliveries. The laundry was in full swing now, the ironer thumping and hissing as the first of the Howard Johnson sheets were fed into its rollers, the washers grinding and making the floor vibrate, the shirt presses going *hissss-shuh!* as Ethel and Rhonda whipped them through.

Peter told him the universal had gone on number four's truck and did he want to look at it before they sent it out to the shop? He said he didn't. He asked Peter if Holiday Inn had gone out yet. Peter said it was being loaded, but the silly ass who ran the place had already called twice about his towels.

He nodded and went back upstairs to look for Vinnie Mason, but Phyllis said Vinnie and Tom Granger had gone out to that new German restaurant to dicker about tablecloths.

"Will you have Vinnie stop in when he gets back?"

"I will, Mr. Dawes. Mr. Ordner called and wanted to know if you'd call him back."

"Thanks, Phyllis."

He went back into the office, got the new things that had collected in the IN box and began to shuffle through them.

A salesman wanted to call about a new industrial bleach, Yello-Go. Where do they come up with the names, he wondered, and put it aside for Ron Stone. Ron loved to inflict Dave with new products, especially if he could wangle a free five hundred pounds of the product for test runs.

A letter of thanks from the United Fund. He put it aside to tack on the announcement board downstairs by the punch-clock.

A circular for office furniture in Executive Pine. Into the wastebasket.

A circular for a Phone-Mate that would broadcast a message and record incoming calls when you were out, up to thirty seconds. *I'm not here, stupid. Buzz off.* Into the wastebasket.

A letter from a lady who had sent the laundry six of her husband's shirts and had gotten them back with the collars burned. He put it aside for later action with a sigh. Ethel had been drinking her lunch again.

A water-test package from the university. He put it aside to go over with Ron and Tom Granger after lunch.

A circular from some insurance company with Art Linkletter telling you how you could get eighty thousand dollars and all you had to do for it was die. Into the wastebasket.

A letter from the smart mick realtor who was peddling the Waterford plant, saying there was a shoe company that was very interested in it, the Tom McAn shoe company no less, no small cheese, and reminding him that the Blue Ribbon's ninety-day option to buy ran out on November 26. *Beware, puny laundry executive. The hour draweth nigh.* Into the wastebasket.

Another salesman for Ron, this one peddling a cleaner with the larcenous name of Swipe. He put it with Yello-Go.

He was turning to the window again when the intercom buzzed. Vinnie was back from the German restaurant.

"Send him in."

Vinnie came right in. He was a tall young man of twenty-five with an olive complexion. His dark hair was combed into its usual elaborately careless tumble. He was wearing a dark red sport coat and dark brown pants. A bow tie. Very rakish, don't you think, Fred? I do, George, I do.

"How are you, Bart?" Vinnie asked.

"Fine," he said. "What's the story on that German restaurant?"

Vinnie laughed. "You should have been there. That old kraut just about fell on his knees he was so happy to see us. We're really going to murder Universal when we get settled into the new plant, Bart. They hadn't even sent a circular, let alone their rep. That kraut, I think he thought he was going to get stuck washing those tablecloths out in the kitchen. But he's got a place there you wouldn't believe. Real beer hall stuff. He's going to murder the competition. The aroma . . . God!" He flapped his hands to indicate the aroma and took a box of cigarettes from the inside pocket of his sport coat. "I'm going to take Sharon there when he gets rolling. Ten percent discount."

In a weird kind of overlay he heard Harry the gun shop proprietor saying: *We give a ten percent discount on orders over three hundred.*

My God, he thought. Did I buy those guns yesterday? Did I really?

That room in his mind went dark.

Hey, Georgie, what are you—

"What's the size of the order?" he asked. His voice was a little thick and he cleared his throat.

"Four to six hundred tablecloths a week once he gets rolling. Plus napkins. All genuine linen. He wants them done in Ivory Snow. I said that was no problem."

He was taking a cigarette out of the box now, doing it slowly, so he could read the label. There was something he could really come to dislike about Vinnie Mason: his dipshit cigarettes. The label on the box said:

PLAYER'S NAVY CUT
CIGARETTES
MEDIUM

Now who in God's world except Vinnie would smoke Player's Navy Cut? Or King Sano? Or English Ovals? Or Marvels or Murads or Twists? If someone put out a brand called Shit-on-a-Stick or Black Lung, Vinnie would smoke them.

"I did tell him we might have to give him two-day service until we get switched over," Vinnie said, giving him a last loving flash of the box as he put it away. "When we go up to Waterford."

"That's what I wanted to talk to you about," he said. Shall I blast him, Fred? Sure. Blow him out of the water, George.

"Really?" He snapped a light to his cigarette with a slim gold Zippo and raised his eyebrows through the smoke like a British character actor.

"I had a note from Steve Ordner yesterday. He wants me to drop over Friday evening for a little talk about the Waterford plant."

"Oh?"

"This morning I had a phone call from Steve Ordner while I was down talking to Peter Wasserman. Mr. Ordner wants me to call him back. That sounds like he's awfully anxious to know something, doesn't it?"

"I guess it does," Vinnie said, flashing his number 2 smile—*Track wet, proceed with caution.*

"What I want to know is who made Steve Ordner so all-at-once fucking anxious. That's what I want to know."

"Well—"

"Come on, Vinnie. Let's not play coy chambermaid. It's ten o'clock and I've got to talk to Ordner, I've got to talk to Ron Stone, I've got to talk to Ethel Gibbs about burnt shirt collars. Have you been picking my nose while I wasn't looking?"

"Well, Sharon and I were over to St—to Mr. Ordner's house Sunday night for dinner—"

"And you just happened to mention that Bart Dawes has been laying back on Waterford while the 784 extension gets closer and closer, is that it?"

"Bart!" Vinnie protested. "It was all perfectly friendly. It was very—"

"I'm sure it was. So was his little note inviting me to court. I imagine our little phone call will be perfectly friendly, too. That's not the point. The point is that he invited you and your wife to dinner in hopes that you'd run off at the mouth and he had no cause to be disappointed."

"Bart—"

He leveled his finger at Vinnie. "You listen to me, Vinnie. If you drop any more shit like this for me to walk in, you'll be looking for a new job. Count on it."

Vinnie was shocked. The cigarette was all but forgotten between his fingers.

"Vinnie, let me tell you something," he said, dropping his voice back to normal. "I know that a young guy like you has listened to six thousand lectures on how old guys like me tore up the world when they were your age. But you earned this one."

Vinnie opened his mouth to protest.

"I don't think you slipped the knife into me," he said, holding up a hand to forestall Vinnie's protest. "If I thought that, I would have had a pink for you when you walked in here. I just think you were dumb. You got in that great big house and had three drinks before dinner and then a soup course and a salad with Thousand Island dressing and then surf and turf for the main course and it was all served by a maid in a black uniform and Carla was doing her lady-of-the-manor bit—but not being the least bit condescending—and there was a strawberry tort or blueberry buckle with whipped cream for dessert and then a couple of coffee brandies or Tia Maria and you just spilled your guts. Is that about how it went?''

"Something like that," Vinnie whispered. His expression was three parts shame and two parts bullish hate.

"He started off by asking how Bart was. You said Bart was fine. He said Bart was a damned good man, but wouldn't it be nice if he could pick his feet up a little on that Waterford deal. You said, it sure would. He said, By the way, how's that going. You said, Well it really isn't my department and he said, Don't tell me, Vincent, you know what's going on. And you said, All I know is that Bart hasn't closed the deal yet. I heard that the Thom McAn people are interested in the site but maybe that's just a rumor. Then he said, Well I'm sure Bart knows what he's doing and you said, Yeah, sure and then you had another coffee brandy and he asked you if you thought the Mustangs would make the play-offs and then you and Sharon were going home and you know when you'll be out there again, Vinnie?''

Vinnie didn't say anything.

"You'll be out there when Steve Ordner needs another snitch. That's when."

"I'm sorry," Vinnie said sulkily. He started to get up.

"I'm not through."

Vinnie sat down again and looked into the corner of the room with smoldering eyes.

"I was doing your job twelve years ago, do you know that? Twelve years, that probably seems like a long time to you. To me, I hardly know where the fuck the time went. But I remember the job well enough to know you like it. And that you do a good job. That reorganization in dry-cleaning, with the new numbering system . . . that was a masterpiece."

Vinnie was staring at him, bewildered.

"I started in the laundry twenty years ago," he said. "In 1953, I was twenty years old. My wife and I were just married. I'd finished two years of business administration and Mary and I were going to wait, but we were using the interruption method, you see. We were going to town and somebody slammed the door downstairs and startled me right into an orgasm. She got pregnant out of it. So whenever I get feeling smart these days I just remind myself that one slammed door is responsible for me being where I am today. It's humbling. In those days there was no slick abortion law. When you got a girl pregnant, you married her or you ran out on her. End of options. I married her and took the first job I could get, which was here. Washroom helper, exactly the same job that Pollack kid is doing downstairs right this minute. Everything was manual in those days, and everything had to be pulled wet out of the washers and extracted in a big Stonington wringer that held five hundred pounds of wet flatwork. If you loaded it wrong, it would take your fucking foot off. Mary lost the baby in her seventh month and the doctor said she'd never have another one. I did the helper's job for three years, and my average take-home for fifty-five hours was fifty-five dollars. Then Ralph Albertson, who was the boss of the washroom in those days, got in a little fender-bender accident and died of a heart attack in the street while he and the other guy were exchanging insurance companies. He was a fine man. The whole laundry shut down the day of his funeral. After he was decently buried, I went to Ray Tarkington and asked for his job. I was pretty sure I'd get it. I knew everything about how to wash, because Ralph had shown me.

"This was a family business in those days, Vinnie. Ray and his dad, Don Tarkington, ran it. Don got it from his father, who started the Blue Ribbon in 1926. It was a nonunion shop and I suppose the labor people would say all three of the Tarkingtons were paternalistic exploiters of the uneducated working man and woman. And they were. But when Betty Keeson slipped on the wet floor and broke her arm, the Tarkingtons paid the hospital bill and there was ten bucks a week for food until she could come back. And every Christmas they put on a big dinner out in the marking-in room—the best chicken pies you ever ate, and cranberry jelly and rolls and your choice of chocolate or mince pudding for dessert. Don and Ray gave every woman a pair of earrings for Christmas and every man a brand-new tie. I've still got my nine ties in the closet at home. When Don Tarkington died in 1959, I wore one of them to his funeral. It was out of style and Mary gave me holy hell, but I wore it anyway. The place was dark and the hours were long and the work was drudgery, but the people cared about you. If the extractor broke down, Don and Ray would be right down there with the rest of us, the sleeves of their white shirts rolled up, wringing out those sheets by hand. That's what a family business was, Vinnie. Something like that.

"So when Ralph died and Ray Tarkington said he'd already hired a guy from outside to run the washroom, I couldn't understand what in hell was going on. And Ray says, My father and I want you to go back to college. And I say, Great, on what? Bus tokens? And he hands me a cashier's check for two thousand dollars. I looked at it and couldn't believe what I was seeing. I say, What is this? And he says, It's not enough, but it'll get your tuition, your room, and your books. For the rest you work your summers here, okay? And I say, is there a way to thank you? And he says, yeah, three ways. First, repay the loan. Second, repay the interest. Third, bring what you learn back to the Blue Ribbon. I took the check home and showed Mary and she cried. Put her hands right over her face and cried."

Vinnie was looking at him now with frank amazement.

"So in 1955 I went back to school and I got a degree in 1957. I went back to the laundry and Ray put me to work as boss of the drivers. Ninety dollars a week. When I paid the first installment on the loan, I asked Ray what the interest was going to run. He says, One percent. I said, *What?* He says, You heard me. Don't you have something to do? So I say, Yeah I think I better go downtown and get a doctor up here to examine your head. Ray laughs like hell and tells me to get the fuck out of his office. I got the last of that money repaid in 1960, and do you know what, Vinnie? Ray gave me a watch. This watch.''

He shot his cuff and showed Vinnie the Bulova watch with its gold expansion band.

"He called it a deferred graduation present. Twenty dollars interest is what I paid on my education, and that son of a bitch turns around and gives me an eighty-buck watch. Engraved on the back it says: *Best from Don & Ray, The Blue Ribbon Laundry.* Don was already a year in his grave then.

"In 1963 Ray put me on your job, keeping an eye on drycleaning, opening new accounts, and running the laundromat branches—only in those days there were just five instead of eleven. I stayed with that until 1967, and then Ray put me in this job here. Then, four years ago, he had to sell. You know about that, the way the bastards put the squeeze on him. It turned him into an old man. So now we're part of a corporation with two dozen other irons in the fire—fast food, Ponderosa golf, those three eyesore discount department stores, the gas stations, all that shit. And Steve Ordner's nothing but a glorified foreman. There's a board of directors somewhere in Chicago or Gary that spends maybe fifteen minutes a week on the Blue Ribbon operation. They don't give a shit about running a laundry. They don't *know* shit about it. They know how to read a cost accountant's report, that's what they know. The cost accountant says, Listen. They're extending 784 through Westside and the Blue Ribbon is standing right in the way, along with half the residential district. And the directors say, Oh, is that right? How much are they allowing us on the property? And that's it. Christ, if Don and Ray Tarkington were alive, they'd have those cheap highway department fucks in court with so many restraining orders on their heads that they wouldn't get out from under until the year 2000. They'd go after them with a good sharp stick. Maybe they were a couple of buck-running paternalistic bastards, but they had a sense of *place,* Vinnie. You don't get that out of a cost accountant's report. If they were alive and someone told them that the highway commission was going to bury the laundry in eight lanes of composition hot-top, you would have heard the scream all the way down to city hall.''

"But they're dead,'' Vinnie said.

"Yeah, they're dead, all right.'' His mind suddenly felt flabby and unstrung, like an amateur's guitar. Whatever he had needed to say to Vinnie had been lost in a welter of embarrassing personal stuff. Look at him, Freddy, he doesn't know what I'm talking about. He doesn't have a clue. "Thank God they're not here to see this.''

Vinnie didn't say anything.

He gathered himself with an effort. "What I'm trying to say, Vinnie, is that there are two groups involved here. Them and us. We're laundry people. That's our business. They're cost accountant people. That's *their* business. They send down orders from on high, and we have to follow them. But that's *all* we have to do. Do you understand?''

"Sure, Bart,'' Vinnie said, but he could see that Vinnie didn't understand at all. He wasn't sure he did himself.

"Okay," he said. "I'll speak to Ordner. But just for your information, Vinnie, the Waterford plant is as good as ours. I'm closing the deal next Tuesday."

Vinnie grinned, relieved. "Jesus, that's great."

"Yes. Everything's under control."

As Vinnie was leaving, he called after him: "You tell me how that German restaurant is, okay?"

Vinnie Mason tossed him his number 1 grin, bright and full of teeth, all systems go. "I sure will, Bart."

Then Vinnie was gone and he was looking at the closed door. I made a mess of that, Fred. I didn't think you did so badly, George. Maybe you lost the handle at the end, but it's only in books that people say everything right the first time. No, I frigged up. He went out of here thinking Barton Dawes has lost a few cards out of his deck. God help him he's right. George, I have to ask you something, man to man. No, don't shut me off. Why did you buy those guns, George? Why did you do that?

Thump, the circuit breaker.

He went down on the floor, gave Ron Stone the salesmen's folders, and when he walked away Ron was bawling for Dave to come over and look at this stuff, might be something in it. Dave rolled his eyes. There was something in it, all right. It was known as work.

He went upstairs and called Ordner's office, hoping Ordner would be out drinking lunch. No breaks today. The secretary put him right through.

"Bart!" Steve Ordner said. "Always good to talk with you."

"Same here. I was talking to Vinnie Mason a little earlier, and he seemed to think you might be a little worried about the Waterford plant."

"Good God, no. Although I did think, maybe Friday night, we could lay out a few things—"

"Yeah, I called mainly to say Mary can't make it."

"Oh?"

"A virus. She doesn't dare go five seconds from the nearest john."

"Say, I'm sorry to hear that."

Cram it, you cheap dick.

"The doctor gave her some pills and she seems to be feeling better. But she might be, you know, catching."

"What time can you make it, Bart? Eight?"

"Yeah, eight's fine."

That's right, screw up the Friday Night Movie, *prick. What else is new?*

"How is the Waterford business progressing, Bart?"

"That's something we'd better talk about in person, Steve."

"That's fine." Another pause. "Carla sends her best. And tell Mary that both Carla and I . . ."

Sure. Yeah. Blah, blah, blah.

November 22, 1973

He woke up with a jerk that knocked the pillow onto the floor, afraid he might have screamed. But Mary was still sleeping in the other bed, a silent mound. The digital clock on the bureau said:

4:23 A.M.

It clicked into the next minute. Old Bea from Baltimore, the one who was into consciousness-raising hydrotherapy, had given it to them last Christmas. He didn't mind the clock, but he had never been able to get used to the click when the numbers changed. 4:23 *click,* 4:24 *click,* a person could go nuts.

He went down to the bathroom, turned on the light, and urinated. It made his heart thump heavily in his chest. Lately when he urinated his heart thumped like a fucking bass drum. Are you trying to tell me something, God?

He went back to bed and lay down, but sleep didn't come for a long time. He had thrashed around while he slept, and the bed had been remolded into enemy territory. He couldn't get it right again. His arms and legs also seemed to have forgotten which way they arranged themselves when he slept.

The dream was easy enough to figure out. No sweat there, Fred. A person could work that circuit breaker trick easy enough when he was awake; he could go on coloring in some picture piece by piece and pretending he couldn't see the whole thing. You could bury the big picture under the floor of your mind. But there was a trapdoor. When you were asleep, sometimes it banged open and something crawled up out of the darkness. *Click.*

4:42 A.M.

In the dream he had been at Pierce Beach with Charlie (funny, when he had given Vinnie Mason that little thumbnail autobiography he had forgotten to mention Charlie—isn't that funny, Fred? No, I don't think it's too funny, George. Neither do I, Fred. But it's late. Or early. Or something.)

He and Charlie were on that long white beach and it was a fine day for the beach—bright blue sky and the sun beaming down like the face on one of those idiotic smiley-smile buttons. People on bright blankets and under umbrellas of many different hues, little kids dibbling around the water's edge with plastic pails. A lifeguard on his whitewashed tower, his skin as brown as a boot, the crotch of his white Latex swim trunks bulging, as if penis and testicle size were somehow a job prerequisite and he wanted everyone in the area to know they were not being let down. Someone's transistor radio blaring rock and roll and even now he could remember the tune:

But I love that dirty water,
Owww, Boston, you're my home.

Two girls walking by in bikinis, safe and sane inside beautiful screwable bodies, never for you but for boyfriends nobody ever saw, their toes kicking up tiny fans of sand.

Only it was funny, Fred, because the tide was coming and there was no tide at Pierce Beach because the nearest ocean was nine hundred miles away.

He and Charlie were making a sand castle. But they had started too near the water and the incoming waves kept coming closer and closer.

We have to build it farther back, Dad, Charlie said, but he was stubborn and kept building. When the tide brought the water up to the first wall, he dug a moat with his fingers, spreading the wet sand like a woman's vagina. The water kept coming.

Goddam it! He yelled at the water.

He rebuilt the wall. A wave knocked it down. People started to scream about something. Others were running. The lifeguard's whistle blew like a silver arrow. He didn't look up. He had to save the castle. But the water kept coming, lapping his ankles, slurping a turret, a roof, the back of the castle, all of it. The last wave withdrew, showing only bland sand, smooth and flat and brown and shining.

There were more screams. Someone was crying. He looked up and saw the lifeguard was giving Charlie mouth-to-mouth. Charlie was wet and white except for his lips and eyelids, which were blue. His chest was not rising and falling. The lifeguard stopped trying. He looked up. He was smiling.

He was out over his head, the lifeguard was saying through his smile. *Isn't it time you went?*

He screamed: *Charlie!* and that was when he had wakened, afraid he might really have screamed.

He lay in the darkness for a long time, listening to the digital clock click, and tried not to think of the dream. At last he got up to get a glass of milk in the kitchen, and it was not until he saw the turkey thawing on a plate on the counter that he remembered it was Thanksgiving and today the laundry was closed. He drank his milk standing up, looking thoughtfully at the plucked body. The color of its skin was the same as the color of his son's skin in his dream. But Charlie hadn't drowned, of course.

When he got back into bed, Mary muttered something interrogative, thick and indecipherable with sleep.

"Nothing," he said. "Go to sleep."

She muttered something else.

"Okay," he said in the darkness.

She slept.

Click.

It was five o'clock, five in the morning. When he finally dozed off, dawn had come into the bedroom like a thief. His last thought was of the Thanksgiving turkey, sitting on the kitchen counter below the glare of the cold fluorescent over-head, dead meat waiting thoughtlessly to be devoured.

November 23, 1973

He drove their two-year-old LTD into Stephan Ordner's driveway at five minutes of eight and parked it behind Ordner's bottle-green Delta 88. The house was a rambling fieldstone, discreetly drawn back from Henreid Drive and partially hid-den behind a high privet that was now skeletal in the smoky butt end of autumn. He had been here before, and knew it quite well. Downstairs was a massive rock-lined fireplace, and more modest ones in the bedrooms upstairs. They all worked. In the basement there was a Brunswick billiard table, a movie screen for home movies, a KLH sound system that Ordner had converted to quad the year before. Photos from Ordner's college basketball days dotted the walls—he stood six foot five and still kept in shape. Ordner had to duck his head going through doorways, and he suspected that Ordner was proud of it. Maybe he had had the doorways lowered so he could duck through them. The dining room table was a slab of pol-ished oak, nine feet long. A wormy-oak highboy complimented it, gleaming richly through six or eight coats of varnish. A tall china cabinet at the other end of the room; it stood—oh, about six foot five, wouldn't you say, Fred? Yes, just about that. Out back there was a sunken barbecue pit almost big enough to broil an uncut dinosaur, and a putting green. No kidney-shaped pool. Kidney-shaped pools were considered jejune these days. Strictly for the Ra-worshiping Southern California middle-classers. The Ordners had no children, but they supported a Korean kid, a South Vietnamese kid, and were putting a Ugandan through engineering school so he could go back home and build hydroelectric dams. They were Democrats, and had been Democrats for Nixon.

His feet whispered up the walk and he rang the bell. The maid opened the door.

"Mr. Dawes," he said.

"Of course, sir. I'll just take your coat. Mr. Ordner is in the study."

"Thank you."

He gave her his topcoat and walked down the hall past the kitchen and the dining room. Just a peek at the big table and the Stephan Ordner Memorial Highboy. The rug on the floor ended and he walked down a hallway floored with white-and-black waxed linoleum checks. His feet clicked.

He reached the study door and Ordner opened it just as he was reaching for the knob, as he had known Ordner would.

"Bart!" Ordner said. They shook hands. Ordner was wearing a brown cord jacket with patched elbows, olive slacks, and Burgundy slippers. No tie.

"Hi, Steve. How's finance?"

Ordner groaned theatrically. "Terrible. Have you looked at the stock market page lately?" He ushered him in and closed the door behind him. The walls were lined with books. To the left there was a small fireplace with an electric log. In the center, a large desk with some papers on it. He knew there was an IBM Selectric buried in that desk someplace; if you pressed the right button it would pop out on top like a sleek-black torpedo.

"The bottom's falling out," he said.

Ordner grimaced. "That's putting it mildly. You can hand it to Nixon, Bart. He finds a use for everything. When they shot the domino theory to hell over in Southeast Asia, he just took it and put it to work on the American economy. Worked lousy over there. Works great over here. What are you drinking?"

"Scotch-rocks would be fine."

"Got it right here."

He went to a fold-out cabinet, produced a fifth of scotch which returned only pocket change from your ten when purchased in a cut-rate liquor store, and splashed it over two ice cubes in a pony glass. He gave it to him and said, "Let's sit down."

They sat in wing chairs drawn up by the electric fire. He thought: *If I tossed my drink in there, I could blow that fucking thing to blazes.* He almost did it, too.

"Carla couldn't be here either," Ordner said. "One of her groups is sponsoring a fashion show. Proceeds to go to some teenage coffeehouse down in Norton."

"The fashion show is down there?"

Ordner looked startled. "In *Norton?* Hell no. Over in Russell. I wouldn't let Carla down in the Landing Strip with two bodyguards and a police dog. There's a priest . . . Drake, I think his name is. Drinks a lot, but those little pick'ninnies love him. He's sort of a liaison. Street priest."

"Oh."

"Yes."

They looked into the fire for a minute. He knocked back half of his scotch.

"The question of the Waterford plant came up at the last board meeting," Ordner said. "Middle of November. I had to admit my pants were a little loose on the matter. I was given . . . uh, a mandate to find out just what the situation is. No reflection on your management, Bart—"

"None taken," he said, and knocked back some more scotch. There was nothing left in there now but a few blots of alcohol trapped between the ice cubes and the glass. "It's always a pleasure when our jobs coincide, Steve."

Ordner looked pleased. "So what's the story? Vin Mason was telling me the deal wasn't closed."

"Vinnie Mason has got a dead short somewhere between his foot and his mouth."

"Then it's closed?"

"Closing. I expect to sign us into Waterford next Friday, unless something comes up."

"I was given to understand that the realtor made you a fairly reasonable offer, which you turned down."

He looked at Ordner, got up, and freshened the blots. "You didn't get that from Vinnie Mason."

"No."

He returned to the wing-back chair and the electric fire. "I don't suppose you'd care to tell me where you did get it?"

Ordner spread his hands. "It's business, Bart. When I hear something, I have to check into it—even if all my personal and professional knowledge of a man indicates that the something must be off-whack. It's nasty, but that's no reason to piss it around."

Freddy, nobody knew about that turn-down except the real estate guy and me. Old Mr. Just Business did a little personal checking, looks like. But that's no reason to piss it around, right? Right, George. Should I blow him out of the water, Freddy? Better be cool, George. And I'd slow down on the firewater.

"The figure I turned down was four-fifty," he said. "Just for the record, is that what you heard?"

"That's about it."

"And that sounded reasonable to you."

"Well," Ordner said, crossing his legs, "actually, it did. The city assessed the old plant at six-twenty, and the boiler can go right across town. Of course, there isn't quite as much room for expansion, but the boys uptown say that since the main plant had already reached pretty much optimum size, there was no need for the extra room. It looked to me as if we might at least break even, perhaps turn a profit . . . although that wasn't the main consideration. We've got to locate, Bart. And damn quick."

"Maybe you heard something else."

Ordner recrossed his legs and sighed. "Actually, I did. I heard that you turned down four-fifty and then Thom McAn came along and offered five."

"A bid the realtor can't accept, in good faith."

"Not yet, but our option to buy runs out on Tuesday. You know that."

"Yes, I do. Steve, let me make three or four points, okay?"

"Be my guest."

"First, Waterford is going to put us three miles away from our industrial contracts—that's an average. That's going to send our operating overhead way up. All the motels are out by the Interstate. Worse than that, our service is going to be slower. Holiday Inn and Hojo are on our backs now when we're fifteen minutes late with the towels. What's it going to be like when the trucks have to fight their way through three miles of crosstown traffic?"

Ordner was shaking his head. "Bart, they're *extending* the Interstate. That's why we're moving, remember? Our boys say there will be no time lost in deliveries. It may even go quicker, using the extension. And they also say the motel corporations have already bought up good land in Waterford and Russell, near what will be the new interchange. We're going to improve our position by going into Waterford, not worsen it.''

I stubbed my toe, Freddy. He's looking at me like I've lost all my marbles. Right, George. Kee-rect.

He smiled. ''Okay. Point taken. But those other motels won't be up for a year, maybe two. And if this energy business is as bad as it looks—''

Ordner said flatly: ''That's a policy decision, Bart. We're just a couple of foot soldiers. We carry out the orders.'' It seemed to him that there was a dart of reproach there.

''Okay. But I wanted my own view on record.''

''Good. It is. But you don't make policy, Bart. I want that perfectly clear. If the gasoline supplies dry up and all the motels fall flat, we'll take it on the ear, along with everyone else. In the meantime, we'd better let the boys upstairs worry about that and do our jobs.''

I've been rebuked, Fred. That you have, George.

''All right. Here's the rest. I estimate it will take two hundred and fifty thousand dollars for renovations before the Waterford plant ever turns out a clean sheet.''

''*What?*'' Ordner set his drink down hard.

Aha, Freddy. Hit a bare nerve there.

''The walls are full of dry rot. The masonry on the east and north sides has mostly crumbled away to powder. And the floors are so bad that the first heavy-duty washer we put in there is going to end up in the basement.''

''That's firm? That two-fifty figure?''

''Firm. We're going to need a new outside stack. New flooring, downstairs and up. And it's going to take five electricians two weeks to take care of that end. The place is only wired for two-forty-volt circuits and we have to have five-fifty loads. And since we're going to be at the far end of all the city utility conduits, I can promise you our power and water bills are going to go up twenty percent. The power increases we can live with, but I don't have to tell you what a twenty percent water-cost increase means to a laundry.''

Ordner was looking at him now, shocked.

''Never mind what I said about the utility increase. That comes under operating overhead, not renovations. So where was I? The place has to be rewired for five-fifty. We're going to need a good burglar alarm and closed circuit TV. New insulation. New roofing. Oh yeah, and a drainage system. Over on Fir Street we're up on high ground, but Douglas Street sits at the bottom of a natural basin. The drainage system alone will cost anywhere from forty to seventy thousand dollars to put in.''

''Christ, how come Tom Granger hasn't told me any of this?''

''He didn't go with me to inspect the place.''

''Why not?''

''Because I told him to stay at the plant.''

''You did *what?*''

''That was the day the furnace went out,'' he said patiently. ''We had orders piling up and no hot water. Tom had to stay. He's the only one in the place that can talk to that furnace.''

"Well Christ, Bart, couldn't you have taken him down another day?''

He knocked back the rest of his drink. "I didn't see the point.''

"You didn't see the—'' Ordner couldn't finish. He set his glass down and shook his head, like a man who has been punched. "Bart, do you know what it's going to mean if your estimate is wrong and we lose that plant? It's going to mean your *job*, that's what it's going to mean. My God, do you want to end up carrying your ass home to Mary in a basket? Is that what you want?''

You wouldn't understand, he thought, because you'd never make a move unless you were covered six ways and had three other fall guys lined up. That's the way you end up with four hundred thousand in stocks and funds, a Delta 88, and a typewriter that pops out of a desk at you like some silly jack-in-the-box. You stupid fuckstick, I could con you for the next ten years. I just might do it, too.

He grinned into Ordner's drawn face. "That's my last point, Steve. That's why I'm not worried.''

"What do you mean?''

Joyously, he lied:

"Thom McAn had already notified the realtor that they're not interested in the plant. They had their guys out to look at it and they hollered holy hell. So what you've got is my word that the place is shit at four-fifty. What you've also got is a ninety-day option that runs out on Tuesday. What you've *also* got is a smart mick realtor named Monohan, who had been bluffing our pants off. It almost worked.''

"What are you suggesting?''

"I'm suggesting we let the option run out. That we stand pat until next Thursday or so. You talk to your boys in cost and accounting about that twenty percent utility hike. I'll talk to Monohan. When I get through with him, he'll be down on his knees for two hundred thousand.''

"Bart, are you sure?''

"Sure I am,'' he said, and smiled tightly. "I wouldn't be sticking out my neck if I thought somebody was going to cut it off.''

George, what are you doing???

Shut up, shut up, don't bother me now.

"What we've got here,'' he said, "is a smart-ass realtor with no buyer. We can afford to take our time. Every day we keep him swinging in the wind is another day the price goes down when we do buy.''

"All right,'' Ordner said slowly. "But let's have one thing clear, Bart. If we fail to exercise our option and then somebody else *does* go in there, I'd have to shoot you out of the saddle. Nothing—''

"I know,'' he said, suddenly tired. "Nothing personal.''

"Bart, are you sure you haven't picked up Mary's bug? You look a little punk tonight.''

You look a little punk yourself, asshole.

"I'll be fine when we get this settled. It's been a strain.''

"Sure it has." Ordner arranged his face in sympathetic lines. "I'd almost forgotten . . . your house is right in the line of fire, too."

"Yes."

"You've found another place?"

"Well, we've got our eye on two. I wouldn't be surprised if I closed the laundry deal and my personal deal on the same day."

Ordner grinned. "It may be the first time in your life you've wheeled and dealed three hundred thousand to half a million dollars between sunrise and sunset."

"Yes, it's going to be quite a day."

On the way home Freddy kept trying to talk to him—scream at him, really—and he had to keep yanking the circuit breaker. He was just pulling onto Crestallen Street West when it burnt out with a smell of frying synapses and overloaded axons. All the questions spilled through and he jammed both feet down on the power brake. The LTD screeched to a halt in the middle of the street, and he was thrown against his seat belt hard enough to lock it and force a grunt up from his stomach.

When he had control of himself, he let the car creep over to the curb. He turned off the motor, killed the lights, unbuckled his seat belt, and sat trembling with his hands on the steering wheel.

From where he sat, the street curved gently, the streetlights making a graceful flashhook of light. It was a pretty street. Most of the houses which now lined it had been built in the postwar period 1946–1958, but somehow, miraculously, it had escaped the Fifties Crackerbox Syndrome, and the diseases that went with it: crumbling foundation, balding lawn, toy proliferation, premature aging of cars, flaking paint, plastic storm windows.

He knew his neighbors—why not? He and Mary had been on Crestallen Street almost fourteen years now. That was a long time. The Upslingers in the house above them; their boy Kenny delivered the morning paper. The Langs across the street; the Hobarts two houses down (Linda Hobart had baby-sat for Charlie, and now she was a doctoral student at City College); the Stauffers; Hank Albert, whose wife had died of emphysema four years ago; the Darbys' and just four houses up from where he was parked and shaking in his car, the Quinns. And a dozen other families that he and Mary had a nodding acquaintance with—mostly the ones with small children.

A nice street, Fred. A nice neighborhood. Oh, I know how the intellectuals sneer at suburbia—it's not as romantic as the rat-infested tenements or the hale-and-hearty back-to-the-land stuff. There are no great museums in suburbia, no great forests, no great challenges.

But there had been good times. I know what you're thinking, Fred. Good times, what are good times? There's no great joy in good times, no great sorrow, no great nothing. Just blah. Backyard barbecues in the summer dusk, everybody a little high but nobody getting really drunk or really ugly. Car pools we got up to go see the Mustangs play. The fucking Musties, who couldn't even beat the Pats the year the Pats were 1–12. Having people in to dinner or going out. Playing golf over at the Westside course or taking the wives to Ponderosa Pines and driving those little go-karts. Remember the time Bill Stauffer drove his right through that board fence and into some guy's swimming pool? Yeah, I remember that, George, we all laughed like hell. But George—

So bring on the bulldozers, right, Fred? Let's bury all of that. There'll be another suburb pretty quick, over in Waterford, where there was nothing but a bunch of vacant lots until this year. The March of Time. Progress in Review. Billion Dollar Babies. So what is it when you go over there to look? A bunch of saltine boxes painted different colors. Plastic pipes that are going to freeze every winter. Plastic wood. Plastic everything. Because Moe at the Highway Commission told Joe down at Joe's Construction, and Sue who works at the front desk at Joe's told Lou at Lou's Construction and pretty soon the big Waterford land boom is on and the developments are going up in the vacant lots, and also the high rises, the condominiums. You get a house on Lilac Lane, which intersects Spain Lane going north and Dain Lane going south. You can pick Elm Street, Oak Street, Cypress Street, White Pine Blister Street. Each house has a full bathroom downstairs, a half-bathroom upstairs, and a fake chimney on the east side. And if you come home drunk you can't even find your own fucking house.

But George—

Shut up, Fred, I'm talking. And where are your neighbors? Maybe they weren't so much, those neighbors, but you knew who they were. You knew who you could borrow a cup of sugar from when you were tapped out. Where are they? Tony and Alicia Lang are in Minnesota because he requested a transfer to a new territory and got it. The Hobarts've moved out to Northside. Hank Albert has got a place in Waterford, true, but when he came back from signing the papers he looked like a man wearing a happy mask. I could see his eyes, Freddy. He looked like somebody who had just had his legs cut off and was trying to fool everybody that he was looking forward to the new plastic ones because they wouldn't get scabs if he happened to bang them against a door. So we move, and where are we? What are we? Just two strangers sitting in a house that's sitting in the middle of a lot more strangers' houses. That's what we are. The March of Time, Freddy. That's what it is. Forty waiting for fifty waiting for sixty. Waiting for a nice hospital bed and a nice nurse to stick a nice catheter inside you. Freddy, forty is the end of being young. Well, actually thirty's the end of being young, forty is where you stop fooling yourself. I don't want to grow old in a strange place.

He was crying again, sitting in his cold dark car and crying like a baby.

George, it's more than the highway, more than the move. I know what's wrong with you.

Shut up, Fred. I warn you.

But Fred wouldn't shut up and that was bad. If he couldn't control Fred anymore, how would he ever get any peace?

It's Charlie, isn't it, George? You don't want to bury him a second time.

"It's Charlie," he said aloud, his voice thick and strange with tears. "And it's me. I can't. I really can't . . ."

He hung his head over and let the tears come, his face screwed up and his fists plastered into his eyes like any little kid you ever saw who lost his candy-nickle out the hole in his pants.

When he finally drove on, he was husked out. He felt dry. Hollow, but dry. Perfectly calm. He could even look at the dark houses on both sides of the street where people had already moved out with no tremor.

We're living in a graveyard now, he thought. Mary and I, in a graveyard. Just like Richard Boone in *I Bury the Living*. The lights were on at the Arlins', but they were leaving on the fifth of December. And the Hobarts had moved last weekend. Empty houses.

Driving up the asphalt of his own driveway (Mary was upstairs; he could see the mild glow of her reading lamp) he suddenly found himself thinking of something Tom Granger had said a couple of weeks before. He would talk to Tom about that. On Monday.

November 25, 1973

He was watching the Mustangs-Chargers game on the color TV and drinking his private drink, Southern Comfort and Seven-Up. It was his private drink because people laughed when he drank it in public. The Chargers were ahead 27–3 in the third quarter. Rucker had been intercepted three times. Great game, huh, Fred? It sure is, George. I don't see how you stand the tension.

Mary was asleep upstairs. It had warmed up over the weekend, and now it was drizzling outside. He felt sleepy himself. He was three drinks along.

There was a time-out, and a commercial came on. The commercial was Bud Wilkenson telling about how this energy crisis was a real bitch and everybody should insulate their attics and also make sure that the fireplace flue was closed when you weren't toasting marshmallows or burning witches or something. The logo of the company presenting the commercial came on at the end; the logo showed a happy tiger peeking at you over a sign that said:

Exxon

He thought that everyone should have known the evil days were coming when Esso changed its name to Exxon. Esso slipped comfortably out of the mouth like the sound of a man relaxing in a hammock. Exxon sounded like the name of a warlord from the planet Yurir.

"Exxon demands that all puny Earthlings throw down their weapons," he said. "Off the pig, puny Earthmen." He snickered and made himself another drink. He didn't even have to get up; the Southern Comfort, a forty-eight ounce bottle of Seven-Up, and a plastic bowl of ice were all sitting on a small round table by his chair.

Back to the game. The Chargers punted. Hugh Fednach, the Mustangs' deep man, collected the football and ran it out to the Mustangs' 31. Then, behind the steely-eyed generalship of Hank Rucker, who might have seen the Heisman trophy once in a newsreel, the Mustangs mounted a six-yard drive . Gene Voreman punted. Andy Cocker of the Chargers returned the ball to the Mustangs' 46. And so it goes, as Kurt Vonnegut had so shrewdly pointed out. He had read all of Kurt Vonnegut's boods. He liked them mostly because they were funny. On the news last week it had beeen reported that the school board of a town called Drake, North Dakota, had burned yea copies of Vonnegut's novel, *Slaughterhouse Five,* which was about the Dresden fire bombing. When you thought about it, there was a funny connection there.

Fred, why don't those highway department fucksticks go build the 784 extension through Drake? I bet they'd love it. George, that's a fine idea. Why don't you write *The Blade* about that? Fuck you, Fred.

The Chargers scored, making it 34–3. Some cheerleaders pranced around on the Astroturf and shook their asses. He fell into a semidoze, and when Fred began to get at him, he couldn't shake him off.

George, since you don't seem to know what you're doing, let me tell you. Let me spell it out for you, old buddy. *(Get off my back, Fred.)* First, the option on the Waterford plant is going to run out. That will happen at midnight on Tuesday. On Wednesday, Thom McAn is going to close their deal with that slavering little piece of St. Patrick's Day shit, Patrick J. Monohan. On Wednesday afternoon or Thursday morning, a big sign that says *SOLD!* is going up. If anyone from the laundry sees it, maybe you can postpone the inevitable by saying: Sure. Sold to us. But if Ordner checks, you're dead. Probably he won't. But *(Freddy, leave me alone)* on Friday a new sign will go up. That sign will say:

SITE OF OUR NEW WATERFORD PLANT
TOM MC AN SHOES
Here We Grow Again!!!

On Monday, bright and early, you are going to lose your job. Yes, the way I see it, you'll be unemployed before your ten o'clock coffee break. Then you can come home and tell Mary. I don't know when that will be. The bus ride only takes fifteen minutes, so conceivably you *could* end twenty years of marriage and twenty years of gainful employment in just about half an hour. But after you tell Mary, comes the explanation scene. You could put it off by getting drunk, but sooner or later—

Fred, shut your goddam mouth.

—sooner or later, you're going to have to explain just how you lost your job. You'll just have to fess up. Well, Mary, the highway department is going to rip down the Fir Street plant in a month or so, and I kind of neglected to get us a new one. I kept thinking that this whole 784 extension business was some kind of nightmare I was going to wake up from. Yes, Mary, yes, I located us a new plant—Waterford, that's right, you *capish*—but somehow I couldn't go through with it. How much is it going to cost Amroco? Oh, I'd say a million or a million-five, depending on how long it takes them to find a new plant location and how much business they lose for good.

I'm warning you, Fred.

Or you could tell her what no one knows better than you, George. That the profit margin on the Blue Ribbon has gotten so thin that the cost accountants might just throw up their hands and say, Let's ditch the whole thing, guys. We'll just take the city's money and buy a penny arcade down in Norton or a nice little pitch 'n' putt out in Russell or Crescent. There's too much potential red ink in this after the sugar that son of a bitch Dawes poured into our gas tank. You could tell her that.

Oh, go to hell.

But that's just the first movie, and this is a double feature, isn't it? Part two comes when you tell Mary there isn't any house to go to and there isn't going to be any house. And how are you going to explain that?

I'm not doing anything.

That's right. You're just some guy who fell asleep in his rowboat. But come Tuesday midnight, your boat is going over the falls, George. For Christ's sweet sake, go see Monohan on Monday and make him an unhappy man. Sign on the dotted line. You'll be in trouble anyway, with all those lies you told Ordner Friday night. But you can bail yourself out of that. God knows you've bailed yourself out of trouble before this

Let me alone. I'm almost asleep.

It's Charlie, isn't it. This is a way of committing suicide. But it's not fair to Mary, George. It's not fair to anybody. You're—

He sat bolt upright, spilling his drink on the rug. "No one except maybe me."

Then what about the guns, George? What about the guns?

Trembling, he picked up his glass and made another drink.

November 26, 1973

He was having lunch with Tom Granger at Nicky's, a diner three blocks over from the laundry. They were sitting in a booth, drinking bottles of beer and waiting for their meals to come. There was a jukebox, and it was playing "Good-bye Yellow Brick Road," by Elton John.

Tom was talking about the Mustangs–Chargers game, which the Chargers had won 37-6. Tom was in love with all the city's sports teams, and their losses sent him into frenzies. Someday, he thought as he listened to Tom castigate the whole Mustangs' roster man by man, Tom Granger will cut off one of his ears with a laundry pin and send it to the general manager. A crazy man would send it to the coach, who would laugh and pin it to the locker room bulletin board, but Tom would send it to the general manager, who would brood over it.

The food came, brought by a waitress in a white nylon pants suit. He estimated her age at three hundred, possibly three hundred and four. Ditto weight. A small card over her left breast said:

GAYLE
Thanks For Your Patronage
Nicky's Diner

Tom had a slice of roast beef that was floating belly up in a plateful of gravy. He had ordered two cheeseburgers, rare, with an order of French fries. He knew the cheeseburgers would be well done. He had eaten at Nicky's before. The 784 extension was going to miss Nicky's by half a block.

They ate. Tom finished his tirade about yesterday's game and asked him about the Waterford plant and his meeting with Ordner.

"I'm going to sign on Thursday or Friday," he said.

"Thought the options ran out on Tuesday."

He went through his story about how Thom McAn had decided they didn't want the Waterford plant. It was no fun lying to Tom Granger. He had known Tom for seventeen years. He wasn't terribly bright. There was no challenge in lying to Tom.

"Oh," Tom said when he had finished, and the subject was closed. He forked roast beef into his mouth and grimaced. "Why do we eat here? The food is lousy here. Even the coffee is. My *wife* makes better coffee"

"I don't know," he said, slipping into the opening. "But do you remember when that new Italian place opened up? We took Mary and Verna."

"Yeah, in August. Verna still raves about that ricotta stuff . . . no, rigatoni. That's what they call it. Rigatoni."

"And that guy sat down next to us? That big fat guy?"

"Big, fat . . . " Tom chewed, trying to remember. He shook his head.

"You said he was a crook."

"Ohhhhh." His eyes opened wide. He pushed his plate away and lit a Herbert Tareyton and dropped the dead match into his plate, where it floated on the gravy. "Yeah, that's right. Sally Magliore."

"Was that his name?"

"Yeah, that's right. Big guy with thick glasses. Nine chins. Salvatore Magliore. Sounds like the specialty in an Italian whorehouse, don't it? Sally One-Eye, they used to call him, on account of he had a cataract on one eye. He had it removed at the Mayo Clinic three or four years ago . . . the cataract, not the eye. Yeah, mhe's a big crook."

"What's he in?"

"What are they all in?" Tom asked, tapping his cigarette ash into his plate. "Dope, girls, gambling, crooked investments, sharking. And murdering other crooks. Did you see that in the paper? Just last week. They found some guy in the trunk of his car behind a filling station. Shot six times in the head and his throat cut. That's really ridiculous. Why would anyone want to cut a guy's throat after they just shot him six times in the head? Organized crime, that's what Sally One-Eye's in."

"Does he have a legitimate business?"

"Yeah, I think he does. Out on the Landing Strip, beyond Norton. He sells cars. Magliore's Guaranteed Okay Used Cars. A body in every trunk." Tom laughed and tapped more ashes into his plate. Gayle came back and asked then if they wanted more coffee. They both ordered more

"I got those cotter pins today for the boiler door," Tom said. "They remind me of my dork."

"Is that right?"

"Yeah, you should see those sons of bitches. Nine inches long and three through the middle."

"Did you mention my dork?" he asked, and they both laughed and talked shop until it was time to go back to work.

He got off the bus that afternoon at Barker Street and went into Duncan's, which was a quiet neighborhood bar. He ordered a beer and listened to Duncan bitch for a little while about the Mustangs–Chargers game. A man came up from the back and told Duncan that the Bowl-a-Score machine wasn't working right. Duncan went back to look at it, and he sipped his beer and looked at the TV. There was a soaper on, and two women were talking in slow, apocalyptic tones about a man named Hank. Hank was coming home from college, and one of the women had just found out that Hank was her son, the result of a disastrous experiment that had occurred after her high school prom twenty years ago.

Freddy tried to say something, and George shut him right up. The circuit breaker was in fine working order. Had been all day.

That's right, you fucking schizo! Fred yelled, and then George sat on him. Go peddle your papers, Freddy. You're persona non grata around here.

"Of course I'm not going to tell him," said one of the women on the tube. "How do you expect me to tell him that?"

"Just . . . tell him," said the other woman.

"Why should I tell him? Why should I knock his whole life out of orbit over something that happened twenty years ago?"

"Are you going to lie to him?"

"I'm not going to tell him anything."

"You *have* to tell him."

"Sharon, I can't afford to tell him."

"If you don't tell him, Betty, I'll tell him myself."

"That fucking machine is all fucked to shit," Duncan said, coming back. "That's been a pain in the ass ever since they put it in. Now what have I got to do? Call the fucking Automatic Industries Company. Wait twenty minutes until some dipshit secretary connects me with the right line. Listen to some guy tell me that they're pretty busy but they'll try to send a guy out Wednesday. *Wednesday!* Then some guy with his brains between the cheeks of his ass will show up on Friday, drink four bucks' worth of free beer, fix whatever's wrong and probably rig something else to break in two weeks, and tell me I shouldn't let the guys throw the weights so hard. I used to have pinball machines. That was good. Those machines hardly ever fucked up. But this is progress. If I'm still here in 1980, they'll take out the Bowl-a-Score and put in an Automatic Blow-Job. You want another beer?"

"Sure," he said.

Duncan went to draw it. He put fifty cents on the bar and walked back to the phone booth beside the broken Bowl-a-Score.

He found what he was looking for in the yellow pages under *Automobiles, New and Used.* The listing there said:MAGLIORE'S USED CARS, Rt. 16, Norton 892-4576

Route 16 became Venner Avenue as you went farther into Norton. Venner Avenue was also known as the Landing Strip, where you could get all the things the yellow pages didn't advertise.

He put a dime in the phone and dialed Magliore's Used Cars. The phone was picked up on the second ring, and male voice said: "Magliore's Used Cars."

"This is Dawes," he said. "Barton Dawes. Can I talk to Mr. Magliore?"

"Sal's busy. But I'll be glad to help you if I can. Pete Mansey."

"No, it has to be Mr. Magliore, Mr. Mansey. It's about those two Eldorados."

"You got a bum steer," Mansey said. "We're not taking any big cars in trade the rest of the year, on account of this energy business. Nobody's buying them. So—"

"I'm buying," he said.

"What's that"

"Two Eldorados. One 1970, one 1972. One gold, one cream. I spoke to Mr. Magliore about them last week. It's a business deal."

"Oh yeah, right. He really isn't here now, Mr. Dawes. To tell you the truth, he's in Chicago. He's not getting in until eleven o'clock tonight."

Outside, Duncan was hanging a sign on the Bowl-a-Score. The sign said:

OUT OF ORDER

"Well he be in tomorrow?"

"Yeah, sure will. Was this a trade deal?"

"No, straight buy."

"One of the specials?"

He hesitated a moment, then said: "Yes, that's right. Would four o'clock be okay?"

"Sure, fine."

"Thanks, Mr. Mansey."

"I'll tell him you called."

"You do that," he said, and hung up carefully. His palms were sweating.

Merv Griffin was chatting with celebrities when got home. There was nothing in the mail; that was a relief. He went into the living room.

Mary was sipping a hot rum concoction in a teacup. There was a box of Kleenex beside her and the room smelled of Vicks.

"Are you all right?" He asked her

"Don'd kiss be," she said, and her voice had a distant foghorning quality. "I cabe downd with sobething."

"Poor kid." He kissed her forehead.

"I hade do ask you, Bard, bud would you ged the groceries tonighd? I was goig with Meg Carder, bud I had to call her ad beg off."

"Sure. Are you running a fever?"

"Dno. Well, baybe a liddle."

"Want me to make an appointment with Fontaine for you?"

"Dno. I will toborrow if I don'd feel bedder."

"You're really stuffy."

"Yes. The Vicks helbed for a while, bud dow—" She shrugged and smiled wanly. "I soud like Dodald Duck."

He hesitated a moment and then said, "I'll be home a little bit late tomorrow night."

"Oh?"

"I'm going out to Northside to look at a house. It seems like a good one. Six rooms. A little backyard. Not too far from the Hobarts."

Freddy said quite clearly: *Why, you dirty low-life son of a bitch.*

Mary brightened. "That's woderful! Cad I go look with you?"

"Better not, with that cold."

"I'll buddle ub."

"Next time," he said firmly.

"Ogay." She looked at him. "Thang God you're finally boving on this," she said. "I was worried."

"Don't worry."

"I wodn't."

She took a sip of the hot rum drink and snuggled against him. He could hear her breath snuffling in and out. Merv Griffin was chatting with James Brolin about his new movie, *Westworld.* Soon to be showing at barbershops all over the country.

After a while Mary got up and put TV dinners in the oven. He got up, switched the TV over to reruns of "F Troop" and tried not to listen to Freddy. After a while,though, Freddy changed his tune.

Do you remember how you got the first TV, Georgie?

He smiled a little, looking not at Forrest Tucker but right through him. I do, Fred. I surely do.

They had come home one evening, about two years after they were married, from the Upshaws, where they had been watching "Your Hit Parade" and "Dan Fortune," and Mary had asked him if he didn't think Donna Upshaw had seemed a little . . . well, off. Now, sitting here, he could remember Mary, slim and oddly, fetchingly taller in a pair of white sandals she had gotten to celebrate summer. She had been wearing white shorts, too; her legs looked long and coltish, as if they really might go all the way up to her chin. In truth, he hadn't been very interested in whether or not Donna Upshaw had seemed a little off; he had been interested in divesting Mary of those tight shorts. That had been where his interest lay—not to put too fine a point on it.

"Maybe she's getting a little tired of serving Spanish peanuts to half the neighborhood just because they're the only people on the street with a TV," he said.

He supposed he had seen the little frown line between her eyes—the one that always meant Mary was cooking something up, but by then they were halfway upstairs, his hand was roaming down over the seat of those shorts—what little seat there was—and it wasn't until later, until after, that she said:

"How much would a table model cost us, Bart?"

Half asleep, he had answered, "Well, I guess we could get a Motorola for twenty-eight, maybe thirty bucks. But the Philco—"

"Not a radio. A TV."

He sat up, turned on the lamp, and looked at her. She was lying there naked, the sheet down around her hips, and although she was smiling at him, he thought she was serious. It was Mary's I-dare-you grin.

"Mary, we can't afford a TV."

"How much for a table model? A GE or a Philco or something?"

"New?"

"New?"

He considered the question, watching the play of lamplight across the lovely round curves of her breasts. She had been so much slimmer then (although she's hardly a fatty now, George, he reproached himself; never said she was, Freddy my boy), so much more alive somehow. Even her hair had crackled out its own message: *alive, awake, aware* . . .

"Around seven hundred and fifty dollars," he said, thinking that would douse the grin . . . but it hadn't.

"Well, look," She said, sitting up Indian-fashion in bed, her legs crossed under the sheet.

"I am," he said, grinning

"Not at *that*." But she laughed, and a flush had spread prettily down her cheeks to her neck (although she hadn't pulled the sheet up, he remembered).

"What's on your mind?"

"Why do men want a TV?" she asked. "To watch all the sports on the weekends. And why do women want one? Those soap operas in the afternoon. You can listen while you iron or put your feet up if your work's done. Now suppose we each found something to do—something that *pays*—during that time we'd otherwise just be sitting around . . . "

"reading a book, or maybe even making love?" he suggested.

"We always find time for *that*," she said, and laughed, and blushed, and her eyes were dark in the lamplight and it threw a warm, semicircular shadow between her breasts, and he knew then that he was going to give in to her, he would have promised her a fifteen-hundred-dollar Zenith console model if she would just let him make love to her again, and at the thought he felt himself stiffening, felt the snake turning to stone, as Mary had once said when she'd had a little too much to drink at the Ridpaths' New Year's Eve party (and now, eighteen years later, he felt the snake turning to stone again—over a memory).

"Well, all right," he said. "I'm going to moonlight weekends and you're going ot moonlight afternoons. But what, dear Mary, Oh-not-so-Virgin Mary, are we going to do?"

She pounced on him, giggling, her breasts a soft weight on his stomach (flat-enough in those days, Freddy, not a sign of a bay window). "That's the trick of it!" she said. "What's today? June eighteenth?"

"That's right."

"Well, you do your weekend things, and on December eighteenth we'll put our money together—"

"—and buy a toaster," he said, grinning.

"—and get that TV," she said solemnly. "I'm sure we can do it, Bart." Then the giggles broke out again. "But the fun part'll be that we won't tell each other what we're up to until after."

"Just as long as I don't see a red light over the door when I come home from work tomorrow," he said, capitulating.

She grabbed him, got on top of him, started to tickle. The tickling turned to caresses.

"Bring it to me," she whispered against his neck, and gripped him with gentle yet excruciating pressure, guiding him and squeezing him at the same time. "Put it in me, Bart."

And later, in the dark again, hands crossed behind his head. he said: "We don't tell each other, right?"

"Nope."

"Mary, what brought this on? What I said about Donna Upshaw not wanting to serve Spanish peanuts to half the neighborhood?"

There were no giggles in her voice when she replied. Her voice was flat, austere, and just a little frightening: a faint taste of winter in the warm June air of their third-floor walkup apartment. "I don't like to freeload, Bart. And I won't. Ever."

For a week and a half he had turned her quirky little proposal over in his mind, wondering just what in the hell he was suppose to do to bring in his half of the seven hundred and fifty dollars (and probably more like three-quarters of it, the way it'll turn out, he thought) on the next twenty or so weekends. He was a little old to be mowing lawns for quarters. And Mary had gotten a look—a smug sort of look—that gave him the idea that she had either landed something or was landing something. Better get on your track shoes, Bart, he thought, and had to laugh out loud at himself.

Pretty fine days, weren't they, Freddy? he asked himself now as Forrest Tucker and "F Troop" gave way to a cereal commercial where an animated rabbit preached that "Trix are for kids." They were, Georgie. They were fucking *great* days.

One day he had been unlocking his car after work, and he had happened to look at the big industrial smokestack behind dry-cleaning, and it came to him

He had put the keys back in his pocket and went in to talk to Don Tarkington. Don leaned back in his chair, looked at him from under shaggy eyebrows that were even then turning white (as were the hairs which bushed out of his ears and curled from his nostrils), hands steepled on his chest.

"Paint the stack," Don said.

He nodded.

"Weekends."

He nodded again.

"Flat fee—three hundred dollars."

And again.

"You're crazy."

He burst out laughing.

Don smiled a little. "You got a dope habit, Bart?"

"No," he said. "But I've got a little thing on with Mary."

"A bet?" The shaggy eyebrows went up half a mile

"More gentlemanly than that. A wager, I guess you'd call it. Anyway, Don, the stack needs the paint, and I need the three hundred dollars. What do you say? A painting contractor would charge you four and a quarter."

"You checked."

"I checked."

"You crazy bastard," Don said, and burst out laughing. "You'll probably kill yourself."

"Yeah, I provably will," he said, and began laughing himself (and here, eighteen years later, as the Trix rabbit gave way to the evening news, he sat grinning like a fool).

And that was how, one weekend after the Fourth of July, he found himself on a shaky scaffolding eighty feet in the air, a paintbrush in his hand and his ass wagging in the wind. Once a sudden afternoon thunderstorm had come up, snapped one of the ropes which held up the scaffolding as easily as you might snap a piece of twine holding a package, and he almost did fall. The safety rope around his waist had held and he had lowered himself to the roof, heart thudding like a drum, sure that no power on earth would get him back up there—not for a lousy table-model TV. But he had gone back. Not for the TV, but for Mary. For the look of the lamplight on her small, uptilted breasts; for the dare-you grin on her lips and in her eyes—her dark eyes which could sometimes turn so light or darken even more, into summer thunderheads.

By early September he had finished the stack; it stood cleanly white against the sky, a chalk mark on a blueboard, slim and bright. He looked at it with some pride as he scrubbed his spattered forearms with paint thinner

Don Tarkington paid him by check. "Not a bad job," was his only comment, "considering the jackass that did it."

He picked up another fifty dollars paneling the walls of Henry Chalmers' new family room—in those days, Henry had been the plant foreman—and painting Ralph Tremont's aging Chris-Craft. When December 18 rolled around, he and Mary sat down at their small dining room table like adversary but oddly friendly gunslingers, and he put three hundred and ninety dollars in cash in front of her— he had banked the money and there had been some interest.

She put four hundred and sixteen dollars with it. She took it from her apron pocket. It made a much bigger wad than his, because most of it was ones and fives.

He gasped at it and then said, "What the Christ did you *do,* Mare?"

Smiling, she said: "I made twenty-six dresses, hemmed up forty-nine dresses, hemmed down sixty-four dresses; I made thirty-one skirts; I crocheted three samplers; I hooked four rugs, one of latch-hook style; I made five sweaters, two afghans and one complete set of table linen; I embroidered sixty-three handkerchiefs; twelve sets of towels and twelve sets of pillowcases, and I can see all the monograms in my sleep."

Laughing, she held out her hands, and for the first time he really noticed the thick pads of calluses on the tips of the fingers, like the calluses a guitar player eventually builds up.

"Oh Christ, Mary," he said, his voice hoarse. "Christ, look at your hands."

"My hands are fine," she said, and her eyes darkened and danced. "And you looked very cute up there on the smokestack, Bart. I thought once I'd buy a slingshot and see if I couldn't hit you in the butt—"

Roaring, he had jumped up and chased her through the living room and into the bedroom. Where we spent the rest of the afternoon, as I recall it, Freddy old man.

They discovered that they not only had enough for a table model TV, but that for another forty dollars they actuallly could have a console model. RCA had jumped the model year, the proprietor of John's TV downtown told them (John's was already buried under the 784 extension of course, long gone, along with the Grand and everything else), and was going for broke. He would be happy to let them have it, and for just ten dollars a week—

"No," Mary said.

John looked pained. "Lady, it's only four weeks. you're hardly signing your life away on easy credit terms."

"Just a minute," Mary said, and led him outside into the pre-Christmas cold where carols tangled in each other up and down the street.

"Mary," he said, "he's right. It's not as if—"

"The first thing we buy on credit ought to be our own house, Bart," she said. That faint line appeared between her eyes. "Now listen—"

They went back inside. "Will you hold it for us?" he asked John.

"I guess so—for a while. But this is my busy season, Mr. Dawes. How long?"

"Just over the weekend," he said. "I'll be in Monday night."

They had spent that weekend in the country, bundled up against the cold and the snow which threatened but did not fall. They drove slowly up and down back roads, giggling like kids, a six-pack on the seat for him and a bottle of wine for Mary, and they saved the beer bottles and picked up more, bags of beer bottles, bags of soda bottles, each one of the small ones worth two cents, the big ones worth a nickle. It had been one hell of a weekend, Bart thought now—Mary's hair had been long, flowing out behind her over that imitation-leather coat of hers, the color flaming in her cheeks. He could see her now, walking up a ditch filled with fallen autumn leaves, kicking through them with her boots, producing a noise like a steady low forest fire . . . then the click of a bottle and she raised it up in triumph, waggled it at him from across the road, grinning like a kid.

They don't have returnable bottles anymore, either, Georgie. The gospel these days is no deposit, no return. Use it up and throw it out.

That Monday, after work, they had turned in thirty-one dollars' worth of bottles, visiting four different supermarkets to spread the wealth around. They had arrived at John's ten minutes before the store closed.

"I'm nine bucks short," he told John

John wrote PAID across the bill of sale that had been taped to the RCA console. "Merry Christmas, Mr. Dawes," he said. "Let me get my dolly and I'll help you out with it."

They got it home, and an excited Dick Keller from the first floor helped him carry it up, and that night they had watched TV until the national anthem had come on the last operating channel and then they had made love in front of the test pattern, both of them with raging headaches from eyestrain.

TV had rarely looked so good since.

Mary came in and saw him looking at the TV, his empty scotch-rocks glass in his hand.

"Your dinner's ready, Bart," she said. "You want it in here?"

He looked at her, wondering exactly when he had seen the dare-you grin on her lips for the last time . . . exactly when the little line between her eyes had begun to be there all the time, like a wrinkle, a scar, a tattoo proclaiming age.

You wonder about some things, he thought, that you'd never in God's world want to know. Now why the hell is that?

"Bart?"

"Let's eat in the dining room," he said. He got up and snapped the TV off.

"All right."

They sat down. He looked at the meal in the aluminum tray. Six little compartments, and something that looked pressed in each one. The meat had gravy on it. It was his impression that the meats in TV dinners *always* had gravy on them. TV dinnermeat would look naked without gravy, he thought, and then he remembered his thought about Lorne Green for absolutley no reason at all : *Boy, I'll snatch you bald-headed.*

It didn't amuse him this time. Somehow it scared him.

"What were you sbiling about in the living roob, Bart?" Mary asked. Her eyes were red from her cold, and her nose had a chapped, raw look.

" I don't remember," he said, and for the moment he thought: *I'll just scream now, I think. For lost things. For your grin, Mary. Pardon me while I just throw back my head and scream for the grin that's never there on your face anymore. Okay?*

"You looked very habby," she said.

Against his will—it was a secret thing, and tonight he felt the needed his secret things, tonight his feelings felt as raw as Mary's nose looked—against his will he said: "I was thinking of the time we went out picking up bottles to finish paying for that TV. The RCA console."

"Oh, that," Mary said, and then sneezed into her hankie over her TV dinner.

He ran into Jack Hobart at the Stop 'n' Shop. Jack's cart was full of frozen foods, heat-and-serve canned products, and a lot of beer.

"Jack!" he said. "What are you doing way over here?"

Jack smiled a little. "I haven't got used to the other store yet, so . . . I thought . . . "

"Where's Ellen?"

"She had to fly back to Cleveland," he said. "Her mother died."

"Jesus, I'm sorry Jack. Wasn't that sudden?"

Shoppers were moving all around them under the cold overhead lights. Muzak came down from hidden speakers, old standards that you could never quite recognize. A woman with a full cart passed them, dragging a screaming three-year-old in a blue parka with snot on the sleeves.

"Yeah, it was," Jack Hobart said. He smiled meaninglessly and looked down into his cart. There was a large yellow bag there that said:

KITTY-PAN KITTY LITTER
Use It, Throw It Away!
Sanitary!

"Yeah, it was. She'd been feeling punk, thank you, but she thought it might have been a, you know, sort of leftover from change of life. It was cancer. They opened her up, took a look, and sewed her right back up. Three weeks later she was dead. Hell of a hard thing for Ellen. I mean, she only twenty years younger."

"Yeah," he said.

"So she's out in Cleveland for a little while."

"Yeah."

"Yeah."

They looked at each other and grinned shamefacedly over the fact of death.

"How is it?" he asked. "Out there in Northside?"

"Well, I'll tell you the truth, Bart. Nobody seems very friendly."

"No?"

"You know Ellen works down at the bank?"

"Yeah, sure."

"Well, a lot of the girls used to have a car pool—I used to let Ellen have the car every Thursday. That was her part. There's a pool out in Northside into the city, but all the women who use it are part of some club that Ellen can't join unless she's been there at least a year."

"That sounds pretty damn close to discrimination, Jack."

"Fuck them," Jack said angrily. "Ellen wouldn't join their goddam club if they crawled up the street on their hands and knees. I got her her own car. A used Buick. She loves it. Should have done it two years ago."

"How's the house?"

"It's fine," Jack said, and sighed. "The electricity's high, though. You should see our bill. That's no good for people with a kid in college."

They shuffled. Now that Jack's anger had passed, the shamefaced grin was back on his face. He realized that Jack was almost pathetically glad to see someone from the neighborhood and was prolonging the moment. He had a sudden vision of Jack knocking around in the new house, the sound from the TV filling the rooms with phantom company, his wife a thousand miles away seeing her mother into the ground.

"Listen, why don't you come back to the house?" he asked. "We'll have a couple of six-packs and listen to Howard Cosell explain everything that's wrong with the NFL."

"Hey, that'd be great."

"Just let me call Mary after we check out."

He called Mary and Mary said okay. She said she would put some frozen pastries in the oven and then go to bed so she wouldn't give Jack her cold.

"How does he like it out there?" she asked.

"Okay, I guess. Mare, Ellen's mother died. She's out in Cleveland for the funeral. Cancer."

"Oh, *no.*"

"So I thought Jack might like the company, you know—"

"Sure, of course." She paused. "Did you tell hib we bight be neighbors before log?"

"No," he said. "I didn't tell him that."

"You ought to. It bight cheer hib ub."

"Sure. Good-bye, Mary."

"Bye."

"Take some aspirin before you go to bed."

"I will."

"Bye."

"Bye, George." She hung up.

He looked at the phone, chilled. She only called him that when she was very pleased with him. Fred-and-George had been Charlie's game originally.

He and Jack Hobart went home and watched the game. They drank a lot of beer. But it wasn't so good.

When Jack was getting into his car to go home at quarter past twelve, he looked up bleakly and said: "That goddam highway. That's what fucked up the works."

"It sure did." He thought Jack looked old, and it scared him. Jack was about his age.

"You keep in touch, Bart."

"I will."

They grinned hollowly at each other, a little drunk, a little sick. He watched Jack's car until its taillights had disappeared down the long, curving hill.

November 27, 1973

He was a little hung-over and a little sleepy from staying up so late. The sound of the laundry washers kicking onto the extract cycle seemed loud in his ears, and the steady *thump-hiss* of the shirt presses and the ironer made him want to wince.

Freddy was worse. Freddy was playing the very devil today.

Listen, Fred was saying. This is your last chance, my boy. You've still got all afternoon to get over to Monohan's office. If you let it wait until five o'clock, it's going to be too late.

The option doesn't run out until midnight.

Sure it doesn't. But right after work Monohan is going to feel a pressing need to go see some relatives. In Alaska. For him it means the difference between a forty-five-thousand-dollar commission and fifty thousand dollars—the price of a new car. For that kind of money you don't need a pocket calculator. For that kind of money you might discover relatives in the sewer system under Bombay.

But it didn't matter. It had gone too far. He had let the machine run without him too long. He was hypnotized by the coming explosion, almost lusted for it. His belly groaned in its own juices.

He spent most of the afternoon in the washroom, watching Ron Stone and Dave run test loads with one of the new laundry products. It was loud in the washroom. The noise hurt his tender head, but it kept him from hearing his thoughts.

After work he got his car out of the parking lot—Mary had been glad to let him have it for the day since he was seeing about their new house—and drove through downtown and through Norton.

In Norton, blacks stood around on street corners and outside bars. Restaurants advertised different kinds of soul food. Children hopped and danced on chalked sidewalk grids. He saw a pimpmobile—a huge pink Eldorado Cadillac—pull up in front of an anonymous brownstone apartment building. The man who got out was a Wilt Chamberlain-size black in a white planter's hat and a white ice cream suit with pearl buttons and black platform shoes with huge gold buckles on the sides. He carried a malacca stick with a large ivory ball on the top. He walked slowly, majestically, around to the hood of the car, where a set of caribou antlers were mounted. A tiny silver spoon hung on a silver chain around his neck and winked in the thin autumn sun. He watched the man in the rearview mirror as the children ran to him for sweets.

Nine blocks later the tenements thinned to ragged, open fields that were still soft and marshy. Oily water stood between hummocks in puddles, their surfaces flat, deadly rainbows. On the left, near the horizon, he could see a plane landing at the city's airport.

He was now on Route 16, traveling past the exurban sprawl between the city and the city limits. He passed McDonald's. Shakey's, Nino's Steak Pit. He passed a Dairy Freez and the Noddy-Time Motel, both closed for the season. He passed the Norton Drive-In, where the marquee said:

FRI—SAT—SUN

RESTLESS WIVES
SOME CAME RUNNING   RATED X
EIGHT-BALL

He passed a bowling alley and a driving range that was closed for the season. Gas stations—two of them with signs that said:

SORRY, NO GAS

It was still four days until they got their gasoline allotments for December. He couldn't find it in himself to feel sorry for the country as a whole as it went into this science-fiction-style crisis—the country had been pigging petroleum for too long to warrant his sympathy—but he could feel sorry for the little men with their peckers caught in the swing of a big door.

A mile farther on he came to Magliore's Used Cars. He didn't know what he had expected, but he felt disappointed. It looked like a cut-rate, fly-by-night operation. Cars were lined up on the lot facing the road under looped lines of flapping banners—red, yellow, blue, green—that had been tied between light standards that would shine down on the product at night. Prices and slogans soaped on the windshields:

$795
RUNS GOOD!

and

$550
GOOD TRANSPORTATION!

and on a dusty old Valiant with flat tires and a cracked windshield:

$75
MECHANIX SPECIAL!

A salesman wearing a gray-green topcoat was nodding and smiling noncommittally as a young kid in a red silk jacket talked to him. They were standing by a blue Mustang with cancer of the rocker panels. The kid said something vehement and thumped the driver's side door with the flat of his hand. Rust flaked off in a small flurry. The salesman shrugged and went on smiling. The Mustang just sat there and got a little older.

There was a combination office and garage in the center of the lot. He parked and got out of his car. There was a lift in the garage, and an old Dodge with giant fins was up on it. A mechanic walked out from under, holding a muffler in both grease-gloved hands like a chalice.

"Say, you can't park there, mister. That's in the right-of-way."

"Where should I park?"

"Take it around back if you're goin in the office."

He drove the LTD around to the back, creeping carefully down the narrow way between the corrugated metal side of the garage and a row of cars. He parked behind the garage and got out. The wind, strong and cutting, made him wince. The heater had disarmed his face and he had to squint his eyes to keep them from tearing.

There was an automobile junkyard back here. It stretched for acres, amazing the eye. Most of the cars had been gutted of parts and now they sat on their wheel rims or axles like the victims of some awful plague who were too contagious to even be dragged to the dead-pit. Grilles with empty headlight sockets gazed at him raptly.

He walked back out front. The mechanic was installing the muffler. An open bottle of Coke was balanced on a pile of tires to his right.

He called to the mechanic: "Is Mr. Magliore in?" Talking to mechanics always made him feel like an asshole. He had gotten his first car twenty-four years ago, and talking to mechanics still made him feel like a pimply teenager.

The mechanic looked over his shoulder and kept working his socket wrench. "Yeah, him and Mansey. Both in the office."

"Thanks."

"Sure."

He went into the office. The walls were imitation pine, the floor muddy squares of red and white linoleum. There were two old chairs with a pile of tattered magazines between them—*Outdoor Life, Field and Stream, True Argosy*. No one was sitting in the chairs. There was one door, probably leading to an inner office, and on the left side, a little cubicle like a theater box office. A woman was sitting in there, working an adding machine. A yellow pencil was poked into her hair. A pair of harlequin glasses hung against her scant bosom, held by a rhinestone chain. He walked over to her, nervous now. He wet his lips before he spoke.

"Excuse me."

She looked up. "Yes?"

He had a crazy impulse to say: *I'm here to see Sally One-Eye, bitch. Shake your tail.*

Instead, he said: "I have an appointment with Mr. Magliore."

"You do?" She looked at him warily for a moment and then riffled through some slips on the table beside the adding machine. She pulled one out. "Your name is Dawes? Barton Dawes?"

"That's right."

"Go right in." She stretched her lips at him and began to peck at the adding machine again.

He was very nervous. Surely they knew he had conned them. They were running some kind of midnight auto sales here, that much had been obvious from the way Mansey had spoken to him yesterday. And they knew he knew. Maybe it would be better to go right out the door, drive like hell to Monohan's office, and maybe catch him before he left for Alaska or Timbuktu or wherever he would be leaving for.

Finally, Freddy said. The man shows some sense.

He walked over to the door in spite of Freddy, opened it, and stepped into the inner office. There were two men. The one behind the desk was fat and wearing heavy glasses. The other was razor thin and dressed in a salmon-pink sports coat that made him think of Vinnie. He was bending over the desk. They were looking at a J.C. Whitney catalogue.

They looked up at him. Magliore smiled from behind his desk. The glasses made his eyes appear faded and enormous, like the yolks of poached eggs.

"Mr. Dawes?"

"That's right."

"Glad you could drop by. Want to shut the door?"

"Okay."

He shut it. When he turned back, Magliore was no longer smiling. Neither was Mansey. They were just looking at him, and the room temperature seemed to have gone down twenty degrees.

"Okay," Magliore said. "What is this shit?"

"I wanted to talk to you."

"I talk for free. But not to shitbirds like you. You call up Pete and give him a line of crap about two Eldorados." He pronounced it "Eldoraydos." "You talk to me, mister. You tell me what your act is."

Standing by the door, he said: "I heard maybe you sold things."

"Yeah, that's right. Cars. I sell cars."

"No," he said. "Other stuff. Stuff like . . . " He looked around at the fake-pine-paneled walls. God knew how many agencies were bugging this place. "Just stuff," he finished, and the words came out on crutches.

"You mean stuff like dope and whores ('hoors') and off-track betting? Or did you want to buy a hitter to knock off your wife or your boss?" Magliore saw him wince and laughed harshly. "That's not too bad, mister, not bad at all for a shitbird. That's the big 'What if this place is bugged' act, right? That's number one at the police academy, am I right?"

"Look, I'm not a—"

"Shut up," Mansey said. He was holding the J.C. Whitney catalogue in his hands. His fingernails were manicured. He had never seen manicured nails exactly like that except on TV commercials where the announcer had to hold a bottle of aspirin or something. "If Sal wants you to talk, he'll tell you to talk."

He blinked and shut his mouth. This was like a bad dream.

"You guys get dumber every day," Magliore said. "That's all right. I like to deal with dummies. I'm *used* to dealing with dummies. I'm good at it. Now. Not that you don't know it, but this office is as clean as a whistle. We wash it every week. I got a cigar box full of bugs at home. Contact mikes, button mikes, pressure mikes, Sony tape recorders no bigger than your hand. They don't even try that much anymore. Now they send shitbirds like you."

He heard himself say: "I'm not a shitbird."

An expression of exaggerated surprise spread across Magliore's face. He turned to Mansey. "Did you hear that? He said he wasn't a shitbird."

"Yeah, I heard that," Mansey said.

"Does he look like a shitbird to you?"

"Yeah, he does," Mansey said.

"Even talks like a shitbird, doesn't he?"

"Yeah."

"So if you're not a shitbird," Magliore said, turning back to him, "what are you?"

"I'm—" he began, not sure of just what to say. What *was* he? Fred, where are you when I need you?

"Come on, come on," Magliore said. "State Police? City? IRS? FBI? He look like prime Effa Bee Eye to you, Pete?"

"Yeah," Pete said.

"Not even the city police would send out a shitbird like you, mister. You must be Effa Bee Eye or a private detective. Which is it?"

He began to feel angry.

"Throw him out, Pete," Magliore said, losing interest. Mansey started forward, still holding the J.C. Whitney catalogue.

"You stupid dork!" He suddenly yelled at Magliore. "You probably see policemen under your bed, you're so stupid! You probably think they're home screwing your wife when you're here!"

Magliore looked at him, magnified eyes widening. Mansey froze, a look of unbelief on his face.

"Dork?" Magliore said, turning the word over in his mouth the way a carpenter will turn a tool he doesn't know over in his hands. "Did he call me a dork?"

He was stunned by what he had said.

"I'll take him around back," Mansey said, starting forward again.

"Hold it," Magliore breathed. He looked at him with honest curiosity. "Did you call me a dork?"

"I'm not a cop," he said. "I'm not a crook, either. I'm just a guy that heard you sold stuff to people who had the money to buy it. Well, I've got the money. I didn't know you had to say the secret word or have a Captain Midnight decoder ring or all that silly shit. Yes, I called you a dork. I'm sorry I did if it will stop this man from beating me up. I'm . . ." He wet his lips and could think of no way to continue. Magliore and Mansey were looking at him with fascination, as if he had just turned into a Greek marble statue before their very eyes.

"Dork," Magliore breathed. "Frisk this guy, Pete."

Pete's hands slapped his shoulders and he turned around.

"Put your hands on the wall," Mansey said, his mouth beside his ear. He smelled like Listerine. "Feet out behind you. Just like on the cop shows."

"I don't watch the cop shows," he said, but he knew what Mansey meant, and he put himself in the frisk position. Mansey ran his hands up his legs, patted his crotch with all the impersonality of a doctor, slipped a hand into his belt, ran his hands up his sides, slipped a finger under his collar.

"Clean," Mansey said.

"Turn around, you," Magliore said.

He turned around. Magliore was still regarding him with fascination.

"Come here."

He walked over.

Magliore tapped the glass top of his desk. Under the glass there were several snapshots: A dark woman who was grinning into the camera with sunglasses pushed back on top of her wiry hair; olive-skinned kids splashing in a pool; Magliore himself walking along the beach in a black bathing suit, looking like King Farouk, a large collie at his heel.

"Dump out," he said.

"Huh?"

"Everything in your pockets. Dump it out."

He thought of protesting, then thought of Mansey, who was hovering just behind his left shoulder. He dumped out.

From his topcoat pockets, the stubs of the tickets from the last movie he and Mary had gone to. Something with a lot of singing in it, he couldn't remember the name.

He took the his topcoat. From his suit coat, a Zippo lighter with his initials— BGD—engraved on it. A package of flints. A single Phillies Cheroot. A tin of Phillips milk of magnesia tablets. A receipt from A&S Tires, the place that had put on his snow tires. Mansey looked at it and said with some satisfaction: "Christ you got burned."

He took off his jacket. Nothing in his shirt breast pocket but a ball of lint. From the right front pocket of his pants he produced his car keys and forty cents in change, mostly in nickles. For some reason he had never been able to fathom, nickles seemed to gravitate to him. There was never a dime for the parking meter; only nickles, which wouldn't fit. He put his wallet on the glass-topped desk with the rest of his things.

Magliore picked up the wallet and looked at the faded monogram on it—Mary had given it to him on their anniversary four years ago.

"What's the *G* for?" Magliore asked.

"George."

He opened the wallet and dealt the contents out in front of him like a solitaire hand.

Forty-three dollars in twenties and ones.

Credit cards: Shell, Sunoco, Arco, Grant's, Sears, Carey's Department Store, American Express.

Driver's license. Social Security. A blood donor card, type A-positive. Library card. A plastic flip-folder. A photostated birth certificate card. Several old receipted bills, some of them falling apart along the fold seams from age. Stamped checking account deposit slips, some of them going back to June.

"What's the matter with you?" Magliore asked irritably. "Don't you ever clean out your wallet? You load a wallet up like this and carry it around for a year, that wallet's hurting."

He shrugged. "I hate to throw things away." He was thinking that it was strange, how Magliore calling him a shitbird had made him angry, but Magliore criticizing his wallet didn't bother him at all.

Magliore opened the flip-folder, which was filled with snapshots. The top one was of Mary, her eyes crossed, her tongue popped out at the camera. An old picture. She had been slimmer then.

"This your wife?"

"Yeah."

"Bet she's pretty when there ain't a camera stuck in her face."

He flipped up another one and smiled.

"Your little boy? I got one about that age. Can he hit a baseball? Whacko! I guess he can."

"That was my son, yes. He's dead now."

"Too bad. Accident?"

"Brain tumor."

Magliore nodded and looked at the other pictures. Fingernail clippings of a life: The house on Crestallen Street West, he and Tom Granger standing in the laundry washroom, a picture of him at the podium of the launderers' convention the year it had been held in the city (he had introduced the keynote speaker), a backyard barbecue with him standing by the grill in a chef's hat and an apron that said: DAD'S COOKIN', MOM'S LOOKIN'.

Magliore put the flip-folder down, bundled the credit cards into a pile, and gave them to Mansey. "Have them photocopied," he said. "And take one of those deposit slips. His wife keeps the checkbook under lock and key, just like mine." Magliore laughed.

Mansey looked at him skeptically. "Are you going to do business with this shitbird?"

"Don't call him a shitbird and maybe he won't call me a dork again." He uttered a wheezy laugh that ended with unsettling suddenness. "You just mind your business, Petie. Don't tell me mine."

Mansey laughed, but exited in a modified stalk.

Magliore looked at him when the door was closed. He chuckled. He shook his head. "Dork," he said. "By God, I thought I'd been called everything."

"Why is he going to photocopy my credit cards?"

"We have part of a computer. No one owns all of it. People use it on a time-sharing basis. If a person knows the right codes, that person can tap into the memory banks of over fifty corporations that have city business. So I'm going to check on you. If you're a cop, we'll find out. If those credit cards are fake, we'll find out. If they're real but not yours, we'll find that out, too. But you got me convinced. I think you're straight. Dork.'' He shook his head and laughed. ''Was yesterday Monday? Mister, you're lucky you didn't call me a dork on Monday.''

''Can I tell you what I want to buy now?''

''You could, and if you were a cop with six recorders on you, you still couldn't touch me. It's called entrapment. But I don't want to hear it now. You come back tomorrow, same time, same station, and I'll tell you if I want to hear it. Even if youre straight, I may not sell you anything. You know why?''

''Why?''

Magliore laughed. ''Because I think you're a fruitcake. Driving on three wheels. Flying on instruments.''

''Why? Because I called you a name?''

''No,'' Magliore said. ''Because you remind me of something that happened to me when I was a kid about my son's age. There was a dog that lived in the neighborhood where I grew up. Hell's Kitchen, in New York. This was before the Second World War, in the Depression. And this guy named Piazzi had a black mongrel bitch named Andrea, but everybody just called her Mr. Piazzi's dog. He kept her chained up all the time, but that dog never got mean, not until this one hot day in August. It might have been 1937. She jumped a kid that came up to pet her and put him in the hospital for a month. Thirty-seven stitches in his neck. But I knew it was going to happen. That dog was out in the hot sun all day, every day, all summer long. In the middle of June it stopped wagging its tail when kids came up to pet it. Then it started to roll its eyes. By the end of July it would growl way back in its throat when some kid patted it. When it started doing that, I stopped patting Mr. Piazzi's dog. And the guys said, Wassa matta, Sally? You chickenshit? And I said, No, I ain't chickenshit but I ain't stupid, either. That dog's gone mean. And they all said, Up your ass, Mr. Piazzi's dog don't bite, she never bit nobody, she wouldn't bite a baby that stuck its head down her throat. And I said, You go on and pat her, there's no law that says you can't pat a dog, but I ain't gonna. And so they all go around saying, Sally's chickenshit, Sally's a girl, Sally wants his mama to walk him past Mr. Piazzi's dog. You know how kids are.''

''I know,'' he said. Mansey had come back in with his credit cards and was standing by the door, listening.

''And one of the kids who was yelling the loudest was the kid who finally got it. Luigi Bronticelli, his name was. A good Jew like me, you know?'' Magliore laughed. ''He went up to pat Mr. Piazzi's dog one day in August when it was hot enough to fry an egg on the sidewalk, and he ain't talked above a whisper since that day. He's got a barbershop in Manhattan, and they call him Whispering Gee.''

Magliore smiled at him.

''You remind me of Mr. Piazzi's dog. You ain't growling yet, but if someone was to pat you, you'd roll your eyes. And you stopped wagging your tail a long time ago. Pete, give this man his things.''

Mansey gave him the bundle.

"You come back tomorrow and we'll talk some more," Magliore said. He watched him putting things back into his wallet. "And you really ought to clean that mess out. You're racking that wallet all to shit.''

"Maybe I will," he said.

"Pete, show this man out to his car.''

"Sure.''

He had the door open and was stepping out when Magliore called after him: "You know what they did to Mr. Piazzi's dog, mister? They took her to the pound and gassed her.''

After supper, while John Chancellor was telling about how the reduced speed limit on the Jersey Turnpike had probably been responsible for fewer accidents, Mary asked him about the house.

"Termites," he said.

Her face fell like an express elevator. "Oh. No good, huh?''

"Well, I'm going out again tomorrow. If Tom Granger knows a good exterminator, I'll take the guy out with me. Get an expert opinion. Maybe it isn't as bad as it looks.''

"I hope it isn't. A backyard and all . . . '' She trailed off wistfully.

Oh, you're a prince, Freddy said suddenly. A veritable prince. How come you're so good to your wife, George? Was it a natural talent or did you take lessons?

"Shut up," he said.

Mary looked around, startled. "What?''

"Oh . . . Chancellor," he said. "I get so sick of gloom and doom from John Chancellor and Walter Cronkite and the rest of them.''

"You shouldn't hate the messenger because of the message," she said, and looked at John Chancellor with doubtful, troubled eyes.

"I suppose so," he said, and thought: *You bastard, Freddy.*

Freddy told him not to hate the messenger for the message.

They watched the news in silence for a while. A commercial for a cold medicine came on—two men whose heads had been turned into blocks of snot. When one of them took the cold pill, the gray-green cube that had been encasing his head fell off in large lumps.

"Your cold sounds better tonight," he said.

"It is. Bart, what's the realtor's name?''

"Monohan," he said automatically.

"No, not the man that's selling you the plant. The one that's selling the house.''

"Olsen," he said promptly, picking the name out of an internal litter bag.

The news came on again. There was a report on David Ben-Gurion, who was about to join Harry Truman in that great Secretariat in the sky.

"How does Jack like it out there?" she asked presently.

He was going to tell her Jack didn't like it at all and heard himself saying, "Okay, I guess."

John Chancellor closed out with a humorous item about flying saucers over Ohio.

He went to bed at half past ten and must have had the bad dream almost at once—when he woke up the digital clock said:

11:22P.M.

In the dream he had been standing on a corner in Norton—the corner of Venner and Rice Street. He had been standing right under the street sign. Down the street, in front of a candy store, a pink pimpmobile with caribou antlers mounted on the hood had just pulled up. Kids began to run toward it from stoops and porches.

Across the street, a large black dog was chained to the railing of a leaning brick tenement. A little boy was approaching it confidently.

He tried to cry out: *Don't pet that dog! Go get your candy!* But the words wouldn't come out. As if in slow motion, the pimp in the white suit and planter's hat turned to look. His hands were full of candy. The children who had crowded around him turned to look. All the children around the pimp were black, but the little boy approaching the dog was white.

The dog struck, catapulting up from its haunches like a blunt arrow. The boy screamed and staggered backward, hands to his throat. When he turned around, the blood was streaming through his fingers. It was Charlie.

That was when he had wakened.

The dreams. The goddam *dreams*.

His son had been dead three years.

November 28, 1973

It was snowing when he got up, but it had almost stopped by the time he got to the laundry. Tom Granger came running out of the plant in his shirtsleeves, his breath making short, stiff plumes in the cold air. He knew from the expression on Tom's face that it was going to be a crummy day.

"We've got trouble, Bart."

"Bad?"

"Bad enough. Johnny Walker had an accident on his way back from Holiday Inn with his first load. Guy in a Pontiac skidded through a red light on Deakman and hit him dead center. *Kapow.*" He paused and looked aimlessly back toward the loading doors. There was no one there. "The cops said Johnny was in a bad way."

"Holy Christ."

"I got out there fifteen or twenty minutes after it happened. You know the intersection—"

"Yeah, yeah, it's a bitch."

Tom shook his head. "If it wasn't so fucking awful you'd have to laugh. It looks like somebody threw a bomb at a washerwoman. There's Holiday Inn sheets and towels everywhere. Some people were stealing them, the fucking ghouls, can you believe what people will do? And the truck . . . Bart, there's nothing left from the driver's side door up. Just junk. Johnny got thrown."

"Is he at Central?"

"No, St Mary's. Johnny's a Catholic, didn't you know that?"

"You want to drive over with me?"

"I better not. Ron's hollering for pressure on the boiler." He shrugged, embarrassed. "You know Ron. The show must go on."

"All right."

He got back into his car and drove out toward St. Mary's Hospital. Jesus Christ, of all the people for it to happen to. Johnny Walker was the only person left at the laundry besides himself who had been working at the Blue Ribbon in 1953—Johnny, in fact, went back to 1946. The thought lodged in his throat like an omen. He knew from reading the papers that the 784 extension was going to make the dangerous Deakman intersection pretty much obsolete.

His name wasn't Johnny at all, not really. He was Corey Everett Walker—he had seen it on enough time cards to know that. But he had been known as Johnny even twenty years ago. His wife had died in 1956 on a vacation trip in Vermont. Since then he had lived with his brother, who drove a sanitation truck for the city. There were dozens of workers at the Blue Ribbon who called Ron "Stoneballs" behind his back, but Johnny had been the only one to use it to his face and get away with it.

He thought: If Johnny dies, I'm the oldest employee the laundry has got. Held over for a twentieth record-breaking year. Isn't that a sketch, Fred?

Fred didn't think so.

Johnny's brother was sitting in the waiting room of the emergency wing, a tall man with Johnny's features and high complexion, dressed in olive work clothes and a black cloth jacket. He was twirling an olive-colored cap between his knees and looking at the floor. He glanced up at the sound of footsteps.

"You from the laundry?" he asked.

"Yes. You're . . . " He didn't expect the name to come to him, but it did. "Arnie, right?"

"Yeah, Arnie Walker." He shook his head slowly. "I dunno, Mr . . . ?"

"Dawes."

"I dunno, Mr. Dawes. I seen him in one of those examinin rooms. He looked pretty banged up. He ain't a kid anymore. He looked bad."

"I'm very sorry," he said.

"That's a bad corner. It wasn't the other guy's fault. He just skidded in the snow. I don't blame the guy. They say he broke his nose but that was all. It's funny the way those things work out, you know it?"

"Yes."

"I remember one time when I was driving a big rig for Hemingway, this was in the early sixties, and I was on the Indiana Toll Road and I saw—"

The outer door banged open and a priest came in. He stamped snow from his boots and then hurried up the corridor, almost running. Arnie Walker saw him, and his eyes widened and took on the glazed look of shock. He made a whining, gasping noise in his throat and tried to stand up. He put an arm around Arnie's shoulders and restrained him.

"Jesus!" Arnie cried. "He had his pyx, did you see it? He's gonna give him the last rites . . . maybe he's dead already. *Johnny—*"

There were other people in the waiting room: a teenage kid with a broken arm, an elderly woman with an elastic bandage around one leg, a man with his thumb wrapped in a giant dressing. They looked up at Arnie and then down, self-consciously, at their magazines.

"Take it easy," he said meaninglessly.

"Let me go," Arnie said. "I got to go see."

"Listen—"

"Let me go!"

He let him go. Arnie Walker went around the corner and out of sight, the way the priest had gone. He sat in the plastic contour seat for a moment, wondering what to do. He looked at the floor, which was covered with black, slushy tracks. He looked at the nurses' station, where a woman was covering a switchboard. He looked out the window and saw that the snow had stopped.

There was a sobbing scream from up the corridor, where the examining rooms were.

Everybody looked up, and the same half-sick expression was on every face.

Another scream, followed by a harsh, braying cry of grief.

Everyone looked back at their magazines. The kid with the broken arm swallowed audibly, producing a small click in the silence.

He got up and went out quickly, not looking back.

At the laundry everyone on the floor came over, and Ron Stone didn't stop them. I don't know, he told them. I never found out if he was alive or dead. You'll hear. I just don't know.

He fled upstairs, feeling weird and disconnected.

"Do you know how Johnny is, Mr. Dawes?" Phyllis asked him. He noticed for the first time that Phyllis, jaunty blue-rinsed hair notwithstanding, was looking old.

"He's bad," he said. "The priest came to give him the last rites."

"Oh, what a dirty shame. And so close to Christmas."

"Did someone go out to Deakman to pick up his load?"

She looked at him a little reproachfully. "Tom sent out Harry Jones. He brought it in five minutes ago."

"Good," he said, but it wasn't good. It was bad. He thought of going down to the washroom and dumping enough Hexlite into the washers to disintegrate all of it—when the extract ended and Pollack opened the machines there would be nothing but a pile of gray fluff. *That* would be good.

Phyllis had said something and he hadn't heard.

"What? I'm sorry."

"I said that Mr. Ordner called. He wants you to call back right away. And a fellow named Harold Swinnerton. He said the cartridges had come in."

"Harold—?" And then he remembered. Harvey's Gun Shop. Only Harvey, like Marley, was as dead as a doornail. "Yes, right."

He went into his office and closed the door. The sign on his desk still said:

THINK!
It May Be A New Experience

He took it off the desk and dropped it into the wastebasket. *Clunk.*

He sat behind his desk, took everything out of the IN basket and threw it into the wastebasket without looking at it. He paused and looked around the office. The walls were wood-paneled. On the left were two framed degrees: one from college, one from the Laundry Institute, where he had gone during the summers of 1969 and 1970. Behind the desk was a large blow-up of himself shaking hands with Ray Tarkington in the Blue Ribbon parking lot just after it had been hot-topped. He and Ray were smiling. The laundry stood in the background, three trucks backed into the loading bay. The smokestack still looked very white.

He had been in this office since 1967, over six years. Since before Woodstock, before Kent State, before the assassination of Robert Kennedy and Martin Luther King, since before Nixon. Years of his life had been spent between these four walls. Millions of breaths, millions of heartbeats. He looked around, seeing if he felt anything. He felt faintly sad. That was all.

He cleaned out his desk, throwing away personal papers and his personal account books. He wrote his resignation on the back of a printed wash formula and slipped it into a laundry pay envelope. He left the impersonal things—the paper clips, the Scotch tape, the big book of checks, the pile of blank time cards held together with rubber bands.

He got up, took the two degrees off the wall, and threw them into the wastebasket. The glass covering the Laundry Institute diploma shattered. The squares where the degrees had hung all these years were a little brighter than the rest of the wall, and that was all.

The phone rang and he picked it up, thinking it would be Ordner. But it was Ron Stone, calling from downstairs.

"Bart?"

"Yeah."

"Johnny passed away a half hour ago. I guess he never really had a chance."

"I'm very sorry. I want to shut it down the rest of the day, Ron."

Ron sighed. "That's best, I guess. But won't you catch hell from the big bosses?"

"I don't work for the big bosses anymore. I just wrote my resignation." There. It was out. That made it real.

A dead beat of silence on the other end. He could hear the washers and the steady thumping hiss of the ironer. The mangler, they called it, on account of what would happen to you if you ever got caught in it.

"I must have heard you wrong," Ron said finally. "I thought you said—"

"I said it, Ron. I'm through. It's been a pleasure working with you and Tom and even Vinnie, when he could keep his mouth shut. But it's over."

"Hey, listen, Bart. Take it easy. I know this has got you upset—"

"It's not over Johnny," he said, not knowing if it was true or not. Maybe he still would have made an effort to save himself, to save the life that had existed under a protective dome of routine for the last twenty years. But when the priest had walked quickly past them down the hall, almost running, to the place where Johnny lay dying or dead, and when Arnie Walker had made that funny whining noise high up in his throat, he had given up. Like driving a car in a skid, or fooling yourself that you were driving, and then just taking your hands off the wheel and putting them over your eyes.

"It's not over Johnny," he repeated.

"Well, listen . . . listen . . . " Ron sounded very upset.

"Look, I'll talk to you later, Ron," he said, not knowing if he would or not. "Go on, have them punch out."

"Okay. Okay, but—"

He hung up gently.

He took the phone book out of the drawer and looked in the yellow pages under GUNS. He dialed Harvey's Gun Shop.

"Hello, Harvey's."

"This is Barton Dawes," he said.

"Oh, right. Those shells came in late yesterday afternoon. I told you I'd have them in plenty of time for Christmas. Two hundred rounds."

"Good. Listen, I'm going to be awfully busy this afternoon. Are you open tonight?"

"Open nights until nine right up to Christmas."

"Okay. I'll try to get in around eight. If not, tomorrow afternoon for sure."

"Good enough. Listen, did you find out if it was Boca Rio?"

"Boca . . . " Oh, yes, Boca Rio, where his cousin Nick Adams would soon be hunting. "Boca Rio. Yeah, I think it was."

"Jesus, I envy him. That was the best time I ever had in my life."

"Shaky cease-fire holds," he said. A sudden image came to him of Johnny

Walker's head mounted over Stephan Ordner's electric log fireplace, with a small polished bronze plaque beneath, saying:

HOMO LAUNDROMAT
November 28, 1973
Bagged on the corner of Deakman

"What was that?" Harry Swinnerton asked, puzzled.

"I said, I envy him too," he said, and closed his eyes. A wave of nausea raced through him. *I'm cracking up,* he thought. *This is called cracking up.*

"Oh. Well, I'll see you, then."

"Sure. Thanks again, Mr. Swinnerton."

He hung up, opened his eyes, and looked around his denuded office again. He flicked the button on the intercom.

"Phyllis?"

"Yes, Mr. Dawes?"

"Johnny died. We're going to shut it down."

"I saw people leaving and thought he must have." Phyllis sounded as if she might have been crying.

"See if you can get Mr. Ordner on the phone before you go, will you?"

"Surely."

He swiveled around in his chair and looked out the window. A road grader, bright orange, was lumbering by with chains on its oversize wheels, lashing at the road. This is their fault, Freddy. All their fault. I was doing okay until those guys down at City Hall decided to rip up my life. I was doing fine, right, Freddy?

Freddy?

Fred?

The phone rang and he picked it up. "Dawes."

"You've gone crazy," Steve Ordner said flatly. "Right out of your mind."

"What do you mean?"

"I mean that I personally called Mr. Monohan this morning at nine-thirty. The McAn people signed the papers on the Waterford plant at nine o'clock. Now what the fuck happened, Barton?"

"I think we'd better discuss that in person."

"So do I. And I think you ought to know that you're going to have to do some fast talking if you want to save your job."

"Stop playing games with me, Steve."

"What?"

"You've got no intention of keeping me on, not even as the sweeper. I've written my resignation already. It's sealed up, but I can quote it from memory. "I quit. Signed, Barton George Dawes.' "

"But why?" He sounded physically wounded. But he wasn't whining like Arnie Walker. He doubted if Steve Ordner had done any whining since his eleventh birthday. Whining was the last resort of lesser men.

"Two o'clock?" he asked.

"Two is fine."

"Good-bye, Steve."

"Bart—"

He hung up and looked blankly at the wall. After a while, Phyllis poked her head in, looking tired and nervous and bewildered beneath her smart Older Person hairdo. Seeing her boss sitting quietly in his denuded office did nothing to improve her state of mind.

"Mr. Dawes, should I go? I'd be glad to stay, if—"

"No, go on, Phyllis. Go home."

She seemed to be struggling to say something else, and he turned around and looked out the window, hoping to spare them both embarrassment. After a moment, the door snicked closed, very softly.

Downstairs, the boiler whined and died. Motors began to start up in the parking lot.

He sat in his empty office in the empty laundry until it was time to go and see Ordner. He was saying good-byes.

Ordner's office was downtown, in one of the new high-rise office buildings that the energy crisis might soon make obsolete. Seventy stories high, all glass, inefficient to heat in winter, a horror to cool in summer. Amroco's offices were on the fifty-fourth floor.

He parked his car in the basement parking lot, took the escalator up to lobby level, went through a revolving door, and found the right bank of elevators. He rode up with a black woman who had a large Afro. She was wearing a jumper and was holding a steno notebook.

"I like your Afro," he said abruptly, for no reason.

She looked at him coolly and said nothing. Nothing at all.

The reception room of Stephan Ordner's office was furnished with free-form chairs and a redheaded secretary who sat beneath a reproduction of Van Gogh's "Sunflowers." There was an oyster-colored shag rug on the floor. Indirect lighting. Indirect Muzak, piping Mantovani.

The redhead smiled at him. She was wearing a black jumper, and her hair was bound with a hank of gold yarn. "Mr. Dawes?"

"Yes."

"Go right in, please."

He opened the door and went right in. Ordner was writing something at his desk, which was topped with an impressive slab of Lucite. Behind him, a huge window gave on a western view of the city. He looked up and put his pen down. "Hello, Bart," he said quietly.

"Hello."

"Sit down."

"Is this going to take that long?"

Ordner looked at him fixedly. "I'd like to slap you," he said. "Do you know that? I'd like to slap you all the way around this office. Not hit you or beat you up. Just slap you."

"I know that," he said, and did.

"I don't think you have any idea of what you threw away," Ordner said. "I suppose the McAn people got to you. I hope they paid you a lot. Because I had you personally earmarked for an executive vice-presidency in this corporation. That would have paid thirty-five thousand a year to start. I hope they paid you more than that."

"They didn't pay me a cent."

"Is that the truth?"

"Yes."

"Then why, Bart? Why in the name of God?"

"Why should I tell you, Steve?" He took the chair he was supposed to take, the supplicant's chair, on the other side of the big, Lucite-topped desk.

For a moment Ordner seemed to be at a loss. He shook his head the way a fighter will when he has been tagged, but not seriously.

"Because you're my employee. How's that for a start?"

"Not good enough."

"What does that mean?"

"Steve, I was Ray Tarkington's employee. He was a real person. You might not have cared for him, but you had to admit he was real. Sometimes when you were talking to him he broke wind or burped or picked dead skin out of his ear. He had real problems. Sometimes I was one of them. Once, when I made a bad decision about billing a motel out in Crager Plaza, he threw me against a door. You're not like him. The Blue Ribbon is Tinkertoys to you, Steve. You don't care about me. You care about your own upward mobility. So don't give me that employee shit. Don't pretend you stuck your cock in my mouth and I bit it."

If Ordner's face was a facade, there was no crack in it. His features continued to register modulated distress, no more. "Do you really believe that?" Ordner asked.

"Yes. You only give a damn about the Blue Ribbon as it affects your status in the corporation. So let's cut the shit. Here." He slid his resignation across the Lucite top of the desk.

Ordner gave his head another little shake. "And what about the people you've hurt, Bart? The little people. Everything else aside, you were in a position of importance." He seemed to taste the phrase. "What about the people at the laundry who are going to lose their jobs because there's no new plant to switch to?"

He laughed harshly and said: "You cheap son of a bitch. You're too fucking high to see down, aren't you?"

Ordner colored. He said carefully: "You better explain that, Bart."

"Every single wage earner at the laundry, from Tom Granger on down to Pollack in the washroom, has unemployment insurance. It's theirs. They *pay* for it. If you're having trouble with that concept, think of it as a business deduction. Like a four-drink lunch at Benjamin's."

Stung, Ordner said, "That's welfare money and you know it."

He reiterated: "You cheap son of a bitch."

Ordners's hands came together and formed a double fist. They clenched together like the hands of a child that has been taught to say the Lord's Prayer by his bed. "You're overstepping yourself, Bart."

"No, I'm not. You called me here. You asked me to explain. What did you want to hear me say? I'm sorry, I screwed up, I'll make restitution? I can't say that. I'm not sorry. I'm not going to make restitution. And if I screwed up, that's between me and Mary. And she'll never even know, not for sure. Are you going to tell me I hurt the corporation? I don't think even you are capable of such a lie. After a corporation gets to a certain size, nothing can hurt it. It gets to be an act of God. When things are good it makes a huge profit, and when times are bad it just makes a profit, and when things go to hell it takes a tax deduction. Now you *know* that."

Ordner said carefully: "What about your own future? What about Mary's?"

"You don't care about that. It's just a lever you think you might be able to use. Let me ask you something, Steve. Is this going to hurt you? Is it going to cut into your salary? Into your yearly dividend? Into your retirement fund?"

Ordner shook his head. "Go on home, Bart. You're not yourself."

"Why? Because I'm talking about you and not just about bucks?"

"You're disturbed, Bart."

"You don't know," he said, standing up and planting his fists on the Lucite top of Ordner's desk. "You're mad at me but you don't know why. Someone told you that if a situation like this ever came up you should be mad. But you don't know why."

Ordner repeated carefully: "You're disturbed."

"You're damn right I am. What are you?"

"Go home, Bart."

"No, but I'll leave you alone and that's what you want. Just answer one question. For one second stop being the corporation man and answer one question for me. Do you care about this? Does any of it mean a damn to you?"

Ordner looked at him for what seemed a long time. The city was spread out behind him like a kingdom of towers, wrapped in grayness and mist. He said: "No."

"All right," he said softly. He looked at Ordner without animosity. "I didn't do it to screw you. Or the corporation."

"Then why? I answered your question. You answer mine. You could have signed on the Waterford plant. After that it would have been someone else's worry. Why didn't you?"

He said: "I can't explain. I listened to myself. But people talk a different language inside. It sounds like the worst kind of shit if you try to talk about it. But it was the right thing."

Ordner looked at him unflinchingly. "And Mary?"

He was silent.

"Go home, Bart," Ordner said.

"What do you want, Steve?"

Ordner shook his head impatiently. "We're done, Bart. If you want to have an encounter session with someone, go to a bar."

"What do you want from me?"

"Only for you to get out of here and go home."

"What do you want from life, then? Where are you hooked into things?"

"Go home, Bart."

"*Answer me!* What do you *want?*" He looked at Ordner nakedly.

Ordner answered quietly, "I want what everyone wants. Go home, Bart."

He left without looking back. And he never went there again.

When he got to Magliore's Used Cars, it was snowing hard and most of the cars he passed had their headlights on. His windshield wipers beat a steady back-and-forth tune, and beyond their sweep snow that had been defrosted into slush ran down the Saf-T-Glass like tears.

He parked in back and walked around to the office. Before he went in, he looked at his ghostly reflection in the plate glass and scrubbed a thin pink film from his lips. The encounter with Ordner had upset him more than he would have believed. He had picked up a bottle of Pepto-Bismol in a drugstore and had chugged half of it on the way out here. Probably won't shit for a week, Fred. But Freddy wasn't at home. Maybe he had gone to visit Monohan's relatives in Bombay.

The woman behind the adding machine gave him a strange speculative smile and waved him in.

Magliore was alone. He was reading *The Wall Street Journal,* and when he came in, Magliore threw it across the desk and into the wastebasket. It landed with a rattling thump.

"It's going right to fucking *hell,*" Magliore said, as if continuing an interior dialogue that had started some time ago. "All these stockbrokers are old women, just like Paul Harvey says. Will the president resign? Will he? Won't he? Will he? Is GE going to go bankrupt with the energy shortage? It gives me a pain in the ass."

"Yeah," he said, but not sure of what he was agreeing to. He felt uneasy, and he wasn't totally sure Magliore remembered who he was. What should he say? *I'm the guy who called you a dork, remember?* Christ, that was no way to start.

"Snowing harder, ain't it?"

"Yes, it is."

"I hate the snow. My brother, he goes to Puerto Rico November first every year, stays until April fifteenth. He owns forty percent of a hotel there. Says he has to look after his investment. Shit. He wouldn't know how to look after his own ass if you gave him a roll of Charmin. What do you want?"

"Huh?" He jumped a little, and felt guilty.

"You came to me to get something. How can I get it for you if I don't know what it is?"

When it was put with such abrupt baldness, he found it hard to speak. The word for what he wanted seemed to have too many corners to come out of his mouth. He remembered something he had done as a kid and smiled a little.

"What's funny?" Magliore asked with sharp pleasantness. "With business the way it is, I could use a joke."

"Once, when I was a kid, I put a yo-yo in my mouth," he said.

"That's funny?"

"No, I couldn't get it out. *That's* funny. My mother took me to the doctor and he got it out. He pinched my ass and when I opened my mouth to yell, he just yanked it out."

"I ain't going to pinch your ass," Magliore said. "What do you want, Dawes?"

"Explosives," he said.

Magliore looked at him. He rolled his eyes. He started to say something and slapped one of his hanging jowls instead. "Explosives."

"Yes."

"I knew this guy was a fruiter," Magliore told himself. "I told Pete when you left, 'There goes a guy looking for an accident to happen.' That's what I told him."

He said nothing. Talk of accidents made him think of Johnny Walker.

"Okay, Okay, I'll bite. What do you want explosives for? You going to blow up the Egyptian Trade Exposition? You going to skyjack an airplane? Or maybe just blow your mother-in-law to hell?"

"I wouldn't waste explosives on her," he said stiffly, and that made them both laugh, but it didn't break the tension.

"So what is it? Who have you got a hardon against?"

He said: "I don't have a hardon against anyone. If I wanted to kill somebody, I'd buy a gun." Then he remembered he *had* bought a gun, had bought *two* guns, and his Pepto-Bismol-drugged stomach began to roll again.

"So why do you need explosives?"

"I want to blow up a road."

Magliore looked at him with measured incredulity. All his emotions seemed larger than life; it was as if he had adopted his character to fit the magnifying properties of his glasses. "You want to blow up a road? What road?"

"It hasn't been built yet." He was beginning to get a sort of perverse pleasure from this. And of course, it was postponing the inevitable confrontation with Mary.

"So you want to blow up a road that hasn't been built. I had you wrong, mister. You're not a fruitcake. You're a psycho. Can you make sense?"

Picking his words carefully, he said: "They're building a road that's known as the 784 extension. When it's done, the state turnpike will go right through the city. For certain reasons I don't want to go into—because I can't—that road has wrecked twenty years of my life. It's—"

"Because they're gonna knock down the laundry where you work, and your house?"

"How did you know that?"

"I told you I was gonna check you. Did you think I was kidding? I even knew you were gonna lose your job. Maybe before you did."

"No, I knew that a month ago," he said, not thinking about what he was saying.

"And how are you going to do it? Were you planning to just drive past the construction, lighting fuses with your cigar and throwing bundles of dynamite out of your car window?"

"No. Whenever there's a holiday, they leave all their machines at the site. I want to blow them all up. And all three of the new overpasses. I want to blow them up, too."

Magliore goggled at him. He goggled for a long time. Then he threw back his head and laughed. His belly shook and his belt buckle heaved up and down like a chip of wood riding a heavy swell. His laughter was full and hearty and rich. He laughed until tears splurted out of his eyes and then he produced a huge comic-opera handkerchief from some inner pocket and wiped them. He stood watching Magliore laugh and was suddenly very sure that this fat man with the thick glasses was going to sell him the explosives. He watched Magliore with a slight smile on his face. He didn't mind the laughter. Today laughter sounded good.

"Man, you're crazy, all right," Magliore said when his laughter had subsided to chuckles and hitchings. "I wish Pete could have been here to hear this. He's never gonna believe it. Yesterday you call me a d-dork and t-today . . . t-t-today . . . " And he was off again, roaring his laughter, mopping his eyes with his handkerchief.

When his mirth had subsided again, he asked, "How were you gonna finance this little venture, Mr. Dawes? Now that you're no longer gainfully employed?"

That was a funny way to put it. *No longer gainfully employed.* When you said it that way, it really sounded true. He was out of a job. All of this was not a dream.

"I cashed in my life insurance last month," he said. "I'd been paying on a ten-thousand-dollar policy for ten years. I've got about three thousand dollars."

"You've really been planning this for that long?"

"No," he said honestly. "When I cashed the policy in, I wasn't sure what I wanted it for."

"In those days you were still keeping your options open, right? You thought you might burn the road, or machine-gun it to death, or strangle it, or—"

"No. I just didn't know what I was going to do. Now I know."

"Well count me out."

"What?" He blinked at Magliore, honestly stunned. This wasn't in the script. Magliore was supposed to give him a hard time, in a fatherly sort of way. Then sell him the explosive. Magliore was supposed to offer a disclaimer, something like: *If you get caught, I'll deny I ever heard of you.*

"What did you say?"

"I said no. N-o. That spells no." He leaned forward. All the good humor had gone out of his eyes. They were flat and suddenly small in spite of the magnification the glasses caused. They were not the eyes of a jolly Neapolitan Santa Claus at all.

"Listen," he said to Magliore. "If I get caught, I'll deny I ever heard of you. I'll never mention your name."

"The fuck you would. You'd spill your fucking guts and cop an insanity plea. I'd go up for life."

"No, listen—"

"*You* listen," Magliore said. "You're funny up to a point. That point has been got to. I said no, I meant no. No guns, no explosive, no dynamite, no nothing. Because why? Because you're a fruitcake and I'm a businessman. Somebody told you I could 'get' things. I can get them, all right. I've gotten lots of things for lots of people. I've also gotten a few things for myself. In 1946, I got a two-to-five bit for carrying a concealed weapon. Did ten months. In 1952 I got a conspiracy rap, which I beat. In 1955, I got a tax-evasion rap, which I also beat. In 1959 I got a receiving-stolen-property rap which I didn't beat. I did eighteen months in Castleton, but the guy who talked to the grand jury got life in a hole in the ground. Since 1959 I been up three times, case dismissed twice, rap beat once. They'd like to get me again because one more good one and I'm in for twenty years, no time off for good behavior. A man in my condition, the only part of him that comes out after twenty years is his kidneys, which they give to some Norton nigger in the welfare ward. This is some game to you. Crazy, but a game. It's no game to me. You think you're telling the truth when you say you'd keep your mouth shut. But you're lying. Not to me, to *you*. So the answer is flat no." He threw up his hands. "If it had been broads, Jesus, I woulda given you two free just for that floor show you put on yesterday. But I ain't going for any of this."

"All right," he said. His stomach felt worse than ever. He felt like he was going to throw up.

"This place is clean," Magliore said, "and I know it's clean. Furthermore, I know *you're* clean, although God knows you're not going to be if you go on like this. But I'll tell you something. About two years ago, this nigger came to me and said he wanted explosives. He wasn't going to blow up something harmless like a road. He was going to blow up a fucking federal courthouse."

Don't tell me any more, he was thinking. I'm going to puke, I think. His stomach felt full of feathers, all of them tickling at once.

"I sold him the goop," Magliore said. "Some of this, some of that. We dickered. He talked to his guys, I talked to my guys. Money changed hands. A lot of money. The goop changed hands. They caught the guy and two of his buddies before they could hurt anyone, thank God. But I never lost a minute's sleep worrying was he going to spill his guts to the cops or the county prosecutor or the Effa Bee Eye. You know why? Because he was with a whole *bunch* of fruitcakes, nigger fruitcakes, and they're the worst kind, and a *bunch* of fruitcakes is a different proposition altogether. A single nut like you, he doesn't give a shit. He burns out like a lightbulb. But if there are thirty guys and three of them get caught, they just zip up their lips and put things on the back burner."

"All right," he said again. His eyes felt small and hot.

"Listen," Magliore said, a little more quietly. "Three thousand bucks wouldn't buy you what you want, anyway. This is like the black market, you know what I mean?—no pun intended. It would take three or four times that to buy the goop you need.''

He said nothing. He couldn't leave until Magliore dismissed him. This was like a nightmare, only it wasn't. He had to keep telling himself that he wouldn't do something stupid in Magliore's presence, like trying to pinch himself awake.

''Dawes?''

''What?''

''It wouldn't do any good anyway. Don't you know that? You can blow up a person or you can blow up a natural landmark or you can destroy a piece of beautiful art, like that crazy shit that took a hammer to the Pietà, may his dink rot off. But you can't blow up buildings or roads or anything like that. It's what all these crazy niggers don't understand. If you blow up a federal courthouse, the feds build two to take its place—one to replace the blown-up one and one just to rack up each and every black ass that gets busted through the front door. If you go around killing cops, they hire six cops for every one you killed—and every one of the new cops is on the prod for dark meat. You can't win, Dawes. White or black. If you get in the way of that road, they'll plow you under along with your house and your job.''

''I have to go now,'' he heard himself say thickly.

''Yeah, you look bad. You need to get this out of your system. I can get you an old whore if you want her. Old and stupid. You can beat the shit out of her, if you want to. Get rid of the poison. I sort of like you, and—''

He ran. He ran blindly, out the door and through the main office and out into the snow. He stood there shivering, drawing in great white freezing gulps of the snowy air. He was suddenly sure that Magliore would come out after him, collar him, take him back into the office, and talk to him until the end of time. When Gabriel trumpeted in the Apocalypse, Sally One-Eye would still be patiently explaining the invulnerability of all systems everywhere and urging the old whore on him.

When he got home the snow was almost six inches deep. The plows had been by and he had to drive the LTD through a crusted drift of snow to get in the driveway. The LTD made it no sweat. It was a good heavy car.

The house was dark. When he opened the door and stepped in, stamping snow off on the mat, it was also silent. Merv Griffin was not chatting with the celebrities.

''Mary?'' He called. There was no answer. *''Mary?''*

He was willing to think she wasn't home until he heard her crying in the living room. He took off his topcoat and hung it on its hanger in the closet. There was a small box on the floor under the hanger. The box was empty. Mary put it there every winter, to catch drips. He had sometimes wondered: Who cares about drips in a closet? Now the answer came to him, perfect in its simplicity. Mary cared. That's who.

He went into the living room. She was sitting on the couch in front of the blank Zenith TV, crying. She wasn't using a handkerchief. Her hands were at her sides.

She had always been a private weeper, going into the upstairs bedroom to do it, or if it surprised her, hiding her face in her hands or a handkerchief. Seeing her this way made her face seem naked and obscene, the face of a plane crash victim. It twisted his heart.

"Mary," he said softly.

She went on crying, not looking at him. He sat down beside her.

"Mary," he said. "It's not as bad as that. Nothing is." But he wondered.

"It's the end of everything," she said, and the words came out splintered by her crying. Oddly, the beauty she had not achieved for good or lost for good was in her face now, shining. In this moment of the final smash, she was a lovely woman.

"Who told you?"

"Everybody told me!" She cried. She still wouldn't look at him, but one hand came up and made a twisting, beating movement against the air before falling against the leg of her slacks. "Tom Granger called. Then Ron Stone's *wife* called. Then Vincent Mason called. They wanted to know what was wrong with you. And I didn't *know!* I didn't know anything *was* wrong!"

"Mary," he said, and tried to take her hand. She snatched it away as if he might be catching.

"Are you punishing me?" she asked, and finally looked at him. "Is that what you're doing? Punishing me?"

"No," he said urgently. "Oh Mary, no." He wanted to cry now, but that would be wrong. That would be very wrong.

"Because I gave you a dead baby and then a baby with a built-in self-destruct? Do you think I murdered your son? Is that why?"

"Mary, he was *our* son—"

"He was yours!" she screamed at him.

"Don't, Mary. Don't." He tried to hold her and she fought away from him.

"Don't you touch me."

They looked at each other, stunned, as if they had discovered for the first time that there was more to them than they had ever dreamed of—vast white spaces on some interior map.

"Mary, I can't help what I did. Please believe that." But it could have been a lie. Nonetheless, he plunged on: "If it had something to do with Charlie, it did. I've done some things I don't understand. I . . . I cashed in my life insurance policy in October. That was the first thing, the first *real* thing, but things had been happening in my mind long before that. But it was easier to do things than to talk about them. Can you understand that? Can you try?"

"What's going to happen to me, Barton? I don't know anything but being your wife. What's going to happen to me?"

"I don't know."

"It's like you raped me," she said, and began to cry again.

"Mary, please don't do that anymore. Don't . . . try not to do that anymore."

"When you were doing all those *things,* didn't you ever think of me? Didn't you ever think that I *depend* on you?"

He couldn't answer. In a strange, disconnected way it was like talking to Magliore again. It was as if Magliore had beaten him home and put on a girdle and Mary's clothes and a Mary mask. What next? The offer of the old whore?

She stood. "I'm going upstairs. I'm going to lie down."

"Mary—" She did not cut him off, but he discovered there were no words to follow that first.

She left the room and he heard her footsteps going upstairs. After that he heard the creak of her bed as she lay down on it. After that he heard her crying again. He got up and turned on the TV and jacked the volume so he wouldn't be able to hear it. On the TV, Merv Griffin was chatting with celebrities.

PART TWO

December

Ah, love, let us be true
To one another! for the world, which seems
To lie before us like a land of dreams,
So various, so beautiful, so new,
Hath really neither joy, nor love, nor light,
Nor certitude, nor peace, nor help for pain;
And we are here as on a darkling plain
Swept with confused armies of struggle and flight,
Where ignorant armies clash by night.

—MATTHEW ARNOLD
"Dover Beach"

December 5, 1973

He was drinking his private drink, Southern Comfort and Seven-Up, and watching some TV program he didn't know the name of. The hero of the program was either a plainclothes cop or a private detective, and some guy had hit him over the head. This had made the plainclothes cop (or private detective) decide that he was getting close to something. Before he had a chance to say what, there was a commercial for Gravy Train. The man in the commercial was saying that Gravy Train, when mixed with warm water, made its own gravy. He asked the audience if it didn't look just like beef stew. To Barton George Dawes it looked just like a loose bowel movement that somebody had done in a red dog dish. The program came back on. The private eye (or plainclothes police detective) was questioning a black bartender who had a police record. The bartender said *dig*. The bartender said *flake off*. The bartender said *dude*. He was a very hip bartender, all right, but Barton George Dawes thought that the private cop (or plainclothes investigator) had his number.

He was quite drunk, and he was watching television in his shorts and nothing else. The house was hot. He had turned the thermostat to seventy-eight degrees and had left it there ever since Mary left. What energy crisis? Fuck you, Dick. Also the horse you rode in on. Fuck Checkers, too. When he got on the turnpike, he drove at seventy, giving the finger to motorists who honked at him to slow down. The president's consumer expert, some woman who looked as if she might have been a child star in the 1930s before passing time had turned her into a political hermaphrodite, had been on a public-service program two nights ago, talking about the ways!! You & I!! could save electricity around the house. Her name was Virginia Knauer, and she was very big on different ways YOU & I could save energy, because this thing was a real bitch and we were all in it together. When the program was over he had gone into the kitchen and turned on the electric blender. Mrs. Knauer had said that blenders were the second-biggest small appliance energy wasters. He had let the blender run on all night and when he got up the next morning—yesterday morning—the motor had burned out. The greatest electricity waster, Mrs. Knauer had said, were those little electric space heaters. He didn't have an electric space heater, but he had toyed with the idea of getting one so he could run it day and night until it burned up. Possibly, if he was drunk and passed out, it would burn him up, too. That would be the end of the whole silly self-pitying mess.

He poured himself another drink and fell to musing over the old TV programs, the ones they had been running when he and Mary were still practically newlyweds and a brand new RCA console model TV—your ordinary, garden-variety RCA

403

console model black-and-white TV—was something to boggle over. There had been "The Jack Benny Program" and "Amos 'n Andy," those original jiveass niggers. There was "Dragnet," the original "Dragnet" with Ben Alexander for Joe Friday's partner instead of that new guy, Harry somebody. There had been "Highway Patrol," with Broderick Crawford growling ten-four into his mike and everybody driving around in Buicks that still had portholes on the side. "Your Show of Shows." "Your Hit Parade," with Gisele MacKenzie singing things like "Green Door" and "Stranger in Paradise." Rock and roll had killed that one. Or how about the quiz shows, how about them? "Tic-Tac-Dough" and "Twenty-One" every Monday night, starring Jack Barry. People going into isolation booths and putting UN-style earphones on their heads to hear fucking incredible questions they had already been briefed on. "The $64,000 Question," with Hal March. Contestants staggering offstage with their arms full of reference books. "Dotto," with Jack Narz. And Saturday morning programs like "Annie Oakley," who was always saving her kid brother Tag from some Christless mess. He had always wondered if that kid was really her bastard. There was "Rin-Tin-Tin," who operated out of Fort Apache. "Sergeant Preston," who operated out of the Yukon—sort of a roving assignment, you might say. "Range Rider," with Jock Mahoney. "Wild Bill Hickok," with Guy Madison and Andy Devine as Jingles. Mary would say Bart, if people knew you watched all that stuff, they'd think you were feeble. Honestly, a man your age! And he had always replied, I want to be able to talk to my kids, kid. Except there had never been any kids, not really. The first one had been nothing but a dead mess—what was that old joke about putting wheels on miscarriages?—and the second had been Charlie, who it was best not to think of. I'll be seeing you in my dreams, Charlie. Every night it seemed he and his son got together in one dream or another. Barton George Dawes and Charles Frederick Dawes, reunited by the wonders of the subconscious mind. And here we are, folks, back in Disney World's newest head trip, Self-Pity Land, where you can take a gondola ride down The Canal of Tears, visit the Museum of Old Snapshots, and go for a ride in The Wonderful NostalgiaMobile, driven by Fred MacMurray. The last stop on your tour is this wonderful replica of Crestallen Street West. It's right here inside this giant Southern Comfort bottle, preserved for all time. That's right, madam, just duck your head as you walk into the neck. It'll widen out soon. And this is the home of Barton George Dawes, the last living resident of Crestallen Street West. Look right in the window here—just a second, sonny, I'll boost you up. That's George all right, sitting in front of his Zenith color TV in his striped boxer shorts, having a drink and crying. Crying? Of course he's crying. What else would he be doing in Self-Pity Land? He cries all the time. The flow of his tears is regulated by our WORLD-FAMOUS TEAM OF ENGINEERS. On Mondays he just mists a little, because that's a slow night. The rest of the week he cries a lot more. On the weekend he goes into overdrive, and on Christmas we may float him right away. I admit he's a little disgusting, but nontheless, he's one of Self-Pity Land's most popular inhabitants, right up there with our recreation of King Kong atop the Empire State Building. He—

He threw his drink at the television.

He missed by quite a bit. The glass hit the wall, fell to the floor, and shattered. He burst into fresh tears.

Crying, he thought: Look at me, look at me, Jesus you're disgusting. You're such a fucking mess it's beyond belief. You spoiled your whole life and Mary's too and you sit here joking about it, you fucking waste. Jesus, Jesus, Jesus—

He was halfway to the telephone before he could stop himself. The night before, drunk and crying, he had called Mary and begged her to come back. He had begged until she began to cry and hung up on him. It made him squirm and grin to think of it, that he had done such a Godawful embarrassing thing.

He went on to the kitchen, got the dustpan and the whiskbroom, and went back to the living room. He shut off the TV and swept up the glass. He took it into the kitchen, weaving slightly, and dumped it into the trash. Then he stood there, wondering what to do next.

He could hear the insectile buzz of the refrigerator and it frightened him. He went to bed. And dreamed.

December 6, 1973

It was half past three and he was slamming up the turnpike toward home, doing seventy. The day was clear and hard and bright, the temperature in the low thirties. Every day since Mary had left he went for a long ride on the turnpike—in a way, it had become his surrogate work. It soothed him. When the road was unrolling in front of him, its edges clearly marked by the low early winter snowbanks on either side, he was without thought and at peace. Sometimes he sang along with the radio in a lusty, bellowing voice. Often on these trips he thought he should just keep going, letting way lead on to way, getting gas on the credit card. He would drive south and not stop until he ran out of roads or out of land. Could you drive all the way to the tip of South America? He didn't know.

But he always came back. He would get off the turnpike, eat hamburgers and French fries in some pickup restaurant, and then drive into the city, arriving at sunset or just past.

He always drove down Stanton Street, parked, and got out to look at whatever progress the 784 extension had made during the day. The construction company had mounted a special platform for rubberneckers—mostly old men and shoppers with an extra minute—and during the day it was always full. They lined up along the railing like clay ducks in a shooting gallery, the cold vapor pluming from their mouths, gawking at the bulldozers and graders and the surveyors with their sextants and tripods. He could cheerfully have shot all of them.

But at night, with the temperatures down in the 20's, with sunset a bitter orange line in the west and thousands of stars already pricking coldly through the firmament overhead, he could measure the road's progress alone and undisturbed. The moments he spent there were becoming very important to him—he suspected that in an obscure way, the moments spent on the observation platform were recharging him, keeping him tied to a world of at least half-sanity. In those moments before the evening's long plunge into drunkenness had begun, before the inevitable urge to call Mary struck, before he began the evening's activities in Self-Pity Land— he was totally himself, coldly and blinkingly sober. He would curl his hands over the iron pipe and stare down at the construction until his fingers became as unfeeling as the iron itself and it became impossible to tell where the world of himself—the world of human things—ended and the outside world of tractors and cranes and observation platforms began. In those moments there was no need to blubber or pick over the rickrack of the past that jumbled his memory. In those moments he felt his *self* pulsing warmly in the cold indifference of the early-winter evening, a real person, perhaps still whole.

Now, whipping up the turnpike at seventy, still forty miles away from the Westgate tollbooths, he saw a figure standing in the breakdown land just past exit 16, muffled up in a CPO coat and wearing a black knitted watchcap. The figure was holding up a sign that said (amazingly, in all this snow): LAS VEGAS. And underneath that, defiantly: OR BUST!

He slammed on the power brake and felt the seat belt strain a groove in his middle with the swift deceleration, a little exhilarated by the Richard Petty sound of his own squealing tires. He pulled over about twenty yards beyond the figure. It tucked its sign under its arm and ran toward him. Something about the way the figure was running told him the hitchhiker was a girl.

The passenger door opened and she got in.

"Hey, thanks."

"Sure." He glanced in the rearview mirror and pulled out, accelerating back to seventy. The road unrolled in front of him again. "A long way to Vegas."

"It sure is." She smiled at him, the stock smile for people that told her it was a long way to Vegas, and pulled off her gloves. "Do you mind if I smoke?"

"No, go ahead."

She pulled out a box of Marlboros. "Like one?"

"No, thanks."

She stuck a cigarette in her mouth, took a box of kitchen matches from her CPO pocket, lit her smoke, took a huge drag and chuffed it out, fogging part of the windshield, put Marlboros and matches away, loosened the dark blue scarf around her neck and said: "I appreciate the ride. It's cold out there."

"Were you waiting long?"

"About an hour. The last guy was drunk. Man, I was glad to get out."

He nodded. "I'll take you to the end of the turnpike."

"End?" She looked at him. "You're going all the way to Chicago?"

"What? Oh, no." He named his city.

"But the turnpike goes through there." She pulled a Sunoco road map, dog-eared from much thumbing, from her other coat pocket. "The map *says* so."

"Unfold it and look again."

She did so.

"What color is the part of the turnpike we're on now?"

"Green."

"What color is the part going through the city?"

"Dotted green. It's . . . oh, Christ! It's under *construction!*"

"That's right. The world-famous 784 extension. Girl, you'll never get to Las Vegas if you don't read the key to your map."

She bent over it, her nose almost touching the paper. Her skin was clear, perhaps normally milky, but now the cold had brought a bloom to her cheeks and forehead. The tip of her nose was red, and a small drop of water hung beside her left nostril. Her hair was clipped short, and not very well. A home job. A pretty chestnut color. Too bad to cut it, worse to cut it badly. What was that Christmas story by O. Henry? "The Gift of the Magi." Who did you buy a watch chain for, little wanderer?

"The solid green picks up at a place called Landy," she said. "How far is that from where this part ends?"

"About thirty miles."

"Oh *Christ*."

She puzzled over the map some more. Exit 15 flashed by.

"What's the bypass road?" she asked finally. "It just looks like a snarl to me."

"Route 7's best," he said. "It's at the last exit, the one they call Westgate." He hesitated. "But you'd do better to just hang it up for the night. There's a Holiday Inn. We won't get there until almost dark, and you don't want to try hitching up Route 7 after dark."

"Why not?" she asked, looking over at him. Her eyes were green and disconcerting; an eye color you read about occasionally but rarely see.

"It's a city bypass road," he said, taking charge of the passing lane and roaring past a whole line of vehicles doing fifty. Several of them honked at him angrily. "Four lanes with a little bitty concrete divider between them. Two lanes west toward Landy, two lanes east into the city. Lots of shopping centers and hamburger stands and bowling alleys and all that. Everybody is going in short hops. No one wants to stop."

"Yeah." She sighed. "Is there a bus to Landy?"

"There used to be a city bus, but it went bankrupt. I guess there must be a Greyhound—"

"Oh, fuck it." She squidged the map back together and stuffed it into her pocket. She stared at the road, looking put out and worried.

"Can't afford a motel room?"

"Mister, I've got thirteen bucks. I couldn't rent a doghouse."

"You can stay at my house if you want," he said.

"Yeah, and maybe you better let me out right here."

"Never mind. I withdraw the offer."

"Besides, what would your wife think?" She looked pointedly at the wedding ring on his finger. It was a look that suggested she thought he might also hang around school play yards after the monitor had gone home for the day.

"My wife and I are separated."

"Recently?"

"Yes. As of December first."

"And now you've got all these hang-ups that you could use some help with," she said. There was contempt in her voice but it was an old contempt, not aimed specifically at him. "Especially some help from a young chick."

"I don't want to lay anybody," he said truthfully. "I don't even think I could get it up." He realized he had just used two terms that he had never used before a woman in his life, but it seemed all right. Not good or bad but all right, like discussing the weather.

"Is that supposed to be a challenge?" she asked. She drew deeply on her cigarette and exhaled more smoke.

"No," he said. "I suppose it sounds like a line if you're looking for lines. I suppose a girl on her own has to be looking for them all the time."

"This must be part three," she said. There was still mild contempt and hostility in her tone, but now it was cut with a certain tired amusement. "How did a nice girl like you get in a car like this?"

"Oh, to hell with it," he said. "You're impossible."

"That's right, I am." She snuffed her cigarette in his ashtray and then wrinkled her nose. "Look at this. Full of candy wrappers and cellophane and every other kind of shit. Why don't you get a litterbag?"

"Because I don't smoke. If you had just called ahead and said, Barton old boy, I intend to be hitching the turnpike today so give me a ride, would you? And by the way, clear the shit out of your ashtray because I intend to smoke—then I would have emptied it. Why don't you just throw it out the window?"

She was smiling. "You have a nice sense of irony."

"It's my sad life."

"Do you know how long it takes filter tips to biodegrade? Two hundred years, that's how long. By that time your grandchildren will be dead."

He shrugged. "You don't mind me breathing in your used carcinogens, screwing up the cilia in my lungs, but you don't want to throw a filter tip out into the turnpike. Okay."

"What's that supposed to mean?"

"Nothing."

"Listen, do you want to let me out? Is that it?"

"No," he said. "Why don't we just talk about something neutral? The state of the dollar. The state of the Union. The state of Arkansas."

"I think I'd rather catch a little nap if you don't mind. It looks like I'm going to be up most of the night."

"Fine."

She tilted the watchcap over her eyes, folded her arms, and became still. After a few moments her breathing deepened to long strokes. He looked at her in short snatches, shoplifting an image of her. She was wearing blue jeans, tight, faded, thin. They molded her legs closely enough to let him know that she wasn't wearing a second pair or long-handles. They were long legs, folded under the dashboard for comfort, and they were probably blushing lobster red now, itching like hell. He started to ask her if her legs itched, and then thought how it would sound. The thought of her hitchhiking all night on Route 7, either getting rides in short hops or not getting rides at all, made him feel uncomfortable. Night, thin pants, temperatures in the 20's. Well, it was her business. If she got cold enough, she could go in someplace and warm up. No problem.

They passed exits 14 and 13. He stopped looking at her and concentrated on his driving. The speedometer needle stayed pegged at seventy, and he stayed in the passing lane. More cars honked at him. As they passed exit 12, a man in a station wagon which bore a KEEP IT AT 50 bumper sticker honked three times and blipped his lights indignantly. He gave the station wagon the finger.

With her eyes still closed she said: "You're going too fast. That's why they're honking."

"I know why they're doing it."

"But you don't care."

"No."

"Just another concerned citizen," she intoned, "doing his part to rid America of the energy squeeze."

"I don't give a tin weasel about the energy squeeze."

"So say we; so say we all."

"I used to drive at fifty-five on the turnpike. No more, no less. That's where my car got the best mileage. Now I'm protesting the Trained Dog Ethic. Surely you read about it in your sociology courses? Or am I wrong? I took it for granted you were a college kid."

She sat up. "I was a sociology major for a while. Well, sort of. But I never heard of the Trained Dog Ethic."

"That's because I made it up."

"Oh. April Fool." Disgust. She slid back down in the seat and tilted the watch-cap over her eyes again.

"The Trained Dog Ethic, first advanced by Barton George Dawes in late 1973, fully explains such mysteries as the monetary crisis, inflation, the Viet Nam war, and the current energy crisis. Let us take the energy crisis as an example. The American people are the trained dogs, trained in this case to love oil-guzzling toys. Cars, snowmobiles, large boats, dune buggies, motorcycles, minicycles, campers, and many, many more. In the years 1973 to 1980 we will be trained to hate energy toys. The American people love to be trained. Training makes them wag their tails. Use energy. Don't use energy. Go pee on the newspaper. I don't object to saving energy, I object to training."

He found himself thinking of Mr. Piazzi's dog, who had first stopped wagging his tail, had then started rolling his eyes, and had then ripped out Luigi Bronticelli's throat.

"Like Pavlov's dogs," he said. "They were trained to salivate at the sound of a bell. We've been trained to salivate when somebody shows us a Bombardier Ski-doo with overdrive or a Zenith color TV with a motorized antenna. I have one of those at my house. The TV has a Space Command gadget. You can sit in your chair and change the channels, hike the volume or lower it, turn it on or off. I stuck the gadget in my mouth once and pushed the on button and the TV came right on. The signal went right through my brain and still did the job. Technology is wonderful."

"You're crazy," she said.

"I guess so." They passed exit 11.

"I think I'll go to sleep. Tell me when we get to the end."

"Okay."

She folded her arms and closed her eyes again.

They passed exit 10.

"It isn't the Trained Dog Ethic I object to anyway," he said. "It's the fact that the masters are mental, moral, and spiritual idiots."

"You're trying to soothe your conscience with a lot of rhetoric," she said with her eyes still closed. "Why don't you just slow down to fifty? You'll feel better."

"*I will not feel better.*" And he spat it out so vehemently that she sat up and looked at him.

"Are you all right?"

"I'm fine," he said. "I lost my wife and my job because either the world has gone crazy or I have. Then I pick up a hitchhiker—a nineteen-year-old kid for Chrissake, the kind that's supposed to take it for granted that the world's gone crazy—and she tells me it's me, the world is doing just fine. Not much oil, but other than that, just fine."

"I'm twenty-one."

"Good for you," he said bitterly. "If the world's so sane, what's a kid like you doing hitchhiking to Las Vegas in the middle of winter? Planning to spend the whole night hitchhiking along Route 7 and probably getting frostbite in your legs because you're not wearing anything under those pants?"

"I am so wearing something underneath! What do you think I *am?*"

"I think you're *stupid!*" he roared at her. "You're going to freeze your *ass* off!"

"And then you won't be able to get a piece of it, right?" she inquired sweetly.

"Oh boy," he muttered. "Oh boy."

They roared past a sedan moving at fifty. The sedan beeped at him. *"Eat it!"* He yelled. *"Raw!"*

"I think you better let me off right now," she said quietly.

"Never mind," he said. "I'm not going to crash us up. Go to sleep."

She looked at him distrustfully for a long second, then folded her arms and closed her eyes. They went past exit 9.

They passed exit 2 at five after four. The shadows stretching across the road had taken on the peculiar blue cast that is the sole property of winter shadows. Venus was already in the east. The traffic had thickened as they approached the city.

He glanced over toward her and saw she was sitting up, looking out at the hurrying, indifferent automobiles. The car directly in front of them had a Christmas tree lashed to its roof rack. The girl's green eyes were very wide, and for a moment he fell into them and saw out of them in the perfect empathy that comes to human beings at mercifully infrequent intervals. He saw that all the cars were going to someplace where it was warm, someplace where there was business to transact or friends to greet or a loom of family life to pick up and stitch upon. He saw their indifference to strangers. He understood in a brief, cold instant of comprehension what Thomas Carlyle called the great dead locomotive of the world, rushing on and on.

"We're almost there?" she asked.

"Fifteen minutes."

"Listen, if I was hard on you—"

"No, I was hard on you. Listen, I've got nothing in particular to do. I'll take you around to Landy."

"No—"

"Or I'll stick you in the Holiday Inn for the night. No strings attached. Merry Christmas and all that."

"Are you really separated from your wife?"

"Yes."

"And so recently?"

"Yes."

"Has she got your kids?"

"We have no kids." They were coming up on the tollbooths. Their green go-lights twinkled indifferently in the early twilight.

"Take me home with you, then."

"I don't have to do that. I mean, you don't have to—"

"I'd just as soon be with somebody tonight," she said. "And I don't like to hitchhike at night. It's scary."

He slid up to a tollbooth and rolled down his window, letting in cold air. He gave the toll taker his card and a dollar ninety. He pulled out slowly. They passed a reflectorized sign that said:

THANK YOU FOR DRIVING SAFELY!

"All right," he said cautiously. He knew he was probably wrong to keep trying to reassure her—probably achieving just the opposite effect—but he couldn't seem to help it. "Listen, it's just that the house is very lonely by myself. We can have supper, and then maybe watch TV and eat popcorn. You can have the upstairs bedroom and I'll—"

She laughed a little and he glanced at her as they went around the cloverleaf.

But she was hard to see now, a little indistinct. She could have been something he dreamed. The idea bothered him.

"Listen," she said. "I better tell you this right now. That drunk I was riding with? I spent the night with him. He was going on to Stilson, where you picked me up. That was his price."

He paused for the red light at the foot of the cloverleaf.

"My roommate told me it would be like that, but I didn't believe her. I wasn't going to fuck my way across the country, not me." She looked at him fleetingly, but he still couldn't read her face in the gloom. "But it's not people *making* you. It's being so disconnected from everything, like spacewalking. When you come into a big city and think of all the people in there, you want to cry. I don't know why, but you do. It gets so you'd spend the night picking some guy's bleeding pimples just to hear him breathe and talk."

"I don't care who you've been sleeping with," he said and pulled out into traffic. Automatically he turned onto Grand Street, heading for home past the 784 construction.

"This salesman," she said. "He's been married fourteen years. He kept saying that while he was humping me. Fourteen years, Sharon, he keeps saying, fourteen years, fourteen years. He came in about fourteen seconds." She uttered a short bark of laughter, rueful and sad.

"Is that your name? Sharon?"

"No. I guess that was his wife's name."

He pulled over to the curb.

"What are you doing?" she asked, instantly distrustful.

"Nothing much," he said. "This is part of going home. Get out, if you want. I'll show you something."

They got out and walked over to the observation platform, now deserted. He laid his bare hands on the cold iron pipe of the railing and looked down. They had been undercoating today, he saw. The last three working days they had put down gravel. Now undercoat. Deserted equipment—trucks and bulldozers and yellow backhoes—stood silently about in the shades of evening like a museum exhibit of dinosaurs. Here we have the vegetarian stegosaurus, the flesh-eating triceratops, the fearsome earth-munching diesel shovel. *Bon appétit.*

"What do you think of it?" he asked her.

"Am I supposed to think something?" She was fencing, trying to figure this out.

"You must think something," he said.

She shrugged. "It's roadwork, so what? They're building a road in a city I'll probably never be in again. What am I supposed to think? It's ugly."

"Ugly," he echoed, relieved.

"I grew up in Portland, Maine," she said. "We lived in a big apartment building and they put this shopping center up across the street—"

"Did they tear anything down to make it?"

"Huh?"

"Did they—"

"Oh. No, it was just a vacant lot with a big field behind it. I was just six or seven. I thought they were going to go on digging and ripping and plowing forever. And all I could think . . . it's funny . . . all I could think was the poor old earth, it's like they're giving it an enema and they never asked if it wanted one or if there was something wrong. I had some kind of an intestinal infection that year, and I was the block expert on enemas."

"Oh," he said.

"We went over one Sunday when they weren't working and it was a lot like this, very quiet, like a corpse that died in bed. They had part of the foundations laid, and there were all of these yellow metal things sticking out of the cement—"

"Core rods."

"Whatever. And there was lots of pipe and bundles of wire covered with clear plastic wrap and there was a lot of raw dirt around. Funny to think of it that way, whoever heard of cooked dirt, but that's how it looked. Just raw. We played hide-and-go-seek around the place and my mother came over and got us and gave me and my sister hell for it. She said little kids can get into bad trouble around construction. My little sister was only four and she cried her head off. Funny to remember all that. Can we get back in the car now? I'm cold."

"Sure," he said, and they did.

As they drove on she said: "I never thought they'd have anything out of that place but a mess. Then pretty soon the shopping center was all there. I can remember the day they hot-topped the parking lot. And a few days after that some men came with a little push-wagon and made all the yellow parking lines. Then they had a big party and some hot-shit cut a ribbon and everybody started using it and it was just like they never built it. The name of the big department store was Mammoth Mart, and my mom used to go there a lot. Sometimes when Angie and I were with her I'd think of all those orange rods sticking through the cement down in the basement. It was like a secret thought."

He nodded. He knew about secret thoughts.

"What does it mean to you?" she asked.

"I'm still trying to figure that out," he said.

He was going to make TV dinners, but she looked in the freezer and saw the roast and said she'd fix it if he didn't mind waiting for it to cook.

"Sure," he said. "I didn't know how long to cook it or even what temperature."

"Do you miss your wife?"

"Like hell."

"Because you don't know how to cook the roast?" she asked, and he didn't answer that. She baked potatoes and cooked frozen corn. They ate in the breakfast nook and she ate four thick slices of the roast, two potatoes, and two helpings of the corn.

"I haven't eaten like that in a year," she said, lighting a cigarette and looking into her empty plate. "I'll probably heave my guts."

"What have you been eating?"

"Animal crackers."

"What?"

"Animal crackers."

"I thought that's what you said."

"They're cheap," she said. "And they fill you up. They've got a lot of nutrients and stuff, too. It says so right on the box."

"Nutrients my ass. You're getting zits, girl. You're too old for those. Come here."

He led her into the dining room and opened Mary's china cupboard. He took out a silver serving dish and pulled a thick pile of paper money out of it. Her eyes widened.

"Who'd you off, mister?"

"I offed my insurance policy. Here. Here's two hundred bucks. Eat on it."

But she didn't touch the money. "You're nuts," she said. "What do you think I'm going to do to you for two hundred dollars?"

"Nothing."

She laughed.

"All right." He put the money on the sideboard and put the silver serving dish back into the cupboard. "If you don't take it with you in the morning, I'll flush it down the john." But he didn't think he would.

She looked into his face. "You know, I think you would."

He said nothing.

"We'll see," she said. "In the morning."

"In the morning," he echoed.

He was watching "To Tell the Truth" on the television. Two of the contestants were lying about being the world's champion female bronc rider, and one was telling the truth. The panel, which included Soupy Sales, Bill Cullen, Arlene Dahl, and Kitty Carlisle, had to guess which one was telling the truth. Garry Moore, television's only three-hundred-year-old game show host, smiled and cracked jokes and dinged a bell when each panelist's time was up.

The girl was looking out the window. "Hey," she said. "Who lives on this street, anyway? All the houses look dark."

"Me and the Dankmans," he said. "And the Dankmans are moving out January fifth."

"Why?"

"The road," he said. "Would you like a drink?"

"What do you mean, the road?"

"It's coming through here," he said. "This house is going to be somewhere in the middle of the median strip, as near as I can figure."

"That's why you showed me the construction?"

"I guess so. I used to work for a laundry about two miles from here. The Blue Ribbon. It's going through there, too."

"That's why you lost your job? Because the laundry was closing?"

"Not exactly. I was supposed to sign an option on a new plant in a suburb called Waterford and I didn't do it."

"Why not?"

"I couldn't bear to," he said simply. "You want a drink?"

"You don't have to get me drunk," she said.

"Oh, Christ," he said, rolling his eyes. "Your mind runs on just one track, doesn't it?"

There was a moment of uncomfortable silence.

"Screwdrivers are about the only drinks I like. Do you have vodka and orange juice?"

"Yes."

"No pot, I guess."

"No, I've never used it."

He went out into the kitchen and made her a screwdriver. He mixed himself a Comfort and Seven-Up and took them back into the living room. She was playing with the Space Command gadget, and the TV switched from channel to channel, displaying its seven-thirty wares: "To Tell the Truth," snow, "What's My Line," "I Dream of Jeannie," "Gilligan's Island," snow, "I Love Lucy," snow, snow, Julia Child making something with avocados that looked a little like dog whoop, "The New Price Is Right," snow, and then back to Garry Moore, who was daring the panel to discover which of the three contestants was the real author of a book about what it was like to be lost for a month in the forests of Saskatchewan.

He gave her her drink.

"Did you eat beetles, number two?" Kitty Carlisle asked.

"What's the matter with you people?" the girl asked. "No 'Star Trek.' Are you heathens?"

"They run it at four o'clock on channel eight," he said.

"Do you watch it?"

"Sometimes. My wife always watches Merv Griffin."

"I didn't see any beetles," number two said. "If I'd seen any, I would have eaten them." The audience laughed heartily.

"Why did she move out? You don't have to tell me if you don't want to." She looked at him warily, as if the price of his confession might be tiresomely high.

"The same reason I got fired off my job," he said, sitting down.

"Because you didn't buy that plant?"

"No. Because I didn't buy a new house."

"I voted for number two," Soupy Sales said, "because he looks like he'd eat a beetle if he saw one." The audience laughed heartily.

"Didn't . . . wow. Oh, wow." She looked at him over her drink without blinking. The expression in her eyes seemed to be a mixture of awe, admiration, and terror. "Where are you going to go?"

"I don't know."

"You're not working?"

"No."

"What do you do all day?"

"I ride on the turnpike."

"And watch TV at night?"

"And drink. Sometimes I make popcorn. I'm going to make popcorn later on tonight."

"I don't eat popcorn."

"Then I'll eat it."

She punched the off button on the Space Command gadget (he sometimes thought of it as a "module" because today you were encouraged to think of everything that zapped on and off as a module) and the picture on the Zenith twinkled down to a bright dot and then winked out.

"Let me see if I've got this straight," she said. "You threw your wife and your job down the drain—"

"But not necessarily in that order."

"Whatever. You threw them away over this road. Is that right?"

He looked at the blank TV uncomfortably. Even though he rarely followed what was happening on it very closely, it made him uncomfortable to have it off. "I don't know if it is or not," he said. "You can't always understand something just because you did it."

"Was it a protest?"

"I don't *know*. If you're protesting something, it's because you think something else would be better. All those people protested the war because they thought peace would be better. People protest drug laws because they think other drug laws would be fairer or more fun or less harm or . . . I don't know. Why don't you turn the TV on?"

"In a minute." He noticed again how green her eyes were, intent, catlike. "Is it because you hate the road? The technological society it represents? The dehumanizing effect of—"

"No," he said. It was so difficult to be honest, and he wondered why he was even bothering when a lie would end the discussion so much more quickly and neatly. She was like the rest of the kids, like Vinnie, like the people who thought education was truth: she wanted propaganda, complete with charts, not an answer. "I've seen them building roads and buildings all my life. I never even thought about it, except it was a pain in the ass to use a detour or have to cross the street because the sidewalk was ripped up or the construction company was using a wrecking ball."

"But when it hit home . . . to *your* house and your job, you said no."

"I said no all right." But he wasn't sure what he had said no to. Or had he said yes? Yes, finally yes to some destructive impulse that had been part of him all along, as much a built in self-destruct mechanism as Charlie's tumor? He found himself wishing Freddy would come around. Freddy could tell her what she wanted to hear. But Fred had been playing it cool.

"You're either crazy or really remarkable," she said.

"People are only remarkable in books," he said. "Let's have the TV."

She turned it on. He let her pick the show.

"What are you drinking?"

It was quarter of nine. He was tipsy, but not as drunk as he would have been by now alone. He was making popcorn in the kitchen. He liked to watch it pop in the tempered glass popper, rising and rising like snow that had sprung up from the ground rather than come down from the sky.

"Southern Comfort and Seven-Up," he said.

"What?"

He chuckled, embarrassed.

"Can I try one?" She showed him her empty glass and grinned. It was the first completely unselfconscious expression she had shown him since he had picked her up. "You make a lousy screwdriver."

"I know," he said. "Comfort and Seven-Up is my private drink. In public I stick to scotch. Hate scotch."

The popcorn was done, and he poured it into a large plastic bowl.

"Can I have one?"

"Sure."

He mixed her a Comfort and Seven-Up, then poured a melted stick of butter over the popcorn.

"That's going to put a lot of cholesterol in your bloodstream," she said, leaning in the doorway between the kitchen and the dining room. She sipped her drink. "Hey, I *like* this."

"Sure you do. Keep it a secret and you'll always be one up."

He salted the popcorn.

"That cholesterol clogs up your heart," she said. "The passageways for the blood get smaller and smaller and then one day . . . *graaag!*" She clutched dramatically at her bosom and spilled some of her drink on her sweater.

"I metabolize it all away," he told her, and went through the doorway. He brushed her breast (primly bra-ed, by the feel) on the way by. It felt a way Mary's breast hadn't felt in years. It was maybe not such a good way to think.

She ate most of the popcorn.

She started to yawn during the eleven o'clock news, which was mostly about the energy crisis and the White House tapes.

"Go on upstairs," he said. "Go to bed."

She gave him a look.

He said, "We're going to get along good if you stop looking like somebody goosed you every time the word 'bed' comes up. The primary purpose of the Great American Bed is sleeping, not intercoursing."

That made her smile.

"You don't even want to turn down the sheets?"

"You're a big girl."

She looked at him calmly. "You can come up with me if you want," she said. "I decided that an hour ago."

"No . . . but you don't have any idea how attractive the invitation is. I've only slept with three women in my entire life, and the first two were so long ago I can hardly remember them. Before I was married."

"Are you kidding?"

"Not at all."

"Listen, it wouldn't be just because you gave me a ride or let me sleep over or anything like that. Or the money you offered."

"It's good of you to say that," he said, and got up. "You better go up now."

But she didn't follow his suit. "You ought to know why you're not doing it."

"I should?"

"Yes. If you do things and can't explain them—like you said—that might be okay because they still get done. But if you decide not to, you ought to know why."

"All right," he said. He nodded toward the dining room, where the money still lay in the silver dish. "It's the money. You're too young to be off whoring."

"I won't take it," she said promptly.

"I know you won't. That's why *I* won't. I want you to take it."

"Because everybody isn't as nice as you?"

"That's right." He looked at her challengingly.

She shook her head in an exasperated way and stood up. "All right. But you're a bourgeois, you know that?"

"Yes."

She came over and kissed him on the mouth. It was exciting. He could smell her, and the smell was nice. He was almost instantly hard.

"Go on," he said.

"If you reconsider during the night—"

"I won't." He watched her go to the stairs, her feet bare. "Hey?"

She turned, her eyebrows raised.

"What's your name?"

"Olivia, if it matters. Stupid, isn't it? Like Olivia De Haviland."

"No, it's okay. I like it. Night, Olivia."

"Night."

She went up. He heard the light click on, the way he had always heard it when Mary went up before him. If he listened closely, he might be able to hear the quietly maddening sound of her sweater against her skin as she pulled it over her head, or the snap of the catch that held her jeans nipped in to her waist . . .

Using the Space Command module, he turned on the TV.

His penis was still fully erect, uncomfortable. It bulged against the crotch of his pants, what Mary had sometimes called the rock of ages and sometimes the snake-that-turned-to-stone in their younger days, when bed was nothing but another playground sport. He pulled at the folds of his underwear and when it didn't go down, he stood up. After a while the erection wilted and he sat down again.

When the news was over, a movie came on—John Agar in *Brain from Planet Arous*. He fell asleep sitting in front of the TV with the Space Command module still clasped loosely in one hand. A few minutes later there was a stirring beneath the fly of his pants as his erection returned, stealthily, like a murderer revisiting the scene of an ancient crime.

December 7, 1973

But he did go to her in the night.

The dream of Mr. Piazzi's dog came to him, and this time he knew the boy approaching the dog was Charlie before the bitch struck. That made it worse and when Mr. Piazzi's dog lunged, he struggled up from sleep like a man clawing his way out of a shallow, sandy grave.

He clawed at the air, not awake but not asleep either, and he lost his sense of balance on the couch, where he had finally curled up. He tottered miserably on the edge of balance for a moment, disoriented, terrified for his dead son who died over and over again in his dreams.

He fell onto the floor, banging his head and hurting his shoulder, and came awake enough to know he was in his own living room and that the dream was over. The reality was miserable, but not actively terrifying.

What was he doing? A sort of gestalt reality of what he had done to his life came to him, a hideous overview. He had ripped it right down the middle, like a cheap piece of cloth. Nothing was right anymore. He was hurting. He could taste stale Southern Comfort in the back of his throat, and he burped up some acid-tasting sour stuff and swallowed it back.

He began to shiver and seized his knees in a futile effort to stop it. In the night everything was strange. What was he doing, sitting on the floor of his living room and holding his knees and shaking like an old drunk in an alley? Or like a catatonic, a fucking psycho, that was more like it. Was that it? Was he a psycho? Nothing sort of funny and whimsical like a fruitcake or a dork or a rubber crutch but an out-and-out psycho? The thought dumped him into fresh terror. Had he gone to a hoodlum in an effort to get explosives? Was he really hiding two guns out in the garage, one of them big enough to kill an elephant? A little whining noise came out of his throat and he got up tentatively, his bones creaking like those of a very old man.

He went up the stairs without allowing himself to think, and stepped into his bedroom. "Olivia?" he whispered. This was preposterous, like an old-time Rudolph Valentino movie. "Are you awake?"

"Yes," she said. She didn't even sound sleepy. "The clock was keeping me awake. That digital clock. It kept going *click*. I pulled the plug."

"That's all right," he said. It was a ludicrous thing to say. "I had a bad dream."

The sound of covers being thrown back. "Come on. Get in with me."

"I—"

"*Will* you shut up?"

He got in with her. She was naked. They made love. Then slept.

In the morning, the temperature was only 10 degrees. She asked him if he got a newspaper.

"We used to," he said. "Kenny Upslinger delivered it. His family moved to Iowa."

"Iowa, yet," she said, and turned on the radio. A man was giving the weather. Clear and cold.

"Would you like a fried egg?"

"Two, if you've got them."

"Sure. Listen, about last night—"

"Never mind last night. I came. That's very rare for me. I enjoyed it."

He felt a certain sneaking pride, maybe what she had wanted him to feel. He fried the eggs. Two for her, two for him. Toast and coffee. She drank three cups with cream and sugar.

"So what are you going to do?" she asked him when they had both finished.

"Take you out to the highway," he said promptly.

She made an impatient gesture. "Not that. About your *life*."

He grinned. "That sounds serious."

"Not for me," she said. "For you."

"I haven't thought about it," he said. "You know, before"—he accented the word *before* slightly to indicate all of his life and all of its parts he had sailed off the edge of the world—"before the ax fell, I think I must have felt the way some condemned man feels in the death house. Nothing seemed real. It seemed I was living in a glass dream that would go on and on. Now everything seems real. Last night . . . that was very real."

"I'm glad," she said, and she looked glad. "But what will you do now?"

"I really don't know."

She said: "I think that's sad."

"Is it?" he asked. It was a real question.

They were in the car again, driving Route 7 toward Landy. The traffic near the city was stop and go. People were on their way to work. When they passed the construction on the 784 extension, the day's operation was already cranking up. Men in yellow hi-impact plastic construction hats and green rubber boots were climbing into their machines, frozen breath pluming from their mouths. The engine of one of the orange city payloaders cranked, cranked, kicked over with a coughing mortar-explosion sound, cranked again, then roared into a choppy idle. The driver gunned it in irregular bursts like the sound of warfare.

"From up here they look like little boys playing trucks in a sandpile," she said.

Outside the city, traffic smoothed out. She had taken the two hundred dollars with neither embarrassment nor reluctance—with no special eagerness, either. She had slit a small section of the CPO coat's lining, had put the bills inside, and had then sewed the slit back up with a needle and some blue thread from Mary's sewing box. She had refused his offer of a ride to the bus station, saying the money would last longer if she went on hitching.

"So what's a nice girl like you doing in a car like this?" he asked.

"Humh?" She looked at him, bumped out of her own thoughts.

He smiled. "Why you? Why Las Vegas? You're living in the margins same as me. Give me some background."

She shrugged. "There isn't much. I was going to college at the University of New Hampshire, in Durham. That's near Portsmouth. I was a junior this year. Living off campus. With a guy. We got into a heavy drug thing."

"You mean like heroin?"

She laughed merrily. "No, I've never known anyone who did heroin. Us nice middle-class druggies stick to the hallucinogens. Lysergic acid. Mescaline. Peyote a couple of times, STP a couple of times. Chemicals. I did sixteen or eighteen trips between September and November."

"What's it like?" he asked.

"Do you mean, did I have any 'bad trips'?"

"No, I didn't mean that at all," he said defensively.

"There were some bad trips, but they all had good parts. And a lot of the good trips had bad parts. Once I decided I had leukemia. That was scary. But mostly they were just strange. I never saw God. I never wanted to commit suicide. I never tried to kill anyone."

She thought that over for a minute. "Everybody has hyped the shit out of those chemicals. The straights, people like Art Linkletter, say they'll kill you. The freaks say they'll open all the doors you need to open. Like you can find a tunnel into the middle of yourself, as if your soul was like the treasure in an H. Rider Haggard novel. Have you ever read him?"

"I read *She* when I was a kid. Didn't he write that?"

"Yes. Do you think your soul is like an emerald in the middle of an idol's forehead?"

"I never thought about it."

"I don't think so," she said. "I'll tell you the best and the worst that ever happened to me on chemicals. The best was topping out in the apartment one time and watching the wallpaper. There were all these little round dots on the wallpaper and they turned into snow for me. I sat in the living room and watched a snowstorm on the wall for better than an hour. And after a while, I saw this little girl trudging through the snow. She had a kerchief on her head, a very rough material like burlap, and she was holding it like this—" She made a fist under her chin. "I decided she was going home, and bang! I saw a whole street in there, all covered with snow. She went up the street and then up a walk and into a house. That was the best. Sitting in the apartment and watching wallovision. Except Jeff called it headovision.''

"Was Jeff the guy you were living with?"

"Yes. The worst trip was one time I decided to plunge out the sink. I don't know why. You get funny ideas sometimes when you're tripping, except they seem perfectly normal. It seemed like I *had* to plunge the sink. So I got the plunger and did it . . . and all this *shit* came out of the drain. I still don't know how much of it was real shit and how much was head shit. Coffee grounds. An old piece of shirt. Great big hunks of congealed grease. Red stuff that looked like blood. And then the hand. Some guy's hand.''

"A what?"

"A *hand.* I called to Jeff and said, Hey, somebody put somebody down the drain. But he had taken off someplace and I was alone. I plunged like hell and finally got the forearm out. The hand was lying on the porcelain, all spotted with coffee grounds, and there was the forearm, going right down the drain. I went into the living room for a minute to see if Jeff had come back, and when I went into the kitchen again, the arm and the hand was gone. It sort of worried me. Sometimes I dream about it.''

"That's crazy," he said, slowing down as they crossed a bridge that was under construction.

"Chemicals make you crazy," she said. "Sometimes that's a good thing. Mostly it isn't. Anyway, we were into this heavy drug thing. Have you ever seen one of those drawings of what an atom looks like, with the protons and neutrons and electrons going around?''

"Yes."

"Well, it was like our apartment was the nucleus and all the people who drifted in and out were the protons and electrons. People coming and going, drifting in and out, all disconnected, like in *Manhattan Transfer.*''

"I haven't read that one."

"You ought to. Jeff always said Dos Passos was the original gonzo journalist. Freaky book. Anyway, some nights we'd be sitting around watching TV with the sound shut off and a record on the stereo, everyone stoned, people balling in the bedroom, maybe, and you wouldn't even know who the fuck everyone *was.* You know what I mean?''

Thinking of some of the parties he had wandered drunkenly through, as bemused as Alice in Wonderland, he said that he did.

"So one night there was a Bob Hope special on. And everybody was sitting around all smoked up, laughing like hell at all those old one-liners, all those same stock expressions, all that good-natured kidding of the power-crazies in Washington. Just sitting around the tube like all the mommies and daddies back home and I thought well, that's what we went through Viet Nam for, so Bob Hope could close the generation gap. It's just a question of how you're getting high.''

"But you were too pure for all that."

"Pure? No, that wasn't it. But I started to think of the last fifteen years or so like some kind of grotesque Monopoly game. Francis Gary Powers gets shot down in his U-2. Lose one turn. Niggers dispersed by fire hoses in Selma. Go directly to jail. Freedom riders shotgunned in Mississippi, marches, rallies, Lester Maddox with his ax handle, Kennedy getting blown up in Dallas, Viet Nam, more marches, Kent State, student strikes, women's liberation, and all for what? So a bunch of heads can sit around stoned in a crummy apartment watching Bob Hope? Fuck that. So I decided to split."

"What about Jeff?"

She shrugged. "He has a scholarship. He's doing good. He says he's going to come out next summer, but I won't look for him until I see him." There was a peculiar disillusioned expression on her face that probably felt like hardy forebearance on the inside.

"Do you miss him?"

"Every night."

"Why Vegas? Do you know someone out there?"

"No."

"It seems like a funny place for an idealist."

"Is that what you think I am?" She laughed and lit a cigarette. "Maybe. But I don't think an ideal needs any particular setting. I want to see that city. It's so different from the rest of the country that it must be good. But I'm not going to gamble. I'm just going to get a job."

"Then what?"

She blew out smoke and shrugged. They were passing a sign that said:

LANDY 5 MILES

"Try to get something together," she said. "I'm not going to put any dope in my head for a long time and I'm going to quit these." She gestured her cigarette in the air, and it made an accidental circle, as if it knew a different truth. "I'm going to stop pretending my life hasn't started yet. It has. It's twenty percent over. I've drunk the cream."

"Look. There's the turnpike entrance."

He pulled over to the side.

"What about you, man? What are you going to do?"

Carefully, he said: "See what develops. Keep my options open."

She said: "You're not in such hot shape, if you don't mind me saying so."

"No, I don't mind."

"Here. Take this." She was holding out a small aluminum packet between the first and second fingers of her right hand.

He took it and looked at it. The foil caught the bright morning sun and heliographed darts of light at his eyes. "What is it?"

"Product four synthetic mescaline. The heaviest, cleanest chemical ever made." She hesitated. "Maybe you should just flush it down the john when you get home. It might fuck you up worse than you are. But it might help. I've heard of it.''

''Have you ever seen it?''

She smiled bitterly. ''No.''

''Will you do something for me? If you can?''

''If I can.''

''Call me on Christmas day.''

''Why?''

''You're like a book I haven't finished. I want to know how a little more of it comes out. Make it a collect call. Here, I'll write down the number.''

He was fumbling a pen out of his pocket when she said, ''No.''

He looked at her, puzzled and hurt. ''No?''

''I can get the number from directory assistance if I need it. But maybe it would be best not to.''

''Why?''

''I don't know. I like you, but it's like someone put a hurtin' on you. I can't explain. It's like you were going to do something really bonkers.''

''You think I'm a fruitcake,'' he heard himself say. ''Well, fuck you.''

She got out of the car stiffly. He leaned over. ''Olivia—''

''Maybe that's not my name.''

''Maybe it is. Please call.''

''Be careful with that stuff,'' she said, pointing at the little aluminum packet. ''You're space walking, too.''

''Good-bye. Be careful.''

''Careful, what's that?'' The bitter smile again. ''Good-bye, Mr. Dawes. Thanks. You're good in bed, do you mind me saying that? You are. Good-bye.''

She slammed the door closed, crossed Route 7, and stood at the base of the turnpike entrance ramp. He watched her show a thumb to a couple of cars. Neither of them stopped. Then the road was clear and he U-turned, honking once. In the rearview mirror he saw a small facsimile of her wave.

Silly twit, he thought, stuffed full of every strange conceit in the world. Still, when he put his hand out to turn on the radio, the fingers trembled.

He drove back to the city, got on the turnpike, and drove two hundred miles at seventy. Once he almost threw the small aluminum packet out the window. Once he almost took the pill inside. At last he just put it in his coat pocket.

When he got home he felt washed out, empty of emotion. The 784 extension had progressed during the day; in a couple of weeks the laundry would be ready for the wrecking ball. They had already taken out the heavy equipment. Tom Granger had told him about that in an odd, stilted phone conversation three nights ago. When they leveled it he would spend the day watching. He would even pack a bag lunch.

There was a letter for Mary from her brother in Jacksonville. He didn't know about the split, then. He put it aside absently with some other mail for Mary that he kept forgetting to forward.

He put a TV dinner in the oven and thought about making himself a drink. He decided not to. He wanted to think about his sexual encounter with the girl the night before, relish it, explore its nuances. A few drinks and it would take on the unnatural, fevered color of a bad sex movie—*Restless Coeds, ID Required*—and he didn't want to think of her like that.

But it wouldn't come, not the way he wanted it. He couldn't remember the precise tight feel of her breasts or the secret taste of her nipples. He knew that the actual friction of intercourse had been more pleasurable with her than with Mary. Olivia had been a snugger fit, and once his penis had popped out of her vagina with an audible sound, like the pop of a champagne cork. But he couldn't really say what the pleasure had been. Instead of being able to feel it, he wanted to masturbate. The desire disgusted him. Furthermore, his disgust disgusted him. She wasn't holy, he assured himself as he sat down to eat his TV dinner. Just a tramp on the bum. To Las Vegas, yet. He found himself wishing that he could view the whole incident with Magliore's jaundiced eye, and that disgusted him most of all.

Later that night he got drunk in spite of all his good intentions, and around ten o'clock the familiar maudlin urge to call Mary rose up in him. He masturbated instead, in front of the TV, and came to climax while an announcer was showing incontrovertibly that Anacin hit and held the highest pain-relief level of any brand.

December 8, 1973

He didn't go riding Saturday. He wandered uselessly around the house, putting off the thing that had to be done. At last he called the home of his in-laws. Lester and Jean Calloway, Mary's parents, were both nearing their seventies. On his previous calls, Jean (whom Charlie had always called "Mamma Jean") had answered the telephone, her voice freezing to ice chips when she realized who was on the line. To her, and to Lester also, undoubtedly, he was like some animal that had run amok and bitten her daughter. Now the animal kept calling up, obviously drunk, whining for their girl to come back so he could bite her again.

He heard Mary herself answer, "Hello?" with enough relief so he could talk normally.

"Me, Mary."

"Oh, Bart. How are you?" Impossible to read her voice.

"Fair."

"How are the Southern Comfort supplies holding out?"

"Mary, I'm not drinking."

"Is that a victory?" She sounded cold, and he felt a touch of panic, mostly that his judgment had been impossibly bad. Could someone he had known so long and whom he thought he knew so well be slipping away so easily?

"I guess it is," he said lamely.

"I understand the laundry had to close down," she said.

"Probably just temporary." He had the weird sensation that he was riding in an elevator, conversing uncomfortably with someone who regarded him as a bore.

"That isn't what Tom Granger's wife said." There, accusation at last. Accusation was better than nothing.

"Tom won't have any problem. The competition uptown has been after him for years. The Brite-Kleen people."

He thought she sighed. "Why did you call, Bart?"

"I think we ought to get together," he said carefully. "We have to talk this over, Mary."

"Do you mean a divorce?" She said it calmly enough, but he thought it was her voice in which he sensed panic now.

"Do you want one?"

"I don't know *what* I want." Her calm fractured and she sounded angry and scared. "I thought everything was fine. I was happy and I thought you were. Now, all at once, that's all changed."

"You thought everything was fine," he repeated. He was suddenly furious with her. "You must have been pretty stupid if you thought that. Did you think I kicked away my job for a practical joke, like a high school senior throwing a cherry bomb into a toilet?"

"Then what is it, Bart? What happened?"

His anger collapsed like a rotten yellow snowbank and he found that there were tears beneath. He fought them grimly, feeling betrayed. This wasn't supposed to happen sober. When you were sober you should be able to keep fucking control of yourself. But here he was, wanting to spill out everything and sob on her lap like a kid with a busted skate and a skinned knee. But he couldn't tell her what was wrong because he didn't precisely know and crying without knowing was too much like it's-time-for-the-loony-bin stuff.

"I don't know," he said finally.

"Charlie?"

Helplessly, he said: "If that was part of it, how could you be so blind to the rest of it?"

"I miss him too, Bart. Still. Every day."

Resentment again. *You've got a funny way of showing it, then.*

"This is no good," he said finally. Tears were trickling down his cheeks but he had kept them out of his voice. *Gentlemen, I think we've got it licked,* he thought, and almost cackled. "Not over the phone, I called to suggest lunch on Monday. Handy Andy's."

"All right. What time?"

"It doesn't matter. I can get off work." The joke fell to the floor and died blood-lessly there.

"One o'clock?" she asked.

"Sure. I'll get us a table."

"Reserve one. Don't just get there at eleven and start drinking."

"I won't," he said humbly, knowing he probably would.

There was a pause. There seemed nothing else to say. Faintly, almost lost in the hum of the open wire, ghostly other voices discussed ghostly other things. Then she said something that surprised him totally.

"Bart, you need to see a psychiatrist."

"I need a what?"

"Psychiatrist. I know how that sounds, just coming out flat. But I want you to know that whatever we decide, I won't come back and live with you unless you agree."

"Good-bye, Mary," he said slowly. "I'll see you on Monday."

"Bart, you need help I can't give."

Carefully, inserting the knife as well as he could over two miles of blind wire, he said: "I knew that anyway. Good-bye, Mary."

He hung up before he could hear the result and caught himself feeling glad. Game, set, and match. He threw a plastic milk pitcher across the room and caught himself feeling glad that he hadn't thrown something breakable. He opened the cupboard over the sink, yanked out the first two glasses his hands came to, and threw them on the floor. They shattered.

Baby, you fucking baby! he screamed at himself. *Why don't you just hold your fucking breath until you turn fucking BLUE?*

He slammed his right fist against the wall to shut out the voice and cried out at the pain. He held his wounded right in his left and stood in the middle of the floor, trembling. When he had himself under control he got a dustpan and the broom and swept the mess up, feeling scared and sullen and hung over.

December 9, 1973

He got on the turnpike, drove a hundred and fifty miles, and then drove back. He didn't dare drive any farther. It was the first gasless Sunday and all the turnpike pit stops were closed. And he didn't want to walk. See? He told himself. This is how they get shitbirds like you, Georgie.

Fred? Is that really you? To what do I owe the honor of this visit, Freddy?

Fuck off, buddy.

On the way home he heard this public service ad on the radio:

"So you're worried about the gasoline shortage and you want to make sure that you and your family aren't caught short this winter. So now you're on your way to your neighborhood gas station with a dozen five-gallon cans. But if you're really worried about your family, you better turn around and go back home. Improper storage of gasoline is dangerous. It's also illegal, but never mind that for a minute. Consider this: When gasoline fumes mix with the air, they become explosive. And one gallon of gas has the explosive potential of twelve sticks of dynamite. Think about that before you fill those cans. And then think about your family. You see— we want you to live.

"This has been a public service announcement from WLDM. The Music People remind you to leave gasoline storage to the people who are equipped to do it properly."

He turned off the radio, slowed down to fifty, and pulled back into the cruising lane. "Twelve sticks of dynamite," he said. "Man, that's amazing."

If he had looked into the rearview mirror, he would have seen that he was grinning.

December 10, 1973

He got to Handy Andy's at just past eleven-thirty and the headwaiter gave him a table beside the stylized batwings that led to the lounge—not a good table, but one of the few empties left as the place filled up for lunch. Handy Andy's specialized in steaks, chops, and something called the Andyburger, which looked a little like a chef's salad stuck between a huge sesame seed roll with a toothpick to hold the whole contraption together. Like all big city restaurants within executive walking distance, it went through indefinable cycles of inness and outness. Two months ago he could have come in here at noon and had his pick of tables—three months hence he might be able to do the same. To him, it had always been one of life's minor mysteries, like the incidents in the books of Charles Fort, or the instinct that always brought the swallows back to Capistrano.

He looked around quickly as he sat down, afraid he would see Vinnie Mason or Steve Ordner or some other laundry executive. But the place was stuffed with strangers. To his left, a young man was trying to persuade his girl that they could afford three days in Sun Valley this February. The rest of the room's conversation was just soft babble—soothing.

"A drink, sir?" The waiter was at his elbow.

"Scotch-rocks, please," he said.

"Very good, sir," the waiter said.

He made the first one last until noon, killed two more by twelve-thirty, and then, just mulishly, he ordered a double. He was just draining it dry when he saw Mary walk in and pause in the door between the foyer and the dining room, looking for him. Heads turned to look at her and he thought: *Mary, you ought to thank me— you're beautiful.* He raised his right hand and waved.

She raised her hand in return greeting and came to his table. She was wearing a knee-length wool dress, soft patterned gray. Her hair was braided in a single thick cable that hung down to her shoulder blades, a way he could not recall having seen her wear it (and maybe worn that way for just that reason). It made her look youthful, and he had a sudden guilty flash of Olivia, working beneath him on the bed he and Mary had shared so often.

"Hello, Bart," she said.

"Hi. You look awful pretty."

"Thanks."

"Do you want a drink?"

"No . . . just an Andyburger. How long have you been here?"

"Oh, not long."

The lunch crowd had thinned, and his waiter appeared almost at once. "Would you like to order now, sir?"

"Yes. Two Andyburgers. Milk for the lady. Another double for myself." He glanced at Mary, but her face showed nothing. That was bad. If she had spoken, he would have canceled the double. He hoped he wouldn't have to go to the bathroom, because he wasn't sure he could walk straight. That would be a wonderful tidbit to carry back to the old folks at home. Carry me back to Ol' Virginnie. He almost giggled.

"Well, you're not drunk, but you're on your way," she said, and unfolded her napkin on her lap.

"That's pretty good," he said. "Did you rehearse it?"

"Bart, let's not fight."

"No," he agreed.

She toyed with her water glass; he picked at his coaster.

"Well?" she said finally.

"Well what?"

"You seemed to have something in mind when you called. Now that you're full of Dutch courage, what is it?"

"Your cold is better," he said idiotically, and tore a hole in his coaster without meaning to. He couldn't tell her what was on the top of his mind: how she seemed to have changed, how she seemed suddenly sophisticated and dangerous, like a cruising secretary who has bartered for a later lunch hour and who would refuse any offer of a drink unless it came from a man inside a four-hundred-dollar suit. And who could tell just by glancing at the cut of the fabric.

"Bart, what are we going to do?"

"I'll see a psychiatrist if you want me to," he said, lowering his voice.

"When?"

"Pretty soon."

"You can make an appointment this afternoon if you want to."

"I don't know any shr—any."

"There's the Yellow Pages."

"That seems like a half-assed sort of way to pick a brainpeeker."

She only looked at him and he looked away, uncomfortable.

"You're angry with me, aren't you?" she asked.

"Yeah, well, I'm not working. Fifty dollars an hour seems sort of high for an unemployed fellow."

"What do you think I'm living on?" she asked sharply. "My folks' charity. And as you'll recall, they're both retired."

"As I recall, your father's got enough shares in SOI and Beechcraft to keep the three of you on easy street well into the next century."

"Bart, that's not so." She sounded startled and hurt.

"Bull*shit* it's not. They were in Jamaica last winter, Miami the year before that, at the Fountainbleau no less, and Honolulu the year before *that*. Nobody does that on a retired engineer's salary. So don't give me that poorbox routine, Mary—"

"Stop it, Bart. The green's showing."

"Not to mention a Cadillac Gran DeVille and a Bonneville station wagon. Not bad. Which one do they use when they go to pick up their food stamps?"

"*Stop it!*" she hissed at him, her lips drawn back a bit from her small white teeth, her fingers gripping the edge of the table.

"Sorry," he muttered.

"Lunch is coming."

The temperature between them cooled a little as the waiter set their Andyburgers and French fries before them, added minuscule dishes of green peas and baby onions, then retired. They ate without speaking for a while, both concentrating on not drooling down their chins or in their laps. I wonder how many marriages the Andyburger has saved? he wondered. Simply by its one providential attribute—when you're eating one you have to shut up.

She put hers down half-eaten, blotted her mouth with her napkin, and said, "They're as good as I remember. Bart, do you have any sensible idea at all about what to do?"

"Of course I do," he said, stung. But he didn't know what his idea was. If he'd gotten in another double, he might have.

"Do you want a divorce?"

"No," he said. Something positive seemed to be called for.

"Do you want me to come back?"

"Do you want to?"

"I don't know," she said. "Shall I tell you something, Bart? I'm worried about myself for the first time in twenty years. I'm *fending* for myself." She started to take a bite of her Andyburger, then set it down again. "Did you know I almost didn't marry you? Had that thought ever crossed your mind?"

The surprise on his face seemed to satisfy her.

"I didn't think it had. I was pregnant, so of course I wanted to marry you. But part of me didn't. Something kept whispering that it would be the worst mistake of my life. So I roasted myself over a slow fire for three days, throwing up every morning when I woke up, hating *you* for that, thinking this, that, and the other. Run away. Get an abortion. Have the baby and put it up for adoption. Have the baby and keep it. But I finally decided to do the sensible thing. The sensible thing." She laughed. "And then lost the baby anyway."

"Yes, you did," he muttered, wishing the conversation would turn from this. It was too much like opening a closet and stepping into puke.

"But I was happy with you, Bart."

"Were you?" he asked automatically. He found he wanted to get away. This wasn't working. Not for him anyway.

"Yes. But something happens to a woman in marriage that doesn't happen to a man. Do you remember when you were a child how you never worried about your parents? You just expected them to be there and they were, same as the food and the heat and the clothes."

"I guess so. Sure."

"And I went and got my silly self pregnant. And for three days a whole new world opened up around me." She was leaning forward, her eyes glowing and anxious, and he realized with dawning shock that this recitation was *important* to her, that it was more than getting together with her childless friends or deciding which pair of slacks to buy in Banberry's or guessing which celebrities Merv would be chatting with at four-thirty. This was *important* to her, and had she really gone through twenty years of marriage with only this one important thought? *Had* she? She had almost said as much. Twenty years, my God. He felt suddenly sick to his stomach. He liked the image of her picking up the empty bottle and waving it at him gleefully from her side of the road so much better.

"I saw myself as an independent person," she was saying. "An independent person with no one to explain myself to or subordinate myself to. No one around to try and change me, because I knew I *could* be changed. I was always weak that way. But also no one to fall back on when I was sick or scared or maybe broke. So I did the sensible thing. Like my mother and *her* mother. Like my friends. I was tired of being a bridesmaid and trying to catch the bouquet. So I said yes, which was what you expected and things went on. There were no worries, and when the baby died and when Charlie died there was you. And you were always good to me. I know that, I appreciate that. But it was a sealed environment. I stopped thinking. I thought I was thinking, but I wasn't. And now it hurts to think. It *hurts*." She looked at him with bright resentment for a minute, and then it faded. "So I'm asking you to think for me, Bart. What do we do now?"

"I'm going to get a job," he lied.

"A job."

"And see a psychiatrist. Mary, things are going to be fine. Honest. I was a little off the beam, but I'm going to get back on. I'm—"

"Do you want me to come home?"

"In a couple of weeks, sure. I just have to get things together a little and—"

"Home? What am I talking about? They're going to tear it down. What am I talking about, home? Jesus," she groaned, "what a mess. Why did you have to drag me into such a shitty mess?"

He couldn't stand her this way. She wasn't like Mary, not at all. "Maybe they won't," he said, taking her hand across the table. "Maybe they won't tear it down, Mary, they might change their minds, if I go and talk to them, explain the situation, they might just—"

She jerked her hand away. She was looking at him, horrified.

"Bart," she whispered.

"What—" He broke off, uncertain. What had he been saying? What could he possibly have been saying to make her look so awful?

"You *know* they're going to tear it down. You knew it a long time ago. And we're sitting here, going around and around—"

"No, we're not," he said. "We're not. Really. We're not. We . . . we . . . " But what *were* they doing? He felt unreal.

"Bart, I think I better go now."

"I'm going to get a job—"

"I'll talk to you." She got up hastily, her thigh bumping the edge of the table, making the silverware gossip.

"The psychiatrist, Mary, I promise—"

"Mamma wanted me to go to the store—"

"*Then go on!*" he shouted at her, and heads turned. "Get out of here, you bitch! You had the best of me and what have I got? A house the city's going to rip down. Get out of my *sight!*"

She fled. The room was horribly quiet for what seemed like eternity. Then the talk picked up again. He looked down at his dripping half-eaten hamburger, trembling, afraid he was going to vomit. When he knew he was not, he paid the check and left without looking around.

December 12, 1973

He made out a Christmas list the night before (drunk) and was now downtown filling an abridged version. The completed list had been staggering—over a hundred and twenty names, including every relative near and distant that he and Mary had between them, a great many friends and acquaintances, and at the bottom—God save the queen—Steve Ordner, his wife, and their for Chrissakes *maid*.

He had pruned most of the names from the list, chuckling bemusedly over some of them, and now strolled slowly past windows filled with Christmas goodies, all to be given in the name of that long-ago Dutch thief who used to slide down people's chimneys and steal everything they owned. One gloved hand patted a five-hundred dollar roll of ten-dollar bills in his pocket.

He was living on the insurance money, and the first thousand dollars of it had melted away with amazing speed. He estimated that he would be broke by the middle of March at this rate, possibly sooner, but found the thought didn't bother him at all. The thought of where he might be or what he might be doing in March was as incomprehensible as calculus.

He went into a jewelry store and bought a beaten-silver owl pin for Mary. The owl had coldly flashing diamond chips for eyes. It cost one hundred and fifty dollars, plus tax. The saleslady was effusive. She was sure his wife was going to love it. He smiled. There goes three appointments with Dr. Psycho, Freddy. What do you think about that?

Freddy wasn't talking.

He went into a large department store and took an escalator up to the toy department, which was dominated by a huge electric train display—green plastic hills honeycombed with tunnels, plastic train stations, overpasses, underpasses, switching points, and a Lionel locomotive that bustled through all of it, puffing ribbons of synthetic smoke from its stack and hauling a long line of freight cars— B&O, SOO LINE, GREAT NORTHERN, GREAT WESTERN, WARNER BROTHERS (WAR- NER BROTHERS??), DIAMOND INTERNATIONAL, SOUTHERN PACIFIC. Young boys and their fathers were standing by the wooden picket fence that surrounded the display, and he felt a warm surge of love for them that was untainted by envy. He felt he could have gone to them, told them of his love for them, his thankfulness for them and the season. He would also have urged them to be careful.

He wandered down an aisle of dolls, and picked one up for each of his three nieces: Chatty Cathy for Tina, Maisie the Acrobat for Cindy, and a Barbie for Sylvia, who was eleven now. In the next aisle he got a GI Joe for Bill, and after some deliberation, a chess set for Andy. Andy was twelve, an object of some worry in the family. Old Bea from Baltimore had confided in Mary that she kept finding stiff places on Andy's sheets. Could it be possible? So early? Mary had told Bea that children were getting more precocious every year. Bea said she supposed it was all the milk they drank, and vitamins, but she *did* wish Andy liked team sports more. Or summer camp. Or horseback riding. Or anything.

Never mind, Andy, he thought, tucking the chess set under his arm. You practice knight's gambits and queen to rook-4 and beat off under the table if you want to.

There was a huge Santa Claus throne at the front of the toy department. The throne was empty, and a sign was propped on an easel in front of it. The sign said:

SANTA IS HAVING LUNCH AT OUR FAMOUS
"MID-TOWN GRILL"

Why Not Join Him?

There was a young man in a denim jacket and jeans looking at the throne, his arms full of packages, and when the young man turned around, he saw it was Vinnie Mason.

"Vinnie!" he said.

Vinnie smiled and colored a little, as if he had been caught doing something a bit nasty. "Hello, Bart," he said, and walked over. There was no embarrassment over shaking hands; their arms were too full of packages.

"Christmas shopping a little?" he asked Vinnie.

"Yeah." He chuckled. "I brought Sharon and Bobbie—that's my daughter Roberta—over to look on Saturday. Bobbie's three now. We wanted to get her picture taken with Santa Claus. You know they do that on Saturdays. Just a buck. But she wouldn't do it. Cried her head off. Sharon was a little upset."

"Well, it's a strange man with a big beard. The little ones get scared sometimes. Maybe she'll go to him next year."

"Maybe." Vinnie smiled briefly.

He smiled back, thinking it was much easier with Vinnie now. He wanted to tell Vinnie not to hate his guts too much. He wanted to tell Vinnie he was sorry if he had fucked up Vinnie's life. "So what are you doing these days, Vinnie?"

Vinnie absolutely beamed. "You won't believe this, it's so good. I'm managing a movie theater. And by next summer I'll be handling three more."

"Media Associates?" It was one of the corporation's companies.

"That's right. We're part of the Cinemate Releasing chain. They send in all the movies . . . proven box-office stuff. But I'm handling the Westfall Cinema completely."

"They're going to add on?"

"Yeah, Cinema II and III by next summer. And the Beacon Drive-In, I'll be handling that, too."

He hesitated. "Vinnie, you tell me if I'm stepping out of line, but if this Cinemate outfit picks the films and books them, then what exactly do you do?"

"Well, handle the money, of course. And order stuff, that's very important. Did you know that the candy stand *alone* can almost pay for one night's film rental if it's handled efficiently? Then there's maintenance and—" He swelled visibly, "and hiring and firing. It's going to keep me busy. Sharon likes it because she's a big movie freak, especially Paul Newman and Clint Eastwood. I like it because all of a sudden I jumped from nine thousand to eleven thousand-five."

He looked at Vinnie dully for a moment, wondering if he should speak. This was Ordner's prize, then. Good doggie. Here's the bone.

"Get out of it, Vinnie," he said. "Get out of it just as quick as you can."

"What, Bart?" Vinnie's brow wrinkled in honest puzzlement.

"Do you know what the word 'gofer' means, Vinnie?"

"Gopher? Sure. It's a little animal that digs holes—"

"No, gofer. G-O-F-E-R."

"I guess I don't know that one, Bart. Is it Jewish?"

"No, it's white-collar. It's a person who does errands. A glorified office boy. Gofer coffee, gofer Danish, gofer a walk around the block, sonny. Gofer."

"What are you talking about, Bart? I mean—"

"I mean that Steve Ordner kicked your special case around with the other members of the board—the ones who matter, anyway—and said, Listen, fellas, we've got to do something about Vincent Mason, and it's a delicate sort of case. He warned us that Bart Dawes was riding a rubber bike, and even though Mason didn't swing quite enough weight to enable us to stop Dawes before he screwed up the waterworks, we owe this Mason something. But of course we can't give him too much responsibility. And do you know why, Vinnie?"

Vinnie was looking at him resentfully. "I know I don't have to eat your shit anymore, Bart. I know that."

He looked at Vinnie earnestly. "I'm not trying to shit you. What you do doesn't mean anything to me anymore. But Chrissakes, Vinnie, you're a young man. I don't want to see him fuck you over this way. The job you've got is a short-term plum, a long-term lemon. The toughest decision you're going to have is when to reorder Buttercup containers and Milky Ways. And Ordner's going to see that it stays that way as long as you're with the corporation."

The Christmas spirit, if that was what it had been, curdled in Vinnie's eyes. He was clutching his packages tightly enough to make the wrappings crackle, and his eyes were gray with resentment. Picture of a young man who steps out his door whistling, ready for the evening's heavy date, only to see all four tires on his new sports car have been slashed. *And he's not listening. I could play him tapes and he still wouldn't believe it.*

"As it turned out, you did the responsible thing," he went on. "I don't know what people are saying about me now—"

"They're saying you're crazy, Bart," Vinnie said in a thin, hostile voice.

"That word's as good as any. So you were right. But you were wrong, too. You spilled your guts. They don't give positions of responsibility to people who spill their guts, not even when they were right to do it, not even when the corporation suffers because of their silence. Those guys on the fortieth floor, Vinnie, they're like doctors. And they don't like loose talk any more than doctors like an intern that goes around blowing off about a doctor who muffed an operation because he had too many cocktails at lunch.''

"You're really determined to mess up my life, aren't you?'' Vinnie asked. "But I don't work for you anymore, Bart. Go waste your poison on someone else.''

Santa Claus was coming back, a huge bag slung over one shoulder, bellowing wild laughter and trailing small children like parti-colored exhaust.

"Vinnie, Vinnie, don't be blind. They're sugar-coating the pill. Sure you're making eleven-five this year and next year when you pick up the other theaters, they'll buck you up to maybe fourteen thousand. And there you'll be twelve years from now, when you can't buy a lousy Coke for thirty cents. Gofer that new carpeting, gofer that consignment of theater seats, gofer those reels of film that got sent across town by mistake. Do you want to be doing that shit when you're forty, Vinnie, with nothing to look forward to but a gold watch?''

"Better than what you're doing.'' Vinnie turned away abruptly, almost bumping Santa, who said something that sounded suspiciously like *watch where the fuck you're going.*

He went after Vinnie. Something about the set expression on Vinnie's face convinced him he was getting through, despite the defensive emplacements. God, God, he thought. Let it be.

"Leave me alone, Bart. Get lost.''

"Get out of it,'' he repeated. "If you wait even until next summer it may be too late. Jobs are going to be tighter than a virgin's chastity belt if this energy crisis goes into high gear, Vinnie. This may be your last chance. It—''

Vinnie wheeled around. "I'm telling you for the last time, Bart.''

"You're flushing your future right down the john, Vinnie. Life's too short for that. What are you going to tell your daughter when—''

Vinnie punched him in the eye. A bolt of white pain flashed up into his head and he staggered backward, arms flying out. The kids who had been following Santa scattered as his packages—dolls, GI Joe, chess set—went flying. He hit a rack of toy telephones, which sprayed across the floor. Somewhere a little girl screamed like a hurt animal and he thought *Don't cry, darling, it's just dumb old George falling down, I do it frequently around the house these days* and someone else—jolly old Santa, maybe—was cursing and yelling for the store detective. Then he was on the floor amid the toy telephones, which all came equipped with battery-powered tape loops, and one of them was saying over and over in his ear: "Do you want to go to the circus? Do you want to go to the circus? Do you . . . ''

December 17, 1973

The shrilling of the telephone brought him out of a thin, uneasy afternoon sleep. He had been dreaming that a young scientist had discovered that, by changing the atomic composition of peanuts just a little, America could produce unlimited quantities of low-polluting gasoline. It seemed to make everything all right, personally and nationally, and the tone of the dream was one of burgeoning jubilation. The phone was a sinister counterpoint that grew and grew until the dream split open and let in an unwelcome reality.

He got up from the couch, went to the phone, and fumbled it to his ear. His eye didn't hurt anymore, but in the hall mirror he could see that it was still colorful.

"Hello?"

"Hi, Bart. Tom."

"Yeah, Tom. How are you?"

"Fine. Listen, Bart. I thought you'd want to know. They're demolishing the Blue Ribbon tomorrow."

His eyes snapped wide. "Tomorrow? It can't be tomorrow. They . . . hell, it's almost Christmas!"

"That's why."

"But they're not up to it yet."

"It's the only industrial building left in the way," Tom said. "They're going to raze it before they knock off for Christmas."

"Are you sure?"

"Yes. They had a news feature on that morning program. 'City Day.' "

"Are you going to be there?"

"Yeah," Tom said. "Too much of my life went by inside that pile for me to be able to stay away."

"Then I guess I'll see you there."

"I guess you will."

He hesitated. "Listen, Tom. I want to apologize. I don't think they're going to reopen the Blue Ribbon, in Waterford or anyplace else. If I screwed you up royally—"

"No, I'm not hurting. I'm up at Brite-Kleen, doing maintenance. Shorter hours, better pay. I guess I found the rose in the shitheap."

"How is it?"

Tom sighed across the wire. "Not so good," he said. "But I'm past fifty now. It's hard to change. It would have been the same in Waterford."

"Tom, about what I did—"

"I don't want to hear about it, Bart." Tom sounded uncomfortable. "That's between you and Mary. Really."

"Okay."

"Uh . . . you getting along good?"

"Sure. I've got a couple of things on the line."

"I'm glad to hear that." Tom paused so long that the silence on the line became thick, and he was about to thank him for calling and hang up when Tom added: "Steve Ordner called up about you. Called me right up at my house."

"Is that so? When?"

"Last week. He's pissed like a bear at you, Bart. He kept asking if any of us had any idea you had been sandbagging the Waterford plant. But it was more than that. He was asking all sorts of other things."

"Like what?"

"Like did you ever take stuff home, office supplies and stuff like that. Did you ever draw from petty cash without putting in a voucher. Or get your laundry done on the company clock. He even asked me if you had any kind of kickback deal going with the motels."

"That son of a bitch," he said wonderingly.

"Like I say, he's hunting around for a nice raw cob to stick up your pump, Bart. I think he'd like to find a criminal charge he could get you on."

"He can't. It's all in the family. And the family's broken up now."

"It broke up a long time ago," Tom said evenly. "When Ray Tarkington died. I don't know anyone who's pissed off at you but Ordner. Those guys downtown . . . it's just dollars and cents to them. They don't know nothing about the laundry business and they don't care to know."

He could think of nothing to say.

"Well . . . " Tom sighed. "I thought you ought to know. And I s'pose you heard about Johnny Walker's brother."

"Arnie? No, what about him?"

"Killed himself."

"What?"

Tom sounded as if he might be sucking back spit through his upper plate. "Ran a hose from the exhaust pipe of his car into the back window and shut everything up. The newsboy found him."

"Holy God," he whispered. He thought of Arnie Walker sitting in the hospital waiting room chair and shivered, as if a goose had walked over his grave. "That's awful."

"Yeah . . . " That sucking noise again. "Listen, I'll be seeing you, Bart."

"Sure. Thanks for calling."

"Glad to do it. Bye."

He hung up slowly, still thinking of Arnie Walker and that funny, whining gasp Arnie had made when the priest hurried in.

Jesus, he had his pyx, did you see it?

"Oh, that's too bad," he said to the empty room, and the words fell dead as he uttered them and he went into the kitchen to fix himself a drink.

Suicide.

The word had a hissing trapped sound, like a snake squirming through a small crevice. It slipped between the tongue and the roof of the mouth like a convict on the lam.

Suicide.

His hand trembled as he poured Southern Comfort, and the neck of the bottle chattered against the rim of the glass. Why did he do that, Freddy? They were just a couple of old farts who roomed together. Jesus Christ, why would *anybody* do that?

But he thought he knew why.

December 18–19, 1973

He got to the laundry around eight in the morning and they didn't start to tear it down until nine, but even at eight there was quite a gallery on hand, standing in the cold with their hands thrust into their coat pockets and frozen breath pluming from their mouths like comic strip balloons—Tom Granger, Ron Stone, Ethel Diment, the shirt girl who usually got tipsy on her lunch break and then burned the hell out of unsuspecting shirt collars all afternoon, Gracie Floyd and her cousin Maureen, both of whom had worked on the ironer, and ten or fifteen others.

The highway department had put out yellow sawhorses and smudge pots and large orange-and-black signs that said:

DETOUR

The signs would route traffic around the block. The sidewalk that fronted the laundry had been closed off, too.

Tom Granger tipped a finger at him but didn't come over. The others from the laundry glanced at him curiously and then put their heads together.

A paranoid's dream, Freddy. Who'll be the first to trot over and scream *j'accuse* in my face?

But Fred wasn't talking.

Around quarter of nine a new '74 Toyota Corolla pulled up, the ten-day plate still taped in the rear window, and Vinnie Mason got out, resplendent and a little self-conscious in a new camel's hair overcoat and leather gloves. Vinnie shot him a sour glance that would have bent steel nails out of plumb and then walked over to where Ron Stone was standing with Dave and Pollack.

At ten minutes of nine they brought a crane up the street, the wrecking ball dangling from the top of the gantry like some disembodied Ethiopian teat. The crane was rolling very slowly on its ten chest-high wheels, and the steady, crackling roar of its exhaust beat into the silvery chill of the morning like an artisan's hammer shaping a sculpture of unknown import.

A man in a yellow hard hat directed it up over the curb and through the parking lot, and he could see the man high up in the cab changing gears and clutching with one blocklike foot. Brown smoke pumped from the crane's overhead stack.

A weird, diaphanous feeling had been haunting him ever since he had parked the station wagon three blocks over and walked here, a simile that wouldn't quite connect. Now, watching the crane halt at the base of the long brick plant, just to the left of what had been the loading bays, the sense of it came to him. It was like stepping into the last chapter of an Ellery Queen mystery where all the participants have been gathered so that the mechanics of the crime could be explained and the culprit unmasked. Soon someone—Steve Ordner, most likely—would step out of the crowd, point at him and scream: *He's the one! Bart Dawes! He killed the Blue Ribbon!* At which point he would draw his pistol in order to silence his nemesis, only to be riddled with police bullets.

The fancy disturbed him. He looked toward the road to assure himself and felt a sinking-elevator sensation in his belly as he saw Ordner's bottle-green Delta 88 parked just beyond the yellow barriers, exhaust pluming from the twin tailpipes.

Steve Ordner was looking calmly back at him through the polarized glass.

At that moment the wrecking ball swung through its arc with a low, ratcheting scream, and the small crowd sighed as it struck the brick wall and punched through with a hollow booming noise like detonating cannon fire.

By four that afternoon there was nothing left of the Blue Ribbon but a jumbled pile of brick and glass, through which protruded the shattered main beams like the broken skeleton of some exhumed monster.

What he did later he did with no conscious thought of the future or consequences. He did it in much the same spirit that he had bought the two guns at Harvey's Gun Shop a month earlier. Only there was no need to use the circuit breaker because Freddy had shut up.

He drove to a gas station and filled up the LTD with hi-test. Clouds had come in over the city during the day, and the radio was forecasting a storm—six to ten inches of new snow. He drove back home, parked the station wagon in the garage, and went down cellar.

Under the stairs there were two large cartons of returnable soda and beer bottles, the top layer covered with a thick patina of dust. Some of the bottles probably went back five years. Even Mary had forgotten about them in the last year or so and had given up pestering him about taking them back for the refund. Most of the stores didn't even accept returnables now. Use them once, throw them away. What the hell.

He stacked the two cartons one on top of the other and carted them out to the garage. When he went back to the kitchen to get a knife, a funnel, and Mary's floor-washing pail, it had begun to spit snow.

He turned on the garage light and took the green plastic garden hose off its nail, where it had been looped since the third week of September. He cut off the nozzle and it fell to the cement floor with a meaningless clink. He paid out three feet and cut it again. He kicked the rest away and looked at the length of hose thoughtfully for a moment. Then he unscrewed his gas cap and slipped the hose gently in, like a delicate lover.

He had seen gas siphoned before, knew the principle, but had never done it himself. He steeled himself for the taste of gasoline and sucked on the end of the hose-length. For a moment there was nothing but an invisible, glutinous resistance, and then his mouth filled with a liquid so cold and foreign that he had to stifle an impulse to gasp and draw some of it down his throat. He spat it out with a grimace, still tasting it on his tongue like some peculiar death. He tilted the hose over Mary's floor-bucket, and a stream of pinkish gasoline spurted into the bottom. The flow fell away to a trickle and he thought he would have to go through the ritual again. But then the flow strengthened a bit and remained constant. Gas flowed into the bucket with a sound like urination in a public toilet.

He spat on the floor, rinsed the inside of his mouth with saliva, spat again. Better. It came to him that although he had been using gasoline almost every day of his adult life, he had never been on such intimate terms with it. The only other time he had actually touched it was when he had filled the small tank of his Briggs & Stratton lawn mower to the overflow point. He was suddenly glad that this had happened. Even the residual taste in his mouth seemed okay.

He went back into the house while the bucket filled (it was snowing harder now) and got some rags from Mary's cleaning cupboard under the sink. He took them back into the garage and tore them into long strips, which he laid out on the hood of the LTD.

When the floor-bucket was half full, he switched the hose into the galvanized steel bucket he usually filled with ashes and clinkers to spread in the driveway when the going was icy. While it filled, he put twenty beer and soda bottles in four neat rows and filled each one three-quarters full, using the funnel. When that was done, he pulled the hose out of the gas tank and poured the contents of the steel pail into Mary's bucket. It filled it almost to the brim.

He stuffed a rag wick into each bottle, plugging the necks completely. He went back to the house, carrying the funnel. The snow filled the earth in slanting, wind-driven lines. The driveway was already white. He put the funnel into the sink and then got the cover that fitted over the top of the bucket from Mary's cupboard. He took it back to the garage and snapped it securely over the gasoline. He opened the LTD's tailgate and put the bucket of gasoline inside. He put his Molotov cocktails into one of the cartons, fitting them snugly one against the other so they would stand at attention like good soldiers. He put the carton on the passenger seat up front, within hand's reach. Then he went back into the house, sat down in his chair, and turned on the Zenith TV with his Space Command module. The "Tuesday

Movie of the Week'' was on. It was a western, starring David Janssen. He thought
David Janssen made a shitty cowboy.

When the movie was over, he watched Marcus Welby treat a disturbed teenager
for epilepsy. The disturbed teenager kept falling down in public places. Welby
fixed her up. After Marcus came station identification and two ads, one for Mir-
acle Chopper and one for an album containing forty-one spiritual favorites, and
then the news. The weather man said it was going to snow all night and most of
tomorrow. He urged people to stay home. The roads were treacherous and most
snow-removal equipment wouldn't be able to get out until after 2:00 A.M. High
winds were causing the snow to drift and generally, the weatherman hinted, things
were going to be an all-around bitch-kitty for the next day or so
    After the news, Dick Cavett came on. He watched half an hour of that, and then
turned the TV off. So Ordner wanted to get him on something criminal, did he?
Well, if he got the LTD stuck after he did it, Ordner would have his wish. Still,
he thought his chances were good. The LTD was a heavy car, and there were studded tires on the back wheels.
    He put on his coat and hat and gloves in the kitchen entry, and paused for a
moment. He went back through the warmly lighted house and looked at it—the
kitchen table, the stove, the dining room bureau with the teacups hung from the
runner above it, the African violet on the mantel in the living room—he felt a warm
surge of love for it, a surge of protectiveness. He thought of the wrecking ball
roaring through it, belting the walls down to junk, shattering the windows, vomiting debris over the floors. He wasn't going to let that happen. Charlie had crawled
on these floors, had taken his first steps in the living room, had once fallen down
the front stairs and scared the piss out of his fumbling parents. Charlie's room was
now an upstairs study, but it was in there that his son had first felt the headaches
and experienced the double vision and smelled those odd aromas, sometimes like
roasting pork, sometimes like burning grass, sometimes like pencil shavings. After
Charlie had died, almost a hundred people had come to see them, and Mary had
served them cake and pie in the living room.
    No, Charlie, he thought. *Not if I can help it.*

He ran the garage door up and saw there was already four inches of snow in the
driveway, very powdery and light. He got in the LTD and started it up. He still
had over three-quarters of a tank. He let the car warm up, and sitting behind the
wheel in the mystic green glow of the dashlights, he fell to thinking about Arnie
Walker. Just a length of rubber hose, that wasn't so bad. It would be like going to
sleep. He had read somewhere that carbon monoxide poisoning was like that. It
even brought the color up in your cheeks so you looked ruddy and healthy, bursting
with life and vitality. It—
    He began to shiver, the goose walking back and forth across his grave again,
and he turned on the heater. When the car was toasty and the shivering had stopped,
he slipped the transmission into reverse and backed out into the snow. He could

hear the gasoline sloshing in Mary's floor-pail, reminding him that he had forgotten something.

He put the car in park again and went back to the house. There was a carton of paper matches in the bureau drawer, and he filled his coat pockets with perhaps twenty folders. Then he went back out.

The streets were very slippery.

There was patch ice under the new snow in places, and once when he braked for a stoplight at the corner of Crestallen and Garner, the LTD slued around almost sideways. When he brought the skid to a stop, his heart was thudding dully against his ribs. This was a crazy thing to be doing, all right. If he got rear-ended with all that gasoline in the back, they could scrape him up with a spoon and bury him in a dog-food box:

Better than suicide. Suicide's a mortal sin.

Well, that was the Catholics for you. But he didn't think he would get hit. Traffic had thinned almost to the vanishing point, and he didn't even see any cops. Probably they were all parked in alleys, cooping.

He turned cautiously onto Kennedy Promenade, which he supposed he would always think of as Dumont Street, which it had been until a special session of the city council had changed it in January of 1964. Dumont/Kennedy Prom ran from Westside all the way downtown, roughly parallel to the 784 construction for almost two miles. He would follow it for a mile, then turn left onto Grand Street. A half mile up, Grand Street became extinct, just like the old Grand Theater itself, might it rest in peace. By next summer Grand Street would be resurrected in the form of an overpass (one of the three he had mentioned to Magliore), but it wouldn't be the same street. Instead of seeing the theater on your right, you would only be able to see six—or was it eight?—lanes of traffic hurrying by down below. He had absorbed a great deal about the extension from radio, TV, and the daily paper, not through any real conscious effort, but almost by osmosis. Perhaps he had stored the material instinctively, the way a squirrel stores nuts. He knew that the construction companies who had contracted the extension were almost through with the actual roadwork for the winter, but he also knew that they expected to complete all the necessary demolitions (*demolitions,* there's a word for you, Fred—but Fred didn't pick up the gauntlet) within the city limits by the end of February. That included Crestallen Street West. In a way it was ironic. If he and Mary had been located a mile farther away, they would not have been liable to demolition until late in the spring—May or early June of 1974. And if wishes were horses, beggars would sit astride golden palominos. He also knew, from personal *conscious* observation, that most of the road machinery was left parked below the point where Grand Street had been murdered.

He turned onto Grand Street now, the rear end of the car trying to wander out from under him. He turned with the skid, jockeying the car, cajoling it with his hands, and it purred on, cutting through snow that was almost virgin—the tracks of the last car to pass this way were already fuzzy and indistinct. The sight of so much fresh snow somehow made him feel better. It was good to be moving, to be *doing*.

As he moved up Grand at a steady unhurried twenty-five, his thoughts drifted back to Mary and the concept of sin, mortal and venial. She had been brought up Catholic, had gone to a parochial grammar school, and although she had given up most religious concepts—intellectually, at least—by the time they met, some of the gut stuff had stuck with her, the stuff they sneak to you in the clinches. As Mary herself said, the nuns had given her six coats of varnish and three of wax. After the miscarriage, her mother had sent a priest to the hospital so that she could make a good confession, and Mary had wept at the sight of him. He had been with her when the priest came in, carrying his pyx, and the sound of his wife's weeping had torn his heart as only one thing had done in the time between then and now.

Once, at his request, she had reeled off a whole list of mortal and venial sins. Although she had learned them in catechism classes twenty, twenty-five, even thirty years before, her list seemed (to him at least) complete and faultless. But there was a matter of interpretation that he couldn't make clear. Sometimes an act was a mortal sin, sometimes only venial. It seemed to depend on the perpetrator's frame of mind. *The conscious will to do evil.* Was that something she had said during those long-ago discussions, or had Freddy whispered it in his ear just now? It puzzled him, worried him. *The conscious will to do evil.*

In the end, he thought he had isolated the two biggies, the two hard and fast mortal sins: suicide and murder. But a later conversation—had it been with Ron Stone? yes, he believed it had—had even blurred half of that. Sometimes, according to Ron (they had been drinking in a bar, it seemed, as long as ten years ago). murder itself was only a venial sin. Or maybe not a sin at all. If you cold-bloodedly planned to do away with somebody who had raped your wife, that might just be a venial sin. And if you killed somebody *in a just war*—those were Ron's exact words, he could almost hear him speaking them in some mental taproom—then it wasn't a sin at all. According to Ron, all the American GI's that had killed Nazis and Japs were going to be okay when the Judgment Trump blew.

That left suicide, that hissing word.

He was coming up to the construction. There were black-and-white barriers with round flashing reflectors on top, and orange signs that glowed briefly and brightly in his headlights. One said:

ROAD ENDS TEMPORARILY

Another said:

DETOUR—FOLLOW SIGNS

Another said:

BLASTING AREA!
TURN OFF 2-WAY RADIOS

He pulled over, put the transmission lever in park, turned on his four-way flashers, and got out of the car. He walked toward the black-and-white barriers. The orange blinkers made the falling snow seem thicker, absurd with color.

He also remembered being confused about absolution. At first he had thought it was fairly simple: If you committed a mortal sin, you were mortally wounded, damned. You could hail Mary until your tongue fell out and you would still go to hell. But Mary said that wasn't always so. There was confession, and atonement, and reconsecration, and so on. It was very confusing. Christ had said there was no eternal life in a murderer, but he had also said whosoever believeth in me shall not perish. *Whosoever*. It seemed that there were as many loopholes in biblical doctrine as there were in a shyster lawyer's purchase agreement. Except for suicide, of course. You couldn't confess suicide or repent suicide or atone for it because that act cut the silver cord and sent you plunging out into whatever worlds there were. And—

And why was he thinking about it, anyway? He didn't intend to kill anybody and certainly he didn't intend to commit suicide. He never even thought about suicide. At least, not until just lately.

He stared over the black-and-white barriers, feeling cold inside.

The machines were down there, hooded in snow, dominated by the wrecking crane. In its brooding immobility it had gained a dimension of awfulness. With its skeletal gantry rising into the snowy darkness, it reminded him of a praying mantis that had gone into some unknown period of winter contemplation.

He swung one of the barriers out of the way. It was very light. He went back to the car, got in, and pulled the transmission lever down into low. He let the car creep forward over the edge and down the slope, which had been worn into smooth ridges by the comings and goings of the big machines. With dirt underneath, the tendency of the heavy car to slip around was reduced. When he got to the bottom he shifted back into park and turned off all the car's lights. He climbed back up the slope, puffing, and put the barrier back in place. He went back down.

He opened the LTD's tailgate and took out Mary's bucket. Then he went around to the passenger seat and set the bucket on the floor beneath his carton of firebombs. He took the white lid off the bucket and, humming softly, dipped each wick in gasoline. That done, he carried the bucket of gas over to the crane and climbed up into the unlocked cab, being careful not to slip. He was excited now, his heartbeat hurrying along, his throat tight and close with bitter exultation.

He splashed gas over the seat, over the controls, over the gearbox. He stepped out on the narrow riveted catwalk that skirted the crane's motor hood and poured the rest of the gas into the cowling. Hydrocarbon perfume filled the air. His gloves had soaked through, wetting his hands and turning them numb almost immediately. He jumped down and stripped the gloves off, putting them into his overcoat pockets. The first packet of matches dropped from his fingers, which felt as distant as wood. He held onto the second pack, but the wind snuffed the first two he had scratched. He turned his back to the wind, hunched over the match folder protectively and got one to stay lighted. He touched it to the rest, and they hissed into flame. He tossed the burning matches into the cab.

At first he thought they must have gone out, because there was nothing. Then there was a soft explosive sound—*flump!*—and fire boiled out of the cab in a furious gust, driving him back two steps. He shielded his eyes from the bright orange flower opening up there.

An arm of fire ran out of the cab, reached the engine hood, paused for a moment as if in reflection, and then sniffed inside. This time the explosion was not soft. KAPLOOM! And suddenly the cowling was in the air, rising almost out of sight, fluttering and turning over. Something whizzed past his head.

It's burning, he thought. *It's really burning!*

He began to do a shuffling dance in the fiery darkness, his face contorted in an ecstasy so great that it seemed his features must shatter and fall in a million smiling pieces. His hands curled into waving fists above his head.

"Hooray!" He screamed into the wind, and the wind screamed back at him. *"Hooray goddam it hooray!"*

He dashed around the car and slipped in the snow and fell down and that might have saved his life because that was when the gas tank of the crane blew debris in a forty-foot circle. A hot piece of metal winged through the right window of the LTD, punching a stellated hole in the safety glass and sending out a drunken spiderweb of cracks.

He picked himself up, frosted with snow all the way down his front, and scrambled behind the wheel. He put his gloves back on—fingerprints—but after that, any thought of caution was gone. He started the car with fingers that could barely feel the ignition key and then heavy-footed the accelerator, "dragging out" they had called it when they had been kids and the world was young, the rear end of the station wagon whipping left and right. The crane was burning furiously, better than he ever would have imagined, the cab an inferno, the big windshield gone.

"Hot damm!" he screamed. "Oh Freddy, *hot damn!*"

He skated the LTD in front of the crane, the firelight sketching his face in two-tone Halloween colors. He rammed his right index finger at the dashboard, hitting the cigarette lighter on the third try. The construction machines were on his left now, and he rolled down his window. Mary's floor-bucket rolled back and forth on the floor, and the beer and soda bottles chattered frantically against one another as the wagon jounced across the gouged and frozen earth.

The cigarette lighter popped out and he slammed both feet down on the power brake. The station wagon looped the loop and came to a stop. He pulled the lighter out of its socket, took a bottle from the carton, and pressed the glowing coil against the wick. It flared alight and he threw it. It shattered against the mud-caked tread of a bulldozer and flame splashed gaudily. He pushed the cigarette lighter back in, drove twenty feet farther, and threw three more at the dark hulk of a payloader. One missed, one struck the side and spilled burning gasoline harmlessly into the snow, and the third arced neatly into the cab.

"Fuckinbullseye!" he screamed.

Another bulldozer. A smaller payloader. Then he came to a house trailer up on jacks. A sign over the door said:

LANE CONSTRUCTION CO.
On-Site Office
NO HIRING DONE HERE!
Please Wipe Your Feet

He pulled the LTD up at point-blank range and threw four burning bottles at the large window beside the door. They all went through, the first shattering the glass of both window and bottle, dragging a burning drape in after it.

Beyond the trailer a pickup truck was parked. He got out of the LTD, tried the pickup's passenger door, and found it unlocked. He lit the wick of one of his bombs and pitched it inside. Flames leaped hungrily across the bench seat.

He got back into his car and saw there were only four or five bottles left. He drove on, shivering in the cold, snot running from his nose, reeking of gasoline, grinning.

A steam shovel. He pitched the rest of the bottles at it, doing no damage until the last, which blew one of the tractor treads loose from its aft cog.

He probed the box again, remembered it was empty, and looked in the rearview mirror.

"Mother-*fuck*," he cried, "Oh, holy mother-*fuck*, Freddy you cock-knocker!"

Behind him, a line of isolated bonfires stood out in the snow-choked darkness like runway landing lights. Flames were belching madly from the windows of the office trailer. The pickup was a ball of fire. The cab of the payloader was an orange cauldron. But the crane was really the masterpiece, because the crane was a roaring yellow beacon of light, a sizzling torch in the middle of the roadwork.

"*Demofuckinlition!*" he screamed.

A semblance of sanity began to return. He dared not go back the way he had come. The police would be on the way soon, maybe already. And the fire department. Could he get out ahead, or was he blocked in?

Heron Place, he might be able to get up to Heron Place. It would be a twenty-five degree angle up the slope, maybe thirty, and he would have to crash the wagon through a highway department barrier, but the guardrails were gone. He thought maybe he could do it. Yes. He *could* do it. Tonight he could do anything.

He drove the LTD up the unfinished roadbed, skidding and slueing, using only his parking lights. When he saw the streetlights of Heron Place above and to the right, he fed the car more and more gas and watched the speedometer needle climb past thirty as he aimed at the embankment. It was near forty when he hit the incline and shot up. About halfway the rear wheels began to lose traction and he dropped the transmission lever into low. The engine dropped a note and the car hitched forward. He was almost nose over the top when the wheels began to spin again, machine-gunning snow and pebbles and frozen clods of earth out behind him. For a moment the issue was in doubt, and then the simple forward inertia of the LTD—coupled with willpower, perhaps—carried it up onto level ground.

The nose of the car bunted the black-and-white barrier aside; it toppled backward into a snowdrift, making a dreamy sugarpuff. He went down over the curb and was almost shocked to realize that he was on a normal street again, as if nothing at all had happened. He shifted back to drive and settled down to a sedate thirty.

He was getting ready to turn toward home when he remembered that he was leaving tracks that plows or new snow might not obliterate for two hours or more. Instead of turning up Crestallen Street, he continued out Heron Place to River Street, and then down River to Route 7. Traffic here had been light ever since the snow had begun to come hard, but there had been enough to chew the snow covering the highway into a loose, churned-up mess.

He merged his tail with that of all the other cars that were moving east and inched his speed up to forty.

He followed Route 7 for almost ten miles, then back into the city and drove toward Crestallen Street. A few plows were out now, moving through the night like gigantic orange mastiffs with glaring yellow eyes. Several times he looked toward the 784 construction, but in the blowing snow he could see nothing.

About halfway home he realized that even though all the windows were rolled up and the heater was on full blast, the car was still cold. He looked back and saw the jagged hole in the rear passenger-side window. There was broken glass and snow on the backseat.

Now how did that happen? he asked himself, bewildered. He honestly had no recollection.

He entered his street from the north and drove directly to his house. It was as he had left it, the single light in his kitchen the only light shining on this whole darkened section of street. There were no police cars parked out front, but the garage door was open and that was just plain stupid. You closed the garage door when it snowed, always. That's why you have a garage, to keep the elements off your stuff. His father used to say that. His father had died in a garage, just like Johnny's brother, but Ralph Dawes had not committed suicide. He had had some kind of stroke. A neighbor had found him with his lawn clippers in his stiffening left hand and a small whetstone by his right. A suburban death. Oh Lord, send this white soul to a heaven where there is no crab grass and the niggers always keep their distance.

He parked the station wagon, pulled the garage door down, and went into the house. He was trembling from exhaustion and reaction. It was quarter past three. He hung his coat and hat in the hall closet and was closing the door when he felt a hot jolt of terror, as riveting as a straight knock of scotch whiskey. He fumbled wildly in his overcoat pockets and let out a whistling sigh when he felt his gloves, still soaked with gasoline, each of them crushed into a soggy little ball.

He thought of making coffee and decided against it. He had a queasy, thumping headache, probably caused by gasoline fumes and helped along by his scary drive through the snowy darkness. In his bedroom he took off his clothes and threw them over a chair without bothering to fold them. He thought he would fall asleep as soon as his head touched the pillow, but it was not so. Now that he was home, and presumably safe, staring wakefulness seized him. It brought fear like a handmaiden. They were going to catch him and put him in jail. His picture would be in the papers. People who knew him would shake their heads and talk it over in cafeterias and lunchrooms. Vinnie Mason would tell his wife that he had known Dawes was crazy all along. Mary's folks would maybe fly her to Reno, where she would first pick up residency and then a divorce. Maybe she would find somebody to fuck her. He wouldn't be surprised.

He lay wakeful, telling himself they weren't going to catch him. He had worn his gloves. No fingerprints. He had Mary's bucket and the white cover that went over the top. He had hidden his tracks, had shaken off possible pursuit just as a fugitive will throw off bloodhounds by walking in a creek. None of these thoughts brought him sleep or comfort. They would catch him. Perhaps someone on Heron Place had seen his car and thought it suspicious that any vehicle should be out so late on such a stormy night. Perhaps someone had jotted down his license plate number and was even now being congratulated by the police. Perhaps they had gotten paint scrapings from the Heron Place construction barrier and were now cajoling his guilty name out of some auto registration computer. Perhaps—

He rolled and thrashed in his bed, waiting for the dancing blue shadows to come in his window, waiting for the heavy knock on his door, waiting for some bodiless, Kafkaesque voice to call: *Okay, open up in there!* And when he finally fell asleep he did it without knowing it, because thought continued without a break, shifting from conscious rumination to the skewed world of dreams with hardly a break, like a car going from drive to low. Even in his dreams he thought he was awake, and in his dreams he committed suicide over and over: burned himself; bludgeoned himself by standing under an anvil and pulling a rope; hanged himself; blew out the stove's pilot lights and then turned on the oven and all four burners; shot himself; defenestrated himself; stepped in front of a speeding Greyhound bus; swallowed pills; swallowed Vanish toilet bowl disinfectant; stuck a can of Glade Pine Fresh aerosol in his mouth, pushed the button, and inhaled until his head floated off into the sky like a child's balloon; committed hara-kari while kneeling in a confessional at St. Dom's, confessing his self-murder to a dumbfounded young priest even as his guts accordioned out onto the bench like beef stew, performing an act of contrition in a fading, bemused voice as he lay in his blood and the steaming sausages of his intestines. But most vividly, over and over, he saw himself behind the wheel of the LTD, racing the engine a little in the closed garage, taking deep breaths and leafing through a copy of *National Geographic*, examining pictures of life in Tahiti and Aukland and the Mardi Gras in New Orleans, turning the pages ever more slowly, until the sound of the engine faded to a fawaway sweet hum and the green waters of the South Pacific inundated him in rocking warmth and took him down to a silver fathom.

December 19, 1973

It was 12:30 in the afternoon when he woke up and got out of bed. He felt as though he had been on a huge bender. His head ached monstrously. His bladder was cramped and full. There was a dead-snake taste in his mouth. Walking made his heart thud like a snare drum. He was not even allowed the luxury of believing (for however short a time) that he had dreamed everything he remembered of the previous night, because the smell of gasoline seemed rubbed into his flesh and it rose, fulsomely fragrant, from the pile of his clothes. The snow was over, the sky was clear, and the bright sunshine made his eyes beg for mercy.

He went into the bathroom, sat on the ring, and a huge diarrhea movement rushed out of him like a mail train highballing through a deserted station. His waste fell into the water with a sickening series of jets and plops that made him groan and clutch his head. He urinated without getting up, the rich and dismaying smell of his digestion's unsavory end product rising thickly around him.

He flushed and went downstairs on his orangewood legs, taking clean clothes with him. He would wait until the godawful smell cleared out of the bathroom and then he would shower, maybe all afternoon.

He gobbled three Excedrin from the green bottle on the shelf over the kitchen sink, then washed them down with two big gulps of Pepto-Bismol. He put on hot water for coffee and smashed his favorite cup by fumbling it off its hook. He swept it up, put out another, dumped instant Maxwell House into it, and then went into the dining room.

He turned on the radio and swept across the dial looking for news, which, like a cop, was never there when you needed it. Pop music. Feed and grain reports. A Golden Nugget 'Cause You Dug It. A call-in talk show. A swap-shop program. Paul Harvey selling Banker's Life Insurance. More pop music. No news.

The water for the coffee was boiling. He set the radio to one of the pop stations and brought his coffee back to the table and drank it black. There was an inclination to vomit with the first two mouthfuls, but after that it was better.

The news came on, first national, then local.

> On the city newsfront, a fire was set at the site of the 784 thruway extension construction near Grand Street in the early hours of this morning. Police Lieutenant Henry King said that vandals apparently used gasoline bombs to fire a crane, two payloaders, two bulldozers, a pickup truck, and the on-site office of the Lane Construction Company, which was entirely gutted.

An exultation as bitter and dark as the taste of his unsweetened coffee closed his throat at the words *entirely gutted.*

Damage done to the payloaders and bulldozers was minor, according to Francis Lane, whose company got a substantial subcontracting bid on the crosstown extension, but the demolition crane, valued at $60,000, is expected to be out of service for as long as two weeks.

Two weeks? Was that *all?*

More serious, according to Lane, was the burning of the on-site office, which contained time sheets, work records, and ninety percent of the company's cost accounting records over the last three months. "This is going to be the very devil to straighten out," Lane said. "It may set us back a month or more."

Maybe that was good news. Maybe an extra month of time made it all worthwhile.

According to Lieutenant King, the vandals fled the construction site in a station wagon, possibly a late-model Chevrolet. He appealed for anyone who may have seen the car leaving the construction area by Heron Street to come forward. Francis Lane estimated total damage in the area of $100,000.
In other local news, State Representative Muriel Reston again appealed for . . .

He snapped it off.
Now that he had heard, and had heard in daylight, things seemed a little better. It was possible to look at things rationally. Of course the police didn't have to give out all their leads, but if they really were looking for a Chevy instead of a Ford, and if they were reduced to pleading for eyewitnesses to come forward, then maybe he was safe, at least for the time being. And if there had been an eyewitness, no amount of worrying would change that.
He would throw away Mary's floor-bucket and open the garage to air out the stink of gasoline. Make up a story to explain the broken back window if anyone asked about it. And most important, he would try to prepare himself mentally for a visit from the police. As the last resident of Crestallen Street West, it might be perfectly logical for them to at least check him out. And they wouldn't have to sniff up his back trail very far to find out he had been acting erratically. He had screwed up the plant. His wife had left him. A former co-worker had punched him out in a department store. And of course, he had a station wagon, Chevrolet or not. All bad. But none of it proof.
And if they did dig up proof, he supposed he would go to jail. But there were worse things than jail. Jail wasn't the end of the world. They would give him a job, feed him. He wouldn't have to worry about what was going to happen when the insurance money ran out. Sure, there were a lot of things worse than jail. Suicide, for instance. That was worse. He went upstairs and showered.

Later that afternoon he called Mary. Her mother answered and went to get Mary with a sniff. But when Mary herself answered, she sounded nearly gay.

"Hi Bart. Merry Christmas in advance."

"No, *Mary* Christmas," he responded. It was an old joke that had graduated from humor to tradition.

"Sure," she said. "What is it, Bart?"

"Well, I've got a few presents . . . just little stuff . . . for you and the nieces and nephews. I wondered if we could get together somewhere. I'll give them to you. I didn't wrap the kids' presents—"

"I'd be glad to wrap them. But you shouldn't have. You're not working."

"But I'm working on it," he said.

"Bart, have you . . . have you done anything about what we talked about?"

"The psychiatrist?"

"Yes,"

"I called two. One is booked up until almost June. The other guy is going to be in the Bahamas until the end of March. He said he could take me then."

"What were their names?"

"Names? Gee, honey, I'd have to look them up again to tell you. Adams, I think the first guy was. Nicholas Adams—"

"Bart," she said sadly.

"It might have been Aarons," he said wildly.

"Bart," she said again.

"Okay." he said. "Believe what you want. You will anyway."

"Bart, if you'd only—

"What about the presents? I called about the presents, not the goddam shrink."

She sighed. "Bring them over Friday, why don't you? I can—"

"What, so your mother and father can hire Charles Manson to meet me at the door? Let's just meet on neutral ground, okay?"

"They're not going to be here." she said. "They're going to spend Christmas with Joanna." Joanna was Joanna St. Claire, Jean Calloway's cousin, who lived in Minnesota. They had been close friends in their girlhood (back in that pleasant lull between the War of 1812 and the advent of the Confederacy, he sometimes thought), and Joanna had had a stroke in July. She was still trying to get over it, but Jean had told him and Mary that the doctors said she could go at any time. That must be nice, he thought, having a time bomb built right into your head like that. Hey, bomb, is it today? Please not today. I haven't finished the new Victoria Holt.

"Bart? Are you there?"

"Yes. I was woolgathering."

"Is one o'clock all right?"

"That's fine."

"Was there anything else?"

"No, huh-uh."

"Well . . ."

"Take good care, Mary."

"I will. Bye, Bart."

"Good-bye."

They hung up and he wandered into the kitchen to make himself a drink. The woman he had just talked to on the phone wasn't the same woman that had sat tearfully on the living room couch less than a month ago, pleading for some reason to help explain the tidal wave that had just swept grandly through her ordered life, destroying the work of twenty years and leaving only a few sticks poking out of the mudflats. It was amazing. He shook his head over it the way he would have shaken his head over the news that Jesus had come down from the sky and had taken Richard Nixon up to heaven upon wheels of fire. She has regained herself. More: She had regained a person he hardly knew at all, a girl-woman he barely remembered. Like an archaeologist she had excavated that person, and the person was a little stiff in the joints from its long storage, but still perfectly usable. The joints would ease and the new-old person would be a whole woman, perhaps scarred by this upheaval but not seriously hurt. He knew her perhaps better than she thought, and he had been able to tell, strictly from the tone of her voice, that she was moving ever close to the idea of divorce, the idea of a clean break with the past . . . a break that would splint well and leave no trace of a limp. She was thirty-eight. Half of her life was ahead of her. There were no children to be casually maimed in the car wreck of this marriage. He would not suggest divorce, but if she did he would agree. He envied her new person and her new beauty. And if she looked back ten years from now on her marriage as a long dark corridor leading into sunlight, he could feel sorry she felt that way, but he couldn't blame her. No, he couldn't blame her.

December 21, 1973

He had given her the presents in Jean Calloway's ticking, ormolu living rooom, and the conversation that followed had been stilted and awkward. He had never been in this room alone with her, and he kept feeling that they should neck. It was a rusty knee-jerk reaction that made him feel like a bad double exposure of his college self.

"Did you lighten you hair?" he asked.

"Just a shade." She shrugged a little.

"It's nice. Makes you look younger."

"You're getting a little gray around the temples, Bart. Makes you look distinguished."

"Bullshit, it makes me look ratty."

She laughed—a little too high-pitched—and looked at the presents on the little side table. He had wrapped the owl pin, had left the toys and the chess set for her to do. The dolls looked blankly at the ceiling, waiting for some little girl's hands to bring them to life.

He looked at Mary. Their eyes caught seriously for a moment and he thought irrevocable words were going to spill out of her and he was frightened. Then the cuckoo jumped out of the clock, announced one-thirty, and they both jumped and then laughed. The moment had passed. He got up so it wouldn't come around again. Saved by a cuckoo bird, he thought. That fits.

"Got to go," he said.

"An appointment?"

"Job interview."

"Really?" She looked glad, "Where? Who? How much?"

He laughed and shook his head. "There's a dozen other applicants with as good a chance as me. I'll tell you when I get it."

"Conceited."

"Sure."

"Bart, what are you doing Christmas?" She looked concerned and solemn, and it suddenly came to him that an invitation to Christmas dinner and not to some new year's divorce court had been the thing on her lips inside. God! He almost sprayed laughter.

"I'm going to eat at home."

"You can come here," she said. "It would be just the two of us."

"No," he said, thoughtfully and then more firmly: "No. Emotions have a way of getting out of hand during the holidays. Another time."

She was nodding, also thoughtfully.

"Will you be eating alone?" he asked.

"I can go to Bob and Janet's. Really, are you sure?"

"Yes."

"Well . . . " But she looked relieved.

They walked to the door and shared a bloodless kiss.

"I'll call you," he said.

"You better."

"And give my best to Bobby."

"I will."

He was halfway down the walk to the car when she called: "Bart! Bart, wait a minute!"

He turned almost fearfully.

"I almost forgot," she said. "Wally Hamner called and invited us to his New Year's party. I accepted for both of us. But if you don't want to—"

"Wally?" He frowned. Walter Hamner was about their only crosstown friend. He worked for a local ad agency. "Doesn't he know we're, you know, separated?"

"He knows, but you know Walt. Things like that don't faze him much."

Indeed they didn't. Just thinking about Walter made him smile. Walter, always threatening to quit advertising in favor of advanced truss design. Composer of obscene limericks and even more obscene parodies of popular tunes. Divorced twice and tagged hard both times. Now impotent, if you believed gossip, and in this case he thought the gossip was probably true. How long had it been since he had seen Walt? Four months? Six? Too long.

"That might be fun," he said, and then a thought stuck him.

She scanned it from his face in her old way and said, "There won't be any laundry people there."

"He and Steve Ordner know each other."

"Well, yes, *him*—" She shrugged to show how unlikely she thought it was that *him* would be there, and the shrug turned into an elbow-holding little shiver. It was only about twenty-five degrees.

"Hey, go on in," he said. "You'll freeze, dummy."

"Do you want to go?"

"I don't know. I'll have to think about it." He kissed her again, this time a little more firmly, and she kissed back. At a moment like this, he could regret everything—but the regret was far away, clinical.

"Merry Christmas, Bart," she said, and he saw she was crying a little.

"Next year will be better," he said, the phrase comforting but without any root meaning. "Go inside before you catch pneumonia."

She went in and he drove away, still thinking about Wally Hamner's New Year's Eve party. He thought he would go.

December 24, 1973

He found a small garage in Norton that would replace the broken back window for ninety dollars. When he asked the garage man if he would be working the day before Christmas, the garage man said: "Hell yes, I'll take it any way I can get it."

He stopped on the way at a Norton U-Wash-It and put his clothes in two machines. He automatically rotated the agitators to see what kind of shape the spring drives were in, and then loaded them carefully so each machine would extract (only in the laundromats they called it "spin-dry") without kicking off on the overload. He paused, smiling a little. You can take the boy out of the laundry, Fred, but you can't take the laundry out of the boy. Right, Fred? Fred? Oh fuck yourself.

"That's a hell of a hole," the garage man said, peering at the spiderwebbed glass.

"Kid with a snowball," he said. "Rock in the middle of it."

"It was," he said. "It really was."

When the window was replaced he drove back to the U-Wash-It, put his clothes in the dryer, set it to medium-hot, and put thirty cents in the slot. He sat down and picked up someone's discarded newspaper. The U-Wash-It's only other customer was a tired-looking young woman with wire-rimmed glasses and blond streaks in her long, reddish-brown hair. She had a small girl with her, and the small girl was throwing a tantrum.

"I want my *bottle!*"

"Goddam it, Rachel—"

"BOTTLE!

"Daddys going to spank you when we get home," the young woman promised grimly. "And no treats before bed."

"BAWWWWTLE

Now why does a young girl like that want to streak her hair? he wondered, and looked at the paper. The headlines said:

SMALL CROWDS IN BETHLEHEM
PILGRIMS FEAR HOLY TERROR

On the bottom of page one, a short news story caught his eye and he read it carefully:

WINTERBURGER SAYS ACTS OF VANDALISM
WILL NOT BE TOLERATED

(Local) Victor Winterburger, Democratic candidate for the seat of the late Donald P. Naish, who was killed in a car crash late last month, said yesterday that acts of vandalism such as the one that caused almost a hundred thousand dollars' worth of damage at the Route 784 construction site early last Wednesday, cannot be tolerated "in a civilized American city." Winterburger made his remarks at an American Legion dinner, and received a standing ovation.

"We have seen what has happened in other cities," Winterburger said. "The defaced buses and subway cars and buildings in New York, the broken windows and senselessly marred schools of Detroit and San Francisco, the abuse of public facilities, public museums, public galleries. We must not allow the greatest country in the world to be overrun with huns and barbarians."

Police were called to the Grand Street area of the construction when a number of fires and explosions were seen by

(Continued page 5 col. 2)

He folded the paper and put it on top of a tattered pile of magazines. The washer hummed and hummed, a low, soporific sound. Huns. Barbarians. They were the huns. They were the rippers and chewers and choppers, turning people out of their homes, kicking apart lives as a small boy might kick apart an anthill—

The young woman dragged her daughter, still crying for a bottle, out of the U-Wash-It. He closed his eyes and dozed off, waiting for his dryer to finish. A few minutes later he snapped awake, thinking he heard fire bells, but it was only a Salvation Army Santa who had taken up his position on the corner out front. When he left the laundry with his basket of clothes, he threw all his pocket change into Santa's pot.

"God bless you," Santa said.

December 25, 1973

The telephone woke him around ten in the morning. He fumbled the extension off the night table, put it to his ear, and an operator said crisply into his sleep, "Will you accept a collect call from Olivia Brenner?"

He was lost and could only fumble, "What? Who? I'm asleep."

A distant, slightly familiar voice said, "Oh for Chrissake," and he knew.

"Yes," he said. "I'll take it." Had she hung up on him? He got up on one elbow to see. "Olivia? You there?"

"Go ahead, please," the operator overrode him, not willing to vary her psalm.

"Olivia, are you there?"

"I'm here." The voice was crackling and distant.

"I'm glad you called."

"I didn't think you'd take the call."

"I just woke up. Are you there? In Las Vegas?"

"Yes," she said flatly. The word came out with curiously dull authority, like a plank dropped on a cement floor.

"Well, how is it? How are you doing?"

Her sigh was so bitter that it was almost a tearless sob. "Not so good."

"No?"

"I met a guy my second . . . no, third . . . night here. Went to a party and go s-o-o-o fucked up—"

"Dope?" he asked cautiously, very aware that this was long distance and the government was everywhere.

"Dope?" she echoed crossly. "Of course it was dope. Bad shit, full of dex or something . . . I think I got raped."

The last trailed off so badly that he had to ask, "What?"

"Raped!" she screamed, so loudly that the receiver distorted. "That's when some stupid jock playing Friday night hippie plays hide the salami with you while your brains are somewhere behind you, dripping off the wall! Rape, do you know what rape is?"

"I know," he said.

"Bullshit, you know."

"Do you need money?"

"Why ask me that? I can't fuck you over the telephone. I can't even hand-job you."

"I have some money," he said. "I could send it. That's all. That's why." Instinctively he found himself speaking, not soothingly, but softly, so she would have to slow down and listen.

"Yeah, yeah."

"Do you have an address?"

"General Delivery, that's my address."

"You don't have an apartment?"

"Yeah, me and this other sad sack have got a place. The mailboxes are all broken. Never mind. You keep the money. I've got a job. Screw, I think I'm going to quit and come back. Merry Christmas to me."

"What's the job?"

"Pushing hamburgers in this fast-food joint. They got slots in the lobby, and people play them and eat hamburgers all night long, can you *believe* it? The last thing you have to do when your shift is over is to wipe off all the handles of the slot machines. They get all covered with mustard and mayo and catsup. And you should see the *people* here. All of them are fat. They've either got tans or burns. And if they don't want to fuck you, you're just part of the furniture. I've had offers from both sexes. Thank God my roomie's about as sex-oriented as a juniper bush, I . . . oh, Christ, why am I telling you all this? I don't even know why I called you. I'm going to hitch out of here at the end of the week, when I get paid."

He heard himself say: "Give it a month."

"*What?*"

"Don't go chickenshit. If you leave now you'll always wonder what you went out there for."

"Did you play football in high school? I bet you did."

"I wasn't even the waterboy."

"Then you don't know anything, do you?"

"I'm thinking about killing myself."

"You don't even . . . what did you say?"

"I'm thinking about killing myself." He said it calmly. He was no longer thinking about long distance and the people who might monitor long distance just for the fun of it—Ma Bell, the White House, the CIA, the Effa Bee Eye. "I keep trying things and they keep not working. It's because I'm a little too old for them to work, I think. Something went wrong a few years ago and I knew it was a bad thing but I didn't know it was bad for me. I thought it just happened and then I was going to get over it. But things keep falling down inside me. I'm sick with it. I keep doing things."

"Have you got cancer?" she whispered.

"I think I do."

"You ought to go to a hospital, get—"

"It's soul cancer."

"You're ego-tripping, man."

"Maybe so," he said. "It doesn't matter. One way or the other, things are set and they'll turn out the way they will. Only one thing that bothers me, and that's a feeling I get from time to time that I'm a character in some bad writer's book and he's already decided how things are going to turn out and why. It's easier to see things that way, even, than to blame it on God—what did He ever do for me, one way or the other? No, it's this bad writer, it's his fault. He cut my son down by writing in a brain tumor. That was chapter one. Suicide or no suicide, that comes just before the epilogue. It's a stupid story."

"Listen," she said, troubled, "if they have one of those Dial Help outfits in your town, maybe you ought to . . . "

"They couldn't do anything for me," he said, "and it doesn't matter. I want to help *you.* For Christsake look around out there before you go chickenshit. Get off dope, you said you were going to. The next time you look around you'll be forty and your options will mostly be gone."

"No, I can't take this. Some other place—"

"All places are the same unless your mind changes. There's no magic place to get your mind right. If you feel like shit, everything you see looks like shit. I *know* that. Newspaper headlines, even the signs I see, they all say yeah, that's right, Georgie, pull the plug. This eats the bird."

"Listen—"

"No, no, *you* listen. Dig your ears out. Getting old is like driving through snow that just gets deeper and deeper. When you finally get in over your hubcaps, you just spin and spin. That's *life.* There are no plows to come and dig you out. Your ship isn't going to come in, girl. There are no boats for nobody. You're never going to win a contest. There's no camera following you and people watching you struggle. This is *it.* All of it. *Everything.*"

"You don't know what it's *like* here!" she cried.

"No, but I know what it's like here."

"You're not in charge of my life."

"I'm going to send you five hundred dollars—Olivia Brenner, c/o General Delivery, Las Vegas."

"I won't be here. They'll send it back."

"They won't. Because I'm not going to put on a return address."

"Throw it away, then."

"Use it to get a better job."

"No."

"Then use it for toilet paper," he said shortly, and hung up. His hands were shaking.

The phone rang five minutes later. The operator said: "Will you accept—"

"No," he said, and hung up.

The phone rang twice more that day, but it was not Olivia either time.

* * *

Around two in the afternoon Mary called him from Bob and Janet Preston's house—Bob and Janet, who always reminded him, like it or not, of Barney and Wilma Flintstone. How was he? Good. A lie. What was he doing for Christmas dinner? Going out to Old Customhouse tonight for turkey with all the trimmings. A lie. Would he like to come over here instead? Janet had all kinds of leftovers and would be happy to get rid of some. No, he really wasn't very hungry at the minute. The truth. He was pretty well looped, and on the spur of the moment he told her he would come to Walter's party. She sounded pleased. Did he know it was BYOB? When did Wally Hamner have a party that wasn't? he asked, and she laughed. They hung up and he went back to sit in front of the TV with a drink.

The phone rang again around seven-thirty, and by that time he was nothing as polite as looped—he was pissy-assed drunk.

"Lo?"

"Dawes?"

"Dozz here; whozzere?"

"Magliore, Dawes. Sal Magliore."

He blinked and peered into his glass. He looked at the Zenith color TV, where he had been watching a movie called *Home for the Holidays*. It was about a family that had gathered at their dying patriarch's house on Christmas Eve and somebody was murdering them one by one. Very Christmasy.

"Mr. Magliore," he said, pronouncing carefully. "Merry Christmas, sir! And the best of everything in the new year!"

"Oh, if you only knew how I dread '74," Magliore said dolefully. "That's the year the oil barons are going to take over the country, Dawes. You see if they don't. Look at my sales sheet for December if you don't believe me. I sold a 1971 Chevy Impala the other day, this car is clean as a whistle, and I sold it for a thousand bucks. *A thousand bucks!* Do you believe that? A forty-five percent knockdown in one year. But I can sell all the '71 Vegas I can get my hands on for fifteen, sixteen hundred bucks. And what are they, I ask you?"

"Little cars?" he asked cautiously.

"They're fucking Maxwell House coffee cans, that's what they are!" Magliore shouted. "Saltine boxes on wheels! Every time you look at the goddam things cross-eyed and say booga-booga at them the engine's outta tune or the exhaust system drops off or the steering linkage is gone. Pintos, Vegas, Gremlins, they're all the same, little suicide boxes. So I'm selling those as fast as I can get them and I can't move a nice Chevy Impala unless I fuckin' give it away. And you say happy new year. Jesus! Mary! Joseph the carpenter!"

"That's seasonal," he said.

"I didn't call about that anyway," Magliore answered. "I called to say congratulations."

"Congratuwhatchens?" He was honestly bewildered.

"You know. Crackle-crackle boom-boom."

"Oh, you mean—"

"Sssst. Not on the phone. Be cool, Dawes."

"Sure. Crackle-crackle boom-boom. That's good." He cackled.

"It was you, wasn't it, Dawes?"

"To you I wouldn't admit my middle name."

Magliore roared. "That's good. *You're* good, Dawes. You're a fruitcake, but you're a *clever* fruitcake. I admire that."

"Thanks," he said, and cleverly knocked back the rest of his drink.

"I also wanted to tell you that everything was going ahead on schedule down there. Rumble and roar."

"What?"

The glass he was holding fell from his fingers and rolled across the rug.

"They've got seconds on all that stuff, Dawes. Thirds on most of it. They're paying cash until they got their bookwork straightened out, but everything is right-on."

"You're crazy."

"No. I thought you ought to know. I told you, Dawes. Some things you can't get rid of."

"You're a bastard. You're lying. Why do you want to call a man up on Christmas night and tell him lies?"

"I ain't lying. It's your play again, Dawes. In this game, it's *always* gonna be your play."

"I don't believe you."

"You poor son of a bitch," Magliore said. He sounded honestly sorry and that was the worst part. "I don't think it's gonna be a very happy new year for you either." He hung up.

And that was Christmas.

December 26, 1973

There was a letter from *them* in the mail (he had begun to see the anonymous people downtown that way, the personal pronoun in italics and printed in drippy, ominous letters like the printing on a horror movie poster), as if to confirm what Magliore had said.

He held it in his hand, looking down at the crisp white business envelope, his mind filled with almost all the bad emotions the human mind can feel: Despair, hatred, fear, anger, loss. He almost tore it into small pieces and threw it into the snow beside the house, and then knew he couldn't do that. He opened it, nearly tearing the envelope in half, and realized that what he felt most was cheated. He had been gypped. He had been rooked. He had destroyed their machines and their records, and they had just brought up a few replacements. It was like trying to fight the Chinese Army singlehanded.

It's your play again, Dawes. In this game it's always gonna be your play.

The other letters had been form jobs, sent from the office of the highway department. *Dear Friend, a big crane is going to come to your house sometime soon. Be on the lookout for this exciting event as WE IMPROVE YOUR CITY!*

This was from the city council, and it was personal. It said:

December 20, 1973

Mr. Barton G. Dawes
1241 Crestallen Street West
M———, W———

Dear Mr. Dawes:

It has come to our attention that you are the last resident of Crestallen Street West who has not relocated. We trust that you are experiencing no undue problems in this matter. While we have a 19642-A form on file (acknowledgment of information concerning City Roads Project 6983-426-73-74-HC), we do not yet have your relocation form (6983-426-73-74-HC-9004, blue folder). As you know, we cannot begin processing your check of reimbursement without this form. According to our 1973 tax assessment, the property at 1241 Crestallen Street West has been valued at $63,500, and so we are sure that you must be as aware of the situation's urgency as we are. By law, you must relocate by January 20, 1974, the date that demolitions work is scheduled to begin on Crestallen Street West.

We must also point out again that according to the State Statute of Eminent Domain (S.L. 19452-36), you would be in violation of the law to remain in your present location past midnight of January 19, 1974. We are sure you understand this, but we are pointing it out once more so that the record will be clear.

If you are having some problem with relocation, I hope you will call me during business hours, or better yet, stop by and discuss the situation. I am sure that things can be worked out; you will find us more than eager to co-sure that things can be worked out; you will find us more than eager to co-operate in this matter. In the meantime, may I wish you a Merry Christmas and a most productive New Year?

Sincerely,

John T. Gordon

For the City Council

JTG/tk

"No," he muttered. "You may not wish it. You may not." He tore the letter to shreds and threw it in the wastebasket.

That night, sitting in front of the Zenith TV, he found himself thinking about how he and Mary had found out, almost forty-two months ago now, that God had decided to do a little roadwork on their son Charlie's brain.

The doctor's name had been Younger. There was a string of letters after his name on the framed diplomas that hung on the warmly paneled walls of his inner office, but all he understood for sure was that Younger was a neurologist; a fast man with a good brain disease.

He and Mary had gone to see him at Younger's request on a warm June afternoon nineteen days after Charlie had been admitted to Doctors Hospital. He was a good-looking man, maybe halfway through his forties, physically fit from a lot of golf played with no electric golf cart. He was tanned a deep cordovan shade. And the doctor's hands fascinated him. They were huge hands, clumsy-looking, but they moved about his desk—now picking up a pen, now riffling through his appointment book, now playing idly across the surface of a silver-inlaid paper-weight—with a lissome grace that was very nearly repulsive.

"Your son has a brain tumor," he said. He spoke flatly, with little inflection, but his eyes watched them very carefully, as if he had just armed a temperamental explosive.

"Tumor," Mary said softly, blankly.

"How bad is it?" he asked Younger.

The symptoms had developed over the space of eight months. First the head-aches, infrequent at the beginning, then more common. Then double vision that came and went, particularly after physical exercise. After that, most shameful to Charlie, some incidence of bedwetting. But they had not taken him to the family doctor until a terrifying temporary blindness in the left eye, which had gone as red as a sunset, obscuring Charlie's good blue. The family doctor had had him ad-mitted for tests, and the other symptoms had followed that: Phantom smells of oranges and shaved pencils; occasional numbness in the left hand; occasional lapses into nonsense and childish obscenity.

"It's bad," Younger said. "You must prepare yourself for the worst. It is in-operable."

Inoperable.

The word echoed up the years to him. He had never thought words had taste, but that one did. It tasted bad and yet juicy at the same time, like rotten hamburger cooked rare.

Inoperable.

Somewhere, Younger said, deep in Charlie's brain, was a collection of bad cells roughly the size of a walnut. If you had that collection of bad cells in front of you on the table, you could squash them with one hard hit. But they weren't on the table. They were deep in the meat of Charlie's mind, still smugly growing, filling him up with random strangeness.

One day, not long after his admission, he had been visiting his son on his lunch break. They had been talking about baseball, discussing, in fact, whether or not they would be able to go to the American League baseball playoffs if the city's team won.

Charlie had said: "I think if their pitching mmmmm mmmm mmmm pitching staff holds up mmmmm nn mmmm pitching mmmm—"

He had leaned forward. "What, Fred? I'm not tracking you."

Charlie's eyes had rolled wildly outward.

"Fred?" George whispered. "Freddy—?"

"Goddam motherfucking mothersucking nnnnnn fuckhole!" his son screamed from the clean white hospital bed. *"Cuntlicking dinkrubbing asswipe sonofa-whoringbitch—"*

"NURSE!" he had screamed, as Charlie passed out. *"OH GOD NURSE!"*

It was the cells, you see, that had made him talk like that. A little bunch of bad cells no bigger, say, than your average-sized walnut. Once, the night nurse said, he had screamed the word *boondoggle* again and again for nearly five minutes. Just bad cells, you know. No bigger than your garden-variety walnut. Making his son rave like an insane dock walloper, making him wet the bed, giving him head-aches, making him—during the first hot week of that July—lose all ability to move his left hand.

"Look," Dr. Younger had told them on that bright, just-right-for-golf June day. He had unrolled a long scroll of paper, an ink-tracing of their son's brain waves. He produced a healthy brain wave as a comparison, but he didn't need it. He looked at what had been going on in his son's head and again felt that rotten yet juicy taste in his mouth. The paper showed an irregular series of spiky mountains and valleys, like a series of badly drawn daggers.

Inoperable.

You see if that collection of bad cells, no bigger than a walnut, had decided to grow on the outside of Charlie's brain, minor surgury would have vacuumed it right up. No sweat, no strain, no pain on the brain, as they had said when they were boys. But instead, it had grown down deep inside and was growing larger every day. If they tried the knife, or laser, or cryosurgery, they would be left with a nice, healthy, breathing piece of meat. If they didn't try any of those things, soon they would be bundling their boy into a coffin.

Dr. Younger said all these things in generalities, covering their lack of options in a soothing foam of technical language that would wear away soon enough. Mary kept shaking her head in gentle bewilderment, but he had understood everything exactly and completely. His first thought, bright and clear, never to be forgiven, was: *Thank God it's not me.* And the funny taste came back and he began to grieve for his son.

Today a walnut, tomorrow the world. The creeping unknown. The incredible dying son. What was there to understand?

Charlie died in October. There were no dramatic dying words. He had been in a coma for three weeks.

He sighed and went out to the kitchen and made himself a drink. Dark night pressed evenly on all the windows. The house was so empty now that Mary was gone. He kept stumbling over little pieces of himself everywhere—snapshots, his old sweatsuit in an upstairs closet, an old pair of slippers under the bureau. It was bad, very bad, to keep doing that.

He had never cried over Charlie after Charlie's death; not even at the funeral. Mary had cried a great deal. For weeks, it seemed, Mary had gone around with a perpetual case of pinkeye. But in the end, she had been the one to heal.

Charlie had left scars on her, that was undeniable. Outwardly, she had all the scars. Mary before-and-after. Before, she would not take a drink unless she considered it socially helpful to his future. She would take a weak screwdriver at a party and carry it around all night. A rum toddy before bed when she had a heavy chest cold. That was all. After, she had a cocktail with him in the late afternoon when he came home, and always a drink before bed. Not serious drinking by anyone's yardstick, not sick-and-puking-in-the-bathroom drinking, but more than before. A little of that protective foam. Undoubtedly just what the doctor would have ordered. Before, she rarely cried over little things. After, she cried over them often, always in private. If dinner was burned. If she had a flat. The time water got in the basement and the sump pump froze and the furnace shorted out. Before, she had been something of a folk music buff—white folk and blues, Van Ronk, Gary Davis, Tom Rush, Tom Paxton, Spider John Koerner. After, her interest just faded away. She sang her own blues and laments on some inner circuit. She had stopped talking about their taking a trip to England if he got promoted a step up. She started doing her hair at home, and the sight of her sitting in front of the TV in rollers became a common one. It was she their friends pitied—rightly so, he supposed. He wanted to pity himself, and did, but kept it a secret. She had been able to need, and to use what was given to her because of her need, and eventually that had saved her. It had kept her from the awful contemplation that kept him awake so many nights after her bedtime drink had lulled her off to sleep. And as she slept, he contemplated the fact that in this world a tiny collection of cells no bigger than a walnut could take a son's life and send him away forever.

He had never hated her for healing, or for the deference other women gave her as a right. They looked on her the way a young oilman might look on an old vet whose hand or back or cheek is shiny with puckered pink burn tissue—with the respect the never-hurt always hold for the once-hurt-now-healed. She had done her time in hell over Charlie, and these other women knew it. But she had come out. There had been Before, there had been Hell, there had been After, and there had even been After-After, when she had returned to two of her four social clubs, had taken up macrame (he had a belt she had done a year ago—a beautiful twisted rope creation with a heavy silver buckle monogrammed BGD), had taken up afternoon TV—soap operas and Merv Griffin chatting with the celebrities.

Now what? he wondered, going back to the living room. After-After-After? It seemed so. A new woman, a whole woman, rising out of the old ashes that he had so crudely stirred. The old oilman with skin grafts over the burns, retaining the old savvy but gaining a new look. Beauty only skin deep? No. Beauty was in the eye of the beholder. It could go for miles.

For him, the scars had all been inside. He had examined his hurts one by one on the long nights after Charlie's death, cataloguing them with all the morbid fascination of a man studying his own bowel movements for signs of blood. He had wanted to watch Charlie play ball on a Little League team. He had wanted to get report cards and rant over them. He wanted to tell him, over and over, to pick up his room. He wanted to worry about the girls Charlie saw, the friends he picked, the boy's internal weather. He wanted to see what his son became and if they could still be in love as they had been until the bad cells, no bigger than a walnut, had come between them like some dark and rapacious woman.

Mary had said, *He was yours.*

That was true. The two of them had fitted so well that names were ridiculous, even pronouns a little obscene. So they became George and Fred, a vaudeville sort of combination, two Mortimer Veeblefeezers against the world.

And if a collection of bad cells no bigger than a walnut could destroy all those things, those things that are so personal that they can never be properly articulated, so personal you hardly dared admit their existence to yourself, what did that leave? How could you ever trust life again? How could you see it as anything more meaningful than a Saturday night demolition derby?

All of it was inside him, but he had been honestly unaware that his thoughts were changing him so deeply, so irretrievably. And now it was all out in the open, like some obscene mess vomited onto a coffee table, reeking with stomach juice, filled with undigested lumps, and if the world was only a demo derby, wouldn't one be justified in stepping out of his car? But what after that? Life seemed only a preparation for hell.

He saw that he had drained his drink in the kitchen; he had come into the living room with an empty glass.

December 31, 1973

He was only two blocks from Wally Hamner's house when he put his hand into his overcoat pocket to see if he had any Canada Mints in there. There were no mints, but he came up with a tiny square of aluminum foil that glinted dully in the station wagon's green dash lights. He spared it a puzzled, absent glance and was about to toss it into the ashtray when he remembered what it was.

In his mind Olivia's voice said: *Synthetic mescaline. Product four, they call it. Very heavy stuff.* He had forgotten all about it.

He put the little foil packet back into his coat pocket and turned onto Walter's street. Cars were lined up halfway down the block on both sides. That was Walter, all right— he had never been one to have anything so simple as a party when there might be a group grope in the offing. The Principle of the Pleasure Push, Wally called it. He claimed that someday he would patent the idea and then publish instructional hand-books on how to use it. If you got enough people together, Wally Hamner main-tained, you were forced into having a good time—pushed into it. Once when Wally was expounding this theory in a bar, he had mentioned lynch mobs. "There," Walter had said blandly, "Bart has just proved my case."

He wondered what Olivia was doing now. She hadn't tried to call back, al-though if she had he would probably have weakened and taken the call. Maybe she had stayed in Vegas just long enough to get the money and had then caught a bus for . . . where? Maine? Did anyone leave Las Vegas for Maine in the middle of winter? Surely not.

Product four, they call it. Very heavy stuff.

He snuggled the wagon up to the curb behind a sporty red GTX with a black racing stripe and got out. New Year's Eve was clear but bitterly cold. A frigid rind of moon hung in the sky overhead like a child's paper cutout. Stars were spangled around it in lavish profusion. The mucus in his nose froze to a glaze that crackled when he flared his nostrils. His breath plumed out on the dark air.

Three houses away from Walter's he picked up the bass line from the stereo. They really had it cranked. There was something about Wally's parties, he re-flected, Pleasure Principle or no. The most well-intentioned of just-thought-we'd-drop-bys ended up staying and drinking until their heads were full of silver chimes that would turn to leaden church bells the next day. The most dyed-in-the-wool rock-music haters ended up boogying in the living room to the endless golden gas-sers that Wally trotted out when everybody got blind drunk enough to look back upon the late fifties and early sixties as the plateau of their lives. They drank and boogied, boogied and drank, until they were panting like little yellow dogs on the

Fourth of July. There were more kisses in the kitchen by halves of differing wholes, more feel-ups per square inch, more wallflowers jerked rudely out of the woodwork, more normally sober folk who would wake up on New Year's Day with groaning hangovers and horridly clear memories of prancing around with lampshades on their heads or of finally deciding to tell the boss a few home truths. Wally seemed to inspire these things, not by any conscious effort, but just by being Wally—and of course there was no party like a New Year's Eve party.

He found himself scanning the parked cars for Steve Ordner's bottle-green Delta 88, but didn't see it anywhere.

Closer to the house, the rest of the rock band coalesced around the persistent bass signature, and Mick Jagger screaming:

> *Ooooh, children—*
> *It's just a kiss away,*
> *Kiss away, kiss away . . .*

Every light in the house was blazing—fuck the energy crisis—except, of course in the living room, where rub-your-peepees would be going on during the slow numbers. Even over the heavy drive of the amplified music he could hear a hundred voices raised in fifty different conversations, as if Babel had fallen only seconds ago.

He thought that, had it been summer (or even fall), it would have been more fun to just stand outside, listening to the circus, charting its progress toward its zenith, and then its gradual fall-off. He had a sudden vision—startling, frightening—of himself standing on Wally Hamner's lawn and holding a roll of EEG graph paper in his hands, covered with the irregular spikes and dips of damaged mental function: the monitored record of a gigantic, tumored Party Brain. He shuddered a little and stuck his hands in his overcoat pockets to warm them.

His right hand encountered the small foil packet again and he took it out. Curious, he unfolded it, regardless of the cold that bit his fingertips with dull teeth. There was a small purple pill inside the foil, small enough to lie on the nail of his pinky finger without touching the edges. Much smaller than, say, a walnut. Could something as small as that make him clinically insane, cause him to see things that weren't there, think in a way he had never thought? Could it, in short, mime all the conditions of his son's mortal illness?

Casually, almost absently, he put the pill in his mouth. It had no taste. He swallowed it.

"BART!" The woman screamed. *"BART DAWES!"* It was a woman in a black off-the-shoulder evening dress with a martini in one hand. She had dark hair, put up for the occasion and held with a glittering rope spangled with imitation diamonds.

He had walked in through the kitchen door. The kitchen was choked, clogged with people. It was only eight-thirty; the Tidal Effect hadn't gotten far yet, then. The Tidal Effect was another part of Walter's theory; as a party continued, he contended, people would migrate to the four corners of the house. "The center does not hold,'' Wally said, blinking wisely. ''T. S. Eliot said that.'' Once, according to Wally, he had found a guy wandering around in the attic eighteen hours after a party ended.

The woman in the black dress kissed him warmly on the lips, her ample breasts pushing against his chest. Some of her martini fell on the floor between them.

''Hi,'' he said. ''Who's you?''

''Tina *Howard,* Bart. Don't you remember the class trip?'' She waggled a long, spade-shaped fingernail under his nose. *''NAUGH-ty BOY!''*

''*That* Tina? By God, you are!'' A stunned grin spread his mouth. That was another thing about Walter's parties; people from your past kept turning up like old photographs. Your best friend on the block thirty years ago; the girl you almost laid once in college; some guy you had worked with for a month on a summer job eighteen years ago.

''Except I'm Tina Howard Wallace now,'' the woman in the black dress said. ''My husband's around here . . . somewhere . . . '' She looked around vaguely, spilled some more of her drink, and swallowed the rest before it could get away from her. ''Isn't it AWFUL, I seem to have lost him.''

She looked at him warmly, speculatively, and Bart could barely believe that this woman had given him his first touch of female flesh—the sophomore class trip at Grover Cleveland High School, a hundred and nine years ago. Rubbing her breast through her white cotton sailor blouse beside . . .

''Cotter's Stream,'' he said aloud.

She blushed and giggled. ''You remember, all right.''

His eyes dropped in a perfect, involuntary reflex to the front of her dress and she shrieked with laughter. He grinned that helpless grin again. ''I guess time goes by faster than we—''

''Bart!'' Wally Hamner yelled over the general party babble. ''Hey buddy, really glad you could make it!''

He cut across the room to them with the also-to-be-patented Walter Hamner Party Zigzag, a thin man, now mostly bald, wearing an impeccable 1962-vintage pinstriped shirt and horn-rimmed glasses. He shook Walter's outstretched hand, and Walter's grip was as hard as he remembered.

''I see you met Tina Wallace,'' Walter said.

''Hell, we go way back when,'' he said, and smiled uncomfortably at Tina.

''Don't you tell my husband that, you naughty boy,'' Tina giggled. '' 'Scuse, please. I'll see you later, Bart?''

''Sure,'' he said.

She disappeared around a clump of people gathered by a table loaded with chips and dips and went on into the living room. He nodded after her and said, ''How do you pick them, Walter? That girl was my first feel. It's like 'This Is Your Life.' ''

Walter shrugged modestly. ''All a part of the Pleasure Push, Barton my boy.'' He nodded at the paper bag tucked under his arm. ''What's in that plain brown wrapper?''

"Southern Comfort. You've got ginger ale, don't you?"

"Sure," Walter said, but grimaced. "Are you really going to drink that down-by-de-Swanee-Ribber stuff? I always thought you were a scotch man."

"I was always a private Comfort-and-ginger-ale man. I've come out of the closet."

Walter grinned. "Mary's around here someplace. She's kinda been keeping an eye out for you. Get yourself a drink and we'll go find her."

"Good enough."

He made his way across the kitchen, saying hi to people he knew vaguely and who looked as if they didn't know him at all, and replying hi, how are you to people he didn't remember who hailed him first. Cigarette smoke rolled majestically through the kitchen. Conversation faded quickly in and out, like stations on late-night AM radio, all of it bright and meaningless.

   . . . Freddy and Jim didn't have their time sheets so I

   . . . said that his mother died quite recently and he's apt to go on a crying jag if he drinks too much

   . . . so when he got the paint scraped off he saw it was really a nice piece, maybe pre-Revolutionary

   . . . and this little kike came to the door selling encyclopedias

   . . . very messy; he won't give her the divorce because of the kids and he drinks like a

   . . . terribly nice dress

   . . . so much to drink that when he went to pay the check he barfed all over the hostess

A long Formica-topped table had been set up in front of the stove and the sink, and it was already crowded with opened liquor bottles and glasses in varying sizes and degrees of fullness. Ashtrays already overflowed with filtertips. Three ice buckets filled with cubes had been crowded into the sink. Over the stove was a large poster which showed Richard Nixon wearing a pair of earphones. The earphone cord disappeared up into the rectum of a donkey standing on the edge of the picture. The caption said:

WE LISTEN BETTER!

To the left, a man in bell-bottomed baggies and a drink in each hand (a water glass filled with what looked to be whiskey and a large stein filled with beer) was entertaining a mixed group with a joke. "This guy comes into this bar, and here's this monkey sitting on the stool next to him. So the guy orders a beer and when the bartender brings it, the guy says, 'Who owns this monkey? Cute little bugger.' And the bartender says, 'Oh, that's the piano player's monkey.' So the guy swings around . . ."

He made himself a drink and looked around for Walt, but he had gone to the door to greet some more guests—a young couple. The man was wearing a huge driving cap, goggles, and an old-time automobile duster. Written on the front of the duster were the words

Keep on Truckin'

Several people were laughing uproariously, and Walter was howling. Whatever the joke was, it seemed to go back a long time.

" . . . and the guy walks over to the piano player and says, 'Do you know your monkey just pissed in my beer?' And the piano player says, 'No, but hum a few bars and I'll fake it.' " Calculated burst of laughter. The man in the bell-bottomed baggies sipped his whiskey and then cooled it with a gulp of beer.

He took his drink and strolled into the darkened living room, slipping behind the turned back of Tina Howard Wallace before she could see him and snag him into a long game of Where Are They Now. She looked, he thought, like the kind of person who could cite you chapter and verse from the lives of classmates who had turned out badly—divorce, nervous disorders, and criminal violations would be her stock in trade—and would have made unpersons out of those who had had success.

Someone had put on the inevitable album of 50's rock and roll, and maybe fifteen couples were jitterbugging hilariously and badly. He saw Mary dancing with a tall, slim man that he knew but could not place. Jack? John? Jason? He shook his head. It wouldn't come. Mary was wearing a party dress he had never seen before. It buttoned up one side, and she had left enough buttons undone to provide a sexy slit to a little above one nyloned knee. He waited for some strong feeling—jealousy or loss, even habitual craving—but none came. He sipped his drink.

She turned her head and saw him. He raised a noncommittal finger in salute: *Go on and finish your dance*—but she broke off and came over, bringing her partner with her.

"I'm so glad you could come, Bart," she said, raising her voice to be heard over the laughter and conversation and stereo. "Do you remember Dick Jackson?"

Bart stuck out his hand and the slim man shook it. "You and your wife lived on our street five . . . no, seven years ago. Is that right?"

Jackson nodded. "We're out in Willowood now."

Housing development, he thought. He had become very sensitive to the city's geography and housing strata.

"Good enough. Are you still working for Piels?"

"No, I've got my own business now. Two trucks. Tri-State Haulers. Say, if that laundry of yours ever needs day-hauling . . . chemicals or any of that stuff . . . "

"I don't work for the laundry anymore," he said, and saw Mary wince slightly, as if someone had knuckled an old bruise.

"No? What are you doing now?"

"Self-employed," he said and grinned. "Were you in on that independent trucker's strike?"

Jackson's face, already dark with alcohol, darkened more. "You're goddam right. And I personally untracked a guy that couldn't see falling into line. Do you know what those miserable Ohio bastards are charging for diesel? 31.9! That takes my profit margin from twelve percent and cuts it right down to nine. And all my truck maintenance has got to come out of that nine. Not to mention the frigging double-nickle speed-limit—''

As he went on about the perils of independent trucking in a country that had suddenly developed a severe case of the energy bends, Bart listened and nodded in the right places and sipped his drink. Mary excused herself and went into the kitchen to get a glass of punch. The man in the automobile duster was doing an exaggerated Charleston to an old Everly Brothers number, and people were laughing and applauding.

Jackson's wife, a busty, muscular-looking girl with carroty red hair, came over and was introduced. She was quite near the stagger point. Her eyes looked like the Tilt signs on a pinball machine. She shook hands with him, smiled glassily, and then said to Dick Jackson: ''Hon, I think I'm going to whoopsie. Where's the bathroom?''

Jackson led her away. He skirted the dance floor and sat down in one of the chairs along the side. He finished his drink. Mary was slow coming back. Someone had collared her into a conversation, he supposed.

He reached into an inside pocket and brought out a pack of cigarettes and lit one. He only smoked at parties now. That was quite a victory over a few years ago, when he had been part of the three-packs a-day cancer brigade.

He was halfway through the cigarette and still watching the kitchen door for Mary when he happened to glance down at his fingers and saw how interesting they were. It was interesting how the first and second fingers of his right hand knew just how to hold the cigarette, as if they had been smoking all their lives.

The thought was so funny he had to smile.

It seemed that he had been examining his fingers for quite a while when he noticed his mouth tasted different. Not bad, just different. The spit in it seemed to have thickened. And his legs . . . his legs felt a little jittery, as if they would like to tap along with the music, as if tapping along with the music would relieve them, make them feel cool and just like legs again—

He felt a little frightened at the way that thought, which had begun so ordinarily, had gone corkscrewing off in a wholly new direction like a man lost in a big house and climbing a tall *crrrrystal* staircase—

There it was again, and it was probably the pill he had taken, Olivia's pill, yes. And wasn't that an interesting way to say crystal? *Crrrrystal*, gave it a crusty, bangled sound, like a stripper's costume.

He smiled craftily and looked at his cigarette, which seemed amazingly *white,* amazingly *round,* amazingly symbolic of all America's padding and wealth. Only in America were cigarettes so good-tasting. He had a puff. Wonderful. He thought of all the cigarettes in America pouring off the production lines in Winston-Salem, a plethora of cigarettes, an endless clean white cornucopia of them. It was the mescaline, all right. He was starting to trip. And if people knew what he had been thinking about the word *crystal* (a/k/a *crrrystal*), they would nod and tap their heads: *Yes, he's crazy, all right. Nutty as a fruitcake.* Fruitcake, there was another good word. He suddenly wished Sal Magliore was here. Together, he and Sally One-Eye would discuss all the facets of the Organization's business. They would discuss old whores and shootings. In his mind's eye he saw Sally One-Eye and himself eating linguini in a small Italian *ristorante* with dark-toned walls and scarred wooden tables while the strains of *The Godfather* played on the soundtrack. All in luxurious Technicolor that you could fall into, bathe in like a bubble bath.

"Crrrrrrystal," he said under his breath, and grinned. It seemed that he had been sitting here and going over one thing and another for a very long time, but no ash had grown on his cigarette at all. He was astounded. He had another puff.

"Bart?"

He looked up. It was Mary, and she had a canapé for him. He smiled at her. "Sit down. Is that for me?"

"Yes." She gave it to him. It was a small triangular sandwich with pink stuff in the middle. It suddenly occurred to him that Mary would be frightened, horrified, if she knew he was on a trip. She might call an emergency squad, the police, God knew who else. He had to act normally. But the thought of acting normal made him feel stranger than ever.

"I'll eat it later," he said, and put the sandwich in his shirt pocket.

"Bart, are you drunk?"

"Just a little," he said. He could see the pores on her face. He could not recall ever having seen them so clearly before. All those little holes, as if God was a cook and she was a pie crust. He giggled and her deepening frown made him say: "Listen, don't tell."

"Tell?" She offered a puzzled frown.

"About the Product four."

"Bart, what in the name of God are you—"

"I've got to go to the bathroom," he said. "I'll be back." He left without looking at her, but he could feel her frown radiating out from her face in waves like heat from a microwave oven. Yet if he didn't look back at her, it was possible she would not guess. In this, the best of all possible worlds, anything was possible, even crrrystal staircases. He smiled fondly. The word had become an old friend.

The trip to the bathroom somehow became an odyssey, a safari. The party noise seemed to have picked up a cyclical beat, IT SEEMED TO fade in and FADE OUT in syllables OF THREE AND even the STEREO faded IN and OUT. He mumbled to people he thought he knew but refused to take up a single thrown conversational gambit; he only pointed to his crotch, smiled, and walked on. He left puzzled faces in his wake. Why is there never a party full of strangers when you need one? he scolded himself.

The bathroom was occupied. He waited outside for what seemed like hours and when he finally got in he couldn't urinate although he seemed to want to. He looked at the wall above the toilet tank and the wall was bulging in and out in a cyclical, three-beat rhythm. He flushed even though he hadn't gone, in case someone outside might be listening, and watched the water swirl out of the bowl. It had a sinister pink color, as if the last user had passed blood. Unsettling.

He left the bathroom and the party smote him again. Faces came and went like floating balloons. The music was nice, though. Elvis was on. Good old Elvis. Rock on, Elvis, rock on.

Mary's face appeared in front of him and hovered, looking concerned. "Bart, what's wrong with you?"

"Wrong? Nothing wrong." He was astounded, amazed. His words had come out in a visual series of musical notes. "I'm hallucinating." He said it aloud, but it was spoken only for himself.

"Bart, what have you taken?" She looked frightened now.

"Mescaline," he said.

"Oh God, Bart. *Drugs? Why?*"

"Why not?" he responded, not to be flip, but because it was the only response he could think of quickly. The words came out in notes again, and this time some of them had flags.

"Do you want me to take you to a doctor?"

He looked at her, surprised, and went ponderously over her question in his mind to see if it had any hidden connotations; Freudian echoes of the funny farm. He giggled again, and the giggles streamed musically out of his mouth and in front of his eyes, crrrrystal notes on lines and spaces, broken by bars and rests.

"Why would I want a doctor?" he said, choosing each word. The question mark was a high quarter-note. "It's just like she said. Not that good, not that bad. But interesting."

"Who?" she demanded. "Who told you? Where did you get it?" Her face was changing, seeming to become hooded and reptilian. Mary as cheap mystery-movie police detective, shining the light in the suspect's eyes—*Come on, McGonigal, whichever way you want it, hard or soft*—and then worse still she began to remind him uneasily of the H. P. Lovecraft stories he had read as a boy, the Cthulu Mythos stories, where perfectly normal human beings changed into fishy, crawling things at the urgings of the Elder Ones. Mary's face began to look scaly, vaguely eellike.

"Never mind," he said, frightened. "Why can't you leave me alone? Stop fucking me up. I'm not bothering you."

Her face recoiled, became Mary's again, Mary's hurt, mistrustful face, and he was sorry. The party beat and swirled around them. "All right, Bart," she said quietly. "You hurt yourself just any way you like. But please don't embarrass me. Can I ask you that much?"

"Of course you c—"

But she had not waited for his answer. She left him, going quickly into the kitchen without looking back. He felt sorry, but he also felt relieved. But suppose someone else tried to talk with him? They would know too. He couldn't talk to people normally, not like this. Apparently he couldn't even fool people into thinking he was drunk.

"Rrrrreet," he said, ruffling the *r*'s lightly off the roof of his mouth. This time the notes came out in a straight line, all of them hurrying notes with flags. He could make notes all night and be perfectly happy, he didn't mind. But not here, where anybody could come along and accost him. Someplace private, where he could hear himself think. The party made him feel as if he were standing behind a large waterfall. Hard to think against the sound of all that. Better to find some quiet backwater. With perhaps a radio to listen to. He felt that listening to music would aid his thinking, and there was a lot to thing about. Reams of things.

Also, he was quite sure that people had begun to glance over at him. Mary must have spread the word. *I'm worried. Bart's on mescaline.* It would move from group to group. They would go on pretending to dance, pretending to drink and have their conversations, but they would really be observing him from behind their hands, whispering about him. He could tell. It was all crrrystal clear.

A man walked past him, carrying a very tall drink and weaving slightly. He twitched the man's sport jacket and whispered hoarsely: "What are they saying about me?"

The man gave him a disconnected smile and blew a warm breath of scotch in his face. "I'll write that down," he said, and walked on.

He finally got into Walter Hamner's den (he could not have said how much later) and when he closed the door behind him, the sounds of the party became blessedly muted. He was getting scared. The stuff he had taken hadn't topped out yet; it just kept coming on stronger and stronger. He seemed to have crossed from one side of the living room to the other in the course of one blink; through the darkened bedroom where coats had been stored in another blink; down the hall in a third. The chain of normal, waking existence had come unclipped, spilling reality beads every which way. Continuity had broken down. His time sense was el destructo. Suppose he never came down? Suppose he was like this forever? It came to him to curl up and sleep it off, but he didn't know if he could. And if he did, God knew what dreams would come. The light, spur-of-the-moment way he had taken the pill now appalled him. This wasn't like being drunk; there was no small kernel of sobriety winking and blinking down deep in the center of him, that part that never got drunk. He was wacky all the way through.

But it was better in here. Maybe he could get control of it in here, by himself. And at least if he freaked out he wouldn't—

"Hi there."

He jumped, startled, and looked into the corner. A man was sitting there in a high-backed chair by one of Walter's bookcases. There was an open book on the man's lap, as a matter of fact. Or was it a man? There was a single light on in the room, a lamp on a small round table to the speaker's left. Its light cast long shadows on his face, shadows so long that his eyes were dark caverns, his cheeks etched in sardonic, malefic lines. For a moment he thought he had stumbled on Satan sitting in Wally Hamner's den. Then the figure stood and he saw it was a man, only a man. A tall fellow, maybe sixty, with blue eyes and a nose that had been repeatedly punched in losing bouts with the bottle. But he wasn't holding a drink, nor was there one on the table.

"Another wanderer, I see," the man said, and offered his hand. "Phil Drake."

"Barton Dawes," he said, still dazed from his fright. They shook. Drake's hand was twisted and scarred by some old wound—a burn, perhaps. But he didn't mind shaking it. *Drake.* The name was familiar but he couldn't remember where he had heard it before.

"Are you quite all right?" Drake asked. "You look a little—"

"I'm high," he said. "I took some mescaline and oh boy am I high." He glanced at the bookcases and saw them going in and out and didn't like it. It was too much like the beating of a giant heart. He didn't want to see things like that anymore.

"I see," Drake said. "Sit down. Tell me about it."

He looked at Drake, slightly amazed, and then felt a tremendous surge of relief. He sat down. "You know about mescaline?" he asked.

"Oh, a little. A little. I run a coffeehouse downtown. Kids wander in off the streets, tripping on something . . . is it a good trip?" he asked politely.

"Good and bad," he said. "It's . . . heavy. That's a good word, the way they use it."

"Yes. It is."

"I was getting a little scared." He glanced out the window and saw a long, celestial highway stretching across the black dome of the sky. He looked away casually, but couldn't help licking his lips. "Tell me . . . how long does this usually go on?"

"When did you drop?"

"Drop?" The word dropped out of his mouth in letters, fell to the carpet, and dissolved there.

"When did you take the stuff?"

"Oh . . . about eight-thirty."

"And it's . . . " He consulted his watch. "It's a quarter of ten now—"

"Quarter of *ten?* Is that *all?*"

Drake smiled. "The sense of time turns to rubber, doesn't it? I expect you'll be pretty well down by one-thirty."

"Really?"

"Oh yes, I should think so. You're probably peaking now. Is it very visual mesc?"

"Yes. A little *too* visual."

"More things to be seen than the eye of man was meant to behold," Drake said, and offered a peculiar, twisted smile.

"Yes, that's it. That's just it." His sense of relief at being with this man was intense. He felt saved. "What do you do besides talk to middle-aged men who have fallen down the rabbit hole?"

Drake smiled. "That's rather good. Usually people on mesc or acid turn inarticulate, sometimes incoherent. I spend most of my evenings at the Dial Help Center. On weekday afternoons I work at the coffee house I mentioned, a place called Drop Down Mamma. Most of the clientele are street freaks and stewbums. Mornings I just walk the streets and talk to my parishioners, if they're up. And in between, I run errands at the county jail.''

"You're a minister?''

"They call me a street priest. Very romantic. Malcolm Boyd, look out. At one time I was a real priest.''

"Not any more?''

"I have left the mother church,'' Drake said. He said it softly, but there was a kind of dreadful finality in his words. He could almost hear the clang of iron doors slammed shut forever.

"Why did you do that?''

Drake shrugged. "It doesn't matter. What about you? How did you get the mesc?''

"I got it from a girl on her way to Las Vegas. A nice girl, I think. She called me on Christmas Day.''

"For help?''

"I think so.''

"Did you help her?''

"I don't know.'' He smiled craftily. "Father, tell me about my immortal soul.''

Drake twitched. "I'm not your father.''

"Never mind, then.''

"What do you want to know about your 'soul'?''

He looked down at his fingers. He could make bolts of light shoot from their tips whenever he wanted to. It gave him a drunken feeling of power. "I want to know what will happen to it if I commit suicide.''

Drake stirred uneasily. "You don't want to think about killing yourself while you're tripping. The dope talks, not you.''

"*I* talk,'' he said. "Answer me.''

"I can't. I don't know what will happen to your 'soul' if you commit suicide. I do, however, know what will happen to your body. It will rot.''

Startled by this idea, he looked down at his hands again. Obligingly, they seemed to crack and molder in front of his gaze, making him think of that Poe story, "The Strange Case of M. Valdemar.'' Quite a night. Poe and Lovecraft. A. Gordon Pym, anyone? How about Abdul Allhazred, the Mad Arab? He looked up, a little disconcerted, but not really daunted.

"What's your body doing?'' Drake asked.

"Huh?'' He frowned, trying to parse sense from the question.

"There are two trips,'' Drake said. "A head trip and a body trip. Do you feel nauseated? Achey? Sick in any way?''

He consulted his body. "No,'' he said. "I just feel . . . busy.'' He laughed a little at the word, and Drake smiled. It was a good word to describe how he felt. His body seemed very active, even still. Rather light, but not ethereal. In fact, he had never felt so *fleshy,* so conscious of the way his mental processes and physical body were webbed together. There was no parting them. You couldn't peel one away from the other. You were stuck with it, baby. Integration. Entropy. The idea burst over him like a quick tropical sunrise. He sat chewing it over in light of his current situation, trying to make out the pattern, if there was one. But—

"But there's the soul," he said aloud.

"What about the soul?" Drake asked pleasantly.

"If you kill the brain, you kill the body," he said slowly. "And vice versa. But what happens to your *soul?* There's the wild card, Fa . . . Mr. Drake."

Drake said: "In that sleep of death, what dreams may come? *Hamlet,* Mr. Dawes."

"Do you think the soul lives on? Is there survival?"

Drake's eyes grayed. "Yes," he said. "I think there is survival . . . in some form."

"And do you think suicide is a mortal sin that condemns the soul to hell?"

Drake didn't speak for a long time. Then he said: "Suicide is wrong. I believe that with all my heart."

"That doesn't answer my question."

Drake stood up. "I have no intention of answering it. I don't deal in metaphysics anymore. I'm a civilian. Do you want to go back to the party?"

He thought of the noise and confusion, and shook his head.

"Home?"

"I couldn't drive. I'd be scared to drive."

"I'll drive you."

"Would you? How would you get back?"

"Call a cab from your house. New Year's Eve is a very good night for cabs."

"That would be good," he said gratefully. "I'd like to be alone, I think. I'd like to watch TV."

"Are you safe alone?" Drake asked somberly.

"Nobody is," he replied with equal gravity, and they both laughed.

"Okay. Do you want to say good-bye to anyone?"

"No. Is there a back door?"

"I think we can find one."

He didn't talk much on the way home. Watching the streetlights go by was almost all the excitement he could stand. When they went by the roadwork, he asked Drake's opinion.

"They're building new roads for energy-sucking behemoths while kids in this city are starving," Drake said shortly. "What do I think? I think it's a bloody crime."

He started to tell Drake about the gasoline bombs, the burning crane, the burning office trailer, and then didn't. Drake might think it was an hallucination. Worse still, he might think it wasn't.

The rest of the evening was not very clear. He directed Drake to his house. Drake commented that everyone on the street must be out partying or to bed early. He didn't comment. Drake called a taxi. They watched TV for a while without talking—Guy Lombardo at the Waldorf-Astoria, making the sweetest music this side of heaven. Guy Lombardo, he thought, was looking decidedly froggy.

The taxi came at quarter to twelve. Drake asked him again if he would be all right.

"Yes, I think I'm coming down." He really was. The hallucinations were draining toward the back of his mind.

Drake opened the front door and pulled up his collar. "Stop thinking about suicide. It's chicken."

He smiled and nodded, but he neither accepted nor rejected Drake's advice. Like everything else these days, he simply took it under advisement. "Happy New Year," he said.

"Same to you, Mr. Dawes."

The taxi honked impatiently.

Drake went down the walk, and the taxi pulled away, yellow light glowing on the roof.

He went back into the living room and sat down in front of the TV. They had switched from Guy Lombardo to Times Square, where the glowing ball was poised atop the Allis-Chalmers Building, ready to start its descent into 1974. He felt weary, drained, finally sleepy. The ball would come down soon and he would enter the new year tripping his ass off. Somewhere in the country a New Year's baby was pushing its squashed, placenta-covered head out of his mother's womb and into this best of all possible worlds. At Walter Hamner's party, people would be raising their glasses and counting down. New Year's resolutions were about to be tested. Most of them would prove as strong as wet paper towels. He made a resolution of his own on the spur of the moment, and got to his feet in spite of his tiredness. His body ached and his spine felt like glass—some kind of hangover. He went into the kitchen and got his hammer off the kitchen shelf. When he brought it back into the living room, the glowing ball was sinking down the pole. There was a split screen, showing the ball on the right, showing the merrymakers at the Waldorf on the left, chanting: "Eight . . . seven . . . six . . . five . . . " One fat society dame caught a glimpse of herself on a monitor, looked surprised, and then waved to the country.

The turn of the year, he thought. Absurdly, goose bumps broke out on his arms.

The ball reached the bottom, and a sign lit up on the top of the Allis-Chalmers Building. The sign said:

1974

At the same instant he swung the hammer and the TV screen exploded. Glass belched onto the carpet. There was a fizz of hot wires, but no fire. Just to be sure the TV would not roast him during the night in revenge, he kicked out the plug with his foot.

"Happy New Year," he said softly, and dropped the hammer to the carpet.

He lay on the couch and fell asleep almost immediately. He slept with the lights on and his sleep was dreamless.

PART THREE

January

If I don't get some shelter,
Oh, I'm gonna fade away . . .
                —Rolling Stones

January 5, 1974

The thing that happened in the Shop 'n' Save that day was the only thing that had happened to him in his whole life that actually seemed planned and sentient, not random. It was as if an invisible finger had written on a fellow human being, expressly for him to read.

He liked to go shopping. It was very soothing, very sane. He enjoyed doing sane things very much after his bout with the mescaline. He had not awakened on New Year's Day until afternoon, and he had spent the remainder of the day wandering disconnectedly around the house, feeling spaced-out and strange. He had picked things up and looked at them, feeling like Iago examining Yorick's skull. To a lesser degree the feeling had carried over to the next day, and even the day after that. But in another way, the effect had been good. His mind felt dusted and clean, as if it had been turned upside down, scrubbed and polished by some maniacally brisk internal housekeeper. He didn't get drunk and thus did not cry. When Mary had called him, very cautiously, around 7:00 P.M. on the first, he had talked to her calmly and reasonably, and it seemed to him that their positions had not changed very much. They were playing a kind of social statues, each waiting for the other to move first. But she had twitched and mentioned divorce. Just the possibility, the veriest wiggle of a finger, but movement for all that. No, the only thing that really disturbed him in the aftermath of the mescaline was the shattered lens of the Zenith color TV. He could not understand why he had done it. He had wanted such a TV for years, even though his favorite programs were the old ones that had been filmed in black and white. It wasn't even the act that distressed him as much as the lingering evidence of it—the broken glass, the exposed wiring. They seemed to reproach him, to say: *Why did you go and do that? I served you faithfully and you broke me. I never harmed you and you smashed me. I was defenseless.* And it was a terrible reminder of what they wanted to do to his house. At last he got an old quilt and covered the front of it. That made it both better and worse. Better because he couldn't see it, worse because it was like having a shrouded corpse in the house. He threw the hammer away like a murder weapon.

But going to the store was a good thing, like drinking coffee in Benjy's Grill or taking the LTD through the Clean Living Car Wash or stopping at Henny's newsstand downtown for a copy of *Time*. The Shop 'n' Save was very large, lighted with fluorescent bars set into the ceiling, and filled with ladies pushing carts and admonishing children and frowning at tomatoes wrapped in see-through plastic that would not allow a good squeeze. Muzak came down from discreet overhead speaker grilles, flowing evenly into your ears to be almost heard.

483

On this day, Saturday, the S&S was filled with weekend shoppers, and there were more men than usual, accompanying their wives and annoying them with sophomoric suggestions. He regarded the husbands, the wives, and the issue of their various partnerships with benign eyes. The day was bright and sunshine poured through the store's big front windows, splashing gaudy squares of light by the checkout registers, occasionally catching some woman's hair and turning it into a halo of light. Things did not seem so serious when it was like this, but things were always worse at night.

His cart was filled with the usual selection of a man thrown rudely into solitary housekeeping: spaghetti, meat sauce in a glass jar, fourteen TV dinners, a dozen eggs, butter, and a package of navel oranges to protect against scurvy.

He was on his way down a middle aisle toward the checkouts when God perhaps spoke to him. There was a woman in front of him, wearing powder-blue slacks and a blue cable-stitched sweater of a navy color. She had very yellow hair. She was maybe thirty-five, good looking in an open, alert way. She made a funny gobbling, crowing noise in her throat and staggered. The squeeze bottle of mustard she had been holding in her hand fell to the floor and rolled, showing a red pennant and the word FRENCH'S over and over again.

"Ma'am?" he ventured. "Are you okay?"

The woman fell backward and her left hand, which she had put up to steady herself, swept a score of coffee cans onto the floor. Each can said:

MAXWELL HOUSE
Good To The Very Last Drop

It happened so fast that he wasn't really scared—not for himself, anyway—but he saw one thing that stuck with him later and came back to haunt his dreams. Her eyes had drifted out into walleyes, just as Charlie's had during his fits.

The woman fell on the floor. She cawed weakly. Her feet, clad in leather boots with a salt rime around the bottoms, drummed on the tiled floor. The woman directly behind him screamed weakly. A clerk who had been putting prices on soup cans ran up the aisle, dropping his stamper. Two of the checkout girls came to the foot of the aisle and stared, their eyes wide.

He heard himself say: "I think she's having an epileptic seizure."

But it wasn't an epileptic seizure. It was some sort of brain hemorrhage and a doctor who had been going around in the store with his wife pronounced her dead. The young doctor looked scared, as if he had just realized that his profession would dog him to his grave, like some vengeful horror monster. By the time he finished his examination, a middling-sized crowd had formed around the young woman lying among the coffee cans which had been the last part of the world over which she had exercised her human perogative to rearrange. Now she had become part of that other world and would be rearranged by other humans. Her cart was half-filled with provisions for a week's living, and the sight of the cans and boxes and wrapped meats filled him with a sharp, agonized terror.

Looking into the dead woman's cart, he wondered what they would do with the groceries. Put them back on the shelves? Save them beside the manager's office until cash redeemed them, proof that the lady of the house had died in harness?

Someone had gotten a cop and he pushed his way through the knot of people on the checkout side. "Look out, here," the cop was saying self-importantly. "Give her air." As if she could use it.

He turned and bulled his way out of the crowd, butting with his shoulder. His calm of the last five days was shattered, and probably for good. Had there ever been a clearer omen? Surely not. But what did it mean? What?

When he got home he shoved the TV dinners into the freezer and then made himself a strong drink. His heart was thudding in his chest. All the way home from the supermarket he had been trying to remember what they had done with Charlie's clothes.

They had given his toys to the Goodwill Shop in Norton, they had transferred his bank account of a thousand dollars (college money—half of everything Charlie had gotten from relatives at birthdays and Christmas went into that account, over his howls of protest) to their own joint account. They had burned his bedding on Mamma Jean's advice—he himself had been unable to understand that, but didn't have the heart to protest; everything had fallen apart and he was supposed to argue over saving a mattress and box springs? But the clothes, that was a different matter. What had they done with Charlie's clothes?

The question gnawed at him all afternoon, making him fretful, and once he almost went to the phone to call Mary and ask her. But that would be the final straw, wouldn't it? She wouldn't have to just guess about the state of his sanity after that.

Just before sunset he went up to the small half-attic, which was reached by crawling through a trapdoor in the ceiling of the master bedroom closet. He had to stand on a chair and shinny up in. He hadn't been in the attic for a long, long time, but the single bare 100-watt bulb still worked. It was coated with dust and cobwebs, but it still worked.

He opened a dusty box at random and discovered all his high school and college yearbooks, laid neatly away. Embossed on the cover of each high school yearbook were the words:

THE CENTURION
Bay High School . . .

On the cover of each college yearbook (they were heavier, more richly bound) were these words:

THE PRISM
Let Us Remember . . .

He opened the high school yearbooks first, flipping through the signed end pages ("Uptown, downtown, all around the town/I'm the gal who wrecked your yearbook/Writing upside down—A.F.A., Connie"), then the photographs of long-ago teachers, frozen behind their desks and beside their blackboards, smiling vaguely, then of classmates he barely remembered with their credits (FHA 1,2; Class Council 2,3,4; Poe Society, 4) listed beneath, along with their nicknames and a little slogan. He knew the fates of some (Army, dead in a car crash, assistant bank manager), but most were gone, their futures hidden from him.

In his senior high yearbook he came across a young George Barton Dawes, looking dreamily toward the future from a retouched photograph that had been taken at Cressey Studios. He was amazed by how little that boy knew of the future and by how much that boy looked like the son this man had come to search out traces of. The boy in the picture had not yet even manufactured the sperm that would become half the boy. Below the picture:

BARTON G. DAWES
"Whizzer"
(Outing Club, 1,2,3,4
Poe Society, 3,4)

Bay High School
Bart, the Klass Klown, helped to lighten our load!

He put the yearbooks back in their box helter-skelter and went on poking. He found drapes that Mary had taken down five years ago. An old easy chair with a broken arm. A clock radio that didn't work. A wedding photograph album that he was scared to look through. Piles of magazines—*ought to get those out*, he told himself. *They're a fire hazard in the summer*. A washing machine motor that he had once brought home from the laundry and tinkered with to no avail. And Charlie's clothes.

They were in three cardboard cartons, each crisp with the smell of mothballs. Charlie's shirts and pants and sweaters, even Charlie's Hanes underwear. He took them out and looked at each item carefully, trying to imagine Charlie wearing these things, moving in them, rearranging minor parts of the world in them. At last it was the smell of the mothballs that drove him out of the attic, shaking and grimacing, needing a drink. The smell of things that had lain quietly and uselessly over the years, things which had no purpose but to hurt. He thought about them for most of the evening, until the drink blotted out the ability to think.

January 7, 1974

The doorbell rang at quarter past ten and when he opened the front door, a man in a suit and a topcoat was standing there, sort of hipshot and slouched and friendly. He was neatly shaved and barbered, carrying a slim briefcase, and at first he thought the man was a salesman with a briefcase full of samples—Amway, or magazine subscriptions, or possibly even the larcenous Swipe—and he prepared to welcome the man in, to listen to his pitch carefully, to ask questions, and maybe even buy something. Except for Olivia, he was the first person who had come to the house since Mary left almost five weeks ago.

But the man wasn't a salesman. He was a lawyer. His name was Philip T. Fenner, and his client was the city council. These facts he announced with a shy grin and a hearty handshake.

"Come on in," he said, and sighed. He supposed that in a half-assed sort of way, this guy *was* a salesman. You might even say he was selling Swipe.

Fenner was talking away, a mile a minute.

"Beautiful house you have here. Just beautiful. Careful ownership always shows, that's what I say. I won't take up much of your time, Mr. Dawes, I know you're a busy man, but Jack Gordon thought I might as well swing out here since it was on my way and drop off this relocation form. I imagine you mailed for one, but the Christmas rush and all, things get lost. And I'd be glad to answer any questions you might have, of course."

"I have a question," he said, unsmiling.

The jolly exterior of his visitor slipped for a moment and he saw the real Fenner lurking behind it, as cold and mechanized as a Pulsar watch. "What would that be, Mr. Dawes?"

He smiled. "Would you like a cup of coffee?"

Back on with the smiling Fenner, cheerful runner of city council errands. "Gee, that'd be nice, if it's not too much trouble. A trifle nippy out there, only seventeen degrees. I think the winters have been getting colder, don't you?"

"They sure have." The water was still hot from his breakfast coffee. "Hope you don't mind instant. My wife's visiting her folks for a while, and I just sort of muddle along."

Fenner laughed good-naturedly and he saw that Fenner knew exactly what the situation was between him and Mary, and probably what the situation was between him and any other given persons or institutions: Steve Ordner, Vinnie Mason, the corporation, God.

"Not at all, instant's fine. I always drink instant. Can't tell the difference. Okay to put some papers on this table?"

"Go right ahead. Do you take cream?"

"No, just black. Black is fine." Fenner unbuttoned his topcoat but didn't take it off. He swept it under him as he sat down, as a woman will sweep her skirt so she doesn't wrinkle the back. In a man, the gesture was almost jarringly fastidious. He opened his briefcase and took out a stapled form that looked like an income tax return. He poured Fenner a cup of coffee and gave it to him.

"Thanks. Thanks very much. Join me?"

"I think I'll have a drink," he said.

"Uh-huh," Fenner said, and smiled charmingly. He sipped his coffee. "Good, very good. Hits the spot."

He made himself a tall drink and said, "Excuse me for just a minute, Mr. Fenner. I have to make a telephone call."

"Certainly. Of course." He sipped his coffee again and smacked his lips over it.

He went to the phone in the hall, leaving the door open. He dialed the Calloway house and Jean answered.

"It's Bart," he said, "Is Mary there, Jean?"

"She's sleeping." Jean's voice was frosty.

"Please wake her up. It's very important."

"I bet it is. I just bet. I told Lester the other night, I said: Lester, it's time we thought about an unlisted phone. And he agreed with me. We both think you've gone off your rocker, Barton Dawes, and that's the plain truth with no shellack on it."

"I'm sorry to hear that. But I really have to—"

The upstairs extension was picked up and Mary said, "Bart?"

"Yes. Mary, has a lawyer named Fenner been out to see you? Kind of slick-talking fellow that tries to act like Jimmy Stewart?"

"No," she said. *Shit, snake-eyes.* Then she added, "He called on the phone." *Jackpot!* Fenner was standing in the doorway now, holding his coffee and sipping it calmly. The half-shy, totally cheerful, aw-shucks expression was gone now. He looked rather pained.

"Mamma, get off the extension," Mary said, and Jean Calloway hung up with a bitter snort.

"Was he asking about me?" he asked.

"Yes."

"He talked to you after the party?"

"Yes, but . . . I didn't tell him anything about that."

"You might have told him more than you know. He comes on like a sleepy tick-hound, but he's the city council's ballcutter." He smiled at Fenner, who thinly smiled back. "You've got an appointment with him?"

"Why . . . yes." She sounded surprised. "But he only wants to talk about the house, Bart—"

"No, that's what he told you. He really wants to talk about me. I think these guys would like to drag me into a competency hearing."

"A . . . what? . . . " She sounded utterly befuddled.

"I haven't taken their money yet, ergo I must be crazy. Mary, do you remember what we talked about at Handy Andy's?"

"Bart, is that Mr. Fenner in the house?"

"Yes."

"The psychiatrist," she said dully. "I mentioned you were going to be seeing a . . . oh, Bart, I'm sorry."

"Don't be," he said softly, and meant it. "This is going to be all right, Mary. I swear. Maybe nothing else, but this is going to be all right."

He hung up and turned to Fenner. "Want me to call Stephan Ordner?" he asked. "Vinnie Mason? I won't bother with Ron Stone or Tom Granger, they'd recognize a cheap prick like you before you even had your briefcase unsnapped. But Vinnie wouldn't and Ordner would welcome you with open arms. He's on the prod for me."

"You needn't," Fenner said. "You've misunderstood me, Mr. Dawes. And you've apparently misunderstood my clients. There is nothing personal in this. No one is out to get you. But there *has* been an awareness for some time that you dislike the 784 extension. You wrote a letter to the paper last August—"

"Last August," he marveled. "You people have a clipping service, don't you?"

"Of course."

He went into a harried crouch, rolling his eyeballs fearfully. "More clippings! More lawyers! Ron, go out and snow those reporters! We have enemies everywhere. Mavis, bring me my pills!" He straightened up. "Paranoia, anyone? Christ, I thought I was bad."

"We also have a public-relations staff," Fenner said stiffly. "We are not nickle-and-diming here, Mr. Dawes. We are talking about a ten-million-dollar project."

He shook his head, disgusted. "They ought to hold a competency hearing on you road guys, not me."

Fenner said: "I'm going to lay all my cards on the table, Mr. Dawes."

"You know, it's been my experience that when anybody says that they're ready to stop screwing around with the little lies and they're about to tell a real whopper."

Fenner flushed, finally angry. "You wrote the newspaper. You dragged your heels on finding a new plant for the Blue Ribbon Laundry and finally got canned—"

"I didn't. I resigned at least a half an hour before they could pink me."

"—and you've ignored all our communications dealing with this house. The consensus is that you may be planning some public display on the twentieth. Calling the papers and TV stations, getting them all out here. The heroic home owner dragged kicking and screaming from his hearth and home by the city's Gestapo agents."

"That worries you, doesn't it?"

"Of course it worries us! Public opinion is volatile, it swings around like a weathervane—"

"And your clients are elected officials."

Fenner looked at him expressionlessly.

"So what now?" he asked. "Are you going to make me an offer I can't refuse?"

Fenner sighed. "I can't understand what we're arguing about, Mr. Dawes. The city is offering you sixty thousand dollars to—"

"Sixty-three five."

"Yes, very good. They are offering you that amount for the house and the lot. Some people are getting a lot less. And what do you get for that money? You get no hassles, no trouble, no heat. The money is practically tax free because you've already paid Uncle the taxes on the money you spent to buy it. All you owe is taxes on the markup. Or don't you think the valuation is fair?"

"Fair enough," he said, thinking about Charlie. "As far as dollars and cents go, it's fair. Probably more than I could get if I wanted to sell it, with the price of loans what they are."

"So what *are* we arguing about?"

"We're not," he said, and sipped his drink. Yes, he had gotten his salesman, all right. "Do you have a house, Mr. Fenner?"

"Yes I do," Fenner said promptly. "A very fine one in Greenwood. And if you are going to ask me what I would do or how I would feel if our positions were reversed, I'll be very frank. I would twist the city's tit for all I could get and then laugh all the way to the bank."

"Yes, of course you would." He laughed and thought of Don and Ray Tarkington, who would have twisted both tits and rammed the courthouse flagpole up the city's ass for good measure. "Do you folks really think I've lost my marbles, then?"

Judiciously, Fenner said: "We don't know. Your resolution to the laundry relocation problem was hardly a normal one."

"Well, I'll tell you this. I have enough marbles left to know I could get myself a lawyer who doesn't like the eminent domain statute—one who still believes in that quaint old adage that a man's home is his castle. He could get a restraining order and we could tie you up for a month, maybe two. With luck and the right progression of judges, we could hold this thing off until next September."

Fenner looked pleased rather than disconcerted, as he had suspected Fenner would. Finally, Fenner was thinking. Here's the hook, Freddy, are you enjoying this? Yes, George, I have to admit I am.

"What do you want?" Fenner asked.

"How much are you prepared to offer?"

"We'll hike the valuation five thousand dollars. Not a penny more. And nobody will hear about the girl."

Everything stopped. Stopped dead.

"What?" he whispered.

"The *girl*, Mr. Dawes. The one you were banging. You had her here December sixth and seventh."

A number of thoughts spiraled through his mind in a period of seconds, some of them extremely sensible, but most of them overlaid and made untrustworthy with a thin yellow patina of fear. But above both fear and sensible thoughts was a vast red rage that made him want to leap across the table and choke this tick-tock man until clocksprings fell out of his ears. And he must not do that; above all, not that.

"Give me a number," he said.

"Number—?"

"Phone number. I'll call you this afternoon and tell you my decision."

"It would be ever so much better if we could wrap it up right now."

You'd like that, wouldn't you? Referee, let's extend this round thirty seconds. I've got this man on the ropes.

"No, I don't think so. Please get out of my house."

Fenner gave a smooth, expressionless shrug. "Here's my card. The number is on it. I expect to be in between two-thirty and four o'clock."

"I'll call."

Fenner left. He watched him through the window beside the front door as he walked down the path to his dark blue Buick, got in, and cruised away. Then he slammed his fist against the wall, hard.

He mixed himself another drink and sat down at the kitchen table to go over the situation. They knew about Olivia. They were willing to use that knowledge as a lever. As a lever to move him it wasn't very good. They could no doubt end his marriage with it, but his marriage was in serious trouble already. But they had *spied* on him.

The question was, how?

If there had been men watching him, they undoubtedly would have known about the world-famous crackle-crackle-boom-boom. If so, they would have used it on him. Why bother with something paltry like a little extramarital boogie-woogie when you can have the recalcitrant home owner slapped in jail for arson? So they had bugged him. When he thought how close he had come to drunkenly spilling the crime to Magliore over the phone, cold little dots of perspiration broke out on his skin. Thank God Magliore had shut him up. Crackle-crackle-boom-boom was bad enough.

So he was living in a bugged house and the question remained: What to do about Fenner's offer and Fenner's clients' methods?

He put a TV dinner in the oven for his lunch and sat down with another drink to wait for it. They had spied on him, tried to bribe him. The more he thought about it, the angrier it made him.

He took the TV dinner out and ate it. He wandered around the house, looking at things. He began to have an idea.

* * *

At three o'clock he called Fenner and told him to send out the form. He would sign it if Fenner took care of the two items they had discussed. Fenner sounded very pleased, even relieved. He said he would be glad to take care of things, and would see he had a form tomorrow. Fenner said he was glad he had decided to be sensible.

"There are a couple of conditions," he said.

"Conditions," Fenner repeated, and sounded instantly wary.

"Don't get excited. It's nothing you can't handle."

"Let's hear them," Fenner said. "But I'm warning you, Dawes, you've squeezed us for about all you can."

"You get the form over to the house tomorrow," he said. "I'll bring it to your office on Wednesday. I want you to have a check for sixty-eight thousand five hundred dollars waiting for me. A *cashier's* check. I'll trade you the release form for the check."

"Mr. Dawes, we can't do business that way—"

"Maybe you're not supposed to, but you *can*. The same way you're not supposed to tap my phone and God knows what else. No check, no form. I'll get the lawyer instead."

Fenner paused. He could almost hear Fenner thinking.

"All right. What else?"

"I don't want to be bothered anymore after Wednesday. On the twentieth, it's yours. Until then it's mine."

"Fine," Fenner said instantly, because of course that wasn't a condition at all. The law said the house was his until midnight on the nineteenth, incontrovertibly the city's property a minute later. If he signed the city's release form and took the city's money, he could holler his head off to every newspaper and TV station in town and not get a bit of sympathy.

"That's all," he said.

"Good," Fenner said, sounding extremely happy. "I'm glad we could finally get together on this in a rational way, Mr.—"

"Fuck you," he said, and hung up.

January 8, 1974

He wasn't there when the courier dropped the bulky brown envelope containing form 6983-426-73-74 (blue folder) through his letter slot. He had gone out into darkest Norton to talk to Sal Magliore. Magliore was not overjoyed to see him, but as he talked, Magliore grew more thoughtful.

Lunch was sent in—spaghetti and veal and a bottle of Gallo red. It was a wonderful meal. Magliore held up his hand to stop him when he got to the part about the five-thousand-dollar bribe and Fenner's knowledge of Olivia. He made a telephone call and spoke briefly to the man on the other end. Magliore gave the man on the other end the Crestallen Street address. "Use the van," he said and hung up. He twirled more spaghetti onto his fork and nodded across the table for the story to go on.

When he finished, Magliore said: "You're lucky they weren't tailing you. You'd be in the box right now."

He was full to bursting, unable to eat another mouthful. He had not had such a meal in five years. He complimented Magliore, and Magliore smiled.

"Some of my friends, they don't eat pasta anymore. They got an image to keep up. So they eat at steak houses or places that have French food or Swedish food or something like that. They got the ulcers to prove it. Why ulcers? Because you can't change what you are." He was pouring spaghetti sauce out of the grease-stained cardboard takeout bucket the spaghetti had come in. He began to mop it up with crusts of garlic bread, stopped, looked across the table with those strange, magnified eyes and said: "You're asking me to help you commit a mortal sin."

He looked at Magliore blankly, unable to hide his surprise.

Magliore laughed crossly. "I know what you're thinkin'. A man in my business is the wrong guy to talk about sin. I already told you that I had one guy knocked off. More than one guy, too. But I never killed anyone that didn't deserve to be killed. And I look at it this way: a guy who dies before God planned him to die, it's like a rain-out at the ball park. The sins that guy committed, they don't count. God has got to let 'em in because they didn't have all the time to repent He meant them to have. So killing a guy is really sparing him the pain of hell. So in a way, I done more for those guys than the Pope himself could have done. I think God knows that. But this isn't any of my business. I like you a lot. You got balls. Doing what you did with those gas bombs, that tooks balls. This, though. This is something different."

"I'm not asking you to do anything. It's my own free will."

Magliore rolled his eyes. "Jesus! Mary! Joseph the carpenter! Why can't you just leave me alone?"

"Because you have what I need."

"I wish to God I didn't."

"Are you going to help me?"

"I don't know."

"I've got the money now. Or will have, shortly."

"It ain't a matter of money. It's a matter of principle. I never dealt with a fruit-cake like you before. I'll have to think about it. I'll call you."

He decided it would be wrong to press further and left.

He was filling out the relocation form when Magliore's men came. They were driving a white Econoline van with RAY'S TV SALES AND SERVICE written on the side, below a dancing TV with a big grin on its picture tube. There were two men, wearing green fatigues and carrying bulky service cases. The cases contained real TV repair tools and tubes, but they also contained sundry other equipment. They "washed" his house. It took an hour and a half. They found bugs in both phones, one in his bedroom, one in the dining room. None in the garage, which made him feel relieved.

"The bastards," he said, holding the shiny bugs in his hand. He dropped the bugs to the floor and ground them under his heel.

On the way out, one of the men said, not unadmiringly: "Mister, you really beat the shit out of that TV. How many times did you have to hit it?"

"Only once," he said.

When they had driven away into the cold late afternoon sunshine, he swept the bugs into a dustpan and dropped their shattered, twinkling remains into the kitchen wastebasket. Then he made himself a drink.

January 9, 1974

There were only a few people in the bank at 2:30 in the afternoon, and he went directly to one of the tables in the middle of the floor with the city's cashier's check. He tore a deposit ticket out of the back of his checkbook and made it out in the sum of $34,250. He went to a teller's window and presented the ticket and the check.

The teller, a young girl with sin-black hair and a short purple dress, her legs clad in sheer nylon stockings that would have brought the Pope to present arms, looked from the ticket to the check and then back again, puzzled.

"Something wrong with the check?" he asked pleasantly. He had to admit he was enjoying this.

"Nooo, but . . . you want to deposit $34,250 and you want $34,250 in *cash*? Is that it?"

He nodded.

"Just a moment, sir, please."

He smiled and nodded, keeping a close eye on her legs as she went to the manager's desk, which was behind a slatted rail but not glassed in, as if to say this man was as human as you or I . . . or almost, anyway. The manager was a middle-aged man dressed in young clothes. His face was as narrow as the gate of heaven and when he looked at the teller (telleress?) in the purple dress, he arched his eyebrows.

They discussed the check, the deposit slip, its implications for the bank and possibly for the entire Federal Deposit System. The girl bent over the desk, her skirt rode up in back, revealing a mauve-colored slip with lace on the hem. *Love o love o careless love*, he thought. Come home with me and we will diddle even unto the end of the age, or until they rip my house down, whichever comes first. The thought made him smile. He had a hard-on . . . well, a semi, anyway. He looked away from her and glanced around the bank. There was a guard, probably a retired cop, standing impassively between the safe and the front doors. An old lady laboriously signing her blue Social Security check. And a large poster on the left wall which showed a picture of the earth as photographed from outer space, a large blue-green gem set against a field of black. Over the planet, in large letters, was written:

GO AWAY

Underneath the planet, in slightly smaller letters:

WITH A FIRST BANK VACATION LOAN

The pretty teller came back. "I'll have to give this to you in five hundreds and hundreds," she said.

"That's fine."

She made out a receipt for his deposit and then went into the bank vault. When she came out, she had a small carrying case. She spoke to the guard and he came over with her. The guard looked at him suspiciously.

She counted out three stacks of ten thousand dollars, twenty five-hundred-dollar bills in each stack. She banded each one and then slipped an adding machine notation between the band and the top bill of each stack. In each case the adding machine slip said:

$10,000

She counted out forty-two hundreds, riffling the bills quickly with the pad of her right index finger. On top of these she laid five ten-dollar bills. She banded the bundle and slid in another adding machine slip which said:

$4,250

The four bundles were lined up side by side, and the three of them eyed them suspiciously for a moment, enough money to buy a house, or five Cadillacs, or a Piper Cub airplane, or almost a hundred thousand cartons of cigarettes.

Then she said, a little dubiously: "I can give you a zipper bag—"

"No, this is fine." He scooped the bundles up and dropped them into his overcoat pockets. The guard watched this cavalier treatment of his *raison d'être* with impassive contempt; the pretty teller seemed fascinated (her salary for five years was disappearing casually into the pockets of this man's off-the-rack overcoat and it hardly made a bulge); and the manager was looking at him with barely concealed dislike, because a bank was a place where money was supposed to be like God, unseen and reverentially regarded.

"Good 'nough," he said, stuffing his checkbook down on top of the ten-thousand-dollar bundles. "Take it easy."

He left and they all looked after him. Then the old woman shuffled up to the pretty teller and presented her Social Security check, properly signed, for payment. The pretty teller gave her two hundred and thirty-five dollars and sixty-three cents.

When he got home he put the money in a dusty beer stein on the top shelf of the kitchen cabinet. Mary had given the stein to him as a gag present on his birthday, five years ago. He had never particularly cared for it, preferring to drink his beer directly from the bottle. Written on the side of the stein was an emblem showing an Olympic torch and the words:

U.S. DRINKING TEAM

He put the stein back, now filled with a headier brew, and went upstairs to Charlie's room, where his desk was. He rummaged through the bottom drawer and found a small manila envelope. He sat down at the desk, added up the new checkbook balance and saw that it came out to $35,053.49. He addressed the manila envelope to Mary, in care of her folks. He slipped the checkbook inside, sealed the envelope, and rummaged in his desk again. He found a half-full book of stamps, and put five eight-centers on the envelope. He regarded it for a moment, and then, below the address, he wrote:

FIRST CLASS MAIL

He left the envelope standing on his desk and went into the kitchen to make himself a drink.

January 10, 1974

It was late in the evening, snowing, and Magliore hadn't called. He was sitting in the living room with a drink, listening to the stereo because the TV was still *hors de combat*. He had gone out earlier with two ten-dollar bills from the beer stein and had bought four rock and roll albums. One of them was called *Let It Bleed* by the Rolling Stones. They had been playing it at the party, and he liked it better than the others he had bought, which seemed sort of sappy. One of them, an album by a group called Crosby, Stills, Nash and Young, was so sappy that he had broken it over his knee. But *Let It Bleed* was filled with loud, leering, thumping music. It banged and jangled. He liked it a great deal. It reminded him of "Let's Make a Deal," which was MC'ed by Monte Hall. Now Mick Jagger was singing:

> *Well we all need someone to cream on,*
> *And if you want to, you can cream on me.*

He had been thinking about the bank poster, showing the whole earth, various and new, with the legend that invited the viewer to GO AWAY. It made him think about the trip he had taken on New Year's Eve. He had gone away, all right. Far away.

But hadn't he enjoyed it?

The thought brought him up short.

He had been dragging around for the last two months like a dog whose balls had been caught in a swinging door. But hadn't there been compensations along the way?

He had done things he never would have done otherwise. The trips on the turnpike, as mindless and free as migration. The girl and the sex, the touch of her breasts so unlike Mary's. Talking with a man who was a crook. Being accepted finally by that man as a serious person. The illegal exhilaration of throwing the gasoline bombs and the dreamy terror, like drowning, when it seemed the car would not lurch up over the embankment and carry him away. Deep emotions had been excavated from his dry, middle-echelon executive's soul like the relics of a dark religion from an archaeological dig. He knew what it was to be *alive*.

Of course there were bad things. The way he had lost control in Handy Andy's, shouting at Mary. The gnawing loneliness of those first two weeks alone, alone for the first time in twenty years with only the dreadful, mortal beat of his own heart for company. Being punched by Vinnie—Vinnie Mason of all people!—in the department store. The awful fear hangover the morning after he had fire-bombed the construction. That lingered most of all.

But even those things, as bad as they had been, had been new and somehow exciting, like the thought that he might be insane or going insane. The tracks through the interior landscape he had been strolling (or crawling?) through these last two months were the only tracks. He had explored himself and if what he had been finding was often banal, it was also sometimes dreadful and beautiful.

His thoughts reverted to Olivia as he had last seen her, standing on the turnpike ramp with her sign, LAS VEGAS . . . OR BUST! held up defiantly into the cold indifference of things. He thought of the bank poster: GO AWAY. Why not? There was nothing to hold him here but dirty obsession. No wife and only the ghost of a child, no job and a house that would be an unhouse in a week and a half. He had cash money and a car he owned free and clear. Why not just get in it and go?

A kind of wild excitement seized him. In his mind's eye he saw himself shutting off the lights, getting into the LTD, and driving to Las Vegas with the money in his pocket. Finding Olivia. Saying to her: *Let's GO AWAY*. Driving to California, selling the car, booking passage to the South Seas. From there to Hong Kong, from Hong Kong to Saigon, to Bombay, to Athens, Madrid, Paris, London, New York. Then to—

Here?

The world was round, that was the deadly truth of it. Like Olivia, going to Nevada, resolving to shake the shit loose. Gets stoned and raped the first time around the new track because the new track is just like the old track, in fact it *is* the old track, around and around until you've worn it down too deep to climb out and then it's time to close the garage door and turn on the ignition and just wait . . . wait . . .

The evening drew on and his thoughts went around and around, like a cat trying to catch and swallow its own tail. At last he fell asleep on the couch and dreamed of Charlie.

January 11, 1974

Magliore called him at quarter past one in the afternoon.

"Okay," he said. "We'll do business, you and I. It's going to cost you nine thousand dollars. I don't suppose that changes your mind."

"In cash?"

"What do you mean in cash? Do you think I'm gonna take your personal check?"

"Okay. Sorry."

"You be at the Revel Lanes Bowladrome tomorrow night at ten o'clock. You know where that is?"

"Yes, out on Route 7. Just past the Skyview Shopping Mall."

"That's right. There'll be two guys on lane sixteen wearing green shirts with Marlin Avenue Firestone on the back in gold thread. You join them. One of them will explain everything you need to know. That'll be while you're bowling. You bowl two or three strings, then you go outside and drive down the road to the Town Line Tavern. You know where that is?"

"No."

"Just go west on 7. It's about two miles from the bowling alley on the same side. Park in back. My friends will park beside you. They'll be driving a Dodge Custom Cab pickup. Blue. They'll transfer a crate from their truck to your wagon. You give them an envelope. I must be crazy, you know that? Out of my gourd. I'll probably go up for this. Then I'll have a nice long time to wonder why the fuck I did it."

"I'd like to talk to you next week. Personally."

"No. Absolutely not. I ain't your father confessor. I never want to see you again. Not even to talk to you. To tell you the truth, Dawes, I don't even want to read about you in the paper."

"It's a simple investment matter."

Magliore paused.

"No," he said finally.

"This is something no one can ever touch you on," he told Magliore. "I want to set up a . . . a trust fund for someone."

"Your wife?"

"No."

"You stop by Tuesday," Magliore said at last. "Maybe I'll see you. Or maybe I'll have better sense."

He hung up.

Back in the living room, he thought of Olivia and of living—the two seemed constantly bound up together. He thought of GOING AWAY. He thought of Charlie, and he could hardly remember Charlie's face anymore, except in snapshot fashion. How could this be possibly happening, then?

With sudden resolution he got up, went to the phone, and turned to TRAVEL in the yellow pages. He dialed a number. But when a friendly female voice on the other end said, "Arnold Travel Agency, how may we help you?" he hung up and stepped quickly away from the phone, rubbing his hands together.

January 12, 1974

The Revel Lanes Bowladrome was a long, fluorescent-lit building that resounded with piped-in Muzak, a jukebox, shouts and conversation, the stuttering bells of pinball machines, the rattle of the coin-op bumper-pool game, and above all else, the lumbering concatenation of falling pins and the booming, droning roll of large black bowling balls.

He went to the counter, got a pair of red-and-white bowling shoes (which the clerk sprayed ceremonially with an aerosol foot disinfectant before allowing them to leave his care), and walked down to Lane 16. The two men were there. He saw that the one standing up to roll was the mechanic who had been replacing the muffler on the day of his first trip to Magliore's Used Car Sales. The fellow sitting at the scoring table was one of the fellows who had come to his house in the TV van. He was drinking a beer from a waxed-paper cup. They both looked at him as he approached.

"I'm Bart," he said.

"I'm Ray," the man at the table said. "And that guy"—the mechanic was rolling now—"is Alan."

The bowling ball left Alan's hand and thundered down the alley. Pins exploded everywhere and then Alan made a disgusted noise. He had left the seven-ten split. He tried to hang his second ball over the right gutter and get them both. The ball dropped into the gutter and he made another digusted noise as the pin-setter knocked them back.

"Go for one," Ray admonished. "Always go for one. Who do you think you are, Billy Welu?"

"I didn't have english on the ball. A little more and *kazam*. Hi, Bart."

"Hello."

They shook hands all around.

"Good to meet you," Alan said. Then, to Ray: "Let's start a new string and let Bart in on it. You got my ass whipped in this one anyhow."

"Sure."

"Go ahead and go first, Bart," Alan said.

He hadn't bowled in maybe five years. He selected a twelve-pound ball that felt right to his fingers and promptly rolled it down the left-hand gutter. He watched it go, feeling like a horse's ass. He was more careful with the next ball but it hooked and he only got three pins. Ray rolled a strike. Alan hit nine and then covered the four pin.

At the end of the five frames the score was Ray 89, Alan 76, Bart 40. But he was enjoying the feeling of sweat on his back and the unaccustomed exertion of certain muscles that were rarely given the chance to show off.

He had gotten into the game enough that for a moment he didn't know what Ray was talking about when he said: "It's called malglinite."

He looked over, frowning a little at the unfamiliar word, and then understood. Alan was out front, holding his ball and looking seriously down at the four-six, all concentration.

"Okay," he said.

"It comes in sticks about four inches long. There are forty sticks. Each one has about sixty times the explosive force of a stick of dynamite."

"Oh," he said, and suddenly felt sick to his stomach. Alan rolled and jumped in the air when he got both pins for his spare.

He rolled, got seven pins, and sat down again. Ray struck out. Alan went to the ball caddy and held the ball under his chin, frowning down the polished lane at the pins. He gave courtesy to the bowler on his right, and then made his four-step approach.

"There's four hundred feet of fuse. It takes an electrical charge to set the stuff off. You can turn a blowtorch on it and it will just melt. It—oh, *good one! Good one, Al!*"

Al had made a Brooklyn hit and knocked them all back.

He got up, threw two gutterballs, and sat down again. Ray spared.

As Alan approached the line, Ray went on: "It takes electricity, a storage battery. You got that?"

"Yes," he said. He looked down at his score. 47. Seven more than his age.

"You can cut lengths of fuse and splice them together and get simultaneous explosion, can you dig it?"

"Yes."

Alan rolled another Brooklyn strike.

When he came back, grinning, Ray said: "You can't trust those Brooklyn hits, boy. Get it over in the right pocket."

"Up your ass, I'm only eight pins down."

He rolled, got six pins, sat down, and Ray struck out again. Ray had 116 at the end of seven.

When he sat down again Ray asked: "Do you have any questions?"

"No. Can we leave at the end of this string?"

"Sure. But you wouldn't be so bad if you worked some of the rust off. You keep twisting your hand when you deliver. That's your problem."

Alan hit the Brooklyn pocket exactly as he had on his two previous strikes, but this time left the seven-ten split and came back scowling. He thought, *this is where I came in.*

"I told you not to trust that whore's pocket," Ray said, grinning.

"Screw," Alan growled. He went for the spare and dropped the ball into the gutter again.

"Some guys," Ray said, laughing. "Honest to God, some guys never learn, you know that? They never do."

The Town Line tavern had a huge red neon sign that knew nothing of the energy crisis. It flicked off and on with mindless, eternal confidence. Underneath the red neon was a white marquee that said:

TONITE

THE FABULOUS OYSTERS

DIRECT FROM BOSTON

There was a plowed parking lot to the right of the tavern, filled with the cars of Saturday night patrons. When he drove in he saw that the parking lot went around to the back in an L. There were several parking slots left back there. He drove in next to an empty one, shut off the car, and got out.

The night was pitilessly cold, the kind of night that doesn't feel that cold until you realize that your ears went as numb as pump handles in the first fifteen seconds you were out. Overhead a million stars glittered in magnified brilliance. Through the tavern's back wall he could hear the Fabulous Oysters playing "After Midnight." J.J. Cale wrote that song, he thought, and wondered where he had picked up that useless piece of information. It was amazing the way the human brain filled up with road litter. He could remember who wrote "After Midnight," but he couldn't remember his dead son's face. That seemed very cruel.

The Custom Cab pickup rolled up next to his station wagon; Ray and Alan got out. They were all business now, both dressed in heavy gloves and Army surplus parkas.

"You got some money for us," Ray said.

He took the envelope out of his coat and handed it over. Ray opened it and riffled the bills inside, estimating rather than counting.

"Okay. Open up your wagon."

He opened the back (which, in the Ford brochures, was called the Magic Doorgate) and the two of them slid a heavy wooden crate out of the pickup and carried it to his wagon.

"Fuse is in the bottom," Ray said, breathing white jets out of his nose. "Remember, you need juice. Otherwise you might just as well use the stuff for birthday candles."

"I'll remember."

"You ought to bowl more. You got a powerful swing."

They got back into their truck and drove away. A few moments later he also drove away, leaving the Fabulous Oysters to their own devices. His ears were cold, and they prickled when the heater warmed them up.

When he got home, he carried the crate into the house and pried it open with a screwdriver. The stuff looked exactly as Ray had said it would, like waxy gray candles. Beneath the sticks and a layer of newspaper were two fat white loops of fuse. The loops of fuse had been secured with white plastic ties that looked identical to the ones with which he secured his Hefty garbage bags.

He put the crate in the living room closet and tried to forget it, but it seemed to give off evil emanations that spread out from the closet to cover the whole house, as though something evil had happened in there years ago, something that had slowly and surely tainted everything.

January 13, 1974

He drove down to the Landing Strip and crawled up and down the streets, looking for Drake's place of business. He saw crowded tenements standing shoulder to shoulder, so exhausted that it seemed that they would collapse if the buildings flanking them were taken away. A forest of TV antennas rose from the top of each one, standing against the sky like frightened hair. Bars, closed until noon. A derelict car in the middle of a side street, tires gone, headlights gone, chrome gone, making it look like a bleached cow skeleton in the middle of Death Valley. Glass twinkled in the gutters. All the pawnshops and liquor stores had accordion grilles across their plate glass windows. He thought: That's what we learned from the race riots eight years ago. How to prevent looting in an emergency. And halfway down Venner Street he saw a small storefront with a sign in Old English letters. The sign said:

DROP DOWN MAMMA COFFEEHOUSE

He parked, locked the car, and went inside. There were only two customers, a young black kid in an oversize pea coat who seemed to be dozing, and an old white boozer who was sipping coffee from a thick white porcelain mug. His hands trembled helplessly each time the mug approached his mouth. The boozer's skin was yellow and when he looked up his eyes were haunted with light, as if the whole man were trapped inside this stinking prison, too deep to get out.

Drake was sitting behind the counter at the rear, next to a two-burner hotplate. One Silex held hot water, the other black coffee. There was a cigar box on the counter with some change in it. There were two signs, crayoned on construction paper. One said:

MENU
Coffee 15¢
Tea 15¢
All soda 25¢
Bologna 30¢
PB&J 25¢
Hot Dog 35¢

The other sign said:

PLEASE WAIT TO BE SERVED!

All Drop In counter help are VOLUNTEERS and when you serve yourself you make them feel useless and stupid. Please wait and remember GOD LOVES YOU!

Drake looked up from his magazine, a tattered copy of *The National Lampoon*. For a moment his eyes went that peculiar hazy shade of a man snapping his mental fingers for the right name, and then he said: "Mr. Dawes, how are you?"

"Good. Can I get a cup of coffee?"

"Sure can." He took one of the thick mugs off the second layer of the pyramid behind him and poured. "Milk?"

"Just black." He gave Drake a quarter and Drake gave him a dime out of the cigar box. "I wanted to thank you for the other night, and I wanted to make a contribution."

"Nothing to thank me for."

"Yes there is. That party was what they call a bad scene."

"Chemicals can do that. Not always, but sometimes. Some boys brought in a friend of theirs last summer who had dropped acid in the city park. The kid went into a screaming fit because he thought the pigeons were coming after him to eat him. Sounds like a *Reader's Digest* horror story, doesn't it?"

"The girl who gave me the mescaline said she once plunged a man's hand out of the drain. She didn't know afterwards if it really happened or not."

"Who was she?"

"I really don't know," he said truthfully. "Anyway, here." He put a roll of bills on the counter next to the cigar box. The roll was secured with a rubber band.

Drake frowned at it without touching it.

"Actually it's for this place," he said. He was sure Drake knew that, but he needed to plug Drake's silence.

Drake unfastened the rubber band, holding the bills with his left, manipulating with that oddly scarred right. He put the rubber band aside and counted slowly.

"This is five thousand dollars," he said.

"Yes."

"Would you be offended if I asked you where—"

"I got it? No, I wouldn't be offended. From the sale of my house to this city. They are going to put a road through there."

"Your wife agrees?"

"My wife has no say in the matter. We are separated. Soon to be divorced. She has her half of the sale to do with as she sees fit."

"I see."

Behind them, the old boozer began to hum. It was not a tune; just humming.

Drake poked moodily at the bills with his right forefinger. The corners of the bills were curled up from being rolled. "I can't take this," he said finally.

"Why not?"

Drake said: "Don't you remember what we talked about?"

He did. "I've no plans that way."

"I think you do. A man with his feet planted in this world does not give money away on a whim."

"This is not a whim," he said firmly.

Drake looked at him sharply. "What would you call it? A chance acquaintance?"

"Hell, I've given money away to people I've never seen. Cancer researchers. A Save-the-Child Foundation. A muscular dystrophy hospital in Boston. I've never been *in* Boston."

"Sums this large?"

"No."

"And cash money, Mr. Dawes. A man who still has a use for money never wants to see it. He cashes checks, signs papers. Even playing nickle-ante poker he uses chips. It makes it symbolic. And in our society a man with no use for money hasn't much use for living, either."

"That's a pretty goddamned materialistic attitude for—"

"A priest? But I'm not that anymore. Not since this happened." He held up the scarred, wounded hand. "Shall I tell you how I get the money to keep this place on its feet? We came too late for the window-dressing charities like the United Fund or the City Appeal Fund. The people who work here are all retired, old people who don't understand the kids who come in here, but want to be something besides just a face leaning out of a third-story window watching the street. I've got some kids on probation that scout up bands to play for free on Friday and Saturday night, bands that are just starting up and need the exposure. We pass the hat. But mostly the grease comes from rich people, the upper crust. I do tours. I speak at ladies' teas. I tell them about the kids on bummers and the Sterno freaks that sleep under the viaducts and make newspaper fires to keep from freezing in the winter. I tell them about the fifteen-year-old girl who'd been on the road since 1971 and came in here with big white lice crawling all over her head and her pubic hair. I tell them about all the VD in Norton. I tell them about the fishermen, guys that hang out in the bus terminals looking for boys on the run, offering them jobs as male whores. I tell them about how these young boys end up blowing some guy in a theater men's room for ten dollars, fifteen if he promises to swallow the come. Fifty percent for him and fifty percent for his pimp. And these women, their eyes go all shocked and then sort of melty and tender, and probably their thighs get all wet and sloppy, but they pony up and that's the important thing. Sometimes you can latch onto one and get more than a ten-buck contribution. She takes you to her house in Crescent for dinner, introduces you to the family, and gets you to say grace after the maid brings the first course. And you say it, no matter how bad the words taste in your mouth and you rumple the kid's hair—there's always one, Dawes, just the one, not like the nasty rabbits down in this part of town that breed a whole tenementful of them—and you say what a fine young man you've got here, or what a pretty girl, and if you're very lucky the lady will have invited some of her bridge buddies or country club buddies to see this sideshow-freak priest, who's probably a radical and running guns to the Panthers or the Algerian Freedom League, and you do the old Father Brown bit, add a trace of the auld Blarney, and smile until your face hurts. All this is known as shaking the money tree, and it's all done in the most elegant of surroundings, but going home it feels just like you were down on your knees and eating some AC/DC businessman's cock in one of the stalls at Cinema 41. But what the hell, that's my game, part of my 'penance' if you'll pardon the word, but my penance doesn't include necrophilia. And that, Mr. Dawes, is what I feel you are offering me. And that's why I have to say no.''

"Penance for what?"

"That," said Drake with a twisted smile. "is between me and God."

"Then why pick this method of finance, if it's so personally repugnant to you? Why don't you just—"

"I do it this way because it's the only way. I'm locked in."

With a sudden, horrible sinking of despair, he realized that Drake had just explained why he had come here, why he had done everything.

"Are you all right, Mr. Dawes? You look—"

"I'm fine. I want to wish you the best of luck. Even if you're not getting anywhere."

"I have no illusions," Drake said, and smiled. "You ought to reconsider . . . anything drastic. There are alternatives."

"Are there?" He smiled back. "Close this place now. Walk out with me and we'll go into business together. I am making a serious proposal."

"You're making sport of me."

"No," he said. "Maybe somebody is making sport of both of us." He turned away, rolling the bills into a short, tight cylinder again. The kid was still sleeping. The old man had put his cup down half empty on the table and was looking at it vacuously. He was still humming. On his way by, he stuffed the roll of bills into the old man's cup, splashing muddy coffee onto the table. He left quickly and unlocked his car at the curb, expecting Drake to follow him out and remonstrate, perhaps save him. But Drake did not, perhaps expecting him to come back in and save himself.

Instead, he got into his car and drove away.

January 14, 1974

He went downtown to the Sears store and bought an automobile battery and a pair of jumper cables. Written on the side of the battery were these words, printed in raised plastic:

DIE-HARD

He went home and put them in the front closet with the wooden crate. He thought of what would happen if the police came here with a search warrant. Guns in the garage, explosives in the living room, a large amount of cash in the kitchen. B. G. Dawes, desperate revolutionary. Secret Agent X-9, in the pay of a foreign cartel too hideous to be mentioned. He had a subscription to *Reader's Digest*, which was filled with such spy stories, along with an endless series of crusades, anti-smoking, anti-pornography, anti-crime. It was always more frightening when the purported spy was a suburban WASP, one of *us*. KGB agents in Willmette or Des Moines, passing microdots in the drugstore lending library, plotting violent overthrow of the republic at drive-in movies, eating Big Macs with one tooth hollowed out so as to contain prussic acid.

Yes, a search warrant and they would crucify him. But he was not really afraid anymore. Things seemed to have progressed beyond that point.

January 15, 1974

"Tell me what you want," Magliore said wearily.

It was sleeting outside; the afternoon was gray and sad, a day when any city bus lurching out of the gray, membranous weather, spewing up slush in all directions with its huge tires, would seem like a figment of a manic-depressive's fantasies, when the very act of living seemed slightly psycho.

"My house? My car? My wife? Anything, Dawes. Just leave me alone in my declining years."

"Look," he said, embarrassed, "I know I'm being a pest."

"He knows he's being a pest," Magliore told the walls. He raised his hands and then let them fall back to his meaty thighs. "Then why in the name of Christ don't you *stop*?"

"This is the last thing."

Magliore rolled his eyes. "This ought to be beautiful," he told the walls. "What is it?"

He pulled out some bills and said, "There's eighteen thousand dollars here. Three thousand would be for you. A finder's fee."

"Who do you want found?"

"A girl in Las Vegas."

"The fifteen's for her?"

"Yes. I'd like you to take it and invest it in whatever operations you run that are good to invest in. And pay her dividends."

"Legitimate operations?"

"Whatever will pay the best dividends. I trust your judgment."

"He trusts my judgment," Magliore informed the walls. "Vegas is a big town, Mr. Dawes. A transient town."

"Don't you have connections there?"

"As a matter of fact I do. But if we're talking about some half-baked hippie girl who may have already cut out for San Francisco or Denver—"

"She goes by the name of Olivia Brenner. And I think she's still in Las Vegas. She was last working in a fast-food restaurant—"

"Of which there are at least two million in Vegas," Magliore said. "Jesus! Mary! Joseph the carpenter!"

"She has an apartment with another girl, or at least she did when I talked to her the last time. I don't know where. She's about five-eight, darkish hair, green eyes. Good figure. Twenty-one years old. Or so she says."

"And suppose I can't locate this marvelous piece of ass?"

"Invest the money and keep the dividends yourself. Call it nuisance pay."

"How do you know I won't do that anyway?"

He stood up, leaving the bills on Magliore's desk. "I guess I don't. But you have an honest face."

"Listen," Magliore said. "I don't mean to bite your ass. You're a man who's already getting his ass bitten. But I don't like this. It's like you're making me executor to your fucking last will and testament."

"Say no if you have to."

"No, no, no, you don't get it. If she's still in Vegas and going under this Olivia Brenner name I think I can find her and three grand is more than fair. It doesn't hurt me one way or the other. But you spook me, Dawes. You're really locked on course."

"Yes."

Magliore frowned down at the pictures of himself, his wife, and his children under the glass top of his desk.

"All right," Magliore said. "This one last time, all right. But no more, Dawes. Absolutely not. If I ever see you again or hear you on the phone, you can forget it. I mean that. I got enough problems of my own without diddling around in yours."

"I agree to that condition."

He stuck out his hand, not sure that Magliore would shake it, but Magliore did.

"You make no sense to me," Magliore said. "Why should I like a guy who makes no sense to me?"

"It's a senseless world," he said. "If you doubt it, just think about Mr. Piazzi's dog."

"I think about her a lot," Magliore said.

January 16, 1974

He took the manila envelope containing the checkbook down to the post office box on the corner and mailed it. That evening he went to see a movie called *The Exorcist* because Max von Sydow was in it and he had always admired Max von Sydow a great deal. In one scene of the movie a little girl puked in a Catholic priest's face. Some people in the back row cheered.

January 17, 1974

Mary called on the phone. She sounded absurdly relieved, gay, and that made everything much easier.

"You sold the house," she said.

"That's right."

"But you're still there."

"Only until Saturday. I've rented a big farmhouse in the country. I'm going to try and get my act back together."

"Oh, Bart. That's so wonderful. I'm so glad." He realized why it was being so easy. She was being phony. She wasn't glad or not glad. She had given up. "About the checkbook . . . "

"Yes."

"You split the money right down the middle, didn't you?"

"Yes I did. If you want to check, you can call Mr. Fenner."

"No. Oh, I didn't mean *that*." And he could almost see her making pushing-away gestures with her hands. "What I meant was . . . you separating the money like that . . . does it mean . . . "

She trailed off artfully and he thought: *Ow, you bitch, you got me. Bull's eye.*

"Yes, I guess it does," he said. "Divorce."

"Have you thought about it?" she asked earnestly, phonily. "Have you *really*—"

"I've thought about it a lot."

"So have I. It seems like the only thing left to do. But I don't hold anything against you, Bart. I'm not mad at you."

My God, she's been reading all those paperback novels. Next she'll tell me she's going back to school. He was surprised at his bitterness. He thought he had gotten past that part.

"What will you do?"

"I'm going back to school," she said, and now there was no phoniness in her voice, now it was excited, shining. "I dug out my old transcript, it was still up in Mamma's attic with all my old clothes, and do you know I only need twenty-four credits to graduate? Bart, that's hardly more than a year!"

He saw Mary crawling through her mother's attic and the image blended with one of himself sitting bewildered in a pile of Charlie's clothes. He shut it out.

"Bart? Are you still there?"

"Yes. I'm glad being single again is going to fulfill you so nicely."

"Bart," she said reproachfully.

But there was no need to snap at her now, to tease her or make her feel bad.

Things had gone beyond that. Mr. Piazzi's dog, having bitten, moves on. That struck him funny and he giggled.

"Bart, are you crying?" She sounded tender. Phony, but tender.

"No," he said bravely.

"Bart, is there anything I can do? If there is, I want to."

"No. I think I'm going to be fine. And I'm glad you're going back to school. Listen, this divorce—who gets it? You or me?"

"I think it would look better if I did," she said timidly.

"Okay. Fine."

There was a pause between them and suddenly she blurted into it, as if the words had escaped without her knowledge or approval: "Have you slept with anyone since I left?"

He thought the question over, and ways of answering: the truth, a lie, an evasion that might keep her awake tonight.

"No," he said carefully, and added: "Have you?"

"Of course not," she said, managing to sound shocked and pleased at the same time. "I wouldn't."

"You will eventually."

"Bart, let's not talk about sex."

"All right," he said placidly enough, although it was she who had brought the subject up. He kept searching for something nice to say to her, something that she would remember. He couldn't think of a thing, and furthermore didn't know why he would want her to remember him at all, at least at this stage of things. They had had good years before. He was sure they must have been good because he couldn't remember much of what had happened in them, except maybe the crazy TV bet.

He heard himself say: "Do you remember when we took Charlie to nursery school the first time?"

"Yes. He cried and you wanted to take him back with us. You didn't want to let him go, Bart."

"And you did."

She was saying something disclaiming in a slightly wounded tone, but he was remembering the scene. The lady who kept the nursery school was Mrs. Ricker. She had a certificate from the state, and she gave all the children a nice hot lunch before sending them home at one o'clock. School was kept downstairs in a made-over basement and as they led Charlie down between them, he felt like a traitor; like a farmer petting a cow and saying Soo, Bess on the way to the slaughterhouse. He had been a beautiful boy, his Charlie. Blond hair that had darkened later, blue, watchful eyes, hands that had been clever even as a toddler. And he had stood between them at the bottom of the stairs, stock-still, watching the other children who were whooping and running and coloring and cutting colored paper with blunt-nosed scissors, so *many* of them, and Charlie had never looked so vulnerable as he did in that instant, just watching the other children. There was no joy or fear in his eyes, only the watchfulness, a kind of *outsiderness*, and he had never felt so much his son's father as then, never so close to the actual run of his thoughts. And

Mrs. Ricker came over, smiling like a barracuda and she said: *We'll have such fun, Chuck,* making him want to cry out: *That's not his name!* And when she put out her hand Charlie did not take it but only watched it so she stole his hand and began to pull him a little toward the others, and he went willingly two steps and then stopped, looked back at them, and Mrs. Young said very quietly: *Go right along, he'll be fine.* And Mary finally had to poke him and say *Come ON, Bart* because he was frozen looking at his son, his son's eyes saying, *Are you going to let them do this to me, George?* and his own eyes saying back, *Yes, I guess I am, Freddy* and he and Mary started up the stairs, showing Charlie their backs, the most dreadful thing a little child can see, and Charlie began to wail. But Mary's footsteps never faltered because a woman's love is strange and cruel and nearly always clear-sighted, love that sees is always horrible love, and she knew walking away was right and so she walked, dismissing the cries as only another part of the boy's development, like smiles from gas or scraped knees. And he had felt a pain in his chest so sharp, so physical, that he had wondered if he was having a heart attack, and then the pain had just passed, leaving him shaken and unable to interpret it, but now he thought that the pain had been plain old prosaic good-bye. Parents' backs aren't the most dreadful thing. The most dreadful thing of all is the speed with which children dismiss those same backs and turn to their own affairs— to the game, the puzzle, the new friend, and eventually to death. Those were the awful things he had come to know now. Charlie had begun dying long before he got sick, and there was no putting a stop to it.

"Bart?" she was saying. "Are you still there, Bart?"

"I'm here."

"What good are you doing yourself thinking about Charlie all the time? It's eating you up. You're his prisoner."

"But you're free," he said. "Yes."

"Shall I see the lawyer next week?"

"Okay. Fine."

"It doesn't have to be nasty, does it, Bart?"

"No. It will be very civilized."

"You won't change your mind and contest it?"

"No."

"I'll . . . I'll be talking to you, then."

"You knew it was time to leave him and so you did. I wish to God I could be that instinctive."

"What?"

"Nothing. Good-bye, Mary. I love you." He realized he had said it after he hung up. He had said it automatically, with no feeling—verbal punctuation. But it wasn't such a bad ending. Not at all.

January 18, 1974

The secretary's voice said: ''Who shall I say is calling?''

''Bart Dawes.''

''Will you hold for a moment?''

''Sure.''

She put him in limbo and he held the blank receiver to his ear, tapping his foot and looking out the window at the ghost town of Crestallen Street West. It was a bright day but very cold, temperature about 10 above with a chill factor making it 10 below. The wind blew skirls of snow across the street to where the Hobarts' house stood broodingly silent, just a shell waiting for the wrecking ball. They had even taken their shutters.

There was a click and Steve Ordner's voice said: ''Bart, how are you?''

''Fine.''

''What can I do for you?''

''I called about the laundry,'' he said. ''I wondered what the corporation had decided to do about relocation.''

Ordner sighed and then said with good-humored reserve: ''A little late for that, isn't it?''

''I didn't call to be beaten with it, Steve.''

''Why not? You've surely beaten everyone else with it. Well, never mind. The board has decided to get out of the industrial laundry business, Bart. The laundromats will stay; they're all doing well. We're going to change the chain name, though. To Handi-Wash. How does that sound?''

''Terrible,'' he said remotely. ''Why don't you sack Vinnie Mason?''

''Vinnie?'' Ordner sounded surprised. ''Vinnie's doing a great job for us. Turning into quite the mogul. I must say I didn't expect such bitterness—''

''Come on, Steve. That job's got no more future than a tenement airshaft. Give him something worthwhile or let him out.''

''I hardly think that's your business, Bart.''

''You've got a dead chicken tied around his neck and he doesn't know it yet because it hasn't started to rot. He still thinks it's dinner.''

''I understand he punched you up a little before Christmas.''

''I told him the truth and he didn't like it.''

''Truth's a slippery word, Bart. I would think you'd understand that better than anyone, after all the lies you told me.''

''That still bugs you, doesn't it?''

"When you discover that a man you thought was a good man is full of shit, it does tend to bug one, yes."

"Bug one," he repeated. "Do you know something, Steve? You're the only person I've ever known in my life that would say that. Bug one. It sounds like something that comes in a fucking aerosol can."

"Was there anything else, Bart?"

"No, not really. I wish you'd stop beating Vinnie, that's all. He's a good man. You're wasting him. And you know goddam well you're wasting him."

"I repeat: why would I want to 'beat' Vinnie?"

"Because you can't get to me."

"You're getting paranoid, Bart. I've got no desire to do anything to you but forget you."

"Is that why you were checking to see if I ever had personal laundry done free? Or took kickbacks from the motels? I understand you even took the petty cash vouchers for the last five years or so."

"Who told you that?" Ordner barked. He sounded startled, off balance.

"Somebody in your organization," he lied joyfully. "Someone who doesn't like you much. Someone who thought I might be able to get the ball rolling a little in time for the next director's meeting."

"Who?"

"Good-bye, Steve. You think about Vinnie Mason, and I'll think about who I might or might not talk to."

"Don't you hang up on me! Don't you—"

He hung up, grinning. Even Steve Ordner had the proverbial feet of clay. Who was it Steve reminded him of? Ball bearings. Strawberry ice cream stolen from the food locker. Herman Wouk. Captain Queeg, that was it. Humphrey Bogart had played him in the movie. He laughed aloud and sang:

> "We all need someone to Queeg on,
> And if you want to, why don'tcha Queeg all over me?"

I'm crazy all right, he thought, still laughing. But it does seem there are certain advantages. It came to him that one of the surest signs of insanity was a man all alone, laughing in the middle of silence, on an empty street filled with empty houses. But the thought could not still his humor and he laughed louder, standing by the telephone and shaking his head and grinning.

January 19, 1974

After dark he went out to the garage and brought in the guns. He loaded the Magnum carefully, according to the directions in the instruction pamphlet, after dry-firing it several times. The Rolling Stones were on the stereo, singing about the Midnight Rambler. He couldn't get over what a fine album that was. He thought about himself as Barton George Dawes, Midnight Rambler, Visits by Appointment Only.

The .460 Weatherbee took eight shells. They looked big enough to fit a medium howitzer. When the rifle was loaded he looked at it curiously, wondering if it was as powerful as Dirty Harry Swinnerton had claimed. He decided to take it out behind the house and fire it. Who was there on Crestallen Street West to report gunshots?

He put on his jacket and started out the back door through the kitchen, then went back to the living room and got one of the small pillows that lay on the couch. Then he went outside, pausing to flick on the 200-watt yard light that he and Mary had used in the summer for backyard barbecues. Back here, the snow was as he had pictured it in his mind a little more than a week ago—untouched, unmarred, totally virgin. No one had foot-fucked this snow. In past years Don Upslinger's boy Kenny sometimes used the backyard express to get up to his friend Ronnie's house. Or Mary used the line he had strung kitty-corner between the house and garage to hang a few things (usually unmentionables) on days when it was too warm for them to freeze. But he himself always went to the garage by the breezeway and now it struck him as sort of marvelous—no one had been in his backyard since snow first fell, in late November. Not even a dog, by the look of it.

He had a sudden crazy urge to stride out into the middle, about where he set the hibachi every summer, and make a snow angel.

Instead he tucked the pillow up against his right shoulder, held it for a moment with his chin, and then pressed the butt plate of the Weatherbee against it. He glared down the sight with his left eye shut, and tried to remember the advice the actors always gave each other just before the gyrenes hit the beaches in the late-night war movies. Usually it was some seasoned veteran like Richard Widmark talking to some green private—Martin Milner, perhaps: *Don't jerk that trigger, son—SQUEEZE it.*

Okay, Fred. Let's see if I can hit my own garage.

He squeezed the trigger.

The rifle did not make a report. It made an explosion. At first he was afraid it had blown up in his hands. He knew he was alive when the recoil knocked him back against the kitchen storm door. The report traveled off in all directions with a curious rolling sound, like jet exhaust. The pillow fell in the snow. His shoulder throbbed.

"Jesus, Fred!" he gasped.

He looked at his garage and was hardly able to believe it. There was a splintered hole in the siding big enough to fit a teacup through.

He leaned the gun against the kitchen storm door and walked through the snow, never minding the fact that he had his low shoes on. He examined the hole for a minute, bemusedly prying up loose splinters with his forefinger, and then he went around and inside.

The exit hole was bigger. He looked at his station wagon. There was a bullet hole in the driver's side door, and the paint had been seared off to show bare metal around the concave hole, which was big enough for him to stick the tips of two fingers in. He opened the door and looked across the seat at the passenger door. Yes, the bullet had gone through there too, just below the door handle.

He walked around to the passenger side and saw where the bullet had exited, leaving another big hole, this time with tines of metal sticking balefully out. He turned and looked at the garage wall opposite where the bullet had entered. It had gone through that too. For all he knew, it was still going.

He heard Harry the gun shop proprietor saying: *So your cousin gut-shoots . . . this baby will spread his insides over twenty feet*. And what would it do to a man? Probably the same. It made him feel ill.

He walked back to the kitchen door, stooped to pick up his pillow, and went back into the house, pausing automatically to stamp his feet so he wouldn't track across Mary's kitchen. In the living room he took off his shirt. There was a red welt in the shape of the rifle's butt plate on his shoulder in spite of the pillow.

He went into the kitchen with his shirt still off and fixed a pot of coffee and a TV dinner. When he finished his meal he went into the living room and laid down on the couch and began to cry, and the crying rose to a jagged, breaking hysteria which he heard and feared but could not control. At last it began to trail off and he fell heavily asleep, breathing harshly. In his sleep he looked old and some of the stubble on his cheeks was white.

January 20, 1974

He woke with a guilty start, afraid it was morning and too late. His sleep had been as sodden and dark as old coffee, the kind of sleep he always woke from feeling stupid and cottonheaded. He looked at his watch and saw it was quarter past two.

The rifle was where he had left it, leaning nonchalantly in the easy chair. The Magnum was on the end table.

He got up, went into the kitchen, and splashed cold water on his face. He went upstairs and put on a fresh shirt. He went back downstairs tucking it in. He locked all the downstairs doors, and for reasons he did not wish to examine too closely, his heart felt a tiny bit lighter as each tumbler clicked. He began to feel like himself again for the first time since that damnable woman had collapsed in front of him in the supermarket. He put the Weatherbee on the floor by the living room picture window and stacked the shells beside it, opening each box as he set it down. He dragged the easy chair over and set it on its side.

He went into the kitchen and locked the windows. He took one of the dining room chairs and propped it under the kitchen doorknob. He poured himself a cup of cold coffee, sipped it absently, grimaced, and dashed it into the sink. He made himself a drink.

He went back into the living room and brought out the automobile storage battery. He put it behind the overturned easy chair, then got the jumper cables and coiled them beside the battery.

He carried the case of explosive upstairs, grunting and puffing. When he got to the landing he set it down with a thump and blew out his breath. He was getting too old for this sort of bullshit, even though a lot of the laundry muscle from the days when he and his partner had lifted four-hundred-pound lots of ironed sheets onto the delivery trucks, was still there. But muscle or no muscle, when a man got to be forty, some things were tempting fate. By forty it was attack time.

He went from room to room upstairs, turning on all the lights: The guest bedroom, the guest bathroom, master bedroom, the study that had once been Charlie's room. He put a chair under the attic trapdoor and went up there, turning on the dusty bulb. Then he went down to the kitchen and got a roll of electrician's tape, a pair of scissors, and a sharp steak knife.

He took two sticks of explosive from the crate (it was soft, and if you pressed it, you left fingerprints) and took them up to the attic. He cut two lengths of fuse and peeled the white insulation back from the copper core with the steak knife. Then he pressed each bare wire into one of the candles. In the closet, standing below the trapdoor now, he peeled the insulation from the other ends of the fuses and carefully attached two more sticks, taping the fuse firmly to each so that the peeled wire wouldn't pull free.

Humming now, he strung more fuse from the attic into the master bedroom and left a stick on each of the twin beds. He strung more fuse from there down the hall and left a stick in the guest bathroom, two more in the guest bedroom. He turned off the lights as he left. In Charlie's old room he left four sticks, taped together in a cluster. He trailed fuse out the door and dropped a coil of it over the stairway railing. Then he went downstairs.

Four sticks on the kitchen counter, beside his bottle of Southern Comfort. Four sticks in the living room. Four in the dining room. Four in the hall.

He trailed fuse back into the living room, a little out of breath from going up and down stairs. But there was one more trip to make. He went back up and got the crate, which was considerably lighter now. There were only eleven sticks of explosive left inside it. The crate, he saw, had once contained oranges. Written on the side, in faded letters, was this word:

POMONA

Beside the word was a picture of an orange with one leaf clinging to the stem.

He took the crate out to the garage, using the breezeway this time, and put the box on the back seat of his car. He wired each stick of malglinite with a short fuse, then joined all eleven to a long length with electrician's tape and strung the long fuse back into the house, being careful to slip the fuse into the crack beneath the side door that opened onto the breezeway and then relocking it.

In the living room he joined the house master fuse with the one that came from the garage. Working carefully, still humming, he cut another length and joined it to the other two with electrician's tape. He payed this final fuse over to the battery and peeled the insulation from the end with the steak knife.

He separated the copper core wires and twisted each bunch into a little pigtail. He took the jumper cables and attached a black alligator clip to one pigtail, a red alligator clip to the other. He went to the storage battery and attached the other black alligator clip to the terminal marked:

POS

He left the red clip unhooked, lying beside the post marked

NEG

Then he went to the stereo, turned it on, and listened to the Rolling Stones. It was five minutes past four. He went to the kitchen, made himself another drink, and went back to the living room with it, suddenly at loose ends. There was a copy of *Good Housekeeping* on the coffee table. There was an article in it about the Kennedy family and their problems. He read the article. After that he read an article titled "Women and Breast Cancer." It was by a woman doctor.

They came at a little past ten, just after the bells of the Congregational Church five blocks over had rung in the hour, calling people to matins, or whatever in hell the Congregationalists called them.

There was a green sedan and a black-and-white police car. They pulled up at the curb and three men got out of the green sedan. One of them was Fenner. He didn't know who the other two were. Each of them had a briefcase.

Two policemen got out of the black-and-white and leaned against it. It was obvious from their attitudes that they expected no trouble; they were discussing something as they leaned against the hood of the black-and-white, and their words came out of their mouths in visible white puffs.

Things stopped.

Stoptime, January 20, 1974

well fred this is it i guess put up or shut up time oh i know in one sense it's too late to shut up i've got explosives strung all over the house like birthday decorations a gun in my hand and another one in my belt like fucking john dillinger well what do you say this is the last decision like climbing a tree i pick this fork then i pick that fork now this now that

(the men frozen in tableau outside in the hallway between seconds fenner in a green suit one foot six inches off the pavement as it steps forward good shoes clad in low fashionable rubbers if there is such a thing as fashionable rubbers his green topcoat flapping open like a crusading attorney in a tv lead-in his head is slightly turned slightly cocked the man in back of him has made some comment and fenner is cocking his head to catch it the man who has spoken has a white plume half out of his mouth this second man is wearing a blue blazer and dark brown pants his topcoat is also open and the wind has caught it stoptime has caught his topcoat in midflap and the third man is just turning from the car and the cops are leaning against their black-and-white with their heads turned to one another they could be discussing anything marriage or a tough case or the shitty season the musties had or the state of their balls and the sun has come through the scud overhead just enough to make a single twinkle on a single shell of one policeman's assigned equipment said shell pushed through one of many little leather loops on said policeman's belt the other cop is wearing shades and the sun has pricked out a compass point on the right lens and his lips are thick sensual caught at the beginning of a smile: this is the photograph)

i'm going ahead freddy my boy do you have anything you'd care to say at this auspicious moment at this point in the proceedings yes says fred you're going to hold out for the newspeople aren't you i sure am says george the words the pictures the newsreels demolition i know has only the point of visibility but freddy does it strike you how lonely this is how all over this city and the world people are eating and shitting and fucking and scratching their eczema all the things they write books about while we have to do this alone yes i've considered that george in fact i tried to tell you something about it if you'll recall and if it's any consolation to you this seems right right now it seems okay because when you can't move you can give them their roadwork but please george don't kill anybody no not on purpose fred but you see the position i am in yes i see i understand by george i'm scared now i'm so scared no don't be scared i'm going to handle this and i'm in perfect control myself

roll it

January 20, 1974

"Roll it," he said aloud, and everything began to move.

He put the rifle to his shoulder, sighted on the right front wheel of the police cruiser, and pulled the trigger.

The gun kicked crushingly against his shoulder and the muzzle jerked upward after the bullet had been fired. The large living room window burst outward, leaving only jagged hunks protruding from the molding like impressionistic glass arrows. The cruiser's front tire did not flatten; it exploded with a loud bang, and the whole car shuddered on its springs like a dog that had been kicked while asleep. The hubcap flew off and rattled aimlessly on the frozen composition surface of Crestallen Street West.

Fenner stopped and looked unbelievingly at the house. His face was raw with shock. The fellow in the blue blazer dropped his briefcase. The other fellow had better reflexes, or perhaps a more developed sense of self-preservation. He wheeled and ran around the green sedan, crouched low, and disappeared from sight.

The policemen moved right and left, behind their own cruiser. A moment later the one wearing sunglasses bounced up from behind the hood, his service revolver held in both hands, and fired three times. The gun made an innocuous popping sound after the Weatherbee's massive crack. He fell behind his chair and heard the bullets pass overhead—you really could hear them, and the noise they made in the air was zzizzz!—and bury themselves in the plaster above the couch. The sound they made entering the plaster reminded him of the sound fists made hitting the heavy bag in a gymnasium. He thought: that's what they'd sound like going into me.

The cop wearing sunglasses was shouting at Fenner and the man in the blue blazer. "Get down! Goddammit, get down! He's got a fucking howitzer in there!"

He raised his head a little more to see better and the cop in the sunglasses saw him do it and fired twice more. The bullets thudded into the wall and this time Mary's favorite picture, "Lobstermen" by Winslow Homer, fell off the wall, hit the couch, and then went to the floor. The glass facing on the picture shattered.

He raised his head again because he had to see what was happening (why hadn't he thought to get a kid's periscope?), he had to see if they were trying to flank him which was how Richard Widmark and Marty Milner always took the Jap pillboxes on the late movies, and if they were trying to do that he would have to try to shoot one, but the cops were still behind their cruiser and Fenner and the guy in the blue blazer were dashing behind the green car. Blue Blazer's briefcase lay on the sidewalk like a small dead animal. He aimed at it, wincing at the recoil of the big rifle even before it came, and fired.

CRRRACKK! and the briefcase exploded into two pieces and jumped savagely into the air, flapping, disgorging a flutter of papers for the wind to stir an invisible finger through.

He fired again, this time at the right front wheel of the green sedan, and the tire blew. One of the men behind the car screamed in soprano terror.

He looked over at the police car and the driver's side door was open. The cop with the sunglasses was lying half in on the seat, using his radio. Soon all the party-goers would be here. They were going to give him away, a little piece for anyone who wanted one, and it would not be personal anymore. He felt a relief that was as bitter as aloes. Whatever it had been, whatever mournful sickness that had brought him to this, the last crotch of a tall tree, it was not his alone anymore, whispering and crying in secret. He had joined the mainstream of lunacy, he had come out of the closet. Soon they could reduce him to safe headline—SHAKY CEASE-FIRE HOLDS ON CRESTALLEN STREET.

He put the rifle down and scrambled across the living room floor on his hands and knees, being careful not to cut himself on the glass from the shattered picture frame. He got the small pillow and then scrambled back. The cop was not in the car anymore.

He picked up the Magnum and put two shots across their bow. The pistol bucked heavily in his hand, but the recoil was manageable. His shoulder throbbed like a rotted tooth.

One of the cops, the one without sunglasses, popped up behind the cruiser's trunk to return his fire and he sent two bullets into the cruiser's back window, blowing it inward in a twisted craze of cracks. The cop ducked back down without firing.

"Hold it!" Fenner bawled. "Let me talk to him!"

"Go ahead," one of the cops said.

"Dawes!" Fenner yelled toughly, sounding like a detective in the last reel of a Jimmy Cagney movie. (The police spotlights are crawling relentlessly back and forth over the front of the sleazy slum tenement where "Mad Dog" Dawes has gone to ground with a smoking .45 automatic in each hand." "Mad Dog" is crouched behind an overturned easy chair, wearing a strappy T-shirt and snarling.) *"Dawes, can you hear me in there!"*

(And "Mad Dog," his face twisted with defiance—although his brow is greased with sweat—screams out:)

"Come and get me, ya dirty coppers!" He bounced up over the easy chair and emptied the Magnum into the green sedan, leaving a ragged row of holes.

"Jesus!" somebody screamed. "Oh Jesus he's nuts!"

"Dawes!" Fenner yelled.

"You'll never take me alive!" he yelled, delirious with joy. "You're the dirty rats who shot my kid brother! I'll see some of ya in *hell* before ya get me!" He reloaded the Magnum with trembling fingers and then put enough shells into the Weatherbee to fill its magazine.

"Dawes!" Fenner yelled again. *"How about a deal?"*

"How about some hot lead, ya dirty screw!" he screamed at Fenner, but he was looking at the police car and when the cop wearing sunglasses put his head stealthily over the hood, he sent him diving with two shots. One of them went through the picture window of the Quinns' house across the street.

"Dawes!" Fenner yelled importantly.

One of the cops said: "Oh shut the fuck up. You're just encouraging him."

There was an embarrassed silence and in it the sound of sirens, still distant, began to rise. He put the Magnum down and picked up the rifle. The joyous delirium had left him feeling tired and achey and needing to shit.

Please let them be quick from the TV stations, he prayed. Quick with their movie cameras.

When the first police car screamed around the corner in a calculated racing drift like something out of *The French Connection* he was ready. He had fired two of the howitzer shells over the parked cruiser to make them stay down, and he drew a careful bead on the grille of the charging cruiser and squeezed the trigger like a seasoned Richard Widmark-type veteran and the whole grille seemed to explode and the hood flew up. The cruiser roared straight over the curb about forty yards up the street and hit a tree. The doors flew open and four cops spilled out with their guns drawn, looking dazed. Two of them walked into each other. Then the cops behind the first cruiser (*his* cops, he thought of them with a trace of propriety) opened fire and he submarined behind the chair while the bullets whizzed above him. It was seventeen minutes of eleven. He thought that now they would try to flank him.

He stuck his head up because he had to and a bullet droned past his right ear. Two more cruisers were coming up Crestallen Street from the other direction, sirens whooping, blue lights flashing. Two of the cops from the crashed cruiser were trying to climb the stake fence between the sidewalk and the Upslingers' backyard and he fired the rifle at them three times, not firing to hit or miss but only to make them go back to their car. They did. Wood from Wilbur Upslinger's fence (ivy climbed on it in the spring and summer) sprayed everywhere, and part of it actually fell over into the snow.

The two new cruisers had pulled up in a V that blocked the road in front of Jack Hobart's house. Police crouched in the apex of the V. One of them was talking to the police in the crash cruiser on a walkie-talkie. A moment later the newest arrivals began laying down a heavy pattern of covering fire, making him duck again. Bullets struck the front door, the front of the house, and all around the picture window. The mirror in the front hall exploded into jumbled diamonds. A bullet punched through the quilt covering the Zenith TV, and the quilt danced briefly.

He scrambled across the living room on his hands and knees and stood up by the small window behind the TV. From here he could look directly into the Upslingers' backyard. Two policemen were trying the flanking movement again. One of them had a nosebleed.

Freddy, I may have to kill one of them to make them stop.

Don't do that, George. Please. Don't do that.

He smashed the window with the butt of the Magnum, cutting his hand. They looked around at the noise, saw him, and began to shoot. He returned their fire and saw two of his bullets punch holes in Wilbur's new aluminum siding (had the city recompensed him for that?). He heard bullets punching into his own house just below the window and on both sides of it. One whined off the frame and splinters flew in his face. He expected a bullet to rip off the top of his head at any moment. It was hard to tell how long the exchange went on. Suddenly one of the cops grabbed his forearm and cried out. The cop dropped his pistol like a child that has grown tired of a stupid game. He ran in a small circle. His partner grabbed him and they began to run back toward their crashed cruiser, the unhurt one with his arm around his partner's waist.

He dropped to his hands and knees and crawled back to the overturned chair and peeked out. Two more cruisers on the street now, one coming from each end. They parked on the Quinns' side of the street and eight policemen got out and ran behind the cruiser with the flat tire and the green sedan.

He put his head down again and crawled into the hall. The house was taking very heavy fire now. He knew he should take the rifle and go upstairs, he would have a better angle on them from up there, could maybe drive them back from their car to cover in the houses across the street. But he didn't dare go that far from the master fuse and the storage battery. The TV people might come at any time.

The front door was full of bullet holes, the dark brown varnish splintered back to show the raw wood underneath. He crawled into the kitchen. All the windows were broken in here and broken glass littered the linoleum. A chance shot had knocked the coffeepot from the stove and it lay overturned in a puddle of brown goo. He crouched below the window for a moment, then bounced up and emptied the Magnum into the V-parked cars. Immediately fire intensified on the kitchen. Two bullet holes appeared in the white enamel of the refrigerator and another struck the Southern Comfort bottle on the counter. It exploded, spraying glass and southern hospitality everywhere.

Crawling back to the living room he felt something like a bee sting in the fleshy part of his right thigh just below the buttocks, and when he clapped his hand to it, his fingers came away bloody.

He lay behind the chair and reloaded the Magnum. Reloaded the Weatherbee. Poked his head up and ducked back down, wincing, at the ferocity of fire that came at him, bullets striking the couch and the wall and the TV, making the quilt shimmy. Poked his head up again and fired at the police cars parked across the street. Blew in one window. And saw—

At the top of the street, a white station wagon and a white Ford van. Written in blue letters on the sides of both was:

WHLM NEWSBEAT
CHANNEL 9

Panting, he crawled back to the window that looked out on the Upslingers' side yard. The news vehicles were crawling slowly and dubiously down Crestallen Street. Suddenly a new police car shot around them and blocked them off, tires smoking. An arm dressed in blue shot out of the cruiser's back window and began waving the newsmobiles off.

A bullet struck the windowsill and jumped into the room at an angle.

He crawled back to the easy chair, holding the Magnum in his bloody right hand and screamed: *"Fenner!"*

The fire slackened a little.

"Fenner!" he screamed again.

"Hold on!" Fenner yelled. *"Stop! Stop a minute!"*

There were a few isolated pops, then nothing.

"What do you want?" Fenner called.

"The news people! Down behind those cars on the other side of the street! I want to talk to them!"

There was a long, contemplative pause.

"No!" Fenner yelled.

"I'll stop shooting if I can talk to them!" That much was true, he thought, looking at the battery.

"No!" Fenner yelled again.

Bastard, he thought helplessly. Is it that important to you? You and Ordner and the rest of you bureaucratic bastards?

The firing began again, tentatively at first, then gaining strength. Then, incredibly, a man in a plaid shirt and blue jeans was running down the sidewalk, holding a pistol-grip camera in one hand.

"I heard that!" the man in the plaid shirt yelled. "I heard every word! I'll get your name, fella! He offered to stop shooting and you—"

A policeman hit him with a waist-high flying tackle and the man in the plaid shirt crunched to the sidewalk. His movie camera flew into the gutter and a moment later three bullets shattered it into winking pieces. A clockspring of unexposed film unwound lazily from the remains. Then the fire flagged again, uncertainly.

"Fenner, let them set up!" he hollered. His throat felt raw and badly used, like the rest of him. His hand hurt and a deep, throbbing ache had begun to emanate outward from his thigh.

"Come out first!" Fenner yelled back. *"We'll let you tell your side of it!"*

Rage washed over him in a red wave at this barefaced lie. *"GODDAMMIT, I'VE GOT A BIG GUN HERE AND I'LL START SHOOTING AT GAS TANKS YOU SHITBIRD AND THERE'LL BE A FUCKING BARBECUE WHEN I GET DONE!"*

Shocked silence.

Then, cautiously, Fenner said: "What do you want?"

"Send that guy you tackled in here! Let the camera crew set up!"

"Absolutely not! We're not giving you a hostage to play games with all day!"

A cop ran over to the listing green sedan bent low and disappeared behind it. There was a consultation.

A new voice yelled: *"There's thirty men behind your house, guy! They've got shotguns! Come out or I'll send them in!"* Time to play his one ratty trump. *"You better not! The whole house is wired with explosive. Look at this!"*

He held the red alligator clip up in the window.

"Can you see it?"

"You're bluffing!" the voice called back confidently.

"If I hook this up to the car battery beside me on the floor, everything goes!" Silence. More consultation.

"Hey!" someone yelled. "Hey, get that guy!" He poked his head up to look and here came the man in the plaid shirt and jeans, right out into the street, no protection, either heroically sure of his own profession or crazy. He had long black hair that fell almost to his collar and a thin dark moustache.

Two cops started to charge around the V-parked cruisers and thought better of it when he put a shot over their heads.

"Jesus Christ what a snafu!" somebody cried out in shrill disgust.

The man in the plaid shirt was on his lawn now, kicking up snow-bursts. Something buzzed by his ear, followed by a report, and he realized he was still looking over the chair. He heard the front door being tried, and then the man in the plaid shirt was hammering on it.

He scrambled across the floor, which was now spotted with grit and plaster that had been knocked out of the walls. His right leg hurt like a bastard and when he looked down he saw his pants leg was bloody from thigh to knee. He turned the lock in the chewed-up door and released the bolt from its catch.

"Okay!" he said, and the man in the plaid shirt burst in.

Up close he didn't look scared although he was panting hard. There was a scrape on his cheek from where the policeman had tackled him, and the left arm of his shirt was ripped. When the man in the plaid shirt was inside he scrambled back into the living room, picked up the rifle, and fired twice blindly over the top of the chair. Then he turned around. The man in the plaid shirt was standing in the doorway, looking incredibly calm. He had taken a large notebook out of his back pocket.

"All right, man," he said. "What shit goes down?"

"What's your name?"

"Dave Albert."

"Has that white van got more film equipment in it?"

"Yes."

"Go to the window. Tell the police to let a camera crew set up on the Quinns' lawn. That's the house across the street. Tell them if it isn't done in five minutes, you got trouble."

"Do I?"

"Sure."

Albert laughed. "You don't look like you could kill time, fella."

"Tell them."

Albert walked to the shattered living room window and stood framed there for a second, obviously relishing the moment.

"He says for my camera crew to set up across the street!" he yelled. *"He say's he's going to kill me if you don't let them!"*

"No!" Fenner yelled back furiously. *"No, no, n—"*

Somebody muzzled him. Silence for a beat.

"All right!" This was the voice that had accused him of bluffing about the explosive. *"Will you let two of our men go up and get them?"*

He thought it over and nodded at the reporter.

"Yes!" Albert called.

There was a pause, and then two uniformed policemen trotted self-consciously up toward where the news van waited, its engine smugly idling. In the meantime two more cruisers had pulled up, and by leaning far to the right he could see that the downhill end of Crestallen Street West had been blocked off. A large crowd of people was standing behind the yellow crash barriers.

"Okay," Albert said, sitting down. "We got a minute. What do you want? A plane?"

"Plane?" he echoed stupidly.

Albert flapped his arms, still holding his notebook. "Fly away, man. Just flyyyyy away."

"Oh." He nodded to show that he understood. "No, I don't want a plane."

"Then what do you want?"

"I want," he said carefully, "to be just twenty with a lot of decisions to make over again." He saw the look in Albert's eyes and said, "I know I can't. I'm not that crazy."

"You're shot."

"Yes."

"Is that what you said it is?" He was pointing at the master fuse and the battery.

"Yes. The main fuse goes to all the rooms in the house. Also the garage."

"Where did you get the explosive?" Albert's voice was amiable but his eyes were alert.

"Found it in my Christmas stocking."

He laughed. "Say, that's not bad. I'm going to use that in my story."

"Fine. When you go back out, tell all the policemen that they better move away."

"Are you going to blow yourself up?" Albert asked. He looked interested, nothing more.

"I am contemplating it."

"You know what, fellow? You've seen too many movies."

"I don't go to the movies much anymore. I did see *The Exorcist*, though. I wish I hadn't. How are your movie guys coming out there?"

Albert peered out the window. "Pretty good. We've got another minute. Your name is Dawes?"

"Did they tell you that?"

Albert laughed contemptuously. "They wouldn't tell me if I had cancer. I read it on the doorbell. Would you mind telling me why you're doing all this?"

"Not at all. It's roadwork."

"The extension?" Albert's eyes glowed brighter. He began to scribble in his book.

"Yes, that's right."

"They took your house?"

"They tried. I'm going to take it."

Albert wrote it down, then snapped his book closed and stuffed it into his back pocket again. "That's pretty stupid, Mr. Dawes. Do you mind my saying that? Why don't you just come out of here with me?"

"You've got an exclusive," he said tiredly. "What are you trying for, the Pulitzer Prize?"

"I'd take it if they offered it." He smiled brightly and then sobered. "Come on, Mr. Dawes. Come on out. I'll see that your side gets told. I'll see—"

"There is no side."

Albert frowned. "What was that?"

"I have no side. That's why I'm doing this." He peered over the chair and looked into a telephoto lens, mounted on a tripod that was sunk into the snow of the Quinns' lawn. "Go on now. Tell them to go away."

"Are you really going to pull the string?"

"I really don't know."

Albert walked to the living room door and then turned around. "Do I know you from somewhere? Why do I keep feeling like I know you?"

He shook his head. He thought he had never seen Albert before in his life.

Watching the newsman walk back across his lawn, slightly at an angle so the camera across the street would get his good side, he wondered what Olivia was doing at that precise second.

He waited fifteen minutes. Their fire had intensified, but no one charged at the back of the house. The main purpose of the fire seemed to be to cover their retreat into the houses across the street. The camera crew remained where it was for a while, grinding impassively away, and then the white Econoline van drove up onto the Quinns' side lawn and the man behind the camera folded the tripod, took it behind the truck, and began to film again.

Something black and tubular whizzed through the air, landed on his lawn about midway between the house and the sidewalk, and began to spurt gas. The wind caught it and carried it off down the street in tattered rifts. A second shell landed short, and then he heard one clunk on the roof. He caught a whiff of that one as it fell into the snow covering Mary's begonias. His nose and eyes filled with crocodile tears.

He scurried across the living room on his hands and knees again, hoping to God he had said nothing to that newsman, Albert, that could be misconstrued as profound. There was no good place to make your stand in the world. Look at Johnny Walker, dying in a meaningless intersection smashup. What had he died for, so that the sheets could go through? Or that woman in the supermarket. The fucking you got was never worth the screwing you took.

He turned on the stereo and the stereo still worked. The Rolling Stones album was still on the turntable and he put on the last cut, missing the right groove the first time when a bullet smacked into the quilt covering the Zenith TV with a thud.

When he had it right, the last bars of "Monkey Man" fading into nothingness, he scurried back to the overturned chair and threw the rifle out the window. He picked up the Magnum and threw that out after it. Good-bye, Nick Adams.

"You can't always get what you want," the stero sang, and he knew that to be a fact. But that didn't stop you from wanting it. A tear gas canister arched through the window, struck the wall over the couch, and exploded in white smoke.

> "But if you try something, you might find,
> You get what you need."

Well, let's just see, Fred. He grasped the red alligator clip in his hand. Let's see if I get what I need.

"Okay," he muttered, and jammed the red clip on the negative pole of the battery.

He closed his eyes and his last thought was that the world was not exploding around him but inside him, and while the explosion was cataclysmic, it was not larger than, say, a good-sized walnut.

Then white.

Epilogue

The WHLM newsteam won a Pultizer Prize for their coverage of what they called "Dawes' Last Stand" on the evening news, and for a half-hour documentary presented three weeks later. The documentary was called "Roadwork" and it examined the necessity—or lack of it—for the 784 extension. The documentary pointed out that one reason the road was being built had nothing to do with traffic patterns or commuter convenience or anything else of such a practical sort. The municipality had to build so many miles of road per year or begin losing federal money on all interstate construction. And so the city had chosen to build. The documentary also pointed out that the city was quietly beginning a litigation against the widow of Barton George Dawes to recover as much of their money as was recoverable. In the wake of the outcry the city dropped its suit.

Still photographs of the wreckage ran on the AP wire and most of the newspapers in the country carried them. In Las Vegas, a young girl who had only recently enrolled in a business school saw the photographs while on her lunch hour and fainted.

Despite the pictures and the words, the extension went ahead and was completed eighteen months later, ahead of schedule. By that time most of the people in the city had forgotten the "Roadwork" documentary, and the city's news force, including Pulitzer winner David Albert, had gone on to other stories and crusades. But few people who had been watching the original newsclip broadcast on the evening news ever forgot that; they remembered even after the facts surrounding it grew blurry in their minds.

That news clip showed a plain white suburban house, sort of a ranch house with an asphalt driveway to the right leading to a one-car garage. A nice-looking house, but totally ordinary. Not a house you'd crane to look at if you happened to be on a Sunday drive. But in the news footage the picture window is shattered. Two guns, a rifle and a pistol, come flying out of it to lie in the snow. For one second you see the hand that has flung them, the fingers held limply up like the hand of a drowning man. You see white smoke blowing around the house, Mace or teargas or something. And then there is a huge belch of orange flame and all the walls of the house seem to bulge out in an impossible cartoon convexity and there is a huge detonation and the camera shakes a little, as if in horror. Peripherally the viewer is aware that the garage has been destroyed in a single ripping blast. For a second it seems (and slow motion replays prove that the eye's split-second impression is correct) that the roof of the house has lifted off its eaves like a Saturn rocket. Then the entire house blows outward and upward, shingles flying, hunks of wood lofted into the

529

air and then returning to earth, something that looks like a quilt twisting lazily in the air like a magic carpet as debris rattle to the ground in a thudding, contrapuntal drum roll.

There is stillness.

Then the shocked, tear-streaming face of Mary Dawes fills the screen; she is looking with drugged and horrified bewilderment at the forest of microphones being thrust into her face, and we have been brought safely back to human things once more.

SIGNET•451-AE1508•$2.50

WELCOME TO AMERICA IN 2025
WHEN THE BEST MEN
DON'T RUN FOR PRESIDENT.
THEY RUN FOR THEIR LIVES.

THE
RUNNING MAN
RICHARD BACHMAN

. . . Minus 100
and COUNTING . . .

She was squinting at the thermometer in the white light coming through the window. Beyond her, in the drizzle, the other highrises in Co-Op City rose like the gray turrets of a penitentiary. Below, in the airshaft, clotheslines flapped with ragged wash. Rats and plump alley cats circulated through the garbage.

She looked at her husband. He was seated at the table, staring up at the Free-Vee with steady, vacant concentration. He had been watching it for weeks now. It wasn't like him. He hated it, always had. Of course, every Development apartment had one—it was the law—but it was still legal to turn them off. The Compulsory Benefit Bill of 2021 had failed to get the required two-thirds majority by six votes. Ordinarily they never watched it. But ever since Cathy had gotten sick, he had been watching the big-money giveaways. It filled her with sick fear.

Behind the compulsive shrieking of the half-time announcer narrating the latest newsie flick, Cathy's flue-hoarsened wailing went on and on.

"How bad is it?" Richards asked.

"Not so bad."

"Don't shit me."

"It's a hundred and four."

He brought both fists down on the table. A plastic dish jumped into the air and clattered down.

"We'll get a doctor. Try not to worry so much. Listen—" She began to babble frantically to distract him; he had turned around and was watching the Free-Vee again. Half-time was over, and the game was on again. This wasn't one of the big ones, of course, just a cheap daytime come-on called *Treadmill to Bucks*. They accepted only chronic heart, liver, or lung patients, sometimes throwing in a crip for comic relief. Every minute the contestant could stay on the treadmill (keeping up a steady flow of chatter with the emcee), he won ten dollars. Every two minutes the emcee asked a Bonus Question in the contestant's category (the current pal, a heart-murmur from Hackensack, was an American history buff) which was worth fifty dollars. If the contestant, dizzy, out of breath, heart doing fantastic rubber acrobatics in his chest, missed the question, fifty dollars was deducted from his winnings and the treadmill was speeded up.

"We'll get along. Ben. We will. Really. I . . . I'll . . . "

"You'll what?" He looked at her brutally. "Hustle? No more, Shelia. She's

533

got to have a real doctor. No more block midwife with dirty hands and whiskey breath. All the modern equipment. I'm going to see to it.''

He crossed the room, eyes swiveling hypnotically to the Free-Vee bolted into one peeling wall above the sink. He took his cheap denim jacket off its hook and pulled it on with fretful gestures.

"No! No, I won't . . . won't allow it. You're not going to—''

"Why not? At worst you can get a few oldbucks as the head of a fatherless house. One way or the other you'll have to see her through this.''

She had never really been a handsome woman, and in the years since her husband had not worked she had grown scrawny, but in this moment she looked beautiful . . . imperious. "I won't take it. I'd rather sell the govie a two-dollar piece of tail when he comes to the door and send him back with his dirty blood money in his pocket. Should I take a bounty on my man?''

He turned on her, grim and humorless, clutching something that set him apart, an invisible something for which the Network had ruthlessly calculated. He was a dinosaur in this time. Not a big one, but still a throwback, an embarrassment. Perhaps a danger. Big clouds condense around small particles.

He gestured at the bedroom. "How about her in an unmarked pauper's grave? Does that appeal to you?''

It left her with only the argument of insensate sorrow. Her face cracked and dissolved into tears.

"Ben, this is just what they want, for people like us, like you—''

"Maybe they won't take me,'' he said, opening the door. "Maybe I don't have whatever it is they look for.''

"If you go now, they'll kill you. And I'll be here watching it. Do you want me watching that with her in the next room?'' She was hardly coherent through her tears.

"I want her to go on living.'' He tried to close the door, but she put her body in the way.

"Give me a kiss before you go, then.''

He kissed her. Down the hall, Mrs. Jenner opened her door and peered out. The rich odor of corned beef and cabbage, tantalizing, maddening, drifted to them. Mrs. Jenner did well—she helped out at the local discount drug and had an almost uncanny eye for illegal-card carriers.

"You'll take the money?'' Richards asked. "You won't do anything stupid?''

"I'll take it,'' she whispered. "You know I'll take it.''

He clutched her awkwardly, then turned away quickly, with no grace, and plunged down the crazily slanting, ill-lighted stairwell.

She stood in the doorway, shaken by soundless sobs, until she heard the door slam hollowly five flights down, and then she put her apron up to her face. She was still clutching the thermometer she had used to take the baby's temperature.

Mrs. Jenner crept up softly and twitched the apron. "Dearie,'' she whispered, "I can put you onto black market penicillin when the money gets here . . . real cheap . . . good quality—''

"Get out!" She screamed at her.

Mr. Jenner recoiled, her upper lip raising instinctively away from the blackened stumps of her teeth. "Just trying to help," she muttered, and scurried back to her room.

Barely muffled by the thin plastiwood, Cathy's wails continued. Mrs. Jenner's Free-Vee blared and hooted. The contestant on *Treadmill to Bucks* had just missed a Bonus Question and had had a heart attack simultaneously. He was being carried off on a rubber stretcher while the audience applauded.

Upper lip rising and falling metronomically, Mrs. Jenner wrote Sheila Richards's name down in her notebook. "We'll see," she said to no one. "We'll just see, Mrs. Smell-So-Sweet."

She closed the notebook with a vicious snap and settled down to watch the next game.

. . . Minus 099
and COUNTING . . .

The drizzle had deepened into a steady rain by the time Richards hit the street. The big Smoke Dokes for Hallucinogenic Jokes thermometer across the street stood at fifty-one degrees. *(Just the Right Temp to Stoke Up a Doke—High to the Nth Degree!)* That might make it sixty in their apartment. And Cathy had the flu.

A rat trotted lazily, lousily, across the cracked and blistered cement of the street. Across the way, the ancient and rusted skeleton of a 2013 Humber stood on decayed axles. It had been completely stripped, even to the wheel bearings and motor mounts, but the cops didn't take it away. The cops rarely ventured south of the Canal anymore. Co-Op City stood in a radiating rat warren of parking lots, deserted shops, Urban Centers, and paved playgrounds. The cycle gangs were the law here, and all those newsie items about the intrepid Block Police of South City were nothing but a pile of warm crap. The streets were ghostly, silent. If you went out, you took the pneumo bus or you carried a gas cylinder.

He walked fast, not looking around, not thinking. The air was sulphurous and thick. Four cycles roared past and someone threw a ragged hunk of asphalt paving. Richards ducked easily. Two pneumo buses passed him, buffeting him with air, but he did not flag them. The week's twenty-dollar unemployment allotment (old-bucks) had been spent. There was no money to buy a token. He supposed the roving packs could sense his poverty. He was not molested.

Highrises, Developments, chain-link fences, parking lots empty except for stripped derelicts, obscenities scrawled on the pavement in soft chalk and now blurring with the rain. Crashed-out windows, rats, wet bags of garbage splashed over the sidewalks and into the gutters. Graffiti written jaggedly on crumbling gray walls: HONKY DON'T LET THE SUN SET ON YOU HEAR. HOME FOLKS BLOW DOKES. YOUR MOMMY ITCHES. SKIN YOUR BANANA. TOMMY'S PUSHING. HITLER WAS COOL. MARY. SID. KILL ALL KIKES. The old G.A. sodium lights put up in the 70s busted with rocks and hunks of paving. No technico was going to replace them down here; they were on the New Credit Dollar. Technicos stay uptown, baby. Uptown's cool. Everything silent except for the rising-then-descending whoosh of the pneumo buses and the echoing clack of Richards's footfalls. This battlefield only lights up at night. In the day it is a deserted gray silence which contains no movement but the cats and rats and fat white maggots trundling across the garbage. No smell but the decaying reek of this brave year 2025. The Free-Vee cables are safely buried under the streets and no one but an idiot or a revolutionary would want to vandalize them. Free-Vee is the stuff of dreams, the bread of life. Scag is twelve oldbucks a bag, Frisco Push goes for twenty a tab, but the Free-Vee will freak you for nothing. Farther along, on the other side of the Canal, the dream machine runs twenty-four hours a day . . . but it runs on New Dollars, and only employed people have any. There are four million others, almost all of them unemployed, south of the Canal in Co-Op City.

Richards walked three miles and the occasional liquor stores and smoke shops, at first heavily grilled, become more numerous. Then the X-Houses *(!!24 Perversions—Count 'Em 24!!)*, the Hockeries, the Blood Emporiums. Greasers sitting on cycles at every corner, the gutters buried in snowdrifts of roach ends. Rich Blokes Smoke Dokes.

He could see the skyscrapers rising into the clouds now, high and clean. The highest of all was the Network Games Building, one hundred stories, the top half buried in cloud and smog cover. He fixed his eyes on it and walked another mile. Now the more expensive movie houses, and smoke shops with no grills (but Rent-A-Pigs stood outside, electric move-alongs hanging from their Sam Browne belts). A city cop on every corner. The People's Fountain Park: Admission 75¢. Well-dressed mothers watching their children as they frolicked on the astroturf behind chain-link fencing. A cop on either side of the gate. A tiny, pathetic glimpse of the fountain.

He crossed the Canal.

As he got closer to the Games Building it grew taller, more and more improbable with its impersonal tiers of rising office windows, its polished stonework. Cops watching him, ready to hustle him along or bust him if he tried to commit loitering. Uptown there was only one function for a man in baggy gray pants and a cheap bowl haircut and sunken eyes. That purpose was the Games.

The qualifying examinations began promptly at noon, and when Ben Richards stepped behind the last man in line, he was almost in the umbra of the Games Building. But the building was still nine blocks and over a mile away. The line stretched before him like an eternal snake. Soon others joined it behind him. The police watched them, hands on either gun butts or move-alongs. They smiled anonymous, contemptuous smiles.

—That one look like a half-wit to you, Frank? Looks like one to me.

—Guy down there ast me if there was a place where he could go to the bathroom. Canya magine it?

—Sons of bitches ain't—

—Kill their own mothers for a—

—Smelled like he didn't have a bath for—

—Ain't nothin like a freak show I always—

Heads down against the rain, they shuffled aimlessly, and after a while the line began to move.

. . . Minus 098
and COUNTING . . .

It was after four when Ben Richards got to the main desk and was routed to Desk 9 (Q-R). The woman sitting at the rumbling plastipunch looked tired and cruel and impersonal. She looked at him and saw no one.

"Name, last-first-middle."

"Richards, Benjamin Stuart."

Her fingers raced over the keys. *Clitter-clitter-clitter* went the machine.

"Age-height-weight."

"Twenty-eight, six-two, one-sixty-five."

Clitter-clitter-clitter

"Certified I.Q. by Weschler test if you know it, and age tested."

"One twenty-six. Age of fourteen."

Clitter-clitter-clitter

The huge lobby was an echoing, rebounding tomb of sound. Questions being asked and answered. People were being led out weeping. People were being thrown out. Hoarse voices were raised in protest. A scream or two. Questions. Always questions.

"Last school attended?"

"Manual Trades."

"Did you graduate?"

"No."

"How many years, and at what age did you leave?"

"Two years. Sixteen years old."

"Reasons for leaving?"

"I got married."
Clitter-clitter-clitter
"Name and age of spouse if any."
"Sheila Catherine Richards, twenty-six."
"Names and ages of children, if any."
"Catherine Sarah Richards, eighteen months."
Clitter-clitter-clitter
"Last question, mister. Don't bother lying; they'll pick it up during the physical and disqualify you there. Have you ever used heroin or the synthetic-amphetamine hallucinogen called San Francisco Push?"
"No."
Clitter
A plastic card popped out and she handed it to him. "Don't lose this, big fella. If you do, you have to start back at go next week." She was looking at him now, seeing his face, the angry eyes, lanky body. Not bad looking. At least some intelligence. Good stats.

She took his card back abruptly and punched off the upper right-hand corner, giving it an odd milled appearance.

"What was that for?"

"Never mind. Somebody will tell you later. Maybe." She pointed over his shoulder at a long hall which led toward a bank of elevators. Dozens of men fresh from the desks were being stopped, showing their plastic I.D.s and moving on. As Richards watched, a trembling, sallow-faced Push freak was stopped by a cop and shown the door. The freak began to cry. But he went.

"Tough old world, big fella," the woman behind the desk said without sympathy. "Move along."

Richards moved along. Behind him, the litany was already beginning again.

. . . Minus 097
and COUNTING . . .

A hard, callused hand slapped his shoulder at the head of the hall beyond the desks. "Card, buddy."

Richards showed it. The cop relaxed, his face subtle and Chinese with disappointment.

"You like turning them back, don't you?" Richards asked. "It really gives you a charge, doesn't it?"

"You want to go downtown, maggot?"

Richards walked past him, and the cop made no move.

He stopped halfway to the bank of elevators and looked back. "Hey. Cop."

The cop looked at him truculently.

"Got a family? It could be you next week."

"Move on!" the cop shouted furiously.

With a smile, Richards moved on.

There was a line of perhaps twenty applicants waiting at the elevators. Richards showed one of the cops on duty his card and the cop looked at him closely. "You a hardass, sonny?"

"Hard enough," Richards said, and smiled.

The cop gave him back his card. "They'll kick it soft again. How smart do you talk with holes in your head, sonny?"

"Just about as smart as you talk without that gun on your leg and your pants down around your ankles," Richards said, still smiling. "Want to try it?"

For a moment he thought the cop was going to swing at him. "They'll fix you," the cop said. "You'll do some walking on your knees before you're done."

The cop swaggered over to three new arrivals and demanded to see their cards.

The man ahead of Richards turned around. He had a nervous, unhappy face and curly hair that came down in a widow's peak. "Say, you don't want to antagonize them, fella. They've got a grapevine."

"Is that so?" Richards asked, looking at him mildly.

The man turned away.

Abruptly the elevator doors snapped open. A black cop with a huge gut stood protecting the bank of push buttons. Another cop sat on a small stool reading a 3-D pervert mag in a small bulletproof cubicle the size of a telephone booth at the rear of the large car. A sawed-off shotgun rested between his knees. Shells were lined up beside him within easy reach.

"Step to the rear!" the fat cop cried with bored importance. "Step to the rear! Step to the rear!"

They crowded in to a depth where a deep breath was impossible. Sad flesh walled Richards on every side. They went up to the second floor. The doors snapped open. Richards, who stood a head taller than anyone else in the car, saw a huge waiting room with many chairs dominated by a huge Free-Vee. A cigarette dispenser stood in one corner.

"Step out! Step out! Show I.D. cards to your left!"

They stepped out, holding out their I.D. cards to the impersonal lens of a camera. Three cops stood close by. For some reason, a buzzer went off at the sight of some dozen cards, and the holders were jerked out of line and hustled away.

Richards showed his card and was waved on. He went to the cigarette machine, got a package of Blams and sat down as far from the Free-Vee as possible. He lit up a smoke and exhaled, coughing. He hadn't had a cigarette in almost six months.

. . . Minus 096
and COUNTING . . .

They called the *A*'s for the physical almost immediately, and about two dozen men got up and filed through a door beyond the Free-Vee. large sign tacked over the door read THIS WAY. There was an arrow below the legend, pointing at the door. The literacy of Games applicants was notoriously low.

They were taking a new letter every fifteen minutes or so. Ben Richards had sat down at about five, and so he estimated it would be quarter of nine before they got to him. He wished he had brought a book, but he supposed things were just as well as they were. Books were regarded with suspicion at best, especially when carried by someone from south of the Canal. Pervert Mags were safer.

He watched the six o'clock newsie restlessly (the fighting in Ecuador was worse, new cannibal riots had broken out in India, the Detroit Tigers had taken the Harding Catamounts by a score of 6–2 in an afternoon game), and when the first of the evening's big-money games came on at six-thirty, he went restlessly to the window and looked out. Now that his mind was made up, the Games bored him again. Most of the others, however, were watching *Fun Guns* with a dreadful fascination. Next week it might be them.

Outside, daylight was bleeding slowly toward dusk. The els were slamming at high speed through the power rings above the second-floor window, their powerful headlights searching the gray air. On the sidewalks below, crowds of men and women (most of them, of course, technicos or Network bureaucrats) were beginning their evening's prowl in search of entertainment. A Certified Pusher was hawking his wares on the corner across the street. A man with a sabled dolly on each arm passed below him; the trio was laughing about something.

He had a sudden awful wave of homesickness for Sheila and Cathy, and wished he could call them. He didn't think it was allowed. He could still walk out, of course; several men already had. They walked across the room, grinning obscurely at nothing, to use the door marked TO STREET. Back to the flat with his daughter glowing fever-bright in the other room? No. Couldn't. Couldn't.

He stood at the window a little while longer, then went back and sat down. The new game, *Dig Your Grave*, was beginning.

The fellow sitting next to Richards twitched his arm anxiously. "Is it true that they wash out over thirty percent just on the physicals?"

"I don't know," Richards said.

"Jesus," the fellow said. "I got bronchitis. Maybe *Treadmill to Bucks* . . . "

Richards could think of nothing to say. The pal's respiration sounded like a faraway truck trying to climb a steep hill.

"I got a fambly," the man said with soft desperation.

Richards looked at the Free-Vee as if it interested him.

The fellow was quiet for a long time. When the program changed again at seven-thirty, Richards heard him asking the man on his other side about the physical.

It was full dark outside now. Richards wondered if it was still raining. It seemed like a very long evening.

. . . Minus 095
and COUNTING . . .

When the R's went through the door under the red arrow and into the examination room it was just a few minutes after nine-thirty. A lot of the initial excitement had worn off, and people were either watching the Free-Vee avidly, with none of their prior dread, or dozing. The man with the noisy chest had a name that began with *L* and had been called over an hour before. Richards wondered idly if he had been cut.

The examination room was long and tiled, lit with fluorescent tubes. It looked like an assembly line, with bored doctors standing at various stations along the way.

Would any of you like to check my little girl? Richards thought bitterly.

The applicants showed their cards to another camera eye embedded in the wall and were ordered to stop by a row of clotheshooks. A doctor in a long white lab coat walked over to them, clipboard tucked under one arm.

"Strip," he said. "Hang your clothes on the hooks. Remember the number over your hook and give the number to the orderly at the far end. Don't worry about your valuables. Nobody here wants them."

Valuables. That was a hot one, Richards thought, unbuttoning his shirt. He had an empty wallet with a few pictures of Sheila and Cathy, a receipt for a shoe sole he had had replaced at the local cobbler's six months ago, a keyring with no keys on it except for the doorkey, a baby sock that he did not remember putting in there, and the package of Blams he had gotten from the machine.

He was wearing tattered skivvies because Sheila was too stubborn to let him go without, but many of the men were buck under their pants. Soon they all stood stripped and anonymous, penises dangling between their legs like forgotten war-clubs. Everyone held his card in one hand. Some shuffled their feet as if the floor were cold, although it was not. The faint, impersonally nostalgic odor of alcohol drifted through.

"Stay in line," the doctor with the clipboard was instructing. "Always show your card. Follow instructions."

The line moved forward. Richards saw there was a cop with each doctor along the way. He dropped his eyes and waited passively.

"Card."

He gave his card over. The first doctor noted the number, then said: "Open your mouth."

Richards opened it. His tongue was depressed.

The next doctor peered into his pupils with a tiny bright light, and then stared in his ears.

The next placed the cold circle of a stethoscope on his chest. "Cough."

Richards coughed. Down the line a man was being hauled away. He needed the money, they couldn't do it, he'd get his lawyer on them.

The doctor moved his stethoscope. "Cough."

Richards coughed. The doctor turned him around and put the stethoscope on his back.

"Take a deep breath and hold it." The stethoscope moved.

"Exhale."

Richards exhaled.

"Move along."

His blood pressure was taken by a grinning doctor with an eyepatch. He was given a short-arm inspection by a bald medico who had several large brown freckles, like liverspots, on his pate. The doctor placed a cool hand between the sac of his scrotum and his upper thigh.

"Cough."

Richards coughed.

"Move along."

His temperature was taken. He was asked to spit in a cup. Halfway, now. Halfway down the hall. Two or three men had already finished up, and an orderly with a pasty face and rabbit teeth was bringing them their clothes in wire baskets. Half a dozen more had been pulled out of the line and shown the stairs.

"Bend over and spread your cheeks."

Richards bent and spread. A finger coated with plastic invaded his rectal channel, explored, retreated.

"Move along."

He stepped into a booth with curtains on three sides, like the old voting booths— voting booths had been done away with by computer election eleven years ago— and urinated in a blue beaker. The doctor took it and put it in a wire rack.

At the next stop he looked at an eye-chart. "Read," the doctor said.

"E—A,L—D,M,F—S,P,M,Z—K,L,A,C,D—U,S,G,A—"

"That's enough. Move along."

He entered another pseudo voting booth and put earphones over his head. He was told to push the white button when he heard something and the red button when he didn't hear it anymore. The sound was very high and faint—like a dog whistle that had been pitch-lowered into just audible human range. Richards pushed buttons until he was told to stop.

He was weighed. His arches were examined. He stood in front of a fluoroscope and put on a lead apron. A doctor, chewing gum and singing something tunelessly under his breath, took several pictures and noted his card number.

Richards had come in with a group of about thirty. Twelve had made it to the far end of the room. Some were dressed and waiting for the elevator. About a dozen more had been hauled out of line. One of them tried to attack the doctor that had cut him and was felled by a policeman wielding a move-along at full charge. The pal fell as if poleaxed.

Richards stood at a low table and was asked if he had had some fifty different diseases. Most of them were respiratory in nature. The doctor looked up sharply when Richards said there was a case of influenza in the family.

"Wife?"

"No. My daughter."

"Age?"

"A year and a half."

"Have you been immunized? Don't try to lie!" the doctor shouted suddenly, as if Richards had already tried to lie. "We'll check your health stats."

"Immunized July 2023. Booster September 2023. Block health clinic."

"Move along."

Richards had a sudden urge to reach over the table and pop the maggot's neck. Instead, he moved along.

At the last stop, a severe-looking woman doctor with close-cropped hair and an Electric Juicer plugged into one ear asked him if he was a homosexual.

"No."

"Have you ever been arrested on a felony charge?"

"No."

"Do you have any severe phobias? By that I mean—"

"No."

"You better listen to the definition," she said with a faint touch of condescension. "I mean—"

"Do I have any unusual and compulsive fears, such as acrophobia or claustrophobia. I don't."

Her lips pressed tightly together, and for a moment she seemed on the verge of sharp comment.

"Do you use or have you used any hallucinogenic or addictive drugs?"

"No."

"Do you have any relatives who have been arrested on charges of crimes against the government or against the Network?"

"No."

"Sign this loyalty oath and this Games Commission release form, Mr., uh, Richards."

He scratched his signature.

"Show the orderly your card and tell him the number—"

He left her in midsentence and gestured at the bucktoothed orderly with his thumb. "Number twenty-six, Bugs." The orderly brought his things. Richards dressed slowly and went over by the elevator. His anus felt hot and embarrassed, violated, a little slippery with the lubricant the doctor had used.

When they were all bunched together, the elevator door opened. The bullet-proof Judas hole was empty this time. The cop was a skinny man with a large wen beside his nose. "Step to the rear," he chanted. "Please step to the rear."

As the doors closed, Richards could see the *S's* coming in at the far end of the hall. The doctor with the clipboard was approaching them. Then the doors clicked together, cutting off the view.

They rode up to the third floor, and the doors opened on a huge, semilit dormitory. Rows and rows of narrow iron-and-canvas cots seemed to stretch out to infinity.

Two cops began to check them out of the elevator, giving them bed numbers. Richards's was 940. The cot had one brown blanket and a very flat pillow. Richards lay down on the cot and let his shoes drop to the floor. His feet dangled over the end; there was nothing to be done about it.

He crossed his arms under his head and stared at the ceiling.

. . . Minus 094
and COUNTING . . .

He was awakened promptly at six the following morning by a very loud buzzer. For a moment he was foggy, disoriented, wondering if Sheila had bought an alarm clock or what. Then it came to him and he sat up.

They were led by groups of fifty into a large industrial bathroom where they showed their cards to a camera guarded by a policeman. Richards went to a blue-tiled booth that contained a mirror, a basin, a shower, a toilet. On the shelf above the basin was a row of toothbrushes wrapped in cellophane, an electric razor, a bar of soap, and a half-used tube of toothpaste. A sign tucked into the corner of the mirror read: *RESPECT THIS PROPERTY!* Beneath it, someone had scrawled: *I ONLY RESPECT MY ASS!*

Richards showered, dried with a towel that topped a pile on the toilet tank, shaved, and brushed.

They were let into a cafeteria where they showed their I.D. cards again. Richards took a tray and pushed it down a stainless steel ledge. He was given a box of cornflakes, a greasy dish of home fries, a scoop of scrambled eggs, a piece of toast as cold and hard as a marble gravestone, a halfpint of milk, a cup of muddy coffee (no cream), an envelope of sugar, an envelope of salt, and a pat of fake butter on a tiny square of oily paper.

He wolfed the meal; they all did. For Richards it was the first real food, other than greasy pizza wedges and government pill-commodities, that he had eaten in God knew how long. Yet it was oddly bland, as if some vampire chef in the kitchen had sucked all the taste out of it and left only brute nutrients.

What were *they* eating this morning? Kelp pills. Fake milk for the baby. A sudden feeling of desperation swelled over him. Christ, when would they start seeing money? Today? Tomorrow? Next week?

Or maybe that was just a gimmick too, a flashy come-on. Maybe there wasn't even any rainbow, let alone a pot of gold.

He sat staring at his empty plate until the seven o'clock buzzer went and they were moved on to the elevators.

. . . Minus 093
and COUNTING . . .

On the fourth floor Richards's group of fifty was herded first into a large, furnitureless room ringed with what looked like letter slots. They showed their cards again, and the elevator doors whooshed closed behind them.

A gaunt man with receding hair with the Games emblem (the silhouette of a human head superimposed over a torch) on his lab coat came into the room.

"Please undress and remove all valuables from your clothes," he said. "Then drop your clothes into one of the incinerator slots. You'll be issued Games coveralls." He smiled magnanimously. "You may keep the coveralls no matter what your personal Games resolution may be."

There was some grumbling, but everyone complied.

"Hurry, please," the gaunt man said. He clapped his hands together twice, like a first-grade teacher signaling the end of playtime. "We have lots ahead of us."

"Are you going to be a contestant, too?" Richards asked.

The gaunt man favored him with a puzzled expression. Somebody in the back snickered.

"Never mind," Richards said, and stepped out of his trousers.

He removed his unvaluable valuables and dumped his shirt, pants, and skivvies into a letter slot. There was a brief, hungry flash of flame from somewhere far below.

The door at the other end opened (there was *always* a door at the other end; they were like rats in a huge, upward-tending maze: an American maze, Richards reflected), and men trundled in large baskets on wheels, labeled S, M, L, and XL. Richards selected an XL for its length and expected it to hang baggily on his frame, but it fit quite well. The material was soft, clingy, almost like silk, but tougher than silk. A single nylon zipper ran up the front. They were all dark blue, and they all had the Games emblem on the right breast pocket. When the entire group was wearing them, Ben Richards felt as if he had lost his face.

"This way, please," the gaunt man said, and ushered them into another waiting room. The inevitable Free-Vee blared and cackled. "You'll be called in groups of ten."

The door beyond the Free-Vee was topped by another sign reading THIS WAY, complete with arrow.

They sat down. After a while, Richards got up and went to the window and looked out. They were higher up, but it was still raining. The streets were slick and black and wet. He wondered what Sheila was doing.

. . . Minus 092 and COUNTING . . .

He went through the door, one of a group of ten now, at quarter past ten. They went through single file. Their cards were scanned. There were ten three-sided booths, but these were more substantial. The sides were constructed of drilled soundproof cork paneling. The overhead lighting was soft and indirect. Muzak was emanating from hidden speakers. There was a plush carpet on the floor; Richards's feet felt startled by something that wasn't cement.

The gaunt man had said something to him.

Richards blinked. "Huh?"

"Booth 6," the gaunt man said reprovingly.

"Oh."

He went to Booth 6. There was a table inside, and a large wall clock mounted at eye level beyond it. On the table was a sharpened G-A/IBM pencil and a pile of unlined paper. Cheap grade, Richards noted.

Standing beside all this was a dazzling computer-age priestess, a tall, Junoesque blonde wearing iridescent short shorts which cleanly outlined the delta-shaped rise of her pudenda. Rouged nipples poked perkily through a silk fishnet blouselet.

"Sit down, please," she said, "I am Rinda Ward, your tester." She held out her hand.

Startled, Richards shook it. "Benjamin Richards."

"May I call you Ben?" The smile was seductive but impersonal. He felt exactly the token rise of desire he was supposed to feel for this well-stacked female with her well-fed body on display. It angered him. He wondered if she got her kicks this way, showing it off to the poor slobs on their way to the meat grinder.

"Sure," he said. "Nice tits."

"Thank you," she said, unruffled. He was seated now, looking up while she looked down, and it added an even more embarrassing angle to the picture. "This test today is to your mental faculties what your physical yesterday was to your body. It will be a fairly long test, and your luncheon will be around three this afternoon—assuming you pass." The smile winked on and off.

"The first section is verbal. You have one hour from the time I give you the test booklet. You may ask questions during the examination, and I will answer them if I am allowed to do so. I will not give you any answers to test questions, however. Do you understand?"

"Yes."

She handed him the booklet. There was a large red hand printed on the cover, palm outward. In large red letters beneath, it said:

STOP!

Beneath this: *Do not turn to the first page until your tester instructs you to proceed.*

"Heavy," Richards remarked.

"Pardon me?" The perfectly sculpted eyebrows went up a notch.

"Nothing."

"You will find an answer sheet when you open your booklet," she recited. "Please make your marks heavy and black. If you wish to change an answer, please erase completely. If you do not know an answer, do *not* guess. Do you understand?"

"Yes."

"Then please turn to page one and begin. When I say stop, please put your pencil down. You may begin."

He didn't begin. He eyed her body slowly, insolently.

After a moment, she flushed. "Your hour has begun, Ben. You had better—"

"Why," he asked, "does everybody assume that when they are dealing with someone from south of the Canal they are dealing with a horny mental incompetent?"

She was completely flustered now. "I . . . I never . . . "

"No, you never." He smiled and picked up his pencil. "My Christ, you people are dumb."

He bent to the test while she was still trying to find an answer or even a reason for his attack; she probably really didn't understand.

The first section required him to mark the letter of the correct fill-in-the-blank answer.

1. One————does not make a summer.
        a. thought
        b. beer
        c. swallow
        d. crime
        e. none of these

He filled in his answer sheet rapidly, rarely stopping to deliberate or consider an answer twice. Fill-ins were followed by vocabulary, then by word-contrasts. When he finished, the hour allotted still had fifteen minutes to run. She made him keep his exam—legally he couldn't give it to her until the hour was up—so Richards leaned back and wordlessly ogled her nearly naked body. The silence grew thick and oppressive, charged. He could see her wishing for an overcoat and it pleased him.

When the time was up, she gave him a second exam. On the first page, there was a drawing of a gasoline carburetor. Below:

You would put this in a

        a. lawnmower
        b. Free-Vee
        c. electric hammock
        d. automobile
        e. none of these

The third exam was a math diagnostic. He was not so good with figures and he began to sweat lightly as he saw the clock getting away from him. In the end, it was nearly a dead heat. He didn't get a chance to finish the last question. Rinda Ward smiled a trifle too widely as she pulled the test and answer sheet away from him. "Not so fast on that one, Ben."

"But they'll all be right," he said, and smiled back at her. He leaned forward and swatted her lightly on the rump. "Take a shower, kid. You done good."

She blushed furiously. "I could have you disqualified."

"Bullshit. You could get yourself fired, that's all."

"Get out. Get back in line." She was snarling, suddenly near tears.

He felt something almost like compassion and choked it back. "You have a nice night tonight," he said. "You go out and have a nice six-course meal with whoever you're sleeping with this week and think about my kid dying of flu in a shitty three-room Development apartment."

He left her staring after him, white-faced.

His group of ten had been cut to six, and they trooped into the next room. It was one-thirty.

... Minus 091
and COUNTING ...

The doctor sitting on the other side of the table in the small booth wore glasses with tiny thick lenses. He had a kind of nasty, pleased grin that reminded Richards of a half-wit he had known as a boy. The kid had enjoyed crouching under the high school bleachers and looking up girls' skirts while he flogged his dog. Richards began to grin.

"Something pleasant?" the doctor asked, flipping up the first inkblot. The nasty grin widened the tiniest bit.

"Yes. You remind me of someone I used to know."

"Oh? Who?"

"Never mind."

"Very well. What do you see here?"

Richards looked at it. An inflated blood pressure cuff had been cinched to his right arm. A number of electrodes had been pasted to his head, and wires from both his head and arm were jacked into a console beside the doctor. Squiggly lines moved across the face of a computer console.

"Two Negro women. Kissing."

He flipped up another one. "This?"

"A sports car. Looks like a Jag."

"Do you like gascars?"

Richards shrugged. "I had a model collection when I was a kid."

The doctor made a note and flipped up another card.

"Sick person. She's lying on her side. The shadows on her face look like prison bars."

"And this last one?"

Richards burst out laughing. "Looks like a pile of shit." He thought of the doctor, complete with his white coat, running around under the bleachers, looking up girls' skirts and jacking off, and he began to laugh again. The doctor sat smiling his nasty smile, making the vision more real, thus funnier. At last his giggles tapered off to a snort or two. Richards hiccupped once and was still.

"I don't suppose you'd care to tell me—"

"No," Richards said. "I wouldn't."

"We'll proceed then. Word association." He didn't bother to explain it. Richards supposed word was getting around. That was good; it would save time.

"Ready?"

"Yes."

The doctor produced a stopwatch from an inside pocket, clicked the business end of his ballpoint pen, and considered a list in front of him.

"Doctor."

"Nigger," Richards responded.

"Penis."

"Cock."

"Red."

"Black."

"Silver."

"Dagger."

"Rifle."

"Murder."

"Win."

"Money."

"Sex."

"Tests."

"Strike."

"Out."

The list continued; they went through over fifty words before the doctor clicked the stem of the stopwatch down and dropped his pen. "Good," he said. He folded his hands and looked at Richards seriously. "I have a final question, Ben. I won't say that I'll know a lie when I hear it, but the machine you're hooked up to will give a very strong indication one way or the other. Have you decided to try for qualification status in the Games out of any suicidal motivation?"

"No."

"What is your reason?"

"My little girl's sick. She needs a doctor. Medicine. Hospital care."

The ballpoint scratched. "Anything else?"

Richards was on the verge of saying no (it was none of their business) and then decided he would give it all. Perhaps because the doctor looked like that nearly forgotten dirty boy of his youth. Maybe only because it needed to be said once, to make it coalesce and take concrete shape, as things do when a man forces himself to translate unformed emotional reactions into spoken words.

"I haven't had work for a long time. I want to work again, even if it's only being the sucker-man in a loaded game. I want to work and support my family. I have pride. Do you have pride, Doctor?"

"It goes before a fall," the doctor said. He clicked the tip of his ballpoint in. "If you have nothing to add, Mr. Richards—" He stood up. That, and the switch back to his surname, suggested that the interview was over whether Richards had any more to say or not.

"No."

"The door is down the hall to your right. Good luck."

"Sure," Richards said.

. . . Minus 090
and COUNTING . . .

The group Richards had come in with was now reduced to four. The new waiting room was much smaller, and the whole group had been reduced roughly by the same figure of sixty percent. The last of the *Y*'s and *Z*'s straggled in at four-thirty. At four, an orderly had circulated with a tray of tasteless sandwiches. Richards got two of them and sat munching, listening to a pal named Rettenmund as he regaled Richards and a few others with a seemingly inexhaustible fund of dirty stories.

When the whole group was together, they were shunted into an elevator and lifted to the fifth floor. Their quarters were made up of a large common room, a communal lavatory, and the inevitable sleep-factory with its rows of cots. They were informed that a cafeteria down the hall would serve a hot meal at seven o'clock.

Richards sat still for a few minutes, then got up and walked over to the cop stationed by the door they had come in through. "Is there a telephone, pal?" He didn't expect they would be allowed to phone out, but the cop merely jerked his thumb toward the hall.

Richards pushed the door open a crack and peered out. Sure enough, there it was. Pay phone.

He looked at the cop again. "Listen, if you loan me fifty cents for the phone, I'll—"

"Screw off, Jack."

Richards held his temper. "I want to call my wife. Our kid is sick. Put yourself in my place, for Christ's sake."

The cop laughed: a short, chopping, ugly sound. "You types are all the same. A story for every day of the year. Technicolor and 3-D on Christmas and Mother's Day."

"You bastard," Richards said, and something in his eyes, the stance of his shoulders suddenly made the cop shift his gaze to the wall. "Aren't you married yourself? Didn't you ever find yourself strapped and have to borrow, even if it tasted like shit in your mouth?"

The cop suddenly jammed a hand into his jumper pocket and came up with a fistful of plastic coins. He thrust two New Quarters at Richards, stuffed the rest of the money back in his pocket, and grabbed a handful of Richards's tunic. "If you send anybody else over here because Charlie Grady is a soft touch, I'll beat your sonofabitching brains out, maggot.''

"Thank you," Richards said steadily. "For the loan."

Charlie Grady laughed and let him go. Richards went out into the hall, picked up the phone, and dropped his money into the horn. It banged hollowly and for a moment nothing happened—*oh, Jesus, all for nothing*—but then the dial tone came. He punched the number of the fifth floor hall phone slowly, hoping the Jenner bitch down the hall wouldn't answer. She'd just as soon yell wrong number when she recognized his voice and he would lose his money.

It rang six times, and then an unfamiliar voice said: "Hello?"

"I want to talk to Sheila Richards in 5C."

"I think she went out," the voice said. It grew insinuating. "She walks up and down the block, you know. They got a sick kid. The man there is shiftless."

"Just knock on the door," he said, cotton mouthed.

"Hold on."

The phone on the other end crashed against the wall as the unfamiliar voice let it dangle. Far away, dim, as if in a dream, he heard the unfamiliar voice knocking and yelling: "Phone! Phone for ya, Missus Richards!"

Half a minute later the unfamiliar voice was back on the line. "She ain't there. I can hear the kid yellin, but she ain't there. Like I say, she keeps an eye out when the fleet's in." The voice giggled.

Richards wished he could teleport himself through the phone line and pop out on the other end, like an evil genie from a black bottle, and choke the unfamiliar voice until his eyeballs popped out and rolled on the floor.

"Take a message," he said. "Write it on the wall if you have to."

"Ain't got no pencil. I'm hangin up. G'bye."

"Wait!" Richards yelled, panic in his voice.

"I'm . . . just a second." Grudgingly the voice said, "She comin up the stairs now."

Richards collapsed sweatily against the wall. A moment later Sheila's voice was in his ear, quizzical, wary, a little frightened: "Hello?"

"Sheila." He closed his eyes, letting the wall support him.

"Ben. Ben, is that you? Are you all right?"

"Yeah. Fine. Cathy. Is she—"

"The same. The fever isn't so bad but she sounds so *croupy*. Ben, I think there's water in her lungs. What if she has pneumonia?"

"It'll be all right. It'll be all right."

"I—" She paused, a long pause. "I hate to leave her, but I had to. Ben, I turned two tricks this morning. I'm sorry. But I got her some medicine at the drug. Some good medicine." Her voice had taken on a zealous, evangelical lilt.

"That stuff is shit," he said. "Listen: No more, Sheila. Please. I think I'm in here. Really. They can't cut many more guys because there's too many shows. There's got to be enough cannon fodder to go around. And they give advances, I think. Mrs. Upshaw—"

"She looked awful in black," Sheila broke in tonelessly.

"Never mind that. You stay with Cathy, Sheila. No more tricks."

"All right. I won't go out again." But he didn't believe her voice. *Fingers crossed, Sheila?* "I love you, Ben."

"And I lo—"

"Three minutes are up," the operator broke in. "If you wish to continue, please deposit one New Quarter or three old quarters."

"Wait a second!" Richards yelled. "Get off the goddam line, bitch. You—"

The empty hum of a broken connection.

He threw the receiver. It flew the length of its silver cord, then rebounded, striking the wall and then penduluming slowly back and forth like some strange snake that had bitten once and then died.

Somebody has to pay, Richards thought numbly as he walked back. Somebody *has* to.

. . . Minus 089
and COUNTING . . .

They were quartered on the fifth floor until ten o'clock the following day, and Richards was nearly out of his mind with anger, worry, and frustration when a young and slightly faggoty-looking pal in a skintight Games uniform asked them to please step into the elevator. They were perhaps three hundred in all: over sixty of their number had been removed soundlessly and painlessly the night before. One of them had been the kid with the inexhaustible fund of dirty jokes.

They were taken to a small auditorium on the sixth floor in groups of fifty. The auditorium was very luxurious, done in great quantities of red plush. There was an ashtray built into the realwood arm of every seat, and Richards hauled out his crumpled pack of Blams. He tapped his ashes on the floor.

There was a small stage at the front, and in the center of that, a lectern. A pitcher of water stood on it.

At about fifteen minutes past ten, the faggoty-looking fellow walked to the lectern and said: "I'd like you to meet Arthur M. Burns, Assistant Director of Games."

"Huzzah," somebody behind Richards said in a sour voice.

A portly man with a tonsure surrounded by gray hair strode to the lectern, pausing and cocking his head as he arrived, as if to appreciate a round of applause which only he could hear. Then he smiled at them, a broad, twinkling smile that seemed to transform him into a pudgy, aging Cupid in a business suit.

"Congratulations," he said. "You've made it."

There was a huge collective sigh, followed by some laughter and back-slapping. More cigarettes were lit up.

"Huzzah," the sour voice repeated.

"Shortly, your program assignments and seventh floor room numbers will be passed out. The executive producers of your particular programs will explain further exactly what is expected of you. But before that happens, I just want to repeat my congratulations and tell you that I find you to be a courageous, resourceful group, refusing to live on the public dole when you have means at your disposal to acquit yourselves as men, and, may I add personally, as true heroes of our time."

"Bullshit," the sour voice remarked.

"Furthermore, I speak for the entire Network when I wish you good luck and Godspeed." Arthur M. Burns chuckled porkily and rubbed his hands together. "Well, I know you're anxious to get those assignments, so I'll spare you any more of my jabber."

A side door popped open, and a dozen Games ushers wearing red tunics came into the auditorium. They began to call out names. White envelopes were passed out, and soon they littered the floor like confetti. Plastic assignment cards were read, exchanged with new acquaintances. There were muffled groans, cheers, cat-calls. Arthur M. Burns presided over it all from his podium, smiling benevolently.

—That Christly *How Hot Can You Take It*, Jesus I hate the heat

—the show's a goddam two-bitter, comes on right after the flictoons, for God's sake

—*Treadmill to Bucks*, gosh, I didn't know my heart was—

—I was hoping I'd get it but I didn't really think—

—Hey Jake, you ever seen this *Swim the Crocodiles*? I thought—

—nothing like I expected—

—I don't think you can—

—Miserable goddam—

—This *Run For Your Guns*—

"Benjamin Richards! Ben Richards?"

"Here!"

He was handed a plain white envelope and tore it open. His fingers were shaking slightly and it took him two tries to get the small plastic card out. He frowned down at it, not understanding. No program assignment was punched on it. The card read simply: ELEVATOR SIX.

He put the card in his breast pocket with his I.D. and left the auditorium. The first five elevators at the end of the hall were doing a brisk business as they ferried the following week's contestants up to the seventh floor. There were four others standing by the closed doors of Elevator 6, and Richards recognized one of them as the owner of the sour voice.

"What's this?" Richards asked. "Are we getting the gate?"

The man with the sour voice was about twenty-five, not bad looking. One arm was withered, probably by polio, which had come back strong in 2005. It had done especially well in Co-Op.

"No such luck," he said, and laughed emptily. "I think we're getting the big-money assignments. The ones where they do more than just land you in the hospital with a stroke or put out an eye or cut off an arm or two. The ones where they kill you. Prime time, baby."

They were joined by a sixth pal, a good-looking kid who was blinking at everything in a surprised way.

"Hello, sucker," the man with the sour voice said.

At eleven o'clock, after all the others had been taken away, the doors of Elevator 6 popped open. There was a cop riding in the Judas hole again.

"See?" The man with the sour voice said. "We're dangerous characters. Public enemies. They're gonna rub us out." He made a tough gangster face and sprayed the bulletproof compartment with an imaginary Sten gun. The cop stared at him woodenly.

. . . Minus 088
and COUNTING . . .

The waiting room on the eighth floor was very small, very plush, very intimate, very private. Richards had it all to himself.

At the end of the elevator ride, three of them had been promptly whisked away down a plushly carpeted corridor by three cops. Richards, the man with the sour voice, and the kid who blinked a lot had been taken here.

A receptionist who vaguely reminded Richards of one of the old tee-vee sex stars (Liz Kelly? Grace Taylor?) he had watched as a kid smiled at the three of them when they came in. She was sitting at a desk in an alcove, surrounded by so many potted plants that she might have been in an Ecuadorian foxhole. "Mr. Jansky," she said with a blinding smile. "Go right in."

The kid who blinked a lot went into the inner sanctum. Richards and the man with the sour voice, whose name was Jimmy Laughlin, made wary conversation. Richards discovered that Laughlin lived only three blocks away from him, on Dock Street. He had held a part-time job until the year before as an engine wiper for General Atomics, and had then been fired for taking part in a sit-down strike protesting leaky radiation shields.

"Well, I'm alive, anyway," he said. "According to those maggots, that's all that counts. I'm sterile, of course. *That* don't matter. That's one of the little risks you run for the princely sum of seven New Bucks a day."

When G-A had shown him the door, the withered arm had made it even tougher to get a job. His wife had come down with bad asthma two years before, was now bed-ridden. "Finally I decided to go for the big brass ring," Laughlin said with a bitter smile. "Maybe I'll get a chance to push a few creeps out a high window before McCone's boys get me."

"Do you think it really is—"

"*The Running Man?* Bet your sweet ass. Give me one of those cruddy cigarettes, pal."

Richards gave him one.

The door opened and the kid who blinked a lot came out on the arm of a beautiful dolly wearing two handkerchiefs and a prayer. The kid gave them a small, nervous smile as they went by.

"Mr. Laughlin? Would you go in, please?"

So Richards was alone, unless you counted the receptionist, who had disappeared into her foxhole again.

He got up and went over to the free cigarette machine in the corner. Laughlin must be right, he reflected. The cigarette machine dispensed Dokes. They must have hit the big leagues. He got a package of Blams, sat down, and lit one up.

About twenty minutes later Laughlin came out with an ash-blonde on his arm. "A friend of mine from the car pool," he said to Richards, and pointed at the blonde. She dimpled dutifully. Laughlin looked pained. "At least the bastard talks straight," he said to Richards. "See you."

He went out. The receptionist poked her head out of her foxhole. "Mr. Richards? Would you step in, please?"

He went in.

... Minus 087
and COUNTING ...

The inner office looked big enough to play killball in.It was dominated by a huge, one-wall picture window that looked west over the homes of the middle class, the dockside warehouses and oil tanks, and Harding Lake itself. Both sky and water were pearl-gray; it was still raining. A large tanker far out was chugging from right to left.

The man behind the desk was of middle height and very black. So black, in fact, that for a moment Richards was struck with unreality. He might have stepped out of a minstrel show.

"Mr. Richards." He rose and extended his hand over the desk. When Richards did not shake it, he did not seem particularly flustered. He merely took his hand back to himself and sat down.

A sling chair was next to the desk. Richards sat down and butted his smoke in an ashtray with the Games emblem embossed on it.

"I'm Dan Killian, Mr. Richards. By now you've probably guessed why you've been brought here. Our records and your test scores both say you're a bright boy."

Richards folded his hands and waited.

"You've been slated as a contestant on *The Running Man*, Mr. Richards. It's our biggest show; it's the most lucrative—and dangerous—for the men involved. I've got your final consent form here on my desk. I've no doubt that you'll sign it, but first I want to tell you why you've been selected and I want you to understand fully what you're getting into."

Richards said nothing.

Killian pulled a dossier onto the virgin surface of his desk blotter. Richards saw that it had his name typed on the front. Killian flipped it open.

"Benjamin Stuart Richards. Age twenty-eight, born August 8, 1997, city of Harding. Attended South City Manual Trades from September of 2011 until December of 2013. Suspended twice for failure to respect authority. I believe you kicked the assistant principal in the upper thigh once while his back was turned?"

"Crap," Richards said. "I kicked him in the ass."

Killian nodded. "However you say, Mr. Richards. You married Sheila Richards, née Gordon, at the age of sixteen. Old-style lifetime contract. Rebel all the way, uh? No union affiliation due to your refusal to sign the Union Oath of Fealty and the Wage Control Articles. I believe that you referred to Area Governor Johnsbury as 'a corn-holing sonofabitch.' "

"Yes," Richards said.

"Your work record has been spotty and you've been fired . . . let's see . . . a total of six times for such things as insubordination, insulting superiors, and abusive criticism of authority."

Richards shrugged.

"In short, you are regarded as antiauthoritarian and antisocial. You're a deviate who has been intelligent enough to stay out of prison and serious trouble with the government, and you're not hooked on anything. A staff psychologist reports you saw lesbians, excrement, and a pollutive gas vehicle in various inkblots. He also reports a high, unexplained degree of hilarity—"

"He reminded me of a kid I used to know. He liked to hide under the bleachers at school and whack off. The kid, I mean. I don't know what your doctor likes to do."

"I see." Killian smiled briefly, white teeth glittering in all that darkness, and went back to his folder. "You held racial responses outlawed by the Racial Act of 2004. You made several rather violent responses during the word-association test."

"I'm here on violent business," Richards said.

"To be sure. And yet we—and here I speak in a larger sense than the Games

Authority; I speak in the national sense—view these responses with extreme disquiet.''

''Afraid someone might tape a stick of Irish to your ignition system some night?'' Richards asked, grinning.

Killian wet his thumb reflectively and turned to the next sheet. ''Fortunately— for us—you've given a hostage to fortune, Mr. Richards. You have a daughter named Catherine, eighteen months. Was that a mistake?'' He smiled frostily.

''Planned,'' Richards said without rancor. ''I was working for G-A then. Somehow, some of my sperm lived through it. A jest of God, maybe. With the world the way it is, I sometimes think we must have been off our trolley.''

''At any rate, you're here,'' Killian said, continuing to smile his cold smile. ''And next Tuesday you will appear on *The Running Man*. You've seen the program?''

''Yes.''

''Then you know it's the biggest thing going on Free-Vee. It's filled with chances for viewer participation, both vicarious and actual. I am executive producer of the program.''

''That's really wonderful,'' Richards said.

''The program is one of the surest ways the Network has of getting rid of embryo troublemakers such as yourself, Mr. Richards. We've been on for six years. To date, we have no survivals. To be brutally honest, we expect to have none.''

''Then you're running a crooked table,'' Richards said flatly.

Killian seemed more amused than horrified. ''But we're not. You keep forgetting you're an anachronism, Mr. Richards. People won't be in the bars and hotels or gathering in the cold in front of appliance stores rooting for you to get away. Goodness! no. They want to see you wiped out, and they'll help if they can. The more messy the better. And there is McCone to contend with. Evan McCone and the Hunters.''

''They sound like a neo-group,'' Richards said.

''McCone never loses,'' Killian said.

Richards grunted.

''You'll appear live Tuesday night. Subsequent programs will be a patch-up of tapes, films, and live tricasts when possible. We've been known to interrupt scheduled broadcasting when a particularly resourceful contestant is on the verge of reaching his . . . personal Waterloo, shall we say.

''The rules are simplicity themselves. You—or your surviving family—will win one hundred New Dollars for each hour you remain free. We stake you to forty-eight hundred dollars running money on the assumption that you will be able to fox the Hunters for forty-eight hours. The unspent balance refundable, of course, if you fall before the forty-eight hours are up. You're given a twelve-hour head start. If you last thirty days, you win the Grand Prize. One billion New Dollars.''

Richards threw back his head and laughed.

''My sentiments exactly,'' Killian said with a dry smile. ''Do you have any questions?''

"Just one," Richards said, leaning forward. The traces of humor had vanished from his face completely. "How would you like to be the one out there, on the run?"

Killian laughed. He held his belly and huge mahogany laughter rolled richly in the room. "Oh . . . Mr. Richards . . . you must excuse m-me—" and he went off into another gale.

At last, dabbing his eyes with a large white handkerchief, Killian seemed to get himself under control. "You see, not only are you possessed of a sense of humor, Mr. Richards. You . . . I—" He choked new laughter down. "Please excuse me. You've struck my funnybone."

"I see I have."

"Other questions?"

"No."

"Very good. There will be a staff meeting before the program. If any questions should develop in that fascinating mind of yours, please hold them until then." Killian pressed a button on his desk.

"Spare me the cheap snatch," Richards said. "I'm married."

Killian's eyebrows went up. "Are you quite sure? Fidelity is admirable, Mr. Richards, but it's a long time from Friday to Tuesday. And considering the fact that you may never see your wife again—"

"I'm married."

"Very well." He nodded to the girl in the doorway and she disappeared. "Anything we *can* do for you, Mr. Richards? You'll have a private suite on the ninth floor, and meal requests will be filled within reason."

"A good bottle of bourbon. And a telephone so I can talk to my w—"

"Ah, no, I'm sorry, Mr. Richards. The bourbon we can do. But once you sign this release form,"—he pushed it over to Richards along with a pen—"you're incommunicado until Tuesday. Would you care to reconsider the girl?"

"No," Richards said, and scrawled his name on the dotted line. "But you better make that two bottles of bourbon."

"Certainly." Killian stood and offered his hand again.

Richards disregarded it again, and walked out.

Killian looked after him and with blank eyes. He was not smiling.

. . . Minus 086
and COUNTING . . .

The receptionist popped promptly out of her foxhole as Richards walked through and handed him an envelope. On the front:

Mr. Richards,

I suspect one of the things that you will not mention during our interview is the fact that you need money badly right now. Is it not true?

Despite rumors to the contrary, Games Authority does *not* give advances. You must not look upon yourself as a contestant with all the glitter that word entails. You are not a Free-Vee star but only a working joe who is being paid extremely well for undertaking a dangerous job.

However, Games Authority has no rule which forbids me from extending you a personal loan. Inside you will find ten percent of your advance salary— not in New Dollars, I should caution you, but in Games Certificates redeemable for dollars. Should you decide to send these certificates to your wife, as I suspect you will, she will find they have one advantage over New Dollars; a reputable doctor will accept them as legal tender, while a quack will not.

Sincerely,
Dan Killian

Richards opened the envelope and pulled out a thick book of coupons with the Games symbol on the vellum cover. Inside were forty-eight coupons with a face value of ten New Dollars each. Richards felt an absurd wave of gratitude toward Killian sweep him and crushed it. He had no doubt that Killian would attach four hundred and eighty dollars of his advance money, and besides that, four-eighty was a pretty goddam cheap price to pay for insurance on the big show, the continued happiness of the client, and Killian's own big-money job.

"Shit," he said.

The receptionist poked attentively out of her foxhole. "Did you say something, Mr. Richards?"

"No. Which way to the elevators?

... Minus 085
and COUNTING ...

The suite was sumptuous.

Wall-to-wall carpeting almost deep enough to breast stroke in covered the floors of all three rooms: living room, bedroom, and bath. The Free-Vee was turned off; blessed silence prevailed. There were flowers in the vases, and on the wall next to the door was a button discreetly marked SERVICE. The service would be fast, too, Richards thought cynically. There were two cops stationed outside his ninth-floor suite just to make sure he didn't go wandering.

He pushed the service button, and the door opened. "Yes, Mr. Richards," one of the cops said. Richards fancied he could see how sour that *Mister* tasted in his mouth. "The bourbon you asked for will be—"

"It's not that," Richards said. He showed the cop the book of coupons Killian had left for him. "I want you to take this somewhere."

"Just write the name and address, Mr. Richards, and I'll see that it's delivered."

Richards found the cobbler's receipt and wrote his address and Sheila's name on the back of it. He gave the tattered paper and the coupon book to the cop. He was turning away when a new thought struck Richards. "Hey! Just a second!"

The cop turned back, and Richards plucked the coupon book out of his hand. He opened it to the first coupon, and tore one tenth of it along the perforated line. Equivalent value: One New Dollar.

"Do you know a cop named Charlie Grady?"

"Charlie?" The cop looked at him warily. "Yeah, I know Charlie. He's got fifth-floor duty."

"Give him this." Richards handed him the coupon section. "Tell him the extra fifty cents is his usurer's fee."

The cop turned away again, and Richards called him back once more.

"You'll bring me written receipts from my wife and from Grady, won't you?" Disgust showed openly on the cop's face. "Ain't you the trusting soul?"

"Sure," Richards said, smiling thinly. "You guys taught me that. South of the Canal you taught me all about it."

"It's gonna be fun," the cop said, "watching them go after you. I'm gonna be glued to my Free-Vee with a beer in each hand."

"Just bring me the receipts," Richards said, and closed the door gently in the cop's face.

The bourbon came twenty minutes later, and Richards told the surprised deliveryman that he would like a couple of thick novels sent up.

"Novels?"

"Books. You know. Read. Words. Movable press." Richards pantomimed flipping pages.

"Yes, sir," he said doubtfully. "Do you have a dinner order?"

Christ, the shit was getting thick. He was drowning in it. Richards saw a sudden fantasy-cartoon: Man falls into outhouse hole and drowns in pink shit that smells like Chanel No. 5. The kicker: It still tastes like shit.

"Steak. Peas. Mashed potatoes." God, what was Sheila sitting down to? A protein pill and a cup of fake coffee? "Milk. Apple cobbler with cream. Got it?"

"Yes, sir. Would you like—"

"No." Richards said, suddenly distraught. "No. Get out." He had no appetite. Absolutely none.

. . . Minus 084
and COUNTING . . .

With sour amusement Richards thought that the Games bellboy had taken him literally about the novels: He must have picked them out with a ruler as his only guide. Anything over an inch and a half is okay. He had brought Richards three books he had never heard of: two golden oldies titled *God Is an Englishman* and *Not as a Stranger* and a huge tome written three years ago called *The Pleasure of Serving*. Richards peeked into that one first and wrinkled his nose. Poor boy makes good in General Atomics. Rises from engine wiper to gear tradesman. Takes night courses (on what? Richards wondered, Monopoly money?). Falls in love with beautiful girl (apparently syphilis hadn't rotted her nose off yet) at a block orgy. Promoted to junior technico following dazzling aptitude scores. Three-year marriage contract follows, and—

Richards threw the book across the room. *God Is an Englishman* was a little better. He poured himself a bourbon on the rocks and settled into the story.

By the time the discreet knock came, he was three hundred pages in, and pretty well in the bag to boot. One of the bourbon bottles was empty. He went to the door holding the other in his hand. The cop was there. "Your receipts, Mr. Richards," he said, and pulled the door closed.

Sheila had not written anything, but had sent one of Cathy's baby pictures. He looked at it and felt the easy tears of drunkenness prick his eyes. He put it in his pocket and looked at the other receipt. Charlie Grady had written briefly on the back of a traffic ticket form:

Thanks, maggot. Get stuffed.
Charlie Grady

Richards snickered and let the paper flitter to the carpet. "Thanks, Charlie," he said to the empty room. "I needed that."

He looked at the picture of Cathy again, a tiny, red-faced infant of four days at the time of the photo, screaming her head off, swimming in a white cradle dress that Sheila had made herself. He felt the tears lurking and made himself think of good old Charlie's thank-you note. He wondered if he could kill the entire second bottle before he passed out, and decided to find out.

He almost made it.

. . . Minus 083
and COUNTING . . .

Richards spent Saturday living through a huge hangover. He was almost over it by Saturday evening, and ordered two more bottles of bourbon with supper. He got through both of them and woke up in the pale early light of Sunday morning seeing large caterpillars with flat, murderous eyes crawling slowly down the far bedroom wall. He decided then it would be against his best interests to wreck his reactions completely before Tuesday, and laid off the booze.

This hangover was slower dissipating. He threw up a good deal, and when there was nothing left to throw up, he had dry heaves. These tapered off around six o'clock Sunday evening, and he ordered soup for dinner. No bourbon. He asked for a dozen neo-rock discers to play on the suite's sound system, and tired of them quickly.

He went to bed early. And slept poorly.

He spent most of Monday on the tiny glassed-in terrace that opened off the bedroom. He was very high above the waterfront now, and the day was a series of sun and showers that was fairly pleasant. He read two novels, went to bed early again, and slept a little better. There was an unpleasant dream: Sheila was dead, and he was at her funeral. Somebody had propped her up in her coffin and stuffed a grotesque corsage of New Dollars in her mouth. He tried to run to her and remove the obscenity; hands grabbed him from behind. He was being held by a dozen cops. One of them was Charlie Grady. He was grinning and saying: "This is what happens to losers, maggot." They were putting their pistols to his head when he woke up.

"Tuesday," he said to no one at all, and rolled out of bed. The fashionable G-A sunburst clock on the far wall said it was nine minutes after seven. The live tricast of *The Running Man* would be going out all over North America in less than eleven hours. He felt a hot drop of fear in his stomach. In twenty-three hours he would be fair game.

He had a long hot shower, dressed in his coverall, ordered ham and eggs for breakfast. He also got the bellboy on duty to send up a carton of Blams.

He spent the rest of the morning and early afternoon reading quietly. It was two o'clock on the nose when a single formal rap came at the door. Three police and Arthur M. Burns, looking potty and more than a bit ridiculous in a Games singlet, walked in. All of the cops were carrying move-alongs.

"It's time for your final briefing, Mr. Richards," Burns said. "Would you—"

"Sure," Richards said. He marked his place in the book he had been reading and put it down on the coffee table. He was suddenly terrified, close to panic, and he was very glad there was no perceptible shake in his fingers.

. . . Minus 082
and COUNTING . . .

The tenth floor of the Games Building was a great deal different from the ones below, and Richards knew that he was meant to go no higher. The fiction of up-ward mobility which started in the grimy street-level lobby ended here on the tenth floor. This was the broadcast facility.

The hallways were wide, white, and stark. Bright yellow go-carts powered by G-A solar-cell motors pottered here and there, carrying loads of Free-Vee tech-nicos to studios and control rooms.

A cart was waiting for them when the elevator stopped, and the five of them--Richards, Burns, and cops—climbed aboard. Necks craned and Richards was pointed out several times as they made the trip. One woman in a yellow Games shorts-and-halter outfit winked and blew Richards a kiss. He gave her the finger.

They seemed to travel miles, through dozens of interconnecting corridors. Richards caught glimpses into at least a dozen studios, one of them containing the infamous treadmill seen on *Treadmill to Bucks*. A tour group from uptown was trying it out and giggling.

At last they came to a stop before a door which read *THE RUNNING MAN: ABSOLUTELY NO ADMITTANCE*. Burns waved to the guard in the bulletproof booth beside the door and then looked at Richards.

"Put your I.D. in the slot between the guard booth and the door," Burns said.

Richards did it. His card disappeared into the slot, and a small light went on in the guard booth. The guard pushed a button and the door slid open. Richards got back into the cart and they were trundled into the room beyond.

"Where's my card?" Richards asked.

"You don't need it anymore."

They were in a control room. The console section was empty except for a bald technico who was sitting in front of a blank monitor screen, reading numbers into a microphone.

Across to the left, Dan Killian and two men Richards hadn't met were sitting around a table with frosty glasses. One of them was vaguely familiar, too pretty to be a technico.

"Hello, Mr. Richards. Hello, Arthur. Would you care for a soft drink, Mr. Richards?"

Richards found he was thirsty; it was quite warm on ten in spite of the many air-conditioning units he had seen. "I'll have a Rooty-Toot," he said.

Killian rose, went to a cold-cabinet, and snapped the lid from a plastic squeeze-bottle. Richards sat down and took the bottle with a nod.

"Mr. Richards, this gentleman on my right is Fred Victor, the director of *The Running Man*. This other fellow, as I'm sure you know, is Bobby Thompson."

Thompson, of course. Host and emcee of *The Running Man*. He wore a natty green tunic, slightly iridescent, and sported a mane of hair that was silvery-attractive enough to be suspect.

"Do you dye it?" Richards asked.

Thompson's impeccable eyebrows went up. "I beg pardon?"

"Never mind," Richards said.

"You'll have to make allowances for Mr. Richards," Killian said, smiling. "He seems afflicted with an extreme case of the rudes."

"Quite understandable," Thompson said, and lit a cigarette. Richards felt a wave of unreality surge over him. "Under the circumstances."

"Come over here, Mr. Richards, if you please," Victor said, taking charge. He led Richards to the bank of screens on the other side of the room. The technico had finished with his numbers and had left the room.

Victor punched two buttons and left-right views of *The Running Man* set sprang into view.

"We don't do a run-through here," Victor said. "We think it detracts from spontaneity. Bobby just wings it, and he does a pretty damn good job. We go on at six o'clock, Harding time. Bobby is center stage on that raised blue dais. He does the lead-in, giving a rundown on you. The monitor will flash a couple of still pictures. You'll be in the wings at stage right, flanked by two Games guards. They'll come on with you, armed with riot guns. Move-alongs would be more practical if you decided to give trouble, but the riot guns are good theater."

"Sure," Richards said.

"There will be a lot of booing from the audience. We pack it that way because it's good theater. Just like the killball matches."

"Are they going to shoot me with fake bullets?" Richards asked. "You could put a few blood bags on me, to spatter on cue. That would be good theater, too."

"Pay attention, please," Victor said. "You and the guards go on when your name is called. Bobby will, uh, interview you. Feel free to express yourself as colorfully as you please. It's all good theater. Then, around six-ten, just before the first Network promo, you'll be given your stake money and exit—*sans* guards—at stage left. Do you understand?"

"Yes. What about Laughlin?"

Victor frowned and lit a cigarette. "He comes on after you, at six-fifteen. We run two contests simultaneously because often one of the contestants is, uh, inadept at staying ahead of the Hunters."

"With the kid as a back-up?"

"Mr. Jansky? Yes. But none of this concerns you, Mr. Richards. When you exit stage left, you'll be given a tape machine which is about the size of a box of popcorn. It weighs six pounds. With it, you'll be given sixty tape clips which are about four inches long. The equipment will fit inside a coat pocket without a bulge. It's a triumph of modern technology."

"Swell."

Victor pressed his lips together. "As Dan has already told you, Richards, you're a contestant only for the masses. Actually, you are a working man and you should view your role in that light. The tape cartridges can be dropped into any mailslot and they will be delivered express to us so we can edit them for airing that night. Failure to deposit two clips per day will result in legal default of payment."

"But I'll still be hunted down."

"Right. So mail those tapes. They won't give away your location; the Hunters operate independently of the broadcasting section."

Richards had his doubts about that but said nothing.

"After we give you the equipment, you will be escorted to the street elevator. This gives directly on Rampart Street. Once you're there, you're on your own." He paused. "Questions?"

"No."

"Then Mr. Killian has one more money detail to straighten out with you."

They walked back to where Dan Killian was in conversation with Arthur M. Burns. Richards asked for another Rooty-Toot and got it.

"Mr. Richards," Killian said, twinkling his teeth at him. "As you know, you leave the studio unarmed. But this is not to say you cannot arm yourself by fair means or foul. Goodness! no. You—or your estate—will be paid an additional one hundred dollars for any Hunter or representative of the law you should happen to dispatch—"

"I know, don't tell me," Richards said. "It's good theater."

Killian smiled delightedly. "How very astute of you. Yes. However, try not to bag any innocent bystanders. That's not kosher."

Richards said nothing.

"The other aspect of the program—"

"The stoolies and independent cameramen. I know."

"They're not stoolies; they're good North American citizens." It was difficult to tell whether Killian's tone of hurt was real or ironic. "Anyway, there's an 800 number for anyone who spots you. A verified sighting pays one hundred New Dollars. A sighting which results in a kill pays a thousand. We pay independent cameramen ten dollars a foot and up—"

"Retire to scenic Jamaica on blood money," Richards cried, spreading his arms wide. "Get your picture on a hundred 3-D weeklies. Be the idol of millions. Just holograph for details."

"That's enough," Killian said quietly. Bobby Thompson was buffing his fingernails; Victor had wandered out and could be faintly heard yelling at someone about camera angles.

Killian pressed a button. "Miss Jones? Ready for you, sweets." He stood up and offered his hand again. "Make-up next, Mr. Richards. Then the lighting runs. You'll be quartered offstage and we won't meet again before you go on. So—"

"It's been grand," Richards said. He declined the hand.

Miss Jones led him out. It was 2:30.

. . . Minus 081
and COUNTING . . .

Richards stood in the wings with a cop on each side, listening to the studio audience as they frantically applauded Bobby Thompson. He was nervous. He jeered at himself for it, but the nervousness was a fact. Jeering would not make it go away. It was 6:01.

"Tonight's first contestant is a shrewd, resourceful man from south of the Canal in our own home city," Thompson was saying. The monitor faded to a stark portrait of Richards in his baggy gray workshirt, taken by a hidden camera days before. The background looked like the fifth floor waiting room. It had been retouched, Richards thought, to make his eyes deeper, his forehead a little lower, his cheeks more shadowed. His mouth had been given a jeering, curled expression by some technico's airbrush. All in all, the Richards on the monitor was terrifying—the angel of urban death, brutal, not very bright, but possessed of a certain primitive animal cunning. The uptown apartment dweller's boogeyman.

"This man is Benjamin Richards, age twenty-eight. Know the face well! In a half-hour, this man will be on the prowl. A verified sighting brings you one hundred New Dollars! A sighting which results in a kill results in one thousand New Dollars for *you*!"

Richards's mind was wandering; it came back to the point with a mighty snap.

" . . . and *this* is the woman that Benjamin Richards's award will go to, if and when he is brought down!"

The picture dissolved to a still of Sheila . . . but the airbrush had been at work again, this time wielded with a heavier hand. The results were brutal. The sweet, not-so-good-looking face had been transformed into that of a vapid slattern. Full, pouting lips, eyes that seemed to glitter with avarice, a suggestion of a double chin fading down to what appeared to be bare breasts.

"You *bastard*!" Richards grated. He lunged forward, but powerful arms held him back.

"Simmer down, buddy. It's only a picture."

A moment later he was half led, half dragged onstage.

The audience reaction was immediate. The studio was filled with screamed cries of "Boo! Cycle bum!" "Get out, you creep!" "Kill him! Kill the bastard!" "You eat it!" "Get out, get out!"

Bobby Thompson held his arms up and shouted good-naturedly for quiet. "Let's hear what he's got to say." The audience quieted, but reluctantly.

Richards stood bull-like under the hot lights with his head lowered. He knew he was projecting exactly the aura of hate and defiance that they wanted him to project, but he could not help it.

He stared at Thompson with hard, red-rimmed eyes. "Somebody is going to eat their own balls for that picture of my wife," he said.

"Speak up, speak up, Mr. Richards!" Thompson cried with just the right note of contempt. "Nobody will hurt you . . . at least, not *yet*."

More screams and hysterical vituperation from the audience.

Richards suddenly wheeled to face them, and they quieted as if slapped. Women stared at him with frightened, half-sexual expressions. Men grinned up at him with blood-hate in their eyes.

"You bastards!" He cried. "If you want to see somebody die so bad, why don't you kill each other?"

His final words were drowned in more screams. People from the audience (perhaps paid to do so) were trying to get onstage. The police were holding them back. Richards faced them, knowing how he must look.

"Thank you, Mr. Richards, for those words of wisdom." The contempt was palpable now, and the crowd, nearly silent again, was eating it up. "Would you like to tell our audience in the studio and at home how long you think you can hold out?"

"I want to tell everybody in the studio and at home that that wasn't my wife! That was a cheap fake—"

The crowd drowned him out. Their screams of hate had reached a near fever pitch. Thompson waited nearly a minute for them to quiet a little, and then repeated: "How long do you expect to hold out, *Mister* Richards?"

"I expect to go the whole thirty," Richards said coolly. "I don't think you've got anybody who can take me."

More screaming. Shaken fists. Someone threw a tomato.

Bobby Thompson faced the audience again and cried: "With those last cheap words of bravado, Mr. Richards will be led from our stage. Tomorrow at noon, the hunt begins. *Remember his face!* It may be next to you on a pneumo bus . . . in a jet plane . . . at a 3-D rack . . . in your local killball arena. Tonight he's in Harding. Tomorrow in New York? Boise? Albuquerque? Columbus? Skulking outside *your* home? *Will you report him?*"

"*YESS!!!*" They screamed.

Richards suddenly gave them the finger—both fingers. This time the rush for the stage was by no stretch of the imagination simulated. Richards was rushed out

the stage-left exit before they could rip him apart on camera, thus depriving the
Network of all the juicy upcoming coverage.

. . . Minus 080
and COUNTING . . .

Killian was in the wings, and convulsed with amusement. "Fine performance,
Mr. Richards. Fine! God, I wish I could give you a bonus. Those fingers . . .
superb!"

"We aim to please," Richards said. The monitors were dissolving to a promo.
"Give me the goddam camera and go fuck yourself."

"That's generically impossible," Killian said, still grinning, "but here's the
camera." He took it from the technico who had been cradling it. "Fully loaded
and ready to go. And here are the clips." He handed Richards a small, surprisingly
heavy oblong box wrapped in oilcloth.

Richards dropped the camera into one coat pocket, the clips into the other.
"Okay. Where's the elevator?"

"Not so fast," Killian said. "You've got a minute . . . twelve of them,
actually. Your twelve hours' leeway doesn't start officially until six-thirty."

The screams of rage had begun again. Looking over his shoulder, Richards saw
that Laughlin was on. His heart went out to him.

"I like you, Richards, and I think you'll do well," Killian said. "You have a
certain crude style that I enjoy immensely. I'm a collector, you know. Cave art
and Egyptian artifacts are my areas of specialization. You are more analogous to
the cave art than to my Egyptian urns, but no matter. I wish you could be preserved—collected, if you please—just as my Asian cave paintings have been collected and preserved."

"Grab a recording of my brain waves, you bastard. They're on record."

"So I'd like to give you a piece of advice," Killian said, ignoring him. "You
don't really have a chance; nobody does with a whole nation in on the manhunt
and with the incredibly sophisticated equipment and training that the Hunters have.
But if you stay low, you'll last longer. Use your legs instead of any weapons you
happen to pick up. And stay close to your own people." He leveled a finger at
Richards in emphasis. "Not these good middle-class folks out there; they hate your
guts. You symbolize all the fears of this dark and broken time. It wasn't all show
and audience-packing out there, Richards. *They hate your guts.* Could you feel
it?"

"Yes," Richards said. "I felt it. I hate them, too."

Killian smiled. "That's why they're killing you." He took Richards's arm; his grip was surprisingly strong. "This way."

Behind them, Laughlin was being ragged by Bobby Thompson to the audience's satisfaction.

Down a white corridor, their footfalls echoing hollowly—alone. All alone. One elevator at the end.

"This is where you and I part company," Killian said. "Express to the street. Nine seconds."

He offered his hand for the fourth time, and Richards refused it again. Yet he lingered a moment.

"What if I could go up?" he asked, and gestured with his head toward the ceiling and the eighty stories above the ceiling. "Who could I kill up there? Who could I kill if I went right to the top?"

Killian laughed softly and punched the button beside the elevator; the doors popped open. "That's what I like about you, Richards. You think big."

Richards stepped into the elevator. The doors slid toward each other.

"Stay low," Killian repeated, and then Richards was alone.

The bottom dropped out of his stomach as the elevator sank toward the street.

. . . Minus 079
and COUNTING . . .

The elevator opened directly onto the street. A cop was standing by its frontage on Nixon Memorial Park, but he did not look at Richards as he stepped out; only tapped his move-along reflectively and stared into the soft drizzle that filled the air.

The drizzle had brought early dusk to the city. The lights glowed mystically through the darkness, and the people moving on Rampart Street in the shadow of the Games Building were only insubstantial shadows, as Richards knew he must be himself. He breathed deeply of the wet, sulphur-tainted air. It was good in spite of the taste. It seemed that he had just been let out of prison, rather than from one communicating cell to another. The air was good. The air was fine.

Stay close to your own people, Killian had said. Of course he was right. Richards hadn't needed Killian to tell him that. Or to know that the heat would be heaviest in Co-Op City when the truce broke at noon tomorrow. But by then he would be over the hills and far away.

He walked three blocks and hailed a taxi. He was hoping the cab's Free-Vee would be busted—a lot of them were—but this one was in A-1 working order, and blaring the closing credits of *The Running Man*. Shit.

"Where, buddy?"

"Robard Street." That was five blocks from his destination; when the cab dropped him, he would go backyard express to Molie's place.

The cab accelerated, ancient gas-powered engine a discordant symphony of pounding pistons and manifold noise. Richards slumped back against the vinyl cushions, into what he hoped was deeper shadow.

"Hey, I just seen you on the Free-Vee!" the cabbie exclaimed. "You're that guy Pritchard!"

"Pritchard. That's right," Richards said resignedly. The Games Building was dwindling behind them. A psychological shadow seemed to be dwindling proportionally in his mind, in spite of the bad luck with the cabby.

"Jesus, you got balls, buddy. I'll say that. You really do. Christ, they'll killya. You know that? They'll killya fuckin-eye dead. You must really have balls."

"That's right. Two of them. Just like you."

"Two of 'm!" the cabby repeated. He was ecstatic. "Jesus, that's good. That's hot! You mind if I tell my wife I hadja as a fare? She goes batshit for the Games. I'll hafta reportcha too, but Christ, I won't get no hunnert for it. Cabbies gotta have at least one supportin witness, y'know. Knowin my luck, no one sawya gettin in."

"That would be tough," Richards said. "I'm sorry you can't help kill me. Should I leave a note saying I was here?"

"Jesus, couldja? That'd be—"

They had just crossed the Canal. "Let me out here," Richards said abruptly. He pulled a New Dollar from the envelope Thompson had handed him, and dropped it on the front seat.

"Gee, I didn't say nothin, did I? I dint meanta—"

"No," Richards said.

"Couldja gimme that note—"

"Get stuffed, maggot."

He lunged out and began walking toward Drummond Street. Co-Op City rose skeletal in the gathering darkness before him. The cabbie's yell floated after him: *"I hope they getya early, you cheap fuck!"*

... Minus 078
and COUNTING ...

Through a backyard; through a ragged hole in a cyclone fence separating one barren asphalt desert from another; across a ghostly, abandoned construction site; pausing far back in shattered shadows as a cycle pack roared by, headlamps glaring in the dark like the psychopathic eyes of nocturnal werewolves. Then over a final fence (cutting one hand) and he was rapping on Molie Jernigan's back door—which is to say, the main entrance.

Molie ran a Dock Street hockshop where a fellow with enough bucks to spread around could buy a police-special move-along, a full-choke riot gun, a submachine gun, heroin, Push, cocaine, drag disguises, a styroflex pseudo-woman, a real whore if you were too strapped to afford styroflex, the current address of one of three floating crap-games, the current address on a swinging Perverto Club, or a hundred other illegal items. If Molie didn't have what you wanted, he would order it for you.

Including false papers.

When he opened the peephole and saw who was there, he offered a kindly smile and said: "Why don't you go away, pal? I never saw you."

"New Dollars," Richards remarked, as if to the air itself. There was a pause. Richards studied the cuff of his shirt as if he had never seen it before.

Then the bolts and locks were opened, quickly, as if Molie were afraid Richards would change his mind. Richards came in. They were in Molie's place behind the store, which was a rat warren of old newsies, stolen musical instruments, stolen cameras, and boxes of black-market groceries. Molie was by necessity something of a Robin Hood; a pawnbroker south of the Canal did not remain in business long if he became too greedy. Molie took the rich uptown maggots as heavily as he could and sold in the neighborhood at close to cost—sometimes lower than cost if some pal was being squeezed hard. Thus his reputation in Co-Op City was excellent, his protection superb. If a cop asked a South City stoolie (and there were hundreds of them) about Molie Jernigan, the informant let it be known that Molie was a slightly senile old-timer who took a little graft and sold a little black market. Any number of uptown swells with strange sexual tendencies could have told the police differently, but there were no vice busts anymore. Everyone knew vice was bad for any real revolutionary climate. The fact that Molie also ran a moderately profitable trade in forged documents, strictly for local customers, was unknown uptown. Still, Richards knew, tooling papers for someone as hot as he was would be extremely dangerous.

"What papers?" Molie asked, sighing deeply and turning on an ancient gooseneck lamp that flooded the working area of his desk with bright white light. He was an old man, approaching seventy-five, and in the close glow of the light his hair looked like spun silver.

"Driver's license. Military Service Card. Street Identicard. Axial charge card. Social Retirement card."

"Easy. Sixty-buck job for anyone but you, Bennie."

"You'll do it?"

"For your wife, I'll do it. For you, no. I don't put my head in the noose for any crazy-ass bastard like Bennie Richards."

"How long, Molie?"

Molie's eyes flashed sardonically. "Knowin your situation as I do, I'll hurry it. An hour for each."

"Christ, five hours . . . can I go—"

"No, you can't. Are you nuts, Bennie? A cop comes pullin up to your Development last week. He's got a envelope for your ol lady. He came in a Black Wagon with about six buddies. Flapper Donnigan was standin on the corner pitchin nicks with Gerry Hanrahan when it transfired. Flapper tells me everythin. The boy's soft, you know."

"I know Flapper's soft," Richards said impatiently. "I sent the money. Is she—"

"Who knows? Who sees?" Molie shrugged and rolled his eyes as he put pens and blank forms in the center of the pool of light thrown by the lamp. "They're four deep around your building, Bennie. Anyone who sent to offer their condolences would end up in a cellar talkin to a bunch of rubber clubs. Even good friends don't need that scam, not even with your ol lady flush. You got a name you want special on these?"

"Doesn't matter as long as it's Anglo. Jesus, Molie, she must have come out for groceries. And the doctor—"

"She sent Budgie O'Sanchez's kid. What's his name."

"Walt."

"Yeah, that's it. I can't keep the goddam spics and micks straight no more. I'm gettin senile, Bennie. Blowin my cool." He glared up at Richards suddenly. "I remember when Mick Jagger was a big name. You don't even know who he was, do ya?"

"I know who he was," Richards said, distraught. He turned to Molie's sidewalk-level window, frightened. It was worse than he thought. Sheila and Cathy were in the cage, too. At least until—

"They're okay, Bennie," Molie said softly. "Just stay away. You're poison to them now. Can you dig it?"

"Yes," Richards said. He was suddenly overwhelmed with despair, black and awful. *I'm homesick*, he thought, amazed, but it was more, it was worse. Everything seemed out of whack, surreal. The very fabric of existence bulging at the seams. Faces, whirling: Laughlin, Burns, Killian, Jansky, Molie, Cathy, Sheila—

He looked out into the blackness, trembling. Molie had gone to work, crooning some old song from his vacant past, something about having Bette Davis eyes, who the hell was *that*?

"He was a drummer," Richards said suddenly. "With that English group, the Beetles. Mick McCartney."

"Yah, you kids," Molie said, bent over his work. "That's all you kids know."

. . . Minus 077
and COUNTING . . .

He left Molie's at ten past midnight, twelve hundred New Dollars lighter. The pawnbroker had also sold him a limited but fairly effective disguise: gray hair, spectacles, mouth wadding, plastic buck-teeth which subtly transfigured his lip line. "Give yourself a little limp, too," Molie advised. "Not a big attention-getter. Just a little one. Remember, you have the power to cloud men's minds, if you use it. Don't remember that line, do ya?"

Richards didn't.

According to his new wallet cards, he was John Griffen Springer, a text-tape salesman from Harding. He was a forty-three year-old widower. No technico status, but that was just as well. Technicos had their own language.

Richards reemerged on Robard Street at 12:30, a good hour to get rolled, mugged, or killed, but a bad hour to make any kind of unnoticed getaway. Still, he had lived south of the Canal all his life.

He crossed the Canal two miles farther west, almost on the edge of the lake. He saw a party of drunken winos huddled around a furtive fire, several rats, but no cops. By 1:15 A.M. he was cutting across the far edge of the no-man's-land of warehouses, cheap beaneries, and shipping offices on the north side of the Canal. At 1:30 he was surrounded by enough uptowners hopping from one sleazy dive to the next to safely hail a cab.

This time the driver didn't give him a second look.

"Jetport," Richards said.

"I'm your man, pal."

The airthrusters shoved them up into traffic. They were at the airport by 1:50. Richards limped past several cops and security guards who showed no interest in him. He bought a ticket to New York because it came naturally to mind. The I.D. check was routine and uneventful. He was on the 2:20 speed shuttle to New York. There were only forty or so passengers, most of them snoozing businessmen and students. The cop in the Judas hole dozed through the entire trip. After a while, Richards dozed, too.

They touched down at 3:06, and Richards deplaned and left the airport without incident.

At 3:15 the cab was spiraling down the Lindsay Overway. They crossed Central Park on a diagonal, and at 3:20, Ben Richards disappeared into the largest city on the face of the earth.

... Minus 076
and COUNTING ...

He went to earth in the Brant Hotel, a so-so establishment on the East Side. That part of the city had been gradually entering a new cycle of chic. Yet the Brant was less than a mile from Manhattan's own blighted inner city—also the largest in the world. As he checked in, he again thought of Dan Killian's parting words: *Stay close to your own people.*

After leaving the taxi he had walked to Times Square, not wanting to check into any hotel during the small morning hours. He spent the five and a half hours from 3:30 to 9:00 in an all-night perverto show. He had wanted desperately to sleep, but both times he had dozed off, he had been snapped awake by the feel of light fingers crawling up his inner thigh.

"How long will you be staying, sir?" the desk clerk asked, glancing at Richards's registration as John G. Springer.

"Don't know," Richards said, trying for meek affability. "All depends on the clients, you understand." He paid sixty New Dollars, holding the room for two days, and took the elevator up to the twenty-third floor. The room offered a somber view of the squalid East River. It was raining in New York, too.

The room was clean but sterile; there was a connecting bathroom and the toilet made constant, ominous noises that Richards could not rectify even by wiggling the ball in the tank.

He had breakfast sent up—a poached egg on toast, orange drink, coffee. When the boy appeared with the tray, he tipped lightly and forgettably.

With breakfast out of the way, he took out the videotape camera and looked at it. A small metal plate labeled INSTRUCTIONS was set just below the viewfinder. Richards read:

1. Push tape cartridge into slot marked A until it clicks home.
2. Set viewfinder by means of crosshairs within the sight.
3. Push button marked B to record sound with video.
4. When the bell sounds, tape cartridge will pop out automatically.

    Recording time: 10 minutes.

    Good, Richards thought. They can watch me sleep.

He set the camera on the bureau next to the Gideon Bible and sighted the crosshairs on the bed. The wall behind was blank and nondescript; he didn't see how anyone could pinpoint his location from either the bed or the background. Street noise from this height was negligible, but he would leave the shower running just in case.

Even with forethought, he nearly pressed the button and stepped into the camera's field of vision with his naked disguise hanging out. Some of it could have been removed, but the gray hair had to stay. He put the pillowslip over his head. Then he pressed the button, walked over to the bed, and sat down facing the lens.

"Peekaboo," Ben Richards said hollowly to his immense listening and viewing audience that would watch this tape later tonight with horrified interest. "You can't see it, but I'm laughing at you shiteaters."

He lay back, closed his eyes, and tried to think of nothing at all. When the tape clip popped out ten minutes later, he was fast asleep.

. . . Minus 075
and COUNTING . . .

When he woke up it was just after 4 P.M.—the hunt was on, then. Had been for three hours, figuring for the time difference. The thought sent a chill through his middle.

He put a new tape in the camera, took down the Gideon Bible, and read the Ten Commandments over and over for ten minutes with the pillow slip on his head.

There were envelopes in the desk drawer, but the name and address of the hotel was on them. He hesitated, and knew it made no difference. He would have to take Killian's word that his location, as revealed by postmarks or return addresses, would not be revealed to McCone and his bird dogs by the Games Authority. He had to use the postal service. They had supplied him with no carrier pigeons.

There was a mail drop by the elevators, and Richards dropped the clips into the out-of-town slot with huge misgivings. Although postal authorities were not eligible for any Games money for reporting the whereabouts of contestants, it still seemed like a horribly risky thing to do. But the only other thing was default, and he couldn't do that, either.

He went back to his room, shut off the shower (the bathroom was as steamy as a tropical jungle), and lay down on the bed to think.

How to run? What was the best thing to do?

He tried to put himself in the place of an average contestant. The first impulse, of course, was pure animal instinct: Go to earth. Make a den and cower in there.

And so he had done. The Brant Hotel.

Would the Hunters expect that? Yes. They would not be looking for a running man at all. They would be looking for a hiding man.

Could they find him in his den?

He wanted very badly to answer no, but he could not. His disguise was good, but hastily put together. Not many people are observant, but there are always some. Perhaps he had been tabbed already. The desk clerk. The bellboy who had brought his breakfast. Perhaps even by one of the faceless men in the perverto show on Forty-second Street.

Not likely, but possible.

And what about his real protection, the false I.D. Molie had provided? Good for how long? Well, the taxi driver who had taken him from the Games Building could put him in South City. And the Hunters were fearfully, dreadfully good. They would be leaning hard on everyone he knew, from Jack Crager to that bitch Eileen Jenner down the hall. Heavy heat. How long until somebody, maybe a head-softie like Flapper Donnigan, let it slip that Molie had forged papers on occasion? And if they found Molie, he was blown. The pawnbroker would hold out long enough to take a belting around; he was canny enough to want a few visible battle scars to sport around the neighborhood. Just so his place didn't have a bad case of spontaneous combustion some night. Then? A simple check of Harding's three jetports would uncover John G. Springer's midnight jaunt to Freak City.

If they found Molie.

You assume they will. You have to assume they will.

Then run. Where?

He didn't know. He had spent his entire life in Harding. In the Midwest. He didn't know the East Coast; there was no place here he could run to and feel that he was on familiar turf. So where? Where?

His teased and unhappy mind drifted into a morbid daydream. They had found Molie with no trouble at all. Pried the Springer name out of him in an easy five minutes, after pulling two fingernails, filling his navel with lighter fluid and threatening to strike a match. They had gotten Richards's flight number with one quick call (handsome, nondescript men in garbardine coats of identical cut and make) and had arrived in New York by 2:30 E.S.T. Advance men had already gotten the address of the Brant by a telex canvass of the New York City hotel-listings, which were computer tabulated day by day. They were outside now, surrounding the place. Busboys and bellboys and clerks and bartenders had been replaced by Hunters. Half a dozen coming up the fire escape. Another fifty packing all three elevators. More and more, pulling up in air cars all around the building. Now they were in the hall, and in a moment the door would crash open and they would lunge in, a tape machine grinding enthusiastically away on a rolling tripod above their muscular shoulders, getting it all down for posterity as they turned him into hamburger.

Richards sat up, sweating. Didn't even have a gun, not yet.

Run. Fast.

Boston would do, to start.

. . . Minus 074
and COUNTING . . .

He left his room at 5:00 P.M. and went down to the lobby. The desk clerk smiled brightly, probably looking forward to his evening relief.

"Afternoon, Mr., uh—"

"Springer." Richards smiled back. "I seem to have struck oil, my man. Three clients who seem . . . receptive. I'll be occupying your excellent facility for an additional two days. May I pay in advance?"

"Certainly, sir."

Dollars changed hands. Still beaming, Richards went back up to his room. The hall was empty. Richards hung the DO NOT DISTURB sign on the doorknob and went quickly to the fire stairs.

Luck was with him and he met no one. He went all the way to the ground floor and slipped out the side entrance unobserved.

The rain had stopped, but the clouds still hung and lowered over Manhattan. The air smelled like a rancid battery. Richards walked briskly, discarding the limp, to the Port Authority Electric Bus terminal. A man could still buy a ticket on a Greyhound without signing his name.

"Boston," he said to the bearded ticket-vendor.

"Twenty-three bucks, pal. Bus pulls out at six-fifteen sharp."

He passed over the money; it left him with something less than three thousand New Dollars. He had an hour to kill, and the terminal was chock-full of people, many of them Vol-Army, with their blue berets and blank, boyish, brutal faces. He bought a Pervert Mag, sat down, and propped it in front of his face. For the next hour he stared at it, turning a page occasionally to try and avoid looking like a statue.

When the bus rolled up to the pier, he shuffled toward the open doors with the rest of the nondescript assortment.

"Hey! Hey, you!"

Richards stared around; a security cop was approaching on the run. He froze, unable to take flight. A distant part of his brain was screaming that he was about to be cut down right here, right here in this shitty bus terminal with wads of gum on the floor and casual obscenities scrawled on the dirt-caked walls; he was going to be some dumb flatfoot's fluke trophy.

"Stop him! Stop that guy!"

The cop was veering. It wasn't him at all. Richards saw. It was a scruffy-looking kid who was running for the stairs, swinging a lady's purse in one hand and bowling bystanders this way and that like tenpins.

He and his pursuer disappeared from sight, taking the stairs three by three in huge leaps. The knot of embarkers, debarkers, and greeters watched them with vague interest for a moment and then picked up the threads of what they had been doing, as if nothing had happened.

Richards stood in line, trembling and cold.

He collapsed into a seat near the back of the coach, and a few minutes later the bus hummed smoothly up the ramp, paused, and joined the flow of traffic. The cop and his quarry had disappeared into the general mob of humanity.

If I'd had a gun. I would have burned him where he stood, Richards thought. Christ. Oh, Christ.

And on the heels of that: *Next time it won't be a purse snatcher. It'll be you.*

He would get a gun in Boston anyway. Somehow.

He remembered Laughlin saying that he would push a few of them out a high window before they took him.

The bus rolled north in the gathering darkness.

. . . Minus 073 and COUNTING . . .

The Boston Y.M.C.A. stood on upper Huntington Avenue. It was huge, black with years, old-fashioned, and boxy. It stood in what used to be one of Boston's better areas in the middle of the last century. It stood there like a guilty reminder of another time, another day, its old-fashioned neon still winking its letters toward the sinful theater district. It looked like the skeleton of a murdered idea.

When Richards walked into the lobby, the desk clerk was arguing with a tiny, scruffy black boy in a killball jersey so big that it reached down over his blue jeans to midshin. The disputed territory seemed to be a gum machine that stood inside the lobby door.

"I loss my nickel, honky. I loss my muh-fuhn nickel!"

"If you don't get out of here, I'll call the house detective, kid. That's all. I'm done talking to you."

"But that goddam machine took my nickel!"

"You stop swearing at me, you little scumbag!" The clerk, who looked an old, cold thirty, reached down and shook the jersey. It was too huge for him to be able to shake the boy inside, too. "Now get out of here. I'm through talking."

Seeing he meant it, the almost comic mask of hate and defiance below the dark sunburst of the kid's afro broke into a hurt, agonized grimace of disbelief. "Lissen, thass the oney muh-fuhn nickel I got. That gumball machine ate my nickel! That—"

"I'm calling the house dick right now." The clerk turned toward the switchboard. His jacket, a refugee from some bargain counter, flapped tiredly around his thin butt.

The boy kicked the plaxteel post of the gum machine, then ran. "Muh-fuhn white honky sum*bitch*!"

The clerk looked after him, the security button, real or mythical unpressed. He smiled at Richards, showing an old keyboard with a few missing keys. "You can't talk to niggers anymore. I'd keep them in cages if I ran the Network."

"He really lose a nickel?" Richards asked, signing the register as John Deegan from Michigan.

"If he did, he stole it," the clerk said. "Oh, I suppose he did. But if I gave him a nickel, I'd have two hundred pickaninnies in here by nightfall claiming the same thing. Where do they learn that language? That's what I want to know. Don't their folks care what they do? How long will you be staying, Mr. Deegan?"

"I don't know. I'm in town on business." He tried on a greasy smile, and when it felt right, he widened it. The desk clerk recognized it instantly (perhaps from his own reflection looking up at him from the depths of the fake-marble counter, which had been polished by a million elbows) and gave it back to him.

"That's $15.50, Mr. Deegan." He pushed a key attached to a worn wooden tongue across the counter to Richards. "Room 512."

"Thank you." Richards paid cash. Again, no I.D. Thank God for the Y.M.C.A.

He crossed to the elevators and looked down the corridor to the Christian Lending Library on the left. It was dimly lit with flyspecked yellow globes, and an old man wearing an overcoat and galoshes was perusing a tract, turning the pages slowly and methodically with a trembling, wetted finger. Richards could hear the clogged whistle of his breathing from where he was by the elevators, and felt a mixture of sorrow and horror.

The elevator clunked to a stop, and the doors opened with wheezy reluctance. As he stepped in, the clerk said loudly: "It's a sin and a shame. I'd put them all in cages."

Richards glanced up, thinking the clerk was speaking to him, but the clerk was not looking at anything.

The lobby was very empty and very silent.

. . . Minus 072
and COUNTING . . .

The fifth floor hall stank of pee.

The corridor was narrow enough to make Richards feel claustrophobic, and the carpet, which might have been red, had worn away in the middle to random strings. The doors were industrial gray, and several of them showed the marks of fresh kicks, smashes, or attempts to jimmy. Signs at every twenty paces advised that there would be NO SMOKING IN THIS HALL BY ORDER OF FIRE MARSHAL. There was a communal bathroom in the center, and the urine stench became suddenly sharp. It was a smell Richards associated automatically with despair. People moved restlessly behind the gray doors like animals in cages—animals too awful, too frightening, to be seen. Someone was chanting what might have been the Hail Mary over and over in a drunken voice. Strange gobbling noises came from behind another door. A country-western tune from behind another (''I ain't got a buck for the phone/and I'm so alone . . . ''). Shuffling noises. The solitary squeak of bedsprings that might mean a man in his own hand. Sobbing. Laughter. The hysterical grunts of a drunken argument. And from behind these, silence. And silence. And silence. A man with a hideously sunken chest walked past Richards without looking at him, carrying a bar of soap and a towel in one hand, wearing gray pajama bottoms tied with string. He wore paper slippers on his feet.

Richards unlocked his room and stepped in. There was a police bar on the inside, and he used it. There was a bed with almost-white sheets and an Army surplus blanket. There was a bureau from which the second drawer was missing. There was a picture of Jesus on one wall. There was a steel rod with two coathangers kitty-cornered in the right angle of two walls. There was nothing else but the window, which looked out on blackness. It was 10:15.

Richards hung up his jacket, slipped off his shoes, and lay down on the bed. He realized how miserable and unknown and vulnerable he was in the world. The universe seemed to shriek and clatter and roar around him like a huge and indifferent jalopy rushing down a hill and toward the lip of a bottomless chasm. His lips began to tremble, and then he cried a little.

He didn't put it on tape. He lay looking at the ceiling, which was cracked into a million crazy scrawls, like a bad potter's-glaze. They had been after him for over eight hours now. He had earned eight hundred dollars of his stake money. Christ, not even out of the hole yet.

And he'd missed himself on Free-Vee. Christ, yes. The bag-over-the-head spectacular.

Where were they? Still in Harding? New York? Or on their way to Boston? No, they couldn't be on their way here, could they? The bus had not passed through any roadblocks. He had left the biggest city in the world anonymously, and he was here under an assumed name. They couldn't be onto him. No way.

The Boston Y might be safe for as long as two days. After that he could move north toward New Hampshire and Vermont, or south toward Hartford or Philadelphia or even Atlanta. Further east was the ocean, and beyond it was Britain and Europe. It was an intriguing idea, but probably out of reach. Passage by plane required I.D., what with France under martial law, and while stowing-away might be possible, discovery would mean a quick and final end to the whole thing. And west was out. West was where the heat was the hottest.

If you can't stand the heat, get out of the kitchen. Who had said that? Molie would know. He snickered a little and felt better.

The disembodied sound of a radio came to his ears.

It would be good to get the gun now, tonight, but he was too tired. The ride had tired him. Being a fugitive tired him. And he knew in an animal way that went deeper than the rational that very soon he might be sleeping in an October-cold culvert or in a weed- and cinder-choked gully.

The gun tomorrow night.

He turned off the light and went to bed.

. . . Minus 071
and COUNTING . . .

It was showtime again.

Richards stood with his buttocks toward the video recorder, humming the theme music to *The Running Man.* A Y.M.C.A. pillowslip was over his head, turned inside out so the name stamped on its hem wouldn't show.

The camera had inspired Richards to a kind of creative humor that he never would have believed he possessed. The self-image he'd always held was that of a rather dour man, with little or no humor in his outlook. The prospect of his approaching death had uncovered a solitary comedian hiding inside.

When the clip popped out, he decided to save the second for afternoon. The solitary room was boring, and perhaps something else would occur to him.

He dressed slowly and then went to the window and looked out.

Thursday morning traffic hustled busily up and down Huntington Avenue. Both sidewalks were crowded with slowly moving pedestrians. Some of them were scanning bright-yellow Help-Wanted Fax. Most of them just walked. There was a cop, it seemed, on every corner. Richards could hear them in his mind: *Move along. Ain't you got someplace to go? Pick it up, maggot.*

So you moved on to the next corner, which was just like the last corner, and were moved along again. You could try to get mad about it, but mostly your feet hurt too much.

Richards debated the risk of going down the hall and showering. He finally decided it would be okay. He went down with a towel over his shoulder, met no one, and walked into the bathroom.

Essence of urine, shit, puke, and disinfectant mingled. All the crapper doors had been yanked off, of course. Someone had scrawled FUK THE NETWORK in foot-high letters above the urinal. It looked as though he might have been angry when he did it. There was a pile of feces in one of the urinals. Someone must have been really drunk, Richards thought. A few sluggish autumn flies were crawling over it. He was not disgusted; the sight was too common; but he was matter-of-factly glad he had worn his shoes.

He also had the shower room to himself. The floor was cracked porcelain, the walls gouged tile with thick runnels of decay near the bottoms. He turned on a rust-clogged showerhead, full hot, and waited patiently for five minutes until the water ran tepid, and then showered quickly. He used a scrap of soap he found on the floor; the Y had either neglected to supply it or the chambermaid had walked off with his.

On his way back to his room, a man with a harelip gave him a tract.

Richards tucked his shirt in, sat on his bed, and lit a cigarette. He was hungry but would wait until dusk to go out and eat.

Boredom drove him to the window again. He counted different makes of cars—Fords, Chevies, Wints, VW's, Plymouths, Studebakers, Rambler-Supremes. First one to a hundred wins. A dull game, but better than no game.

Further up Hunington Avenue was Northeastern University, and directly across the street from the Y was a large automated bookshop. While he counted cars, Richards watched the students come and go. They were in sharp contrast to the Wanted-Fax idlers; their hair was shorter, and they all seemed to be wearing tartan jumpers, which were this year's kampus kraze. They walked through the milling ruck and inside to make their purchases with an air of uncomfortable patronization and hail-fellow that left a curdled amusement in Richards's mouth. The five-minute spaces in front of the store filled and emptied with sporty, flashy cars, often of exotic make. Most of them had college decals in the back windows: Northeastern, M.I.T., Boston College, Harvard. Most of the news-fax bums treated the sporty cars as part of the scenery, but a few looked at them with dumb and wretched longing.

A Wint pulled out of the space directly in front of the store and a Ford pulled in, settling to an inch above the pavement as the driver, a crewcut fellow smoking a foot-long cigar, put it in idle. The car dipped slightly as his passenger, a dude in a brown and white hunting jacket, got out and zipped inside.

Richards sighed. Counting cars was a very poor game. Fords were ahead of their nearest contender by a score of 78 to 40. The outcome going to be predictable as the next election.

Someone pounded on the door and Richards stiffened like a bolt.

"Frankie? You in there, Frankie?"

Richards said nothing. Frozen with fear, he played a statue.

"You eat shit, Frankie-baby." There was a chortle of drunken laughter and the footsteps moved on. Pounding on the next door up. "You in there, Frankie?"

Richards's heart slipped slowly down from his throat.

The Ford was pulling out, and another Ford took its place. Number 79. Shit.

The day slipped into afternoon, and then it was one o'clock. Richards knew this by the ringing of various chimes in churches far away. Ironically, the man living by the clock had no watch.

He was playing a variation of the car game now. Fords worth two points, Studebakers three, Wints four. First one to five hundred wins.

It was perhaps fifteen minutes later that he noticed the young man in the brown and white hunting jacket leaning against a lamppost beyond the bookstore and reading a concert poster. He was not being moved along; in fact, the police seemed to be ignoring him.

You're jumping at shadows, maggot. Next you'll see them in the corners. He counted a Wint with a dented fender. A yellow Ford. An old Studebaker with a wheezing air cylinder, dipping in slight cycles. A VW—no good, they're out of the running. Another Wint. A Studebaker.

A man smoking a foot-long cigar was standing nonchalantly at the bus stop on the corner. He was the only person there. With good reason. Richards had seen the buses come and go, and knew there wouldn't be another one along for forty-five minutes.

Richards felt a coolness creep into his testicles.

An old man in a threadbare black overcoat sauntered down the side of the street and leaned casually against the building.

Two fellows in tartan jumpers got out of a taxi, talking animatedly, and began to study the menu in the window of the Stockholm Restaurant.

A cop walked over and conversed with the man at the bus stop. Then the cop walked away again.

Richards noted with a numb, distant terror that a good many of the newspaper bums were idling along much more slowly. Their clothes and styles of walking seemed oddly familiar, as if they had been around a great many times before and Richards was just becoming aware of it—in the tentative, uneasy way you recognize the voices of the dead in dreams.

There were more cops, too.

I'm being bracketed, he thought. The idea brought a helpless, rabbit terror.

No, his mind corrected. *You've already been bracketed.*

. . . Minus 070
and COUNTING . . .

Richards walked rapidly to the bathroom, being calm, ignoring his terror the way a man on a high ledge ignores the drop. If he was going to get out of this, it would be by keeping his head. If he panicked, he would die quickly.

Someone was in the shower, singing a popular song in a cracked and pitchless voice. No one was at the urinals or the washstands.

The trick had popped effortlessly into his mind as he had stood by the window, watching them gather in their offhand, sinister way. If it hadn't occurred to him, he thought he would be there yet, like Aladdin watching smoke from the lamp coalesce into an omnipotent djinn. They had used the trick as boys to steal newspapers from Development basements. Molie bought them; two cents a pound.

He took one of the wire toothbrush holders off the wall with a hard snap of his wrist. It was a little rusted, but that wouldn't matter. He walked down to the elevator, bending the toothbrush holder out straight.

He pushed the call button, and the cage took a slow eternity to come down from eight. It was empty. Thank Christ it was empty.

He stepped in, looked briefly down the halls, and then turned to the control panel. There was a key slot beside the button marked for the basement. The janitor would have a special card to shove in there. An electric eye scanned the card and then the janitor could push the button and ride down to the basement.

What if it doesn't work?

Never mind that. Never mind that now.

Grimacing in anticipation of a possible electric shock, Richards jammed the toothbrush wire into the slot and pushed the basement button simultaneously.

There was a noise from inside the control panel that sounded like a brief electronic curse. There was a light, tingling jolt up his arm. For a moment, nothing else. Then the folding brass gate slid across, the doors closed, and the elevator lurched unhappily downward. A small tendril of blue smoke curled out of the slot in the panel.

Richards stood away from the elevator door and watched the numbers flash backwards. When the *L* lit, the motor high above made a grinding sound, and the car seemed about to stop. Then, after a moment (perhaps after it thought it had scared Richards enough), it descended again. Twenty seconds later the doors slid open and Richards stepped out into the huge dim basement. There was water dripping somewhere, and the scurry of a disturbed rat. But otherwise, the basement was his. For now.

. . . Minus 069
and COUNTING . . .

Huge, rusted heating pipes festooned with cobwebs crawled crazily all over the ceiling. When the furnace kicked on suddenly, Richards almost screamed in terror. The surge of adrenaline to his limbs and heart was painful, for a moment almost incapacitating.

There were newspapers here, too, Richards saw. Thousands of them, stacked up and tied with string. The rats had nested in them by the thousands. Whole families stared out at the interloper with ruby distrustful eyes.

He began to walk away from the elevator, pausing halfway across the cracked cement floor. There was a large fuse box bolted to a supporting post, and behind it, leaning against the other side, a litter of tools. Richards took the crowbar and continued to walk, keeping his eyes on the floor.

Near the far wall he spied the main storm drain, to his left. He walked over and looked at it, wondering in the back of his mind if they knew he was down here yet.

The storm drain was constructed of vented steel. It was about three feet across, and on the far side there was a slot for the crowbar. Richards slipped it in, levered up the cover, and then put one foot on the crowbar to hold it. He got his hands under the lip of the cover and pushed it over. It fell to the cement with a clang that made the rats squeak with dismay.

The pipe beneath slanted down at a forty-five-degree angle, and Richards guessed that its bore could be no more than two and a half feet. It was very dark. Claustrophobia suddenly filled his mouth with flannel. Too small to maneuver in, almost too small to breathe in. But it had to be.

He turned the storm-drain cover back over and edged it toward the pipe entrance just enough so he could grip it from beneath once he was down there Then he walked over to the fuse box, hammered the padlock off with the crowbar, and shoved it open. He was about to begin pulling fuses when another idea occurred to him.

He walked over to the newspapers which lay in dirty yellow drifts against the whole eastern length of the cellar. Then he ferreted out the folded and dog-eared book of matches he had been lighting his smokes with. There were three left. He yanked out a sheet of paper and formed it into a spill; held it under his arm like a dunce cap and lit a match. The first one guttered out in a draft. The second fell out of his trembling hand and hissed out on the damp concrete.

The third stayed alight. He held it to his paper spill and yellow flame bloomed. A rat, perhaps sensing what was to come, ran across his foot and into the darkness.

A terrible sense of urgency filled him now, and yet he waited until the spill was flaming a foot high. He had no more matches. Carefully, he tucked it into a fissure in the chest-high paper wall and waited until he saw that the fire was spreading.

The huge oil tank which serviced the Y was built into the adjoining wall. Perhaps it would blow. Richards thought it would.

Trotting now, he went back to the fuse box and began ripping out the long tubular fuses. He got most of them before the basement lights went out. He felt his way across to the storm drain, aided by the growing, flickering light of the burning papers.

He sat down with his feet dangling, and then slowly eased in. When his head was below the level of the floor, he pressed his knees against the sides of the pipe to hold himself steady, and worked his arms up above his head. It was slow work. There was very little room to move. The light of the fire was brilliant yellow now, and the crackling sound of burning filled his ears. Then his groping fingers found the lip of the drain, and he slid them up until they gripped the vented cover. He yanked it forward slowly, supporting more and more of the weight with the muscles of his back and neck. When he judged that the far edge of the cover was on the edge of dropping into place, he gave one last fierce tug.

The cover dropped into place with a clang, bending both wrists back cruelly. Richards let his knees relax, and he slid downward like a boy shooting the chutes. The pipe was coated with slime, and he slid effortlessly about twelve feet to where the pipe elbow bent into a straight line. His feet struck smartly, and he stood there like a drunk leaning against a lamppost.

But he couldn't get into the horizontal pipe. The elbow bend was too sharp.

The taste of the claustrophobia became huge, gagging. *Trapped*, his mind babbled. *Trapped in here, trapped, trapped—*

A steel scream rose in his throat and he choked it down.

Calm down. Sure, it's very hackneyed, very trite, but we must be very calm down here. Very calm. Because we are at the bottom of this pipe and we can't get up and we can't get down and if the fucking oil tank goes boom, we are going to be fricasseed very neatly and—

Slowly he began to wriggle around until his chest was against the pipe instead of his back. The slime coating acted as a lubricant, helping his movement. It was very bright in the pipe now, and getting warmer. The vented cover threw prison-bar shadows on his struggling face.

Once leaning against his chest and belly and groin, with his knees bending the right way, he could slip down further, letting his calves and feet slide into the horizontal pipe until he was in the praying position. Still no good. His buttocks were pushing against the solid ceramic facing above the entrance to the horizontal pipe.

Faintly, it seemed that he could hear shouted commands above the heavy crackle of the fire, but it might have been his imagination, which was now strained and fevered beyond the point of trust.

He began to flex the muscles of his thighs and calves in a tiring seesaw rhythm, and little by little his knees began to slide out from under him. He worked his hands up over his head again to give himself more room, and now his face lay solidly against the slime of the pipe. He was very close to fitting now. He swayed his back as much as he could and began to push with his arms and head, the only things left in any position to give him leverage.

When he had begun to think there was not enough room, that he was going to simply hang here, unable to move either way, his hips and buttocks suddenly popped through the horizontal pipe's opening like a champagne cork from a tight bottleneck. The small of his back scraped excruciatingly as his knees slid out from under him, and his shirt rucked up to his shoulderblades. Then he was in the horizontal pipe—except for his head and arms. which were bent back at a joint-twist-ing angle. He wriggled the rest of the way in and then paused there, panting, his face streaked with slime and rat droppings, the skin of his lower back abraded and oozing blood.

This pipe was narrower still; his shoulders scraped lightly on both sides each time his chest rose in respiration.

Thank God I'm underfed.

Panting, he began to back into the unknown darkness of the pipe.

. . . Minus 068
and COUNTING . . .

He made slow, molelike progress for about fifty yards through the horizontal pipe, backing up blindly. Then the oil tank in the Y's basement suddenly blew with a roar that set up enough sympathetic vibrations in the pipes to nearly rupture his eardrums. There was a yellow-white flash, as if a pile of phosphorus had ignited. It faded to a rosy, shifting glow. A few moments later a blast of thermal air struck him in the face, making him grin painfully.

The tape camera in his jacket pocket swung and bounced as he tried to back up faster. The pipe was picking up heat from the fierce explosion and fire that was raging somewhere above him, the way the handle of a skillet picks up heat from a gas-ring. Richards had no urge to be baked down here like a potato in a Dutch oven.

Sweat rolled down his face, mixing with the black streaks of ordure already there, making him look, in the waxing and waning glow of the reflected fire, like an Indian painted for war. The sides of the pipe were hot to the touch now.

Lobsterlike, Richards humped backwards on his knees and forearms, his but-tocks rising to smack the top of the pipe at every movement. His breath came in sharp, doglike gasps. The air was hot, full of the slick taste of oil, uncomfortable to breathe. A headache surfaced within his skull and began to push daggers into the backs of his eyes.

I'm going to fry in here. I'm going to fry.

Then his feet were suddenly dangling in the air. Richards tried to peer through his legs and see what was there, but it was too dark behind and his eyes were too dazzled by the light in front. He would have to take his chance. He backed up until his knees were on the edge of the pipe's ending, and then slid them cautiously over.

His shoes were suddenly in water, cold and shocking after the heat of the pipe. The new pipe ran at right angles to the one Richards had just come through, and it was much larger—big enough to stand in bent over. The thick, slowly moving water came up over his ankles. He paused for just a moment to stare back into the tiny pipe with its soft circle of reflected fireglow. The fact that he could see any glow at all from this distance meant that it must have been a very big bang indeed.

Richards reluctantly forced himself to know it would be their job to assume him alive rather than dead in the inferno of the Y.M.C.A. basement, but perhaps they would not discover the way he had taken until the fire was under control. That seemed a safe assumption. But it had seemed safe to assume that they could not trace him to Boston, too.

Maybe they didn't. After all, what did you really see?

No. It had been them. He knew it. The Hunters. They had even carried the odor of evil. It had wafted up to his fifth floor room on invisible psychic thermals.

A rat dog-paddled past him, pausing to look up briefly with glittering eyes.

Richards splashed clumsily off after it, in the direction the water was flowing.

. . . Minus 067
and COUNTING . . .

Richards stood by the ladder, looking up, dumbfounded by the light. No regular traffic, which was something, but light—

The light was surprising because it had seemed that he had been walking in the sewers for hours piled upon hours. In the darkness, with no visual input and no sound but the gurgle of water, the occasional soft splash of a rat, and the ghostly thumpings in other pipes (what happens if someone flushes a john over my head, Richards wondered morbidly), his time sense had been utterly destroyed.

Now, looking up at the manhole cover some fifteen feet above him, he saw that the light had not yet faded out of the day. There were several circular breather holes in the cover, and pencil-sized rays of light pressed coins of sun on his chest and shoulders.

No air-cars had passed over the cover since he had gotten here; only an occasional heavy ground-vehicle and a fleet of Hondacycles. It made him suspect that, more by good luck and the law of averages than by inner sense of direction, he had managed to find his way to the core of the city—to his own people.

Still, he didn't dare go up until dark. To pass the time, he took out the tape camera, popped in a clip, and began recording his chest. He knew the tapes were "fastlight," able to take advantage of the least available light, and he did not want to give away too much of his surroundings. He did no talking or capering this time. He was too tired.

When the tape was done, he put it with the other exposed clip. He wished he could rid himself of the nagging suspicion—almost a certainty—that the tapes were pinpointing him. There had to be a way to beat that. *Had* to.

He sat down stolidly on the third rung of the ladder to wait for dark. He had been running for nearly thirty hours.

. . . Minus 066
and COUNTING . . .

The boy, seven years old, black, smoking a cigarette, leaned closer to the mouth of the alley, watching the street.

There had been a sudden, slight movement in the street where there had been none before. Shadows moved, rested, moved again. The manhole cover was rising. It paused and something—eyes?—glimmered. The cover suddenly slid aside with a clang.

Someone (or *something,* the boy thought with a trace of fear) was moving out there. Maybe the devil was coming out of hell to get Cassie, he thought. Ma said Cassie was going to heaven to be with Dicky and the other angels. The boy thought that was bullshit. Everybody went to hell when they died, and the devil jabbed them in the ass with a pitchfork. He had seen a picture of the devil in the books Bradley had snuck out of the Boston Public Library. Heaven was for Push freaks. The devil was the Man.

It could be the devil, he thought as Richards suddenly boosted himself out of the manhole and leaned for a second on the seamed and split cement to get his breath back. No tail and no horns, not red like in that book, but the mother looked crazy and mean enough.

Now he was pushing the cover back, and now—

—now holy Jesus he was running toward the alley.

The boy grunted, tried to run, and fell over his own feet.

He was trying to get up, scrambling and dropping things, and the devil suddenly grabbed him.

"Doan stick me wif it!" He screamed in a throat-closed whisper. "Doan stick me wif no fork, you sumbitch—"

"Shhh! Shut up! Shut up!" The devil shook him, making his teeth rattle like marbles in his head, and the boy shut up. The devil peered around in an ecstasy of apprehension. The expression on his face was almost farcical in its extreme fear. The boy was reminded of the comical fellows on that game show *Swim the Crocodiles.* He would have laughed if he hadn't been so frightened himself.

"You ain't the devil," the boy said.

"You'll think I am if you yell."

"I ain't gonna," the boy said contemptuously. "What you think, I wanna get my balls cut off? Jesus, I ain't even big enough to come yet."

"You know a quiet place we can go?"

"Doan kill me, man. I ain't got nothin." The boy's eyes, white in the darkness, rolled up at him.

"I'm not going to kill you."

Holding his hand, the boy led Richards down the twisting, littered alley and into another. At the end, just before the alley opened onto an airshaft between two faceless highrise buildings, the boy led him into a lean-to built of scrounged boards and bricks. It was built for four feet, and Richards banged his head going in.

The boy pulled a dirty swatch of black cloth across the opening and fiddled with something. A moment later a weak glow lit their faces; the boy had hooked a small lightbulb to an old cracked car battery.

"I kifed that battery myself," the boy said. "Bradley tole me how to fix it up. He's got books. I got a nickel bag, too. I'll give it to you if you don't kill me. You better not. Bradley's in the Stabbers. You kill me an he'll make you shit in your boot an eat it."

"I'm not doing any killings," Richards said impatiently. "At least not little kids."

"I ain't no little kid! I kifed that fuckin battery myself!"

The look of injury forced a dented grin to Richards's face. "All right. What's your name, kid?"

"Ain't no kid." Then, sulkily: "Stacey."

"Okay. Stacey. Good. I'm on the run. You believe that?"

"Yeah, you on the run. You dint come outta that manhole to buy dirty pos'cards." He stared speculatively at Richards. "You a honky? Kinda hard to tell wif all that dirt."

"Stacey, I—" He broke off and ran a hand through his hair. When he spoke again, he seemed to be talking to himself. "I got to trust somebody and it turns out to be a kid. A *kid.* Hot Jesus, you ain't even six, boy."

"I'm eight in March," the boy said angrily. "My sister Cassie's got cancer," he added. "She screams a lot. Thass why I like it here. Kifed that fuckin battery myself. You wanna toke up, mister?"

"No, and you don't either. You want two bucks, Stacey?"

"Chris' yes!" Distrust slid over his eyes. "You dint come outta no manhole with two fuckin bucks. Thass bullshit."

Richards produced a New Dollar and gave it to the boy. He stared at it with awe that was close to horror.

"There's another one if you bring your brother," Richards said, and seeing his expression, added swiftly: "I'll give it to you on the side so he won't see it. Bring him alone."

"Won't do no good to try an kill Bradley, man. He'll make you shit in your boot—"

"And eat it. I know. You run and get him. Wait until he's alone."

"Three bucks."

"No."

"Lissen man, for three bucks I can get Cassie some stuff at the drug. Then she won't scream so fuckin much."

The man's face suddenly worked as if someone the boy couldn't see had punched him. "All right. Three."

"New Dollars," the boy persisted.

"Yes, for Christ's sake, *yes*. Get him. And if you bring the cops you won't get anything."

The boy paused, half in and half out of his little cubbyhole. "You stupid if you think I do that. I hate them fuckin oinkers worse than anyone. Even the devil."

He left, a seven-year-old boy with Richards's life in his grubby, scabbed hands. Richards was too tired to be really afraid. He turned off the light, leaned back, and dozed off.

. . . Minus 065
and COUNTING . . .

Dreaming sleep had just begun when his tight-strung senses ripped him back to wakefulness. Confused, in a dark place, the beginning of the nightmare held him for a moment and he thought that some huge police dog was coming for him, a terrifying organic weapon seven feet high. He almost cried aloud before Stacey made the real world fall into place by hissing:

"If he broke my fuckin light I'm gonna—"

The boy was violently shushed. The cloth across the entrance rippled, and Richards turned on the light. He was looking at Stacey and another black. The new fellow was maybe eighteen, Richards guessed, wearing a cycle jacket, looking at Richards with a mixture of hate and interest.

A switchblade clicked out and glittered in Bradley's hand. "If you're heeled, drop it down."

"I'm not."

"I don't believe that sh—" he broke off, and his eyes widened. "Hey. You're that guy on the Free-Vee. You offed the Y.M.C.A. on Hunington Avenue." The lowering blackness of his face was split by an involuntary grin. "They said you fried five cops. That probably means fifteen."

"He come outta the manhole," Stacey said importantly. "I knew it wasn't the devil right away. I knew it was some honky sumbitch. You gonna cut him, Bradley?"

"Just shut up an let men talk." Bradley came the rest of the way inside, squatting awkwardly, and sat across from Richards on a splintery orange crate. He looked at the blade in his hand, seemed surprised to see it still there, and closed it up.

"You're hotter than the sun, man," he said finally.

"That's true."

"Where you gonna get to?"

"I don't know. I've got to get out of Boston."

Bradley sat in silent thought. "You gotta come home with me an Stacey. We gotta talk, an we can't do it here. Too open."

"All right," Richards said wearily. "I don't care."

"We go the back way. The pigs are cruising tonight. Now I know why."

When Bradley led the way out, Stacey kicked Richards sharply in the shin. For a moment Richards stared at him, not understanding, and then remembered. He slipped the boy three New Dollars, and Stacey made it disappear.

. . . Minus 064
and COUNTING . . .

The woman was very old; Richards thought he had never seen anyone as old. She was wearing a cotton print housedress with a large rip under one arm; an ancient, wrinkled dug swayed back and forth against the rip as she went about making the meal that Richards's New Dollars had purchased. The nicotine-yellowed fingers diced and pared and peeled. Her feet, splayed into grotesque boat shapes by years of standing, were clad in pink terrycloth slippers. Her hair looked as if it might have been self-waved by an iron held in a trembling hand; it was pushed back into a kind of pyramid by the twisted hairnet which had gone askew at the back of her head. Her face was a delta of time, no longer brown or black, but grayish, stitched with a radiating galaxy of wrinkles, pouches, and sags. Her toothless mouth worked craftily at the cigarette held there, blowing out puffs of blue smoke that seemed to hang above and behind her in little bunched blue balls. She puffed back and forth, describing a triangle between counter, skillet, and table. Her cotton stockings were rolled at the knee, and above them and the flapping hem of her dress varicose veins bunched in clocksprings.

The apartment was haunted by the ghost of long-departed cabbage.

In the far bedroom, Cassie screamed, whooped, and was silent. Bradley had told Richards with a kind of angry shame that he should not mind her. She had cancer in both lungs and recently it had spread upward into her throat and down into her belly. She was five.

Stacey had gone back out somewhere.

As he and Bradley spoke together, the maddening aroma of simmering ground beef, vegetables, and tomato sauce began to fill the room, driving the cabbage back into the corners and making Richards realize how hungry he was.

"I could turn you in, man. I could kill you an steal all that money. Turn in the body. Get a thousand more bucks and be on easy street."

"I don't think you could do it," Richards said. "I know I couldn't."

"Why're you doing it, anyway?" Bradley asked irritably. "Why you being their sucker? You that greedy?"

"My little girl's name is Cathy," Richards said. "Younger than Cassie. Pneumonia. She cries all the time, too."

Bradley said nothing.

"She could get better. Not like . . . her in there. Pneumonia's no worse than a cold. But you have to have medicine and a doctor. That costs money. I went for the money the only way I could."

"You still a sucker," Bradley said with flat and somehow uncanny emphasis. "You suckin off half the world and they comin in your mouth every night at six-thirty. Your little girl would be better off like Cassie in this world."

"I don't believe that."

"Then you ballsier than me, man. I put a guy in the hospital once with a rupture. Some rich guy. Cops chased me three days. But you ballsier than me." He took a cigarette and lit it. "Maybe you'll go the whole month. A billion dollars. You'd have to buy a fuckin freight train to haul it off."

"Don't swear, praise Gawd," the old woman said from across the room where she was slicing carrots.

Bradley paid no attention. "You an your wife an little girl would be on easy street then. You got two days already."

"No," Richards said. "The game's rigged. You know those two things I gave Stacey to mail when he and your ma went out for groceries? I have to mail two of those every day before midnight." He explained to Bradley about the forfeit clause, and his suspicion that they had traced him to Boston by postmark.

"Easy to beat that."

"How?"

"Never mind. Later. How you gonna get out of Boston? You awful hot. Made 'em mad, blowin up their oinkers at the Y.M.C.A. They had Free-Vee on that tonight. An those ones you took with the bag over your head. That was pretty sharp. Ma!" he finished irritably, "when's that stuff gonna be ready? We're fallin away to shadows right before ya!"

"She comin on," Ma said. She plopped a cover over the rich, slowly bubbling mass and walked slowly into the bedroom to sit by the girl.

"I don't know," Richards said. "I'll try to get a car, I guess. I've got fake papers, but I don't dare use them. I'll do something—wear dark glasses—and get out of the city. I've been thinking about going to Vermont and then crossing over into Canada."

Bradley grunted and got up to put plates on the table. "By now they got every highway going out of Beantown blocked. A man wearin dark glasses calls tention to himself. They'll turn you into monkeymeat before you get six miles."

"Then I don't know," Richards said. "If I stay here, they'll get you for an accessory."

Bradley began spreading dishes. "Suppose we get a car. You got the squeezin green. I got a name that isn't hot. There's a spic on Milk Street that'll sell me a Wint for three hundred. I'll get one of my buddies to drive it up to Manchester. It'll be cool as a fool in Manchester because you're bottled up in Boston. You eatin, Ma?"

"Yes an praise Gawd." She waddled out of the bedroom. "Your sister is sleepin a little."

"Good." He ladled up three dishes of hamburger gumbo and then paused. "Where's Stacey?"

"Said he was goin to the drug," Ma said complacently, shoveling gumbo into her toothless maw at a blinding speed. "Said he goan to get medicine."

"If he gets busted, I'll break his ass," Bradley said, sitting heavily.

"He won't," Richards said. "He's got money."

"Yeah, maybe we don't need no charity money, graymeat."

Richards laughed and salted his meal. "I'd probably be slabbed now if it wasn't for him," he said. "I guess it was earned money."

Bradley leaned forward, concentrating on his plate. None of them said anything more until the meal was done. Richards and Bradley had two helpings; the old woman had three. As they were lighting cigarettes, a key scratched in the lock and all of them stiffened until Stacey came in, looking guilty, frightened, and excited. He was carrying a brown bag in one hand and he gave Ma a bottle of medicine.

"Thass prime dope," he said. "That ol man Curry ast me where I got two dollars and semney-fi cents to buy prime dope an I tole him to go shit in his boot and eat it."

"Doan swear or the devil will poke you," Ma said. "Here's dinner."

The boy's eyes widened. "Jesus, there's meat in it!"

"Naw, we jus shat in it to make it thicker," Bradley said. The boy looked up sharply, saw his brother was joking, giggled, and fell to.

"Will that druggist go to the cops?" Richards asked quietly.

"Curry? Naw. Not if there might be some more squeezin green in this fambly. He knows Cassie's got to have heavy dope."

"What about this Manchester thing?"

"Yeah. Well, Vermont's no good. Not enough of our kind of people. Tough cops. I get some good fella like Rich Goleon to drive that Wint to Manchester and park it in an automatic garage. Then I drive you up in another car." He crushed out his cigarette. "In the trunk. They're only using Jiffy Sniffers on the back road. We'll go right up 495."

"Pretty dangerous for you," Richards said.

"Oh, I wasn't gonna do it free. When Cassie goes, she's gonna go out wrecked."

"Praise Gawd," Ma said.

"Still pretty dangerous for you."

"Any pig grunts at Bradley, he make 'em shit in their boot an eat it," Stacey said, wiping his mouth. When he looked at Bradley, his eyes glittered with the flat shine of hero worship.

"You're dribblin on your shirt, Skinner," Bradley said. He knuckled Stacey's head. "You beatin your meat yet, Skinner? Ain't big enough, are ya?"

"If they catch us, you'll go in for the long bomb," Richards said. "Who's going to take care of the boy?"

"He'll take care of himself if something happens," Bradley said. "Himself and Ma here. He's not hooked on nothin. Are you Stace?"

Stacey shook his head emphatically.

"An he knows if I find any pricks in his arms I'll beat his brains out. Ain't that right, Stacey?"

Stacey nodded.

"Besides, we can use the money. This is a hurtin family. So don't say no more about it. I guess I know what I'm doin."

Richards finished his cigarette in silence while Bradley went in to give Cassie some medicine.

. . . Minus 063
and COUNTING . . .

When he awoke, it was still dark and the inner tide of his body put the time at about four-thirty. The girl, Cassie, had been screaming, and Bradley got up. The three of them were sleeping in the small, drafty back bedroom, Stacey and Richards on the floor. Ma slept with the girl.

Over the steady wheeze of Stacey's deep-sleep respiration, Richards heard Bradley come out of the room. There was a clink of a spoon in the sink. The girl's screams became isolated moans which trailed into silence. Richards could sense Bradley standing somewhere in the kitchen, immobile, waiting for the silence to come. He returned, sat down, farted, and then the bedsprings shifted creakily as he lay down.

"Bradley?"

"What?"

"Stacey said she was only five. Is that so?"

"Yes." The urban dialectic was gone from his voice, making him sound unreal and dreamlike.

"What's a five-year-old kid doing with lung cancer? I didn't know they got it. Leukemia, maybe. Not lung cancer."

There was a bitter, whispered chuckle from the bed. "You're from Harding, right? What's the air-pollution count in Harding?"

"I don't know," Richards said. "They don't give them with the weather anymore. They haven't for . . . gee, I don't know. A long time."

"Not since 2020 in Boston," Bradley whispered back. "They're scared to. You ain't got a nose filter, do you?"

"Don't be stupid," Richards said irritably. "The goddam things cost two hundred bucks, even in the cut-rate stores. I didn't see two hundred bucks all last year. Did you?"

"No," Bradley said softly. He paused. "Stacey's got one. I made it. Ma and Rich Goleon an some other people got em, too."

"You're shitting me," Richards said.

"No, man." He stopped. Richards was suddenly sure that Bradley was weighing what he had said already against a great many more things which he might say. Wondering how much was too much. When the words came again, they came with difficulty. "We've been reading. That Free-Vee shit is for empty-heads."

Richards grunted agreement.

"The gang, you know. Some of the guys are just cruisers, you know? All they're interested in is honky-stomping on Saturday night. But some of us have been going down to the library since we were twelve or so."

"They let you in without a card in Boston?"

"No. You can't get a card unless there's someone with a guaranteed income of five thousand dollars a year in your family. We got some plump-ass kid an kifed his card. We take turns going. We got a gang suit we wear when we go." Bradley paused. "You laugh at me and I'll cut you, man."

"I'm not laughing."

"At first we only read sexbooks. Then when Cassie first started getting sick, I got into this pollution stuff. They've got all the books on impurity counts and smog levels and nose filters in the reserve section. We got a key made from a wax blank. Man, did you know that everybody in Tokyo had to wear a nose filter by 2012?"

"No."

"Rich and Dink Moran built a pollution counter. Dink drew the picture out of the book, and they did it from coffee cans and some stuff they boosted out of cars. It's hid out in an alley. Back in 1978 they had an air pollution scale that went from one to twenty. You understand?"

"Yes."

"When it got up to twelve, the factories and all the pollution-producing shit had to shut down till the weather changed. It was a federal law until 1987, when the Revised Congress rolled it back.'' The shadow on the bed rose up on its elbow. ''I bet you know a lot of people with asthma, that right?''

''Sure,'' Richards said cautiously. ''I've got a touch myself. You get *that* from the air. Christ, everybody knows you stay in the house when it's hot and cloudy and the air doesn't move—''

''Temperature inversion,'' Bradley said grimly.

''—and lots of people get asthma, sure. The air gets like cough syrup in August and September. But lung cancer—''

''You ain't talkin about asthma,'' Bradley said. ''You talkin bout emphysema.''

''Emphysema?'' Richards turned the word over in his mind. He could not assign a meaning to it, although the word was faintly familiar.

''All the tissues in your lungs swell up. You heave an heave an heave, but you're still out of breath. You know a lot of people who get like that?''

Richards thought. He did. He knew a lot of people who had died like that.

''They don't talk about that one,'' Bradley said, as if he had read Richards's thought. ''Now the pollution count in Boston is twenty on a good day. That's like smoking four packs of cigarettes a day just breathing. On a bad day it gets up as high as forty-two. Old dudes drop dead all over town. Asthma goes on the death certificate. But it's the air, the air, the air. And they're pouring it out just as fast as they can, big smokestacks going twenty-four hours a day. The big boys like it that way.

''Those two-hundred-dollar nose filters aren't worth shit. They're just two pieces of screen with a little piece of metholated cotton between them. That's all. The only good ones are from General Atomics. The only ones who can afford them are the big boys. They gave us the Free-Vee to keep us off the streets so we can breathe ourselves to death without making any trouble. How do you like that? The cheapest G-A nose filter on the market goes for six thousand New Dollars. We made one for Stacey for ten bucks from that book. We used an atomic nugget the size of the moon on your fingernail. Got it out of a hearing aid we bought in a hockshop for seven bucks. How do you like that?''

Richards said nothing. He was speechless.

''When Cassie boots off, you think they'll put cancer on the death certificate? Shit they'll put asthma. Else somebody might get scared. Somebody might kife a library card and find out lung cancer is up seven hundred percent since 2015.''

''Is that true? Or are you making it up?''

''I read it in a book. Man, they're killing us. The Free-Vee is killing us. It's like a magician getting you to watch the cakes falling outta his helper's blouse while he pulls rabbits out of his pants and puts 'em in his hat.'' He paused and then said dreamily: ''Sometimes I think that I could blow the whole thing outta the water with ten minutes talk-time on the Free-Vee. Tell em. Show em. Everybody could have a nose filter if the Network wanted em to have em.''

''And I'm helping them,'' Richards said.

"That ain't your fault. You got to run."

Killian's face, and the face of Arthur M. Burns rose up in front of Richards. He wanted to smash them, stomp them, walk on them. Better still, rip out their nose filters and turn them into the street.

"People's mad," Bradley said. "They've been mad at the honkies for thirty years. All they need is a reason. A reason . . . one reason . . ."

Richards drifted off to sleep with the repetition in his ears.

. . . Minus 062
and COUNTING . . .

Richards stayed in all day while Bradley was out seeing about the car and arranging with another member of the gang to drive it to Manchester.

Bradley and Stacey came back at six, and Bradley thumbed on the Free-Vee. "All set, man. We go tonight."

"Now?"

Bradley smiled humorlessly. "Don't you want to see yourself coast-to-coast?"

Richards discovered he did, and when *The Running Man* lead-in came on, he watched, fascinated.

Bobby Thompson stared deadpan at the camera from the middle of a brilliant post in a sea of darkness. "Watch," he said. "This is one of the wolves that walks among you."

A huge blowup of Richards's face appeared on the screen. It held for a moment, then dissolved to a second photo of Richards, this time in the John Griffen Springer disguise.

Dissolve back to Thompson, looking grave. "I speak particularly to the people of Boston tonight. Yesterday afternoon, five policemen went to a blazing, agonized death in the basement of the Boston Y.M.C.A. at the hands of this wolf, who had set a clever, merciless trap. Who is he tonight? *Where* is he tonight? Look! Look at him!"

Thompson faded into the first of the two clips which Richards had filmed that morning. Stacey had dropped them in a mailbox on Commonwealth Avenue, across the city. He had let Ma hold the camera in the back bedroom, after he had draped the window and all the furniture.

"All of you watching this," Richards's image said slowly. "Not the technicos, not the people in the penthouses—I don't mean you shits. You people in the Developments and the ghettos and the cheap highrises. You people in the cycle gangs. You people without jobs. You kids getting busted for dope you don't have and crimes you didn't commit because the Network wants to make sure you aren't meeting together and talking together. I want to tell you about a monstrous conspiracy to deprive you of the very breath in y—''

The audio suddenly became a mixture of squeaks, pops, and gargles. A moment later it died altogether. Richards's mouth was moving, but no sound was coming out.

"We seem to have lost our audio," Bobby Thompson's voice came smoothly, "but we don't need to listen to any more of this murderer's radical ravings to understand what we're dealing with, do we?"

"No!" The audience screamed.

"What will you do if you see him on *your* street?"

"TURN HIM IN!"

"And what are we going to do when we find him?"

"KILL HIM!"

Richards pounded his fist against the tired arm of the only easy chair in the apartment's kitchen-living room. "Those bastards," he said helplessly.

"Did you think they'd let you go on the air with it?" Bradley asked mockingly. "Oh no, man. I'm s'prised they let you get away with as much as they did."

"I didn't think," Richards said sickly.

"No, I guess you didn't," Bradley said.

The first clip faded into the second. In this one, Richards had asked the people watching to storm the libraries, demand cards, find out the truth. He had read off a list of books dealing with air pollution and water pollution that Bradley had given him.

Richards's image opened its mouth. "Fuck every one of you," his image said. The lips seemed to be moving around different words, but how many of the two hundred million people watching were going to notice that? "Fuck all pigs. Fuck the Games Commission. I'm gonna kill every pig I see. I'm gonna—" There was more, enough so that Richards wanted to plug his ears and run out of the room. He couldn't tell if it was the voice of a mimic, or a harangue made up of spliced bits of audio tape.

The clip faded to a split-screen of Thompson's face and the still photo of Richards. "Behold the man," Thompson said. "The man who would kill. The man who would mobilize an army of malcontents like himself to run riot through your streets, raping and burning and overturning. The man would lie, cheat, kill. He has done all these things.

"Benjamin Richards!" The voice cried out with a cold, commanding Old Testament anger. "Are you watching? If so, you have been paid your dirty blood money. A hundred dollars for each hour—now number fifty-four—that you have remained free. And an extra five hundred dollars. One hundred for each of these five men."

The faces of young, clear-featured policemen began appearing on the screen. The still had apparently been taken at a Police Academy graduation exercise. They looked fresh, full of sap and hope, heart-breakingly vulnerable. Softly, a single trumpet began to play Taps.

"And these . . ." Thompson's voice was now low and hoarse with emotion, " . . . these were their families."

Wives, hopefully smiling. Children that had been coaxed to smile into the camera. A lot of children. Richards, cold and sick and nauseated, lowered his head and pressed the back of his hand over his mouth.

Bradley's hand, warm and muscular, pressed his neck. "Hey, no. No, man. That's put on. That's all fake. They were probably a bunch of old harness bulls who—"

"Shut up," Richards said. "Oh shut up. Just. Please. Shut up."

"Five hundred dollars," Thompson was saying, and infinite hate and contempt filled his voice. Richards's face on the screen again, cold, hard, devoid of all emotion save an expression of bloodlust that seemed chiefly to be in the eyes. "Five police, five wives, nineteen children. It comes to just about seventeen dollars and twenty-five cents for each of the dead, the bereaved, the heartbroken. Oh yes, you work cheap, Ben Richards. Even Judas got thirty pieces of silver, but you don't even demand that. Somewhere, even now, a mother is telling her little boy that daddy won't be home ever again because a desperate, greedy man with a gun—"

"Killer!" A woman was sobbing. "Vile, dirty murderer! God will strike you dead!"

"Strike him dead!" The audience over the chant: "Behold the man! He has been paid his blood money—but the man who lives by violence shall die by it. And let every man's hand be raised against Benjamin Richards!"

Hate and fear in every voice, rising in a steady, throbbing roar. No, they wouldn't turn him in. They would rip him to shreds on sight.

Bradley turned off the screen and faced him. "Thass what you're dealing with, man. How about it."

"Maybe I'll kill them," Richards said in a thoughtful voice. "Maybe, before I'm done, I'll get up to the ninetieth floor of that place and just hunt up the maggots who wrote that. Maybe I'll just kill them all."

"Don't talk no more!" Stacey burst out wildly. "Don't talk no more about it!"

In the other room, Cassie slept her drugged, dying sleep.

. . . Minus 061
and COUNTING . . .

Bradley had not dared drill any holes in the floor of the trunk, so Richards curled in a miserable ball with his mouth and nose pressed toward the tiny notch of light which was the trunk's keyhole. Bradley had also pulled out some of the inner trunk insulation around the lid, and that let in a small draft.

The car lifted with a jerk, and he knocked his head against the upper deck. Bradley had told him the ride would be at least an hour and a half, with two stops for roadblocks, perhaps more. Before he closed the trunk, he gave Richards a large revolver.

"Every tenth or twelfth car, they give it a heavy looking over," he said. "They open the trunk to poke around. Those are good odds, eleven to one. If it don't come up, plug you some pork."

The car lurched and heaved over the potholed, cracked-crazed streets of the inner city. Once a kid jeered and there was the thump of a thrown piece of paving. Then the sounds of increasing traffic all around them and more frequent stops for lights.

Richards lay passively, holding the pistol lightly in his right hand, thinking how different Bradley had looked in the gang suit. It was a sober Dillon Street double-breasted, as gray as bank walls. It was rounded off with a maroon tie and a small gold N.A.A.C.P. pin. Bradley had made the leap from scruffy gang-member (pregnant ladies stay away; some of us'ns eat fetuses) to a sober black business fellow who would know exactly who to Tom.

"You look good," Richards said admiringly. "In fact, it's damn incredible."

"Praise Gawd," Ma said.

"I thought you'd enjoy the transformation, my good man," Bradley said with quiet dignity. "I'm the district manager for Raygon Chemicals, you know. We do a thriving business in this area. Fine city, Boston. Immensely convivial."

Stacey burst into giggles.

"You best shut up, nigger," Bradley said. "Else I make you shit in yo boot an eat it."

"You Tom so good, Bradley," Stacey giggled, not intimidated in the least. "You really fuckin funky."

Now the car swung right, onto a smoother surface, and descended in a spiraling arc. They were on an entrance ramp. Going onto 495 or a feeder expressway. Copper wires of tension were stuffed into his legs.

One in eleven. That's not bad odds.

The car picked up speed and height, kicked into drive, then slowed abruptly and kicked out. A voice, terrifyingly close, yelling with monotonous regularity: "Pull over . . . have your license and registration ready . . . pull over . . . have your—"

Already. Starting already.

You so hot, man.

Hot enough to check the trunk on one car in eight? Or six? Or maybe every one?

The car came to a full stop. Richards's eyes moved like trapped rabbits in their sockets. He gripped the revolver.

. . . Minus 060
and COUNTING . . .

"Step out your vehicle, sir," the bored, authoritative voice was saying. "License and registration, please."

A door opened and closed. The engine thrummed softly, holding the car an inch off the paving.

"—district manager for Raygon Chemicals—"

Bradley going into his song and dance. Dear God, what if he didn't have the papers to back it up? What if there was no Raygon Chemicals?

The back door opened, and someone began rummaging in the back seat. It sounded as if the cop (or was it the Government Guard that did this, Richards wondered half coherently) was about to crawl right into the trunk with him.

The door slammed. Feet walked around to the back of the car. Richards licked his lips and held the gun tighter. Visions of dead policemen gibbered before him, angelic faces on twisted, porcine bodies. He wondered if the cop would hose him with machine-gun bullets when he opened the trunk and saw Richards lying here like a curled-up salamander. He wondered if Bradley would take off, try to run. He was going to piss himself. He hadn't done that since he was a kid and his brother would tickle him until his bladder let go. Yes, all those muscles down there were loosening. He would put the bullet right at the juncture of the cop's nose and forehead, splattering brains and splintered skull-fragments in startled streamers to the sky. Make a few more orphans. Yes. Good. Jesus loves me, this I know, for my bladder tells me so. Christ Jesus, what's he doing, ripping the seat out? Sheila, I love you so much and how far will six grand take you? A year, maybe, if they don't kill you for it. Then on the street again, up and down, cross on the corner, swinging the hips, flirting with the empty pocketbook. Hey mister, I go down, this is clean kitty, kid, teach you how—

A hand whacked the top of the trunk casually in passing. Richards bit back a scream. Dust in his nostrils, throat tickling. High school biology, sitting in the back row, scratching his initials and Sheila's on the ancient desk-top: *The sneeze is a function of the involuntary muscles.* I'm going to sneeze my goddam head off but it's pointblank and I can still put that bullet right through his squash and—

"What's in the trunk, mister?"

Bradley's voice, jocular, a little bored: "A spare cylinder that doesn't work half right. I got the key on my ring. Wait, I'll get it."

"If I wanted it, I'd ask."

Other back door opened; closed.

"Drive on."

"Hang tight, fella. Hope you get him."

"Drive on, mister. Move your ass."

The cylinders cranked up. The car lifted and accelerated. It slowed once and must have been waved on. Richards jolted a little as the car rose, sailed a little, and kicked into drive. His breath came in tired little moans. He didn't have to sneeze any more.

. . . Minus 059
and COUNTING . . .

The ride seemed much longer than an hour and a half, and they were stopped twice more. One of them seemed to be a routine license check. At the next one a drawling cop with a dull-witted voice talked to Bradley for some time about how the goddam commie bikers were helping that guy Richards and probably the other one, too. Laughlin had not killed anyone, but it was rumored that he had raped a woman in Topeka.

After that there was nothing but the monotonous whine of the wind and the scream of his own cramped and frozen muscles. Richards did not sleep, but his punished mind did finally push him into a dazed semiconsciousness. There was no carbon monoxide with the air cars, thank God for that.

Centuries after the last roadblock, the car kicked into a lower gear and banked up a spiraling exit ramp. Richards blinked sluggishly and wondered if he was going to throw up. For the first time in his life he felt carsick.

They went through a sickening series of loops and dives that Richards supposed was a traffic interchange. Another five minutes and city sounds took over again. Richards tried repeatedly to shift his body into a new position, but it was impossible. He finally subsided, waiting numbly for it to be over. His right arm, which was curled under him, had gone to sleep an hour ago. Now it felt like a block of wood. He could touch it with the tip of his nose and feel only the pressure on his nose.

They took a right, went straight for a little, then turned again. The bottom dropped out of Richards's stomach as the car dipped down a sharp incline. The echoing of the cylinders told him that they were inside. They had gotten to the garage.

A little helpless sound of relief escaped him.

"Got your check, buddy?" A voice asked.

"Right here, pal."

"Rampway 5."

"Thanks."

They bore right. The car went up, paused, turned right again, then left. They settled into idle, then the car dropped with a soft bump as the engine died. Journey's end.

There was a pause, then the hollow sound of Bradley's door opening and closing. His footsteps clicked toward the trunk, then the chink of light in front of Richards's eyes disappeared as the key slid home.

"You there, Bennie?"

"No," he croaked. "You left me back at the state line. Open this goddam thing."

"Just a second. Place is empty right now. Your car's parked next to us. On the right. Can you get out quick?"

"I don't know."

"Try hard. Here we go."

The trunk lid popped up, letting in dim garage light. Richards got up on one arm, got one leg over the edge, and could go no farther. His cramped body screamed. Bradley took one arm and hauled him out. His legs wanted to buckle. Bradley hooked him under the armpit and half led, half pushed him to the battered green Wint on the right. He propped open the driver's side door, shoved Richards in, and slammed it shut. A moment later Bradley also slid in.

"Jesus," he said softly. "We got here, man. We got here."

"Yeah," Richards said. "Back to Go. Collect two hundred dollars."

They smoked in the shadows, their cigarettes gleaming like eyes. For a little while, neither of them said anything.

. . . Minus 058
and COUNTING . . .

"We almost got it at that first roadblock," Bradley was saying as Richards tried to massage feeling back into his arm. It felt as if phantom nails had been pushed into it. "That cop almost opened it. Almost." He blew out smoke in a huge huff. Richards said nothing.

"How do you feel?" Bradley asked presently.

"It's getting better. Take my wallet out for me. I can't make my arm work just right yet."

Bradley shooed the words away with one hand. "Later. I want to tell you how Rich and I set it up."

Richards lit another cigarette from the stub of the first. A dozen charley horses were loosening slowly.

"There's a hotel room reserved for you on Winthrop Street. The Winthrop House is the name of the place. Sounds fancy. It ain't. The name is Ogden Grassner. Can you remember that?"

"Yes. I'll be recognized immediately."

Bradley reached into the back seat, got a box and dropped it in Richards's lap. It was long, brown, tied with string. To Richards it looked like the kind of box that rented graduation gowns come in. He looked at Bradley questioningly.

"Open it."

He did. There was a pair of thick, blue-tinted glasses lying on top of a drift of black cloth. Richards put the glasses on the dashboard and took out the garment. It was a priest's robe. Beneath it, lying on the bottom of the box, was a rosary, a Bible, and a purple stole.

"A priest?" Richards asked.

"Right. You change right here. I'll help you. There's a cane in the back seat. Your act ain't blind, but it's pretty close. Bump into things. You're in Manchester to attend a Council of Churches meeting on drug abuse. Got it?"

"Yes," Richards said. He hesitated, fingers on the buttons of his shirt. "Do I wear my pants under this rig?"

Bradley burst out laughing.

. . . Minus 057 and COUNTING . . .

Bradley talked rapidly as he drove Richards across town.

"There's a box of gummed mailing labels in your suitcase," he said. "That's in the trunk. The stickers say: After five days return to Brickhill Manufacturing Company, Manchester, N.H. Rich and another guy ran em off. They got a press at the Stabbers' headquarters on Boylston Street. Every day you send your two tapes to me in a box with one of those stickers. I'll mail 'em to Games from Boston. Send the stuff Speed Delivery. That's one they'll never figure out."

The car cozied up to the curb in front of the Winthrop House. "This car will be back in the U-Park-It. Don't try to drive out of Manchester unless you change your disguise. You got to be a chameleon, man."

"How long do you think it will be safe here?" Richards asked. He thought: I've put myself in his hands. It didn't seem that he could think rationally for himself anymore. He could smell mental exhaustion on himself like body odor.

"Your reservation's for a week. That might be okay. It might not. Play it by ear. There's a name and an address in the suitcase. Fella in Portland, Maine.

They'll hide you for a day or two. It'll cost, but they're safe. I gotta go, man. This is a five-minute zone. Money time."

"How much?" Richards asked.

"Six hundred."

"Bullshit. That doesn't even cover expenses."

"Yes it does. With a few bucks left over for the family."

"Take a thousand."

"You need your dough, pal. Uh-uh."

Richards looked at him helplessly. "Christ, Bradley—"

"Send us more if you make it. Send us a million. Put us on easy street."

"Do you think I will?"

Bradley smiled a soft, sad smile and said nothing.

"Then why?" Richards asked flatly. "Why are you doing so much? I can understand you hiding me out. I'd do that. But you must have busted your club's arm."

"They didn't mind. They know the score."

"What score?"

"Ought to naught. That score. If we doan stick out our necks for our own, they got us. No need to wait for the air. We could just as well run a pipe from the stove to the livin room, turn on the Free-Vee and wait."

"Someone'll kill you," Richards said. "Someone will stool on you and you'll end up on a basement floor with your guts beat out. Or Stacey. Or Ma."

Bradley's eyes flashed dimly. "A bad day is comin, though. A bad day for the maggots with their guts full of roast beef. I see blood on the moon for them. Guns and torches. A mojo that walks and talks."

"People have been seeing those things for two thousand years."

The five-minute buzzer went off and Richards fumbled for the door handle. "Thank you," he said. "I don't know how to say it any other way—"

"Go on," Bradley said, "before I get a ticket." A strong brown hand clutched the robe. "An when they get you, take a few along."

Richards opened the rear door and popped the trunk to get the black satchel inside. Bradley handed him a cordovan-colored cane wordlessly.

The car pulled out into traffic smoothly. Richards stood on the curb for a moment, watching him go—watching him myopically, he hoped. The taillights flashed once at the corner, then the car swung out of sight, back to the parking lot where Bradley would leave it and pick up the other to go back to Boston.

Richards had a weird sensation of relief and realized that he was feeling empathy for Bradley—*how glad he must be to have me off his back, finally!*

Richards made himself miss the first step up to the Winthrop House's entrance, and the doorman assisted him.

. . . Minus 056
and COUNTING . . .

Two days passed.

Richards played his part well—that is to say, as if his life depended on it. He took dinner at the hotel both nights in his room. He rose at seven, read his Bible in the lobby, and then went out to his "meeting." The hotel staff treated him with easy, contemptuous cordiality—the kind reserved for half-blind, fumbling clerics (who paid their bills) in this day of limited legalized murder, germ warfare in Egypt and South America, and the notorious have-one-kill-one Nevada abortion law. The Pope was a muttering old man of ninety-six whose driveling edicts concerning such current events were reported as the closing humorous items on the seven o'clock newsies.

Richards held his one-man "meetings" in a rented library cubicle where, with the door locked, he was reading about pollution. There was very little information later than 2002, and what there was seemed to jell very badly with what had been written before. The government, as usual, was doing a tardy but efficient job of double thinking.

At noon he made his way down to a luncheonette on the corner of a street not far from the hotel, bumping into people and excusing himself as he went. Some people told him it was quite all right, Father. Most simply cursed in an uninterested way and pushed him aside.

He spent the afternoons in his room and ate dinner watching *The Running Man*. He had mailed four filmclips while enroute to the library during the mornings. The forwarding from Boston seemed to be going smoothly.

The producers of the program had adopted a new tactic for killing Richards's pollution message (he persisted with it in a kind of grinning frenzy—he had to be getting through to the lip-readers anyway): now the crowd drowned out the voice with a rising storm of jeers, screams, obscenities, and vituperation. Their sound grew increasingly more frenzied; ugly to the point of dementia.

In his long afternoons, Richards reflected that an unwilling change had come over him during his five days on the run. Bradley had done it—Bradley and the little girl. There was no longer just himself, a lone man fighting for his family, bound to be cut down. Now there were all of them out there, strangling on their own respiration—his family included.

He had never been a social man. He had shunned causes with contempt and disgust. They were for pig-simple suckers and people with too much time and money on their hands, like those half-assed college kids with their cute buttons and their neo-rock groups.

Richards's father had slunk into the night when Richards was five. Richards had been too young to remember him in anything but flashes. He had never hated him for it. He understood well enough how a man with a choice between pride and responsibility will almost always choose pride—if responsibility robs him of his manhood. A man can't stick around and watch his wife earning supper on her back. If a man can't do any more than pimp for the woman he married, Richards judged, he might as well walk out of a high window.

He had spent the years between five and sixteen hustling, he and his brother Todd. His mother had died of syphilis when he was ten and Todd was seven. Todd had been killed five years later when a newsie airtruck had lost its emergency brake on a hill while Todd was loading it. The city had fed both mother and son into the Municipal Crematorium. The kids on the street called it either the Ash Factory or the Creamery; they were bitter but helpless, knowing that they themselves would most likely end up being belched out of the stacks and into the city's air. At sixteen Richards was alone, working a full eight-hour shift as an engine wiper after school. And in spite of his back-breaking schedule, he had felt a constant panic that came from knowing he was alone and unknown, drifting free. He awoke sometimes at three in the morning to the rotted-cabbage smell of the one-room tenement flat with terror lodged in the deepest chamber of his soul. He was his own man.

And so he had married, and Sheila had spent the first year in proud silence while their friends (and Richards's enemies; he had made many by his refusal to go along on mass-vandalizing expeditions and join a local gang) waited for the Uterus Express to arrive. When it didn't, interest flagged. They were left in that particular limbo that was reserved for newlyweds in Co-Op City. Few friends and a circle of acquaintances that reached only as far as the stoop of their own building. Richards did not mind this; it suited him. He threw himself into his work wholly, with grinning intensity, getting overtime when he could. The wages were bad, there was no chance of advancement, and inflation was running wild—but they were in love. They remained in love, and why not? Richards was that kind of solitary man who can afford to expend gigantic charges of love, affection, and, perhaps, psychic domination on the woman of his choice. Up until that point his emotions had been almost entirely untouched. In the eleven years of their marriage, they had never argued significantly.

He quit his job in 2018 because the chances of ever having children decreased with every shift he spent behind the leaky G-A old-style lead shields. He might have been all right if he answered the foreman's aggrieved "Why are you quitting?" with a lie. But Richards had told him, simply and clearly, what he thought of General Atomics, concluding with an invitation to the foreman to take all his gamma shields and perform a reverse bowel movement with them. It ended in a short, savage scuffle. The foreman was brawny and looked tough, but Richards made him scream like a woman.

The blackball began to roll. He's dangerous. Steer clear. If you need a man bad, put him on for a week and then get rid of him. In G-A parlance, Richards had Shown Red.

During the next five years he had spent a lot of time rolling and loading newsies, but the work thinned to a trickle and then died. The Free-Vee killed the printed word very effectively. Richards pounded the pavement. Richards was moved along. Richards worked intermittently for day-labor outfits.

The great movements of the decade passed by him ignored, like ghosts to an unbeliever. He knew nothing of the Housewife Massacre in '24 until his wife told him about it three weeks later—two hundred police armed with tommy guns and high-powered move-alongs had turned back an army of women marching on the Southwest Food Depository. Sixty had been killed. He was vaguely aware that nerve gas was being used in the Mideast. But none of it affected him. Protest did not work. Violence did not work. The world was what it was, and Ben Richards moved through it like a thin scythe, asking for nothing, looking for work. He ferreted out a hundred miserable day and half-day jobs. He worked cleaning jellylike slime from under piers and in sump ditches when others on the street, who honestly believed they were looking for work, did nothing.

Move along, maggot. Get lost. No job. Get out. Put on your boogie shoes. I'll blow your effing head off, daddy. Move.

Then the jobs dried up. Impossible to find anything. A rich man in a silk singlet, drunk, accosted him on the street one evening as Richards shambled home after a fruitless day, and told him he would give Richards ten New Dollars if Richards would pull down his pants so he could see if the street freaks really did have peckers a foot long. Richards knocked him down and ran.

It was then, after nine years of trying, that Sheila conceived. He was a wiper, the people in the building said. Can you believe he was a wiper for six years and knocked her up? It'll be a monster, the people in the building said. It'll have two heads and no eyes. *Radiation, radiation, your children will be monsters—*

But instead, it was Cathy. Round, perfect, squalling. Delivered by a midwife from down the block who took fifty cents and four cans of beans.

And now, for the first time since his brother had died, he was drifting again. Every pressure (even, temporarily, the pressure of the chase) had been removed.

His mind and his anger turned toward the Games Federation, with their huge and potent communications link to the whole world. Fat people with nose filters, spending their evenings with dollies in silk underpants. Let the guillotine fall. And fall. And fall. Yet there was no way to get them. They towered above all of them dimly, like the Games Building itself.

Yet, because he was who he was, and because he was alone and changing, he thought about it. He was unaware, alone in his room, that while he thought about it he grinned a huge white-wolf grin that in itself seemed powerful enough to buckle streets and melt buildings. The same grin he had worn on that almost-forgotten day when he had knocked a rich man down and then fled with his pockets empty and his mind burning.

. . . Minus 055
and COUNTING . . .

Monday was exactly the same as Sunday—the working world took no one partic-ular day off anymore—until six-thirty.

Father Ogden Grassner had Meatloaf Supreme sent up (the hotel's cuisine, which would have seemed execrable to a man who had been weaned on anything better than fast-food hamburgers and concentrate pills, tasted great to Richards) with a bottle of Thunderbird wine and settled down to watch *The Running Man*. The first segment, dealing with Richards himself, went much as it had on the two nights previous. The audio on his clips was drowned out by the studio audience. Bobby Thompson was urbane and virulent. A house-to-house search was taking place in Boston. Anyone found harboring the fugitive would be put to death. Richards smiled without humor as they faded to a Network promo. It wasn't so bad; it was even funny, in a limited way. He could stand anything if they didn't broadcast the cops again.

The second half of the program was markedly different. Thompson was smiling broadly. "After the latest tapes sent to us by the monster that goes under the name of Ben Richards, I'm pleased to give you some good news—"

They had gotten Laughlin.

He had been spotted in Topeka on Friday, but an intensive search of the city on Saturday and Sunday had not turned him up. Richards had assumed that Laughlin had slipped through the cordon as he had himself. But this afternoon, Laughlin had been observed by two kids. He had been cowering in a Highway Department road shed. He had broken his right wrist at some point.

The kids, Bobby and Mary Cowles, were shown grinning broadly into the cam-era. Bobby Cowles had a tooth missing. *I wonder if the tooth fairy brought him a quarter*, Richards thought sickly.

Thompson announced proudly that Bobby and Mary, "Topeka's number one citizens," would be on *The Running Man* tomorrow night to be presented Certif-icates of Merit, a life-time supply of FunTwinks cereal, and checks for a thousand New Dollars each, by Hizzoner the Governor of Kansas. This brought wild cheers from the audience.

Following were tapes of Laughlin's riddled, sagging body being carried out of the shed, which had been reduced to matchwood by concentrated fire. There were mingled cheers, boos, and hisses from the studio audience.

Richards turned away sickly, nauseated. Thin, invisible fingers seemed to press against his temples.

From a distance, the words rolled on. The body was being displayed in the rotunda of the Kansas statehouse. Already long lines of citizens were filing past the body. An interviewed policeman who had been in at the kill said Laughlin hadn't put up much of a fight.

Ah, how nice for you, Richards thought, remembering Laughlin, his sour voice, the straight-ahead, jeering look in his eyes.

A friend of mine from the car pool.

Now there was only one big show. The big show was Ben Richards. He didn't want any more of his Meatloaf Supreme.

. . . Minus 054
and COUNTING . . .

He had a very bad dream that night, which was unusual. The old Ben Richards had never dreamed.

What was even more peculiar was the fact that he did not exist as a character in the dream. He only watched, invisible.

The room was vague, dimming off to blackness at the edges of vision. It seemed that water was dripping dankly. Richards had an impression of being deep underground.

In the center of the room, Bradley was sitting in a straight wooden chair with leather straps over his arms and legs. His head had been shaved like that of a penitent. Surrounding him were figures in black hoods. The Hunters, Richards thought with budding dread. Oh dear God, these are the Hunters.

"I ain't the man," Bradley said.

"Yes you are, little brother," one of the hooded figures said gently, and pushed a pin through Bradley's cheek. Bradley screamed.

"Are you the man?"

"Suck it."

A pin slid easily into Bradley's eyeball and was withdrawn dribbling colorless fluid. Bradley's eye took on a punched, flattened look.

"Are you the man?"

"Poke it up your ass."

An electric move-along touched Bradley's neck. He screamed again, and his hair stood on end. He looked like a comical caricature black, a futuristic Stepinfetchit.

"Are you the man, little brother?"

"Nose filters give you cancer," Bradley said. "You're all rotted inside, hon-kies."

His other eyeball was pierced. "Are you the man?"

Bradley, blind, laughed at them.

One of the hooded figures gestured, and from the shadows Bobby and Mary Cowles came tripping gaily. They began to skip around Bradley, singing: " 'Who's afraid of the big bad wolf, the big bad wolf, the big bad wolf?' '

Bradley began to scream and twist in the chair. He seemed to be trying to hold his hands up in a warding-off gesture. The song grew louder and louder, more echoing. The children were changing. Their heads were elongating, growing dark ith blood. Their mouths were open and in the caves within, fangs twinkled like razor-blades.

"I'll tell!" Bradley screamed. "I'll tell! I'll tell! I ain't the man! Ben Richards is the man! I'll tell! God . . . oh . . . G-G-God . . . "

"Where is the man, little brother?"

"I'll tell! I'll tell! He's in—"

But the words were drowned by the singing voices. They were lunging toward Bradley's straining, corded neck when Richards woke up, sweating.

. . . Minus 053
and COUNTING . . .

It was no good in Manchester anymore.

He didn't know if it was the news of Laughlin's brutal midwestern end, or the dream, or only a premonition.

But on Tuesday morning he stayed in, not going to the library. It seemed to him that every minute he stayed in this place was an invitation to quick doom. Looking out the window, he saw a Hunter with a black hood inside every old beaner and slumped taxi driver. Fantasies of gunmen creeping soundlessly up the hall toward his door tormented him. He felt a huge clock was ticking in his head.

He passed the point of indecision shortly after eleven o'clock on Tuesday morning. It was impossible to stay. He knew they knew.

He got his cane and tapped clumsily to the elevators and went down to the lobby.

"Going out, Father Grassner?" The day clerk asked with his usual pleasant, contemptuous smile.

"Day off," Richards said, speaking at the day clerk's shoulder. "Is there a picture show in this town?"

He knew there were at least ten, eight of them showing 3-D perverto shows.

"Well," the clerk said cautiously, "there's the Center. I think they show Disneys—"

"That will be fine," Richards said briskly, and bumped into a potted plant on his way out.

Two blocks from the hotel he went into a drugstore and bought a huge roll of bandage and a pair of cheap aluminum crutches. The clerk put his purchases in a long fiberboard box, and Richards caught a taxi on the next corner.

The car was exactly where it had been, and if there was a stakeout at the U-Park-It, Richards could not spot it. He got in and started up. He had a bad moment when he realized he lacked a driver's license in any name that wasn't hot, and then dismissed it. He didn't think his new disguise would get him past close scrutiny anyway. If there were roadblocks, he would try to crash them. It would get him killed, but he was going to get killed anyway if they tabbed him.

He tossed the Ogden Grassner glasses in the glove box and drove out, waving noncommittally at the boy on duty at the gate. The boy barely looked up from the skin magazine he was reading.

He stopped for a full compressed-air charge on the high-speed urban sprawl on the northern outskirts of the city. The air jockey was in the midst of a volcanic eruption of acne, and seemed pathetically anxious to avoid looking at Richards. So far, so good.

He switched from 91 to Route 17, and from there to a blacktop road with no name or number. Three miles farther along he pulled onto a rutted dirt turnaround and killed the engine.

Tilting the rearview mirror to the right angle, he wrapped the bandage around his skull as quickly as he could, holding the end and clipping it. A bird twitted restlessly in a tired-looking elm.

Not too bad. If he got breathing time in Portland, he could add a neck brace.

He put the crutches beside him on the seat and started the car. Forty minutes later he was entering the traffic circle at Portsmouth. Headed up Route 95, he reached into his pocket and pulled out the crumpled piece of ruled paper that Bradley had left him. He had written on it in the careful script of the self-educated, using a soft lead pencil:

> 94 State Street, Portland
> THE BLUE DOOR, GUESTS
> Elton Parrakis (& Virginia Parrakis)

Richards frowned at it a moment, then glanced up. A black-and-yellow police unit was cruising slowly above the traffic on the turnpike, in tandem with a heavy ground-unit below. They bracketed him for a moment and then were gone, zig-zagging across the six lanes in a graceful ballet. Routine traffic patrol.

As the miles passed, a queasy, almost reluctant sense of relief formed in his chest. It made him feel like laughing and throwing up at the same time.

. . . Minus 052
and COUNTING . . .

The drive to Portland was without incident.

But by the time he reached the edge of the city, driving through the built-up suburbs of Scarborough (rich homes, rich streets, rich private schools surrounded by electrified fences), the sense of relief had begun to fade again. They could be anywhere. They could be all around him. Or they could be nowhere.

State Street was an area of blasted, ancient brownstones not far from an over-grown, junglelike park—a hangout, Richards thought, for this small city's mug-gers, lovers, hypes, and thieves. No one would venture out on State Street after dark without a police dog on a leash, or a score of fellow gang-members.

Number 94 was a crumbling, soot-encrusted building with ancient green shades pulled down over its windows. To Richards the house looked like a very old man who had died with cataracts on his eyes.

He pulled to the curb and got out. The street was dotted with abandoned air cars, some of them rusted down to almost formless hulks. On the edge of the park, a Studebaker lay on its side like a dead dog. This was not police country, obviously. If you left your car unattended, it would gain a clot of leaning, spitting, slate-eyed boys in fifteen minutes. In half an hour some of the leaning boys would have pro-duced crowbars and wrenches and screwdrivers. They would tap them, compare them, twirl them, have mock swordfights with them. They would hold them up into the air thoughtfully, as if testing the weather or receiving mysterious radio transmission through them. In an hour the car would be a stripped carcass, from aircaps and cylinders to the steering wheel itself.

A small boy ran up to Richards as he was setting his crutches under himself. Puckered, shiny burn scars had turned one side of the boy's face into a hairless Frankenstein horror.

"Scag, mister? Good stuff. Put you on the moon." He giggled secretly, the lumped and knobbed flesh of his burnt face bobbing and writhing grotesquely.

"Fuck off," Richards said briefly.

The boy tried to kick one of his crutches out from under him, and Richards swung one of them in a low arc, swatting the boy's bottom. He ran off, cursing.

He made his way up the pitted stone steps slowly and looked at the door. It had once been blue, but now the paint had faded and peeled to a tired desert sky color. There had once been a doorbell, but some vandal had taken care of that with a cold chisel.

Richards knocked and waited. Nothing. He knocked again.

It was late afternoon now, and cold was creeping slowly up the street. Faintly, from the park beyond the end of the block, came the bitter clacking of October branches losing their leaves.

There was no one here. It was time to go.

Yet he knocked again, curiously convinced that there *was* someone in there.

And this time he was rewarded with the slow shuffling of house slippers. A pause at the door. Then: "Who's out there? I don't buy nothin. Go away."

"I was told to visit you," Richards said.

A peephole swung open with a minute squeak and a brown eye peeked through. Then the peephole closed with a snap.

"I don't know you," Flat dismissal.

"I was told to ask for Elton Parrakis."

Grudgingly: "Oh. You're one of those—"

Behind the door locks began to turn, bolts began to be unbolted, one by one. Chains dropped. There was the click of revolving tumblers in one Yale lock and then another. The *chunk-slap* of the heavy-duty TrapBolt being withdrawn.

The door swung open and Richards looked at a scrawny woman with no breasts and huge, knotted hands. Her face was unlined, almost cherubic, but it looked as if it had taken hundreds of invisible hooks and jabs and uppercuts in a no-holds-barred brawl with time itself. Perhaps time was winning, but she was not an easy bleeder. She was almost six feet tall, even in her flat, splayed slippers, and her knees were swollen into treestumps with arthritis. Her hair was wrapped in a bath turban. Her brown eyes, staring at him from under a deep ledge of brow (the eyebrows themselves clung to the precipice like desperate mountain bushes, struggling against the aridity and the altitude), were intelligent and wild with what might have been fear or fury. Later he understood she was simply muddled, afraid, tottering on the edge of insanity.

"I'm Virginia Parrakis," she said flatly. "I'm Elton's mother. Come in."

. . . Minus 051
and COUNTING . . .

She did not recognize him until she had led him into the kitchen to brew tea.

The house was old and crumbling and dark, furnished in a decor he recognized immediately from his own environment: Modern junkshop.

"Elton isn't here now," she said, brooding over the battered aluminum teapot on the gas ring. The light was stronger here, revealing the brown waterstains that blotched the wallpaper, the dead flies, souvenirs of summer past, on the windowsills, the old linoleum creased with black lines, the pile of wet wrapping paper under the leaking drain pipe. There was an odor of disinfectant that made Richards think of last nights in sickrooms.

She crossed the room, and her swollen fingers made a painful search through the heaped junk on the countertop until they found two tea bags, one of them previously used. Richards got the used one. He was not surprised.

"He works," she said, faintly accentuating the first word and making the statement an accusation. "You're from that fellow in Boston, the one Eltie writes to about pollution, aintcha?"

"Yes, Mrs. Parrakis."

"They met in Boston. My Elton services automatic vending machines." She preened for a moment and then began her slow trek back across the dunes of linoleum to the stove. "I told Eltie that what that Bradley was doing was against the law. I told him it would mean prison or even worse. He doesn't listen to *me*. Not to his old mom, he doesn't." She smiled with dark sweetness at this calumny. "Elton was always building things, you know. . . . He built a treehouse with four rooms out back when he was a boy. That was before they cut the elm down, you know. But it was that darky's idea that he should build a pollution station in Portland."

She popped the bags into cups and stood with her back to Richards, slowly warming her hands over the gas ring. "They write each other. I told him the mails aren't safe. You'll go to prison or even worse, I said. He said but Mom, we do it in code. He asks for a dozen apples, I tell him my uncle is a little worse. I said: Eltie, do you think they can't figure that Secret Spy stuff out? He doesn't listen. Oh, he used to. I used to be his best friend. But things have changed. Since he got to pooberty, things have changed. Dirty magazines under his bed and all *that* business. Now this darky. I suppose they caught you testing smogs or carcinogens or something and now you're on the run."

"I—"

"It don't matter!" She said fiercely at the window. It looked out on a backyard filled with rusting pieces of junk and tire rims and some little boy's sandbox that now, many years later, was filled with scruffy October woods.

"It don't matter!" she repeated. "It's the darkies." She turned to Richards and her eyes were hooded and furious and bewildered. "I'm sixty-five, but I was only a fresh young girl of nineteen when it began to happen. It was nineteen seventy-nine and the darkies were everywhere! Everywhere! Yes they were!" she nearly screamed, as if Richards had taken issue with her. "Everywhere! They sent those darkies to school with the whites. They set em high in the government. Radicals, rabble-rousing, and rebellion. I ain't so—"

She broke off as if the words had been splintered from her mouth. She stared at Richards, seeing him for the first time.

"OhGodhavemercy," she whispered.

"Mrs. Parrakis—"

"Nope!" she said in a fear-hoarsened voice. "Nope! Nope! Oh, nope!" She began advancing on him, pausing at the counter to pick up a long, gleaming butcher knife out of the general clutter. "Out! Out! Out!" He got up and began to back away slowly, first through the short hall between the kitchen and shadowy living room, then through the living room itself.

He noticed that an ancient pay telephone hung on the wall from the days when this had been a bona fide inn. The Blue Door, Guests. When was that? Richards wondered Twenty years ago? Forty? Before the darkies had gotten out of hand, or after?

He was just beginning to back down the hall between the living room and the front door when a key rattled in the lock. They both froze as if some celestial hand had stopped the film while deciding what to do next.

The door opened, and Elton Parrakis walked in. He was immensely fat, and his lackluster blond hair was combed back in preposterous waves from his forehead to show a round baby face that held an element of perpetual puzzlement. He was wearing the blue and gold uniform of the Vendo-Spendo Company. He looked thoughtfully at Virginia Parrakis.

"Put that knife down, Mom."

"Nope!" she cried, but already the crumbling of defeat had begun to putty her face.

Parrakis closed the door and began walking toward her. He jiggled.

She shrank away. "You have to make him go, son. He's that badman. That Richards. It'll mean prison or worse. *I don't want you to go!*" She began to wail, dropped the knife, and collapsed into his arms.

He enfolded her and began to rock her gently as she wept. "I'm not going to jail," he said. "Come on, Mom, don't cry. Please don't cry." He smiled at Richards over one of her hunched and shaking shoulders, an embarrassed awfully-sorry-about-this smile. Richards waited.

"Now," Parrakis said, when the sobs had died to sniffles. "Mr. Richards is Bradley Throckmorton's good friend, and he is going to be with us for a couple of days, Mom."

She began to shriek, and he clapped a hand over her mouth, wincing as he did so.

"Yes, Mom. Yes he is. I'm going to drive his car into the park and wire it. And you'll go out tomorrow morning with a package to mail to Cleveland."

"Boston," Richards said automatically. "The tapes go to Boston."

"They go to Cleveland now," Elton Parrakis said, with a patient smile. "Bradley's on the run."

"Oh. Jesus."

"You'll be on the run, too!" Mrs. Parrakis howled at her son. "And they'll catch you, too! You're too fat!"

"I'm going to take Mr. Richards upstairs and show him his room, Mom."

"Mr. Richards? Mr. Richards? Why don't you call him by his right name? Poison!"

He disengaged her with great gentleness, and Richards followed him obediently up the shadowy staircase. "There are a great many rooms up here," he said, panting slightly as his huge buttocks flexed and clenched. "This used to be a rooming house many years ago—when I was a baby. You'll be able to watch the street."

"Maybe I better go," Richards said. "If Bradley's blown, your mother may be right."

"This is your room," he said, and threw open a door on a dusty damp room that held the weight of years. He did not seem to have heard Richards's comment. "It's not much of an accommodation. I'm afraid, but—" He turned to face Richards with his patient I-want-to-please smile. "You may stay as long as you want. Bradley Throckmorton is the best friend I've ever had." The smile faltered a bit. "The *only* friend I've ever had. I'll watch after my Mom. Don't worry."

Richards only repeated: "I better go."

"You can't, you know. That head bandage didn't even fool Mom for long. I'm going to drive your car to a safe place, Mr. Richards. We'll talk later."

He left quickly, lumberingly. Richards noted that the seat of his uniform pants was shiny. He seemed to leave a faint odor of apologia in the room.

Pulling the ancient green shade aside a little, Richards saw him emerge on the cracked front walk below and get into the car. Then he got out again. He hurried back toward the house, and Richards felt a stab of fear.

Ponderously climbing tread on the stairs. The door opened, and Elton smiled at Richards. "Mom's right," he said. "I don't make a very good secret agent. I forgot the keys."

Richards gave them to him and then essayed a joke: "Half a secret agent is better than none."

It struck a sour chord or no chord at all; Elton Parrakis carried his torments with him too clearly, and Richards could almost hear the phantom, jeering voices of the children that would follow him forever, like small tugs behind a big liner.

"Thank you," Richards said softly.

Parrakis left, and the little car that Richards had come from New Hampshire in was driven away toward the park.

Richards pulled the dust cover from the bed and lay down slowly, breathing shallowly and looking at nothing but the ceiling. The bed seemed to clutch him in a perversly damp embrace, even through the coverlet and his clothes. An odor of mildew drifted through the channels of his nose like a senseless rhyme.

Downstairs, Elton's mother was weeping.

... Minus 050
and COUNTING ...

He dozed a little but could not sleep. Darkness was almost full when he heard Elton's heavy tread on the stairs again, and Richards swung his feet onto the floor with relief.

When he knocked and stepped in, Richards saw that Parrakis had changed into a tentlike sports shirt and a pair of jeans.

"I did it," he said. "It's in the park."

"Will it be stripped?"

"No," Elton said. "I have a gadget. A battery and two alligator clips. If anyone puts his hand or a crowbar on it, they'll get a shock and a short blast on a siren. Works good. I built it myself." He seated himself with a heavy sigh.

"What's this about Cleveland?" Richards demanded (it was easy, he found, to demand of Elton).

Parrakis shrugged. "Oh, he's a fellow like me. I met him once in Boston, at the library with Bradley. Our little pollution club. I suppose Mom said something about that." He rubbed his hands together and smiled unhappily.

"She said something," Richards agreed.

"She's . . . . a little dim," Parrakis said. "She doesn't understand much of what's been happening for the last twenty years or so. She's frightened all the time. I'm all she has."

"Will they catch Bradley?"

"I don't know. He's got quite a . . . uh, intelligence network." But his eyes slipped away from Richards's.

"You—"

The door opened and Mrs. Parrakis stood there. Her arms were crossed and she was smiling, but her eyes were haunted. "I've called the police," she said. "Now you'll have to go."

Elton's face drained to a pearly yellowish-white. "You're lying."

Richards lurched to his feet and then paused, his head cocked in a listening gesture.

Faintly, rising, the sound of sirens.

"She's not lying," he said. A sickening sense of futility swept him. Back to square one. "Take me to my car."

"She's lying," Elton insisted. He rose, almost touched Richards's arm, then

620

withdrew his hand as if the other man might be hot to the touch. "They're fire trucks."

"Take me to my car. Quick."

The sirens were becoming louder, rising and falling, wailing. The sound filled Richards with a dreamlike horror, locked in here with these two crazies while—

"Mother—" His face was twisted, beseeching.

"I called them!" She blatted, and seized one of her son's bloated arms as if to shake him. "I had to! For you! That darky has got you all mixed up! We'll say he broke in and we'll get the reward money—"

"Come on," Elton grunted to Richards, and tried to shake free of her.

But she clung stubbornly, like a small dog bedeviling a Percheron. "I had to. You've got to stop this radical business, Eltie! You've got to—"

"Eltie!" He screamed. *"Eltie!"* And he flung her away. She skidded across the room and fell across the bed.

"Quick," Elton said, his face full of terror and misery. "Oh, come quick."

They crashed and blundered down the stairs and out the front door, Elton breaking into gigantic, quivering trot. He was beginning to pant again.

And upstairs, filtering both through the closed window and the open door downstairs, Mrs. Parrakis's scream rose to a shriek which met and mixed and blended with the approaching sirens: "I DID IT FOR YOOOOOOOOOOO—"

. . . Minus 049
and COUNTING . . .

Their shadows chased them down the hill toward the park, waxing and waning as they approached and passed each of the mesh-enclosed G.A. streetlamps. Elton Parrakis breathed like a locomotive, in huge and windy gulps and hisses.

They crossed the street and suddenly headlights picked them out on the far sidewalk in hard relief. Blue flashing lights blazed on as the police car came to a screeching, jamming halt a hundred yards away.

"RICHARDS! BEN RICHARDS!"

Gigantic, megaphone-booming voice.

"Your car . . . up ahead . . . see?" Elton panted.

Richards could just make the car out. Elton had parked it well, under a copse of run-to-seed birch trees near the pond.

The cruiser suddenly screamed into life again, rear tires bonding hot rubber to the pavement in lines of acceleration, its gasoline-powered engine wailing in climbing revolutions. It slammed up over the curb, headlights skyrocketing, and came down pointing directly at them.

Richards turned toward it, suddenly feeling very cool, feeling almost numb. He dragged Bradley's pistol out of his pocket, still backing up. The rest of the cops weren't in sight. Just this one. The car screamed at them across the October-bare ground of the park, self-sealing rear tires digging out great clods of ripped black earth.

He squeezed off two shots at the windshield. It starred but did not shatter. He leaped aside at the last second and rolled. Dry grass against his face. Up on his knees, he fired twice more at the back of the car and then it was coming around in a hard, slewing power turn, blue lights turning the night into a crazy, shadow-leaping nightmare. The cruiser was between him and the car, but Elton had leaped the other way, and was now working frantically to remove his electrical device from the car door.

Someone was halfway out of the passenger side of the police car, which was on its way again. A thick stuttering sound filled the dark. Sten gun. Bullets dug through the turf around him in a senseless pattern. Dirt struck his cheeks, pattered against his forehead.

He knelt as if praying, and fired again into the windshield. This time, the bullet punched a hole through the glass.

The car was on top of him—

He sprang to the left and the reinforced steel bumper struck his left foot, snapping his ankle and sending him sprawling on his face.

The cruiser's engine rose to a supercharged scream, digging through another power turn. Now the headlights were on him again, turning everything stark monochrome. Richards tried to get up, but his broken ankle wouldn't support him.

Sobbing in great gulps of air, he watched the police car loom again. Everything became heightened, surreal. He was living in an adrenaline delirium and everything seemed slow, deliberate, orchestrated. The approaching police car was like a huge, blind buffalo.

The Sten gun rattled again, and this time a bullet punched through his left arm, knocking him sideways. The heavy car tried to veer and get him, and for a moment he had a clear shot at the figure behind the wheel. He fired once and the window blew inward. The car screamed into a slow, digging, sidewards roll, then went up and over, crashing down on the roof and then onto its side. The motor stalled, and in sudden, shocking silence, the police radio crackled clearly.

Richards still could not get to his feet and so he began to crawl toward the car. Parrakis was in it now, trying to start it, but in his blind panic he must have forgotten to lever the safety vents open; each time he turned the key there was only a hollow, coughing boom of air in the chambers.

The night began to fill up with converging sirens.

He was still fifty yards from the car when Elton realized what was wrong and yanked down the vent lever. The next time he turned the key the engine chopped erratically into life and the air car swept toward Richards.

He got to a half-standing position and tore the passenger door open and fell inside. Parrakis banked left onto Route 77 which intersected State Street above the park, the lower deck of the car no more than an inch from the paving, almost low enough to drag and spill them.

Elton gulped in huge swatches of air and let them out with force enough to flap his lips like window blinds.

Two more police cars screamed around the corner behind them, the blue lights flashed on, and they gave chase.

"We're not fast enough!" Elton screamed. "We're not fast—"

"They're on wheels!" Richards yelled back. "Cut through that vacant lot!"

The air car banked left and they were slammed upward violently as they crossed the curb. The battering air pressure shoved them into drive.

The police cars swelled behind them, and then they were shooting. Richards heard steel fingers punching holes in the body of their car. The rear window blew in with a tremendous crash, and they were sprinkled with fragments of safety glass.

Screaming, Elton whipped the air car left and right.

One of the police cars, doing sixty-plus, lost it coming up over the curb. The car veered wildly, revolving blue dome-lights splitting the darkness with lunatic bolts of light, and then it crashed over on its side, digging a hot groove through the littered moraine of the empty lot, until a spark struck its peeled-back gas tank. It exploded whitely, like a road flare.

The second car was following the road again, but Elton beat them. They had cut the cruiser off, but it would gain back the lost distance very shortly. The gas-driven ground cars were nearly three times faster than air drive. And if an air car tried to go too far off the road, the uneven surface beneath the thrusters would flip the car over, as Parrakis had nearly flipped them crossing the curb.

"Turn right!" Richards cried.

Parrakis pulled them around in another grinding, stomach-lurching turn. They were on Route 1; ahead, Richards could see that they would soon be forced up the entranceway to the Coast Turnpike. No evasive action would be possible there; only death would be possible there.

"Turn off! Turn off, goddammit! That alley!" For a moment, the police car was one turn behind them, lost from view.

"NO! No!" Parrakis was gibbering now. "We'll be like rats in a trap!"

Richards leaned over and hauled the wheel around, knocking Elton's hand from the throttle with the same gesture. The air car skidded around in a nearly ninety-degree turn. They bounced off the concrete of the building on the left of the alley's mouth, sending them in at a crooked angle. The blunt nose of the car struck a pile of heaped trash, garbage cans, and splintered crates. Behind these, solid brick.

Richards was pitched violently into the dashboard as they crashed, and his nose broke with a sudden snap, gushing blood with violent force.

The air car lay askew in the alley, one cylinder still coughing a little. Parrakis was a silent lump lolling over the steering wheel. There was no time for him yet.

Richards slammed his shoulder against the crimped passenger door. It popped open, and he hopped on one leg to the mouth of the alley. He reloaded his gun from the crumpled box of shells Bradley had supplied him with. They were greasy-cool to the touch. He dropped some of them around his feet. His arm had begun to throb like an ulcerated tooth, making him feel sick and nauseated with pain.

Headlights turned the deserted city expressway from night to sunless day. The cruiser skidded around the turn, rear tires fighting for traction, sending up the fragrant smell of seared rubber. Looping black marks scored the expansion-joint macadam in parabolas. Then it was leaping forward again. Richards held the gun in both hands, leaning against the building to his left. In a moment they would realize they could see no taillights ahead. The cop riding shotgun would see the alley, know—

Snuffling blood through his broken nose, he began to fire. The range was nearly pointblank, and at this distance, the highpowered slugs smashed through the bulletproof glass as if it had been paper. Each recoil of the heavy pistol pulsed through his wounded arm, making him scream.

The car roared up over the curb, flew a short, wingless distance, and crashed into the blank brick wall across the street. ECHO FREE-VEE REPAIR, a faded sign on this wall read. BECAUSE YOU WATCH IT, WE WON'T BOTCH IT.

The police car, still a foot above the ground, met the brick wall at high speed and exploded.

But others were coming; always others.

Panting, Richards made his way back to the air car. His good leg was very tired.

"I'm hurt," Parrakis was groaning hollowly. "I'm hurt so bad. Where's Mom? Where's my Momma?"

Richards fell on his knees, wriggled under the air car on his back, and began to pull trash and debris from the air chambers like a madman. Blood ran down his cheeks from his ruptured nose and pooled beside his ears.

. . . Minus 048
and COUNTING . . .

The car would only run on five of its six cylinders, and it would go no faster than forty, leaning drunkenly to one side.

Parrakis directed him from the passenger seat, where Richards had manhandled him. The steering column had gone into his abdomen like a railspike, and Richards thought he was dying. The blood on the dented steering wheel was warm and sticky on Richards's palms.

"I'm very sorry," Parrakis said. "Turn left here . . . It's really my fault. I

should have known better. She . . . she doesn't think straight. She doesn't . . .''
He coughed up a glut of black blood and spat it listlessly into his lap. The sirens
filled the night, but they were far behind and off to the west. They had gone out
Marginal Way, and from there Parrakis had directed him onto back roads. Now
they were on Route 9 going north, and the Portland suburbs were petering out into
October-barren scrub countryside. The strip lumberers had been through like lo-
custs, and the end result was a bewildering tangle of second growth and marsh.

"Do you know where you're telling me to go?" Richards asked. He was a huge
brand of pain from one end to the other. He was quite sure his ankle was broken;
there was no doubt at all about his nose. His breath came through it in flattened
gasps.

"To a place I know," Elton Parrakis said, and coughed up more blood. "She
used to tell me a boy's best friend is his Mom. Can you believe that? I used to
believe it. Will they hurt her? Take her to jail?"

"No," Richards said shortly, not knowing if they would or not. It was twenty
minutes of eight. He and Elton had left the Blue Door at ten minutes past seven.
It seemed as if decades had passed.

A far distance off, more sirens were joining in the general chorus. *The unspeak-
able in pursuit of the inedible,* Richards thought disjointedly. *If you can't stand
the heat, get out of the kitchen.* He had dispatched two police cars singlehanded.
Another bonus for Sheila. Blood money. And Cathy. Would Cathy sicken and die
on milk paid for with bounty cash? *How are you, my darlings? I love you. Here
on this twisting, crazy back road fit only for deer jackers and couples looking for
a good make-out spot, I love you and wish that your dreams be sweet. I wish—*

"Turn left," Elton croaked.

Richards swung left up a smooth tarred road that cut through a tangle of denuded
sumac and elm, pine and spruce, scrubby nightmare second growth. A river, ripe
and sulphurous with industrial waste, smote his nose. Low-hanging branches
scraped the roof of the car with skeleton screeches. They passed a sign which read:
SUPER PINE TREE MALL—UNDER CONSTRUCTION—KEEP OUT!—
TRESPASSERS WILL BE PROSECUTED!!

They topped a final rise and there was the Super Pine Tree Mall. Work must
have stopped at least two years ago, Richards thought, and things hadn't been too
advanced when it did. The place was a maze, a rat warren of half-built stores and
shops, discarded lengths of pipe, piles of cinderblock and boards, shacks and rusted
Quonset huts, all overgrown with scrubby junipers and laurels and witchgrass and
blue spruce, blackberry and blackthorn, devil's paintbrush and denuded golden-
rod. And it stretched on for miles. Gaping oblong foundation holes like graves dug
for Roman gods. Rusted skeleton steel. Cement walls with steel core-rods protruding like shadowy cryptograms. Bulldozed oblongs that were to be parking lots
now grassed over.

Somewhere overhead, an owl flew on stiff and noiseless wings, hunting.

"Help me . . . into the driver's seat."

"You're in no condition to drive," Richards said, pushing hard on his door to open it.

"It's the least I can do," Elton Parrakis said with grave and bloody absurdity. "I'll play hare . . . drive as long as I can."

"No," Richards said.

"Let me go!" He screamed at Richards, his fat baby face terrible and grotesque. "I'm dying and you just better let me guh—guh—guh—" He trailed off into hideous silent coughs that brought up fresh gouts of blood. It smelled very moist in the car; like a slaughterhouse. "Help me," he whispered. "I'm too fat to do it by myself. Oh God please help me do this."

Richards helped him. He pushed and heaved and his hands slipped and squelched in Elton's blood. The front seat was an abbatoir. And Elton (who would have thought anyone could have so much blood in him?) continued to bleed.

Then he was wedged behind the wheel and the air car was rising jaggedly, turning. The brake lights blinked on and off, on and off, and the car bunted at trees lightly before Elton found the road out.

Richards thought he would hear the crash, but there was none. The erratic *thumpa-thumpa-thumpa* of the air cylinders grew fainter, beating in the deadly one-cylinder-flat rhythm that would burn out the others in an hour or so. The sound faded. Then there was no sound at all but the faraway buzz of a plane. Richards realized belatedly that he had left the crutches he had purchased for disguise purposes in the back of the car.

The constellations whirled indifferently overhead.

He could see his breath in small, frozen puffs; it was colder tonight.

He turned from the road and plunged into the jungle of the construction site.

. . . Minus 047
and COUNTING . . .

He spied a pile of cast-off insulation lying in the bottom of a cellar hole and climbed down, using the protruding core rods for handholds. He found a stick and pounded the insulation to scare out the rats. He was rewarded with nothing but a thick, fibrous dust that made him sneeze and yelp with the pain-burst in his badly used nose. No rats. All the rats were in the city. He uttered a harsh bray of laughter that sounded jagged and splintered in the big dark.

He wrapped himself in strips of the insulation until he looked like a human igloo—but it was warm. He leaned back against the wall and fell into a half-doze.

When he roused fully, a late moon, no more than a cold scrap of light, hung over the eastern horizon. He was still alone. There were no sirens. It might have been three o'clock.

His arm throbbed uneasily, but the flow of blood had stopped on its own; he saw this after pulling the arm out of the insulation and brushing the fibers gently away from the clot. The Sten gun bullet had apparently ripped a fairly large triangular hunk of meat from the side of his arm just above the elbow. He supposed he was lucky that the bullet hadn't smashed the bone. But his ankle throbbed with a steady, deep ache. The foot itself felt strange and ethereal, barely attached. He supposed the break should be splinted.

Supposing, he dozed again.

When he woke, his head was clearer. The moon had risen halfway up in the sky, but there was still no sign of dawn, true or false. *He was forgetting something—*

It came to him in a nasty, jolting realization.

He had to mail two tape clips before noon, if they were to get to the Games Building by the six-thirty air time. That meant traveling or defaulting the money.

But Bradley was on the run, or captured.

And Elton Parrakis had never given him the Cleveland name.

And his ankle was broken.

Something large (a deer? weren't they extinct in the east?) suddenly crashed through the underbrush off to his right, making him jump. Insulation slid off him like snakes, and he pulled it back around himself miserably, snuffling through his broken nose.

He was a city-dweller sitting in a deserted Development gone back to the wild in the middle of nowhere. The night suddenly seemed alive and malevolent, frightening of its own self, full of crazed bumps and creaks.

Richards breathed through his mouth, considering his options and their consequences.

1. *Do nothing.* Just sit here and wait for things to cool off. Consequence: The money he was piling up, a hundred dollars an hour, would be cut off at six tonight. He would be running for free, but the hunt wouldn't stop, not even if he managed to avoid them for the whole thirty days. The hunt would continue until he was carried off on a board.

2. *Mail the clips to Boston.* It couldn't hurt Bradley or the family, because their cover was already blown. Consequences: (1) The tapes would undoubtedly be sent to Harding by the Hunters watching Bradley's mail, but (2) they would still be able to trace him directly to wherever he mailed the tapes from, with no intervening Boston postmark.

3. *Mail the tapes directly to the Games Building in Harding.* Consequences: The hunt would go on, but he would probably be recognized in any town big enough to command a mailbox.

They were all lousy choices.

Thank you, Mrs. Parrakis. Thank you.

He got up, brushing the insulation away, and tossed the useless head bandage on top of it. As an afterthought, he buried it in the insulation.

He began hunting around for something to use as a crutch (the irony of leaving the real crutches in the car struck him again), and when he found a board that reached approximately to armpit height, he threw it over the lip of the cellar foundation and began to climb laboriously back up the core rods.

When he got to the top, sweating and shivering simultaneously, he realized that he could see his hands. The first faint gray light of dawn had begun to probe the darkness. He looked longingly at the deserted Development, thinking: *It would have made such a fine hiding place—*

No good. He wasn't supposed to be a hiding man; he was a running man. Wasn't that what kept the ratings up?

A cloudy, cataractlike ground mist was creeping slowly through the denuded trees. Richards paused to get his directions and then struck off toward the woods that bordered the abandoned Super Mall on the north.

He paused only once to wrap his coat around the top of his crutch and then continued.

. . . Minus 046
and COUNTING . . .

It had been full daylight for two hours and Richards had almost convinced himself he was going around in large circles when he heard, through the rank brambles and ground bushes up ahead, the whine of air cars.

He pushed on cautiously and then peered out on a two-lane macadam highway. Cars rushed to and fro with fair regularity. About a half a mile up, Richards could make out a cluster of houses and what was either an air station or an old general store with pumps in front.

He pushed on, paralleling the highway, falling over occasionally. His face and hands were a needlepoint of blood from briars and brambles, and his clothes were studded with brown sticker-balls. He had given up trying to brush them away. Burst milkweed pods floated lightly from both shoulders, making him look as if he had been in a pillow fight. He was wet from top to toe; he had made it through the first two brooks, but in the third his "crutch" had slipped on the treacherous bottom and he had fallen headlong. The camera of course was undamaged. It was waterproof and shockproof. Of course.

The bushes and trees were thinning. Richards got down on his hands and knees and crawled. When he had gone as far as he thought he safely could, he studied the situation.

He was on a slight rise of land, a peninsula of the scrubby second-growth weeds he had been walking through. Below him was the highway, a number of ranch-type houses, and a store with air pumps. A car was in there now, being attended to while the driver, a man in a suede windbreaker, chatted with the air jockey. Beside the store, along with three or four gumball machines and a Maryjane vendor, stood a blue and red mailbox. It was only two hundred yards away. Looking at it, Richards realized bitterly that if he had arrived before first light he could have probably done his business unseen.

Well, spilt milk and all that. The best laid plans of mice and men.

He withdrew until he could set up his camera and do his taping without being seen.

"Hello, all you wonderful people out there in Free-Vee land," he began. "This is jovial Ben Richards, taking you on my annual nature hike. If you look closely you may see the fearless scarlet tanager or a great speckled cowbird. Perhaps even a yellow-bellied pig bird or two." He paused. "They may let that part through, but not the rest. If you're deaf and read lips, remember what I'm saying. Tell a neighbor or a friend. Spread the word. The Network is poisoning the air you breathe and denying you cheap protection because—"

He recorded both tapes and put them in his pants pocket. Okay. What next? The only possible way to do it was to go down with the gun drawn, deposit the tapes, and run. He could steal a car. It wasn't as if they weren't going to know where he was anyway.

Randomly, he wondered how far Parrakis had gotten before they cut him down. He had the gun out and in his fist when he heard the voice, startlingly close, seemingly in his left ear: "Come on, Rolf!"

There was a sudden volley of barks that made Richards jump violently and he had just time to think: *Police dogs, Christ, they've got police dogs,* when something huge and black broke cover and arrowed at him.

The gun was knocked into the brush and Richards was on his back. The dog was on top of him, a big German shepherd with a generous streak of mongrel, lapping his face and drooling on his shirt. His tail flagged back and forth in vigorous semaphores of joy.

"Rolf! Hey Rolf! Rol—oh Gawd!" Richards caught an obscured glimpse of running legs in blue jeans, and then a small boy was dragging the dog away. "Jeez, I'm sorry, mister. Jeez, he don't bite, he's too dumb to bite, he's just friendly, he ain't . . . Gawd, ain't you a mess! You get lost?"

The boy was holding Rolf by the collar and staring at Richards with frank interest. He was a good-looking boy, well made, perhaps eleven, and there was none of the pale and patched inner city look on his face. There was something suspicious and alien in his features, yet familiar also. After a moment Richards placed it. It was innocence.

"Yes," he said dryly. "I got lost."

"Gee, you sure must have fallen around some."

"That I did, pal. You want to take a close look at my face and see if it's scratched up very badly? I can't see it, you know."

The boy leaned forward obediently and scanned Richards's face. No sign of recognition flickered there. Richards was satisfied.

"It's all burr-caught," the boy said (there was a delicate New England twang in his voice; not exactly Down East, but lightly springy, sardonic), "but you'll live." His brow furrowed. "You escaped from Thomaston? I know you ain't from Pineland cause you don't look like a retard."

"I'm not escaped from anywhere," Richards said, wondering if that was a lie or the truth. "I was hitchhiking. Bad habit, pal. You never do it, do you?"

"No way," the boy said earnestly. "There's crazy dudes running the roads these days. That's what my dad says."

"He's right," Richards said. "But I just had to get to . . . uh . . ." He snapped his fingers in a pantomime of it-just-slipped-my-mind. "You know, jetport."

"You must mean Voigt Field."

"That's it."

"Jeez, that's over a hundred miles from here, mister. In Derry."

"I know," Richards said ruefully, and ran a hand over Rolf's fur. The dog rolled over obligingly and played dead. Richards fought an urge to utter a morbid chuckle. "I picked up a ride at the New Hampshire border with these three maggots. Real tough guys. They beat me up, stole my wallet and dumped me at some deserted shopping center—"

"Yeah, I know that place. Cripes, you wanna come down to the house and have some breakfast?"

"I'd like to, bucko, but time's wasting. I have to get to that jetport by tonight."

"You going to hitch another lift?" The boy's eyes were round.

"Got to." Richards started to get up, then settled back as if a great idea had struck him. "Listen, do me a favor?"

"I guess so," the boy said cautiously.

Richards took out the two exposed tape-clips. "These are chargeplate cash vouchers," he said glibly. "If you drop them in a mailbox for me, my company will have a lump of cash waiting for me in Derry. Then I'll be on my merry way."

"Even without an address?"

"These go direct," Richards said.

"Sure. Okay. There's a mailbox down at Jarrold's Store." He got up, his inexperienced face unable to disguise the fact that he thought Richards was lying in his teeth. "Come on, Rolf."

He let the boy get fifteen feet and then said: "No. Come here again."

The boy turned and came back with his feet dragging. There was dread on his face. Of course, there were enough holes in Richards's story to drive a truck through.

"I've got to tell you everything, I guess," Richards said. "I was telling you the truth about most of it, pal. But I didn't want to risk the chance that you might blab."

The morning October sun was wonderfully warm on his back and neck and he wished he could stay on the hill all day, and sleep sweetly in fall's fugitive warmth.

He pulled the gun from where it had fallen and let it lie loosely on the grass. The boy's eyes went wide.

"Government," Richards said quietly.

"Jee-*zus!*" The boy whispered. Rolf sat beside him, his pink tongue lolling rakishly from the side of his mouth.

"I'm after some pretty hard guys, kid. You can see that they worked me over pretty well. Those clips you got there have *got* to get through."

"I'll mail em," the boy said breathlessly. "Jeez, wait'll I tell—"

"Nobody," Richards said. "Tell nobody for twenty-four hours. There might be reprisals," he added ominously. "So until tomorrow this time, you never saw me. Understand?"

"Yeah! Sure!"

"Then get on it. And thanks, pal." He held out his hand and the boy shook it awefully.

Richards watched them trot down the hill, a boy in a red plaid shirt with his dog crashing joyfully through the golden-rod beside him. *Why can't my Cathy have something like that?*

His face twisted into a terrifying and wholly unconscious grimace of rage and hate, and he might have cursed God Himself if a better target had not interposed itself on the dark screen of his mind: the Games Federation. And behind that, like the shadow of a darker god, the Network.

He watched until he saw the boy, made tiny with distance, drop the tapes into the mailbox.

Then he got up stiffly, propping his crutch under him, and crashed back into the brush, angling toward the road.

The jetport, then. And maybe someone else would pay some dues before it was all over.

. . . Minus 045
and COUNTING . . .

He had seen an intersection a mile back and Richards left the woods there, making his way awkwardly down the gravel bank between the woods and the road.

He sat there like a man who has given up trying to hook a ride and has decided to enjoy the warm autumn sun instead. He let the first two cars go by; both of them held two men, and he figured the odds were too high.

But when the third one approached the stop sign, he got up. The closing-in feeling was back. This whole area had to be hot, no matter how far Parrakis had gotten. The next car could be police, and that would be the ballgame.

It was a woman in the car, and she was alone. She would not look at him; hitchhikers were distasteful and thus to be ignored. He ripped the passenger door open and was in even as the car was accelerating again. He was picked up and thrown sideways, one hand holding desperately onto the doorjam, his good foot dragging.

The thumping hiss of brakes; the air car swerved wildly. "What—who—you can't—"

Richards pointed the gun at her, knowing he must look grotesque close up, like a man who had been run through a meat grinder. The fierce image would work for him. He dragged his foot in and slammed the door, gun never swerving. She was dressed for town, and wore blue wraparound sunglasses. Good looking from what he could see.

"Wheel it," Richards said.

She did the predictable; slammed both feet on the brake and screamed. Richards was thrown forward, his bad ankle scraping excruciatingly. The air car juddered to a stop on the shoulder, fifty feet beyond the intersection.

"You're that . . . you're . . . R-R-R—"

"Ben Richards. Take your hands off the wheel. Put them in your lap."

She did it, shuddering convulsively. She would not look at him. Afraid, Richards supposed, that she would be turned to stone.

"What's your name, ma'am?"

"A-Amelia Williams. Don't shoot me. Don't kill me. I . . . I . . . you can have my money only *for God sake don't kill meeeeeeee*—"

"Shhhhh," Richards said soothingly. "Shhhhh, shhhhhh." When she had quieted a little he said: "I won't try to change your mind about me, Mrs. Williams. Is it Mrs.?"

"Yes," she said automatically.

"But I have no intention of harming you. Do you understand that?"

"Yes," she said, suddenly eager. "You want the car. They got your friend and now you need a car. You can take it—it's insured—I won't even tell. I swear I won't. I'll say someone stole it in the parking lot—"

"We'll talk about it," Richards said. "Begin to drive. Go up Route 1 and we'll talk about it. Are there roadblocks?"

"N—yes. Hundreds of them. They'll catch you."

"Don't lie, Mrs. Williams. Okay?"

She began to drive, erratically at first, then more smoothly. The motion seemed to soothe her. Richards repeated his question about roadblocks.

"Around Lewiston," she said with frightened unhappiness. "That's where they got that other mag—fellow."

"How far is that?"

"Thirty miles or more."

Parrakis had gotten farther than Richards would have dreamed.

"Will you rape me?" Amelia Williams asked so suddenly that Richards almost barked with laughter.

"No," he said; then, matter-of-factly: "I'm married."

"I saw her," she said with a kind of smirking doubtfulness that made Richards want to smash her. *Eat garbage, bitch. Kill a rat that was hiding in the breadbox, kill it with a whiskbroom and then see how you talk about my wife.*

"Can I get off here?" she asked pleadingly, and he felt a trifle sorry for her again.

"No," he said. "You're my protection, Mrs. Williams. I have to get to Voigt Field, in a place called Derry. You're going to see that I get there."

"That's a hundred and fifty miles!" she wailed.

"Someone else told me a hundred."

"They were wrong. You'll never get through to there."

"I might," Richards said, and then looked at her. "And so might you, if you play it right."

She began to tremble again but said nothing. Her attitude was that of a woman waiting to wake up.

. . . Minus 044
and COUNTING . . .

They traveled north through autumn burning like a torch.

The trees were not dead this far north, murdered by the big, poisonous smokes of Portland, Manchester, and Boston; they were all hues of yellow, red, brilliant starburst purple. They awoke in Richards an aching feeling of melancholy. It was a feeling he never would have suspected his emotions could have harbored only two weeks before. In another month the snow would fly and cover all of it.

Things ended in fall.

She seemed to sense his mood and said nothing. The driving filled the silence between them, lulled them. They passed over the water at Yarmouth, then there were only woods and trailers and miserable poverty shacks with outhouses tacked on the sides (yet one could always spot the Free-Vee cable attachment, bolted on below a sagging, paintless windowsill or beside a hinge-smashed door, winking and heliographing in the sun) until they entered Freeport.

There were three police cruisers parked just outside of town, the cops meeting in a kind of roadside conference. The woman stiffened like a wire, her face desperately pale, but Richards felt calm.

They passed the police without notice, and she slumped.

"If they had been monitoring traffic, they would have been on us like a shot," Richards said casually. "You might as well paint BEN RICHARDS IS IN THIS CAR on your forehead in Day-Glo."

"Why can't you let me go?" she burst out, and in the same breath: "Have you got a jay?"

Rich folks blow Dokes. The thought brought a bubble of ironic laughter and he shook his head.

"You're laughing at me?" she asked, stung. "You've got some nerve, don't you, you cowardly little murderer! Scaring me half out of my life, probably planning to kill me the way you killed those poor boys in Boston—"

"There was a full gross of those poor boys," Richards said. "Ready to kill me. That's their job."

"Killing for pay. Ready to do anything for money. Wanting to overturn the country. Why don't you find decent work? Because you're too lazy! Your kind spit in the face of anything decent."

"Are you decent?" Richards asked.

"Yes!" She stormed. "Isn't that why you picked on me? Because I was defenseless and . . . and decent? So you could use me, drag me down to your level and then laugh about it?"

"If you're so decent, how come you have six thousand New Dollars to buy this fancy car while my little girl dies of the flu?"

"What—" She looked startled. Her mouth started to open and she closed it with a snap. "You're an enemy of the Network," she said. "It says so on the Free-Vee. I saw some of those disgusting things you did."

"You know what's disgusting?" Richards asked, lighting a cigarette from the pack on the dashboard. "I'll tell you. It's disgusting to get blackballed because you don't want to work in a General Atomics job that's going to make you sterile. It's disgusting to sit home and watch your wife earning the grocery money on her back. It's disgusting to know the Network is killing millions of people each year with air pollutants when they could be manufacturing nose filters for six bucks a throw."

"You lie," she said. Her knuckles had gone white on the wheel.

"When this is over," Richards said, "you can go back to your nice split-level duplex and light up a Doke and get stoned and love the way your new silverware sparkles in the highboy. No one fighting rats with broomhandles in your neighborhood or shitting by the back stoop because the toilet doesn't work. I met a little girl five years old with lung cancer. How's that for disgusting? What do—"

"Stop!" she screamed at him. *"You talk dirty!"*

"That's right," he said, watching as the countryside flowed by. Hopelessness filled him like cold water. There was no base of communication with these beautiful chosen ones. They existed up where the air was rare. He had a sudden raging urge to make this woman pull over: knock her sunglasses onto the gravel, drag her through the dirt, make her eat a stone, rape her, jump on her, knock her teeth into the air like startled digits, strip her nude and ask her if she was beginning to see the big picture, the one that runs twenty-four hours a day on channel one, where the national anthem never plays before the sign-off.

"That's right," he muttered. "Dirty-talking old me."

. . . Minus 043
and COUNTING . . .

They got farther than they had any right to, Richards figured. They got all the way to a pretty town by the sea called Camden over a hundred miles from where he had hitched a ride with Amelia Williams.

"Listen," he said as they were entering Augusta, the state capital. "There's a good chance they'll sniff us here. I have no interest in killing you. Dig it?"

"Yes," she said. Then, with bright hate: "You need a hostage."

"Right. So if a cop pulls out behind us, you pull over. Immediately. You open your door and lean out. Just *lean*. Your fanny is not to leave that seat. Understand?"

"Yes."

"You holler: Benjamin Richards is holding me hostage. If you don't give him free passage he'll kill me."

"And you think *that* will work?"

"It better," he said with tense mockery. "It's your ass."

She bit her lip and said nothing.

"It'll work. I think. There will be a dozen freelance cameramen around in no time, hoping to get some Games money or even the Zapruder Award itself. With that kind of publicity, they'll have to play it straight. Sorry you won't get to see us go out in a hail of bullets so they can talk about you sanctimoniously as Ben Richards's last victim."

"Why do you *say* these things?" she burst out.

He didn't reply; only slid down in his seat until just the top of his head showed and waited for the blue lights in the rear-view mirror.

But there were no blue lights in Augusta. They continued on for another hour and a half, skirting the ocean as the sun began to wester, catching little glints and peaks of the water, across fields and beyond bridges and through heavy firs.

It was past two o'clock when they rounded a bend not far from the Camden town line and saw a roadblock; two police cars parked on either side of the road. Two cops were checking a farmer in an old pick-up and waving it through.

"Go another two hundred feet and then stop," Richards said. "Do it just the way I told you."

She was pallid but seemingly in control. Resigned, maybe. She applied the brakes evenly and the air car came to a neat stop in the middle of the road fifty feet from the checkpoint.

The trooper holding the clipboard waved her forward imperiously. When she didn't come, he glanced inquiringly at his companion. A third cop, who had been sitting inside one of the cruisers with his feet up, suddenly grabbed the hand mike under the dash and began to speak rapidly.

Here we go, Richards thought. *Oh God, here we go.*

. . . Minus 042
and COUNTING . . .

The day was very bright (the constant rain of Harding seemed light-years away) and everything was very sharp and clearly defined. The troopers' shadows might have been drawn with black Crayolas. They were unhooking the narrow straps that crossed their gunbutts.

Mrs. Williams swung open the door and leaned out. "Don't shoot, please," she said, and for the first time Richards realized how cultured her voice was, how rich. She might have been in a drawing room except for the pallid knuckles and the fluttering, birdlike pulse in her throat. With the door open he could smell the fresh, invigorating odor of pine and timothy grass.

"Come out of the car with your hands over your head," the cop with the clipboard said. He sounded like a well-programmed machine. General Atomics Model 6925-A9, Richards thought. The Hicksville Trooper. 16-psm Iridium Batteries included. Comes in White Only. "You and your passenger, ma'am. We see him."

"My name is Amelia Williams," she said very clearly. "I can't get out as you ask. Benjamin Richards is holding me hostage. If you don't give him free passage, he says he'll kill me."

The two cops looked at each other, and something barely perceptible passed between them. Richards, with his nerves strung up to a point where he seemed to be operating with a seventh sense, caught it.

"Drive!" he screamed.

She stared around at him, bewildered. "But they won't—"

The clipboard clattered to the road. The two cops fell into the kneeling posture almost simultaneously, guns out, gripped in right hands, left hands holding right wrists. One on each side of the solid white line.

The sheets of flimsy on the clipboard fluttered errantly.

Richards tromped his bad foot on Amelia Williams's right shoe, his lips drawing back into a tragedy mask of pain as the broken ankle grated. The air car ripped forward.

The next moment two hollow punching noises struck the car, making it vibrate. A moment later the windshield blew in, splattering them both with bits of safety glass. She threw both hands up to protect her face and Richards leaned savagely against her, swinging the wheel.

They shot through the gap between the veed cars with scarcely a flirt of the rear deck. He caught a crazy glimpse of the troopers whirling to fire again and then his whole attention was on the road.

They mounted a rise, and then there was one more hollow *thunnn!* as a bullet smashed a hole in the trunk. The car began to fishtail and Richards hung on, whipping the wheel in diminishing arcs. He realized dimly that Williams was screaming.

"Steer!" he shouted at her. "Steer, goddammit! Steer! Steer!"

Her hands groped reflexively for the wheel and found it. He let go and batted the dark glasses away from her eyes with an openhanded blow. They hung on one ear for a moment and then dropped off.

"Pull over!"

"They shot at us." Her voice began to rise. "They shot at us. *They shot at—*"

"*Pull over!*"

The scream of sirens rose behind them.

She pulled over clumsily, sending the car around in a shuddering half-turn that spumed gravel into the air.

"I told them and they tried to kill us," she said wonderingly. "They tried to kill us."

But he was out already, out and hopping clumsily back the way they had come, gun out. He lost his balance and fell heavily, scraping both knees.

When the first cruiser came over the rise he was in a sitting position on the shoulder of the road, the pistol held firmly at shoulder level. The car was doing eighty easily, and still accelerating; some backroad cowboy at the wheel with too much engine up front and visions of glory in his eyes. They perhaps saw him, perhaps tried to stop. It didn't matter. There were no bulletproof tires on these. The one closest to Richards exploded as if there had been dynamite inside. The cruiser took off like a big-ass bird, gunning across the shoulder in howling, uncontrolled flight. It crashed into the hole of a huge elm. The driver's side door flew off. The driver rammed through the windshield like a torpedo and flew thirty yards before crashing into the puckerbrush.

The second car came almost as fast, and it took Richards four shots to find a tire. Two slugs splattered sand next to his spot. This one slid around in a smoking half-turn and rolled three times, spraying glass and metal.

Richards struggled to his feet, looked down and saw his shirt darkening slowly just above the belt. He hopped back toward the air car, and then dropped on his face as the second cruiser exploded, spewing shrapnel above and around him.

He got up, panting and making strange whimpering noises in his mouth. His side had begun to throb in slow, aching cycles.

She could have gotten away, perhaps, but she had made no effort. She was staring, transfixed, at the burning police car in the road. When Richards got in, she shrank from him.

"You killed them. You killed those men."

"They tried to kill me. You too. Drive. Fast."

"THEY DID NOT TRY TO KILL ME!"

"Drive!"

She drove.

The mask of the well-to-do young *hausfrau* on her way back from the market now hung in tatters and shreds. Beneath it was something from the cave, something with twitching lips and rolling eyes. Perhaps it had been there all along.

They drove about five miles and came to a roadside store and air station.

"Pull in," Richards said.

. . . Minus 041
and COUNTING . . .

"Get out."

"No."

He jammed the gun against her right breast and she whimpered. "Don't. Please."

"I'm sorry. But there's no more time for you to play prima donna. Get out."

She got out and he slid after her.

"Let me lean on you."

He slung an arm around her shoulders and pointed with the gun at the telephone booth beside the ice dispenser. They began shuffling toward it, a grotesque two-man vaudeville team. Richards hopped on his good foot. He felt tired. In his mind he saw the cars crashing, the body flying like a torpedo, the leaping explosion. These scenes played over and over again, like a continuous loop of tape.

The store's proprietor, an old pal with white hair and scrawny legs hidden by a dirty butcher's apron, came out and stared at them with worried eyes.

"Hey," he said mildly. "I don't want you here. I got a fam'ly. Go down the road. Please I don't want no trouble."

"Go inside, pop," Richards said. The man went.

Richards slid loosely into the booth, breathing through his mouth, and fumbled

fifty cents into the coin horn. Holding the gun and receiver in one hand, he punched
O.

"What exchange is this, operator?"

"Rockland, sir."

"Put me through to the local newsie hookup, please."

"You may dial that, sir. The number is—"

"You dial it."

"Do you wish—"

"Just dial it!"

"Yes, sir," she said, unruffled. There were clicks and pops in Richards's ear.
Blood had darkened his shirt to a dirty purple color. He looked away from it. It
made him feel ill.

"Rockland Newsie," a voice said in Richards's ear. "Free-Vee Tabloid Number 6943."

"This is Ben Richards."

There was a long silence. Then: "Look, maggot, I like a joke as well as the next
guy, but this has been a long, hard d—"

"Shut up. You're going to get confirmation of this in ten minutes at the outside.
You can get it now if you've got a policeband radio."

"I . . . just a second." There was the clunk of a dropping phone on the other
end, and a faint wailing sound. When the phone was picked up, the voice was hard
and businesslike, with an undercurrent of excitement.

"Where are you, fella? Half the cops in eastern Maine just went through Rockland . . . at about a hundred and ten."

Richards craned his neck at the sign over the store. "A place called Gilly's Town
Line Store & Airstop on U.S. 1. You know it?"

"Yeah. Just—"

"Listen to me, maggot. I didn't call to give you my life story. Get some photogs
out here. Quick. And get this on the air. Red Newsbreak Top. I've got a hostage.
Her name is Amelia Williams. From—" He looked at her.

"Falmouth," she said miserably.

"From Falmouth. Safe conduct or I'll kill her."

"Jesus, I smell the Pulitzer Prize!"

"No, you just shit your pants, that's all," Richards said. He felt lightheaded.
"You get the word out. I want the State Pigs to find out everyone knows I'm not
alone. Three of them at a roadblock tried to blow us up."

"What happened to the cops!"

"I killed them."

"All three? Hot damn!" The voice, pulled away from the phone, yelled distantly: "Dicky, open the national cable!"

"I'm going to kill her if they shoot," Richards said, simultaneously trying to
inject sincerity into his voice and to remember all the old gangster movies he had
seen on tee-vee as a kid. "If they want to save the girl, they better let me through."

"When—"

Richards hung up and hopped clumsily out of the booth. "Help me."

She put an arm around him, grimacing at the blood. "See what you're getting yourself into?"

"Yes."

"This is madness. You're going to be killed."

"Drive north," he mumbled. "Just drive north."

He slid into the car, breathing hard. The world insisted on going in and out. High, atonal music jangled in his ears. She pulled out and onto the road. His blood had smeared on her smart green and black-striped blouse. The old man, Gilly, cracked the screen door open and poked out a very old Polaroid camera. He clicked the shutter, pulled the tape, and waited. His face was painted with horror and excitement and delight.

In the distance, rising and converging, sirens.

. . . Minus 040
and COUNTING . . .

They traveled five miles before people began running out onto their lawns to watch them pass. Many had cameras and Richards relaxed.

"They were shooting at the aircaps at that roadblock," she said quietly. "It was a mistake. That's what it was. A mistake."

"If that maggot was aiming for an aircap when he put out the windshield, there must have been a sight on that pistol three feet high."

"It was a mistake!"

They were entering the residential district of what Richards assumed was Rockland. Summer homes. Dirt roads leading down to beachfront cottages. Breeze Inn. *Private Road.* Just Me'n Patty. *Keep Out.* Elizabeth's Rest. *Trespassers Will Be Shot.* Cloud-Hi. *5000 Volts.* Set-A-Spell. *Guard Dogs on Patrol.*

Unhealthy eyes and avid faces peering at them from behind trees, like Cheshire cats. The blare of battery-powered Free-Vees came through the shattered windshield.

A crazy, weird air of carnival about everything.

"These people," Richards said, "only want to see someone bleed. The more the better. They would just as soon it was both of us. Can you believe that?"

"No."

"Then I salute you."

An older man with silvery barbershop hair, wearing madras shorts that came down over his knees, ran out to the edge of the road. He was carrying a huge camera with a cobra-like telephoto lens. He began snapping pictures wildly, bending and dipping. His legs were fish-belly white. Richards burst into a sudden bray of laughter that made Amelia jump.

"What—"

"He's still got the lens cover on," Richards said. "He's still got—" But laughter overcame him.

Cars crowded the shoulders as they topped a long, slowly rising hill and began to descend toward the clustered town of Rockland itself. Perhaps it had once been a picturesque seacoast fishing village, full of Winslow Homer men in yellow rainslickers who went out in small boats to trap the wily lobster. If so, it was long gone. There was a huge shopping center on either side of the road. A main street strip of honky-tonks, bars, and AutoSlot emporiums. There were neat middle-class homes overlooking the main drag from the heights, and a growing slum looking up from the rancid edge of the water. The sea at the horizon was yet unchanged. It glittered blue and ageless, full of dancing points and nets of light in the late afternoon sun.

They began the descent, and there were two police cars parked across the road. The blue lights flick-flick-flicked jaggedly, crazy and out of sync with each other. Parked at an angle on the left embankment was an armored car with a short, stubby cannon barrel tracking them.

"You're done," she said softly, almost regretfully. "Do I have to die, too?"

"Stop fifty yards from the roadblock and do your stuff," Richards said. He slid down in the seat. A nervous tic stitched his face.

She stopped and opened the car door, but did not lean out. The air was dead silent. *A hush falls over the crowd,* Richards thought ironically.

"I'm scared," she said. "Please. I'm so scared."

"They won't shoot you," he said. "There are too many people. You can't kill hostages unless no one is watching. Those are the rules of the game."

She looked at him for a moment, and he suddenly wished they could have a cup of coffee together. He would listen carefully to her conversation and stir real cream into his hot drink—her treat, of course. Then they could discuss the possibilities of social inequity, the way your socks always fall down when you're wearing rubber boots, and the importance of being earnest.

"Go on, Mrs. Williams," he said with soft, tense mockery. "The eyes of the world are upon you."

She leaned out.

Six police cars and another armored van had pulled up thirty feet behind them, blocking their retreat.

He thought: *Now the only way out is straight up to heaven.*

. . . Minus 039
and COUNTING . . .

"My name is Amelia Williams. Benjamin Richards is holding me hostage. If you don't give us safe conduct, he says he'll kill me."

Silence for a moment so complete that Richards could hear the faraway honk of some distant yacht's air horn.

Then, asexual, blaring, amplified: "WE WANT TO TALK TO BEN RICHARDS."

"No," Richards said swiftly.

"He says he won't."

"COME OUT OF THE CAR, MADAM."

"He'll kill me!" she cried wildly. "Don't you listen? Some men almost killed us back *there!* He says you don't care who you kill. *My God, is he right?*"

A hoarse voice in the crowd yelled "Let her through!"

"COME OUT OF THE CAR OR WE'LL SHOOT."

"Let her through! Let her through!" The crowd had taken up the chant like eager fans at a killball match.

"COME OUT—"

The crowd drowned it out. From somewhere, a rock flew. A police car windshield starred into a matrix of cracks.

There was suddenly a rev of motors, and the two cruisers began to pull apart, opening a narrow slot of pavement. The crowd cheered happily and then fell silent, waiting for the next act.

"ALL CIVILIANS LEAVE THE AREA," the bullhorn chanted. "THERE MAY BE SHOOTING. ALL CIVILIANS LEAVE THE AREA OR YOU MAY BE CHARGED WITH OBSTRUCTION AND UNLAWFUL ASSEMBLY. THE PENALTY FOR OBSTRUCTION AND UNLAWFUL ASSEMBLY IS TEN YEARS IN THE STATE PENITENTIARY OR A FINE OF TEN THOUSAND DOLLARS OR BOTH. CLEAR THE AREA. CLEAR THE AREA."

"Yeah, so no one'll see you shoot the girl!" a hysterical voice yelled. "Screw all pigs!"

The crowd didn't move. A yellow and black newsiemobile had pulled up with a flashy screech. Two men jumped out and began setting up a camera.

Two cops rushed over and there was a short, savage scuffle for the possession of the camera. Then one of the cops yanked it free, picked it up by the tripod, and smashed it on the road. One of the newsmen tried to reach the cop that had done it and was clubbed.

A small boy darted out of the crowd and fired a rock at the back of a cop's head. Blood splattered the road as the cop fell over. A half-dozen more descended on the boy, bearing him off. Incredibly, small and savage fistfights had begun on the sidelines between the well-dressed townfolk and the rattier slum-dwellers. A woman in a ripped and faded housedress suddenly descended on a plump matron and began to pull her hair. They fell heavily to the road and began to roll on the macadam, kicking and screaming.

"My God," Amelia said sickly.

"What's happening?" Richards asked. He dared look no higher than the clock on the dashboard.

"Fights. Police hitting people. Someone broke a newsie's camera."

"GIVE UP, RICHARDS. COME OUT."

"Drive on," Richards said softly.

The air car jerked forward erratically. "They'll shoot for the air caps," she said. "Then wait until you have to come out."

"They won't," Richards said.

"Why?"

"They're too dumb."

They didn't.

They proceeded slowly past the ranked police cars and the bug-eyed spectators. They had split themselves into two groups in unconscious segregation. On one side of the road were the middle- and upper-class citizens, the ladies who had their hair done at the beauty parlor, the men who wore Arrow shirts and loafers. Fellows wearing coveralls with company names on the back and their own names stitched in gold thread over the breast pockets. Women like Amelia Williams herself, dressed for the market and the shops. Their faces were different in all ways but similar in one: They looked oddly incomplete, like pictures with holes for eyes or a jigsaw puzzle with a minor piece missing. It was a lack of desperation. Richards thought. No wolves howled in these bellies. These minds were not filled with rotted, crazed dreams or mad hopes.

These people were on the right side of the road, the side that faced the combination marina and country club they were just passing.

On the other side, the left, were the poor people. Red noses with burst veins. Flattened, sagging breasts. Stringy hair. White socks. Cold sores. Pimples. The blank and hanging mouths of idiocy.

The police were deployed more heavily here, and more were coming all the time. Richards was not surprised at the swiftness and the heaviness of their crunch, despite the suddenness of his appearance. Even here, in Boondocks, U.S.A., the club and the gun were kept near to hand. The dogs were kept hungry in the kennel. The poor break into summer cottages closed for autumn and winter. The poor crash supermarts in subteen gangs. The poor have been known to soap badly spelled obscenities on shop windows. The poor always have itchy assholes and the sight of Naugahyde and chrome and two-hundred-dollar suits and fat bellies have been known to make the mouths of the poor fill with angry spit. And the poor must have their Jack Johnson, their Muhammad Ali, their Clyde Barrow. They stood and watched.

Here on the right, folks, we have the summer people, Richards thought. Fat and sloppy but heavy with armor. On the left, weighing in at only a hundred and thirty— but a scrappy contender with a mean and rolling eyeball—we have the Hungry Honkies. Theirs are the politics of starvation; they'd roll Christ Himself for a pound of salami. Polarization comes to West Sticksville. Watch out for these two contenders, though. They don't stay in the ring; they have a tendency to fight in the ten-dollar seats. Can we find a goat to hang up for both of them?

Slowly, rolling at thirty, Ben Richards passed between them.

. . . Minus 038
and COUNTING . . .

An hour passed. It was four o'clock. Shadows crawled across the road.

Richards, slumped down below eye level in his seat, floated in and out of consciousness effortlessly. He had clumsily pulled his shirt out of his pants to look at the new wound. The bullet had dug a deep and ugly canal in his side that had bled a great deal. The blood had clotted, but grudgingly. When he had to move quickly again, the wound would rip open and bleed a great deal more. Didn't matter. They were going to blow him up. In the face of this massive armory, his plan was a joke. He would go ahead with it, fill in the blanks until there was an "accident" and the air car was blown into bent bolts and shards of metal (" . . . terrible accident . . . the trooper has been suspended pending a full investigation . . . regret the loss of innocent life . . . "—all this buried in the last newsie of the day, between the stock-market report and the Pope's latest pronouncement), but it was only reflex. He had become increasingly worried about Amelia Williams, whose big mistake had been picking Wednesday morning to do her marketing.

"There are tanks out there," she said suddenly. Her voice was light, chatty, hysterical. "Can you imagine it? Can you—" She began to cry.

Richards waited. Finally, he said: "What town are we in?"

"W-W-Winterport, the sign s-said. Oh, I can't! I can't wait for them to do it! *I can't!*"

"Okay," he said.

She blinked slowly, giving an infinitesimal shake of her head as if to clear it. "What?"

"Stop. Get out."

"But they'll kill y—"

"Yes. But there won't be any blood. You won't see any blood. They've got enough firepower out there to vaporize me and the car, too."

"You're lying. You'll kill me."

The gun had been dangling between his knees. He dropped it on the floor. It clunked harmlessly on the rubber floor-mat.

"I want some pot," she said mindlessly. "Oh God, I want to be high. Why didn't you wait for the next car? Jesus! Jesus!"

Richards began to laugh. He laughed in wheezy, shallow-chested heaves that still hurt his side. He closed his eyes and laughed until tears oozed out from under the lids.

"It's cold in here with that broken windshield," she said irrelevantly. "Turn on the heater."

Her face was a pale blotch in the shadows of late afternoon.

. . . Minus 037
and COUNTING . . .

"We're in Derry," she said.

The streets were black with people. They hung over roof ledges and sat on balconies and verandahs from which the summer furniture had been removed. They ate sandwiches and fried chicken from greasy buckets.

"Are there jetport signs?"

"Yes. I'm following them. They'll just close the gates."

"I'll just threaten to kill you again if they do."

"Are you going to skyjack a plane?"

"I'm going to try."

"You can't."

"I'm sure you're right."

They made a right, then a left. Bullhorns exhorted the crowd monotonously to move back, to disperse.

"Is she really your wife? That woman in the pictures?"

"Yes. Her name is Sheila. Our baby, Cathy, is a year and a half old. She had the flu. Maybe she's better now. That's how I got into this."

A helicopter buzzed them, leaving a huge arachnid shadow on the road ahead. A grossly amplified voice exhorted Richards to let the woman go. When it was gone and they could speak again, she said:

"Your wife looks like a little tramp. She could take better care of herself."

"The picture was doctored," Richards said tonelessly.

"They would do that?"

"They would do that."

"The jetport. We're coming up to it."

"Are the gates shut?"

"I can't see . . . wait . . . open but blocked. A tank. It's pointing its shooter at us."

"Drive to within thirty feet of it and stop."

The car crawled slowly down the four-lane access road between the parked police cars, between the ceaseless scream and babble of the crowd. A sign loomed over them: VOIGT AIRFIELD. The woman could see an electrified cyclone fence which crossed a marshy, worthless sort of field on both sides of the road. Straight ahead was a combination information booth and check-in point on a traffic island. Beyond that was the main gate, blocked by an A-62 tank capable of firing one-quarter-megaton shells from its cannon. Farther on, a confusion of roads and parking lots, all tending toward the complex jetline terminals that blocked the runways from view. A huge control tower bulked over everything like an H.G. Wells Martian, the westering sun glaring off its polarized bank of windows and turning them to fire. Employees and passengers alike had crowded down to the nearest parking lot where they were being held back by more police. There was a pulsing, heavy whine in their ears, and Amelia saw a steel-gray Lockheed/G-A Superbird rising into a flat, powerful climb from one of the runways behind the main buildings.

"RICHARDS!"

She jumped and looked at him, frightened. He waved his hand at her nonchalantly. It's all right, Ma. I'm only dying.

"YOU'RE NOT ALLOWED INSIDE," the huge amplified voice admonished him. "LET THE WOMAN GO. STEP OUT."

"What now?" she asked. "It's a stand-off. They'll just wait until—"

"Let's push them a little farther," Richards said. "They'll bluff along a little more. Lean out. Tell them I'm hurt and half-crazy. Tell them I want to give up to the Airline Police."

"You want to do *what?*"

"The Airline Police are neither state enforcement nor federal. They've been international ever since the UN treaty of 1995. There used to be a story that if you gave up to them, you'd get amnesty. Sort of like landing on Free Parking in Monopoly. Full of shit, of course. They turn you over to the Hunters and the Hunters drag you out in back of the barn."

She winced.

"But maybe they'll think I believe it. Or that I've fooled myself into believing it. Go ahead and tell them."

She leaned out and Richards tensed. If there was going to be an "unfortunate accident" which would remove Amelia from the picture, it would probably happen now. Her head and upper body were clearly and cleanly exposed to a thousand guns. One squeeze on one trigger and the entire farce would come to a quick end.

"Ben Richards wants to give up to the Airline Police!" she cried. "He's shot in two places!" She threw a terrified glance over her shoulder and her voice broke, high and clear in the sudden silence the diminishing jet had left. "He's been out of his mind half the time and God I'm so *frightened . . . please . . . please . . . PLEASE!*"

The cameras were recording it all, sending it on a live feed that would be broadcast all over North America and half the world in a matter of minutes. That was good. That was fine. Richards felt tension stiffen his limbs again and knew he was beginning to hope.

Silence for a moment; there was a conference going on behind the check-point booth.

"Very good," Richards said softly.

She looked at him. "Do you think it's hard to sound frightened? We're not in this together, whatever you think. I only want you to go away."

Richards noticed for the first time how perfect her breasts were beneath the bloodstained black and green blouse. How perfect and how precious.

There was a sudden, grinding roar and she screamed aloud.

"It's the tank," he said. "It's okay. Just the tank."

"It's moving," she said. "They're going to let us in."

"RICHARDS! YOU WILL PROCEED TO LOT 16. AIRLINE POLICE WILL BE WAITING THERE TO TAKE YOU INTO CUSTODY!"

"All right," he said thinly. "Drive on. When you get a half a mile inside the gate, stop."

"You're going to get me killed," she said hopelessly. "All I need to do is use the bathroom and you're going to get me killed."

The air car lifted four inches and hummed smoothly forward. Richards crouched going through the gate, anticipating a possible ambush, but there was none. The smooth blacktop curved sedately toward the main buildings. A sign with a pointing arrow informed them that this was the way to Lots 16-20.

Here the police were standing and kneeling behind yellow barricades.

Richards knew that at the slightest suspicious move, they would tear the air car apart.

"Now stop," he said, and she did.

The reaction was instantaneous. "RICHARDS! MOVE IMMEDIATELY TO LOT 16!"

"Tell them that I want a bullhorn," Richards said softly to her. "They are to leave one in the road twenty yards up. I want to talk to them."

She cried his message, and then they waited. A moment later, a man in a blue uniform trotted out into the road and laid an electric bullhorn down. He stood there for a moment, perhaps savoring the realization that he was being seen by five hundred million people, and then withdrew to barricaded anonymity again.

"Go ahead," he told her.

They crept up to the bullhorn, and when the driver's side door was even with it, she opened the door and pulled it in. It was red and white. The letters G and A, embossed over a thunderbolt, were on the side.

"Okay," he said. "How far are we from the main building?"

She squinted. "A quarter of a mile, I guess."

"How far are we from Lot 16?"

"Half that."

"Good. That's good. Yeah." He realized he was compulsively biting his lips and tried to make himself stop. His head hurt; his entire body ached from adrenaline. "Keep driving. Go up to the entrance of Lot 16 and then stop."

"Then what?"

He smiled tightly and unhappily. "That," he said, "is going to be the site of Richards's Last Stand."

. . . Minus 036
and COUNTING . . .

When she stopped the car at the entrance of the parking lot, the reaction was quick and immediate. "KEEP MOVING," the bullhorn prodded. "THE AIRPORT POLICE ARE INSIDE. AS SPECIFIED."

Richards raised his own bullhorn for the first time. "TEN MINUTES," he said. "I HAVE TO THINK."

Silence again.

"Don't you realize you're pushing them to do it?" she asked him in a strange, controlled voice.

He uttered a weird, squeezed giggle that sounded like steam under high pressure escaping from a teapot. "They know I'm getting set to screw them. They don't know how."

"You can't," she said. "Don't you *see* that yet?"

"Maybe I can," he said.

. . . Minus 035
and COUNTING . . .

"Listen:

"When the Games first started, people said they were the world's greatest entertainment because there had never been anything like them. But nothing's that original. There were the gladiators in Rome who did the same thing. And there's another game, too. Poker. In poker the highest hand is a royal straight-flush in spades. And the toughest kind of poker is five-card stud. Four cards up on the table and one in the hole. For nickels and dimes anyone can stay in the game. It costs you maybe half a buck to see the other guy's hole card. But when you push the stakes up, the hole card starts to look bigger and bigger. After a dozen rounds of betting, with your life's savings and car and house on the line, that hole card stands taller than Mount Everest. *The Running Man* is like that. Only I'm not supposed to have any money to bet with. They've got the men, the firepower, and the time. We're playing with their cards and their chips in their casino. When I'm caught, I'm supposed to fold. But maybe I stacked the deck a bit. I called the newsie line in Rockland. The newsies, that's my ten of spades. They *had* to give me safe conduct, because everyone was watching. There were no more chances for neat disposal after that first roadblock. It's funny, too, because it's the Free-Vee that gives the Network the clout that it has. If you see it on the Free-Vee, it must be true. So if the whole country saw the police murder my hostage—a well-to-do, middle-class female hostage—they would have to believe it. They can't risk it; the system is laboring under too much suspension of belief now. Funny, huh? My people are here. There's been trouble on the road already. If the troopers and the Hunters turn all their guns on us, something nasty might happen. A man told me to stay near my own people. He was more right than he knew. One of the reasons they've been handling me with the kid gloves on is because my people are here.

"My people, they're the jack of spades.

"The queen, the lady in the affair, is you.

"I'm the king; the black man with the sword.

"These are my up cards. The media, the possibility of real trouble, you, me. Together they're nothing. A pair will take them. Without the ace of spades it's junk. With the ace, it's unbeatable."

He suddenly picked up her handbag, an imitation alligator-skin clutch purse with a small silver chain. He stuffed it into his coat pocket where it bulged prominently.

"I haven't got the ace," he said softly. "With a little more forethought, I could have had it. But I *do* have a hole card—one they can't see. So I'm going to run a bluff.''

''You don't have a chance,'' she said hollowly. ''What can you do with my bag? Shoot them with a lipstick?''

''I think that they've been playing a crooked game so long that they'll fold. I think they are yellow straight through from the back to belly.''

''RICHARDS! TEN MINUTES ARE UP!''

Richards put the bullhorn to his lips.

. . . Minus 034
and COUNTING . . .

''LISTEN TO ME CAREFULLY!'' His voice boomed and rolled across the flat jetport acres. Police waited tensely. The crowd shuffled. ''I AM CARRYING TWELVE POUNDS OF DYNACORE HI-IMPACT PLASTIC EXPLOSIVE IN MY COAT POCKET—THE VARIETY THEY CALL BLACK IRISH. TWELVE POUNDS IS ENOUGH TO TAKE OUT EVERYTHING AND EVERYONE WITHIN A THIRD OF A MILE AND PROBABLY ENOUGH TO EXPLODE THE JETPORT FUEL STORAGE TANKS. IF YOU DON'T FOL- LOW MY INSTRUCTIONS TO THE LETTER, I'LL BLOW YOU ALL TO HELL. A GENERAL ATOMICS IMPLODER RING IS SET INTO THE EX- PLOSIVE. I HAVE IT PULLED OUT TO HALF-COCK. ONE JIGGLE AND YOU CAN ALL PUT YOUR HEADS BETWEEN YOUR LEGS AND KISS YOUR ASSES GOODBYE.''

There were screams from the crowd followed by sudden tidelike movement. The police at the barricades suddenly found they had no one to hold back. Men and women were tearing across roads and fields, streaming out the gates and scal- ing the cyclone fence around the jetport. Their faces were blank and avid with panic.

The police shuffled uneasily. On no face did Amelia Williams see disbelief.

''RICHARDS?'' The huge voice boomed. ''THAT'S A LIE. COME OUT.''

''I *AM* COMING OUT,'' he boomed back. ''BUT BEFORE I DO, LET ME GIVE YOU YOUR MARCHING ORDERS. I WANT A JET FULLY FUELED AND READY TO FLY WITH A SKELETON CREW. THIS JET WILL BE A LOCKHEED/GA OR A DELTA SUPERSONIC. THE RANGE MUST BE AT LEAST TWO THOUSAND MILES. THIS WILL BE READY IN NINETY MINUTES.''

Cameras reeling and cranking away. Flashbulbs popping. The press looked uneasy too. But, of course, there was the psychic pressure of those five hundred million watchers to be considered. They were real. The job was real. And Richards's twelve pounds of Black Irish might be just a figment of his admirable criminal mentality.

"RICHARDS?" A man dressed only in dark slacks and a white shirt rolled up to the elbows in spite of the fall chill strolled out from behind a gaggle of unmarked cars fifty yards beyond Lot 16. He was carrying a bullhorn larger than Richards's. From this distance, Amelia could see only that he was wearing small spectacles; they flashed in the dying sunlight.

"I AM EVAN McCONE."

He knew the name, of course. It was supposed to strike fear into his heart. He was not surprised to find that it *did* strike fear into his heart. Evan McCone was the Chief Hunter. A direct descendent of J. Edgar Hoover and Heinrich Himmler, he thought. The personification of the steel inside the Network's cathode glove. A boogeyman. A name to frighten bad children with. If you don't stop playing with matches, Johnny, I'll let Evan McCone out of your closet.

Fleetingly, in the eye of memory, he recalled a dream-voice. *Are you the man, little brother?*

"YOU'RE LYING, RICHARDS. WE KNOW IT. A MAN WITHOUT A G-A RATING HAS NO WAY OF GETTING DYNACORE. LET THE WOMAN GO AND COME OUT. WE DON'T WANT TO HAVE TO KILL HER, TOO."

Amelia made a weak, wretched hissing noise.

Richards boomed: "THAT MAY GO OVER IN SHAKER HEIGHTS, LITTLE MAN. IN THE STREETS YOU CAN BUY DYNACORE EVERY TWO BLOCKS IF YOU'VE GOT CASH ON THE LINE. AND I DID. GAMES FEDERATION MONEY. YOU HAVE EIGHTY-SIX MINUTES."

"NO DEAL."

"McCONE?"

"YES."

"I'M SENDING THE WOMAN OUT NOW. SHE'S SEEN THE IRISH." Amelia was looking at him with stunned horror. "MEANWHILE, YOU BETTER GET IT IN GEAR. EIGHTY-FIVE MINUTES. I'M NOT BLUFFING, ASSHOLE. ONE BULLET AND WE'RE ALL GOING TO THE MOON."

"No," she whispered. Her face was an unbelieving rictus. "You can't believe I'm going to *lie* for you."

"If you don't, I'm dead. I'm shot and broken and hardly conscious enough to know what I'm saying, but I know this is the best way, one way or the other. Now listen: Dynacore is white and solid, slightly greasy to the touch. It—"

"No, no! *No!*" She clapped her hands over her ears.

"It looks like a bar of Ivory soap. Very dense, though. Now I'm going to describe the imploder ring. It looks—"

She began to weep. "I can't, don't you *know* that? I have my duty as a citizen. My conscience. I have my—"

"Yeah, and they might find out you lied," he added dryly. "Except they won't. Because if you back me, they'll cave in. I'll be off like a bigass bird."

"*I can't!*"

"RICHARDS! SEND THE WOMAN OUT!"

"The imploder ring is gold," he continued. "About two inches in diameter. It looks like a keyring with no keys in it. Attached to it is a slim rod like a mechanical pencil with a G-A trigger device attached to it. The trigger device looks like the eraser on the pencil."

She was rocking back and forth, moaning a little. She had a cheek in either hand and was twisting her flesh as if it were dough.

"I told them I had pulled out to half-cock. That means you would be able to see a single small notch just above the surface of the Irish. Got it?"

No answer; she wept and moaned and rocked.

"Sure you do," he said softly. "You're a bright girl, aren't you?"

"I'm not going to lie," she said.

"If they ask you anything else, you don't know from Rooty-Toot. You didn't see. You were too scared. Except for one thing: I've been holding the ring ever since that first roadblock. You didn't know what it was, but I had it in my hand."

"Better kill me now."

"Go on," he said. "Get out."

She stared at him convulsively, her mouth working, her eyes dark holes. The pretty, self-assured woman with the wraparound shades was all gone. Richards wondered if that woman would ever reappear. He did not think so. Not wholly.

"Go," he said. "Go. Go."

"I—I—*Ah, God*—"

She lunged against the door and half sprang, half fell out. She was on her feet instantly and running. Her hair streamed out behind her and she seemed very beautiful, almost goddesslike, and she ran into the lukewarm starburst of a million flashbulbs.

Carbines flashed up, ready, and were lowered as the crowd ate her. Richards risked cocking an eyebrow over the driver's side window but could see nothing.

He slouched back down, glanced at his watch, and waited for dissolution.

. . . Minus 033
and COUNTING . . .

The red second hand on his watch made two circles. Another two. Another two.

"RICHARDS!"

He raised the bullhorn to his lips. "SEVENTY-NINE MINUTES, Mc-CONE."

Play it right up to the end. The *only* way to play it. Right up to the moment McCone gave the order to fire at will. It would be quick. And it didn't really seem to matter a whole hell of a lot.

After a long grudging, eternal pause: "WE NEED MORE TIME. AT LEAST THREE HOURS. THERE ISN'T AN L/G-A OR A DELTA ON THIS FIELD. ONE WILL HAVE TO BE FLOWN IN."

She had done it. O, amazing grace. The woman had looked into the abyss and then walked out across it. No net. No way back. Amazing.

Of course they didn't believe her. It was their business not to believe anyone about anything. Right now they would be hustling her to a private room in one of the terminals, half a dozen of McCone's picked interrogators waiting. And when they got her there, the litany would begin. *Of course you're upset, Mrs. Williams, but just for the record . . . would you mind going through this once more . . . we're puzzled by one small thing here . . . are you sure that wasn't the other way around . . . how do you know . . . why . . . then what did he say . . .*

So the correct move was to buy time. Fob Richards off with one excuse and then another. There's a fueling problem, we need more time. No crew is on the jetport grounds, we need more time. There's a flying saucer over Runway Zero-Seven, we need more time. And we haven't broken her yet. Haven't quite gotten her to admit that your high explosive consists of an alligator handbag stuffed with assorted Kleenex and change and cosmetics and credit cards. We need more time.

We can't take a chance on killing you yet. We need more time.

"RICHARDS?"

"LISTEN TO ME," he megaphoned back. "YOU HAVE SEVENTY-FIVE MINUTES. THEN IT ALL GOES UP."

No reply.

Spectators had begun to creep back in spite of Armageddon's shadow. Their eyes were wide and wet and sexual. A number of portable spotlights had been requisitioned and focused on the little car, bathing it in a depthless glow and emphasizing the shattered windshield.

Richards tried to imagine the little room where they would be holding her, probing her for the truth, and could not. The press would be excluded, of course. McCone's men would be trying to scare the tits off her and undoubtedly would be succeeding. But how far would they dare go with a woman who did not belong to the ghetto society of the poor where people had no faces? Drugs. There were drugs, Richards knew, drugs that McCone could command immediately, drugs that could make a Yaqui Indian babble out his entire life story like a babe in arms. Drugs that would make a priest rattle off penitents' confessions like a stenographer's recording machine.

A little violence? The modified electric move-alongs that had worked so well in the Seattle riots of 2005? Or only the steady battering of their questions?

The thoughts served no purpose, but he could not shut them out or turn them off. Beyond the terminals there was the unmistakable whine of a Lockheed carrier being warmed up. His bird. The sound of it came in rising and falling cycles. When it cut off suddenly, he knew the fueling had begun. Twenty minutes if they were hurrying. Richards did not think they would be hurrying.

Well, well, well. Here we are. All the cards on the table but one.

McCone? McCone, are you peeking yet? Have you sliced into her mind yet?

Shadows lengthened across the field and everybody waited.

. . . Minus 032
and COUNTING . . .

Richards discovered that the old cliché was a lie. Time did *not* stand still. In some ways it would have been better if it had. Then there at least would have been an end to hope.

Twice the amplified voice informed Richards that he was lying. He told them if it was so, they had better open up. Five minutes later a new amplified voice told him that the Lockheed's flaps were frozen and that fueling would have to begin with another plane. Richards told them that was fine. As long as the plane was ready to go by the original deadline.

The minutes crept by. Twenty-six left, twenty-five, twenty-two, twenty (*she hasn't broken yet, my God, maybe—*), eighteen, fifteen (the plane's engines again, rising to a strident howl as the ground crews went through fuel-system and pre-flight checks), ten minutes, then eight.

"RICHARDS?"

"HERE."

"WE HAVE SIMPLY GOT TO HAVE MORE TIME. THE BIRD'S FLAPS ARE FROZEN SOLID. WE'RE GOING TO IRRIGATE THE VANES WITH LIQUID HYDROGEN BUT WE SIMPLY HAVE TO HAVE TIME."

"YOU HAVE IT. SEVEN MINUTES. THEN I AM GOING TO PROCEED TO THE AIRFIELD USING THE SERVICE RAMP. I WILL BE DRIVING WITH ONE HAND ON THE WHEEL AND ONE HAND ON THE IM-PLODER RING. ALL GATES WILL BE OPENED. AND REMEMBER THAT I'LL BE GETTING CLOSER TO THOSE FUEL TANKS ALL THE TIME."

"YOU DON'T SEEM TO REALIZE THAT WE—"

"I'M THROUGH TALKING, FELLOWS. SIX MINUTES."

The second hand made its orderly, regular turns. Three minutes left, two, one. They would be going for broke in the little room he could not imagine. He tried to call Amelia's image up in his mind and failed. It was already blurring into other faces. One composite face composed of Stacey and Bradley and Elton and Virginia Parrakis and the boy with the dog. All he could remember was that she was soft and pretty in the uninspired way that so many women can be thanks to Max Factor and Revlon and the plastic surgeons who tuck and tie and smooth out and unbend. Soft. Soft. But hard in some deep place. Where did you go hard, WASP woman? Are you hard enough? Or are you blowing the game right now?

He felt something warm running down his chin and discovered he had bitten his lips through, not once but several times.

He wiped his mouth absently, leaving a tear drop-shaped smear of blood on his sleeve, and dropped the car into gear. It rose obediently, lifters grumbling.

"RICHARDS! IF YOU MOVE THAT CAR, WE'LL SHOOT! THE GIRL TALKED! WE KNOW!"

No one fired a shot.

In a way, it was almost anticlimactic.

. . . Minus 031
and COUNTING . . .

The service ramp described a rising arc around the glassine, futuristic Northern States Terminal. The way was lined with police holding everything from Mace-B and tear gas to heavy armor-piercing weaponry. Their faces were flat, dull, uniform. Richards drove slowly, sitting up straight now, and they looked at him with vacant, bovine awe. In much the same way, Richards thought, that cows must look at a farmer who had gone mad and lies kicking and sunfishing and screaming on the barn floor.

The gate to the service area (CAUTION—EMPLOYEES ONLY—NO SMOK-ING—UNAUTHORIZED PERSONS KEEP OUT) had been swung open, and Richards drove sedately through, passing ranks of high-octane tanker trucks and small private planes pulled up on their chocks. Beyond them was a taxiway, wide oil-blackened cement with expansion joints. Here his bird was waiting, a huge white jumbo jet with a dozen turbine engines softly grumbling. Beyond, runways stretched straight and clean into the gathering twilight, seeming to approach a meeting point on the horizon. The bird's roll-up stairway was just being put into place by four men wearing coveralls. To Richards, it looked like the stairs leading to a scaffold.

And, as if to complete the image, the executioner stepped neatly out of the shadows that the plane's huge belly threw. Evan McCone.

Richards looked at him with the curiosity of a man seeing a celebrity for the first time—no matter how many times you see his picture in the movie 3-D's you can't believe his reality until he appears in the flesh—and then the reality takes on a curious tone of hallucination, as if entity had no right to exist separate from image.

He was a small man wearing rimless glasses, with a faint suggestion of a pot belly beneath his well-tailored suit. It was rumored that McCone wore elevator shoes, but if so, they were unobtrusive. There was a small silver flag-pin in his lapel. All in all, he did not look like a monster at all, the inheritor of such fearsome alphabet-soup bureaus as the F.B.I. and the C.I.A. Not like a man who had mastered the technique of the black car in the night, the rubber club, the sly question about relatives back home. Not like a man who had mastered the entire spectrum of fear.

"Ben Richards?" He used no bullhorn, and without it his voice was soft and cultured without being effeminate in the slightest.

"Yes."

"I have a sworn bill from the Games Federation, an accredited arm of the Network Communications Commission, for your apprehension and execution. Will you honor it?"

"Does a hen need a flag?"

"Ah." McCone sounded pleased. "The formalities are taken care of. I believe in formalities, don't you? No, of course you don't. You've been a very informal contestant. That's why you're still alive. Did you know you surpassed the standing *Running Man* record of eight days and five hours some two hours ago? Of course you don't. But you have. Yes. And your escape from the Y.M.C.A. in Boston. Sterling. I understand the Nielsen rating on the program jumped twelve points."

"Wonderful."

"Of course, we almost had you during that Portland interlude. Bad luck. Parrakis swore with his dying breath that you had jumped ship in Auburn. We believed him; he was so obviously a frightened little man."

"Obviously," Richards echoed softly.

"But this last play has been simply brilliant. I salute you. In a way, I'm almost sorry the game has to end. I suspect I shall never run up against a more inventive opponent."

"Too bad," Richards said.

"It's over, you know," McCone said. "The woman broke. We used Sodium Pentothal on her. Old, but reliable." He pulled a small automatic. "Step out, Mr. Richards. I will pay you the ultimate compliment. I'm going to do it right here, where no one can film it. Your death will be one of relative privacy."

"Get ready, then," Richards grinned.

He opened the door and stepped out. The two men faced each other across the blank service area cement.

. . . Minus 030
and COUNTING . . .

It was McCone who broke the deadlock first. He threw back his head and laughed.

It was a very cultured laugh, soft and velvet. "Oh, you are so good, Mr. Richards. *Par excellence*. Raise, call, and raise again. I salute you with honesty: The woman has not broken. She maintains stubbornly that the bulge I see in your pocket there is Black Irish. We can't S.A.P. her because it leaves a definable trace. A single E.E.G. on the woman and our secret would be out. We are in the process of lifting in three ampoules of Canogyn from New York. Leaves no trace. We expect it in forty minutes. Not in time to stop you, alas.

"She *is* lying. It's obvious. If you will pardon a touch of what your fellows like to call elitism, I will offer my observation that the middle class lies well only about sex. May I offer another observation? Of course I may. I am." McCone smiled. "I suspect it's her handbag. We noticed she had none, although she had been shopping. We're quite observant. What happened to her purse if it isn't in your pocket, Richards?"

He would not pick up the gambit. "Shoot me if you're so sure."

McCone spread his hands sorrowfully. "How well I'd love to! But one does not take chances with human life, not even when the odds are fifty to one in your favor. Too much like Russian roulette. Human life has a certain *sacred* quality. The government—*our* government—realizes this. We are humane."

"Yes, yes," Richards said, and smiled ferally. McCone blinked.

"So you see—"

Richards started. The man was hypnotizing him. The minutes were flying, a helicopter was coming up from Boston loaded with three ampoules of jack-me-up-and-turn-me-over (and if McCone said forty minutes he meant twenty), and here he stood, listening to this man's tinkling little anthem. God, he *was* a monster.

"Listen to me," Richards said harshly, interrupting. "The speech is short, little man. When you inject her, she's going to sing the same tune. For the record, it's all here. Dig?"

He locked his gaze with McCone's and began to walk forward.

"I'll see you, shiteater."

McCone stepped aside. Richards didn't even bother to look at him as he passed. Their coat sleeves brushed.

"For the record, I was told the pull on half-cock was about three pounds. I've got about two and a half on now. Give or take."

He had the satisfaction of hearing the man's breath whistle a little faster.

"Richards?"

He looked back from the stairs and McCone was looking up at him, the gold edges of his glasses gleaming and flashing. "When you get in the air, we're going to shoot you down with a ground-to-air missile. The story for the public will be that Richards got a little itchy on the trigger. R.I.P."

"You won't, though."

"No?"

Richards began to smile and gave half a reason. "We're going to be very low and over heavily populated areas. Add twelve fuel pods to twelve pounds of Irish and you got a very big bang potential. Too big. You'd do it if you could get away with it, but you can't." He paused. "You're so bright. Did you anticipate me on the parachute?"

"Oh, yes," McCone said calmly. "It's in the forward passenger compartment. Such old hat, Mr. Richards. Or do you have another trick in your bag?"

"You haven't been stupid enough to tamper with the chute, either, I'll bet."

"Oh no. Too obvious. And you would pull that nonexistent imploder ring just before you struck, I imagine. Quite an effective airburst."

"Goodbye, little man."

"Goodbye, Mr. Richards. And *bon voyage.*" He chuckled. "Yes, you do rate honesty. So I will show you one more card. Just one. We are going to wait for the Canogyn before taking action. You are absolutely right about the missile. For now, just a bluff. Call and raise again, eh? But I can afford to wait. You see, I am never wrong. Never. And I know you are bluffing. So we can afford to wait. But I'm keeping you. 'Voir, Mr. Richards." He waved.

"Soon," Richards said, but not loud enough for McCone to hear. And he grinned.

. . . Minus 029
and COUNTING . . .

The first-class compartment was long and three aisles wide, paneled with real aged sequoia. A wine-colored rug which felt yards deep covered the floor. A 3-D movie screen was cranked up and out of the way on the far wall between the first class and the galley. In seat 100, the bulky parachute pack sat. Richards patted it briefly and went through the galley. Someone had even put coffee on.

He stepped through another door and stood in a short throat which led to the pilots' compartment. To the right the radio operator, a man of perhaps thirty with a care-lined face, looked at Richards bitterly and then back at his instruments. A few steps up and to the left, the navigator sat at his boards and grids and plastic-encased charts.

"The fellow who's going to get us all killed is coming up fellas," he said into his throat mike. He gazed coolly at Richards.

Richards said nothing. The man, after all, was almost certainly right. He limped into the nose of the plane.

The pilot was fifty or better, an old war-horse with the red nose of a steady drinker, and the clear, perceptive eyes of a man who was not even close to the alcoholic edge. His co-pilot was ten years younger, with a luxuriant growth of red hair spilling out from under his cap.

"Hello, Mr. Richards," the pilot said. He glanced at the bulge in Richards's pocket before he looked at his face. "Pardon me if I don't shake hands. I'm Flight Captain Don Holloway. This is my co-pilot Wayne Duninger."

"Under the circumstances, not very pleased to meet you," Duninger said.

Richards's mouth quirked. "In the same spirit, let me add that I'm sorry to be here. Captain Holloway, you're patched into communications with McCone, aren't you?"

"We sure are. Through Kippy Friedman, our communications man."

"Give me something to talk into."

Holloway handed him a microphone with infinite carefulness.

"Get going on your preflight," Richards said. "Five minutes."

"Will you want the explosive bolts on the rear loading door armed?" Duninger said with great eagerness.

"Tend your knitting," Richards said coldly. It was time to finish it off, make the final bet. His brain felt hot, overheated, on the verge of blowing a bearing. Call and raise, that was the game.

I'm going to sky's the limit right now, McCone.

"Mr. Friedman?"

"Yes."

"This is Richards. I want to talk to McCone."

Dead air for half a minute. Holloway and Duninger weren't watching him any-more; they were going through preflight, reading gauges and pressures, checking flaps, doors, switches. The rising and falling of the huge G-A turbines began again, but now much louder, strident. When McCone's voice finally came, it was small against the brute noise.

"McCone here."

"Come on, maggot. You and the woman are going for a ride. Show up at the loading door in three minutes or I pull the ring."

Duninger stiffened in his bucket seat as if he had been shot. When he went back to his numbers his voice was shaken and terrified.

If he's got guts, this is where he calls. Asking for the woman gives it away. If he's got guts.

Richards waited.

A clock was ticking in his head.

. . . Minus 028
and COUNTING . . .

When McCone's voice came, it contained a foreign, blustery note. Fear? Possibly. Richards's heart lurched in his chest. Maybe it was all going to fall together. Maybe.

"You're nuts, Richards. I'm not—"

"You *listen*," Richards said, punching through McCone's voice. "And while you are, remember that this conversation is being party-lined by every ham operator within sixty miles. The word is going to get around. You're not working in the dark, little man. You're right out on the big stage. You're coming because you're too chicken-shit to pull a double cross when you know it will get you dead. The woman's coming because I told her where I was going."

Weak. Punch him harder. Don't let him think.

"Even if you should live when I pull the ring, you won't be able to get a job selling apples." He was clutching the handbag in his pocket with frantic, maniacal tightness. "So that's it. Three minutes. Signing off."

"Richards, wait—"

He signed off, choking McCone's voice. He handed the mike back to Holloway, and Holloway took it with fingers that trembled only slightly.

"You've got guts," Holloway said slowly. "I'll say that. I don't think I ever saw so much guts."

"There will be more guts than anyone ever saw if he pulls that ring," Duninger said.

"Continue with your preflight, please," Richards said. "I am going back to welcome our guests. We go in five minutes."

He went back and pushed the chute over to the window seat, then sat down watching the door between first class and second class. He would know very soon. He would know very soon.

His hand worked with steady, helpless restlessness on Amelia Williams's handbag.

Outside it was almost full dark.

. . . Minus 027
and COUNTING . . .

They came up the stairs with a full forty-five seconds to spare. Amelia was panting and frightened, her hair blown into a haphazard beehive by the steady wind that rolled this manmade flatland. McCone's appearance was outwardly unchanged; he remained neat and unaffected, unruffled you might say, but his eyes were dark with a hate that was nearly psychotic.

"You haven't won a thing, maggot," he said quietly. "We haven't even started to play our trump cards yet."

"It's nice to see you again, Mrs. Williams," Richards said mildly.

As if he had given her a signal, pulled an invisible string, she began to weep. It was not a hysterical weeping; it was an entirely hopeless sound that came from her belly like hunks of slag. The force of it made her stagger, then crumple to the plush carpet of this plush first-class section with her face cupped in her hands, as if to hold it on. Richards's blood had dried to a tacky maroon smear on her blouse. Her full skirt, spread around her and hiding her legs, made her look like a wilted flower.

Richards felt sorry for her. It was a shallow emotion, feeling sorry, but the best he could manage.

"Mr. Richards?" It was Holloway's voice over the cabin intercom.

"Yes."

"Do we . . . are we green?"

"Yes."

"Then I'm giving the service crew the order to remove the stairs and seal us up. Don't get nervous with that thing."

"All right, Captain. Thank you."

"You gave yourself away when you asked for the woman. You know that, don't you?" McCone seemed to be smiling and scowling at the same time; the overall effect was frighteningly paranoid. His hands were clenching and unclenching.

"Ah, so?" Richards said mildly. "And since you're never wrong, you'll undoubtedly jump me before we take off. That way you'll be out of jeopardy and come up smelling like a rose, right?"

McCone's lips parted in a tiny snarl, and then pressed together until they went white. He made no move. The plane began to pick up a tiny vibration as the engines cycled higher and higher.

The noise was suddenly muted as the boarding door in second class was slammed shut. Leaning over slightly to peer out one of the circular windows on the port side, Richards could see the crew trundling away the stairs.

Now we're all on the scaffold, he thought.

. . . Minus 026
and COUNTING . . .

The FASTEN SEAT BELTS/ NO SMOKING sign to the right of the trundled-up movie screen flashed on. The airplane began a slow, ponderous turn beneath them. Richards had gained all his knowledge of jets from the Free-Vee and from reading, much of it lurid adventure fiction, but this was only the second time he had ever been on one; and it made the shuttle from Harding to New York look like a bathtub toy. He found the huge motion beneath his feet disturbing.

"Amelia?"

She looked up slowly, her face ravaged and tear streaked. "Uh?" Her voice was rusty, dazed, mucus clogged. As if she had forgotten where she was.

"Come forward. We're taking off." He looked at McCone. "You go wherever you please, little man. You have the run of the ship. Just don't bother the crew."

McCone said nothing and sat down near the curtained divider between first and second class. Then, apparently thinking better of it, he pushed through into the next section and was gone.

Richards walked to the woman, using the high backs of the seats for support. "I'd like the window seat," he said. "I've only flown once before." He tried to smile but she only looked at him dumbly.

He slid in, and she sat next to him. She buckled his belt for him so his hand did not have to come out of his pocket.

"You're like a bad dream," she said. "One that never ends."

"I'm sorry."

"I didn't—" she began, and he clamped a hand over her mouth and shook his head. He mouthed the word *No!* at her eyes.

The plane swung around with slow, infinite care, turbines screaming, and began to trundle toward the runways like an ungainly duck about to enter the water. It was so big that Richards felt as if the plane were standing still and the earth itself was moving.

Maybe it's all illusion, he thought wildly. *Maybe they've rigged 3-D projectors outside all the windows and—*

He cut the thought off.

Now they had reached the end of the taxiway and the plane made a cumbersome right turn. They ran at right angles to the runways, passing Three and Two. At One they turned left and paused for a second.

Over the intercom Holloway said expressionlessly: "Taking off, Mr. Richards."

The plane began to move slowly at first, at no more than air-car speed, and then there was a sudden terrifying burst of acceleration that made Richards want to scream aloud in terror.

He was driven back into the soft pile of his seat, and the landing lights outside suddenly began to leap by with dizzying speed. The scrub bushes and exhaust-stunted trees on the desolate, sunset-riven horizon roared toward them. The engines wound up and up and up. The floor began to vibrate again.

He suddenly realized that Amelia Williams was holding on to his shoulder with both hands, her face twisted into a miserable grimace of fear.

Dear God, she's never flown either!

"We're going," he said. He found himself repeating it over and over and over, unable to stop. "We're going. We're going."

"Where?" she whispered.

He didn't answer. He was just beginning to know.

. . . Minus 025
and COUNTING . . .

The two troopers on roadblock duty at the eastern entrance of the jetport watched the huge liner fling itself down the runway, gaining speed. Its lights blinked orange and green in the growing dark, and the howl of its engines buffeted their ears.

"He's going. Christ, he's going."

"Where?" said the other.

They watched the dark shape as it separated from the ground. Its engines took on a curiously flat sound, like artillery practice on a cold morning. It rose at a steep angle, as real and as tangible and as prosaic as a cube of butter on a plate, yet improbable with flight.

"You think he's got it?"

"Hell, I don't know."

The roar of the jet was now coming to them in falling cycles.

"I'll tell you one thing, though." The first turned from the diminishing lights and turned up his collar. "I'm glad he's got that bastard with him. That McCone."

"Can I ask you a personal question?"

"As long as I don't have to answer it."

"Would you like to see him pull it off?"

The trooper said nothing for a long time. The sound of the jet faded, faded, faded, until it disappeared into the underground hum of nerves at work.

"Yes."

"Do you think he will?"

A crescent smile in the darkness. "My friend, I think there's gonna be a big boom."

. . . Minus 024
and COUNTING . . .

The earth had dropped away below them.

Richards stared out wonderingly, unable to drink his fill; he had slept through the other flight as if in wait for this one. The sky had deepened to a shade that hung on the borderline between royal velvet and black. Stars poked through with hesitant brilliance. On the western horizon, the only remnant of the sun was a bitter orange line that illuminated the dark earth below not at all. There was a nestle of lights below he took to be Derry.

"Mr. Richards?"

"Yes." He jumped in his seat as if he had been poked.

"We are in a holding pattern right now. That means we are describing a large circle above the Voigt Jetport. Instructions?"

Richards thought carefully. It wouldn't do to give too much away.

"What's the absolute lowest you can fly this thing?"

There was a long pause for consultation. "We could get away with two thousand feet," Holloway said cautiously. "It's against N.S.A. regs, but—"

"Never mind that," Richards said. "I have to put myself in your hands to a certain extent, Mr. Holloway. I know very little of flying and I'm sure you've been briefed on that. But please remember that the people who are full of bright ideas about how to bamboozle me are all on the ground and out of danger. If you lie to me about anything and I find out—"

"Nobody up here is going to do any lying," Holloway said. "We're only interested in getting this thing back down the way it went up."

"Okay. Good." He gave himself time to think. Amelia Williams sat rigidly beside him, her hands folded in her lap.

"Go due west," he said abruptly. "Two thousand feet. Point out the sights as we go along, please."

"The sights?"

"What we're going over," Richards said. "I've only flown once before."

"Oh." Holloway sounded relieved.

The plane banked beneath their feet and the dark sunset line outside the window tilted on its ear. Richards watched, fascinated. Now it gleamed aslant the thick window, making odd, fugitive sungleams just beyond the glass. *We're chasing the sun,* he thought. *Isn't that amazing?*

It was thirty-five minutes after six.

. . . Minus 023
and COUNTING . . .

The back of the seat in front of Richards was a revelation in itself. There was a pocket with a safety handbook in it. In case of air turbulence, fasten your belt. If the cabin loses pressure, pull down the air mask directly over your head. In case of engine trouble, the stewardess will give you further instructions. In case of sudden explosive death, hope you have enough dental fillings to insure identification.

There was a small Free-Vee set into the seat panel at eye level. A metal card below it reminded the viewer that channels would come and go with a fair degree of speed. A touch-control channel selector was provided for the hungry viewer.

Below and to the right of the Free-Vee was a pad of airline stationery and a G-A stylus on a chain. Richards pulled out a sheet and wrote clumsily on his knee:

"Odds are 99 out of 100 that you're bugged, shoe mike or hair mike, maybe mesh transmitter on your sleeve. McCone listening and waiting for you to drop the other shoe, I bet. In a minute have a hysterical outburst and beg me not to pull the ring. It'll make our chances better. You game?"

She nodded and Richards hesitated, then wrote again:

"Why did you lie about it?"

She plucked the stylus out of his hand and held it over the paper on his knee for a moment and then wrote: "Don't know. You made me feel like a murderer. Wife. And you seemed so"—the stylus paused, wavered and then scrawled—"pitiful."

Richards raised his eyebrows and grinned a little—it hurt. He offered her the stylus but she shook her head mutely. He wrote: "Go into your act in about 5 minutes."

She nodded and Richards crumpled the paper and stuffed it into the ashtray embedded in the armrest. He lit the paper. It puffed into flame and blazed brightly for a moment, kindling a tiny reflective glow in the window. Then it collapsed into ashes which Richards poked thoughtfully.

About five minutes later Amelia Williams began to moan. It sounded so real that for a moment Richards was startled. Then it flashed across his mind that it probably *was* real.

"Please don't," she said. "Please don't make that man . . . have to try you. I never did anything to you. I want to go home to my husband. We have a daughter, too. She's six. She'll wonder where her mommy is."

Richards felt his eyebrow rise and fall twice in an involuntary tic. He didn't want her to be that good. Not *that* good.

"He's dumb," he told her, trying not to speak for an unseen audience, "but I don't think he's that dumb. It will be all right, Mrs. Williams."

"That's easy for you to say. You've got nothing to lose."

He didn't answer her. She was so patently right. Nothing, anyway, that he hadn't lost already.

"Show it to him," she pleaded. "For God's sake, why don't you show it to him? Then he'd have to believe you . . . call off the people on the ground. They're tracking us with missiles. I heard him say so."

"I can't show him," Richards said. "To take it out of my pocket would mean putting the ring on safety or taking the full risk of blowing us up accidentally. Besides," he added, injecting mockery into his voice, "I don't think I'd show him if I could. He's the maggot with something to lose. Let him sweat it."

"I don't think I can stand it," she said dully. "I almost think I'd rather joggle you and have it over. That's the way it's going to end anyway, isn't it?"

"You haven't—" he began, and then the door between first and second was snapped open and McCone half strode, half lunged through. His face was calm, but beneath the calm was an odd sheeny look which Richards recognized immediately. The sheen of fear, white and waxy and glowing.

"Mrs. Williams," he said briskly. "Coffee, if you please. For seven. You'll have to play stewardess on this flight, I'm afraid."

She got up without looking at either of them. "Where?"

"Forward," McCone said smoothly. "Just follow your nose." He was a mild, blinking sort of man—and ready to lunge at Amelia Williams the moment she showed a sign of going for Richards.

She made her way up the aisle without looking back.

McCone stared at Richards and said: "Would you give this up if I could promise you amnesty, pal?"

"*Pal.* That word sounds really greasy in your mouth," Richards marveled. He flexed his free hand, looked at it. The hand was caked with small runnels of dried blood, dotted with tiny scrapes and scratches from his broken-ankle hike through the southern Maine woods. "Really greasy. You make it sound like two pounds of fatty hamburger cooking in the pan. The only kind you can get at the Welfare Stores in Co-Op City." He looked at McCone's well-concealed pot. "That, now. That looks more like a steak gut. Prime cut. No fat on prime cut except that crinkly little ring around the outside right?"

"Amnesty," McCone repeated. "How does that word sound?"

"Like a lie," Richards said, smiling. "Like a fat fucking lie. Don't you think I know you're nothing but the hired help?"

McCone flushed. It was not a soft flush at all; it was hard and red and bricklike. "It's going to be good to have you on my home court," he said. "We've got hi-impact slugs that will make your head look like a pumpkin dropped on a sidewalk from the top floor of a skyscraper. Gas filled. They explode on contact. A gut shot, on the other hand—"

Richards screamed: *"Here it goes! I'm pulling the ring!"*

McCone screeched. He staggered back two steps, his rump hit the well-padded arm of seat number 95 across the way, he overbalanced and fell into it like a man into a sling, his arms flailing the air around his head in crazed warding-off gestures.

His hands froze about his head like petrified birds, splay fingered. His face stared through their grotesque frame like a plaster death-mask on which someone had hung a pair of gold-rimmed spectacles for a joke.

Richards began to laugh. The noise of it was cracked at first, hesitant, foreign to his own ears. How long had it been since he had had a real laugh, an honest one, the kind that comes freely and helplessly from the deepest root of the stomach? It seemed to him that he had never had one in his whole gray, struggling, earnest life. But he was having one now.

You bastard.

McCone's voice had failed him; he could only mouth the words. His face was twisted and scrunched like the face of a badly used teddy bear.

Richards laughed. He held on to one arm of his seat with his free hand and just laughed and laughed and laughed.

. . . Minus 022
and COUNTING . . .

When Holloway's voice informed Richards that the plane was crossing the border between Canada and the state of Vermont (Richards supposed he knew his business; he himself could see nothing but darkness below them, interrupted by occasional clusters of light), he set his coffee down carefully and said:

"Could you supply me with a map of North America, Captain Holloway?"

"Physical or political?" A new voice cut in. The navigator's, Richards supposed. Now he was supposed to play obligingly dumb and not know which map he wanted. Which he didn't.

"Both," he said flatly.

"Are you going to send the woman up for them?"

"What's your name, pal?"

The hesitant pause of a man who realizes with sudden trepidation that he has been singled out. "Donahue."

"You've got legs, Donahue. Suppose you trot them back here yourself."

Donahue trotted them back. He had long hair combed back greaser fashion and pants tailored tight enough to show what looked like a bag of golf balls at the crotch. The maps were encased in limp plastic. Richards didn't know what Donahue's balls were encased in.

"I didn't mean to mouth off," he said unwillingly. Richards thought he could peg him. Well-off young men with a lot of free time often spent much of it roaming the shabby pleasure areas of the big cities, roaming in well-heeled packs, sometimes on foot, more often on choppers. They were queer-stompers. Queers, of course, had to be eradicated. Save our bathrooms for democracy. They rarely ventured beyond the twilight pleasure areas into the full darkness of the ghettos. When they did, they got the shit kicked out of them.

Donahue shifted uneasily under Richards's long gaze. "Anything else?"

"You a queer-stomper, pal?"

"Huh?"

"Never mind. Go on back. Help them fly the plane."

Donahue went back at a fast shuffle.

Richards quickly discovered that the map with the towns and cities and roads was the political map. Pressing one finger down from Derry to the Canada-Vermont border in a western-reaching straightedge, he located their approximate position.

"Captain Holloway?"

"Yes."

"Turn left."

"Huh?" Holloway sounded frankly startled.

"South, I mean. Due south. And remember—"

"I'm remembering," Holloway said. "Don't worry."

The plane banked. McCone sat hunched in the seat he had fallen into, staring at Richards with hungry, wanting eyes.

. . . Minus 021
and COUNTING . . .

Richards found himself drifting in and out of a daze, and it frightened him. The steady drone of the engines were insidious, hypnotic. McCone was aware of what-was happening, and his leaning posture became more and more vulpine. Amelia was also aware. She cringed miserably in a forward seat near the galley, watching them both.

Richards drank two more cups of coffee. Not much help. It was becoming increasingly difficult to concentrate on the coordination of his map and Holloway's toneless commentary on their outlaw flight.

Finally he drove his fist into his side where the bullet had taken him. The pain was immediate and intense, like a dash of cold water in the face. A whistling half-whispered screech issued from either side of his clenched mouth, like stereo. Fresh blood wet his shirt and sieved through onto his hand.

Amelia moaned.

"We'll be passing over Albany in about six minutes," Holloway said. "If you look out, you'll see it coming up on your left."

"Relax," Richards said to no one, to himself. "Relax. Just relax."

God, will it be over soon? Yes. Quite soon.

It was quarter to eight.

. . . Minus 020
and COUNTING . . .

It could have been a bad dream, a nightmare that had crawled out of the dark and into the unhealthy limelight of his half-awake mind—more properly a vision or an hallucination. His brain was working and concentrating on one level, dealing with the problem of navigation and the constant danger of McCone. On another, something black was taking place. Things were moving in the dark.

Track on. Positive.

Huge, whining servomechanisms turning in the dark, in the night. Infrared eyes glowing in unknown spectrums. Pale green foxfire of dials and swinging radar scopes.

Lock. We have a lock.

Trucks rumbling along back-country roads, and on triangulated flatbeds two hundred miles apart, microwave dishes swing at the night sky. Endless streams of electrons fly out on invisible batwings. Bounce, echo. The strong blip and the fading afterimage lingering until the returning swing of light illuminates it in a slightly more southerly position.

Solid?

Yeah. Two hundred miles south of Newark. It could be Newark.

Newark's on Red, also southern New York.

Executive Hold still in effect?

That's right.

We had him dead-bang over Albany.

Be cool, pal.

Trucks thundering through closed towns where people look out of cardboard-patched windows with terrified, hating eyes. Roaring like prehistoric beasts in the night.

Open the holes.

Huge, grinding motors slide huge concrete duncecaps aside, shunting them down gleaming steel tracks. Circular silos like the entrances to the underworld of the Morlocks. Gasps of liquid hydrogen escaping into the air.

Tracking. We are tracking, Newark.

Roger, Springfield. Keep us in.

Drunks sleeping in alleys wake foggily to the thunder of the passing trucks and stare mutely at the slices of sky between close-leaning buildings. Their eyes are faded and yellow, their mouths are dripping lines. Hands pull with senile reflex for newsies to protect against the autumn cold, but the newsies are no longer there, the Free-Vee has killed the last of them. Free-Vee is king of the world. Hallelujah. Rich folks smoke Dokes. The yellow eyes catch an unknown glimpse of high, blinking lights in the sky. Flash, flash. Red and green, red and green. The thunder of the trucks has faded, ramming back and forth in the stone canyons like the fists of vandals. The drunks sleep again. Bitchin'.

We got him west of Springfield.

Go-no-go in five minutes.

From Harding?

Yes.

He's bracketed and braced.

All across the night the invisible batwings fly, drawing a glittering net across the northeast corner of America. Servos controlled by General Atomics computers function smoothly. The missiles turn and shift subtly in a thousand places to follow the blinking red and green lights that sketch the sky. They are like steel rattlesnakes filled with waiting venom.

Richards saw it all, and functioned even as he saw it. The duality of his brain was oddly comforting, in a way. It induced a detachment that was much like insanity. His bloodcrusted finger followed their southward progress smoothly. Now south of Springfield, now west of Hartford, now—

Tracking.

. . . Minus 019
and COUNTING . . .

"Mr. Richards?"

"Yes."

"We are over Newark, New Jersey."

"Yes," Richards said. "I've been watching. Holloway?"

Holloway didn't reply, but Richards knew he was listening.

"They've got a bead drawn on us all the way, don't they?"

"Yes," Holloway said.

Richards looked at McCone. "I imagine they're trying to decide if they can afford to do away with their professional bloodhound here. Imagine they'll decide in the affirmative. After all, all they have to do is train a new one."

McCone was snarling at him, but Richards thought it was a completely unconscious gesture, one that could probably be traced all the way to McCone's ancestors, the Neanderthals who had crept up behind their enemies with large rocks rather than battling to the death in the honorable but unintelligent manner.

"When do we get over open country again, Captain?"

"We won't. Not on a due south heading. We will strike open sea after we cross the offshore North Carolina drilling derricks, though."

"Everything south of here is a suburb of New York City?"

"That's about the size of it," Holloway said.

"Thank you."

Newark was sprawled and groined below them like a handful of dirty jewelry thrown carelessly into some lady's black-velvet vanity box.

"Captain?"

Wearily: "Yes."

"You will now proceed due west."

McCone jumped as if he had been goosed. Amelia made a surprised coughing noise in her throat.

"West?" Holloway asked. He sounded unhappy and frightened for the first time. "You're asking for it, going that way. West takes us over pretty open country. Pennsylvania between Harrisburg and Pittsburgh is all farm country. There isn't another big city east of Cleveland."

"Are you planning my strategy for me, Captain?"

"No, I—"

"Due west," Richards repeated curtly.

Newark swung away beneath them.

"You're crazy," McCone said. "They'll blow us apart."

"With you and five other innocent people on board? This honorable country?"

"It will be a mistake," McCone said harshly. "A mistake on purpose."

"Don't you watch *The National Report?*" Richards asked, still smiling. "We don't make mistakes. We haven't made a mistake since 1950."

Newark was sliding away beneath the wing; darkness took its place.

"You're not laughing anymore," Richards said.

. . . Minus 018
and COUNTING . . .

A half-hour later Holloway came on the voice-com again. He sounded excited.

"Richards, we've been informed by Harding Red that they want to beam a high-intensity broadcast at us. From Games Federation. I was told you would find it very much worth your while to turn on the Free-Vee."

"Thank you."

He regarded the blank Free-Vee screen and almost turned it on. He withdrew his hand as if the back of the next seat with its embedded screen was hot. A curious sense of dread and *déjà vu* filled him. It was too much like going back to the beginning, Sheila with her thin, worked face, the smell of Mrs. Jenner's cabbage cooking down the hall. The blare of the games. *Treadmill to Bucks. Swim the Crocodiles.* Cathy's screams. There could never be another child, of course, not even if he could take all this back, withdraw it, and go back to the beginning. Even the one had been against fantastically high odds.

"Turn it on," McCone said. "Maybe they're going to offer us—you—a deal."

"Shut up," Richards said.

He waited, letting the dread fill him up like heavy water. The curious sense of presentiment. He hurt very badly. His wound was still bleeding, and his legs felt weak and far away. He didn't know if he could get up to finish this charade when the time came.

With a grunt, Richards leaned forward again and pushed the ON button. The Free-Vee sprang to incredibly clear, amplified-signal life. The face that filled the screen, patiently waiting, was very black and very familiar. Dan Killian. He was sitting at a kidney-shaped mahogany desk with the Games symbol on it.

"Hello there," Richards said softly.

He could have fallen out of his seat when Killian straightened up, grinned, and said, "Hello there yourself, Mr. Richards."

. . . Minus 017
and COUNTING . . .

"I can't see you," Killian said, "but I can hear you. The jet's voice-com is being relayed through the radio equipment in the cockpit. They tell me you're shot up."

"It's not as bad as it looks," Richards said. "I got scratched up in the woods."

"Oh yes," Killian said. "The famous Run Through the Woods. Bobby Thompson canonized it on the air just tonight—along with your current exploit, of course. Tomorrow those woods will be full of people looking for a scrap of your shirt, or maybe even a cartridge case."

"That's too bad," Richards said. "I saw a rabbit."

"You've been the greatest contestant we've ever had, Richards. Through a combination of luck and skill, you've been positively the greatest. Great enough for us to offer you a deal."

"What deal? Nationally televised firing squad?"

"This plane hijack has been the most spectacular, but it's also been the dumbest. Do you know why? Because for the first time you're not near your own people. You left them behind when you left the ground. Even the woman that's protecting you. You may think she's yours. *She* may even think it. But she's not. There's no one up there but us, Richards. You're a dead duck. Finally."

"People keep telling me that and I keep drawing breath."

"You've been drawing breath for the last two hours strictly on Games Federation say-so. I did it. And I'm the one that finally shoved through the authorization for the deal I'm going to offer you. There was strong opposition from the old guard—this kind of thing has never been done—but I'm going through with it.

"You asked me who you could kill if you could go all the way to the top with a machine gun. One of them would have been me. Richards. Does that surprise you?"

"I suppose it does. I had you pegged for the house nigger."

Killian threw back his head and laughed, but the laughter sounded forced—the laughter of a man playing for high stakes and laboring under a great tension.

"Here's the deal, Richards. Fly your plane to Harding. There will be a Games limo waiting at the airport. An execution will be performed—a fake. Then you join our team."

There was a startled yelp of rage from McCone. "You black bastard—"

Amelia Williams looked stunned.

"Very good," Richards said. "I knew you were good, but this is really great. What a fine used-car salesman you would have made, Killian."

"Did McCone sound like I was lying?"

"McCone is a fine actor. He did a little song and dance at the airport that could have won an Academy Award." Still, he was troubled. McCone's hustling away of Amelia for coffee when it appeared she might trip the Irish, McCone's steady, heavy antagonism—they didn't fit. Or did they? His mind began to pinwheel. "Maybe you're springing this on him without his knowledge. Counting on his reaction to make it look even better."

Killian said: "You've done your song and dance with the plastic explosive, Mr. Richards. We know—*know*—that you are bluffing. But there is a button on this desk, a small red button, which is not a bluff. Twenty seconds after I push it, that plane will be torn apart by surface-to-air Diamondback missiles carrying clean nuclear warheads."

"The Irish isn't fake, either." But there was a curdled taste in his mouth. The bluff was soured.

"Oh, it is. You couldn't get on a Lockheed G-A plane with a plastic explosive. Not without tripping the alarms. There are four separate detectors on the plane, installed to foil hijackers. A fifth was installed in the parachute you asked for. I can tell you that the alarm lights in the Voigt Field control tower were watched with great interest and trepidation when you got on. The consensus was that you probably had the Irish. You have proved so resourceful all the way up the line that it seemed like a fair assumption to make. There was more than a little relief when none of those lights went on. I assume you never had the opportunity to pick any up. Maybe you never thought of it until too late. Well, doesn't matter. It makes your position worse, but—"

McCone was suddenly standing beside Richards. "Here it goes," he said, grinning. "Here is where I blow your fucking head off, donkey." He pointed his gun at Richards's temple.

. . . Minus 016
and COUNTING . . .

"You're dead if you do," Killian said.

McCone hesitated, fell back a step, and stared at the Free-Vee unbelievingly. His face began to twist and crumple again. His lips writhed in a silent effort to gain speech. When it finally came, it was a whisper of thwarted rage.

"I can take him! Right now! Right here! We'll all be safe! We'll—"

Wearily, Killian said: "You're safe now, you God damned fool. And Donahue could have taken him—if we wanted him taken."

"This man is a criminal!" McCone's voice was rising. "He's killed police officers! Committed acts of anarchy and air piracy! He's . . . he's publicly humiliated me and my department!"

"Sit down," Killian said, and his voice was as cold as the deep space between planets. "It's time you remembered who pays your salary, Mr. Chief Hunter."

"I'm going to the Council President with this!" McCone was raving now. Spittle flew from his lips. "You're going to be chopping cotton when this is over, nig! You goddam worthless night-fighting sonofabitch—"

"Please throw your gun on the floor," a new voice said. Richards looked around, startled. It was Donahue, the navigator, looking colder and deadlier than ever. His greased hair gleamed in the cabin's indirect lighting. He was holding a wire-stock Magnum/Springstun machine pistol, and it was trained on McCone. "Robert S. Donahue, old-timer. Games Council Control. Throw it on the floor."

. . . Minus 015
and COUNTING . . .

McCone looked at him for a long second, and then the gun thumped on the heavy pile of the carpet. "You—"

"I think we've heard all the rhetoric we need," Donahue said. "Go back into second class and sit down like a good boy."

McCone backed up several paces, snarling futilely. He looked to Richards like a vampire in an old horror movie that had been thwarted by a cross.

When he was gone, Donahue threw Richards a sardonic little salute with the barrel of his gun and smiled. "He won't bother you again."

"You still look like a queer-stomper," Richards said evenly.

The small smile faded. Donahue stared at him with sudden, empty dislike for a moment, and then went forward again.

Richards turned back to the Free-Vee screen. He found that his pulse rate had remained perfectly steady. He had no shortness of breath, no rubber legs. Death had become a normality.

"Are you there, Mr. Richards?" Killian asked.

"Yes I am."

"The problem has been handled?"

"Yes."

"Good. Let me get back to what I was saying."

"Go ahead."

Killian sighed at his tone. "I was saying that our knowledge of your bluff makes your position worse, but makes our credibility better. Do you see why?"

"Yes," Richards said detachedly. "It means you could have blown this bird out of the sky anytime. Or you could have had Holloway set the plane down at will. McCone would have bumped me."

"Exactly. Do you believe we know you are bluffing?"

"No. But you're better than McCone. Using your planted houseboy was a fine stroke."

Killian laughed. "Oh, Richards. You are such a peach. Such a rare, iridescent bird." And yet again it sounded forced, tense, pressured. It came to Richards that Killian was holding information which he wanted badly not to tell.

"If you really had it, you would have pulled the string when McCone put the gun to your head. You knew he was going to kill you. Yet you sat there."

Richards knew it was over, knew that they knew. A smile cracked his features. Killian would appreciate that. He was a man of a sharp and sardonic turn of mind. Make them pay to see the hole card, then.

"I'm not buying any of this. If you push me, everything goes bang."

"And you wouldn't be the man you are if you didn't spin it out to the very end. Mr. Donahue?"

"Yes, sir." Donahue's cool, efficient, emotionless voice came over the voice-com and out of the Free-Vee almost simultaneously.

"Please go back and remove Mrs. Williams's pocketbook from Mr. Richards's pocket. You're not to harm him in any way."

"Yes, sir." Richards was eerily reminded of the plastipunch that had stenciled his original I.D. card at Games headquarters. *Clitter-clitter-clitter.*

Donahue reappeared and walked toward Richards. His face was smooth and cold and empty. *Programmed.* The word leaped into Richards's mind.

"Stand right there, pretty boy," Richards remarked, shifting the hand in his coat pocket slightly. "The Man there is safe on the ground. You're the one that's going to the moon."

He thought the steady stride might have faltered for just a second and the eyes seemed to have winced the tiniest uncertain bit, and then he came on again. He might have been promenading on the Côte d'Azur . . . or approaching a gibbering homosexual cowering at the end of a blind alley.

Briefly Richards considered grabbing the parachute and fleeing. Hopeless. Flee? Where? The men's bathroom at the far end of the third class was the end of the line.

"See you in hell," he said softly, and made a pulling gesture in his pocket. This time the reaction was a little better. Donahue made a grunting noise and threw his hands up to protect his face in an instinctive gesture as old as man himself. He lowered them, still in the land of the living, looking embarrassed and very angry.

Richards took Amelia Williams's pocketbook out of his muddy, torn coat pocket and threw it. It struck Donahue's chest and plopped at his feet like a dead bird. Richards's hand was slimed with sweat. Lying on his knee again, it looked strange and white and foreign. Donahue picked up the bag, looked in it perfunctorily, and handed it to Amelia. Richards felt a stupid sort of sadness at its passage. In a way, it was like losing an old friend.

"Boom," he said softly.

. . . Minus 014
and COUNTING . . .

"Your boy is very good," Richards said tiredly, when Donahue had retreated again. "I got him to flinch, but I was hoping he'd pee his pants." He was beginning to notice an odd doubling of his vision. It came and went. He checked his side gingerly. It was clotting reluctantly for the second time. "What now?" he asked. "Do you set up cameras at the airport so everyone can watch the desperado get it?"

"Now the deal," Killian said softly. His face was dark, unreadable. Whatever he had been holding back was now just below the surface. Richards knew it. And suddenly he was filled with dread again. He wanted to reach out and turn the Free-Vee off. Not hear it anymore. He felt his insides begin a slow and terrible quaking—an actual, literal quaking. But he could not turn it off. Of course not. It was, after all, Free.

"Get thee behind me, Satan," he said thickly.

"What?" Killian looked startled.

"Nothing. Make your point."

Killian did not speak. He looked down at his hands. He looked up again. Richards felt an unknown chamber of his mind groan with psychic presentiment. It seemed to him that the ghosts of the poor and the nameless, of the drunks sleeping in alleys, were calling his name.

"McCone is played out," Killian said softly. "You know it because you did it. Cracked him like a soft-shelled egg. We want you to take his place."

Richards, who thought he had passed the point of all shock, found his mouth hanging open in utter, dazed incredulity. It was a lie. Had to be. Yet—Amelia had her purse back now. There was no reason for them to lie or offer false illusions. He was hurt and alone. Both McCone and Donahue were armed. One bullet administered just above the left ear would put a neat end to him with no fuss, no muss, or bother.

Conclusion: Killian was telling God's truth.

"You're nuts," he muttered.

"No. You're the best runner we've ever had. And the best runner knows the best places to look. Open your eyes a little and you'll see that *The Running Man* is designed for something besides pleasuring the masses and getting rid of dangerous people. Richards, the Network is always in the market for fresh new talent. We have to be."

Richards tried to speak, could say nothing. The dread was still in him, widening, heightening, thickening.

"There's never been a Chief Hunter with a family," he finally said. "You ought to know why. The possibilities for extortion—"

"Ben," Killian said with infinite gentleness, "your wife and daughter are dead. They've been dead for over ten days."

. . . Minus 013
and COUNTING . . .

Dan Killian was talking, had been perhaps for some time, but Richards heard him only distantly, distorted by an odd echo effect in his mind. It was like being trapped in a very deep well and hearing someone call down. His mind had gone midnight dark, and the darkness served as the background for a kind of scrapbook slide show. An old Kodak of Sheila wiggling in the halls of Trades High with a loose-leaf binder under her arm. Micro skirts had just come back into fashion then. A freeze-frame of the two of them sitting at the end of the Bay Pier (Admission: Free), backs to the camera, looking out at the water. Hands linked. Sepia-toned photo of a young man in an ill-fitting suit and a young woman in her mother's best dress—specially taken up—standing before a J.P. with a large wart on his nose. They had giggled at that wart on their wedding night. Stark black and white action photo of a sweating, bare-chested man wearing a lead apron and working heavy engine gear-levers in a huge, vaultlike underground chamber lit with arc lamps. Soft-toned color photo (soft to blur the stark, peeling surroundings) of a woman with a big belly standing at a window and looking out, ragged curtain held aside, watching for her man to come up the street. The light is a soft cat's paw on her cheek. Last picture: another old-timey Kodak of a thin fellow holding a tiny scrap of a baby high over his head in a curious mixture of triumph and love, his face split by a huge winning grin. The pictures began to flash by faster and faster, whirling, not bringing any sense of grief and love and loss, not yet, no, bringing only a cool Novocain numbness.

Killian assuring that the Network had nothing to do with their deaths, all a horrible accident. Richards supposed he believed him—not only because the story sounded too much like a lie not to be the truth, but because Killian knew that if Richards agreed to the job offer, his first stop would be Co-Op City, where a single hour on the streets would get him the straight of the matter.

Prowlers. Three of them. (Or tricks? Richards wondered, suddenly agonized. She had sounded slightly furtive on the telephone, as if holding something back—) They had been hopped up, probably. Perhaps they had made some threatening move toward Cathy and Sheila had tried to protect her daughter. They had both died of puncture wounds.

That had snapped him out of it. "Don't feed me that shit!" He screamed suddenly. Amelia flinched backward and suddenly hid her face. "What happened? Tell me what happened!"

"There's nothing more I can say. Your wife was stabbed over sixty times."

"Cathy," Richards said emptily, without thought, and Killian winced.

"Ben, would you like some time to think about all this?"

"Yes. Yes, I would."

"I'm desperately, desperately sorry, pal. I swear on my mother that we had nothing to do with it. Our way would have been to set them up away from you, with visiting rights if you agreed. A man doesn't willingly work for the people who butchered his family. We know that."

"I need time to think."

"As Chief Hunter," Killian said softly, "you could get those bastards and put them down a deep hole. And a lot of others just like them."

"I want to think. Goodbye."

"I—"

Richards reached out and thumbed the Free-Vee into blackness. He sat stonelike in his seat. His hands dangled loosely between his knees. The plane droned on into darkness.

So, he thought. It's all come unraveled. All of it.

. . . Minus 012
and COUNTING . . .

An hour passed.

The time has come, the walrus said, to talk of many things . . . of sailing ships and sealing-wax, And whether pigs have wings.

Pictures flitted in and out of his mind. Stacey. Bradley. Elton Parrakis with his baby face. A nightmare of running. Lighting the newspapers in the basement of the Y.M.C.A. with that last match. The gas-powered cars wheeling and screeching, the Sten gun spitting flame. Laughlin's sour voice. The pictures of those two kids, the junior Gestapo agents.

Well, why not?

No ties now, and certainly no morality. How could morality be an issue to a man cut loose and drifting? How wise Killian had been to see that, to show Richards with calm and gentle brutality just how alone he was. Bradley and his impassioned air-pollution pitch seemed distant, unreal, unimportant. Nose-filters. Yes. At one time the concept of nose-filters had seemed large, very important. No longer so.

The poor you will have with you always.

True. Even Richards's loins had produced a specimen for the killing machine. Eventually the poor would adapt, mutate. Their lungs would produce their own filtration system in ten thousand years or in fifty thousand, and they would rise up, rip out the artificial filters and watch their owners flop and kick and drum their lives away, drowning in an atmosphere where oxygen played only a minor part, and what was futurity to Ben Richards? It was all only bitchin.

There would be a period of grief. They would expect that, provide for it. There would even be rages, moments of revolt. Abortive tries to make the knowledge of deliberate poison in the air public again? Maybe. They would take care of it. Take care of him—anticipation of a time when he would take care of them. Instinctively he knew he could do it. He suspected he might even have a certain genius for the job. They would help him, heal him. Drugs and doctors. A change of mind.

Then, peace.

Contentiousness rooted out like bitterweed.

He regarded the peace longingly, the way a man in the desert regards water.

Amelia Williams cried steadily in her seat long after the time when all tears should have gone dry. He wondered indifferently what would become of her. She couldn't very well be returned to her husband and family in her present state; she simply was not the same lady who had pulled up to a routine stop sign with her mind all full of meals and meetings, clubs and cooking. She had Shown Red. He supposed there would be drugs and therapy, a patient showing off. The Place Where Two Roads Diverged, a pinpointing of the reason why the wrong path had been chosen. A carnival in dark mental browns.

He wanted suddenly to go to her, comfort her, tell her that she was not badly broken, that a single crisscrossing of psychic Band-Aids should fix her, make her even better than she had been before.

Sheila. Cathy.

Their names came and repeated, clanging in his mind like bells, like words repeated until they are reduced to nonsense. Say your name over two hundred times and discover you are no one. Grief was impossible; he could feel only a fuzzy sense of embarrassment: they had taken him, run him slack-lunged, and he had turned out to be nothing but a horse's ass after all. He remembered a boy from his grammar school days who had stood up to give the Pledge of Allegiance and his pants had fallen down.

The plane droned on and on. He sank into a three-quarter doze. Pictures came and went lazily, whole incidents were seen without any emotional color at all.

Then, a final scrapbook picture: a glossy eight-by-ten taken by a bored police photographer who had perhaps been chewing gum. Exhibit C, ladies and gentlemen of the jury. One ripped and sliced small body in a blood-drenched crib. Splatters and runnels on the cheap stucco walls and the broken Mother Goose mobile bought for a dime. A great sticky clot on the secondhand teddy bear with one eye.

He snapped awake, full awake and bolt upright, with his mouth propped wide in a blabbering scream. The force expelled from his lungs was great enough to make his tongue flap like a sail. Everything, everything in the first-class compartment was suddenly clear and plangently real, overpowering, awful. It had the grainy reality of a scare tabloid newsie clip. Laughlin being dragged out of that shed in Topeka, for instance. Everything, everything was very real and in Technicolor.

Amelia screamed affrightedly in unison, cringing back in her seat with eyes as huge as cracked porcelain doorknobs, trying to cram a whole fist in her mouth.

Donahue came charging through the galley, his gun out. His eyes were small enthusiastic black beads. "What is it? What's wrong? McCone?"

"No," Richards said, feeling his heart slow just enough to keep his words from sounding squeezed and desperate. "Bad dream. My little girl."

"Oh." Donahue's eyes softened in counterfeit sympathy. He didn't know how to do it very well. Perhaps he would be a goon all his life. Perhaps he would learn. He turned to go.

"Donahue?"

Donahue turned back warily.

"Had you pretty scared, didn't I?"

"No." Donahue turned away on that short word. His neck was bunched. His buttocks in his tight blue uniform were as pretty as a girl's.

"I can scare you worse," Richards remarked. "I could threaten to take away your nose filter."

Exeunt Donahue.

Richards closed his eyes tiredly. The glossy eight-by-ten came back. Opened them. Closed them. No glossy eight-by-ten. He waited, and when he was sure it was not going to come back (right away), he opened his eyes and thumbed on the Free-Vee.

It popped on and there was Killian.

. . . Minus 011
and COUNTING . . .

"Richards." Killian leaned forward, making no effort to conceal his tension.
"I've decided to accept," Richards said.
Killian leaned back and nothing smiled but his eyes. "I'm very glad," he said.

. . . Minus 010
and COUNTING . . .

"Jesus," Richards said. He was standing in the doorway to the pilot's country.

Holloway turned around. "Hi." He had been speaking to something called Detroit VOR. Duninger was drinking coffee.

The twin control consoles were untended. Yet they swerved, tipped, and turned as if in response to ghost hands and feet. Dials swung. Lights flashed. There seemed to be a huge and constant input and output going on . . . to no one at all.

"Who's driving the bus?" Richards asked, fascinated.

"Otto," Duninger said.

"Otto?"

"Otto the automatic pilot. Get it? Shitty pun." Duninger suddenly smiled. "Glad to have you on the team, fella. You may not believe this, but some of us guys were rooting for you pretty hard."

Richards nodded noncommittally.

Holloway stepped into the slightly awkwark breach by saying: "Otto freaks me out, too. Even after twenty years of this. But he's dead safe. Sophisticated as hell. It would make one of the old ones look like . . . well, like an orange crate beside a Chippendale bureau."

"Is that right?" Richards was staring out into the darkness.

"Yes. You lock on P.O.D.—point of destination—and Otto takes over, aided by Voice-Radar all the way. Makes the pilot pretty superfluous, except for take-offs and landings. And in case of trouble."

"Is there much you *can* do if there's trouble?" Richards asked.

"We can pray," Holloway said. Perhaps it was meant to sound jocular, but it came out with a strange sincerity that hung in the cabin.

"Do those wheels actually steer the plane?" Richards asked.

"Only up and down," Duninger said. "The pedals control sideside motion."

"Sounds like a kid's soapbox racer."

"A little more complicated." Holloway said. "Let's just say there are a few more buttons to push."

"What happens if Otto goes off his chump?"

"Never happens," Duninger said with a grin. "If it did, you'd just override him. But the computer is never wrong, pal."

Richards wanted to leave, but the sight of the turning wheels, the minute, mindless adjustments of the pedals and switches, held him. Holloway and Duninger went back to their business—obscure numbers and communications filled with static.

Holloway looked back once, seemed surprised to see him still there. He grinned and pointed into the darkness. "You'll see Harding coming up there soon."

"How long?"

"You'll be able to see the horizon glow in five to six minutes."

When Holloway turned around next, Richards was gone. He said to Duninger: "I'll be glad when we set that guy down. He's a spook"

Duninger looked down morosely, his face bathed in the green, luminescent glow of the controls. "He didn't like Otto. You know that?"

"I know it," Holloway said.

. . . Minus 009
and COUNTING . . .

Richards walked back down the narrow, hip-wide corridor. Friedman, the communications man, didn't look up. Neither did Donahue. Richards stepped through into the galley and then halted.

The smell of coffee was strong and good. He poured himself a cup, added some instant creamer, and sat down in one of the stewardesses's off-duty chairs. The Silex bubbled and steamed.

There was a complete stock of luxury frozen dinners in the see-through freezers. The liquor cabinet was fully stocked with midget airline bottles.

A man could have a good drunk, he thought.

He sipped his coffee. It was strong and fine. The Silex bubbled.

Here I am, he thought, and sipped. Yes, no question about it. Here he was, just sipping.

Pots and pans all neatly put away. The stainless steel sink gleaming like a chromium jewel in a Formica setting. And, of course, that Silex on the hotplate, bubbling and steaming. Sheila had always wanted a Silex. A Silex lasts, was her claim.

He was weeping.

There was a tiny toilet where only stewardess bottoms had squatted. The door was half ajar and he could see it, yes, even the blue, primly disinfected water in the bowl. Defecate in tasteful splendor at fifty thousand feet.

He drank his coffee and watched the Silex bubble and steam, and he wept. The weeping was very calm and completely silent. It and his cup of coffee ended at the same time.

He got up and put his cup in the stainless steel sink. He picked up the Silex, holding it by its brown plastic handle, and carefully dumped the coffee down the drain. Tiny beads of condensation clung to the thick glass.

He wiped his eyes with the sleeve of his jacket and went back into the narrow corridor. He stepped into Donahue's compartment, carrying the Silex in one hand.

"Want some coffee?" Richards asked.

"No," Donahue said curtly, without looking up.

"Sure you do," Richards said, and swung the heavy glass pot down on Donahue's bent head with all the force he could manage.

. . . Minus 008
and COUNTING . . .

The effort ripped open the wound in his side for the third time, but the pot didn't break. Richards wondered if it had been fortified with something (Vitamin B-12, perhaps?) to keep it from shattering in case of high level turbulence. It did take a huge, amazing blot of Donahue's blood. He fell silently onto his map table. A runnel of blood ran across the plasticoating of the top one and began to drip.

"Roger five-by, C-one-niner-eight-four," a radio voice said brightly.

Richards was still holding the Silex. It was matted with strands of Donahue's hair.

He dropped it, but there was no clunk. Carpeting even here. The glass bubble of the Silex rolled up at him, a winking, bloodshot eyeball. The glossy eight-by-ten of Cathy in her crib appeared unbidden and Richards shuddered.

He lifted Donahue's dead weight by the hair and rummaged inside his blue flight jacket. The gun was there. He was about to drop Donahue's head back to the map table, but paused, and yanked it up even further. Donahue's mouth hung un-hinged, an idiot leer. Blood dripped into it.

Richards wiped blood from one nostril and stared in.

There it was—tiny, very tiny. A glitter of mesh.

"Acknowledge E.T.A. C-one-niner-eight-four," the radio said.

"Hey, that's you!" Friedman called from across the hall. "Donahue—"

Richards limped into the passage. He felt very weak. Friedman looked up. "Will you tell Donahue to get off his butt and acknowledge—"

Richards shot him just above the upper lip. Teeth flew like a broken, savage necklace. Hair, blood, and brains splashed a Rorschach on the wall behind the chair, where a 3-D foldout girl was spreading eternal legs over a varnished mahogany bedpost.

There was a muffled exclamation from the pilot's compartment, and Holloway made a desperate, doomed lunge to shut the door. Richards noticed that he had a very small scar on his forehead, shaped like a question mark. It was the kind of scar a small, adventurous boy might get if he fell from a low branch while playing pilot.

He shot Holloway in the belly and Holloway made a great shocked noise: *"Whoooo-OOO!* His feet flipped out from under him and he fell on his face.

Duninger was turned around in his chair, his face a slack moon. "Don't shoot me, huh?" he said. There was not enough wind in him to make it a statement.

"Here," Richards said kindly, and pulled the trigger. Something popped and flared with brief violence behind Duninger as he fell over.

Silence.

"Acknowledge E.T.A., C-one-niner-eight-four," the radio said.

Richards suddenly whooped and threw up a great glut of coffee and bile. The muscular contraction ripped his wound open further, implanting a great, throbbing pain in his side.

He limped to the controls, still dipping and sliding in endless, complex tandem. So many dials and controls.

Wouldn't they have a communications link constantly open on such an important flight? Surely.

"Acknowledge," Richards said conversationally.

"You got the Free-Vee on up there, C-one-niner-eight-four? We've been getting some garbled transmission. Everything okay?"

"Five-by," Richards said.

"Tell Duninger he owes me a beer," the voice said cryptically, and then there was only background static.

Otto was driving the bus.

Richards went back to finish his business.

... Minus 007
and COUNTING ...

"Oh dear God," Amelia Williams moaned.

Richards looked down at himself casually. His entire right side, from ribcage to calf, was a bright and sparkling red.

"Who would have thought the old man had so much blood in him?" Richards said.

McCone suddenly dashed through into first class. He took in Richards at a glance. McCone's gun was out. He and Richards fired at the same time.

McCone disappeared through the canvas between first and second class. Richards sat down hard. He felt very tired. There was a large hole in his belly. He could see his intestines.

Amelia was screaming endlessly, her hands pulling her cheeks down into a plastic witch-face.

McCone came staggering back into first class. He was grinning. Half of his head appeared to be blown away, but he was grinning all the same.

He fired twice. The first bullet went over Richards's head. The second struck him just below the collarbone.

Richards fired again. McCone staggered around twice in an aimless kind of dipsy-doodle. The gun fell from his fingers. McCone appeared to be observing the heavy white styrofoam ceiling of the first class compartment, perhaps comparing it to his own in second class. He fell over. The smell of burned powder and burned flesh was clear and crisp, as distinctive as apples in a cider press.

Amelia continued to scream. Richards thought how remarkably healthy she sounded.

. . . Minus 006
and COUNTING . . .

Richards got up very slowly, holding his intestines in. It felt as if someone was lighting matches in his stomach.

He went slowly up the aisle, bent over, one hand to his midriff, as if bowing. He picked up the parachute with one hand and dragged it behind him. A loop of gray sausage escaped his fingers and he pushed it back in. It hurt to push it in. It vaguely felt as if he might be shitting himself.

"Guh," Amelia Williams was groaning. "Guh-Guh-Guh-God. Oh God. Oh dear God."

"Put this on," Richards said.

She continued to rock and moan, not hearing him. He dropped the parachute and slapped her. He could get no force into it. He balled his fist and punched her. She shut up. Her eyes stared at him dazedly.

"Put this on," he said again. "Like a packsack. You see how?"

She nodded. "I. Can't. Jump. Scared."

"We're going down. You have to jump."

"Can't."

"All right. Shoot you then."

She popped out of her seat, knocking him sideways, and began to pull the pack-sack on with wild, eye-rolling vigor. She backed away from him as she struggled with the straps.

"No. That one goes uh-under."

She rearranged the strap with great speed, retreating toward McCone's body as Richards approached. Blood was dripping from his mouth.

"Now fasten the clip in the ringbolt. Around. Your buh-belly."

She did it with trembling fingers, weeping when she missed the connection the first time. Her eyes stared madly into his face.

She skittered momentarily in McCone's blood and then stepped over him.

They backed through second class and into third class in the same way. Matches in his belly had been replaced by a steadily flaming lighter.

The emergency door was locked with explosive bolts and a pilot controlled bar. Richards handed her the gun. "Shoot it. I . . . can't take the recoil."

Closing her eyes and averting her face, she pulled the trigger of Donahue's gun twice. Then it was empty. The door stood closed, and Richards felt a faint, sick despair. Amelia Williams was holding the ripcord ring nervously, giving it tiny little twitches.

"Maybe—" she began, and the door suddenly blew away into the night, sucking her along with it.

. . . Minus 005
and COUNTING . . .

Bent haglike, a man in a reverse hurricane, Richards made his way from the blown door, holding the backs of seats. If they had been flying higher, with a greater difference in air pressure, he would have been pulled out, too. As it was he was being badly buffeted, his poor old intestines accordioning out and trailing after him on the floor. The cool night air, thin and sharp at two thousand feet, was like a slap of cold water. The cigarette lighter had become a torch, and his insides were burning.

Through second class. Better. Suction not so great. Now over McCone's sprawled body (step *up*, please) and through first class. Blood ran loosely from his mouth.

He paused at the entrance to the galley and tried to gather up his intestines. He knew they didn't like it on the Outside. Not a bit. They were getting all dirty. He wanted to weep for his poor, fragile intestines, who had asked for none of this.

He couldn't pack them back inside. It was all wrong; they were all jumbled. Frightening images from high school biology books jetted past his eyes. He realized with dawning, stumbling truth, the fact of his own actual ending, and cried out miserably through a mouthful of blood.

There was no answer from the aircraft. Everyone was gone. Everyone but himself and Otto.

The world seemed to be draining of color as his body drained of its own bright fluid. Leaning crookedly against the galley entrance, like a drunk leaning against a lamppost, he saw the things around him go through a shifting, wraithlike grayout.

This is it. I'm going.

He screamed again, bringing the world back into excruciating focus. Not yet. Mustn't.

He lunged through the galley with his guts hanging in ropes around him. Amazing that there could be so much in there. So round, so firm, so fully packed.

He stepped on part of himself, and something inside *pulled*. The flare of pain was beyond belief, beyond the world, and he shrieked, splattering blood on the far wall. He lost his balance and would have fallen, had not the wall stopped him at sixty degrees.

Gutshot. I'm gutshot.

Insanely, his mind responded: *Clitter-clitter-clitter.*

One thing to do.

Gutshot was supposed to be one of the worst. They had had a discussion once about the worst ways to go on their midnight lunch break; that had been when he was a wiper. Hale and hearty and full of blood and piss and semen, all of them, gobbling sandwiches and comparing the relative merits of radiation poisoning, freezing, falling, bludgeoning, drowning. And someone had mentioned being gutshot. Harris, maybe. The fat one who drank illicit beer on the job.

It hurts in the belly, Harris had said. *It takes a long time.* And all of them nodding and agreeing solemnly, with no conception of Pain.

Richards lurched up the narrow corridor, holding both sides for support. Past Donahue. Past Friedman and his radical dental surgery. Numbness crawling up his arms, yet the pain in his belly (what *had* been his belly) growing worse. Still, even through all this he moved, and his ruptured body tried to carry out the commands of the insane Napoleon caged inside his skull.

My God, can this be the end of Rico?

He would not have believed he had so many death-bed cliches inside him. It seemed that his mind was turning inward, eating itself in its last fevered seconds.

One. More. Thing.

He fell over Holloway's sprawled body and lay there, suddenly sleepy. A nap. Yes. Just the ticket. Too hard to get up. Otto, humming. Singing the birthday boy to sleep. Shhh, shhh, shhh. The sheep's in the meadow, the cow's in the corn.

He lifted his head—tremendous effort, his head was steel, pig iron, lead—and stared at the twin controls going through their dance. Beyond him, in the plexiglass windows, Harding.

Too far.

He's under the haystack, fast asleep.

. . . Minus 004
and COUNTING . . .

The radio was squawking worriedly: "Come in, C-one-niner-eight-four. You're too low. Acknowledge. Acknowledge. Shall we assume Guidance control? Acknowledge. Acknowledge Ack—"

"Eat it," Richards whispered.

He began to crawl toward the dipping, swaying controls. In and out went the pedals. Twitch-twitch went the wheels. He screamed as new agony flared. A loop of his intestines had caught under Holloway's chin. He crawled back. Freed them. Started to crawl again.

His arms went slack and for a moment he floated, weightless, with his nose in the soft, deep-pile carpet. He pushed himself up and began to crawl again.

Getting up and into Holloway's seat was Everest.

. . . Minus 003
and COUNTING . . .

There it was. Huge, bulking square and tall into the night, silhouetted black above everything else. Moonlight had turned it alabaster.

He tweaked the wheel just a little. The floor fell away to the left. He lurched in Holloway's seat and almost fell out. He turned the wheel back, overcorrected again, and the floor fell away to the right. The horizon was tilting crazily.

Now the pedals. Yes. Better.

He pushed the wheel in gingerly. A dial in front of his eyes moved from 2000 to 1500 in the wink of an eye. He eased the wheel back. He had very little sight left. His right eye was almost completely gone. Strange that they should go one at a time.

He pushed the wheel in again. Now it seemed that the plane was floating, weightless. The dial slipped from 1500 to 1200 to 900. He pulled it back out.

"C-one-niner-eight-four." The voice was very alarmed now. "What's wrong? Acknowledge!"

"Speak, boy," Richards croaked. "Rowf! Rowf!"

. . . Minus 002
and COUNTING . . .

The big plane cruised through the night like a sliver of ice and now Co-Op City was spread out below like a giant broken carton.

He was coming at it, coming at the Games Building.

... Minus 001
and COUNTING ...

Now the jet cruised across the canal, seemingly held up by the hand of God, giant, roaring. A Push freak in a doorway stared up and thought he was seeing a hallucination, the last dope dream, come to take him away, perhaps to General Atomics heaven where all the food was free and all the piles were clean breeders.

The sound of its engines drove people into doorways, their faces craning upwards like pale flames. Glass show-windows jingled and fell inward. Gutter litter was sucked down bowling-alley streets in dervishes. A cop dropped his move-along and wrapped his hands around his head and screamed and could not hear himself.

The plane was still dropping and now it moved over rooftops like a cruising silver bat; the starboard wingtip missed the side of the Glamour Column Store by a bare twelve feet.

All over Harding, Free-Vees went white with interference and people stared at them with stupid, fearful incredulity.

The thunder filled the world.

Killian looked up from his desk and stared into the wall-to-wall window that formed one entire side of the room.

The twinkling vista of the city, from South City to Crescent, was gone. The entire window was filled with an oncoming Lockheed TriStar jet. Its running lights blinked on and off, and for just a moment, an insane moment of total surprise and horror and disbelief, he could see Richards staring out at him. His face smeared with blood, his black eyes burning like the eyes of a demon.

Richards was grinning.

And giving him the finger.

"—Jesus—" was all Killian had time to get out.

000

Heeling over slightly, the Lockheed struck the Games Building dead on, three quarters of the way up.Its tanks were still better than a quarter full. Its speed was slightly over five hundred miles an hour.

The explosion was tremendous, lighting up the night like the wrath of God, and it rained fire twenty blocks away.

Ø

SIGNET Titles by Stephen King You'll Want to Read